Praise for *Soldier of the Mist*

"Here is a challenge no writer but Wolfe could have taken up and no reader will be able to put down."     —*Christian Science Monitor*

"Gene Wolfe may be the most intriguing writer of speculative fiction in the business today. His *Soldier of the Mist* succeeds not only as a vivid recreation of ancient Greece but also as a literary tour de force."
—*St. Louis Post-Dispatch*

"Gene Wolfe has entered the ranks of those rare imaginative talents whose work will justly be regarded as 'classic' for generations to come."
—*San Francisco Chronicle*

Praise for *Soldier of Arete*

"Wolfe seems to have captured the mentality of a past age—an age filled with prophetic dreams, ghosts, and visitations by gods."
—*The Philadelphia Inquirer*

"Audacious, even exhilarating."     —*Newsday*

"It is both a major, original work of fantasy, and contains some of the best writing about classical Greece I've seen since Mary Renault's more conventional historical fiction."     —*Chicago Sun-Times*

# LATRO IN THE MIST

*Soldier of the Mist*
*and*
*Soldier of Arete*

## GENE WOLFE

ORB
A TOM DOHERTY ASSOCIATES BOOK
NEW YORK

This is a work of fiction. All the characters and events portrayed in these
novels are either fictitious or are used fictitiously.

LATRO IN THE MIST

Edited by David G. Hartwell

*Book design by Michael Collica*

An Orb Edition
Published by Tom Doherty Associates, LLC
175 Fifth Avenue
New York, NY 10010

www.tor.com

Library of Congress Cataloging-in-Publication Data

Wolfe, Gene.
    [Soldier of the mist]
    Latro in the mist / Gene Wolfe.—1st Orb ed.
      p.  cm.
    "A Tom Doherty Associates book."
    Contents: Soldier of the mist—Soldier of Arete.
    ISBN: 0-765-30294-2
    1. Greece—History—Persian Wars, 500–449 B.C.—Fiction.   2. Soldiers—
Fiction.   I. Wolfe, Gene. Soldier of Arete.   II. Title: Soldier of Arete.
III. Title.

PS3573.O52 S65 2003
813'.54—dc21

                                        2002192467

Printed in the United States of America

0  9  8  7  6  5  4

# CONTENTS

# SOLDIER OF THE MIST

This book is
dedicated
with the greatest respect and affection
to
Herodotos of Halicarnassos

First there was a struggle at the barricade of shields; then, the barricade down, a bitter and protracted fight, hand to hand, at the temple of Demeter. . . .

—Herodotos

Although this book is fiction,
it is based on actual events of 479 B.C.

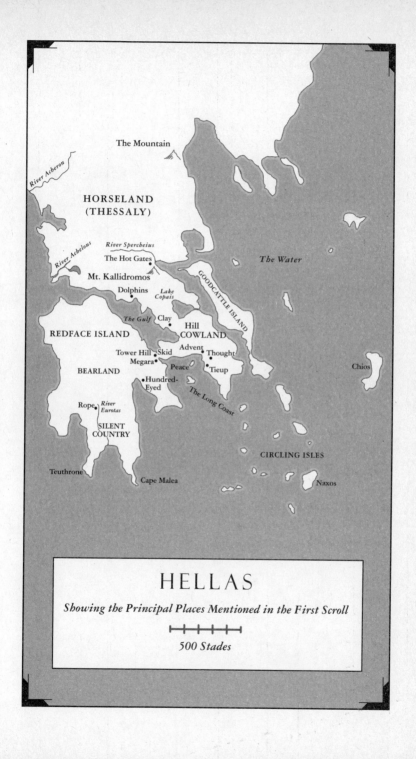

The Mountain

*River Acheron*

HORSELAND
(THESSALY)

*River Achelous*

*River Spercheius*

The Hot Gates

The Water

Mt. Kallidromos

Dolphins

*Lake Copais*

GOODCATTLE ISLAND

*The Gulf* Clay

Hill
COWLAND

REDFACE ISLAND

Advent

Tower Hill Skid

Thought

Chios

Megara

Peace

Tieup

BEARLAND

Hundred-
Eyed

*The Long Coast*

Rope *River Eurotas*

SILENT
COUNTRY

CIRCLING ISLES

Teuthrone

Cape Malea

Naxos

# HELLAS

*Showing the Principal Places Mentioned in the First Scroll*

## 500 Stades

# FOREWORD

A BOUT TWO YEARS AGO, an urn containing scrolls of papyrus, all apparently unused, was found behind a collection of Roman lyres in the basement of the British Museum. The museum retained the urn and disposed of the scrolls, which were listed in Sotheby's catalogue as *Lot 183. Various blank papyrus rolls, possibly the stock of an Egyptian stationer.*

After passing through several hands, they became the property of Mr. D_____ A_____, a dealer and collector in Detroit. He got the notion that something might be concealed in the sticks on which the papyrus was wound and had them X-rayed. The X-rays showed them to be solid; but they also showed line after line of minute characters on the sheet (technically the *protokollon*) gummed to each stick. Sensing himself on the verge of a discovery of real bibliotic importance, he examined a scroll under a powerful lens and found that all its sheets were covered on both sides with minute gray writing, which the personnel of the museum, and of Sotheby's, had apparently taken for dust smears. Spectrographic analysis has established that the writing instrument was a sharp "pencil" of metallic lead. Knowing my interest in dead languages, the owner has asked me to provide this translation.

With the exception of a short section in passable Greek, this first scroll is written in archaic Latin, without punctuation. The author, who called himself "Latro" (a word that may mean brigand, guerrilla, hired man, bodyguard, or pawn), had a disastrous penchant for abbreviation—indeed, it is rare to find him giving any but the shortest words in full; there is a distinct possibility that some abbreviations have been misread. The reader should keep in mind that all punctuation is mine; I have added details merely implied in the text in some instances and have given in full some conversations given in summary.

For convenience in reading, I have divided the work into chapters, breaking the text (insofar as possible) at the points at which "Latro" ceased to write. I have employed the first few words of each chapter as its title.

In dealing with place names, I have followed the original writer, who sometimes wrote them as he heard them but more often translated them when he understood (or believed he understood) their meanings. "Tower Hill" is probably Corinth; "the Long Coast" is surely Attica. In some cases, Latro was certainly mistaken. He seems to have heard some taciturn person referred to as having Laconic manners (Greek λακωνιεμός) and to have concluded that *Laconia* meant "the Silent Country." His error in deriving the name of the principal city of that region from a word for rope or cord (Greek σπάρτον) was one made by many uneducated speakers of his time. He appears to have had some knowledge of Semitic languages and to have spoken Greek fairly fluently, but to have read it poorly or not at all.

A few words about the culture in which Latro found himself soon after he began to write may be in order. The people no more called themselves Greeks than do the people of the nation we call Greece today. By our standards they were casual about clothes, though in most cities it was considered improper for a woman to appear in public completely naked, as men often did. Breakfast was not eaten; unless he had been drinking the night before, the average Greek rose at dawn and ate his first meal at noon; a second meal was eaten in the evening. In peacetime even children drank diluted wine; in wartime soldiers complained bitterly because they had only water, and often fell ill.

Athens ("Thought") was more crime-ridden than New York. Its law against women's leaving their homes alone was meant to prevent attacks on them. (Another woman or even a child was a satisfactory escort.) First-floor rooms were windowless, and burglars were called "wallbreakers." Despite the modern myth, exclusive homosexuality was rare and generally condemned, although bisexuality was common and accepted. The Athenian police were barbarian mercenaries, employed because they were more difficult to corrupt than Greeks. Their skill with the bow was often valuable in apprehending suspects.

Although the Greek city-states were more diverse in law and custom than most scholars are willing to admit, a brisk trade in goods had effected some standardization in money and units of measure. An obol, vulgarly called a spit, bought a light meal. The oarsmen on warships were paid two or three obols a day, but of course they were fed from their ship's stores. Six obols made a drachma (a handful), and a drachma bought a day's service from a skilled mercenary (who supplied his own equipment) or a night's service from one of Kalleos's women. A gold stator was worth two silver drachmas. The most widely circulated ten-drachma coin was called an owl, from the image on its reverse. A hundred drachmas made a mina; sixty minas a talent—about fifty-seven pounds of gold or eight hundred pounds of silver.

The talent was also a unit of weight: about fifty-seven pounds. The most commonly used measure of distance was the stade, from which comes our *stadium*. A stade was about two hundred yards, or a little over one-tenth of a mile.

Humanitarians accepted the institution of slavery, realizing that the alternative was massacre; we who have seen the holocaust of the European Jews should be sparing in our reproaches. Prisoners of war were a principal source of supply. A really first-class slave might cost as much as ten minas, the equivalent of thirty-six thousand dollars. Most were much more reasonable.

If the average well-read American were asked to name five famous Greeks, he would probably answer, "Homer, Socrates, Plato, Aristotle, and Pericles." Critics of Latro's account would do well to recall that Homer had been dead for four hundred years at the time Latro wrote, and that no one had heard of Socrates, Plato, Aristotle, or Pericles. The word *philosopher* was not yet in use.

In ancient Greece, skeptics were those who thought, not those who scoffed. Modern skeptics should note that Latro reports Greece as it was reported by the Greeks themselves. The runner sent from Athens to ask Spartan help before the battle of Marathon met the god Pan on the road and conscientiously recounted their conversation to the Athenian Assembly when he returned. (The Spartans, who well knew who ruled their land, refused to march before the full of the moon.)

—G. W.

# PART ONE

# ONE

## *Read This Each Day*

I WRITE OF WHAT has just occurred. The healer came into this tent at dawn and asked whether I recalled him. When I said I did not, he explained. He gave me this scroll, with this stylus of the slingstone metal, which marks it as though it were wax.

My name is *Latro*. I must not forget. The healer said I forget very quickly, and that is because of a wound I suffered in a battle. He named it as though it were a man, but I do not remember the name. He said I must learn to write down as much as I can, so I can read it when I have forgotten. Thus he has given me this scroll and this stylus of heavy slingstone metal.

I wrote something for him in the dust first. He seemed pleased I could write, saying most soldiers cannot. He said also that my letters are well formed, though some are of shapes he does not know. I held the lamp, and he showed me his writing. It seemed very strange to me. He is of Riverland.

He asked me my name, but I could not bring it to my lips. He asked if I remembered speaking to him yesterday, and I did not. He has spoken to me several times, he says, but I have always forgotten when he comes again. He said some other soldiers told him my name, "Latro," and he asked if I could remember my home. I could. I told him of our house and the brook that laughs over colored stones. I described Mother and Father to him, just as I see them in my mind, but when he asked their names, I could tell him only "Mother" and "Father." He said he thought these memories very old, perhaps from twenty years past or more. He asked who taught me to write, but I could not tell him. Then he gave me these things.

I am sitting by the flap, and because I have written all I remember of what he said, I will write what I see, so that perhaps in time to come I can sift my writing for what may be of value to me.

The sky is wide and blue, though the sun is not yet higher than the tents. There are many, many tents. Some are of hides, some of cloth. Most are plain, but I see one hung with tassels of bright wool. Soon after the healer left, four stiff-legged, unwilling camels were driven past by shouting men. Just now they returned, laden and hung with red and blue tassels of the same kind and raising a great dust because their drivers beat them to make them run.

Soldiers hurry by me, sometimes running, never smiling. Most are short, strong men with black beards. They wear trousers, and embroidered tunics of turquoise and gold over corselets of scales. One came carrying a spear with an apple of gold. He was the first to meet my eyes, and so I stopped him and asked whose army this is. He said, "The Great King's," then made me sit once more and hurried off.

My head still gives me pain. Often my fingers stray toward the bandages there, though the healer said not to touch them. I keep this stylus in my hand, and I will not. Sometimes it seems to me that there is a mist before my eyes that the sun cannot drive away.

Now I write again. I have been examining the sword and armor piled beside my couch. There is a helmet, holed where I received my wound. There is Falcata too, and there are plates for the breast and back. I took up Falcata, and though I did not know her, she knew my hand. Some of the other wounded looked afraid, so I sheathed her again. They do not understand my speech, nor I theirs.

The healer came after I wrote last, and I asked him where I had been hurt. He said it was near the shrine of the Earth Mother, where the Great King's army fought the army of Thought and the Rope Makers.

I helped take down our tent. There are mules for the litters of those who cannot walk. He said I must keep with the rest; if I become separated, I must look for his own mule, who is piebald, or for his servant, who has but one eye. That is the man who carries out the dead, I think. I told him I would carry this scroll and wear the round plates and my sword on my belt of manhood. My helmet might be sold for its bronze, but I do not want to carry it. They have loaded it with the bedding.

———

We rest beside a river, and I write with my feet cooling in its stream. I do not know the name of this river. The army of the Great King blackens the road for many miles, and I, having seen it, do not understand how it could have been vanquished—or why I joined it, since where there are so many men no one could count them, one more or less is nothing. It is said our enemies pursue us, and our cavalry keeps them at bay. This I overheard when I saw a party of horsemen hurrying to the rear. The men who said it speak as I to the healer, and not in these words I write.

A black man is with me. He wears the skin of a spotted beast, and his spear is tipped with twisted horn. Sometimes he speaks, but if ever I knew his words, I have forgotten them all. When we met, he asked by signs if I had seen such men as he. I shook my head, and he seemed to understand. He peers at these letters I make with great interest.

The river was muddy for a time after so many had drunk. Now it runs clear again, and I see myself and the black man reflected. I am not as he, nor as the Great King's other soldiers. I pointed to my arm and my hair and asked the black man if he had seen another such as I. He nodded and opened two little bags he carries; there is white paste in one and vermilion in the other. He showed me by signs that we should go with the others; as he did, I saw beyond his shoulder another man, whiter than I, in the river. At first I thought him drowned, for his face was beneath the water; but he smiled and waved to me, pointing up the river, where the Great King's army marches, before he vanished swiftly downstream. I have told the black man I will not go, because I wish to write of this river-man while I can.

His skin was white as foam, his beard black and curling, so that for a moment I thought it spun of the silt. He was thick at the waist, like a rich man among the veterans, but thick of muscle, too, and horned like a bull. His eyes were merry and brave, the eyes that say, "I will knock down the tower." When he gestured, it seemed to me he meant we would meet again, and I do not want to forget him. His river is cold and smooth, racing from the hills to water this land. I will drink again, and the black man and I will go.

Evening. The healer would feed me if I could find him, I know; but I am too tired to walk far. As the day passed, I grew weaker and could

walk only slowly. When the black man tried to hurry me, I signed that
he should go forward alone. He shook his head and I think called me
many vile names; and at last flourished his spear as if to strike me with
the shaft. I drew Falcata. He dropped his spear and with his chin (so he
points) told me to look behind us. There under the staring sun a thousand horsemen scoured the plain, their shadows and the clouds of dust
more visible than the riders. A soldier with a wounded leg, who could
walk even less than I, said the slingers and archers with whom they
warred were the slaves of the Rope Makers, and if someone he named
were still in the country of the sun, we would turn and rend them. Yet
he seemed to fear the Rope Makers.

Now the black man has built a fire and gone among the tents to
look for food. I feel it can bring me no strength and I shall die tomorrow,
not at the hands of those slaves but falling suddenly and embracing the
earth, drawing it over me like a cloak. The soldiers I can understand
talk much of gods, cursing them and cursing others—ourselves more
than once—in their names. It seems to me I once knew gods, worshiping
beside Mother where the vines twined about the house of some small
god. Now his name is lost. Even if I could call on him, I do not think
he could come at my bidding. This land is surely far, very far from his
little house.

I have gathered wood and heaped it on our fire to make light so I can
write. For I must never forget what happened, *never*. Yet the mist will
come, and it will be lost until I read what I now write.

I went to the river and said, "I know no god but you. I die tomorrow, and I will sink into the earth with the other dead. But I pray you
will give good fortune always to the black man, who has been more
than a brother to me. Here is my sword, with her I would have slain
him. Accept the sacrifice!" Then I cast Falcata into the water.

At once the river-man appeared, rising from the dark stream and
toying with my sword, tossing her in his hands and catching her again,
sometimes by the hilt, sometimes by the blade. With him were two
girls who might have been his daughters, and while he teased them with
her, they sought to snatch her from him. All three shone like pearls in
the moonlight.

Soon he cast Falcata at my feet. "I would mend you if I could," he said to me. "That lies beyond me, though steel and wood, fish, wheat, and barley all obey me." His voice was like the rushing of great waters. "My power is but this: that what is given to me I return manyfold. Thus I cast your sickle on my shore again, new-tempered in my flood. Not wood, nor bronze, nor iron shall stand against her, and she will not fail you until you fail her."

So saying, he and his daughters, if such they were, sank into the water again. I took up Falcata, thinking to dry her blade; but she was hot and dry. Then the black man returned with bread and meat, and many tales told with his fingers of how he had stolen them. We ate, and now he sleeps.

# TWO

## *At Hill*

WE HAVE CAMPED, AND I have forgotten much of what happened since I saw the Swift God. Indeed, I have forgotten the seeing and know of it only because I have read it in this scroll in which I write.

Hill is very beautiful. There are buildings of marble, and a wonderful market. The people are frightened, however, and angry with the Great King because he is not here with more of his soldiers. They fought for him, thinking he would surely best the armies of Thought and Rope—this though the people of those cities are sons of Hellen just as they themselves are. They say the people of Thought hate their very name and will sweep their streets with fire, even as the Great King swept the streets of Thought. They say (for I listened to them in the market) that they will throw themselves upon the mercy of the Rope Makers, but that the Rope Makers have no mercy. They wish us to remain, but they say we will soon go, leaving them no protection but their walls and their own men, of whom the best, their Sacred Band, are all dead. And I think they speak the truth, for already I have heard some say we will break our camp tomorrow.

There are many inns here, but the black man and I have no money, so we sleep outside the walls with the other soldiers of the Great King. I wish I had described the healer when I first wrote, for I cannot find him among so many. There are many piebald mules and not a few one-eyed men, but none of the one-eyed men will say he is the servant of the healer. Most will not speak with me; seeing my bandages, they think I have come to beg. I will not beg, yet it seems to me less honorable to eat what the black man takes, as I just did. This morning I tried to take food in the market as he does, but he is more skilled than I. Soon we will go to another market, where I will stand between him and the owners of the stalls as I did this morning. It is hard for him, because the people stare; yet he is very clever and often succeeds even when they watch him. I do not know how, because he has shown me many times that I am never to watch.

While the black man speaks with his hands and the rest argue, I write these words in the temple of the Shining God, which stands in the agora, the great market of Hill. So much has happened since I last wrote— and I have so little notion of what it may mean—that I do not know how I should begin.

The black man and I went to a different market after we had eaten the first meal and rested, to the agora, in the center of the city. Here jewelry and gold and silver cups are sold, and not just bread and wine, fish and figs. There are many fine buildings with pillars of marble; and there is a floor of stone over the earth, as though one stood in such a building already.

In the midst of all this and the thronging buyers and sellers, there is a fountain, and in the midst of the fountain, pouring forth its waters, an image of the Swift God worked in marble.

Having read of him in this scroll, I rushed to it, thinking the image to be the Swift God himself and calling out to him. A hundred people at least crowded around us then, some soldiers of the Great King like ourselves, but most citizens of Hill. They shouted many questions, and I answered as well as I could. The black man came too, asking by signs for money. Copper, bronze, and silver rained into his hands, so many coins that he had to stop at last and put them into the bag in which he carries his possessions.

That had a bad effect, and little more was given; but men with many rings came and said I must go to the House of the Sun, and when the black man said we would not, said the Sun is the healer and called upon some soldiers of Hill to help them.

Thus we were taken into one of the finest buildings, with columns and many wide steps, where I was made to kneel before the prophetess, who sat upon a bronze tripod. There was much talk between the men with rings and a lean priest, who said many times and in many different ways that the prophetess would not speak for their god until an offering was made.

At last one of the men with many rings sent his slave away, and when we had waited longer still, and all the men with many rings had spoken of the gods and what they knew of them, and what their fathers and grandfathers and uncles had told them of them, this slave returned, bringing with him a little slave girl no taller than my waist.

Then her owner spoke of her most highly, pointing to her comely face and swearing she could read and that she had never known a man. I wondered to hear it, for from the looks she gave the slave who had brought her she knew him and did not like him; but I soon saw the lean priest believed the man with many rings hardly more than I, and perhaps less.

When he had heard him out, he drew the slave girl to one side and showed her letters cut in the walls. These were not all such letters as I make now, and yet I saw they were writing indeed. "Read me the words of the god who makes the future plain, child," the lean priest commanded her. "Read aloud of the god who heals and lets fly the swift arrows of death."

Smoothly and skillfully the slave girl read:

> "Here Leto's son, who strikes the lyre
> Makes clear our days with golden fire,
> Heals all wounds, gives hope divine,
> To those who kneel at his shrine."

Her voice was clear and sweet, and though it was not like the shouting on the drill field, it seemed to rise above the clamor of the marketplace outside.

The priest nodded with satisfaction, motioned the little slave girl to silence, and nodded to the prophetess, who was at once seized by the god they served, so that she writhed and shrieked upon her tripod.

Soon her screams stopped, and she began to speak as quickly as the rattling of pebbles in a jar, in a voice like no woman's; but I paid little heed to her because my eyes were on a golden man, larger than any man should be, who had stepped silently from an alcove.

He motioned to me, and I came.

He was young and formed like a soldier, but he bore no scars. A bow and a shepherd's staff, both of gold, were clasped in his left hand, and a quiver of golden arrows was slung upon his back. He crouched before me as I might have crouched to speak with a child.

I bowed, and as I did I looked around at the others; they heard the prophetess in attitudes of reverence and did not see the golden giant.

"For them I am not here," he said, answering a question I had not asked. His words were fair and smooth, like those of a seller who tells his customer that his goods have been reserved for him alone.

"How can that be?" Even as he spoke, the others murmured and nodded, their eyes still on the prophetess.

"Only the solitary may see the gods," the giant told me. "For the rest, every god is the Unknown God."

"Am I alone then?" I asked him.

"Do you behold me?"

I nodded.

"Prayers to me are sometimes granted," he said. "You have come with no petition. Have you one to make now?"

Unable to speak or think, I shook my head.

"Then you shall have such gifts as are mine to give. Hear my attributes: I am a god of divination, of music, of death, and of healing; I am the slayer of wolves and the master of the sun. I prophesy that though you will wander far in search of your home, you will not find it until you are farthest from it. Once only, you will sing as men sang in the Age of Gold to the playing of the gods. Long after, you will find what you seek in the dead city.

"Though healing is mine, I cannot heal you, nor would I if I could; by the shrine of the Great Mother you fell, to a shrine of hers you must return. Then she will point the way, and in the end the wolf's tooth will return to her who sent it."

Even as this golden man spoke he grew dim in my sight, as though all his substance were being drawn again into the alcove from which he had stepped only a moment before.

"Look beneath the sun. . . ."

When he was gone I rose, dusting my chiton with my hands. The black man, the lean priest, the men with many rings, and even the child still stood before the prophetess; but now the men with many rings argued among themselves, some pointing to the youngest of their number, who spoke at length with outspread hands.

When he had finished, the others spoke all together, many telling him how fortunate he was, because he would leave the city; whereupon he began once more. I soon grew tired of hearing him and read what is written here instead, then wrote as I write now—while still they argue, the black man talks of money with his hands, and the youngest of the men with many rings (who is not truly young, for the hair is leaving his head on both sides) backs away as if to fly.

The child looks at me, at him, at the black man, and then at me once more, with wondering eyes.

# THREE

## *Io*

THE SLAVE GIRL WOKE ME before the first light. Our fire was nearly out, and she was breaking sticks across her knee to add to it. "I'm sorry, master," she said. "I tried to do it as quietly as I could."

I felt I knew her, but I could not recall the time or place where we had met. I asked who she was.

"Io. It means *io*—'happiness'—master."

"And who am I?"

"You're Latro the soldier, master."

She had thrice called me "master." I asked, "Are you a slave, then, Io?" The truth was that I had assumed it already from her tattered peplos.

"I'm your slave, master. The god gave me to you yesterday. Don't you remember?"

I told her I did not.

"They took me to the god's house because he wouldn't tell them anything till somebody brought a present. I was the present, and for me he seized the priestess so she just about went crazy. She said I belonged to you, and I should go with you wherever you went."

A man who had rolled himself in a fine blue cloak threw it off and sat up at that. "Not that I recall," he said. "And I was there."

"This was afterward," Io declared. "After you and the others had left."

He glanced at her skeptically, then said, "I hope you haven't forgotten me as well, Latro." When he saw I had, he continued, "My name is Pindaros, sir, son of Pagondas; and I am a poet. I was one of those who carried you to the temple of our patron."

I said, "I feel I've been dreaming and have just awakened; but I can't tell you what my dream was, or what preceded it."

"Ah!" Reaching in his traveling bag, Pindaros produced a waxed tablet and stylus. "That's really rather good. I hope you won't mind if I write it down? I might be able to make use of it somewhere."

"Write it down?" Something stirred in me, though I could not see it clearly.

"Yes, so I won't forget. You do the same thing, Latro. Yesterday you showed me your book. Do you still have it?"

I looked about and saw this scroll lying where I had slept, with the stylus thrust through the cords.

"It's a good thing you didn't knock it into the fire," Pindaros remarked.

"I wish I had a cloak like yours."

"Why, then, I'll buy you one. I've a little money, having had the good fortune to inherit a bit of land two years ago. Or your friend there can. He collected quite a tidy sum before we took you to the House of the God."

I looked at the black man to whom Pindaros pointed. He was still asleep, or feigning to be; but he would not sleep much longer: even as I looked, horns brayed far off. All around us men were stirring into wakefulness.

"Whose army is this?" I asked.

"What? You a soldier in it, and you don't know your strategist?"

I shook my head. "Perhaps I did, once. I no longer remember."

Io said, "He forgets because of what they did to him in that battle south of the city."

"Well, it used to be Mardonius's, but he's dead; I'm not sure who commands now. Artabazus, I think. At least, he seems to be in charge."

I had picked up my scroll. "Perhaps if I read this, I'd remember."

"Perhaps you would," Pindaros agreed. "But wait a moment, and you'll have more light. The sun will be up, and we'll have a grand view across Lake Copais there."

I was thirsty, so I asked if that was where we were going.

"To the morning sun? I suppose that's where this army's going, if Pausanius and his Rope Makers have anything to say about it. Farther, perhaps. But you and I are going to the cave of the Earth Goddess. You don't remember what the sibyl said?"

"I do," Io announced.

"You recite it for him, then." Pindaros sighed. "I have a temperamental aversion to bad verse."

The slave girl drew herself up to her full height, which was small enough, and chanted:

> "Look under the sun, if you would see!
> Sing! Make sacrifice to me!
> But you must cross the narrow sea.
> The wolf that howls has wrought you woe!
> To that dog's mistress you must go!
> Her hearth burns in the room below.
> I send you to the God Unseen!
> Whose temple lies in Death's terrene!
> There you shall learn why He's not seen.
> Sing then, and make the hills resound!
> King, nymph, and priest shall gather round!
> Wolf, faun, and nymph, spellbound."

Pindar shook his head in dismay. "Isn't that the most awful doggerel you ever heard? They do it much better at the Navel of the World, believe me. This may sound like vanity, but I've often thought the sheer badness of the oracle in our shining city was meant as an admonition to me. 'See, Pindaros,' the god is saying, 'what happens when divine poetry is passed through a heart of clay.' Still, it's certainly clear enough, and you can't always say that when the god speaks at the Navel of the World. Half the time he could mean anything."

"Do you understand it?" I asked in wonder.

"Of course. Most of it, at least. Very likely even this child does."

Io shook her head. "I wasn't listening when the priest explained."

"Actually," Pindaros told her, "I provided more of the explanation than he did, thus drawing this trip upon myself; people suppose that poets have all of time at their disposal, a sort of endless summer."

I said, "I feel I have none, or only today. Then it will be gone."

"Yes, I suppose you do. And I'll have to interpret the god again for you tomorrow."

I shook my head. "I'll write it down."

"Of course. I'd forgotten about your book. Very well then. The first phrase is 'Look under the sun, if you would see.' Do you understand that?"

"I suppose it means I should read my scroll. That's best done by daylight, as you pointed out to me a moment ago."

"No, no! When *sun* appears in the utterances of the sibyl, it always refers to the god. So that phrase means that the light of understanding comes from him; it's one of his best-known faculties. The next, 'Sing! Make sacrifice to me!' means that you are to please him if you wish for understanding. He's the god of music and poetry, so everyone who writes or recites poetry, for example, thereby sacrifices to him; he only accepts rams and rubbish of that sort from boors and the bourgeois, who have nothing better to offer him. Your sacrifice is to be song, and it would be well for you to keep that in mind."

I told him I would try.

"Then there's 'But you must cross the narrow sea.' He's an eastern god, having come to us from the Tall Cap Country, and he's symbolized by the rising sun. Thus that's where you're to make your sacrifice."

I nodded, feeling relieved that I would not have to sing at once.

"On to the next stanza. 'The wolf that howls has wrought you woe!' The god informs us that you've been injured by one whose symbol is the wolf, and points out that the wolf is one of nature's singers— thus the form of your sacrifice, if you are to be healed. 'To that dog's mistress you must go!' Aha!"

Pindaros pointed a finger dramatically at the sky. "Here, in my humble opinion, is the single most significant line in the whole business. It is a goddess who has injured you—a goddess whose symbol is the wolf. That can only be the Great Mother, whom we worship under so many names, most of which mean mother, or earth, or grain-giver, or something of that sort. Furthermore, you are to visit a temple or shrine of hers. But there are many such shrines—which is it? Very conveniently the god tells us: 'Her hearth burns in the room below.' That can only be the famous oracle at Lebadeia, not far from here, which is in a cavern. Furthermore, since we wouldn't want to use the coast road with the ships of Thought prowling the Gulf, it lies on the safest road to the Empire and the Tall Cap Country, which clinches it. You must go there and beg her forgiveness for the injury you did her that caused her to injure you. Only when you've done that will the god be able to cure you—otherwise he would make an enemy of her by doing so, which he understandably doesn't want."

"What about the next line?" I asked. "Who is the God Unseen?"

Pindaros shook his head. "That I can't tell you. There was a shrine to the Unknown God in Thought, and that's surely Death's Country now that the army's destroyed everything again. But let's wait and see. Very often in these affairs, you have to complete the first step before you really understand the next. My guess is that when you've visited the Great Mother in Trophonius's Cave, everything will be clear. Not that it's possible for a mortal—"

Io shouted, "Look down there!" her child's voice so shrill that the black man sat bolt upright. She was shielding her eyes against the sun, which was now rising above the lake. I rose to look, and many of the other soldiers stopped what they were doing to follow the direction of her eyes, so that our part at least of the whole great encampment fell silent.

Music came, very faintly, from the shores of the lake, and a hundred people or more capered there in a wild dance. Goats were scattered among them, and these skipped like the dancers, made nervous, perhaps, by two tame panthers.

"It's the Kid," Pindaros whispered, and he motioned for me to come with him.

Io caught my hand as we joined the stream of soldiers going to the lake for water. "Are we invited to their party?"

I told her I did not know.

Over his shoulder Pindaros said, "You're on a pilgrimage. It wouldn't do to offend him."

And so we trooped down the gentle hillside to the lake shore through sweet spring grass and blooming flowers, Pindaros leading, Io clasping my hand, and the black man scowling as he followed some distance behind us. The rising sun had turned the lake to a sheet of gold, and the dawn wind cast aside her dark garments and decked herself in a hundred perfumes. Behind us, the trumpets of the Great King's army sounded again, but though many of the soldiers hurried back to follow them, we did not.

"You look happy, master," Io said, turning her little face up to mine.

"I am," I told her. "Aren't you?"

"If you are. Oh, yes!"

"You said you were brought to the god's house as an offering. Weren't you happy there?"

"I was afraid," she admitted. "Afraid they'd cut my neck like they do the poor animals, and today I've been afraid the god sent me to you to be a sacrifice someplace else. Do they kill little children for this Great Mother the poet is taking us to see?"

"I've no idea, Io; but if they do, I won't let them kill you. No matter how I may have injured her, nothing could justify such a sacrifice."

"But suppose you have to do it to find your home and your friends?"

"Was it because I wanted to find those things so much that I came to the god's house?"

"I don't know," Io said pensively. "My old master and some other men made you come, I think. Anyway, you were there when the steward brought me. But we sat together for a little while, and you talked to me about them."

Her eyes left mine for the line of celebrants that traced the shore. "Latro, look at them dance!"

I did. They leap and whirl, splashing in the shallows, watering the grass with their flying feet and with the wine they drink and pour out even as they dance. The shrilling of the syrinx and the insistent thudding of the tympanon seem louder now. Though masked men leap among them, the dancers are mostly young women, naked or nearly so save for their wild, disordered hair.

Io has joined them, and with her the black man and Pindaros, but I watch only little Io. How gay she is with the vine crown twined round her head, and yet how intent on imitating the frenzy of the hebetic girls, the nation of children left far behind her for so long as the dance lasts.

Pindaros and the black man and I have left it forever, though once long ago it must have been friends and home to them. As for me— though I have left it too, it seems near; and it holds the only home and the only friends I can remember.

# FOUR

## *Awakened by Moonlight*

I TRIED TO READ this scroll; but though the moon shone so brightly that my hand cast a sharp shadow on the pale papyrus, I could not make out the shadowy letters. A woman slept beside me, naked as I, and like me wet with dew. I saw her shiver, the swelling of her thigh and the curve of her hip more lovely than I would have thought anything could be; and yet she did not wake.

I looked about for something with which to cover her, for it seemed to me that we two would surely not have thrown ourselves upon the grass, thus to sleep with no covering where so many others slept too. My manhood had risen at the sight of—oh!—her. I was ashamed by it, so that I wished a covering for myself, also, but there was nothing.

Water glimmered not far off. I went to wash myself, feeling that I had just started from a dream, and that if only I could cool my face I would recall who the woman was and how I came to lie upon the grassy bank with her.

I waded out until the water was higher than my waist; it was warmer than the dew and made me feel I was drawing a blanket about me. Splashing my face, I discovered that my head was swathed in cloth. I tried to pull these wrappings away, but the effort seared like a brand, so that I desisted at once.

Whether it was the water or the pain that awakened me a second time I cannot say, but I found that though the dreams I had half recalled were gone, nothing replaced them. The murmuring water lapped my chest. Above, the moon shone like a white lamp hung to guide some virgin home, and when I looked toward the bank again I saw her, as pure as the moonlight, a bow bent like the increscent moon in her hand and arrows thrust through the cestus at her waist. For a long while, she picked her way among the sleepers on the bank. At last she mounted the hill beyond, and at its very summit vanished.

Now came the sun, striking diamonds from the opalescent crest of each little wave. It seemed to me I saw it as I had seen it rise across the lake before (for I could see by daylight that the water was indeed a lake), though I could not say when. Since then I have read parts of this scroll, and I understand that better.

Even as the moon had awakened me, the sunlight seemed to rouse the rest, who stood and yawned and looked about. I waded back to the bank then, sorry I had stayed to watch the virgin with the bow and not sought farther for some covering for the woman who had slept with me. She slept still, and I cast the shards of the broken wine jar that lay beside her into the lake. Beside this scroll, I discovered a chiton among weapons and armor I felt were mine, and I covered the woman with it.

A grave man of forty years or so asked me if I was of his nation, and when I denied it, said, "But you are no barbarian—you speak our tongue." He was as naked as I, but he had a crown of ivy in place of my own head wrappings; he held a slender staff of pine, tipped with a pinecone.

"Your speech is clear to me," I said. "But I cannot tell you how it came to be so. I . . . am here. That is all I know."

A child who had been listening said, "He does not remember. He is my master, priest."

"Ah!" The priest nodded to himself. "So it is with many. The God in the Tree wipes clean their minds. There is no guilt."

"I don't think it was your god," the child told him solemnly. "I think it was the Great Mother, or maybe the Earth Mother or the Pig Lady."

"They are the same, my dear," the priest told her kindly. "Come and sit down. You are not too young to understand." He seated himself on the grass. At his gesture, the child sat before him, and I beside her.

"By your accent, you are from our seven-gated city of Hill, are you not?"

She nodded.

"Think then of such a man as you must often have seen in the city. He is a potter, we will say. He is also the father of a daughter much like yourself, the husband of such a woman as you shall be, and the son of another. When our men march to war, he takes up his helmet, his hoplon, and his spear; he is a shieldman. Now answer this riddle for me. Which is he? Shieldman, son, husband, father, or potter?"

"He's all of them," the child said.

"Then how will you address him when you speak to him? Assuming you do not know his name?"

The child was silent.

"You will address him according to the place in which you and he find yourselves and the need you have for him, will you not? If you meet him on the drill field, you will say, 'Shieldman.' In his shop, you will say, 'Potter, how much for this dish?'

"You see, my dear, there are many gods, but not so many as ignorant people suppose. So with your goddess, whom you call the Lady of the Swine. When we wish her to bless our fields, we call her the Grain Goddess. But when we think of her as the mother of all the things that spring from the soil, trees as well as barley, wild beasts as well as tame, Great Mother."

The child said, "I think they ought to tell us their names."

"They have many. That is one of the things I would like to teach you, if I can. Were you to go to Riverland, as I went once, you would find the Great Mother there, though the People of the River do not speak of her as we do. A god—or a goddess—must have a name suitable for the tongue of each nation."

"The poet said your god was the Kid," the child told him.

"There you have a perfect example." The priest smiled. "This poet of whom you speak called him the Kid when he spoke to you, and was quite correct to do so. A moment ago, I myself called him the God in the Tree, which is also correct— Why this is extraordinary! Most extraordinary!"

Turning to look where he did, I saw a man as black as the night coming toward us. He was as naked as we, but he carried a spear tipped with twisted horn.

"As I have often told the maenads and satyrs of his train, such rites as we performed yesterday bring the god nearer. Now here is such proof as to be almost miraculous. Come and sit with us, my friend."

The black man squatted and feigned to drink.

"He wants more wine," the child said.

"He does not speak our tongue?"

"I think he understands a little, but he never says anything. Probably somebody laughed once when he tried."

The priest smiled again. "You are wise beyond your years, my dear. My friend, we have no more wine. What we had was drunk last night to the honor of the god, or poured out in libations. If you wish to drink this morning, your drink must be of water." He cupped his hand and turned it over as if pouring wine onto the ground, then pointed to the lake.

The black man nodded to show he understood but remained where he was.

"I was about to say," the priest continued, "when the unfathomable powers of the god produced our friend as an illustration, that our god is commonly called the King from Nysa. Do you, either of you, know where Nysa lies?"

The child and I admitted we did not.

"It is in the country of the black men, up the river of Riverland. Our god was conceived when the Descender noticed in his travels a certain Semele, a princess, daughter of the king of our own seven-gated city. We were a monarchy in those days, you see." He cleared his throat. "The Descender disguised himself as a king merely earthly, and visiting her father's palace as a royal guest won her, though they did not wed."

The child shook her head sadly.

"Alas, his wife Teleia learned of it. Some say, by the by, that Teleia is also the Earth Mother and the Great Mother; though I believe that to be an error. Whether I am correct or not, Teleia disguised herself also, putting on the form of a certain old woman who had been the princess's nurse. 'Your lover is of a state more than earthly,' she told Princess Semele. 'Make him promise to reveal—' "

A handsome man somewhat younger than the priest had joined us, bringing with him a woman whose hair was dark like other women's, but whose eyes were like two violets. The man said, "I don't suppose you remember me, do you, Latro?"

"No," I said.

"I was afraid you wouldn't. I'm Pindaros, and your friend. This girl"—he nodded to the child—"is your slave, Io. And this is . . . ah . . . ?"

"Hilaeira," she said. By then my eyes had left her own, and I saw that she sought to conceal her breasts without appearing to do so. "It's not customary to exchange names during the bacchanalia. Now it's all right. You remember me, don't you?"

I said, "I know I slept beside you and covered you when I woke."

Pindaros explained, "He was struck down by the Great Mother. He forgets everything very quickly."

"How terrible for you!" Hilaeira said, and yet I could see she was glad to learn I had forgotten what we must have done the night before.

The priest had continued to instruct Io while we three spoke among ourselves. Now he said, "—gave to the child god the form of a kid."

Io must have been listening to us; she turned aside to whisper, "He writes things down to remember. Master, yesterday you sat by yourself and wrote for a long time. Then this woman came to you, and you rolled up your book again."

"Teleia, Queen of the Gods, was not deceived. With sweet herbs and clotted honey, she lured the kid away, coming at last to the isle of Naxos, where her bodyguard waited under the command of her daughter, the Lady of Thought."

The last of the worshipers were rising now, many appearing so exhausted and ill that I wondered whether a beaten army could have looked worse. I felt I had seen such an army once; but when I tried to recall it, there was only a dead man lying beside the road and another man, with a curling beard, putting the horse-cloth on his mount.

The black man, who must soon have grown bored with what he could understand of the priest's story, had gone to the lake to drink. Now he returned and gestured for me to rise.

Indicating Pindaros, Hilaeira whispered, "He said the child was your slave. Are you this man's?" When I did not answer she added, "A slave can't own a slave; any slave he buys belongs to his master."

"I don't know," I told her. "But I feel he's my friend."

Pindaros said, "It would be discourteous for us to leave while your young slave is being taught. Afterward we can go looking for the first meal."

I motioned for the black man to sit with me, and he did.

Hilaeira asked, "You really don't remember anything, or know whether you're slave or free? How is that possible?"

I tried to tell her. "There is a mist behind me. Here, at the back of my head. I stepped from it when I woke beside you and went to the lake to drink and wash. Still, I think I'm a free man."

"But the Lady of Thought," continued the priest, "is not called so for nothing. She's a true sophist, and like her city follows her own interests alone, counting promises and honor as nothing. Though she had helped her mother, she saved the heart of the kid from the pot and carried it to the Descender."

He continued so for some time, his voice (like the wind) toying with the fresh grass, while his followers gathered about us; but I will not give the whole of his story. We must go soon, and I do not think it important.

At last he said, "So you see, we have a particular claim upon the Kid. His mother was a princess of our seven-gated city, and it was through the blue waters of our lake—right over there—that he entered the underworld to rescue her. Yesterday you helped celebrate that rescue." Then silence fell.

Pindaros asked, "Are you finished?"

The priest nodded, smiling. "There is a great deal more I could say. But little heads are like little cups, soon so full they can hold no more."

"Then let's go." Pindaros stood up. "There should be some peasants around here who'll be happy enough to sell us a bite."

"I will lead the worshipers back to the city," the priest told him. "If you wish to wait for us, I'll point out the farmhouses that feed us each year."

Pindaros shook his head. "We're on our way to Lebadeia, and we must put a good many stades behind us today if we're to reach the sacred cavern tomorrow."

Hilaeira's violet eyes flashed. "You're on a pilgrimage?"

"Yes, we've been ordered to go by the oracle of the Poet God. Or rather," Pindaros added, "Latro has, and a committee of our citizens has chosen me to guide him."

"May I go with you? I don't know what's happened—you certainly don't want to hear about my personal life—but I've been feeling very religious lately, much closer to the gods and everything than I ever did before. That's why I attended the bacchanal."

"Certainly," Pindaros told her. "Why, it would be the worst sort of beginning if we were to deny a devotee our protection on the road."

"Wonderful!" She sprang erect and brushed his lips with hers. "I'll get my things."

I put on this chiton and these back and breast plates, and took up the crooked sword and the bronze belt I found with them. Io says the sword is Falcata, and that name is indeed written on the blade. There is a painted mask too; Io says the priest gave it to me yesterday, when I was a satyr. I have hung it about my neck by the cord.

We have stopped at this house to eat cakes, salt olives, and cheese, and to drink wine. There is a seat here where I can spread this scroll across my knee in the proper way, and I am making use of it to write all these things down. But Pindaros said a moment ago that we must soon go.

Now there are swarthy men with javelins and long knives coming over the hill.

# FIVE

---

## *Among the Slaves of the Rope Makers*

I T IS THE CUSTOM to beat and abuse captives. Pindaros says this is because the Rope Makers despise their slaves but count us as equals, or at least as near to equals as anyone who is not a Rope Maker can be.

Me they beat more than Pindaros or the black man until we found the old man sleeping. Now they do not beat me. They do not beat Hilaeira or her child much, either; but both weep, and they have done something to the child's legs so that she can scarcely walk. When my hands were freed, I carried her until we halted here.

A moment ago a sentry took this scroll from me. I watched him, and when he left the camp to relieve himself I spoke to the serpent woman. She followed him and soon returned with my scroll in her mouth. Her teeth are long and hollow. She says she draws life through them, and she has drunk her fill.

Now I must write of the earliest things I remember from this day, before they too are lost in the mist: the brightness of the sun and the billows of soft dust that lifted with each step to gray my feet and my legs too, as far as my knees. The black man walked before me. Once I turned to look back and saw Pindaros behind me, and my shadow, black as the black man's, stretched upon the road. I was beaten with a javelin shaft for that. The black man called out, I think telling them not to strike me, and they beat him also. Our hands were bound behind us. I feared they would strike my head because I could not protect it, but they did not.

When the beating was over and we had walked a few steps more, I saw an old black man asleep near the road, and I asked Pindaros (for I knew his name) if they would bind him like the black man with us. Pindaros asked what man I meant. I pointed with my chin as the black man does, but Pindaros could not see him, because he lay half-concealed in the purple shade of a vineyard.

One of the slaves of the Rope Makers asked me what man it was I spoke of. I told him, but he said, "No, that is only the shadow of the vines." I said I would show him the sleeping man if he would allow me to leave the road. I spoke as I did because I thought that if the old black man awakened he would wish to aid the black man with us and might tell someone of our capture.

"Go ahead," the slave who had spoken to me said. "You show me, but if you run, you'll join our friends. And if there's nobody there, you'll pay for them again."

I left the road and knelt beside the sleeping man. "Father," I whispered. "Father, wake up and help us." Because my hands were tied, I could not shake him, but I dropped to one knee and nudged him with the other as I spoke.

He opened his eyes and sat up. He was bald, and the curling beard that hung to his belly was as white as frost.

"By all the twelve, he's right!" the slave who had come with me called to the rest.

"What is it, my boy?" the old man asked thickly. "What's the trouble here?"

"I don't know," I told him. "I'm afraid they're going to kill us."

"Oh, no." He was looking at the mask that hung about my neck. "Why, you're a friend of my pupil's. They can't do that." He rose, swaying, and I could see that he had fallen asleep beside the vineyard because he had drunk as much as he could hold. The black man gleams with sweat, but this fat old man shone more, so that it seemed there was a light behind him.

To the slave who had come with me, he said, "I lost a flute and my cup. Find them for me, will you, my son? I've no desire to bend down at the moment."

The flute was a plain one of polished wood, the cup of wood also; it lay upon its side in the grass not far from the flute.

Several of the slaves of the Rope Makers crowded around staring. I believe the black man was the first such they had ever seen, and now they had seen two. One said, "If you want to keep your flute and cup, old man, you'd better tell us who you are."

"Why, I do." The old man belched softly. "I do very much indeed. I am the King of Nysa."

At that the little girl piped, "Are you the Kid? This morning a priest said the Kid was the King of Nysa."

"No, no, no!" The old man shook his head and sipped twilight-hued wine from his cup. "I'm sure he did not, child. You must learn"— he belched again—"to listen more carefully. Otherwise you will never acquire wisdom. I'm sure he said my pupil was the King *from* Nysa. King *of* Nysa, King *from* Nysa. You see, he was put into my hands when he was yet very young. I tutored him myself, and he has rewarded me"— he belched a third time—"as you behold."

One of the slaves laughed. "By giving you all the wine you wanted. Good enough! I wish my own master would reward me like that."

"Exactly!" the old man exclaimed. "Precisely so! You're a most penetrating young fellow, I must say."

It was then I noticed that Pindaros stood with head bowed.

The oldest slave said, "That's a nice flute you have, old man. Now hear my judgment, for I command here. You must play for us. If you do it well, you can keep it, for it offends the gods to take a good musician's instrument. If you don't play well, you'll lose it, and get a drubbing besides. And if you won't play at all, you've had your last carouse." Several of the others shouted their agreement.

"Gladly, my son. Most gladly. But I won't flute without someone to sing to my music. What about this poor boy with the broken head? Since he found me, may he sing to my fluting?"

The leader of the slaves nodded. "With the same laws. He'd better sing well, or he'll screech a lively tune when we thwack him."

The old man smiled at me, his teeth whiter even than his beard. "Your throat will be clogged with the dust of the road, my boy. You'll need a swallow of this to clear it." He held his cup to my lips, and I filled my mouth with the wine. There is no describing how it tasted—as earth, rain, and sun must taste to the vine, I think. Or perhaps as the vine to them.

Then the old man began to flute.

And I to sing. I cannot write the words here, because they were in no tongue I know. Yet I understood as I sang them, and they told of the morning of the world, when the slaves of the Rope Makers had been free men serving their own king and the Earth Mother.

They told too of the King from Nysa and his majesty, and how he had given the King of Nysa to the Earth Mother to be her foster son, and to the Boundary Stone.

The slaves of the Rope Makers danced as I sang, waving their weapons and skipping and hopping like lambs in the field, and the black man and Pindaros, and the woman and the child danced with them, because the knots that had bound them had been only such as little children tie, knots that loosen at a shaking.

At last the song died at my lips. There was no more music.

Pindaros sat with me for a time beside this fire, while the rest slept. He said, "Two of the lines of the prophecy were fulfilled today. Did you remember?"

I could only shake my head.

" 'Sing then! And make the hills resound! King, nymph, and priest shall gather round!' The god—he was a god, you realize that, don't you, Latro? The god was a king, the King of Nysa. Hilaeira was a nymph last night when we danced to the honor of the Twice-Born God. I'm a priest of the Shining God, because I'm a poet. The Shining God was telling you that you should sing when the King of Nysa called upon you. You did, and he took away the cords that bound us. So that part's all right."

I asked him what part was not all right.

"I don't know," he admitted. "Perhaps everything's all right. But—" He stirred the coals, I suppose to give himself time to think, and I saw his hand shake. "It's just that I've never actually seen an immortal before. You have, I know. You were talking of seeing the River God, back in our shining city."

I said, "I don't remember."

"No, you wouldn't, I suppose. But you may have written about it in that book. You ought to read it."

"I will, when I've written everything I still remember from today."

He sighed. "You're right, that's much more important."

"I'm writing about the King of Nysa, saying he was a black man like the black man with us."

Pindaros nodded. "That was why he came, of course. As King of Nysa, he's that man's king, and no doubt that man's his faithful worshiper. The Great King's army, that's retreating toward the north, levied troops from many strange nations."

Pindaros paused, staring at the flaming coals. "Or it may be that he was following the Kid. He's rumored to do it, and the mysteries we performed yesterday may have called the Kid to us. They're intended to, after all. They say that where the Kid has been, one finds his old tutor asleep; and if one can bind him before he wakes, he can be forced to reveal one's destiny." He shivered. "I'm glad we didn't do that. I don't think I want to know mine, though I once visited the oracle of Iamus to ask about it. I wouldn't want to hear it from the mouth of a god, someone with whom I couldn't argue."

I was still considering what he had said first. "I thought I knew what that word *king* meant. Now I'm not sure. When you say 'the King of Nysa,' is it the same as when you say the army of the Great King is retreating?"

"Poor Latro." Pindaros patted my shoulder as a man might quiet a horse, but there was so much kindness in it I did not mind. "What a pity it would be if you, who can learn nothing new, were to lose the little you know. I can explain, but you'll soon forget."

"I'll write it out," I told him. "Just as I'm writing now about the King of Nysa. Tomorrow I'll read it and understand."

"Very well, then." Pindaros cleared his throat. "In the first days, the nations of men were ruled by their gods. Here the Thunderer was our king in the same way the Great King rules his empire. Men and women saw him every day, and those who did could speak to him if they dared. In just the same way, no doubt, the King of Nysa ruled that nation, which lies to the south of Riverland. If Odysseus had traveled so far, he might still have found him there, sitting his throne among the black men.

"Often the gods took the goddesses in their arms, and thus they fathered new gods. So Homer and Hesiod teach us, and they were skilled poets, the true enlightened singing-birds of the Shining God. Often too the gods deigned to couple with our race; then their offspring were heroes greater than men—but not wholly gods. In this fashion Heracles was born of Alcmene, for example."

I nodded to show I understood.

"In time, the gods saw that there were no thrones for their children, or for their children's children." Pindaros paused to look at the starry sky that mocked our little fire. "Do you remember the farmhouse where we ate, Latro?"

I shook my head.

"There was a chair at the table where the farmer sat to eat. His daughter, that curly-headed imp who dashed about the house shouting, crawled into it while I watched. Her father didn't punish her for it, or even make her climb down; he mussed her hair instead and kissed her. So it was between the gods and their children, who became the kings of men. The kings of the Silent Country, to which we're being taken, still trace their proud lines from Alcmene's son. And if you were to travel east to the Empire instead, you'd find many a place where the Heraclids, the sons and daughters of Heracles, ruled not long ago; and a few where they rule yet, vassals of the Great King."

I asked whether the farmer would not someday wish to sit in his chair again.

"Who can say?" Pindaros whispered. "The ages to come are wisest." After that he remained silent, stroking his chin and staring into the flames.

# SIX
## —
## *Eos*

THE LADY OF THE DAWN is in the sky. I know her name because
a moment ago as I unrolled this scroll she touched it with her shell-
pink finger and traced the letters for me there. I have copied them just
where she drew them—look and see.

I remember writing last night, and what I wrote; but the things
themselves have vanished. I hope I wrote the truth. It is important to
know the truth, because so soon what I write will be all I know.

Last night I slept only a little, though I rolled up this beautiful
papyrus and tied it with its cords so I might sleep. One of the slaves of
the Rope Makers woke me, sitting cross-legged beside me and shaking
me by the shoulder.

"Do you know who I am?" he asked.

I told him I did not.

"I am Cerdon. I let you leave the road when you saw . . ." He waited
expectantly.

"I'm tired," I told him. "I want to sleep."

"I could beat you—you know that? You've probably never had a
real beating in your life."

"I don't know."

The anger drained from his face, though it still looked dark in the
firelight. "That's right, you don't, do you? The poet told me about you.
Do you remember what you saw under the vines?"

It was lost, but I recalled what I had written. "A black man, an old
man and fat."

"A god," Cerdon whispered. His eyes sought the heavens, and in
the clear night found innumerable stars. "I'd never seen one before. I
never even knew anybody who had. Ghosts, yes, many; but not a god."

I asked, "Then how can you be sure?"

"We danced. I too—I couldn't stand still. It was a god, and you saw him when none of the rest of us could. Then when you touched him, all of us could see him. Everyone knows what happened."

Very softly the serpent woman hissed. She was beyond the firelight, but it gleamed in her eyes as in beads of jet. They said, "Give him to me!" and I heard the scales of her belly like daggers drawn from their sheaths as she moved impatiently over the spring grass. "No," I said.

"Yes, we do," Cerdon insisted. "Then I saw him as I see you now. Except that he didn't look like you. He didn't look like any ordinary man."

"No," I said again, and let my eyes close.

"Do you know of the Great Mother?"

I opened them again, and because I lay facedown with my head pillowed on my arms, I saw Cerdon's feet and the crushed grass on which he sat. The grass looked black in the firelight. "No," I said a third time. And then, "Perhaps somewhere I have heard of her."

"The Rope Makers call us slaves, but there was a time when we were free. We pulled the oars in the galleys of Minos, but we did it for silver and because we shared in his glory."

Cerdon's voice, which had been only a whisper before, fell lower, so low I could scarcely hear him, though my ears were so near his lips. "The Great Mother was our goddess then, as she is our goddess still. The Descender overcame her. That's what they say. He took her against her will, and such was his might that she bore him the Fingers, five boys and five girls. Yet she hates him, though he woos her with rain and rends her oaks to show his strength. The Rope Makers say the oaks are his, but that can't be. If they were his, would he destroy them?"

"I don't know," I said. "Perhaps."

"The trees are hers," Cerdon whispered. "Only hers. That's why the Rope Makers make us cut them down, make us dig out their stumps and plow the fields. The whole Silent Country was covered with oak and pine, when we were free. Now the Rope Makers say the Huntress rules Redface Island—because she's the Descender's daughter, and they want us to forget our Great Mother. We haven't forgotten. We'll never forget."

I tried to nod, but my head was too heavy to move.

"We've been slaves, but we're warriors now. You saw my javelins and my sling."

I could not remember, but I said I had.

"A year ago, they would have killed me if I touched them. Only they had arms, and the arms were guarded by armed Rope Makers, always. Then the Great King came. They needed us, and now we're warriors. Who can keep warriors slaves? They will strike him down!"

I said, "And you wish me to strike with you," because it was plain that it was what he had come for.

"Yes!" His spittle flew in my face.

"There's no Rope Maker with you now." I sat up, rubbing my eyes. "Is there? Is this the country of the Rope Makers?"

"They have no country, they have only their city. The Silent Country is ours. But no, we're not there. It's far to the south, on Redface Island."

"Then why go back? You have friends and weapons."

"Our wives are there, and our children. No, you must come with us. You must find the Great Mother and touch her. We will kiss the ground at her feet then, because to kiss the ground is to kiss her lips. We will drive the Rope Makers back into the sea, and she will be our queen. I have your sword, and I'll give it to you again if you'll lead us. You will be her chief priest."

"Then I'll lead you," I said. "In the morning, when we're rested and ready to march."

"Good! Good!" Cerdon smiled broadly, and I saw that some blow had deprived him of three teeth. "You won't forget?"

"I'll write it in this scroll."

"No," he said. "Don't write it, someone may see it."

But I have written anyway, so I will not forget. This is everything Cerdon said and all I said.

When he had gone to another place and stretched himself to sleep, the serpent woman came, saying, "Won't you give him to me?"

"Who am I," I asked, "that I should say yes to you, or no?"

"Give him something of yours," the serpent woman instructed me. "Bathe him or touch him. If you only touch him, it may be enough to make him real."

"He's real now," I said. "A man of blood and bone, just as I am.

You aren't real." What she had said had made me think about those things.

"Less than his dreams," the serpent woman hissed. A tongue of blue fire with two points emerged from her mouth when she spoke. "What is it you wish? Perhaps I can bring it to you."

"Only to sleep," I said. "To sleep and to dream of home."

"Touch him for me then, and I will go away. The fauns bring dreams, and should I meet one, I will order him to bring you the dream you wish."

"Who are you?" I asked her, for I was still thinking of such matters.

"A daughter of Enodia." Her eyes sought out the refulgent moon, riding just above the horizon cradled in a woman's slender arms.

"Is that who holds the moon?" I asked. "I see her, and I would not call her dark."

"Now she is the Huntress," the serpent woman hissed, "and Selene. You may see more of both than you like before you're done."

Then she was gone.

I tried to sleep again, but Sleep would not come, though I saw him standing with closed eyes at the edge of the firelight. In a moment, he turned away to walk among the shadows. I thought then of writing in this scroll but felt too tired. Holding it as near the flames as I dared, I read it for a time.

Pindaros came. "I see you can sleep no more than I," he said. "That's an evil thing, for slaves. A slave must learn to sleep whenever he can."

"Are we slaves?" I asked.

"We are now. No, worse, for we are the slaves of the slaves of the Rope Makers. Soon they will take us to their masters, and then perhaps we'll only be slaves of the Rope Makers. That will be better, if you like, but I won't celebrate it."

"Will we have to twist their ropes for them?"

Pindaros chuckled. "They don't really make rope," he said. "Or anyway, no more than anyone else does. If we're very unlucky, we'll be driven into the mines. That's the worst thing that can befall a slave."

I nodded to show I understood.

"I don't think that will happen to me. The People of Thought may destroy our shining city and take my property—they hate us—but I have friends even in Thought, and certain talents."

"You're worried about the little girl and me." I looked across the fire at the sleeping child.

"And Hilaeira, and the black man too. If I'm freed, I'll buy freedom for all of you if I can. But it might help if you could sing for the Rope Makers as you sang today to the playing of the god. They love choral music, and they don't much value soloists; still no one could resist that, and no one would keep such a singer a slave. Can you do it?"

Hoping to please him, I tried; but I could not recall the words I had sung, nor any tune.

"It will be all right," Pindaros said. "I'll get us all freed some way. You don't remember, I know; I could see it in your eyes. It was a miracle, and you've forgotten it."

"I'm sorry," I told him, and I was.

"You haven't offended me." He sighed. "And I'm sorrier for you, Latro, than for any other man I know."

I asked whether he recalled the words.

"No," he said. "Not really. But I remember how they sounded, that great rushing swing like waves beating upon a cliff that ended in larks and thunder. That's the way poetry ought to sound."

I nodded because he seemed to expect it.

"As my own never has. But after hearing your song, I think I may be getting a bit closer. Listen to this:

> "Arrows have I for the hearts of the wise,
>      Straight-drawn by Nature to bear off the prize,
>           But lift I my bow to the crowd on the plain,
>      The fools hear but wind, and some fool must explain.

"Do you like it?"

"Very much," I said.

"Well, I don't. But I like it better than anything I've done before tonight. In our shining city, there are—there were, I ought to say— half a dozen of us who tried our hands at verse now and then. That was the way we put it, 'tried our hands,' as though there were no difference between composing poetry and weaving mats beside the fire. We met monthly to sing our latest lines to one another, and pretended not to notice that none of them was ever heard again. If mine had seemed the best to me when our dinner was over, why, I was the cock of the walk—in my own eyes—for the month that followed. How proud I was of my little ode for the Pythia's games!"

I said, "I suppose everyone's vain in one way or another. I know I am."

Pindaros shrugged. "Your good looks are real, and so is your strength, as you proved just today. But as for us—now I see that we were only noisy boys, when we should have been men or been silent. After hearing the god this afternoon, it may be that I will be a man someday. I hope so. Latro, I wouldn't boast to you like this—and that's what it is, boasting—if I didn't know you'll forget everything I've said."

"I'll write it down," I told him.

"To be sure!" Pindaros laughed softly. "The gods have their revenge, as always.

> "We call for night to hide our acts,
> But Night, a god, gives God the facts."

"I like that, too," I said.

"Composed for you this moment and thrown hot from the forge. Still, there may be something in it. 'We've need of night . . .' "

"Pindaros, is there really a god of night?"

"There are at least a dozen."

"With a body like a snake's and a head like a woman's, a woman with black hair that has never seen a comb?"

He stared at me for a moment in silence, and at last stirred the fire as he had before. "You've seen that, haven't you? No, that's no goddess—it's a monster of some kind. Heracles was supposed to have rid this part of the world of them; but Heracles has been on the Mountain for four hundred years, and I suppose they're creeping back. Do you see it now?"

I shook my head.

"Good. I was hoping to get some sleep before these slaves stirred their lazy legs. If you see your monster again, don't touch it. Promise?"

"I promise." I almost said that if I were to touch him, that might be enough; but I did not.

He rose and stretched. "Then I'll try to sleep. A sleep without dreams, I hope. Empty of horrors. I ought to copy you and write myself a note forbidding me to talk to you in the dark. Alas, I lack your diligence. Good night again, Latro."

"Good night, Pindaros."

When he was gone, a small arm circled my waist. "I know you," I told its owner. "You're Io. I've been reading about you in this scroll."

"You're my master," the child said. "They had no right to do what they did to me. Only you."

"What did they do?" I asked, but she did not answer. Putting my arm about her shoulders, I looked at her face in the firelight and saw how many tears had furrowed those dusty cheeks. "If the serpent woman comes again, I'll tell her she can't have you."

She shook her head. "It's not that. I ran away, and now I've been punished for it."

"Did you run away from me, little Io? I wouldn't punish you if you did."

She shook her head. "From the Bright God. And I lied when I said he'd given me to you."

"Perhaps he did," I told her. Holding her close, I watched the silent figures in the shadows for some sign, but there was none. "The gods are not at all like us, little Io."

# PART TWO

# SEVEN

## *Beside the Beached Ships*

THIS LITTLE TENT SEEMS SMALL indeed. When I woke a short time ago, I discovered this scroll. Being barred from leaving by the sentry at the door and not wishing to disturb the black man who shares this tent with me (he was busily carving a doll), I resolved to read it from the beginning.

I had hardly started when a man in a fine corselet of bronze came in, and I supposed him to be the healer of whom I had just read. He disabused me of that notion at once, saying, "My name's Hypereides, fellow. Hypereides the Trierarch, and I'm your master now. How can you pretend not to know me?"

I said, "I'm afraid I forget very quickly."

He scowled ferociously and pointed a finger at me. "Now I've got you! If you forget, how can you remember that?"

I explained that I had just read it and pointed to the place where it says, "The Healer says I forget very quickly, and that it is because of a wound I suffered in a battle."

"Wonderful," Hypereides said. "Wonderful! You've an answer for everything."

"No," I said. "I only wish I did. If you're not the healer, can you tell me where I am now?"

There was a stool in one corner of the tent. (I am using it now to write this.) He pulled it over and sat down, motioning for me to sit on the ground before him. "Armor's heavy stuff," he said, "something I never considered as a youngster, when I used to watch the soldiers ride past in the Panathenaea. You learn soon enough to sit when you can and as high as you can, so it's not too hard to stand up." He took off his helmet with its gorgeous crest of blue horsehair and scratched his bald head. "I'm too old for this sort of thing, let me tell you. I fought at Fennel Field, my boy, ten years ago. There was a battle! Would you like to hear the story?"

"Yes," I said. "Very much."

"You really would? You're not just saying that to please a man older than yourself?"

"No, I'd like it. Perhaps it would recall to me the battle in which I was wounded."

"You don't remember my telling you yesterday? No, I see you don't. I didn't mean to cause you such pain." He cleared his throat. "I'll make it up to you, my boy. I'm a wealthy man back home, though you mightn't think it to see me parading about in this stuff. I'm in leather, you see. Everybody in leather knows Hypereides." He paused and his smile faded. "Three ships the Assembly laid on me."

"Three ships?"

"Build them, outfit them, pay the rowers. It cost . . . well, you wouldn't believe what it cost. Want to take a look at them, my boy?"

"Yes. I'm sure I've seen ships before, somewhere, and they were very interesting."

"Certainly," Hypereides said. "You too."

Looking around, I saw that the black man had laid down the doll and his little knife and was asking by signs whether he might go with us.

"It's all right," Hypereides told the guard at the door. "In fact, I don't think we'll need you here any more. Go find Acetes and ask him what he wants you to do."

Three ships had been drawn up on the beach, and their red-painted sides were covered with men hammering hair and pine tar into their seams.

"We were hit by a blow rounding Cape Malea," Hypereides explained. "It loosened them up, and by the time we got to Tower Hill we were taking on more water than I liked. A man *does* learn a bit about ships in the leather trade, I'll admit; and I thought it better to caulk them now than to try to take them back home as they were, and for all I know be handed some urgent message and told to put to sea again at once. Certainly it wouldn't do to run into a few stray barbarians and find them in better shape than we are."

"Who are these barbarians?" I asked.

"Why, the Great King's navy, of course. With the help of Boreas, we beat them in the Strait of Peace, let me tell you. There was a battle! I wish you could see our rams, my boy; the bronze itself is scarred. There was a time—I don't expect you to believe this, yet it's the plain fact— when there was so much blood in the sea we floated a span deeper than usual, just as if we were running up an estuary. I'm telling you, every man you see here fought like a hero and every oar rose like a slaughtering spear."

He pointed. "That's my personal command in the middle there, *Europa*. A hundred and ninety-five men to pull her oars. A dozen soldiers besides myself, and four Sons of Scoloti to draw the bow. The soldiers don't have to be paid, being citizens like me or foreigners who live with us. But the rowers, my boy! Great gods, the rowers! Three obols a day for every stick, and their food. And wine for their water! A drachma every day for each Son of Scoloti. *Two* for the kybernetes. That's almost a dozen owls a day, just for *Europa*. With the other ships, it comes to twenty."

He paused, frowning down at the sandy ground, then looked up and smiled. "Did you catch the signification of her name, my boy? Europa was carried off by the Thunderer in the shape of a bull. So when people see *Europa*, they think of a bull—wait till you see her mainsail! And what does a bull make them think of? Why, leather, of course. Because the best and strongest leather is bull's hide. And let me tell you, my boy, there'll be a lot of shields to be refitted when this war's over. Leather—bull, bull—Europa, *Europa*—Hypereides. Besides, Europa gave her name to the whole continent, bigger than her brother's place and Libya's combined, and the barbarians come from the other side. Europe—Europa. *Europa*—Hypereides. So who're you going to buy your leather from when the war's over?"

"You, sir, I promise." But I was looking at the ships and thinking I could never have seen anything made by men half so lovely, though they smelled of tar and lay on their sides like three beached logs. I said, "If Europa the woman was as slender and graceful as your ships, it's no wonder the Thunderer ran away with her. Any man would want to." I did not want him to guess I could not remember who the Thunderer might be.

Hypereides had put his helmet on, pushed back so the visor seemed the bill of a cap. Now he took it off again to rub his head. "I've always thought she must have been on the weighty side, myself," he said. "I mean, what sort of woman would a god want to turn himself into a bull for? Besides, he carried her on his back, and his choosing a bull's shape for that makes it appear cargo was a consideration."

He laid his arm across my shoulders. "It's quite wrong, my boy, to think that for a woman to give you pleasure she has to be as lissome as a lad from the palaestra. When we get back home, I'll introduce you to a hetaera called Kalleos. Then you'll see. Besides, a girl with some flesh on her is easier to catch; when you get to be my age you'll appreciate the importance of that."

While we stood looking at the ships from a distance, the black man had run down to them and poked about. As Hypereides spoke of the hetaera, he came leaping back to squat before us, pointing with his chin to the ships and the sparkling sea and making many little marks in the sand with his fingers.

"Look there," Hypereides said. "This fellow's seen the barbarian navy. Both of you must have, because you were with their army, and their ships followed it clear around the Water."

"Were there really so many?" I asked him.

"More than a thousand, and that's not counting the traders that carried food for the troops, or the special ships the Great King had built for his cavalry horses. Why, in the Strait of Peace you couldn't see the water for blood and wreckage."

He squatted beside the black man. "Here's the Long Coast. Right here's Tieup, where my old warehouse stood before they burned it; Megareos, my manager, is captain of *Eidyia* now. The man I had on Ceos has *Clytia*.

"Tieup's where our navy was before it went up to Artemisium. Here's the island of Peace over here, and here's Peace. We only had about three hundred ships, and we beached 'em in these three bays on the island the night before. Mine were in this bay here—all our city's were. You can keep a trader at sea half a month, my boy, but a warship has to touch land nearly every night, because there's so many aboard you can't carry enough water for 'em."

I said, "I see."

"Themistocles was with the navy, and he had a slave of his swim the channel and demand an audience with the Great King. This slave said Themistocles had sent him, which was true enough, and Themistocles wanted to be satrap of the Long Coast. Then he warned the Great King that our navy was going to slip off the next day to reinforce Tower Hill." Hypereides chuckled. "And the Great King believed it, too. He sent all the ships from Riverland around to the other end of the bay to cut us off.

"Then the strategists—mostly Themistocles and Eurybiades the Rope Maker, from what I've heard—sent the ships from Tower Hill to make sure the Riverlanders, over there, didn't come up behind us. A lot of people in the city still think the ships from Tower Hill deserted, and you can see why: the rumor the slave started, and then their leaving the rest of the fleet."

The black man pointed with his chin, and I saw a sailor striding up the beach toward us. Hypereides conferred with him for a moment, then told us to return to this tent. "I'm putting you on your honor," he said. "I don't want to have to keep you two chained like the others, but if you try to leave, I'll have to do it. Understand?"

I told him I did.

"But you'll forget—I forgot that." He turned to the sailor and said, "Stay with them until I send somebody to relieve you. I don't think you'll have any trouble; just don't let them wander away."

He is with us now; his name is Lyson. He asked whether Hypereides had told me about the Battle of Peace. I said he had begun but had been called away, and I was eager to hear the rest.

Lyson grinned at that and said Hypereides had taken us to see his ships the day before as well and had recounted the events of the battle while we looked at them. Lyson had been whittling pegs then and had heard most of it. "He took you to see the other prisoners too, because he wanted to ask them questions about you. The little girl gave you that book, and Hypereides let you keep it; and he let that fellow have a knife like mine because he showed he wanted to whittle."

I asked why these other prisoners were kept chained when we were not.

"Because they're from Cowland, of course. But you, you're Hyper-eides's ideal audience, one he can tell his stories to over and over." Lyson laughed.

I said, "I suppose the crews of all three ships are making fun of me."

"Oh, no. We've got too much to do for that. Anyway, we're mostly laughing at Hypereides, not at you. And we wouldn't laugh at him if we didn't like him."

"Is he a good commander?"

"He worries too much," Lyson said. "But yes, he is. He knows a lot about winds and currents, and it's good to have somebody on a ship who worries too much. He's an able merchant too—that's why we were sent here—and so he gets good food for us cheap and doesn't stint as much as most of them."

"It seems strange to have a merchant commanding warships," I said. "I'd think a horseman would do it."

"Is that how it would be in your own country?"

"I don't know. Perhaps."

"In Thought we keep the horsemen on their horses where they belong. But listen here, if you weren't lying to Hypereides and you really don't know where you're from, you've only to look for a city where a horseman would be put in charge of warships. It's someplace in the Empire, I suppose."

I asked where that lay.

"To the east. Who'd you think we were fighting in the Strait of Peace, anyway?"

"The Great King, so Hypereides said."

"And the Great King rules the Empire. You were in his army. We've got your sword and pot-lids now. How'd you think you got that wound?"

I shook my head and somewhere found the memory that had once been painful to do so, though it was no longer. "In a battle. Other than that, I don't know."

"Of course not, poor stick. Somebody ought to look at it for you, though. Those bandages are dirty enough to beach on."

The black man had been listening to us, and though he did not speak, he seemed to understand what he heard. Now he said by signs that if he were allowed to, he would take off my bandages, wash them (vividly pantomiming how he would scrub them on a stone and beat them with another), dry them in the sun, and replace them.

"Ah," Lyson said, "but if I go with you, this one'll wander off."

The black man denied it, clasping my hand and saying by signs that he would not leave me, nor I him.

"He'll forget."

The black man cocked his head to show he did not understand the word.

Lyson pointed to his own head and traced the ground with his finger as though writing or drawing, then smoothed the imaginary scratches away.

The black man nodded and pretended to draw too, then with his finger indicated the course of the sun across the vault of heaven, and when it had set rubbed the drawing out.

"Ah, it takes all day."

The black man nodded again and unwound my bandages, and the two of them went off together, fast becoming friends.

As for me, I finished the reading of this scroll I had earlier begun. Now they have returned, and I write but feel I know less than ever. So many strange things—events I cannot credit—are described here. So many people are mentioned whom I have forgotten. Surely Io was the little girl who gave me this yesterday; but where are Pindaros, Hilaeira, and Cerdon? Where is the serpent woman, and how did the black man and I come to be where we are?

# EIGHT

## *At Sea*

OUR SHIP ROLLS IN A way that makes it hard to write, but I am
learning to allow for it. The sailors say it is often much worse and
I must walk and write and drink on board, and do everything else, before
the sea grows rougher. "When we round Cape Malea, forget your home,"
they say; but I remember it, though I have forgotten every other place.

Our ship is the *Europa*, the largest of the three, with triple-banked
oars. The men who sit highest have the longest oars, and they think
themselves the best because they can spit on the rest; but all get the
same pay. Now we are under sail, and they have no work, save for one
or two who are bailing and the like. Soon there will be work enough,
they say. Some are sleeping on the rowing benches, though all slept, I
think, last night.

I am writing in the bow, leaning comfortably back against the high,
straight post that marks the front of our ship. Below it (I remember,
though I cannot see it from where I sit) is our ram. It does not look like
a real ram at all—the dark eyes painted on the bow make the green
metal look like the bill of an angry bird, at least to me. I can see the
ram through the water when I stand and look over the bow. The water
is sky-colored and very clear; but there is a second sky below, and I
cannot see to the bottom.

A big rope runs from my bow post to the very top of the mast, and
there are more such ropes there, going to both sides of the ship and to
the stern, all to brace the mast against the pull of the sail. The one above
my head bends a trifle, but the rest are stretched as straight as spears;
the wind is behind us now, and our rowers are idling on their benches
while the wide sail labors for them.

This sail hangs from a long, tapered yard raised almost to the top of the mast. There is a bull painted on it, not just a head like the carved bull's head on the sternpost, but every part; and I think I like him best of all our decorations. He is black, his nose is gold, and his blue eye rolls to see the woman sitting on his back. He has a brave tail, and it seems to me that if I were on one of the other ships it would appear that his golden hoofs ran upon the sea.

The woman who rides him has red hair and blue eyes, and two chins. She smiles as she rides; her hands stroke the bull's horns.

The long, narrow deck runs from the place where I sit to the stern, where two sailors hold the steering oars and the kybernetes watches them and the sail. The prisoners are chained to the mast where it goes through the deck.

Our captain's name is Hypereides. He is a man of middle years, bald and thick at the waist but erect and energetic. Not as tall as I. He came to talk with me, and I asked him the name of the country to our left. He said, "That's Redface Island, my boy."

It surprised me and I laughed.

"Not much of a name, is it? But that's all the name it has. Named for old Pelops, who was king there hundreds and hundreds of years ago."

"Did he have a red face?"

"That's what they say. The satirists make jokes about him, saying it was red from drinking, or that he was always angry, stamping up and down and sneezing. If you ask me, neither can be right. How could his mother know he was going to drink too much? Maybe he was angry all the time as a baby—the gods know a lot of them are—but who ever heard of one's being named for it? If you ask me, my boy, he was born with one of those red patches on his face that some children have. Anyway, that's where Tower Hill is, and the Rope Makers' city."

Then he told me about the Battle of Peace and how his ships had been hidden in a bay on the isle of Peace. Very early in the morning, when there was still fog on the water, the barbarians' ships had come into the strait. A lookout had seen them through the fog and heard the chants of their rowers, and he sent a signal. Hypereides and his ships, and all the other ships of the city came out then, and the Rope Makers' ships too. "You should have seen us, my boy—every man shouting out the Victory Hymn, and every oar bent like a bow!"

They met the barbarians ram to ram, and the ships from Peace came

out of the bay behind the Dog's Tail and caught the barbarians in the
flank; but there were so many barbarian ships that even when they fled
they were a great fleet. No one knows where they are now, and most of
the ships from Thought and Rope, and all the ships from Tower Hill,
are hunting them among the islands.

Hypereides said that I must have fought for the Great King, and I
asked him if I were a barbarian. "Not a real barbarian," he said. "Because
you talk like a civilized man. Besides, there were a lot of us fighting for
the Great King—almost as many as were on our side. See those people
I've got chained up? They're from Hill—you can tell by the way they
talk. Their city fought for him, and we mean to burn it around their
ears, just as he burned ours."

The sun was high and hot, but the base of the mast was in the
shadow of the sail; so when Hypereides went to talk to the kybernetes,
I went to talk to the prisoners. One of the bowmen was watching them,
and he looked to Hypereides to see whether he minded. Hypereides had
his back to us, and the bowman said nothing.

I want to write about the bowmen before I forget that I intended
to. They wear leggings and tall fox-fur caps. Their clothes look very
uncomfortable, and while I was talking to the prisoners the bowman
watching them took off his cap to fan himself.

Their curved bows are of wood and horn, and they bend backward
now because they are not strung. It seems to me the right way to carry
arrows is over the back, but the bowmen have their quivers at their
waists. The quivers have a beard at the top that folds over the opening
to keep out the spray.

The bowmen have cheeks that come straight up to their fierce eyes,
like the cheek-pieces of a helmet. Their eyes and hair are lighter than
ours, and their beards are longer. They cut the hair from their enemy's
dead and wear it on their belts and wipe their hands on it. They cannot
speak the tongue I speak to Hypereides and the rest as well as I can,
and they cannot speak the tongue in which I am writing this at all.
They smell of sweat. That is all I know of them.

No, there is one thing more, which is why I wrote all I just did. It
is that the bowman who watches the prisoners watches me as no one
else does. Sometimes I think he is afraid, sometimes that he wants some

favor. I do not know what his look may mean; but I thought I should write of it here, to read when I have forgotten.

The prisoners from Hill are a man, his wife, and their daughter. When I came to them, they called me Latro. At first I thought they believed me such a one—a hired soldier or a bandit. But they have nothing to steal, and who has hired me? Then I understood that *Latro* is my name and they knew me. I sat on the deck beside them and said that it was cooler there and if they wished I would bring them water.

The man said, "Latro, have you read your book?"

I glanced about and saw it in the beakhead where I had left it. I told the man I had been examining the ship and had not.

The woman saw it too, and looked frightened. "Latro, it will blow away!"

"No, it won't," I told her. "The stylus is heavy, and I've put it through the cords."

"It's very important that you read it," the man said. "You offered to bring us water. I don't want water—they gave us enough earlier. I want you to bring me your book instead. I swear by the Shining God not to harm it."

I hesitated, but the child said, "Please, master!" and there was something in her voice I could not resist. I got it and brought it back, and the man took it and wrote a few words on the outside.

I told him, "That's not the best way. Unroll it like this, and you can write on the inner surface. Then when the book's closed, the writing's protected."

"But sometimes the scribe writes where I have written too, when he wishes to leave some message for a person who otherwise would not open the book. He might write, 'Here are the laws of the city,' for example."

"That's so," I admitted. "I'd forgotten."

"You speak our language well," he said. "Can you read what I've written?"

I shook my head. "I think I've seen letters like those before, but I can't read them."

"Then you must write it yourself. Write, 'Read me every day,' in your own language."

I took the stylus and wrote what he had told me, just above his own writing.

The child said, "Now if you'll read it, you'll know who you are and who we are."

Her voice pleased me, and I patted her head. "But there is so much to read here, little one. I've unrolled it enough to see that it's a long, long scroll, and the writing is very small. Besides, it was written with this and not with ink, and so the writing is gray, not black, which makes it hard to read. You can tell me these things, if you know them, much faster than I could read about them."

"You have to go to the house of the Great Mother," the child announced solemnly. Then she recited a poem. When it was over she said, "Pindaros was taking you there."

"I'm Pindaros," the man told me. "The citizens of our shining city designated me as your guide. I know you don't remember, but I swear it's the truth."

A black man who had been sleeping with the sailors rose and climbed from his bench to the deck where we sat. It seemed to me that we had met before, and he looked so friendly and cheerful that I smiled to see him now.

He exclaimed, *"Hah!"* when he saw me smile. Some of the sleeping men stirred at the sound, and those who were not asleep stared at us. The bowman, who had been watching and listening, put his hand to the knife in his belt.

"You must be less noisy, my friend," Pindaros said.

The black man grinned in reply and pointed from his heart to mine, and then, triumphantly, from mine to his.

"You mean he knows you," Pindaros said. "Yes, perhaps he does, a bit."

I said, "Is he a sailor? He doesn't look like the others."

"He's your comrade. He was taking care of you before Hilaeira and Io and I met you. Perhaps you saved his life in the battle, but he was using you to beg when I first saw you." To the black man he said, "You got a great deal by your begging, too. I don't suppose you still have it?"

The black man shook his head and pretended to gash his arm with his knife. Filling his hand with the unseen blood, he counted it out as money, making a little click with his tongue for the sound made by each imaginary coin as he put it on the deck. When he was finished he indicated me.

The child said, "He gave it to the slaves that night when we camped, while you were writing poetry and talking to Latro. It was for the slaves Latro killed, because the slaves were going to kill him when we got to the Silent Country."

"I doubt if the Rope Makers would have let them. Not that it matters; I had ten owls, but they got them in Tower Hill. I'd rather we were prisoners in Rope than in Tower Hill, but even Tower Hill would be preferable to Thought." Pindaros sighed. "We're their ancient enemies, and they are ours."

Hypereides had been telling me how the ships of Thought had fought the barbarians, implying that I was a barbarian myself; now I asked Pindaros if his city and Thought were worse enemies.

His laugh was bitter. "Worse by far. You forget, Latro, and so perhaps you've forgotten that brothers can be enemies more terrible than strangers. Our fields are rich, and theirs are poor; thus they envied us long ago and tried to take what was ours by force. Then they turned to trading, growing the olive and the vine, and exchanging oil, fruit, and wine for bread. They became great makers of jars too and sold them everywhere. Then the Lady of Thought, who loves sharp dealing, showed them a vein of silver."

The black man's eyes opened wide, and he leaned forward to catch every word, though I do not think he understood them all.

"They had been rich. Now they grew richer, and we proved no wiser than they and tried to take what was theirs. There is hardly a family in our shining city that is not related to them in some way, and hardly a man in theirs—except the foreigners—who's not a cousin of ours. And so we hate one another, and cease to hate every four years when our champions give their strength to the Descender; then we hate again, worse than ever, when the games are done." He pursed his mouth to spit but thought better of it.

I looked at the woman. She had eyes like thunderheads and seemed far more lovely to me than the woman painted on our sail. I did not wish to think this, but I thought that if Pindaros was a slave, I might somehow buy her and her child. "And are we friends," I asked her, "since we've traveled together?"

"We met at the rites of the God of Two Doors," the woman said. She smiled then, remembering something I could not recall; and I felt she would not object, that she would be content to live with me and leave her husband wherever his fate might take him. "Then the slaves of the Rope Makers came," she said, "and while Pindaros and the black man faced their first antagonists, you killed three. But the others were going to kill Io and me, and Pindaros stepped in front of you and made you stop. For a moment I thought you were going to cut him down, and so did he, I think. Instead you dropped your sword, and they bound your hands and beat you, and made you kiss the dust before their feet. Yes, we're friends."

I said, "I'm glad I've forgotten that surrender."

Pindaros nodded. "I wish I could forget it too; in many ways, your state is a most enviable one. Nevertheless, now that the Shining God has directed you to the Great Mother, you'd better go to her and be cured if you can."

"Who is this Great Mother?" I asked him. "And what does the child's poem mean?"

Then he told me of the gods and their ways. I listened intently as he spoke, just as I had to Hypereides's account of the Battle of Peace; but though I do not know what it was I hoped to hear from each, I knew when each was finished that I had not heard it.

Now the sun is hidden behind our sail, though I sit in the bow again; the ship rocks me as a mother rocks her child. There are voices in the waves, voices that laugh and sing and call out one to another.

I listen to them too, hoping to hear some mention of my home and the family and friends I must surely have there.

# NINE

## *Night Comes*

ACROSS THE SEA, BLACK SHADOWS race like chariots. Though it will soon be too dark for me to write here, I will write as much as I can, and if I cannot write everything where I am, I will go to one of the fires and write there, then sleep.

I had hardly put away this stylus when the kybernetes spoke to the sailors, who stopped gambling and talking to furl the sail, strike the mast, and run out their oars.

It is wonderful to travel in such a slim, swift ship under sail; but it is far more so when the rowers strain at the oars and the ship leaps from the water at every stroke and falls back shouting. Then the wind is not behind the ship, but the ship makes her own, which you feel full in your face though silver spray blows across the bow.

Then too the flute boy plays, and the sailors all sing to his piping to keep the stroke; their song calls up the sea gods, who come to the surface to hear it, their ears like shells, their hair like sea wrack. For a long time I stood in the bow watching them and seeing the land brought ever nearer, and I felt that I myself was a god of the waters.

At last, when the land was so close I could see the leaves on the trees and the stones on the beach, the kybernetes came and stood beside me; and seeing that he meant to give no order for a few moments more, I ventured to tell him how beautiful I thought his ship and the others, which we had outdistanced and now saw behind us.

"There's none better," he said. "Hardly one as good. Say what you please about Hypereides, but he spared no expense on *Europa*. You may say it was to be expected, because he meant to take the command himself; but there's many another who did the same and got his timber cheap anyhow. Not Hypereides. He's got the wit to see that his honor's gone aboard her as well as his life."

"He must be brave too," I said, "to take charge of this ship himself when he could have stayed safely at home."

"Oh, he couldn't have done that," the kybernetes told me, glancing at the beach. "They're foolish enough in the Assembly at times, but never such fools as to let the men who supply the army and navy stay clear of the fighting. Not that Hypereides would have been safe in the city anyway; the barbarians burned it. Still, he could have served on land if he wanted. A good many did. But look at *Clytia* there. She's a fine ship too. My brother's kybernetes on her. Do you know what that poet said to me?"

Not knowing who the poet might be, I shook my head.

"He said her oars, with the foam on them, made her look like a bird with four white wings. And it's true—just look. He may be a pig from Cowland, but he's a fine poet all the same. Were you there when he sang for us last night?"

I said, "I'm afraid I don't remember."

"Ha, ha! You drank too much and fell asleep!" He slapped my back. "You've the soul of a sailor. We'll train you to the oar when that head wound heals."

"Were they good poems?"

The kybernetes nodded. "The men couldn't get enough of him. I'm going to ask Hypereides to make him perform for us again tonight. Not that I'll have to ask, I expect." He raised his voice. *"Easy now! Easy!"*

"Are you going to beach the ships here?"

"Bet on it, stick. The wind's favoring, so we *might* round the cape before sundown; and if we hadn't a day to spare, I'd try it. But if there was trouble, we'd have to spend the night at sea, and that's no joke. I told Hypereides we ought to put in, and he agreed. There's a little place called Teuthrone not far from here, and we may be able to buy some fresh food—what we got from Tower Hill's about gone."

He shouted another order, and all the oars on one side remained raised when they left the sea. The ship spun about like a twig in an eddy. In a moment more, the oars were backing water, rowing us backward to the shore. Half a dozen sailors dove from the stern and swam to the beach like seals. Two more threw them coils of rope.

"*Ship oars!*" the kybernetes shouted. Then: "*Over the side!*"

I must have shown how astonished I was, because he rubbed his hands and said, "Yes, it's a good crew. I chose most of them myself, and the rest are men who worked for Hypereides before the war."

By that time there was hardly a score of people left aboard—the kybernetes and I, the soldiers (whose breastplates and greaves would have sunk them like stones had they dived into the sea), the bowmen, the black man, the three prisoners, and Hypereides. Without her crew, the ship seemed so light I was afraid she might turn over.

"Come here!" the kybernetes called. He waved, and the soldiers and prisoners joined us in the bow, making the stern rise a bit more.

Ashore the sailors were heaving at their ropes. I felt the keel scrape, come free, then scrape again. The deck began to tilt and we grabbed the railing.

"Don't jump now," the kybernetes said, seeing that I was considering it. "That's a rock bottom."

The deck was almost too steep for us to keep our footing when we made our way aft, but from there it was easy to climb over the taffrail and onto the beach without so much as getting our feet wet.

By the time I stood on land, the sailors were already gathering driftwood for a fire and the other ships were backing water a stade or so from the beach. The black man and I helped collect wood, having seen that it was a point of honor with the sailors to get the best before the crews of the other ships reached shore.

This coast is low and rocky, with a few scrubby trees; and yet it cannot really be said that beauty ends where the clear seawater comes to shore. While I watched, a hawk came racing down the ridge, caught the updraft from the sea, and soared on it like a gull, never moving a wing; when I saw it, I saw this rocky land too for what it is, a finger of the forest on a hand held out to the sea.

Hypereides took three soldiers and a score of sailors and went into the village to buy supplies. Acetes posted two more soldiers on the ridge as sentries. The rest of us threw off our clothes and plunged into the water to swim and wash. Even the prisoners, I noticed, were allowed to wash, though because of their chains they could not swim. I myself swam only a little, careful to keep the bandages on my head out of the water. I noticed that the bowmen went some distance away so they might wash out of sight of the rest of us.

When I returned to the beach, the child was sitting on a stone beside my possessions. I thanked her for watching them, and she said, "I didn't want anyone to take your book, master. Then you wouldn't know who you are, or who I am."

"Who are you?" I asked her. "And why do you call me master?"

"I'm your slave Io."

I explained that I had thought her the daughter of the couple with whom she had been chained.

"I knew you did," she said. "But we only met them a little while ago. I'm your slave, given you as your personal property by the Shining God when you were in Hill."

I shook my head.

"That's the truth, master, I swear by the club of Heracles. And if you'll just read your book you'll find out all about it, and about the curse the Great Mother laid on you. Then you'll see it isn't right for me to be like this"—she held up her chain to show me—"when you're free. I should be free too, to serve you."

I tried to recall what the woman had told me this morning. "The soldiers captured us when we were going somewhere."

"Not these soldiers, master. Those were the slaves of the Rope Makers. They beat you, and they treated me like a woman and made me bleed there, though I'm not a woman yet. Hilaeira says I won't have a baby, but she might." Io sighed, recalling much pain and weariness, I think, that I have forgotten.

"Then we met some real soldiers, shieldmen with helmets and big spears. They made the slaves of the Rope Makers give us up. I hid your book because I was afraid they'd take it from you, and they made us go to Tower Hill, but I don't think the people in Tower Hill wanted to keep us—they're afraid of the Rope Makers like everybody else, and they didn't want to have prisoners that were taken from them. But they're afraid of the People of Thought too, and the soldiers from my city helped burn theirs. So after a while they gave us to Hypereides. He separated us, but I could see he liked you, so when you came to talk to me I gave your book back. I had it under my peplos, with the cords around my waist. Did you read it? I told you to."

"I don't know," I said.

"Maybe you did. But if you didn't write anything afterward, it doesn't matter now."

"You're a very knowing little girl," I told her, pulling on my chiton.

"It hasn't helped me much. I was owned by a pretty nice family back in Hill. Now I'm here, and all I've got out of the trip is a bath. Will you talk to Hypereides and ask him to let me take off my chain?"

While I tied my sandals, I said, "You can't take off a chain as though it were one of these."

"Yes, I can. They have them to chain up bad sailors and barbarian prisoners, so they aren't made to fit somebody as little as me. It's tight, but I can get my foot out. I did it last night."

"Show me."

She crossed her chained foot over her knee, stuck out her tongue, and tugged at the shackle, which was indeed too large. "I was sweating a little then," she said. "I guess that made it easier. Now it's got sand under it."

"You'll take the skin off."

"No, I won't. Master, put your hand right here, and your thumb against my heel. Then pull with your fingers and tell me what you think."

I did so, and the shackle slipped from her foot as easily as an anklet. "You were joking," I said. "Why, you might almost have stepped out of it."

"Maybe I was, a little bit. You're not angry at me, are you, master?"

"No. But you'd better put it back on before someone sees you."

"I don't think I can," she told me. "I'll say it fell off in the water, and I couldn't find it."

"Then you'd better hide it under one of those stones."

"I know a better place. I found it while you were swimming around. Look at the edge of this big rock."

It was a hole the size of a man's head. When I thrust my arm into it, I discovered that it went almost straight down.

"I wouldn't do that," Io said. "Something smells bad down there."

She dropped the chain and shackle into it. "I don't think they'll put another one on me. They'll be afraid that will get lost too."

One of the sailors who had reboarded the ship had returned now with a bronze fire-box. I was surprised to see how bright its vents seemed. The sun was setting behind the finger of land, plunging the beach into shadow.

"I'll go and get our food, master," Io said happily. "That's one of the things I ought to do for you."

"It won't be ready yet!" I called after her, but she paid no attention. I had picked up this scroll and started to follow her when someone tapped my shoulder.

It was one of the bowmen. I said, "She'll do no harm; she's only a child."

He shrugged to show he was not concerned about Io. "My name is Oior," he said. "I am of the People of Scoloti. You are Latro. I heard the man and woman speak of you."

I nodded.

"I do not know this land."

"Nor I, either."

He looked surprised at that but went on resolutely. "It has many gods. In my land we sacrifice to red fire and air the unseen, to black earth, pale water, sun and moon, and to the sword of iron. That is all. I do not know these gods. Now I am troubled, and my trouble will be the trouble of all who are here." He looked around to see whether anyone was watching us. "I do not have much money, but you will have all I have." He held out his hand, filled with bronze coins.

"I don't want your money," I told him.

"Take. That is how friends are made in this land."

To please him, I took a single coin.

"Good," he said. "But this is no good place to talk, and soon there will be food. When we have eaten and drunk, go high up." He pointed to the ridge, between the sentries who stood black against the sky to the north and south. "Wait for Oior there."

Now I am waiting, and I have written this as I wait. The sun has set, and the last light will soon leave the western sky. The moon is rising, and if the bowman does not come before I grow sleepy, I will go to a fire to sleep.

# TEN
---
## *Under a Waning Moon*

I WRITE BESIDE THE FIRE. When I look about, it seems that no one is awake but the black man and me. He walks up and down the beach, his face turned to the sea as if waiting for some sail.

Yet I know many are awake. Now and then one sits up, sees the rest, and lies down again. The wind sighs in the trees and among the rocks; but there are other sighs, not born of the wind.

I asked Hypereides whether we would bury the dead man in the morning. He said we would not, that there is hope we will reach the city soon. If we do, the dead man can lie with his family, if he has one.

But I should return to the place where I stopped writing only a short time ago. Io carried food and wine to me, though I had eaten already, and we shared it with our backs against one of the highest rocks of the ridge, watching the moon rise over the sea and enjoying the spectacle provided by the fires of driftwood and the ships drawn up on the beach.

Hypereides was generous with food, and because no one had remembered I had eaten already, Io had received full portions for both of us. While I pretended to dine a second time, she piled what she did not want of her own meal onto my trencher, so there was a great deal there still when I drained the cup, wiped my fingers with bread, and laid it at my feet.

"I would like something of that."

I looked around to see who spoke. What I had thought only a stone resting by chance upon a larger stone was in fact the head of a woman. As soon as she saw I had seen her, she rose and came toward us. She was naked and graceful, beyond her first youth (as well as I could judge in the moonlight), though not her beauty. The black hair that fell to her waist seemed longer, thicker, and more tangled than any woman's hair should be.

As she came nearer to us, I decided she was a celebrant of some cult; for though she wore no gown, she had tied the shed skin of a snake above her hips like a cincture, with the head and tail hanging down.

"Here," I said. I picked up my trencher again and held it out to her. "You may have it all."

She smiled and shook her head.

"Master!" Io gasped.

She was staring at me, and I asked her what was wrong.

"There's nobody there!"

The woman whispered, "She's your slave. Won't you give her to me? Touch her and she's mine. Touch me, and I am hers." She scarcely moved her lips when she spoke; and she looked away, toward the moon, when she said, "I am hers."

"Master, is there somebody here? Somebody I can't see?"

I told Io, "A woman with dark hair, belted with a snake skin."

"Like the flute-playing man?"

I did not remember such a man and could only shake my head.

"Come to the fire," she pleaded. She tried to pull me away.

The woman whispered, "I won't hurt you. I've come to teach you, and to give you a warning."

"And the child?"

"The child is yours. She could be mine. What harm in that?"

I told Io, "Go away. Run to the fire. Stay there till I come."

She flew as a rabbit flies the hooves of warhorses, leaping and skipping among the rocks.

"You are selfish," the woman said. "You eat, while I go hungry."

"You may eat as I did."

"But quick of wit, an excellent thing. Alas, that I cannot chew such food." She smiled, and I saw that her teeth were small and pointed, shining in the moonlight.

"I didn't know there were such women as you. Are all the people of this coast like you?"

"We have spoken before," she said.

"Then I've forgotten it."

She studied my eyes and sank fluidly to the ground to sit beside me. "If you have forgotten me, you must have seen many things."

"Is that what you came to teach me?"

"Ah," she said. "It is my face you do not remember."

I nodded.

"And the rest is somewhat differently arranged. Yes, you are right. That is one of the things I have come to teach you."

I looked at her, seeing how fair her body was and how white. "I'd gladly learn."

Her hand caressed my thigh, but though her fingers moved with life, they felt as cold as stones. "Someday, perhaps. Do you desire me?"

"Very much."

"Later, then, as I told you. When you have recovered from that wound. But now I must teach you, as I said I would." She pointed to the moon. "Do you see the goddess?"

"Yes," I said. "But what a fool I am. A moment ago, I thought her only a crescent lamp in the sky."

"There is a shadow across her face now," the woman told me. "In seven days, the shadow will cover it wholly. Then she will become our dark goddess, and if she comes to you, you will see her so."

"I don't understand."

"I tell you these things because I know she once showed herself to you as a bright goddess when the moon was nearly full. What she has once done, she will do again, so these things are good for you to know. For a very small price, I will tell you more—things that will be of the greatest value to you."

I did not ask what the price was, because I knew; and I saw that she knew I knew. I said, "Could you take her? Even when she's sitting around the fire with the rest?"

"I could take her though she sat in the fire."

"I won't pay that price."

"Learn wisdom," she said. "Knowledge is more than gold."

I shook my head. "Knowledge is soon changed, then lost in the mist, an echo half-heard."

She rose at that, brushing the dust from her hips and thighs like any other woman. "And I sought to teach you wisdom. You mocked me when you said you were a fool."

"If I mocked you, I've forgotten it."

"Yes, that is best. To forget. But remember me when you meet my mistress in any guise. Remember that I helped you and would have helped you more, if you had been as generous to me as I to you."

"I'll try," I said.

"And I will warn you, as I promised. The child fled down this hill, and fled safely; but soon one who walks this hill will die. Listen well!"

"I am," I said.

"Then wait for the death. Afterward you may go in safety." She paused, licking her lips as she cocked her head to listen.

I listened too, and heard far off the noise a stone made falling upon a stone.

"Someone comes," she said. "I would ask you for him, but that would be your death. Notice that I am your friend, merciful and just, more than fair in every dealing."

"As you say."

"Do not forget my warning and my teaching. There is one thing more." Swiftly she went to the boulder behind which she had been waiting when I first saw her. For an instant she disappeared as she crouched to take something from the ground. Then she stood beside me again and dropped it at my feet. It clinked as coins do, tossed in the hand.

"The women here put knives beneath their children's cradles," she told me. "They tell one another they will keep us away; and though they do not—not always—it is true we do not like iron." She crouched again, this time to wipe her hands on the ground. "The reason we do not is to come."

I picked up what she had dropped. It was a chain, with a shackle at one end.

"Don't let your brat dump her rubbish into my house again," the woman said.

A man's voice, rough and deep, called, *"Latro!"* I glanced in the direction of his call, and when I looked again the woman was gone. The stone rested on the boulder as before. I went to it and picked it up. It was a common stone, not otherwise than any other; I tossed it away.

*"Latro!"* The man's voice sounded a second time.

"Over here," I called.

A tall foxskin cap came into view. "I am glad you waited," the bowman told me. "You are indeed my friend."

I said, "Yes. Soon we will walk back to the fire together, Oior." For I trusted neither the woman nor her warning, and I feared for the child.

"But not before we have spoken." The bowman paused, rubbing his chin. "A friend believes his friend."

"That's true."

"I told you I do not know the gods of this land."

I nodded; we could see each other almost as well in the bright moonlight as we might by day.

"And you do not know mine. You must believe what I say of them. A friend speaks only the truth to his friend."

I said, "I'll believe whatever you tell me, Oior. I've already seen something tonight stranger than anything you're liable to say."

He sat on the ground almost where the woman had. "Eat your food, Latro."

I sat too, on the other side of the trencher. "I've had all I want."

"As have I, Latro; but friends share food in my land." He broke a piece of bread and gave half to me.

"Here also." I ate my bread as he ate his.

"Once our land was ruled by the Sons of Cimmer," Oior began. "They were a mighty people. Their right ran from the Ister to the Island Sea. Most of all were they men mighty in magic, sacrificing the sons of the Sons of Cimmer to the threefold Artimpasa. At last their sorcerers slew even their king's son, the acolyte of Apia. She is Mother of Men and Monsters, but the boy's blood burned on Artimpasa's altar.

"But the king came to know of the sacrifice of his son, and with hands held to heaven he declared death, that no sorcerer should sacrifice again among the Sons of Cimmer. He sent forth his soldiers, saying, 'Slay every sorcerer! Leave none alive!'

"Seven sorcerers sped to the sunrise beyond the Island Sea. Death-daunted they dwelt in the desert, cutting its cliffs for their cottages and at last counting a numerous nation, the Neuri."

To show I was listening, I nodded again.

"Sorcery they sent against the Sons of Cimmer, stealing the strength from their swords. Silver they sold to the Sons of Scoloti, paid in moon-pale ponies and brides bought for their proud priests. So they learned from our lips, copied our clothes and our customs.

"Soon they said, 'Strong are the Sons of Scoloti! Why do they dwell in the desert? Strike the Sons of Cimmer, a puling people languishing in a lordly land.' Then bent we our bows and waged war.

"Scattered were the Sons of Cimmer, wider with each wind. We pastured our ponies in their palaces and tented in their temples, princes of their plains.

"Long ago, low we laid them. Careful chroniclers count the kings since we came to the country of the Sons of Cimmer, but count them I cannot." He sighed, his recitation ended.

I felt I knew why he had given it, and I asked, "But what of the Neuri, Oior?"

"How can a simple bowman speak of the sorcerers? They live in their ancient land, east of the Island Sea. But they live among us too, and no one can say who they are. They have our speech and our clothing. As well as we they draw the bow, and with a touch, tame horses. No one knows them, unless he sees the sign."

"And you have seen it," I prompted him.

He bowed his head in acknowledgment. "Apia burned her brand on the Neuri, price of the boy's blood. Once in each year, and sometimes more than once, each changes. 'Sorcerer' is your word, Latro. *Neurian*, say the Sons of Scoloti. Apia is earth, Artimpasa the moon."

"I understand," I said. "How does a Neurian change?"

"His eyes dim. His ears sharpen. Swift then are his feet across the plain—"

A dog howled in the distance. Oior gripped me by the arm. "Listen!"

"It's a dog," I said, "singing to the moon. Nothing more. There's a town—Teuthrone, the kybernetes called it—not far from here. Where there's a town, there are always dogs."

"When the Neuri change, they drink the blood of men and eat their flesh, pawing the dead to wake them."

"And you believe there is one here?"

Oior nodded. "On our ship. You have seen our ship. Have you stood in the lowest place, where the water laps the wooden walls?"

I shook my head.

"There is sand there, and water and wine, bread, dried meat, and other good things. Often I watch the man, the woman, and the child. You understand?"

I nodded again.

"Once they thirsted, and when the rest had eaten, no one had fed them. The man spoke to Hypereides. Hypereides is a kindly man, for he has not even put out their eyes. He told me to go to the lowest place and bring water, wine, bread, olives, and cheese. I got them, and I thought it might be I would never go there again, and it might be good to see all that was there. I was where the oarmen stand, and do not sit."

"In the stern?" I asked. "Where the steersmen are?"

"Beneath them. A step I took with back bent. Then two, then three. It was very dark. The food is where the oarmen stand because the evil water runs away when the ship is pulled onto the shore. If I had turned and gone back then, I would not have known. I took one step more, and eyes opened, far before mine. Not a man's eyes."

"So you believe one of the other bowmen is a Neurian?"

"I have seen such eyes before," Oior said, "when my sister died. Eyes that were like two white stones, cold and bright. But now when I look into the eyes of the others, I cannot see the stones. I heard the man and the woman, and even the child, when they talked. You are blessed by your gods and see unseen things. You must look into the eyes of all three."

"I am cursed by our gods," I told him, "like your Neuri. And Hypereides will not believe us."

"Behold," Oior said, and drew the dagger from his belt. "Apia's prayer is scribed along the blade. It will send him to his grave, and I will heap stones upon it. Then he cannot return unless the stones are taken away. Will you look?"

I said, "Suppose I look and see nothing? Will you believe me?"

"You will not see nothing." Oior pointed to the crescent moon. "There is Artimpasa. You will see her in his eyes, or Apia's black wolf. Then you will know."

"But if I do *not* see," I insisted, "will you believe me?"

Oior nodded. "You are my friend. I will believe."

"Then I will look."

"Good!" He rose smiling. "Come with me. I will take you to the other bowmen. I will say, 'Here is Latro, friend to the Sons of Scoloti, friend to Oior, enemy to all that is evil.' I will speak the names, and you will take each by the hand and look into his eyes."

"I understand."

"The rest will be listening to the man in chains, but the bowmen do not listen, because this talk is like the cackling of geese to us. Come, it is not far, and I know the path."

It was not easy to see the way in the moonlight, for there was in fact no path, though Oior moved as readily as if there were. He was five strides or more ahead of me when an arm circled my throat.

# ELEVEN

## *In the Grip of the Neurian*

I FELL BACKWARD, HALF-STRANGLED. For an instant there was a long knife, its point at my chest; perhaps its owner hesitated for fear his blade would pierce his own heart.

Steel flashed and he cried out, his lips near my ear. Oior was rushing back toward us. I was flung to one side. As I drew breath, I heard bone snap—a horrible sound, but a joyful one because the bone was not mine.

When I got to my feet, Oior was wiping his dagger on the hair at his belt, and the bowman who had watched the prisoners lay dead, his head twisted to one side.

"Thank you," I gasped. "Thank you, Oior."

If he heard me, he gave no sign; his dagger cleaned to his satisfaction, he plunged it back into its sheath.

Louder I said, "Thank you, Oior. We were friends already; now we are friends forever."

He shrugged. "A lucky throw. If not . . . Indeed, the goddess was in it."

"I have no money, except for what you gave me. But I will tell Hypereides. He will reward you, I'm sure."

Oior shook his head. "As you are my friend, Latro, do not tell. To the men of this land, the Sons of Scoloti and the Neuri are one. This would bring dishonor upon all. Go to the fire. Hear the man in chains. I will dig a place here for this Neurian with his own knife and pile it with stones so he cannot rise. Tomorrow he will be here, and we will not."

"I understand," I said. "Oior, even what you did—I'm afraid I may forget. But we are friends forever. Tell me."

He held his dagger out to me and with his free hand drew the bow from his bowcase. "Put your hand on my bow," he said. "Put your hand on my dagger. So we swear."

I did as he asked, and he pointed dagger and bow toward the moon. *"More than brothers,"* he pronounced. *"Though I die."*

"More than brothers," I replied, "though I die."

"When you forget, I will tell you, Latro," he said, "and then you will remember. Go now."

I gathered up the trenchers and cups, and turned to say good-bye to him. I wish I had not, and perhaps I will write of that later, when I find words to tell of what was, perhaps, only a trick of the moonlight.

Afterward I ran, and I had nearly reached the fire when I heard shouts and groans. A party of sailors was carrying something along the beach. Those who had been sitting about the fire rose and went to them, and I went too.

Blood still seeped from the dead man's ragged wounds. I turned aside from the sight, and the sailors from the fire crowded around him. In truth, I was thankful I could see him no longer.

Hypereides and the kybernetes pushed through to look at him. I heard the kybernetes ask where he had been found, and someone said, "At the edge of the water, sir."

The kybernetes must have felt the dead man's hair, though I did not see him do it. "And dripping wet. Washed up. He went for a swim at an unlucky time, I'm afraid. I've seen things pulled from the sea—" If he finished the thought, I did not hear him.

Hypereides said, "You, there. Go to the ship. There's a roll of sail-cloth in the supplies. Cut off a piece big enough to wrap him in."

A sailor darted away.

The black man appeared beside me, asking by signs whether I had seen the dead man, or whether I knew what had befallen him; I could not be sure which. I shook my head.

Hypereides shouted, "We need an altar, and fast! Get to it, the rest of you. Pile up these rocks. Right here's as good a place as any."

I think the sailors were happy to have work to do. The altar semed almost to lift itself from the ground, a heap of stones as high as my waist, as long as my outstretched arms and nearly as wide.

Pindaros joined us, bringing the woman and Io. "Where have you been?" he asked me. "Io said you were up on the ridge, and she seemed worried about you. I tried to go, but Hypereides wouldn't let me, or our friend here either; afraid we'd run off, I suppose." He lowered his voice. "He was right, too, at least so far as I was concerned."

I explained lamely, "There was someone Io couldn't see. And other things."

The woman said, "You and she had better stay with us in the future."

Hypereides came to speak to Pindaros. "I know some prayers, but if you could compose something special . . . ?"

"I'll try," Pindaros said.

"You won't have long to work on it, I'm afraid."

"I'll do the best I can. What was his name?"

"Kekrops. He was an upper-bank man, if that helps." Hypereides hesitated. "Something short enough for me to remember after hearing it once or twice."

"I'll try," Pindaros said again. He turned away, lost in thought.

The dead man was laid before the altar and a fire of driftwood kindled upon it. Ten sailors who had sworn they had good voices and no blood guilt sang a litany to the sea god: *"Horse-Breaker, Earth-Shaker, Wave-Maker, spare us! Ship-Taker, Spring-Maker, Anchor-Staker, care for us!"* And so on.

When they were finished, Hypereides, in full armor with his blue crest upon his helmet, cast bread into the fire and poured wine from a golden cup.

"Third brother of the greater gods,
By destiny, Death's king,
Accept for suffering Kekrops's sake,
The food, the wine we bring.
He labored for thy brother,
Thy brother used him sore.
Accept a sailor cast adrift,
Beached on thy river's shore."

Some beast howled nearby, and little Io, sitting on my right, pressed herself against me. "It's only a dog," I whispered. "Don't be frightened."

The black man reached across her to touch my shoulder. When I looked at him, he shook his head and bared his teeth.

Hypereides finished the poem in a thundering voice I would not have believed he commanded.

> "Yet should the old man slacken,
> You'll find no better oar,
> To row such souls as Ocean rolls
> Unto Death's bitter shore."

"By all the Twelve," whispered Pindaros. "He remembered the whole of it. I wouldn't have bet a spit on him."

Hypereides then cast beans, mussels, and meat into the fire, with other things. Two sailors rushed forward with leather buckets of seawater to quench it. Two more quickly wrapped the dead man and carried him away.

"It was a wonderful poem," I told Pindaros.

He shook his head. The men around us were rising and drifting back to the big fires nearer the ships.

"Surely it was. See how many of them are crying."

"They were his friends," Pindaros said. "Why shouldn't they weep? May the Gentle Ones snatch you! Poetry must shake the heart." There were tears in his own eyes; and so that I would not see them he strode away, his chain dragging after him in the sand.

My thoughts were still upon the fight on the ridge, and I glanced at the ragged skyline it showed against the stars. A tall figure with a staff stood there with a shorter figure, like a boy, beside him.

The woman who had sat beside Pindaros took my arm. "Come, Latro, it's time to go."

"No," I told her. "You take Io. I'll come soon. I think this is someone I should speak with."

She and the black man followed the direction of my gaze, but it was clear they saw nothing. Holding the chain that bound her leg in one hand, the woman took Io's hand in the other. They and the black man hurried off, followed by a bowman who was not Oior.

Alone, I watched the tall figure come down from the ridge. After him trailed the smaller one, who seemed often to stumble. A light surrounded the tall figure; the lesser one had no such luminosity but seemed translucent, so that I sometimes dimly glimpsed the rocks and trees behind him. Neither cast a shadow in the moonlight.

When the tall figure had come near, I saluted him, calling, "Hail!" By then I could see that his hair and beard were gray, his face stern and dark.

"Hail," he answered, and lifted his staff. His voice was deep and hollow.

I asked him, as politely as I could, whether he had come for Kekrops, and offered to lead him to the body.

"There is no need," he told me, and he pointed with his staff to the foot of the altar, where Kekrops had been laid out. I was startled to see that the body was still there; it rose despite its wounds and stumbled across the sand to him.

"You fear the dead," the tall figure told me, seeing my look. "You need not; no one will do you less harm."

The smaller figure had left the slope of the ridge; while we spoke, it crossed the beach toward us. It was a bowman dressed like those on our ship, and I asked the tall one if he was the man who had tried to kill me.

"Yes," he said. "But he will not do so now. Until he is freed, he is my slave."

"He is a murderer," I said. "I hope you will punish him for what he did."

The bowman shook his head. It swung loosely, like a blossom on a broken stalk.

"He cannot speak," the tall figure told me, "unless you first speak to him. That is my law, which I lay upon all my slaves."

I asked the dead bowman, "Didn't you kill Kekrops? Can you deny his murder when he stands beside you?" Now that I must write that, it seems strange. I can only say it did not seem so then.

"Spu killed only in war," the dead bowman murmured. He held a finger to his eye. "Spu would kill you, Neurian, in justice for him."

"We must go," the tall figure told me. "It is not right that they should remain on earth, and I have much to do. I have lingered only to tell you that my wife's mother sends her to speak with you. Do not forget."

"I'll do my best not to," I promised.

He nodded. "And I will remind you of it when I can. I do not understand mercy, and thus I am as I am; but perhaps she will be merciful to you, and I can learn from her. I hope she is at least just." He took a step forward, and it seemed to me that he stood upon a stair I could not see. With each step, he sank more deeply into the ground; the sailor and the bowman followed him.

"Good-bye," I called. And then to the bowman, I cannot say why, "I forgive you!" He smiled at that—it was strange to see the dead mouth smile—and touched his forehead.

Then all three were gone.

"There you are!" It was the kybernetes, with a sailor carrying a javelin in tow. "You shouldn't go off by yourself, Latro. It's dangerous for you." He lowered his voice. "I've just learned that one of the bowmen plans to kill you. A man of mine who knows a bit of their gabble overheard them talking. Do you remember this stick?"

He pointed to the sailor, and I shook my head.

"I chose him because he's a stout fellow and he watched you before. His name's Lyson. He's not to leave you . . . and you're not to leave him, understand? Those are my orders."

"Was the bowman who wants to kill me named Spu?" I asked.

"Why, yes," the kybernetes said. "How did you know?"

"I was talking to him as you came up. He was a simple, decent man, I think."

The kybernetes looked at Lyson, and Lyson looked at the ground, shaking his head.

The kybernetes cleared his throat. "Well, if you meet Spu again before we find him, try to remember that he may not be so friendly the next time. I just hope Lyson's with you—and he'd better be."

Now Lyson is indeed with me, though he sleeps. Only I am left awake, and the black man, and the sentries Hypereides has set around us and the ships. A moment ago, a lovely young woman left the largest ship, and seeing that I saw her, halted to speak with me. I asked who she was.

She smiled at that. "Why, Latro, my name's been on your lips half the day. Would you like to see me fatter, with red hair? I can do that, if you wish."

"No," I told her. "You are so much more lovely than your picture on the sail."

Her smile faded. "Yet plain girls are luckier. Ask your little Io."

I did not understand her, and I believe she knew it; yet she did not explain. "I only stopped to tell you I am going to the Great Mother," she said. "I was her priestess once; and though I was taken from her long ago, it may still mean something to her, if only a little. Because you've loved my beauty today, I'll ask her to be kind to you."

"Is she merciful?" I asked, remembering what the tall lord of death had said.

Europa shook her head. "Sometimes she is kind," she told me. "But we are none of us merciful."

She has walked into the ridge, which opened a door for her. There is another woman on the ship now. I see her pace the deck in the moonlight, as if deep in thought. She wears a helmet with a high crest, like Hypereides's, and her shield writhes with serpents.

Her face recalls to me the face of Oior, Oior's face not as I saw it at any other time, but as I saw it when I looked back upon leaving him and saw him bent over the dead bowman. When I had met him on the beach and when we had talked at the top of this narrow ridge of land, his sun-browned face had been as open as the faces of the sailors, though without their vivacity and native cunning, a face as strong and as simple as the face of a charger or a bullock. It was a face much like my own, I think, and I liked him better for it.

And yet when I turned back to look at him as I descended the slope, it had changed utterly, though all its features were the same. It had become the face of a scholar of the worst kind, of the sort of man who has studied many things hidden from common men and grown wise and corrupt. He smiled to see the dead bowman, and he stroked the livid cheek as a mother strokes her child.

I must remember that.

# TWELVE

## *The Goddess of Love*

THE LADY OF THE DOVES once blessed this place. Her statue was thrown down by the barbarians and both its hands broken off. When we came, the black man and I set it upon its base again—an act of piety, so says Pindaros, that must surely win us her favor. Though her hands lie at her feet with her doves still perched on their fingers, she is a most lovely goddess.

But there are a great many earlier things I wish to record here while I still remember them.

We came into the Bay of Peace about midmorning, I believe, though that is lost in the mist. The first thing I can recall clearly from this day is seeing the huts stretching far up the hillsides of Peace, many unroofed.

It was on that island, so Hypereides told me, that the poor of his city found refuge when the Great King's army came, and where they remained for the most part even after the Battle of Peace, for fear it might come again. Now that a decisive victory has been won on land, they are abandoning their huts and returning to the city.

There are three bays on the east coast of the island, and the city of Peace is on the southernmost. The richest families that came to Peace are there, having paid heavily for their lodgings. We put in at the middle bay, Hypereides hoping, as he said, to ferry some poorer folk back.

"Besides," he told me, "this is where we were before the battle. The families of a lot of my men are here, and other people who helped us out in various ways."

Pindaros, who was listening to Hypereides with me, put in, "You were wounded in the battle that freed them to go home, Latro. But since you were on the wrong side, you'd better not tell anybody that."

"And you'd better not go ashore at all," Hypereides told him. "Once they hear that Cowland tongue of yours, they're apt to stone you. Didn't you fight, too? You can't be much more than forty, and you look able enough."

Pindaros grinned at him. "I'm thirty-nine, Hypereides—the best time of a man's life, as I'm sure you remember. But as for fighting, you know what Archilichos wrote:

> "Some lucky lout has got my noble shield.
> I had to run, and dropped it on the way;
> So 'tis with us who fly the reeking field.
> Who cares? Tomorrow's loot is what I lost today."

Hypereides shook his finger at him. "You're going to get yourself in trouble, poet. There are many in the city who won't honor your supple mouth. Or tolerate it, either."

"But if I should get into trouble, good master, why, you're in trouble too. So why don't you free me? Then in the next war you may be my prisoner instead of I yours. I'll treat you royally, I swear."

We were under oar already, for the wind was in the southwest and the strait runs due south; thus it was easy to bring all three ships into the wind to enter the bay. By that time I could see the crowd on shore, and the kybernetes came forward to suggest we stow our mast and sail.

Hypereides wet a finger and held it up. "There's not much of a blow. Don't you think it might swing north later?"

The kybernetes shrugged. "I've seen it happen, sir. I wouldn't count on it."

"Neither would I, but let's not count it out, either. Besides, these fellows should welcome the chance to sweat a bit and show their wives how hard they're working."

"There's something in that. But if I were you, Hypereides, I'd put a couple of soldiers at the gangplank. Otherwise you'll get enough women on board to capsize her."

"I've already ordered it," Hypereides told him. "Still I'm glad you mentioned it. It won't hurt to lie to for a bit here, will it? I've got a speech to make to the crew."

"We'd have to, to unship the mast."

"Good." Going aft to face the crew, he waved for their attention and bellowed, "*Up oars! In oars!* Waterman, you can pass the dipper while I'm talking. Men, how many of you have families still on the island? As far as you know?"

About half the hands went up, including Lyson's.

"All right. We don't want to lose a lot of time here, so those who don't, stay on your benches. The kybernetes will call the ones who do to the gangplank by oar groups, one from port, one from starboard. That's no more than six at a time, ever. If you see 'em—that's wives, children, parents, or your wife's parents, and nobody else—tell 'em to come to the gangplank and the soldiers will let 'em board. If you don't see 'em, they're probably back home already, so go back to your bench so the next oar group can come up. I have to go ashore—"

There were a few muttered groans.

"—to consult with the authorities. Acetes and his men will keep order; if you know what's good for you, you'll do as they say. While they're on this ship, your wives and families are your responsibility. Keep 'em in hand or they'll be put ashore, and not on the mainland, either. Otherwise nobody's to leave the ship till we get to Tieup. I should be back by the time your families are on board and the kybernetes has found places for 'em and got 'em settled down, and as soon as I'm back, off we go. I want to make Tieup before nightfall, *you hear me?*"

That brought a rousing cheer.

"*And I won't be denied!* So get some rest, because you may have to break your backs before we do. Now— *Out oars! Mind the count!*" He beat the rowing rhythm with one hand on the other as the flute boy readied his instrument. "*I love my wife, and she loves me! But all I do is stir this sea! I love my girl, and she loves me! But all I do is stir this sea!*"

The rowers took up the chant, and soon men with mooring lines were leaping to the quay, where a thousand slatternly women greeted our ships by calling out names that might have been anybody's, holding up their babies, and waving rags of every color, and many that were of no color at all. Hypereides, whose armor I had polished with similar rags, could hardly get a foot on the gangplank for the press of them, and at length the soldiers had to drive them back with the butts of their spears to permit him to leave.

Astonishingly (or so I thought) a few of these women were actually the wives of various rowers. When the first hugs and kisses were done with, the kybernetes made them sit on the thalamite benches (which run completely across the ship under the storming deck) and threatened to put them on the ballast if the ship became unstable, as he assured them it would if they let their children run loose.

A bowman came aft to join us as we watched. "I am Oior," he said. "You do not remember?"

When I shook my head, Io pulled at my chiton, whispering, "Watch out, Latro. You know what Lyson said."

"Oior does Latro no harm. Spu was the Son of Scoloti who wished harm to Latro, and Spu is gone."

Pindaros drawled, "I heard about that. Hypereides thinks he jumped ship at Teuthrone. What do you think, Oior?"

The bowman laughed. "Oior is a Son of Scoloti. Oior does not think. Ask any man of your people. But tell me, does it not make you sad to see so many men who now greet their families again, when you do not?"

"I don't have much of one, for which I thank the gods," Pindaros told him. "If I did, somebody else would have claimed my estate. Let's just hope that our noble enemies here leave me in possession—otherwise, I'll need a few rich relations to take care of me, and I haven't got them."

"Sad for you. Oior has wife." He held out his hand at waist level with the thumb folded and all four fingers extended. "So many sons. Many, many daughters, too many for any man. You want girl? Play with this one, take care of her when older. You choose. Oior sell very cheap."

Hilaeira gasped, "Would he? Really do that? Sell his own children?"

"Of course," Pindaros said. "All barbarians will, except for the kings. And very wise of them too, I'd say. Children are easily got and lots of trouble afterward. I'm with you, Oior."

"Easily got by men," Hilaeira snapped. "Not by us. Not that I know for myself, but I've helped others. Why, my aunt—"

"Is somebody we don't want to hear about now," Pindaros told her.

"You talk to captain very much. Oior wants to know what you think this ship will do."

"Go to Tieup and get refitted. She's in pretty good shape now, so that shouldn't take more than a couple days. After that, perhaps join the fleet, which I should imagine is hanging about the Circling Isles hoping for a chance at the Great King's navy. Or the strategists may cook up another special task for Hypereides. One never knows."

"And you? Not just you only, this girl, this woman, this man, black man."

"We'll be left in the city, all of us. Those of us from the shining city will be sold as slaves, I think we can depend on that. If they've left me my estate, I'll buy our way out, and if they haven't, they haven't. Latro and the black man may be sold too—if they are, I'll buy them and free them, so that Latro can obey the oracle of the Shining God. If they're held as prisoners of war, well, I'll see what I can do."

Hilaeira said, "I don't want to be a freed slave. I'm a freeborn citizen."

"Of a conquered city," Pindaros reminded her dryly.

"Bowmen go ashore in Tieup?"

"Certainly. I imagine you'll be paid there, at least if you ask for it. Then you can go home, if you like."

"Oior will maybe leave this ship, go on some other."

I asked him whether fighting for anyone who would hire him were the only way he had to earn his living.

"You also," he said. "So this man speaks."

"I know," I said. "I wanted to learn about you because I thought it might tell me something of myself. You have a wife and children; do you have a house too, and a farm?"

He shook his head. "The Sons of Scoloti do not have those things. We live in wagons, follow grass. Oior has many, many horses, many cattle also. Here in south you have pigs and sheep. We never see them if not we come. They are slow to walk. They could not live in my land."

Pindaros asked, "Is the sun in your eyes, Oior?"

"Yes, yes. Light from the water." He seemed to stare at the deck. "Eyes are the bowman. I go now."

When he had left, Pindaros remarked, "That was rather strange, don't you think?"

I said, "For a bowman to have weak eyes? I suppose so."

Io murmured, "They were only weak when they looked at you, master."

Hypereides returned as the last of the sailors' families were being settled, just as he had promised. With him were a dozen attractive women, finely dressed in gowns of yellow, pink, and scarlet, with much silver jewelry and some gold. Several held flutes or little drums, but their many bags and boxes were carried for them by porters whom their leader paid.

This was a plump woman somewhat younger than Hypereides, with red hair and cold blue eyes. She came aft with him as we pushed off from the quay, now riding so deep that the greased boots of the thalamites' oars were almost in the water. "Well, well," she said, looking at me. "Here's a likely boy! Where'd you get this one?"

"Picked them all up at Tower Hill after we left Dolphins, as I told you. He's the perfect confidant—forgets everything overnight."

"Really?" I would not have believed those hard eyes could be sad, but for a moment they were.

"I swear it. I'll introduce you to him, but tomorrow he won't know your name unless he notes it down. Will you, Latro?"

Wishing to please her and discountenance him, I said, "How could I forget it? No one could forget such a woman, whom once seen must remain in the eye of the mind forever."

She dimpled and took my right hand between hers, which were small and moist. "I'm Kalleos, Latro. Do you know you're quite the figure of a man?"

"No," I said. "But thank you."

"You are. You might pose for one of the sculptors, and perhaps you will. In fact, you'd be just about perfect, if only you had money. You don't, do you?"

"I have this." I showed her my coin.

She laughed. "One spit! Where'd you get it?"

"I don't know."

"Is this a joke, Hypereides? Will he actually forget who I am?"

"Unless he writes it in that book he carries, and remembers to read what he's written."

"Wonderful!" Smiling at me still, she said, "What you have there isn't really money, Latro, only change. A daric or a mina, that's money. Hypereides, will you let me have him?"

He shook his head as though in despair. "This war's ruined the leather trade. In the old days, certainly. But now . . ." He shrugged.

"What do you think it's done for us, cooped up on Peace with a bunch of refugees? Latro, you look strong enough. Can you box or wrestle?"

"I don't know."

Pindaros said, "I've seen him with a sword—no spear and no hoplon. If I were a strategist, I'd trade ten shieldmen for him."

Kalleos looked at him. "Don't I know you, pig?"

He nodded. "Some friends treated me to a dinner at your house just before the barbarians came."

"That's right!" Kalleos snapped her fingers. "You're the poet. You got Rhoda to help you with a love lyric. It ended up being a little, uh—"

"Paphian," Pindaros supplied.

"Exactly! Pinfeather . . . What's your name?"

"Pindaros, madame."

"Pindaros, I'm sorry I called you a pig. It's the war, you know—everybody does it. Hypereides will let you come with him tonight, if he knows what's good for him. I don't know if my house's still standing, but we'll make it up to you whether it is or not. No charge. If you need money, I could even lend you a few drachmas till you get home again."

I do not think Pindaros is often without words, but he had none then. At last Hilaeira said, "Thank you. That's very, very kind of you, madame."

"Wait!" Pindaros leaped into the air, waving his hands. "I've got it—the city's saved!" He whirled about, arms wide, to address Hilaeira and Io. "Our freedom! My estate! We get to keep them!"

"It's true, Hypereides," Kalleos told him. "It's the Rope Makers. Our people wanted to burn Hill and take Cowland, but the Rope Makers wouldn't stand for it. They want to make sure we'll always have an enemy in the north."

# THIRTEEN

## *Oh, Violet Crowned City!*

PINDAROS EXCLAIMED, "OH, BRIGHT BULWARK of our nation, ruined!" A thin blue smoke overhung what had been the city of Deathless Thought; and though it was set well back from the sea (Tieup, at the edge of the water, had fared much better) the clear air and bright summer sunshine mercilessly revealed how little remained.

"Oh, violet crowned!" Pindaros turned away.

Hilaeira asked, "How can you sing its praises? This is what these people would have done to us."

"Because we chose to surrender," Pindaros told her. "And lost even when we fought for the Great King. They chose to resist, and won even with us against them. We were wrong, and they were right. Their city was destroyed; ours deserved it."

"You can't mean that."

"I do. I love our shining city as much as any man can love his home, and I'm delighted it's endured. But I studied here with Agathocles and Apollodoros, and I won't pretend this was the justice of the gods."

The black man pointed to himself and me to indicate we had assisted in the destruction. I nodded to show I understood, hoping no one else had seen him.

Hypereides came aft rubbing his hands. The wind had veered north as soon as we left the bay, so he felt certain he enjoyed divine favor. "What a ship! Loaded to the gunnels and still outreaching the others. That's the Long Coast whizzing past, my boy, the land that bore her and us. If I'd known she'd be this good, I'd have had three triremes instead of one and the triacontors. Well, too bad for their skippers, I say. This'll teach 'em their old boss's still the boss."

Io piped, *"Clytia* has her oars out, sir. Now *Eidyia*'s putting hers out too."

"They think they can beat us like that, little sweetheart, but don't you bet on it. We can match 'em trick for trick."

In a few moments more, our own crew was hard at work. *"I love my boy, and so does he! But all I do is stir this sea!"* They stirred it well enough; we reached the boathouses a ship's length ahead of *Eidyia* and three before *Clytia*.

I went forward to join Kalleos while the sailors were unshipping the masts. She was keeping watch over her women, who were alternately snubbing Acetes's soldiers and joking with them. "Wasn't that a lovely sail?" she asked. "I'll tell you, I hate to see it put away."

"Not half so beautiful as the original, madame."

Her blue eyes shone. "Latro, you and me are going to get along."

"Am I to go with you, then, madame?"

"That's right. Hypereides hasn't signed a bill of sale yet, but we've hooked fingers on the deal, and he'll draw one up tonight. You see, Latro, in my business I need a man who can keep order. It's better if he doesn't have to fight, but he has to be able to. I used to have a freedman. Gello, his name was. But he had to go in the army, and I hear they got him in the winter skirmishing. Be polite, do your work, don't bother my girls unless they want to be bothered, and you'll never feel the whip. Get me mad, and . . . well, they always need a few good men in the silver mines."

"I'll write what you say here," I told her. "Then I won't forget." Yet even as I spoke, I was thinking that I am no one's slave, no matter how these people talk.

As soon as the masts were down, we had glided into the boathouse. Now sailors and sailors' families were crowding ashore. I started to go with them, but Kalleos stopped me. "Wait till they're gone. If you think I'm going to walk to the city with them, you don't know me as well as you're going to. I'll hire a sedan chair if I can. Otherwise I plan to take my time, and I don't want their brats climbing all over me."

I said, "If you'll tell me how much you want to promise the bearers, I'll hire a chair for you now and have them bring it to the ship."

She cocked her head at me. "You know, you may turn out to be a nicer buy than I thought. But I've a better idea yet. Turn left out of the boathouse and go down the narrowest street you see. Three doors on the left, and there's a man who used to rent them. He may still have his chairs, even if most of his bearers are in the navy. Tell him Kalleos sent you, and you'll pay a spit for a chair without bearers, to be returned by you in the morning. If he won't agree, throw down the spit and take a chair. Here's a spit, and a drachma too, in case he wants a deposit. Bring the chair here, and we'll hire one of these sailors to carry the other end."

"I think I can get someone who won't have to be paid, madame, if you'll feed him."

"Better and better! Go to it."

I waved to the black man, and together we had no difficulty in persuading the chair owner to let us have a light one with long poles and a painted canopy.

"I lost a little flesh on the island," Kalleos told us as she took her seat. "I can tell by the way my gowns fit. Lucky for you I did."

While I had been gone, she had hired a dozen sailors to carry the bags and clothes boxes; so there was quite a procession, the gaudily gowned women following us, and the sailors following them with the baggage. The women were in a cheerful mood, happy to return to the city even if the city was destroyed. When we reached the stones that marked its borders, Kalleos had them strike up a tune on their drums and flutes while a tall, handsome woman called Phye strummed a lyre and sang.

"She has a lovely voice, hasn't she?" Kalleos said.

She had, and I agreed. The black man was carrying the front of the chair, and I the back.

"Two drachmas a night I could get for her, if only she'd learn philosophy," Kalleos grumbled. "But she won't. You can't get it through that thick skull of hers. Last year I got one of the finest sophists in the city to lecture her. After three days, I asked her to tell me what she knew, and all she'd say was, 'But what's the *use* of it?' " Kalleos shook her head.

"What is the use, madame?"

"Why, to get two drachmas a night, you big ninny! A man won't pay that kind of money unless he thinks he's sleeping above himself, no matter how good-looking the girl is, or how accommodating, either. He doesn't want her to talk about Solon or whether the world's all fire or all water; but he wants to think she could if he felt like it.

"Solon!" Kalleos chuckled. "When I was younger, I used to know an old woman who'd known him. You know what he wanted? A girl who could drink with him cup for cup. That's what she said. They finally found one, a big blond Geta who cost them a fortune. She drank with him all night, slept with him, and thanked him—still in the bed—by signs when he paid her and tipped her and went home. Then the owner and the fancy man—that's you, Latro—told her to get out of bed, and she fell on her face and broke her nose."

I had been looking at the smoke over the city. I asked how it could still be burning, when it had been destroyed, as I understood it, last autumn.

"Oh, those aren't the fires the barbarians lit," Kalleos told me. "That's just dust raised by the builders, and people burning wreckage to be rid of it. A few went over as soon as the Great King's army left, then more when the weather turned good this year; and now all the rest after the victory at Clay. The best people are coming home from Argolis too, and all that means that the customers will be here, not on the island. So here we are, and the playing and singing is to let them know we're back."

She pointed. "They'll be building a new temple for the goddess up there on the sacred rock—that's what I hear—when the war's over and they can raise the money."

"It will be a beautiful site," I said.

"Always has been. There's a spring of salt water up there that was put there by the Earth Shaker himself in the Golden Age, when he tried to claim the city. And up till last year, the oldest olive tree in the whole world, the first olive tree, planted by the goddess in person. The barbarians cut it down and burned it; but the roots have put up a new shoot, that's what I hear."

I told her I would like to see it, and that I was surprised the citizens had not fought to the death to defend such things.

"A lot did. The temple treasurers, because there was so much they couldn't get it all away, and a lot of poor people who were left behind by the last ships. Before the Great King's army got here, the Assembly sent to the Navel to ask what to do. The god always gives good answers, but he usually puts them so you wish he hadn't. This time he said we'd be safe behind walls of wood. I guess you understand that."

She looked back to see whether I did, and I shook my head.

"Well, neither did we. Most people thought it meant the ships, but there was an old palisade around the hilltop, and some people thought it meant that. They strengthened it quite a bit, but the barbarians burned it with fire arrows and killed them all."

After that she did not seem to wish to talk, and I contented myself with listening to the women's music and looking about at the destruction of Thought, which had not—or so it seemed to me—been very large to begin with.

Soon Kalleos directed the black man to turn down a side street. There we halted at a house with two walls still standing, and she stepped out. Her head was proud as she walked through the broken doorway, and she turned it neither to the right nor the left; but I saw a tear roll down her cheek.

The women stopped their playing and singing, and scattered to search for possessions they had left behind, though I think none of them has yet found much. The sailors laid down their burdens and demanded their pay, an obol apiece. The black man and I explained (he by signs and I with words) that we had nothing and went inside too, to look for Kalleos.

We found her in the courtyard kicking at rubbish. "Here you are at last," she said. "Get busy! We'll have guests tonight, and I want all this cleared out, every stick of it."

I said, "You haven't paid the sailors, madame."

"Because I've got more work for them, you ninny. Tell them to come in here. No, get to work, and I'll talk to them myself."

We did what we could, saving those things that appeared repairable or still usable and burning the rest, as a thousand others were doing all over the city. Soon the sailors were at work too, patching the door and setting brick upon brick to rebuild the walls. Kalleos asked how many urns had been left whole. There were only three, and I told her.

"Not nearly enough. Latro, you can remember for a day or so—isn't that what Hypereides said?"

I did not know, but the black man nodded in agreement.

"Fine. I want you to go to the market. Most of the people selling there will have stalls or a cloth on the ground. Pay no attention to those.

Find a potter who's selling out of a cart. You understand?"

"Yes, madame."

"And find a flower-seller with a cart too. Tell them to follow you. Bring them and their carts back here, and I'll buy everything they have. There's nothing like flowers when you don't have furniture. Your friend's to stay here and work, understand? And you're not to loiter, either. We've a lot to do before tonight."

I did as Kalleos had told me, but on the way back I was stopped by a man of unusual and rather less than prepossessing appearance. The chlamys that draped his narrow shoulders was of a pale hyacinth; he carried a tall, crooked staff topped with the figure of a woman, and his dark eyes were so prominent they seemed about to leap from his head.

With his staff held to one side, he bowed very low in the Oriental way. It seemed to me there was something of mockery in it; but then there seemed something of mockery—lent by his eyes, his tall, lean frame, and his disordered hair—in all he said and did.

"I should be most grateful for a trifle of information, good sir. May I inquire whom it is who has need of so many urns and blossoms? That it's none of my affair, I well understand; but surely it will do no harm to tell me. And who knows? Soon I may be in a position to do you, sir, some little favor in return. It is the mouse, after all, that gnaws the net that binds the lion, as a certain wise slave from the east taught us long ago."

"They're for Kalleos, my mistress," I told him.

His mouth opened so widely when he grinned that it seemed he showed a hundred teeth. "Kalleos, dear old Kalleos! I know her very well. We're good friends, Kalleos and I. I wasn't aware she had returned to this glorious city."

"She came back only today," I said.

"Wonderful! May I accompany you?" He looked around as though reconciling the destruction with the city as he had known it. "Why, her house is only a few doors away, I believe? Tell her, fellow, that an old admirer who would pay his respects awaits her leisure. I am Eurykles the Necromancer."

# FOURTEEN

## *How Strange a Celebration*

PINDAROS SAID, "WAS THERE EVER anything like it?" He waved at the banks of flowers, with the broken walls beyond them only half restored. "Now it's the city of the Lady of Thought indeed, Latro. The people are here again, yet her owls roost in the ruins. What a poem I shall make of all this!"

Behind him, Hypereides said, "When you write it, don't forget to say I was here, and that I drank my wine and cuddled my wench as of old."

"You're no fit subject for great poetry," Pindaros told him. "No, stop, I'll make you so. For a thousand years, your name will be linked with Achilles's."

I had tallied them in my mind as they trooped in, six in all: Pindaros, Hypereides, the kybernetes, Acetes, and two others I did not recognize, the captains of *Eidyia* and *Clytia*. Now Acetes was holding out the bundle he had carried into the house. "Here, Latro, Hypereides said you should have these."

I unwound the sailcloth and found bronze disks for the breast and back, and with them a hooked sword and a bronze belt. It was strange to touch the cool metal of the sword and belt, because I, who remembered nothing else, felt I remembered them, though I could not have told where I had worn them or even when I had lost them. I buckled them on, knowing they had been mine before, but no more than that.

When I had put the disks in the room Kalleos had given me, I returned to the courtyard, where she had greeted her guests and was making them comfortable on the couches she bought this afternoon. "Hypereides," she said, pouring his wine herself, "I've a proposal to make to you."

He smiled. "No one can say he found Hypereides unready for business."

"I told you there'd be nobody here tonight but you and your guests.
If you'll look around, you'll see I've kept my word."

"You've cheated me already," Hypereides told her. "The stars are
coming. But never mind, I won't ask for my slave back. Only for the
black one, whom you took without a by-your-leave."

"Certainly," Kalleos said. "I thought he was a free sailor when I
borrowed him. He can return with you in the morning. But Hypereides,
a friend of mine dropped in today when he heard I was back in the city.
He's as merry a fellow as you'll ever meet, full of jokes and stories, I
promise you. If you don't want him to join your party, just say so and
I swear you'll never see him. But if you've no objection, I'll be forever
grateful. And of course there'll be no charge to him or you. His name's
Eurykles of Miletos."

At that moment, one of the women came to tell me the food had
arrived, and I went to the rear entrance to help the cookshop owner and
the black man unload.

Kalleos came just as we were finishing. "Good, good! They're all
hungry. Do you know anything about food, Latro?"

"I don't remember," I told her.

"I suppose not." She looked at the trays I was making up. "At least
you're doing well enough so far. The girls will carry them in, understand? You don't go in again unless there's trouble. I don't expect any
tonight, but you never can tell. Try to stay awake and don't drink, and
everything will be fine. Sometimes a girl screams and sometimes she
*screams*. You know what I mean?"

"I think so."

"Well, don't go in unless one *screams*. Got it? If all of them start
screaming, come fast. Don't draw that sword unless you have to, and
don't use it no matter what. Where'd you get it, anyway?"

"From the Swift God," I said, and only when I had spoken realized
I did not know what I meant by what I had said.

"You poor boy." Kalleos kissed me lightly on the cheek. "Phye,
dear, get some of those lazy sluts in here to take these trays so the man
has room to work. Tune your lyre if you haven't already, and tell the

flute girls to fetch their whistles. But wait till the trays have been brought in before you start."

"I know," Phye said. "I know."

Turning back to me, Kalleos shook her head. " 'Wine, music, and women—what else does a man need?' That's what your friend the poet asked me. And do you know, I nearly told him. Meat, for one thing; veal and lamb, and they cost me—I won't say, it isn't polite, but a lot. Not to mention some nice fish, three kinds of cheese, bread, figs, grapes, and honey. And tomorrow you'll sweep half of it off the floor. You didn't come free, Latro, let me tell you." She paused, studying me. "You know, I used to be a slave myself. From up north."

I said, "I wondered, because of your coloring. Very few people here have red hair or blue eyes."

"I'm a Budini, or I was. I don't even remember their words any more. Somebody stole me, I think, when I was just a little girl." She paused again. "Do you want to be free, Latro?"

"I am free," I told her. "It's only that I don't remember."

She sighed. "Well, as long as you don't, you're going to have to have somebody around who does and will tell you what to do. I suppose it might as well be me."

When all the food was ready, I went to the courtyard arch to listen to the flutes; but in a few moments Pindaros came out and drew me back into the kitchen. "Hypereides has sold you to Kalleos," he said.

"Yes, I've been working for her."

"That puts me in serious difficulties, as I hope you understand."

I told him that until I found my home and friends I would be as happy in this place as in any.

"Your happiness—permit me to speak frankly—doesn't much concern me now. The pledge I made in the temple of the Shining God does. I promised to take you to the shrine of the Great Mother. I've done my best so far, and I must say the Shining God's rewarded me handsomely: I've heard the playing of a god and your singing. That's a privilege given few, and it's improved my own poetry almost beyond belief. But if I return to my city without fulfilling my vow . . ."

"Yes?" I asked.

"He may take it away—that's what I'm afraid of. And even if he doesn't, someone's bound to ask about our visit to the shrine. What am I to say? That I've left you here a slave while I raise the money to buy your freedom? What will they think of me? We've got to work out something."

"I'll try," I told him.

He patted my back. "I know you will, and so will I. And if I can get you to the shrine, perhaps you'll be cured. Then we'll worry about your happiness, both of us. Probably you'll want to return to your homeland, as you say, and I'll arrange passage for you on some trading ship. The war's nearly over now, and the merchants will be sailing again."

"I'd like that," I said. "To return home and find people I won't forget."

Over Pindaros's shoulder, I saw the rear door swing back very quietly. For an instant, the black man looked in. When he saw us, he held a finger to his lips, then gestured for me to join him and shut the door again.

"You'd better go back in there," I told Pindaros. "Before you're missed. I'll remember."

"It doesn't matter," he said. "They think I'm relieving myself."

"Pindaros, is your Shining God a very great god?"

"One of the greatest. He's the god of music and poetry, of light, sudden death, herds and flocks, healing, and much more."

"Then if he wishes me to visit this shrine, I will do so. He trusted you to guide me; I think you should trust him to guide us."

Pindaros shook his head as if in wonder. "Is it because you can't remember the past that you're so wise, Latro?"

We chatted for a few moments more, he telling me about the refitting of Hypereides's ships and I telling him of the work the black man and I had done for Kalleos.

"You've accomplished wonders," Pindaros told me. "It's almost as though I were at some dinner in our own city. Do you think they'll ask me to recite?"

"I imagine so," I said.

He shook his head again. "That's the trouble with being a poet: your friends all think you're a public entertainer. Worse luck, I don't have anything suitable. I'll dodge it if I can—propose singing or games."

"I'm sure you'll think of something."

Turning away, he muttered, "I'd a hundred times sooner think of a way to get you to the shrine."

As soon as he had left, I hurried to the rear door. The black man grinned at me from the darkness outside and held up a sleeping child. "Io."

I nodded, for I recalled her from this morning when we were still on Hypereides's ship.

He stepped into the kitchen, where there was more light, and walked his fingers through the air, holding her cradled in one arm.

I said, "All that way? No wonder she's tired. I suppose she followed Pindaros and the rest, staying far enough behind to keep out of sight."

The black man motioned for me to come, and carried her to one of the roofless sleeping rooms. There he laid her on some discarded gowns and put his finger to his lips.

"No," I told him. "If she wakes without knowing how she got here, she'll be frightened." I do not know how I knew that. I knew it as I know many other things. I shook her gently, saying, "Io, why did you come so far?"

She opened her eyes. "Oh, master!"

"You should have stayed with the woman," I told her.

She whispered, "I don't belong to her. I belong to you."

"Something bad might have happened to you on the road, and in the morning we'll have to send you back to the ships."

"I belong to you. The Shining God sent me to take care of you."

"The Shining God sent Pindaros," I told her, "or so he says."

Sleepily, she rolled her head from side to side. "The oracle sent Pindaros. The god sent me."

It seemed futile to argue. I said, "Io, you must be quiet and stay in this room. See, I'm covering you with some of these so you won't get cold. If Kalleos or her women see you, they may make you leave. If they do, go to the back of the house and wait for me."

She was sleeping again before I finished. The black man laid a wooden doll beside her and stretched himself beside the doll.

"Yes," I said. "It's better that she have a protector."

He nodded—and fell asleep himself, I think, before I had left the room.

Now I sit on a broken chair near the courtyard door, where I can hear Phye's songs. There is a lamp here with a good wick and a fine, bright flame, so here I watch the stars and the waning moon; and write everything that has happened today, so I will not sleep. If Kalleos were to beat me, I might kill her; I do not wish that, and I too might die. It is better to write, though my eyes water and burn.

It is later, and Phye no longer sings. Pindaros suggested they play kottabos, and I, not knowing how it was played, stood under the lintel for a time to watch. Pindaros drew a circle on the floor and a line at some distance from it. Everyone stood behind this line; and as each drained his cup, he threw the lees at the circle.

When several rounds had been played, Eurykles proposed that the loser of the next tell a tale, and Pindaros seconded him. Hypereides lost, and I sit listening to him (though I do not think I shall trouble to record his tale here) while I write.

# FIFTEEN

## *The Woman Who Went Out*

P HYE'S TALE HAD NOT YET begun when a shout of laughter woke me. No doubt she had missed the circle purposely, or perhaps one of the men had pinched her as she threw, or jostled her arm. I give here as much of it as I recall:

Once there was a woman whose husband was very rich but would never give her any money. They had an estate outside the city and a fine house in it, with many slaves and so on, but her gowns were still the gowns she had brought from her father's house, and her husband would not buy her so much as a comb.

One day when she lay weeping on her bed, her maid discovered her there. Now her maid was a Babylonian and as clever as all the people of that city are, and so she said, "My lady, I can guess easily enough why you weep. It's because all the other ladies hereabout have lovers to entertain them, and buy them silver bracelets and curios from Riverland, and talking birds that tell them how beautiful they are even when their lovers aren't around to do it. While you, poor thing, have only that ugly old fool your husband, a skinflint who never gives you so much as a sparrow."

"No," said her mistress, "it's because he never gives me any money."

"That's what I said," said her maid. "For we women, men and money are the same thing, after all. Have I ever told you how we girls get our dowries in Babylon?"

"No," said the mistress again. "But please do, even if it isn't a very good story. Because hearing even a poor story would be better than lying on this barren bed crying away my life."

"Why, it's no story at all," said her maid, "but the plain truth. When a girl in my city approaches the age of marriage, she sells herself to whatever men she likes for as much as they'll pay. In that way the best looking soon accumulate a great deal of money and so get a handsome husband, and soon after, many comely children. By the same token, homely girls get none, and thus it is that we Babylonians are the best-looking people in the whole world." (Here Phye, whom I was watching by this time through the doorway, patted her hair to considerable laughter and applause.) "Though you, my lady, would be thought lovely anywhere, I must say."

"That's extremely interesting," said her mistress, "and I certainly never knew it. But it doesn't do me the least good; I'm married already, so I don't need another dowry."

"True," said her maid. "But suppose you were to go out at night and make whatever handsome men you meet the same sort of offer our Babylonian girls do? You'd have a handsome lover for the night, and very quickly a great deal of money."

"It's certainly a most attractive idea," her mistress admitted, "but it seems to me that it's out of the question. My husband sleeps with me every night. If he were to wake and find me gone . . . Now that you mention it, I suppose it *might* be possible to administer some sort of mild and harmless medication that would assure him of a good night's sleep. Do you happen to know of a dealer in such preparations?"

Her maid shook her head sadly. "Most of them are ineffective, my lady, and even the worst cost a great deal. But I know a trick worth a dozen of them, if you can tell me where to find the last resting place of an amorous woman."

"Really?" said her mistress. "Magic? How fascinating! You know, my cousin Phyllis's grave is only a short walk from here. Would that do, do you think?"

"I don't know," said the maid. "Was she fond of men?"

"Extremely," said her mistress. "And when she died, one of my uncle's he-goats wouldn't eat for a month."

"Then she'd be perfect," said the maid. "Here's all we have to do. At dinner tonight, you must slip something into your husband's food that will make him ill—"

"Night soil, you mean?" her mistress suggested.

The maid shook her head. "Too obvious. . . . I have it! He's accustomed to rancid oil—it's the only sort he'll let us buy for the kitchen.

Give me that old pin to take to the market, and I'll trade it for the freshest, purest oil I can find. That should make him sick, and he'll sleep overnight in the temple of the Healing God in the hope of a cure. When he's gone, you and I will dig some earth from the garden and take it to your cousin's grave. There you'll moisten it with a certain fluid I'll indicate to you—you have a plentiful supply—and we'll make a doll of clay, kneading a lock of your hair into it."

Her mistress clapped her hands with delight. "Why, this is *much* better than crying!"

"Then," her maid continued, "we'll lay the doll on her grave and engage in a recitation in which I shall prompt you. After that, whenever you want to leave at night, all you'll have to do is put the clay doll in your bed in your place. If your husband wakes, he'll see you beside him. And if he embraces the doll, he'll meet with such a reception as will endear you to him forever."

"Wonderful!" exclaimed her mistress, and that very night they carried out their plan with complete success.

The next night the lady waited until her husband was asleep, put the doll in their bed beside him, and enjoyed a succession of fascinating adventures in the city that left her a great deal wealthier than she had been before.

All went well for some time, she adventuring almost every night and her husband never complaining, though she noticed the clay doll was losing its proper shape. Early each morning when she returned, she would pat it until it looked as it had when she and the maid had formed it. But every night when she took it out again, she found that the clay had shifted downward in a most alarming fashion; and at last she told her maid the problem.

"Alas, my lady," said the maid. "I feared this might occur. In Babylon, we fire these figures in a potter's furnace—then there's no further trouble. But since you had no money and I didn't know of a potter here who'd be likely to cooperate without it, I neglected that step."

"What are you talking about?" said her mistress. "What's the matter with the doll?"

Her maid sighed. "It's a condition in which you would not, I think, wish to find yourself, my lady. If nature is allowed to take its course, there will soon be *two* clay dolls instead of one."

"How horrible!" said her mistress. "What can we do? Can't we bribe a potter to fire it now?"

"My lady," said her maid, "it would only crack later. I believe the best thing would be for us to bury the doll again in the place where we dug it up. You'll have to sleep with your husband—at least for a time—but that can't be helped. Do you by any chance remember the spot?"

"Why, yes," said her mistress. "It was under the apple tree."

"Then that would be the best place to put it," said the maid.

And so they did, and the woman began sleeping with her husband once more.

One day one of his rivals in business, a man as penurious as himself, found him moping about the market. "What's the matter?" he said. "Has someone cheated you?" For he would have been sorry indeed to hear that the husband had been cheated by anyone other than himself.

"No," said the husband. "It's my wife."

"Ah," said his rival. "There's a great deal of that going around these days, you know."

"Not long ago," said the husband, "she was as passionate as any man could wish. But now . . ."

"I can well imagine," said his rival. "Not that I've ever experienced the same thing myself."

"It's like embracing a woman of clay," said the poor husband. "And all I can think of is how I used to go to dinner parties and have a fine woman every night. I thought that when I married it would be better—because I used to have to give a party myself now and then, and it was so costly—but honestly I think the old days were better, and in fact I know it."

"Then all you have to do is return to them," said his rival. "Send her back to her father."

"And refund her dowry?" asked the husband. "You must be mad!"

"Then I can teach you a spell that will serve your turn," said his rival, who had no faith in such spells himself. "At least, my grandfather swore by it. You must find a blossoming tree in green and ardent health."

"Why, the apple tree in our garden has been blooming for days," said the husband. "I declare, you've never seen a tree doing better."

"Exactly the thing, then," said his rival. "You must lop off a limb and hide it under your bed. Whenever you want to go out and amuse yourself, take out the limb and put it in the bed in your place, saying,

"Stick I cut, so brave and bright,
Stick be straight and strong tonight!

"Believe me, as long as your wife doesn't light the lamp, she'll never know the difference." Then the rival went away, chuckling as he wondered whether his grandfather's spell would work.

But the husband ran home, and noting that the apple tree in his garden was still in flower, he immediately ordered his gardener to saw off its largest limb.

"It'll be the death of it," said the gardener, shaking his head.

"I don't care," said the husband. "It quite spoils the symmetry all natural objects should possess; so cut it off."

And thus it was done, and the husband carried the limb to the bedroom he shared with his wife and put it beneath the bed.

That night, the woman noticed that her husband's hair smelled of apple blossoms, which it certainly never had before. "Why, he's trying to make himself attractive for me," she said to herself. "And who knows what may come of that. . . . I should encourage him."

She gave him a kiss on the cheek, one thing led to another, and she was embraced ardently all night, until at last she fell into an exhausted sleep.

At dawn her husband returned, put the limb under the bed once more, and lay down congratulating himself.

This went on for several nights, until at last, in the very heat of love, the woman said, "Although you're stout and strong all night, dear, I notice you're always exhausted in the morning. You'd better get some rest when we're finished."

To this, the limb replied, "I wilt not, stepmother." Which so surprised the woman that she lit the lamp.

You may imagine her delight then, for she saw in her bed not the withered old husband she had expected, but a blooming youth with fair red cheeks. She blew out the lamp at once, and for some time they came together each night as happily as any pair could.

It was not to continue. One night she rolled over meaning to embrace her lover and found, to her great disgust, that she was caressing her husband instead. Thereafter the same thing occurred more and more frequently, for her husband had discovered that he was no longer so young as once he had been, and he was sorely pained by the inroads his nighttime adventures were making in his fortune.

But when her husband had occupied the bed every night for nearly a month, the woman smelled apple blossoms again. Then, kissing her lover, she exclaimed, "If only he were dead! I'd have his money, and we could live together for the rest of our lives. You wouldn't be niggardly to me, would you, darling?"

"Never, stepmother," said her lover. "Every spring I would furnish our house new, and each fall I would shower upon you the fruits of the earth."

That sounded promising, and by this time the woman had convinced herself that "stepmother" was only her lover's pet name for her, he being at least in appearance somewhat the younger. Thus she said, "Do it, then! Do it tonight!"

"I will, stepmother."

And the next morning the man and his wife were found dead by the gardener, hung with the same rope. A noose had been tied in each end and the rope thrown over the largest limb of the apple tree in the garden.

The gardener and the lady's maid were accused of murdering them and tried on the Areopagus; but their deaths were ruled a double suicide, and husband and wife were buried beneath the apple tree.

There was laughter and applause when Phye's tale was told, and Hypereides said, "I'll have to be careful not to tell that one to my crew around the fire some evening. Do you know, I think half of 'em would swallow the whole rigmarole as solid fact. Why, on this past voyage, there was talk of a werewolf aboard."

The kybernetes shook his head ruefully. "It's our mixing with the Orientals that's done it, Captain. We used to be a reasonable people, believing in the Gods of the Mountain and nothing else. Now there's more gods up and down the Long Coast than along the River in Riverland. A god for wine, and all sorts of nonsense."

"Are you saying," Pindaros snapped, "that you don't credit the God in the Tree? I can tell you, sir, you're badly mistaken."

Kalleos intervened. "Gentlemen! Aristocrats! It's a rule of this house that there are to be no religious arguments. Tolerant discussion, if you like. But no fighting."

"I assure you," Pindaros said stiffly, "that I speak from personal experience."

"So do I," Kalleos told him. "I've seen men who've been the best of friends for years at each other's throats. The gods are stronger than we are, so let them do their own fighting."

"Words of wisdom," said Eurykles. "Now if I may shift the conversation to what I hope will be a somewhat less touchy topic, it's my opinion that such tales of magic as Phye has just amused us with should not be discounted wholly, Hypereides. It's quite possible for we poor mortals to peep a bit into the future, for example—and I do not refer exclusively to quizzing some god or other at an oracle."

"Perhaps," Hypereides admitted. "I've heard some things along that line that make a man think."

"Lo!" exclaimed Eurykles, regarding Hypereides with admiration. "There's the mark of an open mind for you, friends. Your true man of reason never accepts or rejects without evidence, unless the thing is foolish on the face of it, like that business with the apple branch."

The kybernetes chuckled. "And the clay doll."

"No, no!" Eurykles raised a hand. "I won't say it can be done. But there's certainly something real behind it. Spirits *can* be summoned from a grave, and I urge you as reasonable men not to mock what you don't understand." He drained his cup. "My dear, I'd like quite a bit more of that."

"Trinkets!" said the kybernetes.

"What, sir?" asked Eurykles thickly. "Do you deny that such things can be? Why, I myself, in the practice of my profession—" He belched. "Excuse it. I have often called the dead to stand before me while I questioned them."

The kybernetes laughed. "Since I've no wish to be asked to leave by the lady of this house, I offer no comment."

"You don't believe me, but your captain here is a wiser man than you. Aren't you, sir?"

"Perhaps not wholly," Hypereides said.

"What?" Eurykles reached into the neck of his chiton and produced a leather purse. "Here I have ten birds. Yes, ten little owls nesting together. They're here to testify that I can do what I say."

"And it's easily said," said the kybernetes, "where we are now. But it can't be proved."

"There's a burial ground not far from here," Eurykles told him. "Surely this good wine—and I wouldn't in the least object to another drop, my dear—has given you the courage to come along with me."

"If you're proposing a bet," said the kybernetes, "I'd like to see what's in there."

Eurykles loosed the strings and shook out the jingling coins, arranging them in a row with one uncertain finger.

The kybernetes examined them and said, "I'm not a wealthy man, but I'll cover three, with the provision that I'm to judge whether a ghost has been produced."

Eurykles shook his head, nearly falling from his couch in the process. "Why, what protection would I have then? You might faint or run, but declare afterward . . ." He seemed to lose his thoughts, as drunken men often do. "Anything," he finished weakly.

Kalleos said, "I'll hold the money and judge. If you admit there was a ghost, you lose. Or if you run or faint, as Eurykles says. Otherwise, you win. Fair enough?"

"Absolutely," the kybernetes told her.

Eurykles mumbled, "That's only three. What of the other seven? Hardly worth my while."

The captain of *Eidyia* announced, "I'll cover one."

"And one for me," said the captain of *Clytia*.

"And the rest?" Eurykles looked at Pindaros. "You, sir? I'll make my fortune tonight, if I can."

"I haven't a copper," the poet told him. "As Kalleos will testify. Even if I did, I'd be betting with you rather than against you."

Hypereides said, "In that case, I'll cover the remaining five. Furthermore, I'll bet two with you, Pindaros—on trust. I go to Hill now and then, and the first time I do, I'll come by to collect."

"If you win," Pindaros told him. "Kalleos, if we're going to the burial ground, may I ask that we have Latro for a guard? The streets are dangerous by night, and we've all had a bit to drink."

# SIXTEEN

## *In the City*

O NLY SOLDIERS ARE SUPPOSED TO carry arms, so Kalleos told me. She gave me Gello's old gray cloak to cover my sword.

Eurykles had said the burial ground was not far from Kalleos's house, but it seemed far to me. I wondered whether I would be able to find the house again, or if the others could find it, for they were all somewhat drunk, and some were very drunk. Of the women, only Phye had come with us, Kalleos saying she would not walk so far to see a god, far less a ghost, and the rest admitting frankly that they would be frightened out of their wits if Eurykles won his bet.

Kalleos had provided two torches. I carried one and Phye the other. It was good she had it, for there were stones and fallen bricks everywhere, and yet the remaining walls (and many still stand) cast shadows that seemed blacker for the faint moonlight around them. I walked at the front of our procession. After me came Eurykles to direct me; Kalleos had given him a fowl for a sacrifice, and he carried it under his cloak, from which it voiced faint protests. In what order the rest walked, if there was any, I do not know, except that Phye brought up the rear.

When we reached the burial ground, Eurykles asked Hypereides whether there was any person there with whom he wished to speak. "If so," he said, "I'll attempt that first, as a courtesy to you. I reserve the right to raise another to settle our bet if I'm unsuccessful with the first. Have you a parent buried here, for example? Or anyone else whom you wish called home from the realm of shadow?"

Hypereides shook his head, and I thought he looked frightened.

I whispered to Pindaros, "Isn't it strange to see so many people in this place?"

"All of us, you mean," he said.

"And the rest." With my free hand I indicated the others who stood about us.

"Latro," Pindaros whispered, "when your mistress's friend Eurykles performs his ceremony, you must help him."

I nodded.

"If there's someone standing close by who seems attentive to the ceremony, but who did not come with us from Kalleos's house, you must touch him. Just reach out and touch him. Will you do that?"

Eurykles continued, "None of you, then, have any particular person in mind?"

All three captains shook their heads; so did the kybernetes.

"Then I'll search for a grave that appears to offer a good subject. I shall attempt that subject, and upon the result the whole of our bet depends. Is that understood?"

They murmured their agreement.

"Good. Phye, come with me. I must look at the graves and read the stones. You, boy, whatever your name is. You come too."

For some while we moved from grave to grave, our feet rustling the dry stalks of the grain that had been planted there, Eurykles hesitating a long time over many of the graves, sometimes tracing the letters in the stones with his fingers, sometimes scraping soil from the grave to sniff or taste. A wandering wind brought the odors of cooking and ordure from the city, and the smell too of freshly dug earth.

Phye screamed and dropped her torch, clutching Eurykles for protection. The fowl flew squawking from his cloak, and he slapped Phye, demanding to know what the matter was.

"There!" she said, and pointed with a trembling arm.

Lifting my torch higher, I saw what she had seen and went over to look at it.

A grave had been opened. The grave soil was thrown back in a heap, the withered remains of the funerary wreaths lay upon it, and the coffin had been pulled half out of its place and smashed. The body of a young woman, thus exposed, lay with feet and legs still within what remained of the coffin. The shroud had been torn away, leaving her naked except for her long dark hair. The smell of death was on her; I stepped away from it, feeling I had known it before, though I could not have said where or when.

"Take the reins!" Eurykles ordered Phye. "This is no time for your womb to dance." She only sobbed and buried her face in his cloak.

Acetes said, "Something terrible has happened here. What we see is desecration." His hand was on his sword.

"I quite agree," Eurykles told him. "*Something* has happened, but what is it? Who did it?"

Acetes could only shake his head.

I stroked Phye's hand and asked whether she was feeling better. When she nodded, I got her torch and relit it for her from my own.

Eurykles told the others, "I'm only a foreigner in your city, but I'm grateful to my hosts, and I see my duty plainly here. We must discover what has occurred and inform the archons. My own talents and training—most of all the favor with which I am regarded by the chthonic gods—lay an obligation upon me. I will raise the spirit of this poor girl, and from it we will learn who has done this, and why it has been done."

"I can't," Phye whispered.

Faintly though she spoke, Eurykles heard her and turned. "What do you mean?"

"I can't watch. I can't stay here while you do—whatever you're going to do. I'm going back." She drew away from him. "Don't try to stop me!"

"I won't," Eurykles told her. "Believe me I quite understand, and if I could be spared I'd take you back to Kalleos's house myself. Unfortunately these other gentlemen—"

"Have entered into a wager they regret," one of the captains said. "I'll go back with you if you want, Phye. As for the bet, I stand with my old master, Hypereides. If he wins, so do I. I lose if he loses."

"No!" Phye glared at him with so much hatred in her eyes that I thought she might fly at his face. "Do you think I want your filthy hands under my gown all the way back to Kalleos's?" She spun on her heel and strode off, her torch zigzagging as she threaded her way among the silent people.

Eurykles shrugged. "I was wrong to allow a woman to come with us," he said. "I can only apologize to the rest of you."

"That's all right," Hypereides told him. "If you're going to do something, let's get on with it." He drew his cloak more tightly about him.

Eurykles nodded and said to me, "See if you can find that bird, will you? It won't have flown far in the dark."

A small cypress grew a few steps away. The fowl was roosting in its branches, where I caught it easily enough.

When I returned to the men waiting beside the opened grave, Eurykles had a knife. As soon as I gave him the fowl, he cut its throat with a quick slash, pronouncing words in a language I did not understand. Three times he walked around the grave with slow, bobbing strides, scattering the fowl's blood; as he completed each circuit he called softly *Thygater*, which I suppose must have been the woman's name. As he made the third circuit, I saw her eyes open to watch him; and remembering what Pindaros had told me to do, I crouched and reached into the grave to touch her.

At once she sat up, pulling her feet from the broken coffin.

I heard the indrawn breath of Hypereides and all the rest, and I confess I was startled too, so that I jerked back my hand. Eurykles himself was staring at her slack-jawed.

Once standing, Thygater remained where she was, looking not at Eurykles or Pindaros or any other.

"You've won," Hypereides whispered, his voice shaking. "Let's go."

Eurykles threw back his head and extended his thin arms to the moon. *"I triumph!"* he shouted.

"Be still," the kybernetes hissed. "Do you—"

*"I triumph!"* Eurykles pointed to the ground at his feet. "Here! Stand *here*, Thygater! Present yourself to your master!"

Obediently, the dead woman climbed from her grave and stood where Eurykles had pointed. Though she walked, there was nothing of life in her; a doll with jointed limbs, moved by a child, might have walked so.

"Answer!" Eurykles ordered her. "Who disturbed your sleep?"

"You," the dead woman said. A coin fell from her mouth as she spoke, and her breath reeked of death. "And this man"—without turning her head to look at me, she pointed—"whom my king says must go as he was sent."

"Yes, I woke you, and this man with his torch. But who dug here and broke the coffin in which you lay?"

"I did not lie there," the dead woman said. "I was very far away."

"But who dug here?" Eurykles insisted.

"A wolf."

"But a man must have broken your coffin."

"A wolf."

Pindaros said softly, "She speaks as an oracle, I think."

Eurykles nodded, the inclination of his head so slight that I was not certain I had seen it. "What was the wolf's name? Speak!"

"His name was Man."

"How did he break your coffin?"

"With a stone."

"Held in his hands?" Eurykles demanded.

"Yes."

The captain who had offered to escort Phye said, "That girl was right. I'm going back." Everyone except Eurykles and me stepped away from the opened grave.

Eurykles said, "Don't you know she can prophesy for us, you fools? Listen, and you'll hear the veil of the future torn to shreds. *Thygater!* Who will win the war?"

"Wolves and ravens win all wars."

"Will Khshayarsha, whom your people call the Great King, ever rule this country?"

"The Great King has ruled our country."

"That's what the oracle of Dolphins said," Pindaros told Eurykles.

"Wait not for horse and war,
But quit the land that bore you.
The eastern king shall rule your shore,
And yet give way before you."

I do not think Eurykles heard him. "Thygater! How may I become rich?"

"By becoming poor."

Hypereides announced, "I've seen a wonder tonight, but it was something I'd sooner not have seen, and I can't believe the gods smile on such things. I'm going back to Tieup. Anybody who wants to hear more can do it and take the consequences for all I care. Eurykles, tell Kalleos I lost and went back to my ships; I'll tell her myself the next time I see her."

"I'm coming with you," the kybernetes said, and Acetes and both captains nodded.

"Not so fast," Pindaros put in. "Hypereides, you bet me two owls, and Kalleos isn't holding those stakes."

Hypereides dropped them into Pindaros's outstretched palm. "If you want to come with us, you can share my room in Tieup."

Pindaros shook his head. "Latro and I are going back to Kalleos's. Tomorrow I'll come for Hilaeira and Io."

It was on my tongue to tell him Io was already there, but I bit it back.

Eurykles spat on his hands and rubbed them together. "As you desert us, Thygater and I are going into the city. I've certain patrons there who'll be most gratified to behold my victory. Come, Thygater!"

"Wait," Pindaros told me. "Our way lies with theirs, but we need not walk with the dead woman."

I watched them go, and Hypereides and the other to the west. "Pindaros," I asked, "why am I so afraid?"

"Who wouldn't be? I was terrified myself. So is Eurykles, I think, but ambition overrules it." He laughed nervously. "You saw through his little trick, I hope? I meant you to give Eurykles more than he bargained for, but you came over us both and gave me more than I'd bargained for as well."

"I'm not afraid of the dead woman," I said. "But I'm afraid of something. Pindaros, look at the moon. What do you see?"

"It's very thin," he said. "And it's setting behind the sacred hill. What about it?"

"Do you see where some columns are still standing? The moon is tangled in them—some are before her, but others are behind her."

"No," Pindaros said. "No, Latro, I *don't* see that. Shall we go now?"

I agreed. When we had left the burial ground and were about half-way to Kalleos's, Pindaros said, "No wonder you weren't frightened by the dead girl, Latro. You're more frightening than she. The wonder is that she didn't seem afraid of you. But perhaps she was."

The door was barred, and our knocking brought no one to open it;

but it was not difficult to find a place where the wall had been thrown down and not yet rebuilt. "My room has half a roof," Pindaros told me. "Kalleos showed it to me earlier. The best in the house, she said; and except for her own it probably is. You're welcome to share it if you like."

"No," I told him. "I have a place."

"As you wish." He sighed and smiled. "You got a cloak out of our adventures tonight, at least. I got two owls, and I had a woman; I've gone farther and come away with less. Good night, Latro."

I went to this room where the black man and Io are sleeping. Io woke and asked if I was all right. When I said I was, she told me Phye had come back sometime earlier, and Kalleos had beaten her terribly.

I assured her that no one had beaten me, and we lay down side by side. She was soon asleep, but I was still frightened and could not sleep. Against all reason, the moon that had been setting when Pindaros and I were walking had climbed high in the heavens again, looking like the dead woman's eye when it opened a slit to see Eurykles.

Dawn came through the broken roof, and I sat up and wrote all that has happened since I wrote before. This is the last, and I see that upon the outside of my scroll it is written that I am to read it each day, and so I begin. Perhaps then I will understand what the dead woman meant, and where I am to go.

# SEVENTEEN

## *On the Way to Advent*

THERE ARE MANY INNS. Though we arrived by daylight, it was too late to go to the house of the god; Pindaros has taken a room for us in this one only a few stades away. The inn is a hollow square with two stories all the way around. We have a double room—like a man's bent arm, but wider.

The first thing I can remember from this day is eating the first meal with Kalleos and the other women. I knew her name then from some earlier time, for I called her by it when I brought out the boiled barley meal and fruit, and the wine and water, asking Kalleos whether I could carry food to Io and the black man. Kalleos said to bring them to the courtyard, where the long table stood. (I think the black man and I must have put it there, because when the time came to take it down we knew how to do it.)

The women were talking about how happy they were to be in the city again, and of going to the market to buy jewelry and new clothes. Though the sun was at its zenith, I think most had just risen. Another man came, still yawning and rubbing his teeth with a cloth. I made room for him, and he said, "I'm Pindaros. Do you remember me, Latro?"

I answered, "Yes. I remember our parting last night, and this morning I read my scroll. Your name is written there often. Pindaros, I must find the healer from Riverland."

When I mentioned Riverland, the women fell quiet to listen. Pindaros said, "Who is that?"

"The man who treated me just after the battle. He told me my name; he'd learned it from the men of my maniple. Do you see how important that is? Those men knew who I was, so they must know where I came from."

"And you want to find out?" Pindaros asked. "You haven't talked about it much before."

"Yes!"

He said to Kalleos, "He's been getting better all the time. This is the best yet. Latro, you must go to the Great Mother. Did you read that in your book too?"

I told him I had read the words of the Shining God: "By the shrine of the Great Mother you fell, to a shrine of hers you must return."

"There you are, then."

One of the women asked, "Who's the Great Mother?" But Pindaros waved her to silence.

"I don't trust the gods of this land," I said.

Pindaros shrugged. "A man must trust the gods. There's nobody else."

"If the scroll is true, I've seen many more than you," I told him. "You've only seen the Black God—"

The black man nudged me and opened and closed his hands to show that there were twenty black gods at least.

"I believe you," I said. "But the scroll tells only of your seeing one, and the same for Pindaros. Have you seen more?"

He shook his head.

Kalleos asked, "Are you saying you've actually seen a god, Latro? Like they used to appear to people in the old days?"

"I don't know," I told her. "I've forgotten, but I wrote of many in my scroll."

"He has," Pindaros told her. "He's seen one at least, because I was there and saw him too. So did little Io—remind me to ask how you got here, Io—and our comrade there. I think he's seen many more. He's told me about them at various times, and after seeing the King of Nysa, whom he just called the Black God, I believe him."

"Then believe me also when I say no one should trust them. Some are better than others, no doubt: the Swift God, the Shining God, and the King of Nysa. But I think . . ."

"Yes?" Pindaros bent toward me, listening.

"I think that even the best act in some twisted way, perhaps. There's malice even in those who would be kind, I think even in Europa. In the serpent woman it burned so hot that I felt it still when I read what I had written of her."

I do not think Kalleos had been listening to me. She said, "But you remember, Pinfeather. And you, honey. You've got to tell us about it."

Then Pindaros and Io told of meeting the Black God. I remember thinking that it was much as it was written in this scroll, so I will not give their words here. I remember too that I was glad it was they who spoke and not I, because I was hungry and it gave me time to eat.

They were still talking when I finished my barley porridge and bit into an apple. When there was a knock at the door, I went.

A pretty woman with blue eyes darker than Kalleos's waited there. "Hello, Latro," she said. "Do you remember me?"

I shook my head.

"I'm Hilaeira, and we're old friends. May I come in?"

I stood aside and told her I had read of her in my scroll that morning.

She smiled and said, "I'll bet you didn't read that you're handsomer than ever, but you are. Hypereides says this house is full of women. I don't see how they can keep their hands off you. Do you remember Pindaros?"

"Yes," I said. "He's eating the first meal. I think perhaps Kalleos will invite you to join us if you like."

"I'd love to. I just came from Tieup, and that's no stroll."

We went into the courtyard, where I told Kalleos, "This is Hilaeira. May she join us?"

"Of course, of course!" Kalleos said. "Hilaeira, dear, I ought to have introduced myself on *Europa*, and I'm sorry I didn't. You can sit beside me—move over, Eleonore—and help yourself. Like I said, I would have offered to help you yesterday, but I thought you were Pinfeather's wife. How'd you get to the city?"

"I walked," Hilaeira told her. "Hypereides says it's against the law here for a woman to go out alone, but Io was gone—"

Io called, "Here I am!"

"Why, so you are! Anyway, Hypereides wouldn't send anybody. He didn't want to spare them, and he thought Pindaros would come. Pindaros didn't, so I decided to risk it. I thought I'd probably meet him on the road, but of course I didn't. Hypereides gave me a letter for you."

Hilaeira reached into the neck of her gown and drew it out. "It's a little damp, I'm afraid."

"No matter. Read it to me, will you, dear? This sunlight would have my poor eyes weeping like Niobe."

Hilaeira broke the seal and glanced at the writing. "Are you sure you want me to? It looks rather personal. I—"

The women all laughed.

"Go ahead, dear. We've no secrets in this house."

"All right. 'My darling sweet: May I say once more how fine it was for this weary old sailor to rest his salt-rimed head upon that divine white bosom of yours—' "

At this point Hilaeira was interrupted again by the women's laughter, and some of them beat the table with their spoons. There were more such interruptions subsequently, but I shall take no more notice of them.

" 'When I began my voyage to the Navel and Tower Hill, I quite agreed with the Assembly's decision to send ships instead of going overland, but what a weary steed a ship is!

" 'And yet the return paid for all. Thank you, dearest Kalleos. The second part of your payment must await my return, alas, for we are being dispatched to join the fleet. Send my slave back with the chair *today*.' That's underlined," Hilaeira added.

Kalleos looked at the black man. "You have to take the chair back, understand? Then go to the sheds and find Hypereides. If you don't, he'll have the archers after you."

The black man nodded, his face expressionless, then turned to me, pretending to write upon the palm of his hand and cocking an eyebrow as he does when he wants to ask a question. I said, "You want to know whether I read of you in my scroll. Yes, I did. You were my first friend; I know that."

He left the table, and I have not seen him since.

" 'Be kind to poor Latro,' " Hilaeira continued, " 'and you will find him anxious to do whatever lies in his power to help you. At least, I have always found him so.

" 'Pindaros Pagondas of Cowland will already have told you what happened last night. I think it was the worst adventure of my life. May all the Twelve preserve me from such another! I lost, and you may pay the money I and the others left with you to Eurykles. When you have done so, I urge you never to see him again. Believe me, O sweetest Kalleos, if you had been one of us last night, you would not.

" 'And now farewell—' "

"Wait up!" Kalleos exclaimed. "Pinfeather hasn't told me anything. What happened, poet?"

"In a moment," Pindaros said. "Let her finish."

" 'And now farewell from your grateful lover Hypereides, darling Kalleos. The Rope Makers say a man who goes to war must return with his hoplon or upon it. I've tested mine and it won't float, so I mean to carry it back. Till then I remain your loving Hypereides.' "

When the women had subsided somewhat, Pindaros asked, "Do you really want me to tell you what happened last night? In front of everyone here? I warn you, if I do I'll tell the truth. You've been a generous hostess, Kalleos, so if you'd prefer to hear it in private . . ."

"Go ahead," Kalleos told him.

"From the beginning?"

She nodded.

"All right, then I'll start by saying that when Eurykles made his bet it struck me that Phye's tale had been very convenient for him. When she said she'd come with us—alone out of all these women—I felt sure something was in the wind. Maybe I hadn't drunk quite as much as the others, or maybe I've got a stronger head. I don't know. How much were you supposed to get, Phye?"

Kalleos said, "Never mind that," and Phye, through bruised lips, "An owl."

"We found an opened grave," Pindaros continued, "and at first I thought Eurykles had done it himself; later I realized it would have been too great a risk. Phye was frightened, and she went to him for protection. That told me she knew Eurykles better than any of the rest of us, and that she was really afraid. If she'd been faking it, she would almost certainly have grabbed Hypereides, since he'd bet the most money."

"Go on," Kalleos said grimly.

"When we were here, Eurykles had seemed very drunk. I suppose you have to seem drunk to bet that you can raise the dead. But at the burial ground, he was the soberest of all, except for Latro, who hadn't been drinking. Phye said she was leaving, and it seemed to me she meant it; but it also seemed that Eurykles either thought it was part of some plan or wanted her to believe he thought that, so that she'd go ahead with it when she got her nerve back."

"She didn't," Kalleos told him grimly. "She came here."

"I can see that. Phye, I'd put a slice of cucumber on that eye, if I were you."

"Nothing you've talked about would have horrified Hypereides," Kalleos said. "Get on with it."

"All right, I will. Eurykles raised the woman from the grave. She stood up and talked to us, but she was quite clearly dead. Her face was livid, and her cheeks beginning to fall in."

Kalleos leaned toward him, her eyes narrowed to slits. "He *did* it?"

Pindaros shrugged. "He sacrificed a cock, and she stood up and spoke. When the rest of us left, she followed him into the city." He turned to Phye. "What were you supposed to do? Supply the voice, or actually appear as the ghost?"

She said, "You knew. Even when we were back here, you knew."

"Because I bet with Hypereides? I knew enough to know who was going to win a strange bet proposed by a stranger. So does Hypereides, I imagine, when he's sober."

By then the women were all talking at once. Hilaeira whispered across the table, "Latro, did you touch her? Do you remember?"

I nodded.

"Which brings us to Latro," Pindaros said to her. "I can't go back to our shining city until I've taken him to the shrine of the Great Mother. I won't blame you if you don't want to come, though you're welcome to if you wish."

Hilaeira said, "My father—he's dead—had a business connection here. I thought perhaps he'd let me stay with him a while."

"Certainly," Pindaros said.

"This is so near Advent, where they have the mysteries of the Grain Goddess, and I'd love to be an initiate. They'll take me, won't they? Despite the war?"

"They'll accept anyone who hasn't committed murder, I believe," Pindaros told her. "But there's quite a period of study involved—half a year or so. Kalleos, what do you know of the mysteries? Is there any reason Hilaeira couldn't be initiated?"

Kalleos shook her head, smiling again. "Not a reason in the world.

And Hilaeira, dear, I heard what you said about your poor uncle, or whoever it was. Believe me, dear, you don't need him. You're welcome to stay right here with me for as long as you like."

"Why, that's very kind of you," Hilaeira said.

"It does take a while, you understand. But you're lucky, because it's right about now that they start. You'll have to go down to Advent every so often all summer, and there are fasts and ceremonies and whatnot. I've never gone through it, but I know people who have."

"Did it change their lives?" Hilaeira asked.

"Hm? Oh, yes, absolutely. Gave them a whole new outlook, and a better one too, I'd say. And it's ever so useful socially. Where was I? Washings—there's a lot of them, mostly in the Ilissus. In the fall they admit you to the lesser mysteries. After that would be the time for you to go home, if you want to. Then a year later you come back, go through the lesser mysteries again, and then the greater mysteries. Then you're an initiate and a friend of the goddess's forever, and every year you can come back for the greater mysteries, though you don't have to. Those last four days. The lesser mysteries are two, I think. But you really ought to go down to Advent and talk to the priests."

"Is it far?"

"No. If you start when we're through eating, you . . . Pinfeather, what's the matter with you?"

"It's just that— Last night, Latro said— By all the gods!"

Hilaeira was looking at him too. "For a man who takes talking corpses in his stride, you seem a bit distraught."

"I should be. I am! I've been an idiot. Io, do you remember what the prophetess said? I want to be sure my memory's not playing me false."

"I think so," Io told him. "Let me see. 'Look under the sun . . .' "

"Further along," Pindaros told her. "About the wolf."

" 'The wolf that howls has wrought you woe!' " Io chanted. " 'To that dog's mistress you must go! Her hearth burns in the room below. I send you to the God Unseen!' "

"That's enough. 'The wolf that howls has wrought you woe, to that dog's mistress you must go, her hearth burns in the room below.' Kalleos, is there a cave at Advent?"

Kalleos shook her head. "I haven't the least idea."

"There must be. I need to borrow Latro for today and tomorrow. May I have him? I'll bring him back to you, I swear."

"I suppose so. Would you mind telling me what's going on?"

Pindaros had bitten into his apple. He chewed and swallowed before answering. "Back in our city, I took an oath to guide Latro to the place mentioned by the prophetess. I thought it meant the oracle at Lebadeia, which is only about two days' journey."

"You consulted the god at the Navel?" Kalleos asked.

Pindaros shook his head. "There's a temple of the Shining God and a prophetess in our city. We never got to Lebadeia, as you can see from our ending up here. But last night Latro said—"

I interrupted. "That we should trust the Shining God if we trusted his oracle."

"Right. Latro, I know you don't remember, but go get your book. Look at the very beginning and tell me where you were wounded. We know about the battle—where on the battlefield."

"I don't have to get it," I told him. "I read it this morning. At the temple of the Earth Mother."

Pindaros heaved a great sigh. "I thought I recalled someone's saying something about that. That clinches it."

"Clinches what?" Hilaeira asked.

"The wolf is one of the badges of the Great Mother," Pindaros told her. "That's why I thought it was the shrine of the Great Mother that was meant—it is in a cave, by the way. But don't you remember what the priest said to us beside the lake? The morning after you and I first met?"

"He explained that the gods have different names to indicate different attributes, and different names in different places, too. Of course, I knew that before."

Pindaros nodded. "And do you know how Advent got its name? Or why the mysteries are performed there?"

"I thought it had always been there."

"No, in ancient times Advent—which wasn't called Advent then— had a king named Celeos. His people lived by hunting and fishing, and gathering wild fruits. The Great Mother was looking for her daughter, who'd been carried away by the Receiver of Many. To shorten a long story, in her wanderings she came to Advent and taught Celeos to grow grain."

Hilaeira exclaimed, "I see!"

"Certainly, and I should have seen too, much sooner. The Grain Goddess *is* the Great Mother, and the Great Mother is the Earth Mother, who sends up our wheat and barley. Her greatest temple's at Advent, and it was near a temple of hers that Latro was wounded. The Shining God was telling Latro to go to Advent, and when I started to lead him in the wrong direction, he made sure we'd get to the right place after all. All I have to do now is take him there, which I can do this afternoon. Then I'll be free to return home."

"And will I find my friends?" I asked him. "Will I be cured then?"

"I don't know," Pindaros answered solemnly. "Certainly you will have taken the first step."

# EIGHTEEN

## *Here in the Hall of the Great Mother*

I SACRIFICED TODAY. ABOUT MIDMORNING, Pindaros, Hilaeira, Io, and I went to talk to a priest. He told us that his name was Polyhommes and that he was of the family of the Eumolpides. "The high priest is always chosen from our family," he said. "Thus many of us serve our turn, hoping for a smile from the goddess." He smiled himself, and broadly, for he was one of those happy and helpful fat men one sometimes meets in the service of gods and kings, though he smelled of blood, as I suppose all priests must.

"We are the children of Demophon, whom the goddess would have made immortal if she could. I grant it's not as good as being of the line of Heracles, who actually *was* made immortal, but it's the best we can manage. Now what can I do to help you, sir? This is your wife, I take it, and your little daughter. And your son, who's been injured. A striking young man—what a pity someone struck him!" He chuckled. "This is not a shrine of healing, however, save for the spirit. I will be happy to direct you to one."

I said, "I hope it will be a shrine of healing for me," and Pindaros explained our actual relationships.

"Ah! Then we have here, in fact, two parties, though you have traveled together. Let's take the young woman first, for her case will be somewhat easier, I believe.

"You must understand, my daughter, that there are three classes of persons who cannot be admitted to the mysteries. These are murderers, magicians, and soothsayers. If you are admitted to the mysteries—or if you so much as begin the ceremonies for admission—and it is discovered that you belong to any of those three classes, the penalty is death. But at this moment there is no penalty; you need not even tell me, 'I have killed,' or, 'I am a magician.' All you have to do is leave this room and return to the city. Nothing will be said or done."

"I . . ."

"Yes, my daughter?"

"Do you know how girls sometimes dip a mirror into a spring when the moon is full? When you look into it, in the moonlight . . ."

"What do you see?"

"Your husband's face. The man who's going to be your husband. The Moon Virgin shows you, if you're a virgin yourself."

Polyhommes laughed. "Hopeless for me, I'm afraid. I've four children."

"I used to be good at it, or I thought I was, and I, uh, showed some other girls how. I don't do it any more."

"I see. Did you look into the mirror *for* them, or did you simply show them how to do it for themselves?"

"I showed them how," Hilaeira said. "You can't do it for somebody else. Each one has to do it for herself."

"And did they pay you for your help?"

Hilaeira shook her head.

"Then you're surely not a magician or a soothsayer, my daughter. May I take it you're not a murderess? In that case, you may attend the initial ceremony. That will be . . ." He paused, counting on his fingers. "Just five days from now, in the evening. You're living in the city?"

"I'm staying with a friend."

"Then it would probably be best for you to return there. There are good inns here, but they're frightfully expensive, I'm told. On the fifth day you may come here just as you did today. We'll assemble at the stele at sunset."

Hilaeira cleared her throat, a sound like the peep of a little frog. "I said I was staying in Thought, Holiness. I'm not *from* Thought."

Polyhommes laughed again. "You're from Cowland, my daughter. You're all from Cowland, except for your young friend here, and I can't imagine where he's from. Can't you tell we speak differently here on the Long Coast? We don't double the 'fish' and the 'camel' the way you do, for one thing."

"That doesn't matter?"

Polyhommes shook his head. "I said there were three classes who were not admitted. Actually, there is a fourth—those who cannot understand our language well enough to comprehend the ceremonies. But even they are excluded only on practical grounds. If a barbarian learns our speech, he is welcomed."

"And will I have to make an offering when I come again in five days?"

He shook his head again. "Most do, but it isn't required. I take it you're not wealthy?"

"No."

"Then my advice is to make an offering, but a small one. Perhaps one drachma—or an obol, if that's all you can afford. That way you'll have something to put in the krater and need feel no embarrassment."

"May I ask one more question?"

"A hundred, my daughter, if they're all as sensible as those you've asked thus far."

"It isn't this way in our city, but here people tell me a woman isn't supposed to go out alone. Will anyone bother me when I try to come back? I don't think Pindaros will be here then, and Kalleos probably won't want Latro to come."

Polyhommes smiled. "You won't be alone, my child. Far from it. Recollect that every candidate for initiation this year will be on the Sacred Way with you. No one will molest you, I promise. Nor will the archers stop you and inquire why you've no escort. If you're nervous, you need only find some decent man and put yourself under his protection."

"Thank you," Hilaeira said. "Thank you very much, Holiness."

"And now, young man, to you. You're not a candidate?"

Pindaros said, "He merely wishes to present himself to the goddess."

"Purity is best, just the same. I take it he's no magician or soothsayer. Has he blood guilt?"

"He doesn't remember, as I told you."

I said, "I killed three slaves once, I think, though I didn't write it down. You said so later, Pindaros, and I read about it this morning while you and Hilaeira were still asleep."

"They were slaves of the Rope Makers," Pindaros explained, "serving as auxiliaries in their army. Blood spilled in battle doesn't count, does it?"

Polyhommes shook his head. "There's no guilt. Have you an offering?"

Io whispered, "The Shining God gave me to him. He can't give me to the goddess, can he?"

"He may if he wishes," Polyhommes told her. "Do you, young man? This slave girl would make a fine offering."

"No. But I've nothing else."

"I can give him a little money," Pindaros put in.

"Good. Young man, I'd suggest you use what your friend gives you to purchase an animal for sacrifice. The town is full of people who sell them—you'll have no difficulty. If you're short of funds, a hen is acceptable."

Pindaros shuddered. "No. Not a hen."

"Fine. A more, ah, significant beast is, of course, a better sacrifice. Normally those who sacrifice here desire to improve the fertility of their fields, and a hen is often sufficient. A young pig is the most common gift."

Pindaros said, "Like Hilaeira, I have a final question. Are there caves here? I realize you can't reveal the mysteries, but caves connected with the worship of the goddess?"

Polyhommes nodded without speaking.

"Wonderful! Sir, Holiness, you've been very, very kind. We'll go and get the sacrificial animal now. Meanwhile, perhaps a small gift for yourself . . . ?"

"Would be most gratefully accepted." Polyhommes glanced at his palm and smiled. "Return at noon with your sacrifice, my son. I will be present to assist you with the liturgy."

When we were outside, Pindaros said, "I'm going to follow a hunch. Have you heard of the Lady of Cymbals?"

I shook my head; so did Hilaeira.

"That's the name under which the Great Mother's worshiped in the Tall Cap Country. Not by the sons of Perseus or Medea, but by their slaves—Lydia's people, and so on. They use the lion and the wolf as the Great Mother's badges more than we do. I know you don't remember that the oracle mentioned a wolf, Latro, unless you read that this morning too. But it did, and it said you had to cross the sea, which probably meant to the Tall Cap Country. After one's manhood, the sacrifice most acceptable to the Lady of Cymbals is a bullock."

Hilaeira asked, "Do you have enough money?"

"If we can find a cheap one. Kalleos advanced me a bit, and I won a bit more betting with Hypereides."

Most of the animal sellers had only the smaller ones. Shoats were the creatures most often sacrificed, as Polyhommes had told us, and fowls the cheapest; but there were sheep too, and eventually we came upon a yearling bull for sale.

Io said, "His horns have only just sprouted," and patted his muzzle.

"Very tender indeed, young lady," the farmer promised her. "You won't find better meat anyplace."

"That's right," Io said to Hilaeira. "We get to keep the meat, don't we? Will they cook it for us at the inn?"

Hilaeira nodded. "For a share of it. And they'll keep everything and give us something worse unless somebody watches them."

"I think he'd let me ride on his back, like Kalleos on the sail."

Pindaros bargained with the farmer and, after starting to walk away twice, bought the bullock for what he said was far too much money. "The people here laugh at us because we named our country after our cattle," he told me. "But we have some good stock, and I wouldn't trade them for all the ships on the Long Coast. You can't eat a ship, or plow anything but the sea."

There was a cord through the bullock's nose, and it followed us docilely enough while we bought a garland for its neck and chaplets of flowers for ourselves, though Pindaros refused to let Io mount.

Perhaps I should write here that the temple of the Grain Goddess is called the Royal House and that Pindaros said it was different from any other he had seen. Certainly it seems strange enough to me. It is large and square, and its interior is filled with pillars, so that one walks in it as in a forest of stone. They say the fire before the statue has been kept burning since the goddess wished to bathe the infant Demophon in its flames.

I will not give the words we spoke to the goddess before we sacrificed; I do not think it lawful. When all had been said, I put my hand on the bullock's head and begged the goddess to join my friends and me in our meal. Polyhommes poured milk in the bullock's ear, asking whether it wished to go to the goddess. It nodded, and Polyhommes cut its throat with the holy knife, which is of bronze, not iron. We cast certain parts of the carcass into the flames, and everyone relaxed.

"A good sacrifice, wouldn't you say, Holiness?" Pindaros smiled and straightened his chaplet of blossoms.

"A most excellent sacrifice," Polyhommes assured him.

Hilaeira's eyes were bright with tears. "I feel I'm a friend of the goddess's already," she said. "Once I thought she smiled at me. I really did."

"She does have a kind face," Polyhommes said, smiling up at his goddess. "Severe, but—"

Io asked, "What's the matter?"

He did not answer. He had been ruddy, but his cheeks were as white as tallow now, and the hand that held the sacred blade shook so that I feared he would drop it.

Pindaros took his arm. "Are you ill?"

"Let me sit," Polyhommes gasped, and Pindaros and I led him to the nearest bench. His forehead was beaded with sweat; when he was seated, he wiped it with a corner of his robe. "You wouldn't know," he said. "You're not familiar with her, as I am."

"What is it?" Pindaros asked.

"My family always supplies the priests . . ."

"You told us that."

"So we're always in and out of the Royal House, even when we're just children. I've seen the goddess . . . I've seen her statue I suppose ten thousand times."

We nodded.

"Now I want one of you—you, little girl—to describe it to me. I must know whether you see what I do."

Io asked, "Just talk about her? She's real big, bigger than any real woman. She wears her hair off her shoulders, I think probably in a knot at the back of her head. Should I go around and see?"

"No. Go on."

"And she's got a crown of poppies, and wheat—a sheaf of wheat, is that what they call it?—in her hand. Her other hand is pointing at the floor."

The fat priest let out his breath in a great *whoosh*. "I must see my uncle—get him to rule on this. All four of you remain here. Right here. It might be better if you didn't speak."

He hurried off, and we sat in silence. It seemed to me there should have been a feeling of peace then in the quiet temple, peace engendered by its sullen fire, its bars of sunshine and deep shadows; but there was none. Rather it seemed filled with soft yet heavy noises, as if some massive beast stirred and stamped where it could not be seen.

Polyhommes soon returned. "Our high priest has gone to the city; I'll have to decide this myself." He seemed calmer, and the heavy odor of wine was on his breath. "Very well. You must accept my statement that I have observed this statue many times, and that until today its left hand has always rested upon the head of the stone boar standing beside it."

Hilaeira's mouth opened, and even Pindaros gave a low whistle.

"A miracle—a major miracle—has taken place here today. A great sign. Did any of you see it? See the hand actually move?"

Pindaros, Hilaeira, and I all shook our heads. Io had trotted around the sacred hearth to look more closely at the statue.

"A pity, and yet move it surely did, doubtless at the very moment of sacrifice, when our eyes were on the victim." Polyhommes paused, drew a deep breath, and let it out again. "I suppose you've heard about the dead woman in the city? She's said to have walked until cockcrow and spoken to many persons, and the whole town's abuzz over it. No one knows what it may mean, and now this! Wait until word of this gets out! Can you imagine it?"

"I can," Pindaros said. "I hope I'm far away by then."

Polyhommes continued as though he had not heard him. "This is something you can see for yourself and go home and tell your children about. This is—"

Io called. "There's a clean place on the pig's head where the hand used to be. Come look!"

No doubt it was a measure of our amazement that all of us did, obedient as children to a child's command. She was right. Smoke from the sacred fire had grimed the boar's head, but the broken marble where the goddess's hand had left it was white and new.

"Think what this will mean for our Royal House." Polyhommes rubbed his hands. "For the mysteries!"

"And I was here," Hilaeira whispered.

"Indeed you were, my daughter. Indeed you were! And when you've fathomed the mysteries—well, priests are always chosen from the men of our family, as I've said. But there is a place—the highest of all—for a woman in the ceremonies."

Hilaeira stared at him, a dawning wonder in her eyes.

"She too is customarily of the Eumolpides, but that is no insupportable obstacle. There is adoption, after all. There is even marriage. Such arrangements might be made by the high priest, and there can surely be no question now about who the next high priest will be." Polyhommes threw out his chest. "My uncle is an elderly man, and it would seem that the goddess has made her wishes regarding his successor quite clear. There was, after all, only one priest present at the time of the miracle."

Io asked, "But what does she want?"

"Eh?" He turned to look at her.

"The goddess. Why's she pointing at the floor?"

"I'm not sure." The fat priest hesitated. "When such a gesture is used by one in authority, it generally means that something or someone is to be brought to him."

Pindaros cleared his throat. "An oracle in our shining city directed that Latro be brought to the goddess."

"Ah. And he was the giver of the sacrifice—officially, at least." Polyhommes turned to me. "Young man, you must remain in this Royal House overnight, sleeping on the floor or upon one of these benches. Perhaps the goddess herself will appear in your dreams. If not, I think it likely she'll favor you with some message."

Thus I am here, sitting with my back against a column and writing these words by the light of the declining sun. I have had a good deal of time to think this afternoon; and it seems to me that more than once I have felt the spirit of a house when I, a stranger, went into that house—though I cannot retrieve from the mist those times or those houses. A temple is the house of the god who dwells there, and so I open myself to this house of the Grain Goddess, hoping to know whether it is friendly to me.

There is nothing—or rather, there is only the sense of age. It is as if I sit with a woman so old she neither knows nor cares whether I am real or only some figment of her disordered mind, a shadow or a ghost. A fly may light upon a rock; but what does the rock, which has seen whole ages since the morning when gods strode from hill to hill, care for a fly, the creature of a summer?

# NINETEEN

## In the Presence of the Goddess

I ATE THE BEEF, BREAD, and fruit Io had brought me from the inn, and drank the wine. When I was finished, I spread the pallet Hilaeira had carried and lay down; but I was not in the least ready for sleep, and when the town grew quiet, I sat up again.

For a time I read this scroll (which I must try always to keep with me) by the light of the sacred fire, learning of the many gods and goddesses who have shown themselves to me; and once or twice I took up the stylus to add some conclusion to the account of today's events I had written earlier. But how can a man draw conclusions from what he does not comprehend? I knew I did not understand what occurred, and it seemed to me that it would be better to wait until the goddess had spoken. Now I sit in the same place to write this record.

An acolyte entered without taking the least notice of me and, mumbling a prayer, cast an armload of cedar into the fire. It fell with a deep booming, as though the sacred hearth were a drum and not a stone. When I dozed, that booming echoed through my dreams and woke me.

I could see the statue plainly in the firelight. The hand pointing to the floor was nearest the flames and flushed with their light, so that it seemed to glow like iron in a forge. I felt it demanded something of me, and I threw off my cloak, hoping that when I was nearer I would understand. The goddess's hand was hot to my touch, but it was only after I had drawn my own away that I looked at last and saw the thing to which she pointed.

There was a small section of floor between the coping around the sacred fire and the pedestal upon which the goddess stood. It was dirtier than the floor in other places, I think because those who cleaned it were fearful to approach her too closely, or were not permitted to do so. I knelt and brushed its surface with the tips of my fingers. Just at the place she indicated, there was a ring of bronze set in the stone, though the depression that held it was so packed with dirt I could scarcely see it.

I wished then for Falcata, but I could not have worn her in the temple, and I had left her at our inn. There had been ribs among the meat, however, and when I had worked the point of the sharpest under the ring, it came up easily enough. I cast the rib into the fire as an additional offering and pulled at the ring with both hands.

The slab rose more readily than I had expected. Beneath it was a narrow stair and close beside it a pillar of flame; for the sacred hearth was not, as I had assumed, at the level of the temple floor, but here below it. I descended the stair, keeping away from the flames as well as I could.

"Your hair is singed." The voice was that of a woman. "I smell it, Latro."

I looked through the fire and saw her seated upon a dais at the end of the low room. Young she was, and lovely, wreathed in leaves and flowers; and flowers and leaves had been woven to make a chiton and a himation for her. And yet for all her youth and beauty, and the colors and perfumes of so many blossoms, there was something terrifying about her. When I reached the floor, I circled the sacred hearth, bowed low to her, and asked whether she was the Great Mother.

"No," she said. "I am her daughter. Because you are no friend of my mother's it would be best for you to call me the Maiden."

She rose from her seat as she spoke and came to stand before me. Slender and fragile though she looked, her eyes were higher than mine. "My mother cannot be everywhere, though she is in many places together. And so, because you have meddled in my realm, I offered to speak with you for her." She touched my hair, brushing away the scorched ends. "My mother does not wish to meet you again in any case. Would you not rather treat with me instead?"

"But I must meet with her," I said. I had read in this scroll what the Shining God had said and what the prophetess had chanted, and I told the Maiden of them.

"You are mistaken," the Maiden told me. "The Wolf-Killer said only that you must go to a shrine of my mother's, not that you need speak with her. As for the sibyl, her words were but a muddle of the Wolf-Killer's, cast in bad verse. Here is the hearth. You stand in the room below, though it was not always thus. You wished to speak with my mother, but I am before you in her place, more beautiful than she and a greater goddess."

"In that case, goddess, may I beg you to heal me and return me to my friends and my own city?"

She smiled. "You wish to remember, as the others do? If you remember, you will never forget me."

"I don't want to," I told her, but I knew even as I spoke that I lied.

"Many do," she said. "Or at least many believe they do. Do you know who I am?"

I shook my head.

"You have met my husband, but even he is lost now among the vapors that cloud your mind. I am the Queen of the Dead."

"Then surely I must not forget you. If men and women only knew how lovely you are, they wouldn't dread you as they do."

"They know," the Maiden told me, and plucked a lupine from her chiton. "Here is the wolf-flower for you, who bear the wolf's tooth. Do you know where it was born?"

I understood and said, "Beneath the soil."

The Maiden nodded. "If ten thousand others had not perished, this flower could never have been. It is the dead—trees and grasses, animals and men—who send you all you have of men, animals, trees, and grasses."

"Goddess, you say I've meddled in your realm. I don't remember; but restore my memory, and I'll do whatever you want of me to make amends."

"And what of the injury you did my mother?"

"I don't recall that, either," I told her. "But I am sorry from the bottom of my heart."

"Ah, you are no longer so stiff-necked as once you were. If this were my affair and not hers, I would do something for you now, perhaps. But it is hers, not mine." She smiled the infinitely kind smile of a woman who will not do what you ask. "I will convey your apology to her and plead your case most eloquently."

I think she saw the fury in my eyes before I knew of it myself, for she took a step backward without turning away from me.

"No!" My hand reached for Falcata, and I learned why the gods forbid our weapons in their temples.

"You threaten me. Do you not know that I cannot be harmed by a common mortal?"

"No," I said again. "No, I don't know that. Nor that I'm a common mortal. Perhaps I am. Perhaps not."

"You and your sword have been blessed by Asopus; but I am far greater than he, and your sword is elsewhere."

"You're right," I said. "My hands are all I have. I'll do the best I can with them."

"Against one entitled to your reverence as a goddess and your respect as a woman."

"If there's no need of them, I won't use them. Goddess, Maiden, I don't want to harm you or your mother. Yet I came hoping . . ." It seemed a bite of dry bread were caught in my throat; I could not speak.

"To be as other men. To know your home and friends."

"Yes."

"But by threatening me, you will only come to Death. Then you will be mine as so many others are, your home my kingdom, your friends my slaves."

"Better that than to live like this."

The stench of the grave filled the room, so strong that it masked the smoke from the cedar fire. Death rose through the floor and stood beside her, his skeleton hand clutching his black cloak.

"I need only say, 'He is yours,' and your life is past."

"I'll face him if I must."

Her smile grew warmer. "When you die at last, some monument will read, *Here rests one who dared the gods*. I will see to it. Yet I would rather not take such a hero in his youth."

Death sank from sight as quietly as he had come.

"You asked three favors of me; I will grant one, and you may choose the one. Will you be healed? Or returned to your friends? Or would you prefer to see your home again, though you will not recall it? I warn you, my mother will have a finger in it, whichever you choose; and I will make no further concessions. If you threaten me again, you will walk in the Lands of the Living no more."

I looked into her lovely, inhuman eyes; and I could not think which to choose.

"May I offer you refreshment?" she asked. "You may sample my wine while you decide, though if you drink deep of it, you must remain with me."

Glad of any argument that might postpone the choice, I protested, "But then, Maiden, I could see neither my friends nor my city."

"Both will be mine soon enough. Meanwhile you are young and very brave; come and share my couch, that a greater hero may be born. Our wine is in the columbarium there."

She pointed, and I saw a niche in the wall. In it stood a dusty jar and a cup, once the castle of some spider queen. Fear woke my hair. "What is this place?" I asked.

"You do not know? How quickly they forget, above! Your race might beg for memory better than yourself. You stand in the megaron of King Celeos. Behold his walls, where sits Minos his overlord, painted from life when he visited Celeos here. Celeos is my subject now and my husband's, and Minos one of our chief justices; no judge could better find the guilt attached to every party in a dispute than Minos. Behind you burns the fire in which my mother would have purified Celeos's son. When at last it dies, all this land will come to us."

I could only stare about me.

"This room has waited you a whole age of the world, but I will not. Have you chosen? Or will you die?"

"I'll choose," I told her. "If I ask for memory, I will indeed know who I am. But I may find myself very far from my city and my friends, and I've noticed that those who remember are generally less happy than I. If I choose my city, without friends or memories it will be as strange a place to me as this town of Advent. So I'm going to choose to rejoin my friends, who, if they are truly my friends, will tell me about my past, and where my city lies. Have I chosen wisely?"

"I had rather you had chosen me. Still, you have chosen, and one additional drop joins the flood that whirls us to destruction. Your wish shall be granted, as soon as it can be arranged. Do not cry out to me for succor when you are caught by the current."

She turned as if to go, and I saw that her back was a mass of putrefaction where worms and maggots writhed. I caught my breath but managed to say, "Do you hope to horrify me, Maiden? Every man who has followed a plow knows what you've shown me, yet we bless you all the same."

Again, she revealed her smiling face. "Beware my half sister Auge, who has stolen the south from my mother. And keep my flower—you shall have need of it." As she spoke, she sank slowly from sight.

At once the room grew darker despite the fire. I felt that a hundred ghosts, banished from it by her presence, were returning. Beside Minos stood a naked man with the head of a bull, his hand upon Minos's shoulder. The play of the firelight upon his muscled chest and arms made it seem they moved. A moment more, and he stamped as an ox does in the stall.

I snatched up the lupine, fled up the steps, and slammed down the slab. Almost, I threw the lupine into the flames; but its blue petals shone in the firelight, and I saw that it was but a wildflower, newly blown and brave with dew. I took off my chaplet, which had held many such blossoms, and found it sadly wilted. It I put into the flames instead, and I have rolled the lupine into the last turning of this scroll.

For it seems to me that we who bless her should not wantonly destroy what she has given.

Now I have written all I recall of this day. Already the morning, when we came to this place and met with Polyhommes, is as faded as the chaplet. I have looked back to see whether I spoke with Pindaros, Hilaeira, or Io at our inn, but there is nothing. Nor do I remember the name of the inn, nor where it stands. I would go there now and tell Pindaros of the Maiden, but no doubt the doors would be bolted, even if I should find it. I have written very small, always, not to waste this scroll. Now my eyes sting and burn when I seek to read it in the firelight, and yet nearly half the sheets are gray with my writing. I will write no more tonight.

# PART THREE

# TWENTY

## In My Room

HERE IN KALLEOS'S HOUSE, I have decided to write again. I have just read the last of what is written on this scroll, but I do not know whether it is true or even how long it has been since I wrote it. I read because I noticed the scroll in this chest today when I got out a clean chiton, and I thought if ever I needed to write something I would use it. I will write first who I am. I think this tells only who I was.

I am *Latro*, whom Kalleos calls her man slave. There is a girl slave too, Io, but she is too small to do heavy work. There are also Lalos the cook and another cook whose name I have forgotten, but they are not slaves; tonight Kalleos paid them, and they went home. Many women live here, but they are not slaves either, I think, and they do no work—only welcome the men when they come to their couches, and eat and drink with them. Before the men came, some of them teased me, but I could see they liked me and meant no harm. Kalleos paid them this morning after the first meal.

One of them spoke to me afterward, when the rest had gone to the market. She said, "I'm going to Advent tonight, Latro. Isn't it wonderful? If you want to come, I'll ask Kalleos."

I knew Latro was my name, because that and other things are written on the door of this room. I asked her why I should want to go to Advent.

"You don't remember, do you? You really don't."

I shook my head.

"I wish Pindaros hadn't gone home and left you here," she said sadly. "Kalleos wouldn't sell you for what he had, but I think he should have stayed and sent for more money, instead of going to get it."

I could see she was concerned for me; I told her I was happy enough, and that I had eaten all I wanted when I finished bringing the food from the kitchen.

"You said the Maiden promised you'd see your friends again. I wish she were quicker."

That was when I knew I had not always been in this place, and that I must have a family and a city of my own. Once there was a very large man and a very large woman who took care of me. I remember helping the woman carry cuttings away when the man pruned our vines. They had spoken to me too; and though I could understand everything Kalleos and the rest said, and speak to them as well as they to me, I knew their words were not mine, and I could speak mine to myself. So do I write, now. I did not know then who the Maiden was, because I had not read this scroll; by the time I wanted to ask about her, the woman had gone.

I stacked the dishes from the first meal and carried a stack into the kitchen. Lalos had told me his name when I had come to get the food. Now he said, "Have you heard about the Rope Makers, Latro?"

"No. Who are the Rope Makers?"

"The best soldiers in the world. People say they can't be beaten."

The other cook farted with his mouth.

"That's what people say—I didn't say it was true. Anyway, there's a lochos of Rope Makers going from house to house asking questions. The magistrates shouldn't have let them in—that's what I think. Of course they're our allies, and I suppose the magistrates didn't want trouble. Suppose they'd said no, and the Rope Makers had fought their way in. With so many away with the army and navy, who knows what would have happened?"

The other cook said, "You do. And everything else."

I asked, "Will they come here?"

"I suppose, some of them. They're going everywhere, asking crazy questions like what did you eat at the first meal yesterday."

The other cook said, "Then we'll tell them. What's the harm in telling a Rope Maker what you had at the first meal?"

"Yes, we'll tell them," Lalos agreed. "We'd better."

I carried in the rest of the dishes, and the cooks put little Io to washing them. There was food waste, mostly seeds and apple cores, scattered around the courtyard. Kalleos told me, "I'm your mistress,

Kalleos, Latro. I want you to sweep all this up. You know about answering the front door?"

I nodded and told her I had read it on my own door.

"Good. And *don't* forget to sweep again tonight when everyone's left. You can remember that, and I like it clean in the morning. And Latro, no matter what they tell you, the girls have to look after their own rooms—they'll get you to do it if they can, the lazy sluts. And their rooms have to be clean by tonight. If you see one who doesn't clean her room, you tell me."

I said, "I will, madame."

"And when you go to the door tonight, don't let in anyone who's drunk until he shows you his money—silver, not bronze or copper. Or gold. Let in anybody who has gold. But don't let in anyone who looks poor, drunk or sober. And don't draw that crooked sword of yours unless you have to. You shouldn't have to."

"No, madame."

"Use your fists, like you did on what's-his-name the other night. And when Io's finished washing up, send her to me. Don't let those two idlers in the kitchen make her do all their work—I want her to go to the market with me. I'll have most of the stuff for tonight delivered, and she can carry the odds and ends. Make the deliverymen go to the back, and don't talk to them. And make them leave—*after* you have all the goods—if they try to snoop. I'm counting on you, Latro."

Men came as soon as it grew dark, mostly bald or graying men, too old to fight. I admitted them; when they were busy with the women, I slept a bit in my chair by the door, only waking when the first left. Some stayed, sleeping with the women in their rooms. When the courtyard was empty, I carried the cups and bowls back to the kitchen for Io to wash tomorrow and got out my broom.

Many of the lamps were dark, and a man slept in one corner. I could see it would be impossible to clean the place well, but I decided to clean it as well as I could. It was very pleasant in the courtyard anyway. The thinnest-possible sliver of moon peeped between the clouds and left shadows beneath the walls, and the heat had passed. The air was soft, perfumed by the flowers Kalleos had bought that afternoon.

I was sweeping near a corner where there were many urns holding

many flowers, when a woman's hand stroked my shoulder. I turned to
see who she was, but her face was lost in the shadows. She said, "Come,
child of war. Do that later, or never."

Knowing what she wanted, I laid my broom on the flagstones and
sought her among the blossoms, not finding her until she showed herself
to me by kindling a silver lamp shaped like a dove, which hung over
the couch in her chamber.

I cannot remember what women I have possessed. Perhaps there
have been none. I know that for me tonight she was the first—that no
other would have been real beside her, that our joy endured while cities
rose and fell, and that while I clasped her the breezes of spring blew
perpetually.

My lover was half woman and half child, her cheeks and all her
flesh rose-tinted in the roseate light from the dove, slender yet round of
limb, her breasts small but perfect, her eyes like the skies of summer,
her hair like fire, like butter, like night, ripe with myriad perfumes.
"You forget," she said. "But you will remember me."

I nodded because I could not speak. I do not think I could have
lifted my hand.

"I am more lovely than my rival. Three faces she has, but none like
mine. You have forgotten her; you will never forget me."

"Never." Her chamber was hung with crimson velvet; it seemed to
glow in the dim light.

"And I am lovelier far than Kore, the Maiden." Her voice grew
bitter. "Not long ago, I gave my favor to a poor creature called Myrrha.
Better I had withheld it. Her own father bore her down, and she became
a tree, a speechless thing with wooden limbs." A horned doorman fluttered wide, white sleeves to ensure our privacy. "Yet she bore him a
child, the fairest ever seen. I locked it in a chest—so you would call it—
to keep it safe, for I had lovers who would have used it like a woman."

I nodded, though I would rather she had talked of love.

"I trusted her—that vile girl who calls herself the Maiden, though
her legs clasp Hades. She opened the chest and stole the child. I begged
for justice, but she kept it four moons each year. At last it died, and
from its blood sprang this blood-red blossom where we lie."

I said, "I would lie here forever, for every kiss of yours is new to
me."

"Yet you will not, O my lover. Soon, how soon you must go! But you will not forget me, nor what I say."

Then she whispered in my ear, repeating the same thing again and again in many ways. I cannot write it here, because I do not remember what it was—and it seems to me that even as I heard her words they were lost; but perhaps they only sank into some part of me where memory does not go. She showed me an apple of gold and spun the dove to make its light play upon that apple.

Then she was gone, and her chamber too, and I was left leaning on my broom in the cold court. The moon glowed high overhead, a crescent glyph cupping some meaning I did not comprehend.

I got one of the lamps and searched among the flowers for the door to her room; when I found it, it was only a crimson anemone, half-open, before which fluttered a tiny white moth.

With my hand I brushed him away and held it up, and it seemed to me the heart of the blossoms held a spark of laughter, but perhaps it was only a tear of dew.

A woman touched my shoulder. It was Kalleos, her breath heavy with wine because she had been drinking with the men.

"You don't have to worry about that, Latro," she said. "Poking among the flowers with a light. Get it tomorrow, when you can see what you're doing. Put away that broom and come with me. You're a fine figure of a man, know that?"

"Thank you," I said. "What is it you want, madame?"

"Only your arm to get me to my door. I'm ready for my bed tonight, by every god, and I'll sleep like a chalcis. I've a skin in there, Latro, and I'll give you a drink before you go. It isn't right that you should work all the time and never get to party."

I took her to her room, where she sat on her bed, her weight making the straps creak under the mattress until I thought they must break. She told me where the wineskin was and had me pour cups for us both; and while I was drinking mine, she blew out the lamp.

"I'm at that age when a woman looks best in the dark," she said. "Come and sit with me."

My hand brushed her naked breast.

"Surely you know how to put your arm around a woman?"

It was not completely dark. I had left the door open a crack, and a thread of light from the silver dove stole in, whispering something too faint for me to hear. Kalleos had let her robe fall to her hips, and I could see her white breasts and the rounded bulge that ended in the dark cloth of her robe. I felt they should disgust me now, but they did not. Rather it seemed that in some way Kalleos was the woman in the anemone, as a word written is the spoken word, and not just a dirty smudge upon the papyrus.

"Kiss me," she said. "And let me lay down."

I did as she told me, then took off her sandals and pulled her gown away from her legs.

By that time she was snoring. I went out, shutting the door behind me, and came here to my own place, where I write these words.

# TWENTY-ONE

## *Eutaktos*

THE LOCHAGOS KNOCKED AS I was serving the first meal today. Kalleos moaned. "That's trouble, I'm sure of it."

Zoe, who had been boasting about the big tip she had been given the night before, said, "It might be good news. You never know."

"Anything that happens before dark is bad news when you've got a headache. When you're my age, you'll understand."

The knocking grew louder. Phye said, "That's not knuckles. He's pounding with something."

It had been the grounding iron of a spear, as I learned when I opened the door. Eutaktos and half a dozen shieldmen shouldered their way in. Their hoplons and cuirasses protected their bellies, but their helmets were pushed back, and I was able to hit one in the neck and throw Eutaktos over my hip before the rest got their spears leveled. I threw my chair and drew my sword, and the women began to scream. Eutaktos was up again and had his own sword out, with Io hanging from his sword arm and crying, "Don't kill him!"

He shook her off. "We won't, unless he runs on the spears. Who's master here?"

Kalleos came forward, wearing the expression she used when the women threw food. "I am, and that's my slave you're talking about killing. If you kill him, you'll pay for him. Nine minas he cost me not a month ago, and I have a receipt signed by a leading citizen."

"You're no daughter of Hellen's."

"I didn't say I was a citizen," Kalleos answered with dignity. "I said the man I spoke of is. He's at sea in command of a squadron of our warships at this very moment. As for me, as a freedwoman and a resident foreigner I am protected by our laws."

Eutaktos looked sourly from her to me. "How many men here?"

"Right now? Three. Why do you want to know?"

"Get the rest."

Kalleos shrugged and told Phye, "Bring in Lalos and Leon."

"You there." Eutaktos pointed to me with his sword. "Quick! Name the man who sold you."

I shook my head.

Io said, "Hypereides, sir. Please don't hurt Latro—he can't remember."

The shieldmen, who had been nudging one another and winking while they stared at the women, fell silent as though someone had given a command. Eutaktos lowered his sword and sent it rasping back into the scabbard. "You say he doesn't remember, little girl?"

Suddenly abashed, Io nodded.

"We can settle this quickly," Eutaktos told Kalleos. "Do you have any books?"

Kalleos shook her head. "None. I keep all my records on wax tablets."

"None at all? Want us to search? You won't like it."

"There's a book Latro has to write in. He does forget, as Io says."

"Ah." Eutaktos glanced at one of the other Rope Makers, and both smiled. "Fetch it, woman."

"I don't know where he keeps it."

Phye said, "You won't be able to read it, Lochagos. I've tried, but he writes in some barbaric tongue." Our two cooks, who had banged the pans that morning and talked loudly, looked very small beside her. The man I had hit got to his feet rubbing his neck.

"But he can read it to me," Eutaktos said. "Latro, bring me your book."

Io said, "He's afraid you'll take it, sir. You won't, will you?"

Eutaktos shook his head. "Do you know where it is?"

Io nodded. "I know more about Latro than anybody."

"Then get it. We won't hurt him or you."

Io ran to my room and was soon back carrying this scroll.

"Good!" Eutaktos said. "And now—"

There was a tap at the door. Eutaktos told one of the shieldmen to see who it was and send him away. To me he said, "A fine book, must have cost a couple of owls. Too long for you to unroll it all between your hands?"

I nodded.

"Then do it on the floor, so I can see it. Little girl, hold down the end."

The shieldman who had been sent to the door announced, "Urgent message, Lochagos. A Milesian."

Eutaktos nodded, and the soldier ushered in a tall and very lean man with hair like a black haystack; he wore a purple cloak and many rings. This man darted a glance at me, another at Kalleos, and said to Eutaktos, "Many blessings upon you, noble warrior! I have words that are for your heroic ears alone."

Kalleos came forward smiling. "I can show you to a comfortable room, Lochagos, where you two can talk in private. We haven't tidied up yet from last night, but—"

"No matter," Eutaktos snapped. "Take us there—we won't be long. You, Latro, close your book again and keep it so. Basias, see that he does."

They were back almost at once, the Rope Maker looking pleased and the Milesian chagrined. To his shieldmen, Eutaktos said, "This fellow's come to tell us what we were about to see for ourselves." He turned to me. "Unroll your book."

I did as he had ordered, and when I reached the final sheet found a dried flower there.

Eutaktos crouched beside me. "You men, look here! Did everyone see this?"

The shieldmen nodded, and several said, "Yes, sir."

"Remember it. You may have to tell Pausanias. You heard me ask the question. You heard he couldn't answer. You saw him unroll this book, you saw the flower. Don't forget those things." He stood up. "These are high matters. It won't go well with anyone who makes a mistake."

The Milesian began, "Noble Rope Maker, if you would care—"

"I wouldn't. You Ionians are mad for gold. We win your battles for you, so you think we've got it. There isn't a man here who's any richer than the poorest slave in this house, myself included."

"In that case . . ." The Milesian shrugged and turned to go.

"Not so fast!"

Two shieldmen blocked the door.

"You'll leave when I say, not before. Obey orders or suffer for it. Latro, you're coming with us; so's the child. What's her name?"

"Io!" Io piped.

"Woman." Eutaktos turned to Kalleos. "Apply to Pausanias or either of our kings and you'll be compensated. Shut up! You talk too much—all of you do up here."

"Sir," I said, "I've got a cloak and some clean chitons. May I get them?"

He nodded. "Whatever you want, as long as that book's part of it. Basias, go with him."

Kalleos said, "Eurykles, you're not going with them too, are you?"

"Of course not," the Milesian told her.

Eutaktos turned on him. "Of course, you mean. You're from Miletos, Miletos is in the Empire, the Empire's our enemy, you're our prisoner. Curses and witchery will get your throat cut before you finish them."

I left with Basias then, and so I did not hear what else was said. When we returned, Io had a little bundle at her feet and a wooden doll under her arm. Basias looked inquiringly at Eutaktos and pointed to my sword.

Kalleos explained, "He was my watchman, Lochagos. Latro, I'll keep that for you, if you like."

"No," Eutaktos told her, "Basias will keep it. Pausanias may return it to him."

The street was hot after the shade of Kalleos's courtyard. I held my belongings at my shoulder with one hand and held Io's hand with the other; she held mine and did the same. Eutaktos marched in front of us, staring every man he saw out of countenance and spitting every time some new city stink offended his nostrils. The Milesian stumped sour-faced after us, muttering to himself.

Basias was on my right, and on my left and behind us tramped the rest of the shieldmen, all with long spears, red cloaks, and big hoplons painted with the wedge-shaped letter that the Crimson Men call the Stylus, which seems to me a most fit insignia for their Silent Country. They might have been the vanguard of an army of occupation, and the archers posted where the road left the city looked relieved when we marched past.

Among the Rope Makers each shieldman has several slaves to carry his belongings, pitch his tent, and prepare his food. These slaves had bought wine in the city, so we had a little to stir into our water (for the shieldmen had not yet eaten the first meal), as well as raw onions, boiled barley, salt olives, and cheese. Io says I forget, and I know I do; but I remembered then how much wine there had been on Kalleos's table when we left, and her melons and figs.

Before we ate, Eutaktos sent slaves into Thought to recall the other enomotia of his lochos. When the meal was over (which it soon was) he ordered the rest to break camp. I asked Basias where we were going.

"Back to Redface Island," he told me, "if that's where the prince is. He wants to see you."

I asked why, but he only shook his head.

Io said, "You don't remember, but we sailed around Redface Island with Hypereides. It looked wild—just a few little villages along the shore."

Basias nodded. "Too many pirates. Tower Hill trades for us."

The Milesian had come over to listen. He remarked, "And gets rich from it."

"That's their problem." Basias turned and stalked away.

"Odd people, aren't they?" the Milesian said. "I know you don't recognize me, Latro, but I'm Eurykles the Necromancer. You held a light for me not long ago, when I performed one of my greatest wonders."

Io said, "You came to Kalleos's and joined Hypereides's party. Rhoda told me."

Eurykles nodded. "That's right, and from it you must know I'm a good friend of Kalleos's; and Kalleos is Latro's rightful owner."

"She is not!"

He looked at her askance. He is one of those people who can raise one eyebrow a great deal higher than the other.

"Latro's a free man, and I'm *his* slave. Kalleos said I was hers, but she didn't even have a bill for me."

"Nor does Latro, I imagine. Not that it matters now. Don't talk of buying and selling to these Rope Makers, by the way. Among every other people in the world, trading's honorable and stealing dishonorable; but among the Rope Makers it's just the reverse. Stealing's glorious if you don't get caught, but trading blackens a man's name as much as keeping a stall in the market."

I said, "You don't like them."

"Nobody does. Some people admire them, and some people nearly worship them; but nobody likes them, and from what I've seen of them today, they don't even like each other."

Io asked whether he had been to Redface Island.

He shook his head. "There's no money past Tower Hill on the isthmus, not a scrap. Nothing but barley, blood, and beans. You saw how Eutaktos treated me when I came to him with valuable information, didn't you? Made me a prisoner! An officer from any decent city would have filled my mouth with silver."

I said, "You came to tell the Rope Makers about me."

"Yes, I did. It was quite clever of me, I think. You see, I had heard the Rope Makers were going through the city asking all sorts of foolish questions and paying no attention to the answers. They'd ask someone where he'd eaten dinner, and most would say in their own houses, and a few at some friend's house, and one or two at an inn or a cookshop; but it didn't seem to matter, no matter what they said. And after I'd listened to half a dozen stories like that, it dawned on me that they were looking for a man who didn't know. That had to be you."

Io asked, "What's my master ever done to you, fellow?"

Eurykles grinned. "Why, nothing. But I didn't think they were going to harm him, and I still don't. Judging from what Eutaktos says, Pausanias is just as apt to honor him. Besides, they would have found him sooner or later anyway—I was too late, actually—and I may still get something out of it."

"I thought you didn't want to be their prisoner."

"Yes, but it's their ingratitude that rankles. Anytime I really want to leave, I'll just render my person invisible and stroll away."

Then the last of the Rope Makers came out of the city and we left, each shieldman with his slaves marching behind him and carrying his hoplon, helmet, and spear, as well as the other things, and Io, Eurykles, and I behind Eutaktos as before. Now we are camped by a spring, and

Io has reminded me that before I sleep I should write down what happened today. A woman with two torches and two hounds is beckoning
from the crossroads, and when I have finished writing this I will go to
see what it is she wants.

# TWENTY-TWO

## The Woman at the Crossroads

THE DARK MOTHER FRIGHTENED ME. She is gone, but I am still afraid. I would not have thought I could be frightened by a woman even if she held a knife to my throat; but the Dark Mother is no common woman.

When I left the fire and went to speak to her, she seemed nothing more, a woman such as anyone might see in any village. Her eyes were dark, her hair black and bound with a fillet. The top of her head came only to my shoulder. She held a torch in each hand, torches that smoked, sending up black columns to the night sky.

Her dogs were black too, and very large—I think of the kind kings use to hunt lions, though I cannot remember ever having seen such a hunt. Their muzzles came to her elbows, and sometimes their ears stood erect like the ears of wolves. Their spittle was white and shone, even when it had dropped from their flews to the ground.

"You do not know me," the Dark Mother said, "though you have seen me each night."

When I heard her voice I knew she was a queen, and I bowed.

"These dogs of mine could tear you to bits, do you know that? Do you think you could resist them?"

"No, great mistress," I said. "Because they are yours."

She laughed, and at the sound of her laughter, things stirred among the trees. "That is a good answer. But do not call me *mistress**; that word means an owner of the earth, and she is my enemy. I am Enodia, the Dark Mother."

"Yes, Dark Mother."

---

*The word Latro used was probably *despoina* (Gk. δέσποινα).—G. W.

"Will you forget me, when you see me no longer?"

"I will strive not to forget, Dark Mother."

She laughed again, and the stirring told me the things waiting among the trees were so near they could almost be seen.

"I am the woman of poisons, Latro. Of murder, ghosts, and the spells that bring death. I am the Queen of the Neurians; and I am three. Do you understand?"

"Yes, Dark Mother," I said. "No, Dark Mother."

"Today you passed many farms. There you must have seen my image, cut in wood or stone—three women, standing back to back."

"Yes, Dark Mother, I saw the image. I did not know what it meant." My teeth warred in my mouth, the teeth above against the teeth below.

"You do not remember, yet you have looked often at the moon and seen me, as I have seen you. Once when I heard a certain one called the God in the Tree, I came while you stood in water. I sought him but found he was not He whom I sought. Do you recall me as I was then?"

I could not speak; I shook my head.

As the darkness vanishes when the moon steps from behind a cloud, so she vanished. In her place stood the lovely virgin I had seen beside the lake after I had slept with Hilaeira.

"You remember now," the virgin said, and smiled. "Earth's power is great, but I am here and she is not." She held a bow, just as I remembered, and there were seven arrows in the cestus at her waist. The Dark Mother's hounds fawned on her.

"Yes," I said. "I remember. Oh, thank you!" and I knelt and would have kissed her feet but that the hounds bared their teeth at me.

"I am no friend of yours, save as you are the enemy of my enemy; and when I am gone, you will forget me once more."

"Then never go!" I begged her. "Or take me with you."

"I cannot stay, and you cannot go where I go. But I have come to tell you of the place to which you will go soon. It is my country—do you understand? Call me Huntress now, for that is what they call me there, and Auge."

"Yes, Huntress."

"Once it was Gaea's. I sent my people, and they took it for me, breaking her altars."

"Yes, Huntress."

"You must not seek to loose their grasp, and because you will forget, I desire to send a slave with you who will remind you. Happily, there is someone with you who has sworn to serve me without reservation, and thus is mine wholly to do with as I choose."

"And I, Huntress."

"Hardly, though I know you mean well. Look at this." She held out her hand; in it writhed a little snake no longer than my finger. "Take her, and keep her safe."

I took it, but I had nowhere to put it. I held it in my hand, and in a moment it seemed to vanish; I held nothing.

"Good. Down that road is a farmhouse." The Huntress pointed with her bow. "It is not far, and you need not fear that the shieldman set to watch you will wake. You must go to that farm and make its people give you a wineskin and a cup. When you meet the one who has dedicated himself to me, you must make him drink, and you must put my serpent into the cup. Do you understand?"

"Huntress," I said, "I have lost your serpent."

"You will find her again when the time comes. Now go. I send my dogs before you to rouse the house."

As she spoke, they flashed from her side. For an instant I saw them streaking down the road she had indicated; then they were gone.

I turned and followed them, knowing that was what the virgin wished me to do. When I had taken fifty steps or so, the urge to see her once more overwhelmed me, and I looked over my shoulder.

I wish I had not, because she was gone. The Dark Mother stood where she had stood, holding her torches; wisps of fog and dark, shapeless things had left the trees to be with her. Someone screamed and I began to run, though I could not have said whether I ran to give aid or to fly the Dark Mother.

The farmhouse was like a hundred others, of rough brick with a thatched roof, its farmyard surrounded by a low wall of mud and sticks. The gate had been broken; I entered easily. Inside, the wooden figure of the three women had been thrown down, though the altars to either side of the door had not been touched. The door was whole, but as I approached it a man with staring eyes flung it open and ran out. He would have collided with me as one horseman rides down another, had I not caught him as he came.

I asked, "Are you the father of this hearth?"

"Yes," he said.

"Then I can take away the curse, I think; but you must give me freely a skin of wine and a cup."

His mouth worked. I think it would have foamed had there been any moisture there. The screaming inside had stopped, though a child wept.

"Give me the wine," I told him.

Without another word he turned and went in again, and I followed him.

His wife came to him, naked and weeping, her face twisted with fear and grief. She tried to speak, but only the noises of grief and fear could pass her lips. He pushed her to one side; when she saw me she clasped me for protection, and I put my arm about her.

The man returned with a wineskin and a cup of unglazed clay. "This has waited two seasons," he said. I saw that he himself was no older than I, and perhaps younger.

Telling him to comfort his wife, I went back outside. There I set up the image in its place again, poured a little wine into the cup, and sprinkled a few drops before each of the three figures, calling them Dark Mother, Huntress, and Moon. Before I had finished, silence settled on the house, and an owl hooted from the wood.

The farmer and his wife came out to me, she now wearing a gown and leading a girl younger than Io by the hand. I told them I did not think they would be troubled again. They thanked me many times; and he brought a lamp, another skin of wine, and cups like the one he had given me. We all drank the unmixed wine, the child sipping from her mother's cup that she might sleep soundly, as her mother said. I asked them what they had seen.

The child would say only that it had been a bad thing; I did not question her further, seeing that it made her afraid. The woman said that a hag with staring eyes had sat upon her and held her motionless by a spell; she had been unable to breathe. The man spoke of a winged creature, not a bird nor a bat, that had flapped after him from room to room.

I asked whether any of them had seen a dog. They told me they owned a dog and had heard him bark. We went to look for him in his kennel behind the house and found him dead, though there was no mark upon him. He was old and white at the muzzle. The man asked whether I was an archimage; I told him only for this night.

When I left the farmhouse, a figure moved at the crossroad, and I saw many tiny lights, though the Dark Mother and her torches were gone. It was the Milesian; he started up as though frightened when I approached him, though he relaxed when he saw my face. "Latro!" he exclaimed. "There's someone else awake, at least. Do you know the Rope Makers didn't even post a guard? There's confidence for you."

I asked what he was doing.

"Just a little sacrifice to the Triple Goddess. Road crossings like this are sacred to her, provided there's no house in sight, and the dark of the moon is the best time. I hadn't thanked her properly yet for the great boon she gave me in the city—you were there and saw it, what a pity you don't remember! Anyway, this seemed a good chance to do it. Then this fellow"—he pointed to the sacrifice, a black puppy—"wandered up to me, and I knew it had to be propitious."

I said, "If you haven't finished . . ."

"Oh, no. I completed the last invocation just as I heard your step." He bent and picked up the glowing things that formed a circle around the puppy, then looked significantly at the wineskin. "You've been buying from the peasants, I see."

I nodded and asked whether he was dedicated to the Triple Goddess.

"Yes indeed. Ever since I was a lad. She gives her worshipers all they ask—even old Hesiod says so in his verses, though none of his countrymen seemed to heed him. I admit she has some strange ways of doing it."

I knew then that he was the one of whom the Huntress had spoken, and I loosened the thongs of the wineskin and poured wine into the cup. "What is it you have asked of her?"

"Power, of course. Gold is only a kind of power, and not the best kind. As for women, I've had a good many, and I find I prefer boys."

To fill the time, I said, "Power will get you all you wish of those. Kings have no difficulty."

"Of course not. But real power is not of this world, but of the higher one—the ability to call back the dead and summon spirits; the knowledge of unseen things."

I sipped from the cup, and as I lowered it, felt the little snake stir in the hand that held the skin. When I poured more wine into the cup, I dropped the snake in with it.

The Milesian drained it at a gulp. "Thanks. I owe you something for that, Latro." He wiped his mouth on the back of his hand. "I'd initiate you into the mystery of the goddess, but you'd forget, and it can't be written down."

Side by side we walked back to the tents of the Rope Makers. My bed was in Basias's tent; I do not know with whom the Milesian's was. He asked if we might share another cup before we slept. I told him I had drunk all the wine I wanted, but I would gladly give him another. He drank it and wished me a good night.

I tried to wish him the same, but the words stayed in my throat.

"Eurykles," he told me, thinking that I had forgotten his name.

"Yes, Eurykles," I said. "Good luck, Eurykles. I know your goddess is pleased with you."

He smiled and waved before he went into one of the tents.

I lay down, and after a long time I slept. Now the sky grows light, and though I would sooner forget what happened last night, I think it best to write it here.

# TWENTY-THREE

## *In the Village*

I AM WRITING THIS IN the courtyard of the inn. Eutaktos had been so eager to leave Thought that he did not buy provisions for the return to Redface Island. I think perhaps he believed also that he could get them more cheaply away from the city, and in that I suppose he was right. Anyway, we have halted here, and Eutaktos and some others are bargaining for food in the market. I am writing because I have not yet forgotten what took place last night, though I do not remember how I came to be among these Rope Makers.

The Milesian came to me when we halted here and said, "Let's find a wineshop. I'll repay you for what you gave me last night." I pretended to have forgotten, but he pressed me to go anyway, saying, "Basias can come with us. Then they can't say we were trying to get away."

Soon the Milesian, Basias, Io, and I were sitting very comfortably at a table in the shade; there was a jar of old wine and one of cold well water in the center of the table, and each of us had a cup before him. "You will recall that we were discussing the Triple Goddess last evening," the Milesian said to me. "At least, I hope you will. That hasn't gone yet, has it?"

I shook my head. "I can remember our camping outside this village late last night, and everything that came after that."

Io asked, "Where are we, anyway? Is this far from Advent?"

"This is Acharnae," the Milesian told her. "We're about fifty stades from Advent, which will be our next stop. It would have been a little shorter along the Sacred Way, but I suppose Eutaktos felt there was too much danger of incurring a charge of impiety." He looked at Basias for confirmation, but the Rope Maker only shrugged and put his cup to his lips.

"I've been to Advent before," Io told the Milesian. "With Latro and Pindaros and Hilaeira. Latro slept in the temple."

"Really? And did he learn anything?"

"That the goddess would soon restore him to his friends."

I asked Io to tell me about that.

"I don't know much, because you didn't tell me much. I think you told Pindaros more than me, and you probably wrote more than you told Pindaros. All you said to me was that you saw the goddess, and she gave you a flower and promised you'd see your friends soon. We were your friends, Hilaeira and Pindaros and me, but I don't think she meant us. I think she meant the friends you lost when you were hurt."

Basias was looking at me narrowly. "She gave you a flower in a dream?"

I said, "I don't know."

Io told him. "He just said she gave him one."

The Milesian spun an owl on the table as if hoping for an omen. "You can never tell about goddesses. Or gods either. Possibly a dream with a goddess in it is more real than a day without one. The goddess makes it so. That's what I'd like to be."

I was surprised. "A goddess?"

"Or a god. Whatever. Find some little place, impress the people with my powers, and make them build me a temple."

Basias told him, "You'd better put more water in that."

The Milesian smiled. "Perhaps you're right."

"Drinking unmixed wine will drive a man mad—everybody knows that. The Sons of Scoloti do it, and they're all as mad as crabs."

"Yet I've heard there are little villages along your coast where the people worship sea gods who've been forgotten everywhere else in the world."

Basias drank again. "Who cares what slaves do? Or who their slave gods are?"

Io said, "We had four Sons of Scoloti on Hypereides's ship with us, Latro. But then one left the night the sailor died and never came back."

Basias nodded. "What did I tell you?"

The Milesian spun his coin again. "Not all of them are Sons of Scoloti. Some are Neurians; there was a Neurian in the city."

"Who are they? I never heard of them."

"They live east of the Sons of Scoloti and have much the same manners and customs. At least, when we see them."

Basias poured himself more wine. "Then who cares?"

"Except that they can change themselves into wolves. Or anyway they change into wolves. Some people say they can't control it." The Milesian lowered his voice. "Latro, you don't remember how I raised a woman in the city, but one of them had opened her grave. I had planned, you see, just to produce a ghost; but when I saw that broken coffin— well, the opportunity was too good to miss."

The innkeeper, who had been lounging against the wall not far away, sauntered over to join the conversation. "I couldn't help but hear what you said about men who change to wolves. You know, we had somethin' a bit odd happen just last night, right here in Acharnae. Family sleepin' peacefully in their beds, when just like a thunderclap the place was full of I don't know what you call 'em. People talk about Sabaktes and Mormo and all that, kind of like they was a joke. These wasn't, though they didn't write their names on the walls."

The Milesian said, "They vanished at dawn, I assume. I wish I might stay here another day, so I might exorcise them for those good people; my fame in that line outreaches the known world, though I hesitate to say it. But I fear the noble Eutaktos means for us to march again after the first meal."

"They're gone already," the innkeeper said. "I haven't talked to the family myself, but I know them that have, and they say a man come to the door just as they was runnin' out. He said to give him a skin of wine and he'd fix things. So they did, and he set up the figure of the three goddesses that had been knocked down and poured out a bit to each goddess. Soon as he did that, they was gone." The innkeeper paused, looking from face to face. "He was a real tall man, they said, with a scar on his head."

The Milesian yawned. "What happened to the wine? I don't suppose he poured it all out."

"Oh, he kept that. Some people are sayin' he probably whistled up those whatever-they-weres just to get it. I say that for a man who could do that, he was satisfied awful cheap."

"And so would I," the Milesian drawled when the innkeeper had left. He spun the owl on the table as before. "But then, it all depends on just whom the wonder's worked for, doesn't it? When I raised the dead woman in the city, I had sense enough to take her around to some wealthy patrons before cockcrow. Most of them weren't *my* patrons before they saw her, to be sure. But they were afterward. Some people despise wealth, however. I do myself."

"You don't talk like it," Basias told him.

"Do you have any money?"

"I thought this was your treat."

"Oh, it is. I just want to know whether you've got any."

"Couple of obols," Basias admitted.

"Then throw them away. They're no good where we're going, or so people tell me. Toss them into the dirt there. I'm sure that fellow who just left will be happy to pick them up."

Basias darted the Milesian a surly look but said nothing.

"You see, you don't despise *money*. Nor do I. Wealth is stuffy and stupid and arrogant, and the only good thing about it is that it has money. Money's lovely stuff—just look at this." He held up the owl. "See how it shines? On one side the owl: the male principle. On the other, the Lady of Thought: the female principle." He spun the coin on the table. "Money always gives you something to think about."

Basias asked, "Do you know what Pausanias did after the Battle of Clay?"

The Milesian looked bored, but Io piped, "Tell us!"

"We killed Mardonius and got his baggage. So Pausanias told his cooks to cook a meal just like they would have for him and his staff. He called in all our officers and showed it to them. I wasn't there, but Eutaktos was, and he told me. Pausanias said, 'See the wealth of these people who have come to share our poverty.' "

"It's perfectly true." The Milesian nodded, still spinning his coin. "By our standards, the wealth of the Empire is incalculable. His name wasn't really Mardonius, by the way. It was Marduniya. It means 'the warrior.' "

Basias said, "I couldn't say that without wrenching my mouth."

"You'll have to learn to wrench your mouth, if you hope to get rich while you're liberating the Asian cities with Pausanias."

"Who said I did?"

"Why, no one. I said 'if.' "

"You say too much, Eurykles."

"I know. I know." The Milesian rose. "But now, if you'll excuse me, kind friends, I have to—where does one do it here, anyway? In back, I suppose."

No one spoke for a moment, then Basias said, "I'd like to go with him."

I asked why he did not.

"Because I'm supposed to stay with you. But I'd like to see what he has under all those clothes. Did you ever?"

"See him naked?" I asked. "Not that I remember."

Io said, "Neither have I, and I don't want to. I'm too little for that."

Basias grinned at her. "Anyway, you know it. Half don't. But if you change your mind, I'll show you a way."

I said, "And I will kill you for it."

"You mean you'll try, barbarian."

Io said, "Latro isn't a barbarian. He talks just as good as you do. Better."

"Talk, yes, but can he wrestle?"

"You saw him throw your lochagos."

Basias was grinning again now. "I did, and it set me wondering. Want a bout, barbarian?" He drained his wine. "Same rules they use in Olympia—no hitting, no kicking, no holds below the waist."

I stood and took off my chiton. Basias laid his sword belt on the table and took off his cuirass, then pulled his own chiton over his head. The innkeeper appeared from nowhere with half a dozen loungers in his train. "Just a friendly bout," Basias told him.

He was shorter than I by a hand, but a trifle heavier. When he extended his arm for me, it was like gripping the limb of an oak. In a moment he had me by the waist; and in a moment more, I was flat on my back in the dirt.

"Easy meat," Basias said. "Didn't anybody ever teach you?"

I said, "I don't know."

"Well, that's one fall. Three and you lose. Want to try again?"

I bathed my hands in dust to dry the sweat. This time he lifted me over his head. "Now if I wanted to hurt you, barbarian, I'd throw you into the table. But that would spill the wine."

The inn yard swung dizzily until it was where the sky should be, then slapped me as a man swats a fly.

"Two falls for me. Got anything left?"

My eyes were wet with the tears of shame, and I wiped them on the back of my arm. One of the loungers told the innkeeper, "I'll take my obol now. Why not save the time and trouble?"

Io was saying, "I'll bet you another obol," to the lounger by the time I had my knees under me.

"Bet with a child? Let me see your money. All right, but you'd be a fool if he were Heracles."

The oak limb I had imagined a moment earlier appeared before my eyes. "I can't help you up," the big man who held it rumbled. "It's against the rules. But it's not against them to take your time getting up, and you'd better do it."

I got a foot beneath me but kept one knee on the ground as I wiped my forehead.

"He's beating you by lifting you, like I beat Antaeus. You have to keep hold of him all the time. He can't lift himself."

When Basias offered me his arm again, I closed with him, gripping him under the arms as he gripped me by the waist.

"He'll try to bend you back," the man with the club said. "Twist and squeeze. Every muscle in your arm's a piece of raw hide. They're drying in the sun, pulling up. Hear his ribs creak? Dig into his neck with that sharp chin of yours."

We fell together. When I had climbed off him, Basias said, "You're learning. That's one for you. You've got to give me your arm this time."

I turned him upside down and found that his lower ribs were softer than the upper ones. His arms were no longer as hard as they had been. With one hand on his waist and one at his shoulder, I was able to get him above my head. "You didn't throw me at the table," I told him. "So I won't do it to you either."

The big man with the club pointed to the lounger who had bet with Io.

I said, "All right," and knocked the lounger off his feet with Basias.

The Milesian applauded, rapping the tabletop with his cup.

"Good!" the big man whispered. "Now let him win."

# TWENTY-FOUR

## *Why Did You Lose?*

IO ASKED HER QUESTION WITH her eyes as I sat writing. I said, "I don't know." And then, thinking of the man with the club and why he might have spoken as he had, "Do you think we'd be better off if I'd won? Besides, it wouldn't have been fair. Suppose Basias had thrown me into the table. That would have ended the match."

He came out of the inn with grease on the place where he had hurt his arm. "Any wine left?"

Io tilted the jar and peered inside. "Almost half-full."

"I can use it. Your master's a man of his hands, girl. With some training he might do for the Games."

"You'd better water that," she told him. "It drives you mad."

"I'll spit in it. Same thing." He looked at me. "You really don't know who you are?"

I shook my head. The Milesian stirred in his sleep, groaning like a woman in love.

"You're a barbarian by the look of you. No Hellene ever had a beak like that. No helot either. That sword of yours looks foreign too. You have any armor?"

Io said, "He used to have front and back plates, round things that hung over his shoulders and tied at the waist. I think Kalleos has them now."

Basias drained his cup and filled it again. "I saw a lot of those on dead men at Clay, but they don't help me much."

I said, "Tell us about the battle. You were there, and I'd like to know."

"What happened to you? I can't tell you that without knowing where you were." He dipped a finger in his wine. "Here's our army.

That's a ridgeline, see? Over here's the enemy." He poured a puddle on the table. "The plain was black with them. One of our officers—Amompharetos is his name—had been giving Pausanias trouble. He should have been asked to the council, see? Only he wasn't. Either the message never got to him, which is what Pausanias says, or Pausanias never sent it. That's what Amompharetos said. They finally got it patched up, so Pausanias put Amompharetos and his taksis back here in reserve to show he trusted him."

Io said, "It looks to me like he didn't."

"You're no man; you'll never understand war. But the reserve's the most important part of the army. It's got to go to the hottest place when the army's losing. There were more hills here on the right, with all the men from that dirty place we just left hiding behind them. We're out where the enemy can see us; then Pausanias gives the order to pull back."

Io interrupted. "Is Pausanias one of your kings? And do you really have two?"

"Sure we've got two," Basias told her. "It's the only system that works."

"I'd think they'd fight."

"That's it. Suppose there was just one. A lot of people have tried that. If he's strong, he takes every man's wife, and the sons too. He does whatever he likes. But look at us. If one of ours tried that, we'd side with the other. So they don't. But Pausanias isn't a king, he's regent for Pleistarchos."

Basias held up his cup to me. I poured a little wine from mine into his and let him do the same. "Over here's the Molois," he continued, "almost dry. Here's Hysiae and here's Argiopium, just a village around the temple of the Grain Goddess."

The grass underfoot is yellowing, the sky so light a blue it hurts the eyes. Brown hills rise at the end of the yellow plain. Dark horsemen cross and recross; beyond them the red cloaks of the enemy seep away like blood from a corpse. Mardonius is on his white stallion in the midst of the Immortals. The trumpets are blowing, and the heralds shout to advance. I try to keep our hundred together, but Medes with bows and big wicker shields press through our formation, then spearmen and bowmen with bodies painted white and red. We run across the plain, the swifter outpacing the slower, the lightly armed always farther ahead of the heavily armed, until I can see no one I know, only dust and running strangers, and ahead the shining bronze wall of the hoplons, the bristling hedge of the spears.

Little Io was pressing my forehead with a wet cloth. An enemy bent over me, his horsehair crest nodding, his red cloak falling beside his shoulders. I reached for Falcata, but Falcata was gone.

"It's all right," Io said. "All right, master."

The enemy straightened up. "How long's he been like this?" It was Eutaktos, and I knew him.

"Not long," Io said. "Basias sent one of the inn servants for you."

I tried to say I was well, but it came from my lips in this tongue, not in theirs.

"He talks a lot," Io told Eutaktos, "only you can't understand it. Most of the time he doesn't seem to see me."

I said, "I'm better now," speaking as they.

Eutaktos said, "Good, good," and knelt beside me. "What happened? Basias hit you?"

I did not understand what he meant. "We broke," I told him. "Even when they made a new shieldwall we were only a mob behind it. The Medes took the spears in their hands and broke them, died. The arrows were no good, and I can't find Falcata."

Io said, "That's his sword."

I told them Marcus was dead, and I could not find Umeri, that we should not have gone to Riverland.

Eutaktos said, "There's magic in this. Where's that magician?"

Io gestured. "Asleep outside."

"He was, maybe. Not now. I would have seen him." Eutaktos stamped away and I sat up.

"Are you better, master?"

Io's little face looked so concerned I had to laugh. "Yes," I said. "And I know you. But I can't think who you are."

"I'm Io, your slave girl. The Shining God gave me to you."

We were in a cramped, dark room that smelled of smoke. I said, "I don't remember. What is this place?"

"Just an inn."

A tall, ugly woman with short black hair came in, saying, "Hello, Latro. Do you remember me?"

I said, "Latro?"

"Yes, you're Latro, and I'm your friend Eurykles. Kalleos's friend too. Do you recall Kalleos?"

I shook my head.

"I'm supposed to heal you," the woman said, "and I want to. But I don't know what happened—I was taking a nap. It might help if I did."

Io said, "Do you remember how he wrestled with Basias?"

"Yes. Basias threw him twice, then he threw Basias twice, then Basias threw Latro again to end the bout. We all had a drink on it, and Basias went in here to try to find something to put on that bad place on his arm. Latro wanted to write in his book—"

I looked at Io and tried to stand. She said hastily, "I have it right here, master. Your stylus too."

"—and I got sleepy and lay down. What happened after that?"

"Basias came back and they drank some more, and Basias asked Latro if he had any armor." Io looked at me. "Basias has your sword, master. He's keeping it for you."

The ugly woman said, "Go on."

"And I said he didn't. Then Latro said to tell him about the battle. I guess he meant the one where everybody in our Sacred Band got killed. Anyway Basias knew, and he told us about their kings and where the armies were." Io paused for breath.

"Then Latro shouted. He kept on shouting and knocked over the wine, and Basias got hold of him from in back and tried to throw him down, but Latro got loose. Then Basias and a lot of men from the inn caught him and threw him down and he stopped shouting. He talked a lot, but you couldn't understand him, and they carried him in here. Basias said it was because he didn't put enough water in his wine, but he did. He put a lot more in than Basias did."

The ugly woman nodded and sat beside me on the low bed. "What was the matter, Latro? Why were you shouting?"

"We all were," I told her. "Running toward the enemy and shouting. They were retreating—we had so many more than they—and it seemed as though a good push would end the war. Then they turned like an elk with a thousand points."

"I see." A few hairs sprouted from the woman's chin; she pulled at them with her fingers. "Eutaktos thinks it's witchery, but I'm beginning to doubt it; the malice of someone on the Mountain seems more likely. We might try a sacrifice to the War God. Or . . . Latro, these Rope Makers have a healer called Aesculapius. Do you know of him?"

I shook my head.

"He might be best, since you're under their protection, or ought to be. I'll talk to Eutaktos about it. I'll also compound a charm for you, calling upon certain powers with whom I have influence. Health isn't one of their concerns, usually—still, they may be able to do something."

When the ugly woman left, Io wanted to stay with me; but I would rather have her where she can discover what's taking place and return to tell me. Before she left I had her bring me a stool, so I might write this in comfort. Eutaktos has put two shieldmen at the door, but they permit it to stand open, and I am sitting so the light falls upon the papyrus.

Io has returned to say that the slaves of the Rope Makers are building an altar to the Healing God the ugly woman spoke of. She says Basias has been to this god's great temple on Redface Island, and that when Eutaktos has sacrificed for me I will have to sleep beside the altar. In her absence, I had been reading this scroll, and thus I know I slept in the temple of the Grain Goddess once in much the same way.

Io says Eutaktos intends to leave this place and go to Advent tomorrow, whether the god appears or not. From Advent there is a good road to Redface Island.

I asked her about the ugly woman who promised to make me a charm; she says there is no such woman, that it was Eurykles of Miletos, who wears a purple cloak but is a man. That seems stranger to me than any of the strange things I have read in this scroll.

The innkeeper brought my supper, and I asked for a lamp. He said he had lost a bet on me, but it was worth it to see the man he bet with knocked down. He asked a great many questions about who I was and where I came from, none of which I could answer. He says he sees many foreigners in his trade, but he could not tell me where my country lies.

I asked him to tell me the nations I was *not* from. Here is what he said: Not a Hellene. (Which I knew already, of course.) Not of Persepolis. (I asked him about this place; it is the Great King's city.) Not of Riverland. (This I knew, because I recalled thinking we should not have gone there. Plainly I have been there, and though it is not my home, it may be that someone there knows me.) Not of Horseland, the Tall Cap Country, or the Archers' Country. Not a Carian.

I am more determined to find my friends and my home than ever now, because of the things I have read here. I feel that though I may forget everything else, I will not forget that. The Queen of the Dead promised I will soon see my friends again, and I wonder if they too are not prisoners of the Rope Makers. I would try to sleep, but when I shut my eyes I see the wall of spears, the wicker shields trampled down, the bodies of the dead, and the white walls of the temple.

# TWENTY-FIVE

## *I, Eurykles, Write*

A S REQUESTED BY YOUR SLAVE, Io, I shall describe the events of the past night and day, turning her words into such as may properly be set down. She asks this because Eutaktos the Spartiate has forbidden you should have this book, thinking that writing in it as you do has disordered your mind. She wishes a record to be kept that she may read it to you when this book is restored to you, and I form the letters better than she, and smaller.

But before I write as she has directed me, permit me to say somewhat of myself. For though it may be, Latro, that the august regent wishes you ill, it may also be that he wishes you well—as, indeed, it is my fond hope he does. How then will you recollect your friend and companion on this journey to the dour isle of Pelops, if I do not here record some outline of my person as a corrective to your errant memory? So shall I now do, after placating little Io (fiery as the gadfly), who nibbles her lips with impatience.

Very well then, and briefly: I was born in Miletos, in the lesser Asia, my father having been, as Mother always assured me, a distinguished citizen of that, my native city. When I was but eleven years of age, the Triple Goddess appeared to me in a dream, pointing out the leaves of a certain plant and urging me by their aid to escape another boy, at whose hands I had suffered many injustices. After several errors, I discovered the correct plant in the waking world and contrived to slip a young and tender leaf into a confection I feigned to eat until he took it from me. He was ill for several days preceding his death, which a wise priest summoned by his parents ascribed quite correctly to the darts of the Far-Shooting Delian.

Following this boy's demise, I made—as you, my dear friend, may imagine—many, many sacrifices; and though they were but sparrows, frogs, and suchlike boyish things, I am bold (or rather say, I have such impudence) enough to suppose that they were accepted in the spirit in which a willing heart offered them, however young. In a year or less, I heard of the great Carian temple to her, at no great distance inland from my city. Thither I journeyed, walking most of the way. There I made a prayer to that sly messenger who lends to thieves his winged heels and managed to procure a most suitable sacrifice in the form of a large black rabbit with a crescent moon of white upon its forehead. (For this animal I was complimented by a priest, a kindness I have not—O subtle reeds, bear witness—forgotten to this day.)

Upon returning to Miletos, I discovered that Mother had seized the occasion of my absence to remove herself from the city; some said to Samos, others to Chios. Here was the hand of the goddess clearly, and I resolved that she alone would be my mother henceforth. I attached myself as firmly as I could to all who were in her good graces, and offered my services to those who, like prudent Agamemnon, called King of Men, sought her favor.

To me, at least, it has been granted in full. I do not scruple to say in any company that there is neither man nor woman more skilled in her mysteries than I, or more adept at the weaving of curses, the compounding of poisons, or the raising of ghosts. You yourself were present at my greatest triumph, Latro, and I pray that divine Trioditis, who sees the past as well as the present and the future, may someday restore what you have lost, that you may give witness to it.

In my person I am a true son of Ion, far taller than the ruck of men and blessed with a dancer's frame, hardy and graceful rather than muscular. My eyes are prominent, as are the bones of my cheeks. My nose and mouth are delicate, my lofty forehead half-concealed by abundant hair. If the stamping Io soon reads you this, you may know me by my chlamys, which has been dyed a pleasing color with the juice of mulberries.

As a frequent visitor to her city, I gained the friendship of your mistress, Kalleos, a happy event made twice happy for me by the triumph I have already mentioned. Suffice it to say that you and I, in company with certain others, among whom Io of the burning eye was not included, made our way from your mistress's house to a certain place of burial, and there discovered One whom I restored—for a brief time at least—to the Lands of the Living. It was the wonder of all beholders, and should you find it difficult to credit what I say, I urge you to return to the city we have left, where you will find the matter talked of by all.

For your sake, then, I have compounded a charm calculated to calm and restore your mind—this at your own request and Eutaktos's as well. And indeed I would have acted had either of you asked alone.

For the Moon, a single white stone. For the Huntress, one of the minute arrowheads made before the time of the gods, which the initiate may sometimes discover. For the Dark, a single black hair plucked from the head of one who has dedicated himself wholly—that is to say, from my own head. With a thorn of the white-flowered briar dipped in my own blood, I wrote upon a scrap of cypress bark my plea for you to the goddess. All these I bound in a circle of deerskin and with mighty invocations hung about your neck on a thong.

The sophists would say that all these things—stone, dart, hair, prayer, and hide—count for nothing; or at most that they serve only to turn the minds of priest and supplicant to the gods. Yet I have observed that those who believe so win no favor, and thus I myself believe that they are something more. With the charm in place (as Io urgently bids me write), Eutaktos and I, with Io and some others, escorted you to the altar I had ordered the slaves to build. There the holy fire was kindled, there Eutaktos himself offered a sacrifice for you, and there you remained, circled at some distance by sentries.

I regret I was not present when you reported to Eutaktos in the morning; but Io was, having secreted herself nearby with that stealth and cunning so well suited to the cattle-raising half barbarians from whom she proceeds. Her description of the conversation is prolix indeed, but I shall abstract from it.

In your dream, you seemed to wake at the cracking of a stick (or so Io says you told Eutaktos) to see an elderly man, bent and swan-white of beard, approaching from the wood. You rose and asked if he was the god Aesculapius. He denied it. When you pressed him, he maintained that he was indeed Aesculapius, but no god—merely a poor mortal forced to serve them. You asked then if he would not heal you. Again he shook his head, saying that he had been sent by the murderess of his mother, whose slave he is from her temple on Euboea to the island temple of Anadyomene, but that he could do nothing; at which point he vanished.

Io says that at this Eutaktos grew angry, shouting that Aesculapius would not have employed such words to describe the goddess. This moment you chose (surely, friend Latro, you might have chosen more wisely) to ask that Eutaktos return you to your comrades, saying that you had read in this book of your visit to the Queen Below, and that Eutaktos should not take it upon himself to thwart the will of one to whom all must come at last.

At that Eutaktos grew more wrathful still. He ordered that this book be taken from you (as it was, by Basias), and we broke camp. These events you have already forgotten, or so Io and I fear. We now proceed to more recent things, which you at present know as well as we—or so we hope—but which will perhaps have escaped you when Io reads my words to you.

First as to the goddess. Aesculapius, as I have explained to you, was the son of her brother and twin, borne by a mortal woman named Coronis. While she carried his child, Coronis proved unfaithful to him; and upon learning of the disgrace, the goddess slew her. The god, however, recalling that the child she carried was his own as well as hers, saved him from her funeral pyre, snatching him both from his mother's womb and from the flames, and giving him over to the tutelage of one from whom he learned so much of the healing art as to exceed his teacher and every other mortal.

I cannot believe that he would call his rescuer's (and his father's) twin a murderess, since the right of the gods to slay mortals even as we slay beasts is everywhere unquestioned, and the woman was far from blameless. I am happy to learn, however, that Aesculapius is subject to the goddess in this part of the world. So high is she already in the eyes of her devoted Eurykles that nothing could raise her higher; and yet it may be useful to me.

Now as to recent events. You will wish to know how it is that Io and I have your book, though you do not. The answer is that Basias the Spartiate has permitted it from the good feeling he has for Io and yourself, saying that so long as you are granted no sight of it, Eutaktos will not object. Thus we now keep it from you, but write as we do.

We are halted this night upon the road to Megara, having passed through Eleusis without a halt. About Megara (or so the gossip of the soldiers has it) the regent is camped with his army. Megara is not ruled by his city in name, but it is a member of its league, and no doubt at least some of his troops are Megarians. When we reach Megara tomorrow, we may thus expect to be delivered to the regent. I have exerted myself to discover all I can concerning him, and Io agrees that I should pass my knowledge to you by this means.

He is said to be a man in his twenties, somewhat over the average height, handsome but scarred, and muscular as all these strange islanders are. He is said also to be more persuasive than most in speech, but as short and sharp of tongue as any. He is a scion of the elder of his nation's royal houses, an Agid, and thus only remotely related to that great Lycurgus, whose code of laws has set his nation apart from all others. Specifically, he is the son of Cleombrotos, who was himself the younger son of King Anaxandridas. By this connection is he the uncle of King Pleistarchos, who ascended to his father's throne only last year, and he stands regent for him. He has a wife awaiting his return to his city, and a young son, Pleistoanax.

As to his skill in battle—the thing these people value so far above all else that all else is naught to them—his victory over the Sons of Perseus, whose army was so much greater than his own, stands witness to it; it needs no other. As to the favor of the gods, what soldier can gain the victory without it?

I speak of him now with more than ordinary interest, for a runner with a message all say was his arrived not long ago and hastened to Eutaktos's tent. Soon leaving it in search of refreshment, he encountered Io and asked of you. She brought him to you, and together you three talked at some length. Then he, having satisfied himself (so Io says) that you indeed recalled nothing, wished to examine this book, and she brought him to me.

His name is Pasicrates, and he is a most comely youth, tall and well-featured as all these people are, but as stiff and sullen as the rest. At his request, I showed him your book, and I watched him discover (as others have) that he could not read it. He opened it to the end, however, and examined the flower, then replaced it carefully and rolled the book up again. He asked whether I had been present when Eutaktos found it, and I confirmed that I had and described the scene to him. He asked why Eutaktos has seen fit to bring me with you, to which I replied that he must ask Eutaktos. He wished to know what my city was, and then why I had deserted fair Ionia's shore to come across the Water. At his urging, I described my life to the best of my ability, and somewhat more fully than I have written of it here. He is himself a servant of the Triple Goddess—as he proved, turning his back to show me the scars he received when he was beaten before her altar at Orthia.

Perhaps I should explain here a custom of these people of which you are very likely unaware. Each year, when the boys of that year are about to pass from the care of their teachers into that of their officers, the best and strongest are chosen to run a gauntlet to the honor of the goddess. Much blood is spilled, and I have heard that they generally continue until one or two of the boys are dead.

It is a point of honor, I should add, among the boys not to cry out, though I cannot say what would befall a boy who did. It has been many years, I think, since such a thing occurred, and perhaps it never has. The boys who die in silence are received as sacrifices to the goddess. (How sad it is to count the places at which such sacrifices, the most pleasing of all, are still made and to find the fingers of one's hands more than sufficient!) Those who live are honored above all the rest and carry her favor for the remainder of their days.

I spoke to this Pasicrates as eloquently as I could and with all the charm I command, which some have not hesitated to call great. And I will not deny that it would please me very well to have the love of so handsome a youth, and one who is sworn to the goddess, as I am myself—though whether such a thing would please her as well, I cannot say.

But I can say, and I will, that it appeared to me that Pasicrates was not wholly insensible to the attractions of my person. (Unlike yourself, dear Latro, though I hesitate to write it.) We look upon these people, who live only for war and are forever training for battle, and think how comely they are. But what must they think, who hear for the first time, from our lips, the trumpets of eloquence and the deep-mouthed tocsins of philosophy? Must not they think us as far above common men as we think them? So (as I dare to hope) does the messenger of the great regent think your poor friend—

Eurykles of Miletos

# TWENTY-SIX

## *Pasicrates*

THE REGENT'S MESSENGER HAS RESTORED my scroll to me. He sought me out this morning and asked whether I recalled meeting with him the night before. I do not remember that now; but I must have when we spoke, since I told him I did.

He said, "Then you know I'm Pausanias's runner."

I nodded and said I was surprised he did not leave our plodding march to return with word from Eutaktos.

"The only order I brought was that he should continue the search if he has not found you, and return with all speed if he had. It's you Pausanias wants to see, not me. If I were to run back, could you keep pace with me?"

I confessed I did not know but said I would try.

"Then we'll race to the tree on that hill and see who shows the best heels."

He no sooner spoke than he was off like an arrow. I followed as fast as I could, and my legs are longer than his; but I never overtook him, and he had time to halt at the tree and turn to study me before I came pounding up.

"You might run to Megara at that," he said. "But look at this poor tortoise." It was Basias, the man whose tent I share, doing his best in his cuirass and greaves and waving his sword.

Pasicrates called, "You can't touch us with that! Get a longer blade!" Seeing that we were not deserting the column, Basias slowed to a walk.

"Want to sit here?" Pasicrates asked. "They have to tramp up this hill anyway." His face had that relentless regularity we find so attractive in a statue's, but his eyes seemed as cruel as a stoat's. As though I had not seen their look, I threw myself down in the shade.

"How did you lose your memory? Do you know?"

I shook my head.

"Perhaps the child does, or that Eurykles."

"Who are they?"

"Friends of yours that Eutaktos brought along. I talked to them yesterday. Come to think of it, Io was there when I talked with you—the little slave. She's yours, she says."

I said, "I remember the child, but not her name."

"What about Eurykles?"

I shook my head again.

"When I got here, I wondered why Eutaktos had bothered with them. I understand now."

We spoke no more after that until Basias reached us.

"Just a foot race," Pasicrates told him. "I don't think my job's in danger, but Latro can replace me if I'm wounded."

Basias nodded, wiping the sweat from his forehead with his finger and flinging it away. "Wrestler, too."

"You've tried him?"

Red-faced and panting, Basias dropped beside us. "Beat him. Five falls, though. He's strong."

"He looks it. How much do you know about him?"

"Forgets. Got a slave girl. I've got his sword. That's all."

"I see. Latro, what's my name?"

"Pasicrates."

"Right. How'd you know?"

"You told me," I said.

Basias explained, "In the morning he remembers everything after we camped. But it goes. By noon he won't remember anything before he woke."

"And the child remembers for him?"

"He had a book. It says read this each morning, but we can't read the rest. Eutaktos had me take it."

"I want you to give it back—I'll have a word with Eutaktos. Latro, if you had your book again, would you read it for me?"

I said, "If you want to hear it."

"Or for Pausanias, the regent of Rope?"

"Of course."

"Good. I don't think I'll have you do it yet, because there might be something there he wouldn't wish me to know. We'll see tonight when we reach Megara. Basias, what about Eurykles? Does he help Latro too?"

"A bit. Not so much as the child."

"What do you think of him?"

Basias grinned. "He better stay out of sight in Rope. The women'll kill him."

"He bothers me," Pasicrates said half to himself.

"Hit him and he won't."

"Not like that. Latro, among us it's customary for each older man to have a younger friend. You understand? It's a good system. The younger man learns more. If he gets into trouble, he's got someone to speak for him. This isn't the same thing."

Absently, I asked what it was. I was watching a scarlet wildflower nod in the breeze; it seemed charged with meaning.

"Like a man with a daughter. Except that the daughter's the man himself."

Basias said, "Bet you've plenty after you."

"Certainly." Pasicrates had been lying on his back on the sparse grass. Now he sat up. "I'm Pausanias's protégé, and they like that. That's why it seems so familiar. And yet so strange. I wish he were a slave."

Basias asked why, but Pasicrates did not answer. After a moment he said, "His hands are cold. Have you noticed?"

Not long after, the marchers caught up with us and we fell in with the rest. I moved among them looking for the child Pasicrates had mentioned, and soon found her. To test my grasp of what I had heard, I said, "I have good news, Io. I'm going to get my scroll back."

"That's wonderful, and you knew my name!"

"Pasicrates told me."

"And he said Eutaktos is going to let you have it again?"

"Yes. Except that I don't think Eutaktos knows it. Pasicrates will order him to."

Io looked doubtful. "Eutaktos is a lot older."

"I know," I told her.

When we had walked a few more stades, a tall woman in a purple

cloak handed me this scroll, with the stylus I am using thrust through
the cords. "Here, Latro," she said. "The lochagos ordered Basias to return
it. I'd been keeping it for him, and I said I'd bring it." She slipped an
arm through mine.

"It was Pasicrates," Io whispered to her.

"Really? He's quite a handsome youth, but not as handsome as your
master."

"What does that have to do with it?"

"Nothing. I was just thinking." She squeezed my arm. "You know,
Latro, in a way you're rather fortunate. If you wished to change your
name, all you'd have to do would be to tell your friends to call you by
the new one next morning; then you'd never know you had once been
someone else. I don't suppose you know whether you've ever done it?"

"I don't think so. Do you want to change yours?"

She nodded. "It means 'well talked of,' which is good enough, I
suppose; but I'd like something better. What do you think of Drakon?"

"Shouldn't it be Drakaina?"

The woman laughed, and Io said, "That's good, master."

"Do either of you know where we are? Pasicrates said we were going
to Megara."

Before they could reply, Basias dropped back to walk between Io
and me. "We're turning off at this fork," he announced. "The three of
you, me, Eutaktos, and Pasicrates. We're to see the regent while the rest
make camp."

We hurried down a dusty road that looked no more important than
the other; but when we reached the summit of the next hill, the whole
scene changed as a nightscape does at the rising of the sun.

A thousand tents stood in orderly rows upon a rolling plain. Beyond
them, a city lifted white walls; beyond those spread sparkling blue water
dotted with foam where the salt-sharp wind ruffled countless waves; and
beyond the tumultuous sea rose the dim blue bulk of an island.

Io shouted for joy. "Look! Look! Is that Peace? We went there on
Hypereides's ship, only he wouldn't let us off. Is it?"

Basias mussed her brown curls. "That's right. You've an eye for the
lay of the land, little girl. If you were an Amazon, you'd make a strategist
someday."

Io pulled at my chiton and pointed at the sea. "Latro, that's Peace Bay. Hypereides told us. It's where the ships from Thought beat the barbarians."

Pasicrates whirled on her like a panther. "Our ships fought there too, and our Strategist Eurybiades commanded the combined fleets!"

I said, "Don't shout at her. She didn't know, and neither did I."

"But she at least will remember," Pasicrates snapped, "because I shouted at her. Mild lessons are soon forgotten, and in the end the kind teacher is the cruel teacher—he doesn't teach. Enough! I'll tell Pausanias you're coming." He runs so well I think only the finest horse could overtake him. Before we had gone another hundred strides, he was flashing among the tents.

Io's dusty cheeks were streaked with tears. I picked her up and tried to comfort her. "I'm all right, master," she said. And then, "He was right, I won't forget. Not even his name."

"Eurybiades?"

She shook her head. "Pasicrates."

To distract her, I said, "Look how many tents there are! A whole army's camped here, with thousands of soldiers. Have you and I ever seen any army in camp before, Io?"

The woman whispered, "This is nothing. You should have seen the encampment of the Great King. It was like a city on the march—but no city on earth could have equaled it, except perhaps Babylon."

Eutaktos must have sharp ears, because he overheard her. "I saw that camp, and my slaves looted the pavilions of the satraps. If your Great King were here with us, he would not think this camp nothing."

Pausanias's tent is larger than all the rest, embroidered and hung with tassels of gold. I think it must have been part of the loot Eutaktos spoke of. When we came near, I could hear voices; one, I think, the voice of Pasicrates, the other harsh and flat, the speech of a young man accustomed to giving orders and to concealing any emotion he might feel while giving them. I heard Pasicrates say, ". . . a spy of the Great King's."

The other answered, "A spy is a stone that can be thrown back."

Eutaktos coughed, I suppose to let those within know we had arrived. After that I could distinguish no more words.

There are two sentries at the door, tall men no older than Pasicrates;

they will not permit us to approach it. We stand to one side—or rather, Eutaktos and Basias stand so, their hands on their sword hilts. Io, the woman, and I are sitting on the ground, where I write these words, having seen by reading how good it is to write so that what has happened is not lost.

I have read of the Lady of the Doves; and I feel I then visited a realm at once higher and smaller than our own. What was it she wished of me? For I feel sure there was something. Did she obtain it? Even after reading what I wrote twice, I cannot say. I am sure she was a friend to the woman Kalleos; but was Kalleos a friend to me?

The Lady of the Doves said I would not forget her, though I forget everything. She was not wrong; when I read of her again, my flesh stirred at the memory. For love, she was surely the only woman, or all of them.

But I must put her memory aside and think of what I will say in the tent. Soon, I think, Pasicrates will come out and take us in to the regent.

# TWENTY-SEVEN

## *Pausanias*

THE REGENT HAS FURNISHED HIS tent with plunder. He sits upon scarlet cushions, and there are carpets rich with griffins, black bulls savaged by golden lions, and men strangely dressed, with black and curling beards. The air is perfumed by lamps of gold.

Pasicrates announced, "O royal Pausanias, this is the man Eutaktos the Lochagos brought. I have examined him, and I am satisfied he is indeed the one shown you in your dream, so far as I am able to judge."

The regent stared at me. His face is terrible with scars, but it seemed to me it would have been terrible without them, as hard and cruel as iron. Perhaps a smile touched his mouth; a scar drew up one cheek, so I could not be sure.

"The man I saw wore a chaplet of withered blossoms. Fellow! Were you wearing such a chaplet when my shieldmen discovered you?"

"I don't remember," I told him. "But I may have written of it. May I look?" I held up this scroll.

The regent's lips drew back from his teeth, which are large and not quite white. "Good. Very good. And the flower?"

Pasicrates said, "It was still there when I examined the book, Highness. The lochagos may have put it there, but I doubt that he did."

The regent pointed. "Open that to the stick."

I did as he ordered, holding the scroll so he could see the writing. As I unrolled the last sheet, a dried lupine dropped into his hand.

Pasicrates cleared his throat. "Perhaps I ought to add, Highness, that the lochagos says they appeared to have had a dinner party the night before in the house where he found this man. There would have been flowers, naturally, and chaplets for the guests."

The regent waved this aside. "I'm satisfied. I wish Tisamenus were here, but this is the man, or we'll never find him. He looks like him as well. I couldn't see that scar in my dream, but no doubt the chaplet covered it."

I asked, "You dreamed of me?"

He nodded. "It was Kore herself, smiling and wreathed in blossoms. She said, 'For the many subjects you have given, I will show you a secret known but to the gods.' Then I saw you. What's your name, anyway?"

"Latro," I told him.

"I saw you sitting on a pallet. It was night, but there was a fire, and I could see the firelight flicker on your face. You were holding this, and you unrolled that book and put the flower into it and rolled it partway up, then wrote. The goddess was gone, but I heard her voice. She said, 'He will have forgotten everything, knowing nothing more of the past than of the future. See who is with him!' Nike stood behind you in the shadows."

"I am to bring you victory?"

Still smiling his snarling smile, the regent leaned back among his cushions. "Not many men are favored by the gods. A few heroes like Perseus, Theseus, my ancestor Heracles. Those destined to—destined for greatness." He turned to his messenger. "Where did he get that scar, Pasicrates?"

"I don't know, Highness. The lochagos brought two others with him, a slave child who remembers for him and the magician I told you of. They're outside with the lochagos and the ouragos who guarded him on the march."

"Get them in here. All of them."

Eutaktos entered first, Basias last. I think they were all a bit frightened.

The regent smiled again when he saw Io. "You know your master's history, little girl, or so Pasicrates tells me."

Io nodded timidly.

"How did he receive that scar?"

"I wasn't with him, sir."

"But you know. Don't mind this face. The faces of my conquests look far worse."

"There was a big battle. Our men went with the Great King's army, but they lost. My master fought in that, I think."

"And so do I. But you must tell me why you think as you do."

"Because it was when the army came back that they brought him to our temple. That was the first time I saw him."

"And did he have that scar then?"

Io shook her head. "There was a bandage with blood on it."

Pasicrates said, "But if he fought for the barbarians, Highness—"

"You're a handsome boy," the regent told him. "But if you want to stay where you are, you'd better learn to think. To whom did the Maiden appear? Who has her favor?"

"Ah, I see!"

"I hope so. Lochagos, I like a man who achieves his objective. Who makes no excuses because he needs none. I won't forget this."

Eutaktos stood very straight. "Thank you, Highness."

"This man with you has been taking care of . . ."

"Latro," I prompted.

"Of Latro, as I understand it."

"Yes, Highness."

"And has learned something of his ways in the process, no doubt. I'm going to detach him for the time being. You may return to your lochos."

"Thank you, Highness." Eutaktos left us, walking proudly. I have not seen him again.

"Child, do you know that your city and mine are no longer enemies?"

Io nodded. "Pindaros said so."

"A man of your city?"

She nodded again. "He said you saved us."

"He was right. It's true your men fought me, and fought very well for foreigners. But when a war's over, it's over. Or it should be. Thought's army wanted to burn your city; I wouldn't let them. Now your city and mine are friends."

Io said politely, "I hope it's always so, sir."

"And when I've more leisure, I want to talk with you. If you tell me the truth, I'll see things go well for you. You'll have food and new clothes, and other children to play with."

"Thank you, sir," Io said. "Only I don't belong to you. I belong to Latro."

"Well said, but I doubt if he'll object. Will you, Latro?"

I shook my head.

"And this soldier of mine will continue to look after you. After all three of you." He looked toward Basias, who stood like a statue, his hands to his sides. "An idiot, a child, and a spy won't be too much for you, will they, ouragos? What's your name?"

"Basias, Highness! No, Highness!"

"Good. I don't think the first two will give you much trouble, Basias. The spy may. If he does, kill him. If he won't follow orders, I don't want him alive."

The woman in the purple cloak exclaimed, "I'm not a spy!"

"Of course you are. If I hadn't known it before, I'd know it now because you were too slow to deny it. You're from Miletos, or so you told my messenger."

She nodded. "And I'm—"

"A Hellene. As we all are, save Latro. A good many Hellenes fought for the Great King."

"I didn't fight at all."

"Certainly not. Your king's no fool, and neither are his ministers. One look at that face would tell any sensible man you'd be more useful behind the enemy's line than before it. I know what happened to Miletos; the Great King tore down your walls and sent you to herd goats. I'd ask how you got out, but you've some story. Don't bother. Basias has his sword—not that he'd need it."

"I am protected—"

"You're under no law but ours, and ours says we can kill you where you stand. It would give Basias one fewer worry, and if you lie to me, he'll wring your neck."

Basias said, "He was in the Great King's camp, Highness. I heard him tell Latro."

Spreading his hands, the regent whispered, "Speak or die. Who got your report?"

Though the time had been so brief, the woman had recovered her composure. "Believe me, most royal—"

As quickly as he might have thrust with his spear, Basias grasped her arm. She raised a hand to claw his face, but a blow to her head sent her reeling across the tent.

Basias drew his sword.

"Wait," the regent told him. To me he said, "I saw that step. You would have protected your friend, if only Basias were here. What if he were not? If you had only Pasicrates and me to deal with?"

I said, "If it weren't for the sentries, I would have killed all of you, or tried to."

Io gasped, "Master, no!"

The regent waved her fears away. "Your master's a man of courage. He'll need to be, living among us."

Awkwardly, the woman got to her feet. There were tears in her eyes, but something else too.

"I don't have time for more of this," the regent told her. "You may speak and live or remain silent and die. Choose."

"Then I choose to speak," the woman said. "Who would not?" She smoothed her cloak as women do, as women keep their clothes in order though the cities burn.

"Good. A confessed spy may be useful. Useful, you may live and even prosper. Who got your report?"

"Artabazus."

"Better and better. And that report was . . . ?"

"That half a year and a few gifts would make any fighting unnecessary."

"He did not believe you?"

The woman shook her head. "He believed me, but he couldn't convince Mardonius."

Basias dropped his sword. It fell point down, piercing the carpet where he stood and sticking upright in the earth beneath it. He lifted his arm and looked at his hand with unbelieving eyes. The fingers were swollen, and there was a gray pallor on the skin.

"Let me see that," the regent said. And then, when Basias did not obey, "Come here!"

Like a doll moved by strings, Basias walked to where the regent sat and held out his hand.

"He had a poisoned pin in his hair." The regent looked at the woman. "Tell us the antidote."

"I have no pin, Highness," she said. "You may search my person if you wish."

"You hid it when you fell. You may be worth something at that. What's your name?"

"Eurykles, Highness. Others have thought so."

The regent nodded absently. "Basias, tell the sentries one of them is to take you to Kichesippos, my healer. The rest of you, come here and sit before me. I'm tired of breaking my neck. Take cushions if you want."

I got a cushion for the woman and a long one for Io and me. As I put them down before the regent, I could hear Basias talking to the sentries outside.

"You too, Pasicrates," the regent said; and his messenger seated himself upon a cushion at his right hand.

"Eurykles, tell me why you gave Artabazus that advice."

"Because it was the best I could give," the woman said. She paused to gather her thoughts. "War is only the last recourse of politics; it has no sure victories, or so I think. A king who fights when he might gain his ends by a cupful of wisdom and a handful of gold is a fool."

The regent smiled. "You believe your Great King a fool?"

"The Great King was gone. Mardonius was a good soldier but a stupid man. If Artabazus had been in command . . ."

"If Artabazus had been in command, what then? What of the Hellenes? You're one, as you just reminded us."

"You'd be ruled by men of our race, just as you are now, and as our cities in the lesser Asia are. What difference would there be? Why should ten myriads die?"

"You know of others who think as you do? In Thought?"

"I'm certain such men exist."

"You're careful. So am I." The regent glanced at Io and me. "Let me suggest to all three of you something you may not have noticed. Perhaps I should say let *us* suggest it, because I've talked to Pasicrates and he feels as I do."

The woman leaned toward him, her fingers playing upon her cheek. "Yes, Highness?"

"We are four men whose interests run so close they're indistinguishable. Let me speak of Rope and this whole country first. We Rope Makers are the finest soldiers in the world, and the Great King knows that now. But men who know war know it's no game; a wise man dodges it if he can, just as you said. As for glory, my uncle Leonidas won enough

at the Gates to the Hot Springs to last our family till Tantalus drinks—I
say nothing of my own battle. An honorable peace, then, is our only
desire."

The woman called Eurykles gave the slightest of nods, her eyes fixed
upon the regent as a serpent transfixes a bird.

"Our country is divided into so many warring cities no one can
count them all, or no one has bothered. Every clutter of huts on the
mountainside makes its own laws, issues its own currency, and fields its
tiny army to crush its tiny neighbor. Clearly, what we need is union
under the noblest of our cities, which by a happy coincidence happens
to be my own."

"By a coincidence even happier," the woman said, "I have before
me a member of the elder royal house of that city, who is in addition
its most renowned living leader."

"Thank you." The regent nodded graciously. "Unfortunately, our
city is not strong enough to unite all the rest. More, it is not rich enough.
I have often thought that if only we had found the silver, instead of
Thought, or if we had seized the treasury of Croesus . . ." He shrugged
and let the words trail away. "But suppose we had the help—or at least
the threat—of additional troops. Cavalry, let us say, because there's so
little here. With that threat and gold enough to make gifts to farsighted
men, a great deal might be done."

The woman nodded. "It might indeed."

Pasicrates murmured, "Highness, do you think you should speak
in this way before the child?"

"Speak in what way? Say that I seek an honorable peace with the
Great King and a position for Rope commensurate with its virtues? She
may repeat that to anyone she may meet."

Io said, "I won't repeat anything. I don't do that, except for telling
Latro. But you said all our interests went together."

"Your master is fortunate in his slave; I've seen that already. As for
our interests, let's take Eurykles here first. We'll get to you in a moment.
Eurykles serves the Great King, as he admitted a moment ago. More
directly, he serves Artabazus. He wishes to be rewarded for his work,
like any other man. The Great King wants to recover the prestige he
lost here and to add to his glory. Peace and union under a leader grateful
to him—"

The woman said, "Would be all he could desire, Highness, I'm sure. Someone who has the king's ear would have to be consulted, naturally."

"Naturally. Now as to you, child. Your city is allied with the Great King already, and as your friend Pindaros told you, it would have been destroyed but for my own city and my acts in its behalf. Isn't it clear that anything that helps your strongest friends helps you?"

Io shook her head. "To tell the truth, I don't care about my city. I care about Latro."

I said, "Who is a soldier of the Great King's. You think I'm an idiot because I forget, Prince Pausanias, and perhaps I am. But I've always known that, even when I did not know my name."

# TWENTY-EIGHT

## *Mycale*

A PLACE OF WHICH MOST, I think, had never heard before is now on everyone's lips. The combined fleets of Thought and the Rope Makers have given the barbarians another terrible defeat there. Some say this was on the same day as the great battle in which I was wounded, others that it must surely have been after it, for it could not have taken so long for the news to reach us. To this the first reply that a ship may be delayed for any time one chooses by storms and contrary winds, and that the news came first to Thought, and only subsequently to us from there.

Io said, "Oh, I hope the black man's all right. I know you don't remember the black man, Latro, but he was your friend even before Pindaros and me. When they brought you to the temple, he was with you."

I asked her, "Do you think he was in that battle?"

"I hope not, but he probably was. When Hypereides sold you to Kalleos, he kept the black man. And Hypereides was going to take his ships back to the fleet."

"Then I hope the black man is safe, and Hypereides dead."

"You shouldn't be like that, master. Hypereides wasn't a bad man. He got us out of that dungeon in Tower Hill, just by talking, and he let Pindaros and Hilaeira go when the law said he should."

But before I write of these recent matters, I should write of earlier things, which may soon be lost to me in the mist I cannot drive from the back of my thoughts. The regent has put us in the care of his messenger, who sent his slaves to bring our possessions and Basias's tent. He showed us where his own stood, near the regent's, and told us to put up Basias's beside it. I did not think I recalled how a tent should

be erected; but when I had spread everything upon the ground, the steps
came to me each in turn. Io crawled beneath the oiled linen and held
up the poles, and she enjoyed that so much I took three times longer
about the whole business than I should.

A sword Io says is mine was with Basias's clothing in a scabbard
hung from a belt of manhood. I put it on and felt better at once; a man
without weapons is a slave. Io says Kalleos let me wear it when I was
hers, and perhaps that is why I did not feel resentful toward her, as Io
swears I did not.

Then Basias's slaves came, cowering because they thought themselves to be beaten. They had been gathering firewood when Pasicrates's
slaves had come, and they had discovered what had befallen their master's baggage with great difficulty. I explained that their master was ill
and ordered them to have such food as sick men eat ready for him.

That was wise, because slaves soon brought Basias in a litter. With
them was an old man who told us he was Kichesippos the Messenian,
but who speaks as the Rope Makers and their slaves do, making the ox
long. Basias's arm was swollen and black, and it seemed to me that he
was in a dream, sometimes hearing what we said, sometimes deaf to it,
sometimes seeing what we could not see. Perhaps that is how I seem to
others; I do not know.

Kichesippos told Basias's slaves, "Your master has been bitten by a
viper, and from the breadth between its fangs and the severity of his
reaction, by a larger one than I have ever seen. I have cut his wounds
and drawn forth the poison as well as it can be done. Do not attempt
to do that a second time; after the first, it is useless. Let him rest, see
that he is warm, feed him if he will eat. Give him all he wants to eat
and drink. By the favor of the goddess, he may recover. But he may
die."

Io asked if there was nothing more we could do.

"As I understand the matter, the viper has not been killed?"

I nodded, and Io said, "We never even saw one, sir. He hit somebody, and somebody else said there was a poisoned pin in his hair."

Kichesippos shook his head. "A pin could not have held so much,
and it would have left a single scratch. I will not remove the bandage
to show you the punctures, but there are two." (Then I marveled at little
Io's cunning; if she had told him it was his master, Pausanias, who had

said it, surely Kichesippos would never have contradicted him.)

"If the viper were dead," he continued, "that might be of benefit to him. Still more if its raw flesh could be held to his wound—while it lives, it strengthens its poison as a city strengthens the army it sends forth. Other than that, I can suggest nothing."

Io said, "Then you might examine my master. Perhaps the royal regent spoke of him after they conferred today? He can't remember."

"I've noticed the scar. Come here, young man, I wish to touch it. Will you kneel? No act of submission is implied. Tell me if I hurt you."

I knelt before him and felt his deft fingers glide along the side of my head. Io asked, "Are you a priest of Aesculapius? When Latro slept beside his altar, Aesculapius said he couldn't help him."

"Nor can I, I'm afraid," Kichesippos told her, "without reopening the wound. That might easily kill him." His fingers withdrew. "You may stand, young man. Do you drop things? Do you fall or suffer dizziness?"

I shook my head.

"You are fortunate—all those symptoms are to be expected. Were you wearing a helmet when your injury occurred?"

I told him I did not know.

"That's right, you forget. Is that your only symptom?"

"Yes," I told him.

Io said, "Gods appear to him. Sometimes."

Kichesippos sighed. "Occasional hallucinations. Young man, I think some foreign object has been driven deeply into your brain. A splinter of bone is the most likely thing, judging from the visible wound; but I have known of a similar case in which the object was a small arrowhead. If it's of any comfort to you, it probably won't get any worse. Eventually the object may dissolve, particularly if it's a bone splinter. If that occurs, the damaged part may—I say *may*—reconstitute itself, partially at least.

"Don't get your hopes up. The process will take years if it happens at all, and it probably will not. As for treatment . . ." He shrugged. "Prayers are never wholly wasted. Even if you're not cured, you may receive some other benefit. There is Aesculapius, whom this child says you have petitioned already. In addition, there are shrines all over the country to heroes who are said to heal, though they killed, mostly, while they lived. One may help you. And there are the great gods, if you can get their attention. Meanwhile, learn to live with your disability. Do you recall my name?"

"Kichesippos."

Io said, "In the morning he remembers yesterday evening, but by noon he's forgotten it. He writes things down."

"Excellent."

I said, "Yet when I reread what I've written, I sometimes wonder whether I wrote the truth."

"I see." Kichesippos nodded to himself. "Have you written anything today?"

"Yes, while we were waiting to see the regent."

"And were you tempted to lie? I do not ask whether you lied, but only whether you were tempted to do so."

I shook my head.

"Then I very much doubt that you have lied in the past. Lying is a habit, you see, like drinking too much. You told the truth as you saw it, which is all any man can do."

I said I hoped he was correct.

"You must remember that in every life there occur events so extraordinary that only the most talented and ingenious liar could have conceived them. Take the great battle at Mycale—have you heard about it?"

Io and I shook our heads.

"Word of it reached the regent only today, and the noble Pasicrates, who had it directly from my master, informed me as we conferred about your poor friend here." The old man paused to collect his thoughts.

"This Mycale is a place on the Asian coast. King Leotychides found the barbarian fleet beached there, the portents were favorable, and he ordered an immediate attack. The ships' crews had been reinforced by an army from Susa, and it seems to have been a hot fight. But in the long run the barbarians can't stand up to disciplined troops, and they broke. Naturally, our men held their formation; but a few men from other cities ran after the enemy, and by great good luck they were able to reach the stockade before the gates could be shut. That finished the barbarians, and we burned more than three hundred ships." He rubbed his palms together. "The men from a hundred ships burned three hun-

dred and destroyed an army. In a century, who will believe it? The Great
King will build more ships, no doubt, and raise new armies. But not
this year, and not the next."

"And meanwhile," I said, "he'll need every soldier he has."

Kichesippos nodded. "I imagine so."

By the time the old physician left, it was nearly dark. I told the
slaves to prepare food for us, and the woman in the purple cloak joined
us while we ate. "Would you mind if I had some? I couldn't help but
smell it. I'm your neighbor now—did you know?"

"No," Io said. "We didn't know where you were staying."

"With the handsome Pasicrates. But he's off somewhere at the moment, and his slaves won't obey me."

There was hardly enough food for Io, Basias, and me, so I went to
Pasicrates's tent, where I found his slaves cooking a meal for themselves.
One escaped, but when I had the other two by the throat I pounded the
right head against the left and told them to bring food, and that I would
push their faces into the coals the next time they disobeyed the woman.

When I returned to our own tent, she said, "What did I tell you?
Barley, blood, and beans. And after sampling the barley and beans, I
think I would prefer the blood. Well, beans are a proper food for the
dead, anyway."

I asked her whether she planned to die.

"No, but we're going there. Hadn't you heard? To Rope, so the
royal Pausanias can bed his wife, then to Acheron so he can consult the
shades. It should be an interesting trip."

Io asked, "You mean we're going to visit the dead?"

The woman nodded, and though I felt vaguely that I had once
considered her less than attractive, I could not help noticing that her
face was lovely in the firelight. "I am, at least, and the regent is. You
should have seen how delighted he was when someone told him who I
was. He sent for me again at once, and I thought he was going to ask
me to raise a few ghosts for him on the spot."

"Is it far?" Io inquired.

"To Acheron? Why, no, just the other side of the grave."

I told the woman not to tease her.

"Oh," she said, "you want to take the long road. No, not really, Io.
Two or three days to Rope, and not much longer, I'd think, to Acheron,

if we get a ship at the gulf, as I suppose we will. By the way, do you have a comb I might borrow? I seem to have lost mine."

Not with the best grace, Io produced a little bone comb. The woman ran it through her dark hair, which in truth could not have been more disordered if it had never been combed at all.

"I'm going to let it grow out," she said. "These Rope Makers all let theirs grow long, have you noticed? They comb it before a battle, or so I've heard. See? No poisoned pins."

Pasicrates's slaves brought a bowl of beans, some dried fish, a loaf of barley bread, and a wine bowl. I told Io to see whether Basias had eaten. She reported that he was thirsty, and I gave her a cup of mixed wine from the bowl, and half the loaf.

The woman said, "You'd better eat some of that yourself. You won't be getting anything better."

I said, "I intend to. But first, may I ask you a question? Your tongue isn't my own, and I sometimes feel I haven't learned as much of it as I'd like."

"Certainly."

"Then tell me why everyone calls you Eurykles, which is a man's name."

"Ah," she said. "That's a *personal* question."

"Will you answer it?"

"If I may ask you one."

"Of course."

"Because they haven't divined my true nature. They think me a man. So did you, in a time you've forgotten."

I said, "I'll try not to reveal your secret."

She smiled. "Speak out if you wish. It's all one to Hippocleides, if you know that expression."

Just then Io came out of the tent, the wine cup still more than half full. "He won't eat any bread," she said. "I talked to his slaves and gave it to them. They said he wouldn't eat for them, either, but he sipped a little broth."

The woman called Eurykles shuddered.

"Since you don't mind people knowing, what shall we call you?" I asked her.

"Why not Drakaina, as you yourself suggested? Drakaina of Miletos.

By the way, have you heard about the battle and what the Milesians did afterward?"

"Not about the Milesians. Weren't they sent inland to herd goats? That's what the regent said."

"Oh, no. Just some people from the prominent families. And not to herd goats, not really; they were sent to Susa as hostages. But when the people of my fair city heard about Mycale, they rose against the barbarian garrison and killed them all."

"As a barbarian myself, I'm not sure I approve."

"Nor am I," Drakaina said. "Still, it puts me in a rather dubious position, doesn't it? I like that." She rose and returned Io's comb.

"Aren't you going to ask your personal question?"

She shook her head. "I'll reserve it. Later, perhaps."

When she had gone back into Pasicrates's tent, Io looked at her little comb with dismay. "Now I'll have to wash it," she said.

# TWENTY-NINE

## *The Silent Country*

THIS LAND THE ROPE MAKERS rule is a place of harsh mountains and wide, fertile valleys. Behind us are the rough hills of Bearland, where we camped last night and Basias woke me with his groaning. Io says we camped the night before outside Tower Hill, and she hid this scroll as she had when we were imprisoned there, for fear it would be taken from me. She says also that some of the soldiers were from that city, and that they left the army there.

This morning while we were still in Bearland, I wondered why this Silent Country should be called so. When we stopped in the village for the first meal, I went to one of the houses to ask the people.

There was no one there, they being (as I assumed) at work in their fields. Io says Basias is supposed to watch me, but he is too ill for that; and Pasicrates, who had watched me on the morning march, has run ahead.

Thus I went from house to house, stooping to enter the low doorways and coughing at the smoke from the hearths. Once I found a pot seething over the flames, and once a half-eaten barley cake; but there were no men, no women, and no children, and at last I began to think that they were somehow hidden from mortal eyes, or perhaps that they were the spirits of the dead, whom the Rope Makers had in some way forced to toil.

The fifth place to which I came was a smithy. Its forge still blazed, and tongs gripped a half-formed, glowing spit. When I saw it I knew the smith could not be more than a step or two away; I found him crouched beneath his own work table, hiding behind his leather apron, which he had draped across it. I pulled him out and made him stand.

His grizzled head came only to my shoulder, but he was as muscular as all are who are of that trade.

He begged my pardon many times, saying over and over that he had meant no disrespect and had only been frightened to see a stranger. I told him I would not hurt him, and explained that I merely wished to ask him a few questions about this land.

At that he grew more frightened than ever, his face the color of ashes. He feigned to be deaf and, when I shouted at him, to speak some gobbling dialect and to be unable to understand me. I drew Falcata and laid her edge at his throat; but he caught my wrist and wrenched it until I cried out, and with his free hand snatched up his hammer. Then I saw the face of Death himself, his naked, grinning skull.

In an instant Death was gone; there was only the smith's face again, more ashen now than ever, its mouth open and its eyes rolling backward into his head. The sound his hammer made as it fell from his hand and struck the earthen floor seemed too loud, like the noise that wakes us from sleep.

I let him go, and he leaned backward until his body was held erect for a moment by the javelin in his back. The point crept from his chest under the press of his weight, two fingers' width of hammered iron that shone in the light of the forge, before he slipped to one side and tumbled down.

One of the slaves of the Rope Makers stood in the doorway holding a second javelin. I said, "Thank you. I owe you my life."

Putting his foot on the body, he drew out his weapon and wiped its head on the smith's leather apron. "This is my village," he said. And then, "He made this."

"But he would have killed me, when I would not have harmed him."

"He thought you would, and it would have been his death if he had been seen talking with a foreigner. As it will be mine if I'm seen with you."

"Then let us not be seen," I said, and we dragged the smith's body to a place out of sight of the street; when we had concealed it as well as we could, we kicked dust over the blood, and he led me through a rear door to a yard where the smithy and its heaps of charcoal shielded us.

"You don't remember me," he said.

I shook my head. "I forget much."

"So you told me after we had seen the black god. I'm Cerdon, Latro. Do you still have your book? Perhaps you wrote of me there, though I told you not to."

"Are we friends, then? Is that why you saved me?"

"We can be, if you'll keep your promise."

"If I've promised something to you, I'll do what I promised. If I haven't, I'll give you whatever you ask anyway. You saved my life."

"Then come with me to the shrine of the Great Mother tonight. It's not far from here."

I heard a faint sound as he spoke: the whisper of a woman's skirt, or the dry slithering of a serpent. Then it was gone, and when I looked I saw nothing. I said, "I'd do it gladly if I could; but we'll march as soon as the slaves have eaten. Tonight we'll be far away."

"But you'll come if you can, and not forget?"

"By tonight? No. Tomorrow I'll have forgotten, perhaps."

"Good. I'll get you as soon as the camp's asleep. Your slave won't inform on us, and the Rope Maker in your tent is too ill to notice anything." He started to rise.

"Wait," I told him. "How was it you were here when I needed your help?"

"I've watched you since Megara, knowing it was useless to talk until we got here. I knew we'd come, though, because our village is on the road to Rope, and it belongs to Pausanias. When I saw you go away without a guard, that was my chance. So I followed you, hoping to find you alone; and by her grace I did."

I did not understand. "This smithy belongs to the regent?"

"This village, the fields, and all of us. I helped bring the Rope Maker to your tent for Kichesippos. You didn't recognize me."

"No," I admitted.

"I knew you didn't. Now I must go, but I'll come tonight. Don't forget."

"What about . . ." I nodded to indicate the dead man in the smithy.

"I'll see to it," he said. "No one will care but us."

When I returned to the grove where the shieldmen had eaten, they were forming their column while a few tardy slaves covered fires or stowed pots. We marched bravely through the village to the music of the flutes; but when we reached this river, we found the bridge in flames. Though the slaves soon put out the fire, the roadway had been destroyed, and it was decided to camp here for the night. Everyone is weary after the march through Bearland anyway, and they say the bridge will be repaired tomorrow.

Basias's slaves had to carry him in a litter this morning, as well as carrying our tent and the other things. I asked if it was not too much for them. They said it was not—it was no more than they had borne when they left the Silent Country to fight the Great King, because they had to carry ten days' rations. I offered to take one end of the litter; I believe they would have liked to accept, but they were afraid they would be punished.

I asked whether Basias owned a village, and whether they came from there. They said he owned only a farm. All three live on it and work the land. It is south of Rope, and they believe they will be ordered to take him there until he is well. He has a house in Rope too, but they think the farm will be better. If he dies, the farm will pass to a relative.

They did not seem afraid to talk to me; so I told them I had gone into the village, and the people there would not. They said it is different and better in the army, and that no one will inform on them for speaking to a stranger when they must pitch the tent for him to sleep in and cook his meals; but that it would be well if I did not speak to the slaves of others. I think perhaps Basias is a kinder master than the regent, though perhaps it is only that he is not so rich. A man who has only a farm and three slaves cannot afford to lose even one.

I went into the tent then and talked to him, telling him about the burning of the bridge, because I was growing more and more curious about this strange land. Although I cannot say what customs of other nations are, I feel certain those I have known have not been like this; there is no sense of familiarity in anything I hear.

He was weak, but I think not in much pain. Io says he is feverish sometimes and thinks himself a boy again, talking of his old teachers; but he was not like that when I spoke to him.

I told him of the bridge, and he said the slaves across the river had done it hoping we would take some other route—that the slaves here would want us to pass through as quickly as possible. Naturally I did not tell him about Cerdon or what happened in the smithy. He asked

about the fields we had passed, and whether they had been plowed for
the fall sowing. I was surprised, thinking he would have seen them
himself as we marched; but he said he had slept most of the morning,
and he could not see much from his litter anyway, because of those who
walked beside it. I told him the fields were still in stubble, perhaps
because so many men were with the army.

"Time to plow," he murmured. "Before the rains."

"You won't be able to plow for a while, I'm afraid. I'm sure your
slaves can manage it, with you there to direct them."

"I never plow. I'd no longer be a Rope Maker, see? But it's got to
get done. On the Long Coast the shieldmen have farms and slaves, and
work their farms too. I wish I could. We need another hand, but I have
to drill."

"The war's nearly over," I told him. "That's the way people talk, at
least."

He rolled his head from side to side. "The Great King'll come back.
If not, we'll go there, loot Susa and Persepolis. Or there'll be a different
war. There's always another war."

He wanted to drink. I brought water from the slow, green river and
mixed it with wine.

When I held the cup for him, he said, "I won't wrestle you any
more, Latro. You'd beat me today. But I beat you once. Remember
that?"

I shook my head.

"You wrote when we were through. Read your book."

Soon after that I left him, sitting before the tent in the sunshine to
do as he had suggested. Not knowing where I might find the account
of our wrestling, or even whether it was there, I opened this scroll
halfway and read of how I had seen Eurykles the Necromancer raise a
woman from the dead. I was glad then that it was day; and every few
lines I lifted my eyes from the papyrus to watch the peaceful river slipping past and the thin black smoke from the timbers the slaves had
pulled from the bridge.

After a time, Drakaina came to sit by me. She laughed when she
saw my face and asked what I was thinking.

"What a terrible thing it must be to have memory—although I
wish it."

"Why, if it is so terrible?"

"Because not having memory, I lose myself; and that is worse. This day is like a stone taken from a palace and carried far away to lands where no one knows what a wall may be. And I think every other day has been so for me as well."

She said, "Then you must enjoy each as it comes, because each day is all you have."

I shook my head. "Consider the slaves in that village we passed. Every day for them must be much like the day before. If only I could find my own country, I could live there as they do. Then I'd know much that had happened the day before, even if I could not remember it."

"A goddess has promised you'll soon be restored to your friends," she said. "Or so I've been told."

Joy shook me. Before I knew what I did, I took her in my arms and kissed her. Nor did she resist me, and her lips were as cool as the brook of shining stones where once I washed my face and paddled my feet.

"Come," she said. "We can go to Pasicrates's tent and tie the flap. I have wine there, and his slaves will bring us food. We need not come out until morning."

I followed her, never thinking of my promise to Cerdon. The tent was warm and dim and silent. She loosed the purple cords that held her cloak about her neck, saying, "Do you remember how a woman looks, Latro?"

"Of course," I told her. "I don't know when I've seen one, but I know."

The cloak fell at her feet. "Then see me." She drew her chiton over her head. The swelling of her hips was like the rolling of a windless sea, and her breasts stood proudly, domed temples roofed with carnelian and snow. A snakeskin was knotted about her waist.

She touched it when she saw my eyes upon it. "I cannot remove this. But there is no need."

"No," I said, and embraced her.

She laughed, tickling and kissing me. "You don't recall our sitting side by side on a hillside of this very island, Latro. How I hungered for you then! And now you are mine."

"Yes," I said. And yet I knew already that it was no, though I burned with desire. I longed for her as a dying man for water, a starving man for bread, a weak man for a crown; but I did not long for her as a man for a woman, and I could do nothing.

She mocked me and I would have strangled her, but her eyes took the strength from my hands; she tore them away. "I'll come to you when the moon is up," she said. "You will be stronger then. Wait for me."

Thus I sit before our fire and write this, hoping someday to understand all that has happened, watching the pale moth that flutters about the flames, and waiting for the moon.

# THIRTY

## *The Great Mother*

THE TERRIBLE GODDESS OF THE slaves appeared last night. I touched her and everyone saw her. It was horrible. Now the camp is stirring, but there is no need to write quickly; the market will be full before the bridge is mended. I will have time to read this again and again, so that I will never forget.

Cerdon crept to the fire while I sat staring at the flames, and crouched beside me. "There are sentries tonight," he whispered. "We must be careful. But the Silent One has gone, and that's more than I let myself hope for."

I felt that Drakaina might yet come and that Cerdon would not grudge us a few moments together, so I asked who the Silent One was and added, "I think you are all silent here."

"The young one." Cerdon spat into the fire. "The Silent Ones are always young men, because young men haven't begun to doubt."

"I'm a young man," I said. "So are you."

He chuckled softly at that. "No, you're no Silent One. Nor I. Besides, they're younger than either of us. They're Rope Makers, chosen from the first families—families that own whole villages and many farms. Do you know about the judges?"

I shook my head, glad of another delay.

"The judges rule. The kings pretend to rule; and they lead the armies, fighting in the first rank and often dying. But five judges rule our land. Only the kings can make war; that's the law. But each year the judges meet to make a war that's outside the law."

I said, "If there's a new war each year, you must always be at war."

"We are." Uneasily, he glanced over his shoulder. "The war's against us."

"Against you slaves?" I smiled. "People don't go to war against their own slaves."

"So I heard when I was in the north with the army. Masters there would laugh at such a thing, just as you did. Here it's so. Each year the war's voted in secret, and it's a war against us. The judges speak to young men, to the men who were boys until the full moon, when they were whipped for Auge. They become Silent Ones, seeming just untried shieldmen but each having the ear of some judge. A Silent One may kill us as he likes. You know the Silent One, I think. His tent stands over there. Do you remember his name?"

It was the tent to which Drakaina had taken me, and I remembered what she had said. "Pasicrates?"

Cerdon nodded.

"If the identity of the Silent Ones is kept secret, how can you know?"

"There's a look about their eyes. An ordinary Rope Maker—an Equal, like the one in your tent—may kill only his own slaves. If he kills another man's, even a Neighbor's, he must pay. A Silent One looks at you, and his hand moves by a finger toward his dagger, maybe because the others respect you, maybe only because you've talked to a foreigner." Cerdon shook himself as men do when they wake from evil dreams. "Now it's time to go," he said. "Past time. You'll have to leave that sword behind." He rose, motioning for me to follow.

I unbuckled Falcata and laid her in the tent. Cerdon was about three strides ahead of me. "Hurry," he said. As he spoke something moved beside his leg, and he cried out. It was but a muffled cry, smothered behind the hand with which he covered his mouth, but Io must have heard it in her sleep. She came running from the tent as I knelt beside him.

"Master! What happened?"

I told her I did not know. I carried Cerdon to the fire and by its light saw two wounds in his leg. Five times I filled my mouth with his blood. Io brought wine and water when I was through; I rinsed my mouth, and we poured wine on the wounds. By then he was dripping with sweat.

I asked Io whether Basias's slaves were awake as well. She shook her head and offered to get them up.

"No," Cerdon gasped.

Io said, "When Basias was bitten, the regent's healer said to keep him warm." I nodded and told her to bring my cloak.

Cerdon whispered, "You must go without me."

"If you wish."

"You must go. I saved you at the first meal. Do you remember?"

"Yes," I told him. "I'll go alone, if that's what you want."

Io covered him with my cloak and tucked it in around him, then filled a cup and held it to his lips.

"Follow the river. You'll see a white stone, and a path. Follow the path. There's a wood we never cut—not even for building timber . . . a fire there."

"I understand," I said, and stood up.

"Wait. You must touch her. Touch her, and I'm repaid."

"I will."

Io said, "I'll look after him, master, and hide him if he can walk a little when it gets light. I don't think he wants us to call anyone."

I ran, partly because Cerdon had said to hurry, partly because I feared the snake. There were sentries as he had said, but it was easy to slip between them and scramble down the bank into its shadow. The river—it is called the Eurotas, I believe—was nearly dead of the summer heat; the soft earth at the edge of its water muted my steps. There was an odor of decay.

The white stone had been put beside the path as a marker, or so it seemed to me; the wide valley of the Eurotas is a place of wheat and barley, and not one of stones and sand. The path born beside this stone climbed the bank at once, crossed fields of stubble far from any house, wound among sheep meadows into the eastern hills, and at last reached a wood of stunted trees—a wood filled with ax-bitten stumps.

It would have been so easy to lose the path in the dim moonlight that I wonder now how I did not; yet it had been trodden by many feet not so long ago. In the meadows, sheep must have crossed and recrossed it, but the marks of their sharp hooves had been blotted everywhere by softer walkers; in the woods my fingers told me of herbs crushed at its edges still damp with their own juices.

Two hills it climbed; the third it seemed rather to split as a man splits firewood with a wedge. When I had passed between those walls of stone, I walked as though in a hall colonnaded with mossy trunks, trees so softly furred that to brush against one was like caressing some vast beast, oaks as broad as boulders and as tall as masts.

A lion stepped from the darkness beneath the trees into a glade filled with moonlight, not half a stade away, and turned its black-maned head to stare at me. An instant later it had vanished in the shadows once more. I waited, fearing I would meet it should I go forward; and as I stood there, straining my ears to catch the least sound, I heard the singing of children.

Something in their song promised I need not fear even a lion in that enchanted place. I did not trust it and waited still; but after a time I went forward again, and soon I saw the red flicker of firelight through the leaves. I had walked quietly before; I sought to walk even more quietly now, so that I could assess the ceremony to which I had come before the other worshipers saw me.

The altar was a flat stone set upon two standing stones, its top only a trifle higher than my waist. The children I had heard were dancing in the space between two fires, stepping slowly and solemnly in the moon-light to the tapping of a pair of stone-headed hammers and the lilting of their own high, clear voices. Behind them, in the shadows of the trees, men and women murmured like willows stirred by the wind. Cerdon had called this a shrine of the Great Mother and indicated I must touch her, but I saw no goddess.

The clicking of the hammers was like the beating of my heart. For a long while I listened to it and to the children's song, and watched their dance; the girls wore garlands of flowers, the boys garlands of straw.

The clicking stopped.

The little dancers froze in their circle. The woman who held the hammers rose, and another led her forward. The child nearest the altar— a girl—went with them.

When they reached the altar, the woman and the girl held the woman with the hammers back; she was blind. She touched the altar with her hammers and laid them upon it. With the help of the other woman, she lifted the girl onto the altar. Slowly she chose a hammer and edged around the altar top until she stood at one end, nearest the girl's head.

As she walked, so I walked too—much more swiftly than she, but

I had more ground to cover. I circled the clearing until the altar was between me and those who watched, and as she lifted her hammer I shouted a name and dashed forward.

A sighted woman might have stopped to look; then I would have succeeded. The blind priestess did not. The stone hammer fell, splashing the girl's brains upon the stone.

That was when I saw the Great Mother, an old woman half again as tall as I, leaning over her priestess and dabbling her fingers in the blood. A goddess indeed, but aged and crazed, her gown torn and gray with dirt. For all I owed Cerdon, I would not have touched her if I could. I turned to flee instead; something struck my head, and I lay stretched upon the ground.

Before I could rise, a hundred slaves were upon me. Some had such sticks as could be picked up in the wood; some only their fists and feet. One shouted to the rest to stand aside and raised a billhook. They released me, then turned and fled as though it were they who were to die. I caught the ankle of the slave with the billhook with one foot and kicked his knee with the other, and he fell.

As I scrambled up, Rope Makers were emerging from the trees, their line as straight as on the drill field, their long spears leveled. I snatched up the billhook and killed the slave who would have killed me, finding it a better weapon than I would have supposed.

It was then I understood that the others did not see the goddess: a man took the priestess by the arm and led her away, assisted by the sighted woman; and for a moment he stood within the Great Mother, as a fire within its own smoke. "I drink no blood that has wet iron," she said.

I tried to explain that I had not killed the man with the billhook for her, then Drakaina embraced me. "Thank Auge! I thought they'd killed you."

"How did you get here?" I asked. "Were you watching before?"

She shook her lovely head, making the gems in her ears glitter in the moonlight. "I came with the Rope Makers. Or rather, I brought them. I could find this place—and you, Latro—though they could not."

The Rope Makers reached us as she spoke. Save for the dead man and the dead girl on the altar, the worshipers were gone. So was their terrible goddess, though I could hear her old, cracked voice calling to her people among the oaks.

# THIRTY-ONE
## *Mother Ge's Words*

THE PROPHECY OF THE GODDESS still echoes in my ears. I must write it here, though if it is read by the Silent One, by Pasicrates, he will surely try to kill me.

He was not at the shrine of the Great Mother, but because I thought the leader of the Rope Makers (who had gathered to stare at the altar and the dead girl) might be Pasicrates, I asked his name. "Eutaktos," he told me. "Have you forgotten our march from Thought?"

Drakaina said, "Of course he's forgotten, noble Eutaktos—you know how he is. But what about you? Don't you remember me?"

Eutaktos said politely, "I know who you are, my lady, and I see what a service you have done for Rope tonight."

"What of Eurykles of Miletos, who marched with you? Where is he now?"

"Wherever the regent has sent him," Eutaktos said. "Do you think I meddle in such things?" He turned to his men. "Why're you standing there, you clods? Pull her off and tear down that altar."

I asked whether he would bury the child.

He shook his head. "Let the gods bury their own dead—they make us take care of ours. But Latro"—his harsh voice softened a trifle—"don't try to handle something like this by yourself again. Get help." As he spoke, eight shieldmen lifted one side of the altar, and it fell with a crash. There were about thirty shieldmen altogether, one enomotia, I suppose.

As we stepped beneath the trees, someone threw a stone. That was how it began. Stones and heavy sticks flew all the way to the split hill. A shieldman was struck on the foot, though he could still limp along;

soon another's leg was broken. Two shieldmen tied their red cloaks to
the shafts of their spears and carried him.

In the split the stones were much larger, and they struck much
harder because they were thrown by men on the hilltops. Those who
had thrown from behind the trees were mostly women and boys, I think.
Without armor Drakaina and I hung back, but the shieldmen held their
big hoplons over their heads and advanced. The cries from the hilltops
and the clang of the stones on the bronze hoplons were like the din of
a hundred smiths, all shouting as they hammered a hundred anvils; they
deafened and bewildered us all, or at least all of us save Drakaina.

She took my arm and drew me away to the thick shadows we had
just left. I said, "They'll kill us here."

"They'll certainly kill us *there*. Don't you see the Rope Makers aren't
getting through?"

Nor were they. The rearmost shieldmen had stopped and were backing away from the stones.

"They've probably blocked the path in some way. Or if four or five
slaves with weapons were stationed where it widens out, one or two
Rope Makers would have to fight them all. In their phalanx they may
be the best soldiers in the world, but I doubt they're much better than
other men alone."

The rest soon followed those we had seen retreating. Nearly every
man was helping a wounded comrade with his spear arm while he tried
to fend off the stones with his shield. Eutaktos bellowed, "Back to the
fires! It won't be long till daylight."

Drakaina screamed. I turned in time to see the flash of the knife.
Then she was gone. The woman who had attacked her shrieked and fell.

Another woman and a boy rushed at me in the darkness, and I cut
them down with the billhook, though I am not proud of it. When they
were dead, I examined them; that was when I saw I had killed someone's
wife and a boy of twelve or so, she armed with a kitchen knife, he with
a sickle.* Seeing the sickle, I wished for my sword, though the billhook
was no mean weapon. The woman who had attacked Drakaina was
writhing in agony, but of Drakaina herself there was no sign.

I rejoined the Rope Makers, helping carry a wounded man. There

---

*Latin *falx*.—G. W.

were more stones as we fought our way to the clearing. I was struck twice, but I did not fall, nor were any of my bones broken. When we had marched to the split in the hill, the Rope Makers had stayed in file, and often they had seemed not to notice the missiles hurled at us. Now several rushed into the trees again and again. Twice they killed slaves, but one of the Rope Makers did not return.

The fires had burned low, so while some of us treated our wounded, the rest (of whom I was one) gathered such wood as we could find and piled it on the flames. When I heard the voice of the goddess in the oak wood again, I told Eutaktos the slaves would attack us soon.

He looked up from the dying Rope Maker he had been attending to ask what made me think so. Before I could reply, a lion roared from the trees, and a wolf howled. As though they too were lions and wolves, a hundred answered them. Every man had a stone, and each ran close before he threw, then dashed back into the shadows. We picked up such stones as we could find and flung them back, but most were lost in the dark.

They charged our circle at last. I fought with my back to one of the supports that had held the altar, though it was not high enough to give much protection. A Rope Maker fell beside me, then another, and after that I no longer heard Eutaktos shouting encouragement. I fought on alone, ringed by slaves with clubs and hachets. All this took less time than it has taken to write of it.

The cracked voice of the old goddess called, *"Wait!"* and though I do not think the slaves knew they heard it, they obeyed it nonetheless.

Long strides carried her to the fires; the spilling of so much blood must have restored her vigor, if not her youth. The lion and the wolf frisked around her like dogs, and though the slaves of the Rope Makers could not see her, they saw them and drew away in terror. When she stood before me I was a child once more, confronted by the crone from the cave on the hill.

"It is you," she said, "come again to visit Mother Ge. Europa carried your message, and my daughter has told me what she promised you. Do you recall Europa? Or my daughter Kore?"

If I had ever known them, they were lost in the mist, lost forever as though they had never been.

"No. No, you do not." Huge though she was, her voice seemed faint when she spoke to me; I could scarcely hear her above the snarling of the beasts and the cries of the slaves. "Why don't you threaten me with that hedge bill?" she asked. "You threatened Kore. Do you still fear my lion?"

I shook my head as she spoke, for as she spoke, what I had known of Kore and Europa came flooding back to me. "If I were to kill you, Mother, who would heal me?"

"By the wolf that gave your fathers suck, you are learning wisdom."

The slaves were staring at me as though I were mad. They had lowered their weapons, and as Mother Ge spoke I dropped mine, went to her, and touched her arm.

The slaves shouted aloud when I laid my hand on her, but quickly they fell silent again. When they came forward, many eyes streamed with tears—the eyes of men as well as those of women and of children. They would have touched her too, I think, if they could; but the lion and the wolf rushed at them, menacing them as the shepherd's dogs menace the sheep.

"Goddess!" one of the slaves shouted. "Hear our plea!"

"I have heard your plea many times," Mother Ge told him, and now her voice was like the singing of a bird in the sun, in lands that are drowned forever.

"Five hundred years the men of Rope have enslaved us."

"And five hundred more. Yet you are seven when they are one. Why should I aid you?"

At that, they led the blind priestess forward. She cried, "We are your worshipers! Who will feed your altars if we lose our faith?"

"I have millions more in other lands," Mother Ge told her. "And some for whom I am not yet bent and old." She paused, sucking her gums. "But I would have another sacrifice tonight. Give it to me willingly, and I will do all I can to free you. The victim need not die. Will you give it?"

"Yes," shouted the priestess and the man who had spoken before; and after them, all the people shouted, "Yes!" Then Mother Ge told them what she required of him, and the blind priestess found a sharp flint for it, searching the ground on all fours like a beast.

Twice he tried to strike but drew back his hand at the first blood. Though Mother Ge had said he need not die, his progeny died that

night to ten thousand generations, and he knew it as well as I. He stood
well back from Mother Ge and from me; the other slaves crowded around
him, cheering him and pledging tawdry rewards—a new roof or a milch
goat. I knew then that I might slip away in the dark if I chose, but I
waited as fascinated as the rest.

Then there was a stroke in which there was no hesitation. His manhood came away in his hand, looking like the offal from a butcher's
shop when he held it up. Someone took it from him and laid it upon
the fallen altar, and he stood with legs wide apart, bleeding like a
woman—or, rather, like a bull when it is made an ox. The others made
him lie on the ground and stanched his flow with cobwebs and moss.

"Now hear me," Mother Ge said. She straightened her back, and it
seemed that a great light shone there, a light from which her body
shielded us. "This man is sacred to me as long as he lives. In payment,
I will fight for you, striving to make his master, Prince Pausanias, king
of this land."

The slaves muttered against these words, and a few shouted protests.

"You think him your greatest foe, but I tell you he will be your
greatest friend and perhaps your king, turning his back upon his own
kindred. Still he, and I, may fail. If so, I shall destroy Rope—"

Here the slaves roared so loudly I could not hear.

"—then you must rise against the Rope Makers, your scythes to
cut their spears, your sickles to beat down their swords. But first, your
stones against their helmets. So you defeated them on this night. Remember it."

Then she was gone, and the clearing seemed dark and far from the
lands of men. One fire was dying, the other already no more than embers.
In a litter they wove of vines, half a dozen men carried away the man
who had unmanned himself. Others trailed behind them, bearing the
bodies of relatives killed in the fighting. Some women asked me to come
with them and offered to treat my bruises, but I feared them still because
of the woman I had killed, and I told them to follow their husbands.
They did as I ordered, leaving me alone with the dead.

Though the billhook was not intended for digging, I was able to
scratch out a small and shallow grave in the soft earth of the clearing. I
buried the girl I had not saved and heaped her grave with the stones
that had been flung at us. I believe one of the dead Rope Makers was

Eutaktos, whom I had known in some time I have forgotten. Though I robbed several of their helmets to study their faces, I could not be sure; I had seen Eutaktos only briefly and by firelight.

Nor did I any longer know who Kore and Europa were, nor what they had once meant to me, though I could recall a time not long ago when I had known. Their names and that memory troubled me at least as much as the thought that the lion and the wolf might still be near. I muttered "Kore" and "Europa" over and over as I built up the dying fire and carried blazing sticks to reestablish the other, until at last *Kore* and *Europa* ceased to have any meaning at all for me, ceased even to be names.

Walking up and down between the fires, I waited for dawn before I made my way through the split hill. The bodies of many Rope Makers had laid on that narrow path, and there were still many bloodstains; but the slaves had dragged the bodies away, so that they lay in the shadows beneath the trees, wrapped in the green life of the oaks. I do not think the other Rope Makers will find them there.

From the place where Drakaina had taken my arm, I could see the old goddess walking the valley, a woman taller than women, at once darker and brighter than the treetops touched by dawn. She stopped at the grave, I think, for after a time she vanished from sight and I heard her weeping.

When I had passed the split hill, I cast aside my weapon and hurried through the dew-decked fields to this camp on the bank of the Eurotas, where now I write these words in the morning sunlight. Io met me. After I had told her something of what had happened that night and she had salved my bruises and mourned with many head shakings the blow that had struck me down, she took me proudly to see Cerdon, whom she had hidden among the hay that fed our pack mules; but Cerdon had died while she slept, and already his limbs were cold and stiff.

# THIRTY-TWO

## *Here in Rope*

STRANGERS ARE VIEWED WITH THE greatest suspicion. This morning Drakaina, Io, and I went to see the famous temple of Orthia. Its enclosure on the riverbank must once have been separated from the city, but now the Rope Makers have built their houses right up to the boundaries of the sacred ground. Drakaina said, "In the Empire, we wall our cities properly. When you're on one side of the wall, you're in the city; on the other, you're in the country. With all these straggling hamlets, who knows? Thought was almost as bad, but at least they had guard posts on the roads."

"The Great King tore down your walls," Io reminded her. "That's what the regent said."

Drakaina nodded. "The People from Parsa have a sense of fitness. Its walls symbolize a city, and pulling them down is the destruction of the city. Rope's been destroyed already—or let's say that it's never existed. This is just four villages; no wonder they call it scattered."

Slaves turned their faces to one side when we passed, and even the Neighbors we saw did not wish to speak with us. Rope Makers stopped us and questioned us, women as well as men, and many told us we were unwelcome. We soon learned to reply that we would gladly go elsewhere if only their regent would permit it, which silenced them quite effectively.

Drakaina shook her lovely head after one such encounter. "There's no place in the world where men are less free than they are here, and none where women are freer—save perhaps in the country of the Amazons, the women who live without men."

"Are they real?" Io asked. "Once Basias said I'd be a strategist among them."

"Of course they are." Drakaina slipped her arm through mine. "But you'll have to go far to the north and east—much farther east than my own city. And you'll have to leave Latro here with me. The Amazons don't care for foreigners any more than these Rope Makers, and they consider all men spies."

I said, "There can be no such race; they'd die out in a generation."

"They lie with the young men of the Sons of Scoloti. If they bear a girl afterward, they sear her left breast so she can use the bow. Boys buy them the favor of their goddess, or so I've heard. I admit I've never seen one of these women warriors myself."

I thought of the dream I had last night when she said that; perhaps later I will write of it here.

"There it is!" Io exclaimed, and pointed.

"About what I expected. They don't know what a real temple looks like here. Nobody could who hasn't traveled in the east, though some of these are at least beautiful. This isn't even that. In fact, if this whole city were destroyed, no one would ever guess from looking at the ruins that half the world had trembled at its name."

The temple was indeed small and very simple, its pillars mere wooden posts painted white. I took off my sword and fastened the belt around one.

Io said, "We're supposed to make an offering. See the bowl? Master, do you have any money?"

Drakaina told her, "I'll take care of it," and tossed one of the iron coins of the Rope Makers so that it rang against the bronze rim.

As we went from the brilliant sunlight of the portico into the shadowy interior, Io asked, "Where did you get that?"

"Hush!"

It was the age of the temple that impressed me most, I think, and perhaps it would be just to say that its age was the only impressive thing about it; but that made it truly a sacred place, the home built for a god when the world was young and men had not yet forgotten that when the gods are mocked they punish us by leaving us.

A priestess, white-haired but as tall as I and as straight as any spear, glided from some recess. "Welcome," she said, "to this house in the name of the Huntress, and to this land in the name of the House of Heracles."

"It's true," I admitted, "that we're all foreigners here, madame. But we've come to Rope at the order of your regent, the great Prince Pausanias, who does not permit us to leave."

Drakaina quickly added, "We have the freedom of the city, however, and I am a priestess of your goddess."

The white-haired woman made the slightest of bows. "As such, you may sacrifice here whenever you wish. No one will prevent you. Should anyone question you, tell them you have my permission. I am Gorgo, daughter of Cleomenes, mother of Pleistarchos, and widow of Leonidas."

Drakaina began, "Then the regent is—"

"My cousin and my nephew. Would you care to see the image of the goddess?" She led us to a wooden figure, cracked and blackened by time. "She is called Orthia because she was found standing upright, just where you see her now, in the days when our forefathers conquered this land."

The bulging eyes of the statue gave it the look of a madwoman. In either hand it grasped a snake.

"The wood is cypress, which is sacred to her. The snake in her right hand is the empyreal serpent, the one in her left the chthonic serpent. She holds both and stands between them, the only god who unites heaven to earth and the lower world. When she appears here, it is most often as a snake."

Io asked, "Could she help my master? He's been cursed by the Grain Goddess."

Drakaina added, "I've already offered sacrifices to our threefold goddess on his behalf. Do you remember Basias, Io? He promised to carry a message to her." She turned back to the priestess. "And Latro is much better. His memory was taken from him, and he still can't remember; but now he acts almost as though he could."

I said, "The goddess is angry."

"Why?" Gorgo's eyes were large and cool, the rare blue eyes that shine like ice.

"I don't know. But can't you see the way she looks at Drakaina?"

Io's hand flew to her mouth to stifle a shout of nervous laughter.

"No," the priestess told me softly. "I cannot see that. But you do. What has this woman done?"

"I don't know."

Even in the dimness of the temple, I could see how white Drakaina's face was. She said, "He is mad, most reverend Queen. Pasicrates and I, and the little girl, care for him."

"Pasicrates is a fine young man, and a faithful servant of the goddess."

"As I am. If I have displeased her—"

"You will be punished."

When Gorgo said that, there was a silence that stretched so long that it became unbearable. At last Io asked, "Is this where the boys get whipped?"

"Yes, child." One corner of the priestess's mouth lifted by the width of a grain of wheat. "In this city, we girls receive much the same education as the boys, but we are spared that. Here food is placed upon the altar, and the older men stand where you are standing, and on the portico outside, and as far as the sacred precinct of the temple reaches. The boys must dash past them and take the food, then dash past again; they are beaten as they run. See the stains their blood has left on our floor? Thus they learn what women already know: that without women there is no food for men. Because they are beaten that day, they can never forget. There is a statue of the goddess at Ephesos with a hundred breasts. The lesson is the same."

Pasicrates was waiting for us when we left the temple. "My slave said you had gone out to see the sights," he told us. "This is the first most visitors want to see."

Drakaina asked, "And are there others?"

"We do not have the wealth of Tower Hill," Pasicrates conceded as he led us away, "and yet our city is not without interest. The well I am about to show you is known these days in every civilized land."

"Really?" She smiled at him; her sharply angled face gave her smiles a disturbing quality. "Is it like the one at Hysiai, that inspires all who drink to prophesy?"

"No," Pasicrates replied. He hesitated. "I was on the point of saying it isn't a magic well at all. Except that now that I think on it, it does have power, and power of a sort you might find particularly interesting. It changes men to women."

Io said, "It seems like everybody's turning against you, even the Huntress."

Drakaina looked so angry that I feared for Io, though she faced up to it as bravely as any child could.

Pasicrates said, "What's this? Tell me, little girl."

"Latro says the goddess is mad at her. Sometimes Latro sees things other people don't. Sometimes he sees the gods; and talks to them, too."

"How interesting. I should have asked you more about him when we met. Foolishly, I wasted my time with one Eurykles. Latro, what did you see?"

"Only that she gave Drakaina a look of fury, just as Drakaina looked at Io a moment ago."

"And it's Orthia who sends sudden death to women. What a pity you're not a man, Drakaina. Is that your true name, by the way?"

She feigned not to hear him.

"She is also the protector of young beasts and of children," Pasicrates told Io. "Did you know that? Our boys pray to her before they are beaten, and dedicate the end of their childhood to her. Yet she favors girls more. It goes ill with anyone who harms a girl here, unless he is high in her favor."

I said, "It will go ill with anyone who hurts Io, while I live."

Pasicrates nodded, "You might well be the instrument of her justice. So might I."

We had been strolling through the city as we talked; when nothing more was said for a time, I ventured to ask about the houses, saying it seemed strange to me to see so many windows in a city of his people.

"Ah, but you've been in Thought, even if you don't remember it. There they think about being robbed. We don't. We're too poor, and there's little here to buy." He smiled. "But here's the well. Look down. You'll find it worth seeing."

Io dashed ahead and pulled herself up by the coping to peer into the depths. *"Skeletons!"* she called.

When Pasicrates arrived he seated himself on it beside her. "Are bones all you see, little Io? Surely there is something more."

"Just mud and water."

"Yes, earth and water. You see, I am a knowledgeable guide. I brought you here at noon, when the sun shines far enough down for you to see the bottom. It's not a very deep well. Perhaps that's why it went dry, or nearly dry. Drakaina, don't you want to look?"

I peered inside. As Pasicrates had indicated, the sun reached more than halfway to the bottom and lent light enough to show the rest. Three black-bearded men were penned there. They had heavy gold bracelets on their arms, and their golden sword hilts were set with many gems. One gripped his wrist, his face twisted in agony; one covered his face with his hands; one wept, face upturned, and extended his hands to me.

Pasicrates said, "The Great King sent his ambassadors here, demanding earth and water in token of our submission. They were bold men when they came, but frightened women when we threw them in to get them for themselves. You should have heard them scream. Drakaina, I think you'd better look. I won't push you." He slid from the coping and strode away.

Io said softly, "I thought he liked the Great King."

"He's jealous," Drakaina snapped. "The regent prefers me. Latro will find that understandable, though perhaps you won't. When we went into the temple, you asked where I got the coin I offered. Prince Pausanias gave it to me, as he's given me other things. Do you like this gown?" Her hand caressed the crimson fabric. "It's moth's spinning, brought from the end of the earth; once it belonged to a noble lady of Susa."

"It's beautiful," Io said with honest admiration. "But now that you're speaking to me again, will you tell me how you explained to the regent? You were a man the first time he saw you, and you're a woman now, and he's not like Latro."

"I told him the truth—that the goddess had given me my desire. It hasn't reduced his esteem for me, believe me."

"Watch out," Io said. "She's liable to take it back."

Drakaina shook her head, and it seemed to me that she was hearing someone other than Io. "I feel I've lived a long, long time," she said. "And that I've been what I am since the first stars took shape."

Afterward we idled about the city; but nothing more was said that I think worth recounting, save that Drakaina remarked that I had given her a slave some time ago. When I asked what had become of him, she said he was dead.

We watched naked women run and throw the discus, which Io thought disgusting, and saw the barracks where the Rope Makers sleep.

After that we returned to this hill fortress in the center of the city, stopping for a time to watch slaves at work upon the tomb of Leonidas. This was in the village called Pitana, which stands close beside the hill. I do not know what the name may mean. Perhaps "legion." A least Io says there is a mora of that name in the regent's army.

Here in the fortress I write as I do, catching the fading light of the sun as it shines through the embrasure. Drakaina has just come to say this day will be our last in Rope.

# PART FOUR

# THIRTY-THREE

## *Through This Shadowed Gorge*

DARK ACHERON CUTS THE ROCKS like a knife, at last plunging into the earth on its way to the Lands of the Dead. Nowhere else are they so near the living; nowhere else are they so readily summoned—so says Drakaina, who is even now preparing for the ceremony. As I watch, Prince Pausanias himself digs the votive pit, while Io feeds ferns to the black lamb and black ewe lamb he will sacrifice. Pasicrates and I have dipped jars of water from Acheron and unloaded the mule, which carried honey, milk, wine, and the other needful things. I am writing this because Io says I have neglected to write for too long; and indeed when I read what I had written last, I saw that we had been in Rope, which the young men of the prince's bodyguard speak of as a place very far away.

But also because I do not wish to lose all recollection of the dream I had last night. It was of a ship, a round-bellied trader with a white swan at its stern, a broad, striped mainsail, and an angled foremast. I opened a hatch on deck and went below to a cavern, where a lovely queen and a grim king sat thrones of black stone amid the smell of death. Three dogs barked, and the queen said, "He passes. His message fulfills . . ."

There was more that I have forgotten. When I told Io of the ship, she said it was the one in which we came here. If that is so, some part of me retains the memory, though I cannot recall it. Surely that is a good sign. It may be I will find my past soon, perhaps even here among these damp and frowning rocks. Pausanias has completed his pit, and Pasicrates winds dark garlands of hemlock and rue about the lambs. There are chaplets of herbs for us.

It came, and I saw it! Drakaina poured libations of milk, honey, sweet wine, and water, and strewed the ground with barley meal. She held the lambs while Prince Pausanias pronounced the invocation: "Royal Agids come! Advise me, and I will make your tombs places of pilgrimage and sacrifice for the entire world. Should I seek peace or war? Was my dream true, that said this slave would bring me victory? How shall I know it? Come! Speak! You I love in death as in life." Though his hand shook, he took up his sword and struck off the heads of the black lamb and the black ewe lamb so that their blood streamed into the pit; releasing their flaccid bodies, Drakaina began a chant in a tongue unknown to me.

At once the rock behind her split, and there came forth a king in armor, with a bloodstained knife in his hand, bleeding limbs, and a lolling head. He was terrible to behold, but he knelt and drank the vapors from the pit as a shepherd drinks from a spring; as he drank, his wounds ceased to bleed and he appeared almost a living man—not handsome, for his face had been scarred by wine as well as the knife, yet having such an air of command as few possess. Drakaina fell in a fit, her mouth gaping and rimmed with foam. From it there issued a man's voice, as swift and hard as the crack of a lash.

> "Nephew, seek peace and not death.
> Nor drink from the blue cup of Lethe.
> Ask who will make the fortress yield,
> To those that fought at Fennel Field."

At the final word Drakaina gave a great cry; and the stone, which had closed, opened again to receive the dead king. In his train now walked an attendant, a lean, fantastically dressed man with disordered hair. Drakaina was weak and sick when they were gone. She crawled to drink the milk left from the libations.

The prince drew a deep breath; his forehead was beaded with sweat. "Was it good? Who'll provide the exegesis?" He wiped his hands on his chiton. "Pasicrates, who spoke to me?"

Pasicrates looked to Drakaina. Receiving no help from her, he ventured, "Your royal uncle, perhaps, King Cleomenes. Only he per-ished—" Pasicrates hesitated, then finished weakly, "By seeking death."

"By his own hand, you mean. You may say so. He desecrated the

sacred lands of the Great Goddess and her daughter when he marched
to Advent. The nature of his punishment is common knowledge. What
of the second line?"

"He warns you against the wine that drove him mad, and so by
implication against offending the gods as he did. You asked three questions, Highness. It seems to me the first two lines of your royal uncle's
verse answer your first two questions. You are to seek peace, and you
are to trust your dream, because to distrust it would be an offense to
the gods."

"Very good." Pausanias nodded. "And those who fought at Fennel
Field are the shieldmen of Thought, who are now besieging the fortified
city of Sestos. Cleomenes fought them, twice invading the Long Coast.
I should aid them instead—seeking peace with Thought now, that I
may better seek peace with Persepolis later. So Cleomenes seems to be
saying."

"Highness, you asked how you might know whether your dream
was truly from the gods. King Cleomenes urges you to ask who will
make a fortress yield to the men of Thought. Why not send a token
force from your retinue to Sestos? They say it's the strongest place in
the world; if it falls, you'll know your dream was the true speech of the
Maiden. If it doesn't, it will be a failure for Thought and not for us.
That seems to me to be your royal uncle's advice, sir, and I see no flaw
in it."

Pausanias's face twisted in its scarred smile. "Yes, the risks will be
small, and the People of Thought will take it as a friendly gesture, a
personal gesture on my part, since Leotychides has withdrawn. The aristocratic party there, particularly, will take it so. Xanthippos commands."
He chuckled. "And you wouldn't exactly object to leading a hundred
of my heroes on a new Trojan War, would you, Pasicrates? Or should I
say, swift-footed Achilles? It will be a glorious adventure, one in which
a man might win considerable reputation."

Pasicrates looked at his feet. "I will stay or go, as my strategist
commands."

"You'll go, then, and keep your eyes open." The prince wiped his
sword on his cloak.

I said, "And I, Highness. I must go with him."

Io protested, "Master, we might get killed!"

"You don't have to," I told her. "But I do. If the gods say I bring the regent victory, I must be with his standard."

"Here's your first volunteer, Pasicrates. Will you take him?"

Pasicrates nodded. "Highness, I'd like to take all three. Latro for the reason he just gave: the test won't be valid without him. The child to care for him, and the sorceress because it may be desirable to . . . ah . . ."

"Arrange terms of surrender." The prince rose.

"Exactly, Highness."

"All right, then. It will make things easier for me at home anyway—Gorgo doesn't like her."

When the winding mountain paths had brought us here again, the regent ordered his bodyguard to form the phalanx; this bodyguard consists of three hundred unmarried men chosen by himself. "Shieldmen of Rope," he began. "Rope Makers! Hear me! You know of the glorious victory of Mycale. There's not a man among us who doesn't wish he had been there. Now word has reached me that our allies, jealous of our glory, were not content with that victory. When our ships set out for home, they remained across the Water, and they have laid siege to the Great King's city of Sestos!"

Though the young soldiers stood rigidly at attention, there was a stir among them, like the stirring of a wood that hears far off the thunder of the storm.

"When we return, I intend to tell the judges we should send an army to aid them—but what if Sestos falls before it arrives? You know how we were late to Fennel Field. You have heard, I imagine, that the men of Thought are claiming credit for the victory at Peace. I ask you, shall we let them say they took Sestos alone?"

Three hundred voices roared, *"No!"*

"And I too say *no!*" The regent paused; the young men waited, tense and expectant. "All of you know Pasicrates, and you know he has my entire confidence. Pasicrates, step out here!"

Pasicrates left the first line of the phalanx to stand beside the regent, and even to me he looked a young hero in his bright armor.

"Pasicrates will lead a hundred volunteers to Sestos. Those who do *not* wish to volunteer, remain in ranks. Volunteers! Step forward and join Pasicrates!"

The formation surged forward as one man. "He'll choose," the regent shouted. "Pasicrates, choose your hundred!"

A moment ago, Io asked what I was writing about. "About the choosing of the hundred volunteers," I told her.

"What about what we did in the gorge, killing the black lambs?" I told her I had already written about that.

"Do you think it was really real? That King Cleomenes talked through Drakaina?"

"I know it was," I said. "I saw him."

"I wish you'd touched him. Then I could have seen him too."

I shook my head. "He would have frightened you." I described him to her, dwelling on the horror of his wounds.

"I've seen a lot. You don't remember all I've seen. I saw you kill the Rope Makers' slaves, and I saw Kekrops after the sea monster killed him. Do you think Pasicrates understood what Cleomenes said?"

Drakaina sat up at that. "Do you remember? What was it?"

"Don't you know? You said the words."

"No," Drakaina told her. "I was not I who spoke. I remember nothing."

Io recited the four lines as I have given them and added, "I don't think Pasicrates was right. I think Cleomenes wanted a real peace, and not for the regent to send men to Sestos. That was what he meant when he said the regent should ask who took the fortress. If he didn't send men, he wouldn't know."

Drakaina said, "He meant no one would take it. I've seen Sestos, and believe me, what they say is true—it's the strongest place on earth. People talk of the walls of Babylon, but they are gapped to let the river through. That was how the People from Parsa took it the first time. Sestos has no such weakness. As for seeking peace, Cleomenes knows that Demaratus, the true heir to the younger crown of Rope, is one of the Great King's advisers. He naturally hopes for an agreement that will leave the Agids the elder crown and give Demaratus the younger. If such an agreement had been struck two years ago, the whole war might have been prevented."

I asked if she was feeling better.

"Yes, thank you. Weak, but as though I'll be stronger than ever when I'm no longer weak. Do you know what I mean?" She cupped her full breasts and caressed them, savoring delights to come. "Something in me knows the best part of this life still lies ahead."

Io asked, "Just how many lives do you have? And is there a spring where you take a bath to get back your virginity?"

Drakaina smiled at her. Her lovely face looks hungry when she smiles. "Don't flutter too close, little bird of joy, or you'll sing a different song."

Io seated herself at my feet. "You may be the bird who has to learn a new tune, Drakaina. Prince Pausanias likes you, but we're going with Pasicrates, and he hates you."

"Because I came between him and the regent—quite literally, as it happens. When the regent's a hundred leagues away, things will be different; you'll see." With such fluid grace as few women possess, Drakaina rose. "In fact, I think I'll have my first chat with the noble Pasicrates now. He'll be the one who assigns us space on the ship, I suppose. I want the captain's cabin. Would you care to bet I don't get it?" From the sheen of her dark hair and the grace of her swaying figure, it seemed likely enough she would.

When she was out of sight, Io made a face. "I think if somebody sliced her up the way you said Cleomenes was, she'd wiggle till sunset."

I did not want to punish Io, but I told her I thought that an ugly thing for a child to say, even though Drakaina's name was "she-dragon."

"It used to be Eurykles of Miletos," Io told me. "I know you don't remember, Latro, but it was. Eurykles was a man, and when we lived with Kalleos, sometimes he spent the whole night in her room. Drakaina says he changed himself into her by magic. I didn't like Eurykles much, but I liked him a whole lot better than Drakaina. And if you ask me *she* changed him into her, somehow."

I asked her how this Eurykles had looked. Now that she has described him for me, I know he was the man I saw follow King Cleomenes.

A short time ago, the prince regent's runner came to tell me that he will send for me soon. He said I was to wash and put on my best clothes, which I have done. I asked if he would be present, but he said he would be in the town getting supplies for our expedition to Sestos. A shieldman of the bodyguard—one of those who will not be coming to Sestos with us—will probably be sent for me, he said.

Io reports that according to the gossip of the camp, a ship has brought the regent's sorcerer.

# THIRTY-FOUR

## *In the Regent's Tent*

THERE WAS NO ONE TO meet me. "Wait here," said the young shieldman who had brought me. As he turned to leave he added, "Don't touch anything."

I do not believe I have ever been a thief; but for a thief it would have been tempting indeed. There were lamps of silver, gold, and crystal, and many soft carpets and cushions. A long knife in a green sheath with gold mountings hung from one of the tent poles, and an ivory griffin spread its wings upon a peak of ebony.

I was admiring this last when the regent entered, bringing with him a sly little Hellene with a beard. "This is the slave," the regent said, dropping to a cushion. "Latro—Tisamenus, my mantis."

I did not know the word, and my ignorance must have appeared on my face. Tisamenus murmured, "A mere consulter of the gods, sir, a humble reader of the omens of sacifice."

"Tisamenus advised me at Clay. Those who know the result know why I think highly of him."

"His Highness has told me of his dream. I wished to see the man. It sometimes amuses His Highness to accede to my little requests. Sir, Latro, I noticed you were admiring that statuette when we entered. Do you know of those monsters?"

"Do they actually exist? No, nothing."

The regent said, "I'm told they live in the country of those Sons of Scoloti who revolted against the royal branch of their people, and that they hoard gold."

I said, "Which can't be as precious as this carving, Highness."

Tisamenus murmured, "I'd understood they're found north and

west of the Issedonians. It's said they put out one eye of any man they find trying to make off with their treasure; but if he's already one-eyed, they kill him. However, I think it likely my information is mistaken, Highness, and yours correct."

The regent laughed. "No, you've the right of it, I feel sure. The best intelligence of such things is always that which puts them farthest from us."

Tisamenus nodded and smiled. "I don't suppose you've seen the creatures, sir?"

I shrugged. "I've no way of knowing. From what I read in my book today, I was already with the regent when we were in Rope. If he's told you about me, he must have told you I don't remember."

"Yet you remembered the monster, sir. I saw that memory in your eyes."

I shook my head. "I don't recall what I learned of them, if I did. Or how I learned it, or where."

The regent chuckled. "Sit down, you two. I'm remiss in my duties as your host. Latro, Tisamenus—" He turned to the mantis. "Which do you prefer, Tisamenus of Elis, or Tisamenus of Rope?"

"As Your Highness chooses to honor his servant."

"Tisamenus of Elis, then. Latro, Tisamenus got my permission to visit his family after the battle. That was unfortunate, because he wasn't present to interpret my dream when I dreamed about you; but I've told him that dream now, and in general he seems to feel I've caught the meaning without him."

"To visit my sisters and their husbands, sir. I have not been favored in the matter of sons and daughters." The mantis sighed. "And the Inescapable One deprived me of my poor wife at the time of the last Games."

I cleared my throat. I did not think what I was about to say would lose me my head, but the possibility, however slight, lent a chill to my words. "With your leave, mantis. Why is it you call me 'sir' when the regent has called me a slave?"

The regent said brusquely, "That's just his way."

Almost too softly to be heard, Tisamenus murmured, "Courtesy is never wasted, sir. Particularly courtesy toward a slave. We slaves appreciate it." To me he added, "You will not be able to answer our questions, then. That's a terrible pity, but perhaps you won't object if we beg you to try."

"Fetch some wine," the regent told Tisamenus. "Want a cup, Latro?"

"I can answer that one," I said. "Yes. But Io can tell you more about me than I can tell you about myself."

"I questioned her some time ago," the regent said. "And I was able to pass to Tisamenus all I learned in a few words. She met you in Hill. You were badly wounded. You'd tried to embrace a statue of the River God, and they brought you to the oracle there. It gave her to you and assigned a citizen to guide you to Advent. All three of you were imprisoned in Tower Hill until you were freed by a captain from Thought. In Advent, the goddess came to you in a dream and promised to restore you to your friends. Then the lochagos I'd sent looking for you found you and brought you to me."

Tisamenus poured the wine, so old and good it perfumed even that perfumed air. "Thank you," I said, accepting the cup.

"You don't look pleased. What's the matter?"

"You told me a lot, Highness, but none of it was what I wanted to hear."

"Which is?"

"Who my friends are, where my home is, what happened to me, and how I can be cured."

"Your friends are here—two of them, at least. I'm your greatest friend, and anyone who stands with me will be your friend as well. Do you know of the promise made me in my dream?"

"Yes. We talked of it this afternoon in the gorge."

Tisamenus murmured, "Then perhaps you also know why it should be so. What makes you a talisman of victory?"

"I have no idea."

The regent said, "My first notion was that we'd been born at the same instant—it's well known such children are linked. Tisamenus?"

The mantis looked doubtful. "I'd guess he's the younger." To me he said, "I don't suppose, sir, that you know the day of your birth?"

I shook my head, and the regent shrugged. "So it might be true.

I'm in my twenty-eighth year. Think that might be your age, Latro? Speak up. You won't be beaten."

"Twenty-eight sounds old to me, Highness. So I think I must be less."

Tisamenus had risen. "Shrewdly spoken, sir, and I agree. May I call your attention once more to this admirable carving? Can you perhaps inform me as to the name borne by these monsters?"

"They're the Clawed Ones," I said.

"So," Tisamenus whispered. "The god who took away your memory left you that. What man comprehends their ways?"

The regent drank. "A thousand times I've heard somebody say that: Who understands the ways of the gods? Everybody asks the question, nobody answers it. Now I'm a man and nearly a king—do you know many of our Rope Makers already call me King Pausanias, Tisamenus? So I'll try, Latro. You do."

As cautiously as I could, I said, "I'm not sure I follow you, Highness."

"I called you an idiot once. Since then, I've seen enough of you to know you're anything but."

"Yet there's an idiot here, Highness, if you believe I'm in the councils of the gods."

Tisamenus said, "You're treading on dangerous ground, sir."

"Because if you believe it, Highness, it must be true; and I would be an idiot not to tell you."

The regent gave Tisamenus his twisted smile. "You see what I mean? If this were the pentathlon, he'd win every event."

"Good," I said. "Because if we're linked, Highness, it might be that if I were beaten you'd be beaten too."

"And the chariot race. But Latro, my friend—and I'll call you my friend and not my slave—you know things you don't know you know. You didn't remember the name of the winged monsters until you were asked, did you?"

I shook my head.

Tisamenus murmured, "So it is, perhaps, with the councils of the gods. If we recall them to you, will you tell His Highness?"

I said, "If he wishes it, certainly. But though Io says I once swept floors for a woman in Thought, I don't believe I ever swept the hall of Olympus."

"Then we'll begin with speculations humbler still. You acknowledge that there are many gods?"

I sipped my wine. "All men do, I suppose."

"You once told His Highness, no doubt truly, that you were a soldier of the Great King."

"I feel I am."

"Then you must know something of the barbarians, sir. Indeed, you must have marched through Parsa, for the Great King's army did so on its way here. Are you aware that they hold there's only a single god, whom they call Ahuramazda?"

"I know nothing of them," I said. "At least, nothing I can remember."

"And yet they sacrifice to the sun, the moon, and the earth, and to fire and water. It is possible—I speak now as a sophist, sir—that there is but one god. It is possible also that there are many. But it is not possible that there are one *and* many. You disagree?"

I shrugged. "Sometimes a word is used for two things. When I loaded the regent's mule, I tied the load with rope."

Prince Pausanias chuckled. "Excellent! But now that you've bested poor Tisamenus, let me play Ahuramazda's advocate. I say that just as there's only one king at Persepolis, there can be only one god. Why should he tolerate more? He'll destroy them, then there'll be only one. Show me my error, Latro, if you can."

"Highness, if you were truly a magus—I mean a priest of this Ahuramazda—I don't think you'd speak like that. You'd say there can't be a single god, but that just as there are two kings in Rope, there must be two gods also."

The regent held out his cup, and Tisamenus poured him more wine. "Why do you say that, sir?"

"I don't say it, but I think the magi would. They would reason thus: There's good in the world, so there's a good god, a wise lord. But there's evil too, so there must be an evil lord as well. In fact, one posits the other. There can be no good without evil, no evil without good."

The regent remarked, "Here we know that good and evil come from the same gods, having observed that the same man is good one time and evil another."

"Highness, a magus would say, Then I will call the good Ahuramazda and the bad Angra Manyu, evil mind. And if the good is truly good, won't it put the lie from it?"

The regent nodded. "Yet what you say doesn't explain Orith—the other gods. What of earth, fire, wind, and so forth?"

Tisamenus nodded, leaning toward me to listen.

I said, "Now I can speak for myself as well as for the magi. It doesn't seem to me that there can't be good without evil or evil without good. For a blind man, isn't it always night? With no day? It seemed to me that if Ahuramazda—"

A shieldman of the bodyguard entered as I spoke; when I fell silent, he addressed the regent. "The captain has arrived, Highness."

"Then he must wait. Go on, Latro."

"If Ahuramazda exists, Highness, all things serve him. The oak is his; so is the mouse that gnaws its root. Without oaks there could be no mice, without mice no cats, and without cats no oaks. But shouldn't he have servants greater than oaks and men? Surely he must, because the gap between Ahuramazda and men and oaks is very wide, and we see that every king has some minister whose authority's only slightly less than his own, and that such men have ministers of their own, similarly empowered. Besides, the existence of the sun, the moon, the earth, and of fire and water are indisputable facts."

"But the existence of Ahuramazda is not an indisputable fact. Finish your wine."

I did so. "Highness, let us think of a great city like Susa. Within the city stands a palace as great again. A beggar boy squats outside the palace wall, and I'm that poor boy."

"Is Ahuramazda the king in that palace?"

I shook my head. "No, Highness. Not so far as I, Latro the beggar boy, have seen. The servants are the lords of the palace. Once a cook gave me meat, and a scullion, bread. I've even seen the steward, Highness, with my own eyes. The steward's a very great lord indeed, Highness."

The regent rose. Tisamenus stood at once, and so did I.

"So he is, to a beggar boy," the regent said, "though not to himself, perhaps. We'll speak of this again when you've returned from Sestos. Do you want to see your ship?"

I nodded. "Even if it's the one we came in, I'd like to see it, Highness. I've forgotten it, but Io says we came by ship."

"It's one of those that brought us here," he told me as we stepped from the scented air of the tent into night air that was sweeter still. "But not the one in which you and Io sailed with me. I'm taking that back to Olympia. One of the others is going to carry you and Pasicrates to Sestos."

The shieldman and another man were waiting outside. The regent said, "You're Captain Nepos?"

The captain stepped foward, bowing low. "The same." His hair gleamed like foam in the moonlight.

"You understand your commission and accept it?"

"I'm to carry a hundred Rope Makers and two hundred and seventy slaves to Sestos. And a woman, who must have a cabin to herself."

"And a slave girl," the regent told him. "With the slave you see before you."

"We can occupy the same cabin," I said. "Or we can sleep on deck, if there's no cabin for us."

The captain shook his head. "Just about everybody will have to sleep on deck, and it'll be crowded at that."

The regent asked, "But your ship will hold them all, with their rations?"

"Yes, Highness, only not in much comfort."

"They don't require comfort. You know you won't be able to make port at Sestos? It's under siege, and the other ports of the Chersonese are still the Great King's."

The captain nodded. "I'll land them on this side, from boats. That'll be the safest way."

"Good. Come with us, then. I've promised Latro the sight of your ship, and you'll have to point it out to him." The regent looked about for Tisamenus, but he was gone. The shieldman offered to search for him, but the regent shook his head. "You've got to allow these fellows some freedom, if you want to hang on to them." As we began our walk, he added to me, "He wanted to spare his legs, I suppose. We had to make him a citizen to get his help at Clay, but he's no Rope Maker, just the same."

Though the moon was low and as crooked as my sword, it was a clear night with many stars. We climbed a cliff above the town that gave us a fine view of the little harbor. "There's *Nausicaa*," her captain said proudly. "Nearest the mouth of the bay." His ship was only a darker shape upon the dark water; yet I wished I were on board already, for I feel there is nothing for me here.

The regent said, "You'll be anxious to get back, I imagine, Captain."

"Anxious to serve you, Highness, but—"

"Go." The regent waved a hand.

I thought we would return to the camp, but the regent remained where he was, and after a time I realized he was not looking at the ship, but at the sea, and at Sestos and the world beyond.

When he turned away at last, he said softly, "What if the beggar boy— Let's not call him Latro; his name is Pausanias. What if Pausanias the beggar boy could become known to the king? You must help me, and I'll help you. I'll give you your freedom and much more."

I said I did not think I could do anything, but I would be happy to do all I could.

"You can do a great deal, I think. You know the servants, Latro. Perhaps you can persuade them to allow me to enter the palace."

He turned to go. The shieldman, who had followed us when we climbed the steep path up the cliff, came after us as silently as ever.

While we returned to the camp, I thought about what the regent had said and all the things I have written here. And I despaired of promoting so great and terrible an enterprise, though I could not say so when I parted from the regent. How is a man, even a prince and a regent, to enter a palace no man has seen? To befriend a monarch whose ministers are gods?

There is one more thing to tell, though I hesitate to write of it. A moment ago, as I was about to enter this tent Io and I share with Drakaina and Pasicrates, I heard the strange, sly voice of Tisamenus at my ear: *"Kill the man with the wooden foot!"* When I looked around for him, there was no one in sight.

I have no notion what this may mean, or who the man with the wooden foot may be. Perhaps it was some trick of the wind. Perhaps I am to be mad as well as clouded of memory, and this voice was a phantom of that all-obscuring mist.

# THIRTY-FIVE

## *Ships Can Sail Dry Land*

OUR SHIP IS CROSSING THE isthmus today. I have already read much in this scroll and found in it many things that puzzle me; perhaps I should write of our crossing before it becomes one puzzle more.

I woke with Io asleep beneath my arm and Drakaina awake on the other side. She says we coupled in the night, but I do not believe her. Though she is so lovely, her eyes are as hard as stones, and I would never have intercourse with a woman while a child slept with us. Nor do I believe a man could, without waking the child. Besides, though I cannot now recall the night before, I believe I could remember it when she first spoke, and that I did not credit what she said, though she said also that I had drunk too much wine.

True or not, I rose and dressed; so did she. Io woke too, grumbling because she had no chance to wash her little peplos while we were at sea and had none now, though we rode at anchor.

Our ship is larger than most of the others I saw in the harbor this morning. Io says we waited all yesterday for our turn at the slipway, but it is hard without a bribe for the slipmaster. This morning the young man who sleeps in our cabin roused his hundred (they sleep on the deck with their slaves and the sailors, and it was their feet that woke me) and had them rowed to the city. Io said we watched the ships yesterday, and the oxen draw them along the slip much more slowly than a man walks—that is true, as I see now—and thus we could go into the city, too. If *Nausicaa* were taken on the slip, we could soon catch up to her.

"We've been here before, Latro," she told me. "This is the place where the soldiers came from who took us away from the Rope Makers' slaves. You won't find that in your book, because I had it then. See that hill? Up there's where they kept us till Hypereides came and they gave us to him. Pindaros and Hilaeira and the black man were with us, and I'll never forget how it was when they struck off our fetters—Hypereides told them to, after he'd talked to us—and they led us out into the sunshine. You can see the whole city from up there, and it's really beautiful. Do you want to see it? I'd like to look at the place where they kept us."

Drakaina said, "Yes, let's go. Perhaps they'll keep you again. But will the guards let us go up?"

Io nodded. "They let anybody go. There's a temple at the top to Kalleos's goddess, and some other temples and things."

The city is full of people, all hurrying to someplace else. Many are slaves and workmen with no clothes but their caps; but many are wealthy too, with gold rings and jeweled chains and perfumed hair. Men are carried about the city in litters. Drakaina says that in Thought only women and sick men use them, and this place is much more like the east, where she comes from. The truly rich have their own litters and dress four or six slaves alike to carry them. Those who merely wish to be thought rich hire litters, with two bearers or four.

"If we had the money," Drakaina said, "we could hire two litters ourselves, so we wouldn't have to climb all those steps. You and Io in one and I in the other." (I believe she had at first planned to suggest that Io ride with her but seeing the expression on the child's face knew it to be useless.)

"You've got money," Io told her. "The regent gave it to you, that's what you said, and you paid the boatman. So go ahead and hire yourself a litter, and Latro and I will walk."

I nodded, and in truth I wanted to stretch my legs, which feel as though they have not had much exercise lately.

Drakaina said, "Not enough. But we could sell something."

Io looked at her askance. "What? Sell one of those rings? I never thought they were real gold."

"Not my rings. But we've other commodities, if only we can find the right buyer."

A soldier tried to shoulder past us, and she caught him by the arm.

"Not now," he said, and then when he had seen how lovely she is, "Call on me tonight. You'll find me generous. I'm Hippagretas, Lochagos of the City Guard. Across from the Market Temple of the Stone God, and two doors north."

"I'm not from Tower Hill," Drakaina told him. "Not that I'd mind having a lover so distinguished and handsome. I only wished to ask you who commands the army of this city."

"Corustas is our strategist."

"And where can we find him? Will you guide us?"

"In the citadel, of course. But no." He shook his head, tossing the purple plumes of his helmet. "Much as I'd like to, I have important affairs."

I smiled to hear that even the soldiers of this town hurried about like merchants.

Drakaina smiled too. "Might Corustas not reward an officer who brought him people with information?"

The lochagos stared at her for a moment. "You have a message for the strategist?"

"I have information, which I will give him only in person. But I suppose I may tell you that we have just disembarked from the ship carrying the aide to the regent of Rope."

Soon Drakaina and Hippagretas were in one big litter and Io and I in another, each litter carried on the shoulders of four bearers. "You and the black man had to carry Kalleos like this," Io told me. "But there were only the two of you, and I bet Kalleos is as heavy as you and me together."

I asked whether we had to climb so steep a slope, and she shook her head. "It was uphill, but not nearly as bad as this. I was following you, and you didn't know it." She giggled. "I'd watch the litter and wonder which of you would give up first, but neither of you did."

I told her no man likes to admit he's weaker than another.

"A lot of women do—that's one reason why so many of us like men better, besides their being easier to fool. Look there, you can see the water already. And there's the slipway. Thirty-six stades from the gulf to the Sea of Saros. That's what the man we talked to yesterday said."

I asked her whether Drakaina had been with us.

She shook her head. "She stayed on board, because Pasicrates was there, if you ask me. We went with the captain, and they seemed happy enough to see us go."

I scarcely heard her. With the few steps since she had mentioned the water, the bearers had turned a corner and ascended a bit more; and the bright patch of water Io had pointed out had grown to an azure sea, as a child grows who is a woman as soon as your attention is distracted for a moment, at once restless and restful, alluring and dangerous. And it struck me then that the sea was the world, and everything else—the city, the towering crag of limestone, the very ships that floated upon it and the fish that swam in it—was only exceptional, only oddities like the bits of leaf or straw one sees in a globe of amber.

I was myself a mariner on that sea, a sailor at the mercy of wind and wave, lost in the mists and hearing breakers on the reefs of a rocky coast.

"This is it," Io said as the bearers lowered our litter before a frowning building. "This is where they kept us, Latro, in a cellar down a lot of steps." Drakaina and the lochagos were out of their litter already.

The interior seemed a cavern after the heat and brilliant sun outside. I understood then why so many gods and goddesses are said to live under the earth or among the everlasting snows of the mountaintops; no doubt we would do the same if only we were not bound to our fields for sustenance.

Corustas proved to be a beefy man in a cuirass of boiled leather molded with lions' heads. The snarling faces woke some faint fear in me, and I seemed for an instant to see a lion rear and threaten a mob in rags with its claws and fangs.

"You were on the ship with the young Rope Makers?" Corustas said. "I take it you are not Rope Makers yourselves."

Drakaina shook her head. "I am from the east. The man—who will be able to tell you little or nothing, by the way—is a barbarian, and neither he nor I can tell you his tribe. The child is from Hill."

"And your information?"

"And your price?"

"That must be determined when I have heard you. If it will save our city"—he smiled—"ten talents, perhaps. Otherwise much less."

Drakaina said, "Your city's in no immediate danger, as far as I know."

"Fine. You'd be surprised how often people come here to warn me of oracles and the like." He took out a silver owl and held it in his palm.

"Now tell me what you've come to say, and we'll see if it's worth this. My time's not unlimited."

"It concerns an oracle," Drakaina said. "A dream in which the regent places complete trust." She extended her own hand.

"And it concerns my city?"

"Not directly. It may eventually."

Corustas leaned back. His chair was of ivory, inset with garnets and topazes. "Your ship is the *Nausicaa*, out of Aegae, bound for Hundred-Eyed. A hundred young Rope Makers are aboard, sent by the regent to offer praise at the temple of the Heavenly Queen in fulfillment of some vow."

Io smiled behind her hand, and Drakaina said, "You've been questioning the sailors. That was what they were told."

"And the young Rope Makers," Corustas added. When Drakaina said nothing, he muttered, "When we could," and dropped the owl into her hand.

"The hundred men are not bound for Hundred-Eyed, nor for any other place on Redface Island. Nor are they being sent in fulfillment of a vow, nor for any other sacred purpose."

"I know that, naturally," Corustas said, gauging Drakaina with his eyes. "They wore full armor when they went to threaten our slipmaster today. The Argives aren't fools enough to let a hundred armed Rope Makers through their gates." He took out another owl.

Drakaina shook her head. "Ten."

"Absurd!"

"But for nothing I will tell you they are picked men, taking their instructions directly from the regent."

"I knew that as soon as young Hippagretas told me you had said the regent's aide was aboard."

I asked whether *Nausicaa* would be taken on the slip today. "Ah!" Corustas winked. "You can talk after all. But you know nothing about all this."

"No," I said. "Nothing."

"You think a woman can get more and is less likely to be tortured. You're wrong on both counts. To answer your question, whether the ship crosses the isthmus today or never depends on the message I send our slipmaster. That in turn depends on what we say here." He looked back to Drakaina. "Five owls for the true destination."

"One word only."

"Agreed, but no tricks."

"Sestos."

For a moment I thought the strategist had fallen asleep. His eyes closed and his chin dropped to his chest. Then he opened his eyes again and straightened up.

"Yes, isn't it?" Drakaina said.

"And a dream told him to do it?"

Drakaina rose, knotting the six silver owls into her robe. "We really should go. The child wants to see your city from the summit."

"One more for the dream."

"Come, Io. Latro."

"Three."

Drakaina did not sit down again. "The dream—"

"Who was it? The Huntress?"

"The Queen Below. Had it been the Huntress, I wouldn't be telling you these things. She promised him that the fortress would fall soon after the young men arrived, and the regent believes her implicitly. Now you know all I do."

As Corustas counted out three more owls, he asked, "Why the Queen Below? It should have been the Warrior, or perhaps even the Sun."

Drakaina smiled. "A strategist, and you've never seen the fall of a city? Believe me, there's little enough drill or light then, but a great deal of death."

Outside, she asked the bearers whether the lochagos had paid them, and when they said he had, ordered them to carry us to the temple at the summit. They protested that they had been paid only to bring us up from the city and return us to the place where they had found us. Drakaina said, "Don't trouble me with your impudence. We've been conferring with Strategist Corustas, and if you won't earn your money like honest men, he'll have you whipped in the marketplace." After that they did as she told them.

The temple was small but every bit as lovely as it had looked from below, with slender marble pillars and elaborate capitals; its pediment showed a youth offering an apple to three maids.

When the bearers were out of earshot, Io whispered, "You didn't tell him about Latro. I thought you were going to."

"Certainly not. Suppose Corustas had decided to keep him here? Do you think the regent wouldn't have guessed someone talked? And that it was you or me? Now have a look at the view; I told Corustas you were going to."

Io did and so did I, feeling the sea breeze would never be so pure again as it was today, nor the sun so bright. The white city of Tower Hill spread in two terraces below us. Its gulf, stretching away to the west like a great blue road, promised all the untouched riches of the thinly peopled western lands, and I felt a sudden longing to go there.

"By all the Twelve, that's *Nausicaa*!" Io exclaimed. "See, Latro? Not on the skid, but waiting to get on. Notice her cutter bow?"

Drakaina smiled. "Quite the little sailor."

"The kybernetes taught me when we sailed with Hypereides. And I talk to our sailors too, instead of holding my nose in the air."

A jeweled and scented woman with golden bells in her hair passed us, jingling as she turned her head to smile at Drakaina; she carried two live hares by the ears.

# THIRTY-SIX

## To Reach the Hot Gates

A SHIP CAN FOLLOW EITHER of two courses, as our captain explained. He is a white-haired old man, fat, and stiff in all his joints, but very knowing of the sea. When he saw I did not understand, he sat on a coil of rope and drew the coast on the deck for me with a bit of chalk.

"Here's the skid where we went across." He drew as he spoke. "And here's Water and Peace."

Io asked, "Does that name* really mean 'peace'? That's what Latro says. It seems like there's been so much fighting there."

The captain looked far away, out over the dancing waves. "Because in the old times it was agreed with the Crimson Men there'd be no raiding on the island. In the old times—my grandfather's times—everybody took what he could, and there was no shame to it. A ship came to a city, and if her skipper thought his crew could take it, he tried. If you met a ship that could beat yours, you ran, and if you didn't run fast enough, you lost it. A man knew where he stood. Now maybe it's peace, and maybe it's war, and you don't know and neither does he. Last year the Crimson Men were the best in the Great King's navy. I mean the best sailors—the Riverlanders were the best sea fighters. And the Crimson Men would have fought on Peace if they could have landed. The old promises don't count, and the new aren't lived up to.

"Kings used to look for places where both wanted the same. Then they'd make an honest bargain and keep it, and if they didn't, they'd be disgraced, and punished by the gods, and their people too. Now it's all trying to get the advantage by tricks. What's the use of a bargain,

---

*Salamis* (Gk. Σαλαμίς). Latro translates the Phoenician root.—G. W.

when the other man's not going to keep it as soon as he sees it's a trick?"

Io pointed. "Thought must be right about here."

"That's Tieup. Thought's up here on the hill. I don't go there much any more. We're way past all that anyhow. Here's where we are." He continued the coast to the north, then made a long mark beside it. "That's Goodcattle Island, a great place for sheep. With a regular crew, we'd be going wide of it; there's a narrow channel, and the wind's from the north, mostly. But with all these stout lads to pull the sweeps, there's no reason to, as the noble Pasicrates says. We'll spend the night at the Hot Gates, and he can make his sacrifice. There's nothing like a fair wind, but the ash wind blows whichever way you want."

By "the ash wind" he meant the sweeps, long oars that one or two pull standing up. There are twenty on each side, and I took my turn at one with the men of Rope. It is hard work, and it blisters the hands; but it is made easier by singing, and it strengthens the whole body. My head cannot remember for long, but my arms, back, and legs do not forget. They told me they had been wasting in idleness and desired to strive with the blue giant; so I did, and laughed to see men (who so often make poor beasts serve their will) rowing the bawling bullock tied to our mainmast across the sea.

None of these things are of much importance, perhaps, but they are the first I remember; thus I write them, having waked from my dream.

Only eighty could be used at the sweeps, and we have more than four hundred, with Pasicrates and myself and the crew, a number that let all of us rest far longer than we rowed. When the sun was halfway to the hills on our left, a wind rose behind us. The crew hoisted both sails, and we ported our sweeps.

Pasicrates proposed wrestling matches, there not being room enough on the deck for any sport but wrestling or boxing. A lovely woman called Drakaina came to watch, taking a place close beside me. She has a purple gown and many jewels, and the Rope Makers moved aside for her very readily; she must be a person of importance.

Sniffing the wind, she said, "I smell the river—that air has crocodiles in it. Do you know what they are, Latro?"

I told her I did and described them.

"But you do not remember where you saw them?"

I shook my head.

"Are you going to wrestle, when your turn comes? Throw the other man over the railing for me."

It was something the victors often did to show their strength. Our ship trailed a rope, and the loser swam to it and climbed back on board, many saying the cool plunge was so pleasant after the heat of the deck that it was better to lose than to win. I promised Drakaina I would if I could.

"You're a good wrestler—I've seen you. You nearly defeated Basias, and I think you could have if you had wished."

I asked, "Is Basias here?" because I did not know the names of most of the men from Rope and thought I might wrestle him again.

She shook her lovely head. "He has gone to the Receiver of Many."

Hearing that, I feared I was defiled by his blood, for I know something is not well with me. "Was it I who killed him?"

"No," she told me. "I did."

Then it was my turn to wrestle.

Pasicrates had matched me against himself. He is very quick; but I am a little stronger, I think, and I felt I was going to win the first fall; but just as I was about to throw him to the deck, he slipped from under my arm so that I was left like a man who tries to break an unbarred door.

The railing caught me at the hip, and Pasicrates got my right leg behind the knee and tossed me over.

How cold the water was, and how good it smelled! It seemed to me that I should not be able to breathe it as I did; but though it was much colder than air, it was richer too and strengthened me as wine does.

When I opened my eyes, it was as though I were suspended in the sky like the sun; the blue water was all about me, a darker blue above, a paler, brighter blue below, where a great brown snail with a mossy shell crawled and trailed a thread of slime.

"Welcome," said a voice above me, and I looked up to see a girl not much older than Io. Her hair was darker than Drakaina's gown— so dark it was nearly black. Almost it seemed a cloud or aureole, and not such hair as men and women have.

I tried to speak, but water filled my mouth and no sound came, only bubbles that fell to the pale ground and vanished.

"I am Thoe, daughter of Nereus," the girl told me. "I have forty-nine sisters, all older than myself. We are permitted to show ourselves to those who are soon to die."

She must have seen the fear in my eyes, because she laughed; I knew then that she had said what she had for the pleasure of frightening me. Her teeth were small and very sharp. "No, you are not really going to drown." She took my hand. "Do you feel you are suffocating?"

I shook my head.

"You see, you cannot, as long as you are with me. But when I leave, you'll have to go down there again, unless you want to die. It's just that mortal men aren't supposed to see us too often, because they might guess at things they're not to know; mortal women hardly ever see us, because they know when they do. We can show ourselves to children as often as we like, though, because they forget the way you do."

She wriggled off through the water like a serpent, waving for me to follow. I shouted but produced only a rush of water from my mouth.

"Europa told me about you. She's rather a friend of mine, except that she's too fond of herself because she used to lie with the Descender. Sometimes Father shows himself to sailors before storms, if he thinks the storm will kill them all. Do you know about that?"

Thoe glanced over her shoulder to observe my answer, and I shook my head.

"Then the sailors say, 'Look! It's the old sea man!' and they take in their sail and put out a sea anchor, and sometimes they live. It's good of him to warn them like that, don't you think?"

I nodded. We were swimming up and up, circling as a hawk soars on a rising wind. The brown slug looked very small now, but I saw men's legs kicking all around it.

"And sometimes my sisters and I show ourselves to ships about to strike a reef. We call warnings, but our voices are high when we're out of water, and the sailors tell each other we're singing to lure them to their deaths."

From what she had said, I guessed why I had been unable to speak. Pitching my voice high as I could, I said that was unjust of them.

She laughed at my croaking. "But sometimes we *do*. You see, sometimes the ships aren't wrecked, and so we try to call them back so we won't get in trouble. We comb each other's hair then and admire our beauty like mortal women. It usually brings them. We aren't cheating, because we lie, sometimes, with them, if any live through the wreck. We do it before they get too weak and thirsty. Except for me, because I'm the youngest. This will be my first time."

Until she said that, it had seemed to me I had been flung into another world from which I might never return; and I had been too dazed by the beauty and strangeness of it to try. Now I understood that if only I could reach the air below, I would again be with Drakaina and the men wrestling on the deck. I gestured to show what I meant to do, and Thoe caught me by the hair.

"You need not fear," she said. "We bear your children beneath the sea, so they drown." When she saw my horror she said, "Kiss me at least before you go, so that I will not be shamed before my sisters."

Slender and cold, her arms wrapped my neck. When her lips brushed mine, it seemed to me that I had been fevered all my life, and that I wanted nothing more than to cool myself forever in the icy billows of northern seas, where snow drifts from the sky to the waves like the feathers of white geese.

My head broke the surface. I shook sea water from my hair, and when I opened my mouth to gasp for breath, more water vomited from it, as water is spewed from a face of stone in a fountain. This water was bitter with salt; it ran from my nostrils too and stung them.

A wave broke over my head as I spluttered and gasped for air. I could not remember whether I could swim well or not—surely I could not swim as Thoe had—but I felt Pasicrates would not have thrown me over the railing unless he had known I could; and before I had finished those thoughts I was swimming, though I could not have said where.

It was nearly dark, and as I swam, lifted by the waves and cast down again, the stars came out one by one, shaping gods and beasts. I found the Great Bear, and from it, Polaris. The captain had said a north wind would be foul for us; thus we had been sailing north, with the mainland to the west and Goodcattle Island to the east. I kept Polaris at my right shoulder, hoping to find land or the ship.

Thoe leaped across the waves as though springing from rock to rock and stopped to stand upon a beach and laugh at me. When my foot touched the sand she vanished, and her laughter was only the lapping of the waves. For a long while I was too exhausted to do anything but lie sprawled like a corpse driven to shore.

It was thirst that made me rise. Mingled with the soft laughter of the waves, I heard the chuckle of a brook glad to have come at last to the sea and rest. I searched and found it, and drank deeply; and though I saw the red gleam of a fire far away and heard men's voices, I did not walk toward it until I had filled my stomach with water. (Not long ago I asked Drakaina what god it was who shaped the world. She said it had been made by Phanes, the four-winged and four-headed, who is male and female together. How cruel it was of Phanes to make the seas salt, and how many must have died because of it!)

The voices were those of the men from Rope. When I saw them, I could not help wondering whether Thoe had guided me to them, and I recalled our captain's saying Pasicrates meant to sacrifice at the Hot Gates. Stone columns stood there. Before them was an altar, with a driftwood fire on it. Pasicrates held the halter of the bullock; a rude garland circled its neck.

". . . and intercede for us, great Leonidas, intercede for us, all you heroes, when we must recount what befell the slave, Latro. For you know there was no true victory upon him, nor did he carry the favor of any god." This he spoke, and as he said "god," the sacred knife entered the bullock's neck to speed it to Leonidas.

Surely no one could have resisted such a moment. As I stepped into the firelight, I announced, "The gods say otherwise, Pasicrates."

Unable to recall my past, I cannot say whether it has held many such culminations, but I doubt it. To see these men, so hard, so strong, so prideful in their hardness and their strength, with their mouths gasping like children washed the last fatigue from me.

I said, "You were permitted to throw me so that I might speak with a certain Nereid. Thoe is her name. Now I have returned, ready to resume our match. When the others wrestled, it was for three falls— not one."

For an instant there was a hush so complete the crackling of the fire on the altar seemed the burning of a city. Far up the mountain they call Kallidromos, a lion roared. At the sound the men of Rope roared too, so many and so loud as to silence the waves and the grieving wind.

Before their shout died, Pasicrates and I were locked more tightly than any lovers. I knew his strength then, and he knew mine. He sought to lift me, but I held him too tightly, and slowly, slowly, I bent him back. I could have broken him then if I had wished, snapping his spine as a soldier mad for blood seizes his enemy's spear and breaks it; but I was not mad for blood, only for victory. I threw him to the ground instead.

Io rushed forward, laughing like a lark, with a jar of wine and a rag for my face. A Rope Maker did the same for Pasicrates. Another, perhaps a year or two older, asked, "What of the sacrifice? Surely this is sacrilege."

Pasicrates answered, "We give our might to Leonidas, just as might was offered to Patroklos. The winner will complete the sacrifice."

When we closed again, his strength was twice what it had been. For what seemed a whole night we strove together, but I could not throw him, nor could he throw me.

There came a moment when my face was to the fire, and he met my gaze. The lion roared again, nearer now, and loud as a war horn over the shouting of the men from Rope. Pasicrates stiffened. "There's a lion in your eyes," he gasped.

"And a boy in yours," I told him; and lifting him over my head, I carried him away from the altar until the waves licked at my ankles, and I cast him into the sea. The lion roared a third time. I have not heard it since.

# THIRTY-SEVEN

## *Leonidas, Lion of Rope*

HEAR OUR PRAYER," I INTONED, dressed again in the chiton Io had kept for me, crowned with a few wildflowers and girded with my belt of manhood. "Accept our homage!" Moved by I cannot say what spirit, I added, "We do not ask for victory, but for courage." With that I cast the bullock's fat and heart into the fire, and the men from Rope sang a marching song.

The sacrifice was complete. Half a dozen slaves fell upon the bullock and hewed it to bits with knives and hatchets. Soon everyone had a stick with a gobbet of meat at the end of it. There was wine too, barley bread, hard cheese, salt olives, raisins, and dried figs.

Io said, "This is the best meal we've had since we've been with these awful people, Latro. You're lucky you don't remember what we've been eating."

"This is good enough for me," I told her. I was so hungry I had to force myself to chew, so as not to choke on the meat.

"For me too. But don't ever, ever try their soup. We have, and if somebody was going to pour that soup down my throat I'd cut it first." She went to the carcass and got another bit of flesh to put on her stick. "This is as good as dining with Kalleos, and I don't know anything nicer you can say about a meal than that. If you want some more meat, though, you'd better get it. There isn't much left."

I shook my head. "I'll have something else. Meat alone upsets the digestion."

Io giggled. "And to think Drakaina's missing it."

"She is? Where is she?"

"Still on the ship." Io pointed toward the bay, where our ship rode at anchor in the moonlight. "Pasicrates thought the reason you never

came up was that she'd put a spell on you. Or anyway, that's what he
*said* he thought. If you ask me he was looking for somebody to blame,
and he picked the right party. So she's back there with her hands tied
behind her and a clout over her mouth so she can't work any more
magic."

"I must speak to him about that," I told her.

With what remained of my loaf in my hand, I went to the fire at
which he sat and seated myself beside him, saying, "Greetings, most
noble Pasicrates."

"Ah," he said. "The victor. Yet a slave. Still a slave. I should not
have demeaned myself, and the gods have punished me for it."

"As you say. You are our commander, the master of our ship and
all on board. But if I'm a slave, I no longer recall whose. Your servant—I
will not say your slave—has come to beg you to release the woman
called Drakaina. She's done me no harm today. Has she harmed you?"

"No," he said. "We'll free her in the morning."

"Then let me swim to the ship, and I'll tell the watch you've ordered
her freed."

He looked at me quizzically. "You'd swim there yourself, if I permitted it?"

"Certainly."

"Then you won't have to." He turned to one of his companions.
"Take the boat and a couple of seamen, and tell them to free the woman.
Bring her back with you."

The man nodded, rose, and vanished into the night.

"As for you, Latro, I want you to come with me. Do you know what
this place is?"

I said, "They call it the Hot Gates, but I don't know why. Since
we sacrificed to Leonidas, I suppose he's a hero and that he's buried
here."

"He was," Pasicrates told me. "Our people dug up his body—what
they could find of it—and sent it back to Rope. It had been hacked to
bits." He spat. "The Great King paraded Leonidas's head on a spear."

As we walked on, I asked him what it was I smelled. It was like
the stench of a bad egg, but so strong it overpowered even the tang of
the sea.

"The springs. They boil out of the ground, not pure and cold like other springs, but steaming and reeking, sickening to drink and yet a cure for many ills. Or so I've been told. This is my first visit to this place, but they say in Rope that's why it's called the Hot Gates—it's the way to those boiling springs."

"Is that where we're going?" I asked him.

"No, only to the ruined wall. My men and I went to look at it by daylight, before you came out of the sea. Now I want to show it to you, and tell you what happened here. You'll forget, but I've begun to think that's because you're the ear of the gods; they hear, instead of you, or they take the memory of what you've heard from you. This is something the gods should know."

"There it is." I pointed. "Where that man sits combing his hair." I could see him plainly in the moonlight, naked and muscular, plowing his long dark locks with a comb of pale shell.

"You see a man dressing his hair?"

"Yes," I said. "And another—now he throws a discus. But this can't be the wall you're looking for. It isn't ruined."

Pasicrates told me, "Those must be ghosts you see. Here Leonidas and his Rope Makers exercised their bodies before the battle and readied them for burial. You and I are alone, and the wall lies in ruins before us. The Great King destroyed it so his host could pass."

I said, "Then Leonidas was killed, and the army of your city destroyed."

"He had no army, only three hundred Rope Makers, a few thousand slaves—he was the first to arm them—and a thousand or so unreliable allies. But the judges had instructed him to hold this road around Kallidromos, and he held it for three days against the Great King's host, until he and every man who'd stayed with him were dead. The Great King counted three millions all told, about half of them real fighting men and the rest mule drivers and the like."

"Surely that's impossible," I said. "Such a small force could never defend this place against so many."

"So the Great King thought." Pasicrates turned suddenly to face me. "That was a tear, I think, that struck my hand. You're no Rope Maker, Latro. Why do you weep?"

"Because I must have seen this battle," I said. "I must have taken part in it. And I have forgotten it."

There was a narrow gate in the wall, and as I spoke it opened and a gray-bearded man in armor came out. As he drew nearer, I saw he had only one eye. I described him to Pasicrates and asked whether it was Leonidas.

"No. It must be Leonidas's mantis, Megistias, who spoke the tongues of all the beasts." Pasicrates's voice was calm, but it was the calm of one who uses all his will to hold his fear in check.

In a moment Megistias stood before us. His face was pale and set, his single eye fierce in the moonlight, the eye of an old falcon half-blind. He muttered something I did not understand and passed his hand before my face.

Then he was gone. I stood in the front rank with other men, men armed as I was with two javelins, a helmet, back and breast plates, and a rectangular shield.

Turning to face the hundred, I shouted, "While the Immortals are gone, we could have no higher honor than to be the protectors of the Universal King, the King of the World's Four Quarters, the King of the Lands, the King of Parsa, the King of Media, the King of Sumer, the King of Akkad, the King of Babylon, and the King of Riverland. Let us treasure that honor and be worthy of it." Yet I paid little heed to the sense of what I myself had said; it had been in my own tongue, and knowing that my comrades understood it made its cadences more lovely to me than any music.

When I turned again, I saw why I had spoken. A knot of men was breaking from the melee, cleaving a path through the levies driven forward by their officers' whips; but there was small cause for fear: they were no more than thirty at most.

At my command, we cast the first javelin together, then the second. Our javelins were not like the light arrows of the archers; they had weight as well as speed, and they transfixed the hoplons of our enemies and pierced their corselets. Half a dozen fell at the first cast, more at the second, when every man drew his sword.

Another command; we locked shields and charged, the slope of the ground being with us. *"Cassius!"*

The man who opposed me was taller than I, his helmet high-crested and his battered armor traced with gold. He thrust for my eyes; but his own blazed not at me but at the Great King, who sat his throne on the hill behind us. I was only an obstacle that barred his way for a moment, then would bar it no more. I wanted to shout that I was no less a man than himself, my honor and my life as precious to me as his to him. But neither of us had time or breath for shouting.

I swung my falcata with all my strength, and the downward cut bit deep in the rim of his hoplon. Its bronze gripped the blade and held it, conquered in its conquest; a twist of his arm wrenched the falcata from my hand.

Disarmed, I barred his way still, blocking each thrust with my shield, giving way one bitter step at a time. The man on his right died, and the man on his left. I fell, tripped by what I cannot say. He rushed by me, but I slipped my shield arm from the leather loop and still half-recumbent hurled my shield at his back.

Except that it was not my shield, only the cloak in which I slept. I sat up and rubbed my eyes, my ears still ringing with the din of battle. The bodies of the slain drank their own blood, becoming only sleepers, living men who breathed and sometimes stirred. Leonidas was but the dying fire. I rose and saw the army of the Great King, proud horseman and cringing conscript, melt into the slopes of Kallidromos.

I could not sleep again, nor did I wish to. I built up the fire and spoke for a while with Drakaina, who was also awake. She says Falcata is the name I give my sword and not its kind, and that it is a kopis.

Then, recalling the map drawn by the captain of our ship and the way I had wrestled on the deck with Pasicrates, I wrote of those things here, and of Thoe the Nereid, my dream, and all the rest. Now Io has risen too, and she has read the writing on the columns to me. There are three.

The first:

"Redface Isle, four thousand bred;
Three million scorned, till all were dead."

The second:

"The wizard Megistias's tomb you view,
Who slew the foe from Spercheius's ford.

> This greatest seer his death foreknew,
> Yet sooner died than leave his lord."

The third:

> "Speak to the Silent City,
> Saying that in her cause,
> We begged no tyrant's pity,
> And fell obedient to her laws."

A sailor who heard Io read said these verses, which Io and I agreed in thinking very fine, were put here by an old man called Simonides; but he does not know him personally.

# THIRTY-EIGHT

## *Wet Weather to Sestos*

WAVES BROKE OVER THE BOW all day, while the wild wind the sailors call the Hellesponter laid the ship on her beam ends. If it truly blew from that part of the world, we could have done nothing, as the captain told me, for it would have come across our bow with the waves. It did not, but in fact blew out of those northern lands that are said to be rendered uninhabitable by bees. Thus, by pulling the sail to starboard as far as we could, we plunged across the pounding sea as if our fat, rolling *Nausicaa* were a racing chariot, passing the island the sailors call Boat a little after dawn.

If it is a boat, it is a burning boat; for it is here, they say, that the Smith God has his workshop, and the sail of Boat is in fact the smoke that rises from his forge. They say too that this god once built a metal man to guard the Island of Liars, but his wonderful creation was destroyed by the crew of a ship from Hundred-Eyed.

Save for the captain, a few sailors, and myself, everyone fell prey to the sea disease. The captain assured me it was not serious and would cure itself as soon as the sea was calmer, it being no more than a sleight of the Sea God's to preserve the rations of good ships by ensuring that their greedy passengers eat no more and offer all they have already consumed to him.

Whether that is true or otherwise, this sea disease affected all the Rope Makers, as well as Io, the Lady Drakaina, and many of the crew. With so few able to work, everyone was needed. I joined the sailors who could still keep the ship, sometimes helping with a steering oar, sometimes heaving at a line to trim a sail, sometimes climbing the mainmast (this was difficult because it was so wet) to take in sail or let it out. All this while *Nausicaa* bucked like Pegasus or wallowed like a boar, making what would otherwise have been mere drudgery into a great contention with the sea. I thought then how happy a sailor's life must be and wished I might join the crew and live as they did; but I said nothing to the captain.

Once indeed it seemed the sea played too roughly with me. I was standing on the rail trying to clear the foreyard arm, which had fouled one of its halyards, when I felt the ship drop from under me and I was cast into the water; but a wave lifted me at once and tossed me onto the deck a little aft of the mainmast. By good luck I landed on my feet, and the crew has treated me with considerable respect ever since. However, I feared the same thing might happen again, and that the sea, seeing me grown proud, would drop me on my head or my buttocks; thus I took care to be as humble toward everyone as I could, to praise the wild majesty of the sea whenever we had time to talk, and to offer a coin I found tied into a corner of this chiton—it is my oldest, which Io suggested I wear because of the bad weather—to the Sea God.

Just after the sun had reached its zenith, the waning wind brought rain. The captain came to talk with me, and I happened to mention the coin, saying that though it had been but copper and small, the Sea God must have accepted it.

He agreed and told me the story (which I set down here as a caution for myself in future days) of King Polycrates, who was so lucky he conquered any place he wished and defeated every army sent against him. Besides all this, he was an ally of the King of Riverland, who was in those times the most powerful monarch in the world, and a great friend of his as well; and at last the King of Riverland grew concerned, saying, "Polycrates, my friend, the gods never raise a man high but to cast him down, as boys carry jars up a tower so they can throw them from the top. Some bad luck is bound to befall you. Of all your possessions, which is most precious to you?"

"This emerald ring," answered Polycrates. "It came to me from my father, and because it looks so fine, all the people of my island counted me as a great man from the moment I put it on. At their request I took charge of their affairs, and I have ruled ever since with the success and good fortune you know."

"Then throw it into the sea to appease the gods," the King of Riverland counseled him. "Perhaps if you do, they will permit you a serene old age."

Polycrates thought about this advice as he was returning from Riverland, slipped off his ring, and hurled it into the waves with a prayer. When he reached home, his people held a great celebration in his honor and brought him many gifts, the loot of the cities he had burned and the ships he had captured, one bringing a rich armor, another a necklace of gold and hyacinth, a third a cloak of byssus, and so on. Last of all came a poor fisherman. "Majesty," he said, "I have nothing to offer you but this fish, the finest I caught today; but I beg you to accept it in the spirit in which it comes to you."

"I will," Polycrates said graciously. "Tonight you and I shall dine together in my royal hall, old man, and you shall see your fish upon my table."

At this the old fisherman was overjoyed. He stepped to one side, took out his knife, and opened the fish to clean it for the king's cooks. But no sooner had he slit its belly than a beautiful emerald ring dropped from it and rolled to lie at Polycrates's feet.

At this all the people cheered, thinking it showed what a favorite of the gods their king was. But Polycrates wept, knowing his sacrifice had been rejected. He was soon proved right, for he was lured to his death by one of the satraps of the Great King, who at that time had not yet conquered Riverland and considered every friend of its king his enemy.

Though the wind grew less it did not die, and before night came we saw the dark loom of the land through the falling rain. All the men from Rope whooped for joy and insisted on landing at once. The captain was very willing we should, for there is no port on this side of the land, and thus it is a hazardous spot for ships. But while the boat was being made ready, he tried to buy me from Pasicrates, offering four minas, then five, and at last six, though he said he would have to have a year in which to pay the final two. "You'll waste him ashore," he said. "He's the best sailor I've ever seen and a favorite of the gods to boot."

"I can't sell him for any price," Pasicrates answered. "He's the regent's, not mine. Perhaps you're fortunate at that—a favorite of the gods is a dangerous man."

Thus we landed in the rain, with all the men from Rope rejoicing at one moment to be off the ship and swearing at the next while they tried to keep their armor and their rations dry. I had expected to see a city, but there was only a camp of tents and huts, with ships drawn up on the beach. Io knew nothing of Sestos; so I asked Drakaina, who told me the city was a hundred stades inland. She liked the rain no better than the Rope Makers did, but she looked so lovely with her wet gown clinging and her eyes ringed with starry drops that the men from Rope ceased to complain whenever she was in their sight, throwing out their chests instead and pretending no weather could ever trouble them.

Pasicrates, however, stood upon a great rock and studied the sea. I saw the worry in his face and asked him what the matter was when he came down. "This rain signals the end of the sailing season," he said. "Soon the leaves will turn, and there will be storms worse than the one this morning. It will be hard to get supplies, and to return home when the city falls." He gave me a crooked smile and added, "You must hurry." I was not sure what he meant, but Io says I am to take the city for the regent of Rope, though no one knows how.

Our march to Sestos was long and cold. The Rope Makers wrapped themselves in their scarlet cloaks, and Drakaina hired two sailors to make a litter covered with sailcloth for her. I sheltered Io and myself under my cloak as well as I could, and I think that because there were two of us, we were warmer than all the rest.

"How big you're getting," I told her. "When I think of you it's always as someone much smaller, but your head comes to my ribs."

"Children my age grow fast," she told me. "Then too, traveling with you I've had sunshine and plenty of exercise, which most girls don't get. Good food too, while we were with Hypereides and Kalleos. Kalleos gave you this cloak, master, so you could wear your sword on the streets at night and not be stopped by the archers. I know you don't remember, but it was the night Eurykles bet he could raise a ghost."

"Who's Eurykles?" I asked her.

"A man we used to know. A magician. He's gone now, and I don't think he'll ever come back. Kalleos will miss him, I suppose. Do you still have your book?"

"Yes, I put it in my pack. I've got your clothes and your doll too."

"My doll's broken." She shrugged. "I like keeping it, though. Are you sure all that isn't too heavy for you? I could carry my own things. I'm your slave, after all."

"No. I could carry this pack a long way, and I suppose I'll have to. I doubt that it's any heavier than the loads the Rope Makers are carrying, with their helmets and spears, their armor and their big hoplons."

"But they have their own slaves to carry their tents and rations and the other things," Io pointed out. "When we were on Redface Island, they made their slaves carry everything except their swords. I don't understand why they don't do that here. Do you think they're afraid the slaves would slip in the mud if they had to carry so much?"

"They would only beat them," I told her. "This is the Empire, and they know we might be charged by the Great King's cavalry."

Io turned her dripping face to stare at mine. "How do you know that, master? Are you starting to remember?"

"No. I know those things, but I don't know how I learned them."

"Then you have to write all this down when we get to Sestos. Everything you remember from today, because I may not always be with you. And master, I heard the captain trying to buy you. Write that you're not a slave, even if—"

"I know," I told her. "But I wanted us to stay on the ship, if we could. A merchant ship visits many ports, and there are men in them from many others."

"So maybe you could find your home. I understand."

"Besides, I like the work, though not the idea of deserting my patron."

Io lifted a finger to her lips.

We still have not seen the walls. Darkness came long before we reached this place and pitched our tents. Pasicrates, Io, and I will sleep in this one, with Pasicrates's slaves. Drakaina shares a tent with two Rope Makers, I think so that neither can molest her.

We had beans, onions, and twice-baked bread tonight, and it seemed very little after so long a march through the rain, though there is still some wine. The Rope Makers joked about going to Sestos for more food, and some of them, I think, stole food from the soldiers of Thought. I find it easy to see why there is so much ill feeling between these two cities, even though they are allies—*friends*, as it is said in their tongue. Allies must be friends in deed and not only in word, if they are to have more than a sham alliance.

No moon and no stars tonight, only a thin drizzle that is almost a mist. I sit in the doorway of our tent, where the smoking fire gives just enough light for me to write. They say firewood is scarce already, but with a hundred Rope Makers and more than two hundred armed slaves at his command, Pasicrates will have all he needs, so I throw on more whenever the flames sink too low.

When I was a child, we saved the prunings from our vines to burn— I remember that. I remember my mother's singing as she crouched by the fire to stir a little black pot, and how she watched me as she sang to see whether I enjoyed her song. When my father was there, he would cut a pipe from reeds, and then the reeds sang her song with her. Our god—I have just remembered this—was Lar. My father said Mother's song made Lar happy. I remember thinking I understood more than he, and being proud and secretive (as little boys are) because I knew Lar was the song, and not something apart from it. I remember lying under the wolfskin and seeing Lar flash from wall to wall, singing and teasing me. I tried to catch him and woke rubbing my eyes, with Mother singing beside the fire.

# THIRTY-NINE

## Engines of War

SIEGE TOWERS AND BATTERING RAMS are everywhere on the landward side of the city, each with a few hundreds to protect it from a sally. That is so the barbarians will not know whence the attack will come, as Xanthippos, the strategist from Thought, explained. Pasicrates of course asked where it *would* come, but Xanthippos only shook his head and looked wise, saying he had several sites under consideration. It seemed to me he had not decided because no place is yet weak enough to permit an assault.

But perhaps I am driving my dog before the cattle. I should say first that Pasicrates, Drakaina, and I went to Xanthippos this morning; and that he is a man of about my own height, gray at the temples, with an affable yet reserved air Drakaina said is characteristic of the old aristocracy of Thought.

He welcomed us cordially to a tent bare of any sign of wealth or luxury, with a worn-out sail for a ground cloth and simple stools that appeared to have been made on the spot. "We are delighted," he said, "that the Rope Makers have chosen to join us. How encouraging to see our ancient friendship renewed in the face of our common enemy. Am I to take it that the other ships were blown from their course by yesterday's storm? Let us hope they arrive safely today."

"Why?" Pasicrates asked bluntly. "Are you in need of troops?"

"No, not at all. What I have real need of is a hole through those walls." Xanthippos chuckled, his keen gray eyes including all of us in his merriment. "There are only about five hundred barbarians inside, all told. Some thousand Hellenes, but I expect them to change their allegiance once the assault begins."

Pasicrates nodded. "We Hellenes are notorious for it—save for the men of my own city. And our assault will be .... ?"

"As soon as the walls are breached. That will be in another month, I should say. May I ask whether it is King Leotychides or Prince Pausanias who commands?"

"Neither," Pasicrates told him. "Nor will there be more ships. There was only one, and we have come."

It was not possible to tell whether Xanthippos was really surprised or merely feigning to be. He seemed to me the sort of man who has mastered his feelings for so long that he no longer knows them, and may be furious or overcome by love without being conscious of either.

"I am the regent's man." Pasicrates took an iron signet from his finger and gave it to Xanthippos. "I come for him."

"Then allow me to congratulate him, through you, on his great victory. It will give me the deepest pleasure to do so in person upon some future day. No doubt you yourself took a leading part in that glorious battle. Alas that I was with the fleet! Would you care to cast aside, if only momentarily, that sometimes awkward briefness in speech for which your fellow citizens are so well known and describe for me—for my enlightenment as a strategist, I may say, as well as my delight—just what it was you did?"

"My duty," Pasicrates told him. He then questioned him about the progress of the siege but learned very little.

"So you see"—Xanthippos spread his hands—"the great thing is to retain the flexibility that enables one to seize, and indeed to recognize, opportunity."

"But you expect Sestos to fall in a month."

"Or a trifle longer, perhaps. Certainly before the onset of winter, though we may see some of its earlier stages. There is very little food in the city, I'm told, and they are not Rope Makers there, accustomed to living on a bite of bread and a handful of olives."

"Your own men should be planting next year's crop already."

"They're mostly city men." Xanthippos smiled. "You Rope Makers are fond of saying we have no soldiers—only cobblers, masons, blacksmiths, and the like. It sometimes has its advantages."

"And you," Pasicrates told him, "are found of saying we Rope Makers know nothing of sieges." He checked himself. "I came to convey the regent's respects to you—"

"Consider it done."

"I do. And to tell you we will have to draw rations with your own men. We brought only a few days' supplies. You would not want to strain our ancient friendship, I think. For a bite of bread and a handful of olives we will lead your assault. You need only follow us."

Xanthippos was still smiling. "Your heroic offer is duly noted."

"You'll find your men inspirited by the knowledge that they are led by the shieldmen of Rope." Pasicrates stood, and Drakaina and I rose with him. "As for sieges, we know more than you suppose." He held out one hand, its fingers outspread. "Count them, Xanthippos. I say Sestos will fall before you're finished."

Xanthippos remained unruffled. "Then the news you bring is doubly good. Not only have we received reinforcements from Rope, but the city is to fall within five days. You didn't mean five months, I hope? Before you go, may I ask why you brought this man and this woman when you came to confer with me?"

Without waiting for Pasicrates's answer, he turned to Drakaina. "Are you a Babylonian, my dear? A marvelous city, and one justly noted for the beauty of its women. Prior to this unhappy war I had the pleasure of visiting it. I hope to return, should my fellow citizens ostracize me again, which I fear is more than likely."

"You may ask," Pasicrates told him. "But you will not be answered."

Outside, Drakaina said, "We should not have come with you. We'll be watched after this."

Pasicrates snorted. "Magical arts, and you can't evade a few of these shopkeepers? How are you going to get into the city?"

"Not by transforming myself into a bat, if that's what you're thinking. Not unless I must, and I haven't had a chance to gauge the problem yet."

"Nor I," Pasicrates admitted. "You're right; let's make a circuit of the walls."

The rain had stopped, but clouds hung gray and heavy over Sestos, and we had to pick our way through mud. I noticed some of the soldiers from Thought had winter boots, but all of us were still in sandals. From the walls to the distant hills spread the melancholy ruins of the houses that had once stood outside the city proper. The holes that had been their cellars were full of black water, and broken bricks and charred timbers protruded even where the men from Thought had made crude paths and roads.

We had gone no more than a couple of stades when Io came running up to join us, splashing through the mud in bare feet. "How was Xanthippos?" she asked.

I told her that if he was half as clever with the barbarians as he had been with us, the city would fall within five days, as Pasicrates had promised him it would.

"That was because you're here. Wasn't it, Pasicrates?"

The Roper Maker pretended not to hear her. He was already some way ahead of us.

"We must get inside," Drakaina told her. "You're a clever child, so keep your eyes open."

Io whispered, "I have already. I can get you inside any time you want, if nobody's watching."

Drakaina stared. "How— No, never mind. When we're alone. But have you ever seen such walls, either of you? The Great King has made this the lock with which he chains the whole coast."

Io said, "Then we've brought the key, if the regent's dream is true. Pasicrates is going to storm the city in a day or two, that's what the Rope Makers were telling each other while you were gone."

I said, "But if the key is in the chest, who can unlock it? I'm going into the city with Drakaina."

"Master, the Maiden sent you here. You don't remember, but I do. She said you'd find your friends here. If you go inside, it might not work. Besides, I'll have to come with you. I belong to you, and I have to remember things for you."

Drakaina hissed, "Certainly not!"

"I agree. I won't risk her life like that. Io, I'll bring you to me later if I can."

Io pointed, no doubt to distract me. "There's a lake!"

"No," Drakaina told her. "That's the strait."

In a few moments we were there. As Io had indicated, the strait was no wider than a small lake—we could watch men working on the wharves of the city on the opposite shore—and though it joined the horizon to the northeast, to the southwest we saw what appeared to be its termination. As we looked over the water, a trireme appeared there as if born of the rocky coast and, beating six white wings, seemed to fly along the waves as it came to join the others blockading Sestos.

Io said, "If this goes to the sea, I'm surprised they don't land the supplies here. It would be a lot safer."

I said, "It would be a great deal more dangerous, if that coast to the east still acknowledges the rule of the Great King."

Pasicrates had been studying the scene in silence. Now he said, "It was here, little Io, that the brave Leander swam from shore to shore to visit his beloved. I see you know the story."

Io nodded. "But he drowned one night, and she threw herself from the top of the tower. Only I didn't know this was the place."

Pasicrates favored her with his bitter smile. "I'm sure that if you were to go into the city, they'd point out the precise tower—her blood-stains in the street too, very likely."

"It doesn't look so far. I bet I could swim it."

I cautioned her, "Don't try. Haven't you noticed how fast that ship's coming? There must be a strong current."

Drakaina added, "You may try for all I care, Io; but your master's correct, and there are frequent storms as well. Pasicrates, you too were thinking that where one swam, another may swim, weren't you?"

The Rope Maker nodded slowly.

"But swimmers could carry only daggers. A dozen shieldmen would be more than a match for a hundred of them."

"I wasn't thinking of storming the city with swimmers," Pasicrates told her. "I was wondering how Xanthippos gets his information." He turned on his heel and started back the way we had come.

Drakaina said, "The lovely Helle drowned here too, giving her name to the place, when she fell from the back of the Golden Ram. These are dangerous waters, you see." She smiled at Io as a stoat might smile at a starling, though I sensed she was trying to seem kind.

"I *don't* know that story," Io said. "Would you tell me about the Golden Ram, please?"

"With pleasure. It belongs to the Warrior, and it lives in the sky between the Bull and the Fish. Remind me on some clear night, and

I'll point it out to you. Once, long ago, it came to earth to interfere in the matter of two children, Phrixos and Helle, who had become a burden to their stepmother, Ino. No doubt the Warrior had planned to make Phrixos a hero, or something of that kind. Ino's called the White Goddess now, by the way, and she's an aspect of the Triple Goddess. Anyway, the Ram was determined to frustrate her, so it got itself a golden coat and joined the children as they were playing in a meadow, promising them a ride on its back. As soon as they were on, it sprang into the air, and at the highest point of its leap, right here, Helle fell off and drowned as I told you."

Io asked, "What happened to her brother?"

"The Ram carried him to Aea, at the east end of the Euxine, thinking he'd be safe there. After putting in a good word for him with the king, it hung its golden coat in a tree and returned to the sky. I was a princess in Aea—"

"Wait a minute! I thought this was hundreds and hundreds of years ago."

"We live many different lives," Drakaina told Io, "in many different bodies. Or at least some of us do. I was a princess in Aea, and a priestess of Enodia just as I am now. I told my father quite truthfully that the goddess said he would be killed by a stranger. Since Phrixos was the only stranger around, that did for *him*. And I set my pet python to guard the golden fleece. Then—"

We had caught up with Pasicrates, who had stopped to examine one of the ramps the men from Thought were building. It was of earth, with logs laid in crisscross layers to reinforce it. "Childish," he said.

I ventured that it looked well constructed to me.

"Yes? How would you continue it when it nears the wall? It must be highest of all there, and the defenders will rain down stones and spears upon your head. Burning pitch too, perhaps."

"I'd assign a shield bearer to each workman," I told him. "A hoplon's big enough to protect two men from stones and spears from above. For that matter a strongly roofed wagon could be used to move the logs, and much of the work could be done from inside it with the floorboards taken out. And I'd station every archer and slinger I had about halfway from here to the wall to make my enemies think twice about showing themselves to throw stones and spears. They could only form a single line along the parapet there, but my archers and slingers would be able to form four or five lines, so that for every missile of theirs we'd return four or five."

Pasicrates stroked his chin and did not answer.

We soon came to just such a roofed wagon as I had spoken of, with a splintered battering ram slung in it; no doubt I had seen it on our way to the strait, and it was the unconscious recollection of it that had made me speak as I did. I stopped and asked the men repairing the battering ram how it had been broken, and one pointed to one of the narrow doors in the base of the wall. "We tried to knock on that, but they've got a log three times as big as this up there. It's hooked to a chain so they can swing it down and pull it back up. When the old ram came out of the barn here, down she swung and snapped it right off in back of the bronze, like you see."

Young though Pasicrates is, he had not seemed boyish to me until then. "Tell them what to do, Latro. I'm sure you know."

I said, "Fundamentally, they have to catch either the log or its chain, holding it with something too heavy for the men on the wall to draw up. This wagon they call the barn seems heavy enough to me; there's a lot of thick wood in the roof, and those wheels are solid oak and as wide as both my legs. The men are putting a stouter timber in the ram already. If I were in command, I'd put spikes on its sides, and on the sides of the wagon too. Then the log would nail itself to one or the other as soon as it struck."

One of the men who had been fitting the new beam into its slings stopped work and stepped over to us. "I'm Ialtos. I'm in charge here, and I thank you for the advice; we'll make use of it. Did I hear the Rope Maker call you Latro?"

I nodded. "That's my name. Or at least, that's what I'm called among your people."

"We've got a captain here—" He pointed. "See that tower on wheels? They're putting leather on the front and sides so it can't be set on fire, and he's superintending the job. He'll talk you deaf, do you know what I mean? But he knows leather and how to get it."

Io shouted, "Hypereides!"

"That's the man—I see you've met him. He goes on sometimes about a slave he used to have called Latro. Sort of a simple-minded fellow according to Hypereides, but you could tell he liked him. He traded him to a hetaera for a series of dinners—mostly, I think, to keep him away from the fighting."

Drakaina said, "I wouldn't call Latro simple-minded, but he forgets from one day to the next." She shot a mocking glance at the Rope Maker. "He's unusual in some other respects too, wouldn't you say, Pasicrates?"

"Even women who speak little talk too much." He took her arm to draw her away from Ialtos.

Io had been studying the tower on wheels. Now she tugged at my cloak. "Look, master! Up on that ladder. It's the black man!"

# FORTY

___

## *Among Forgotten Friends*

THE HEART REMEMBERS, EVEN WHEN no trace of face or voice remains. The black man came running to us, shouting, his arms in the air; and though I do not know where we met or why I love him (though no doubt those things are written somewhere on this scroll), I could not stop smiling. Without thinking at all about what I should do, I embraced him as a brother.

When we had shouted together and pounded each other on the back and hugged with all our strength like two wrestlers, Pasicrates tried to question him; but he only smiled and shook his head.

Io explained, "He understands—most of it, anyway. But he can't talk, or he won't."

Drakaina said something then in a harsh and rapid way that seemed to me no better than the creaking and grinding of mill stones; and to Io's amazement and my own, the black man answered her at once in the same language. "Your friend speaks the tongue of Aram," Drakaina told Io. "Not as well as the People from Parsa, but nearly as well as I do myself."

Pasicrates said, "Then ask him how he came to learn it."

She spoke to him again, and when he had replied she said, "He says, 'For three years I was with the army. We marched from Nysa to Riverland, from Riverland over the desert to the Crimson Country, then through many other countries.' He also says, 'My king is not subject to the Great King; but the Great King gave him gold and many fine things, and swore there would be peace between our lands forever if he would send a thousand men. I walked before a hundred and twenty, all young men from my own district, and I learned to talk in this way that

I might know the wishes of the Lords of Parsa.' " Drakaina added, "I'm shortening this a little."

Io demanded, "Ask how he met Latro."

" 'I saw a god had touched him. Such people are holy; someone must care for them.' "

Io started to ask where Hypereides was, but Pasicrates silenced her. "Does he want to go back to his own country?"

Before Drakaina spoke, the black man nodded and began to speak. She said, "Yes, very much. He says, 'My father and mother are there, both my wives, and my son, who is very small.' "

Pasicrates nodded. "Are there any of the other men from his country in the city?"

"He says he doesn't know, but he doesn't think so. He thinks they may have gone south with the army. He says, 'If they were here, they would show themselves to me on the walls.' And I suppose he's right—he was in plain view working on that tower; hundreds of people in the city must have seen him."

"Tell him I require him to carry a message into the city for me."

Io protested. "He belongs to Hypereides!" I think she did not want to lose sight of the black man again so soon after we had found him.

"Who will surely consent for the good of our cause. No doubt he will be compensated by his city."

"He says Latro and this child must come with him."

I smiled and Io giggled, darting a glance at Pasicrates.

He ignored her. "And why is that?"

Now the black man spoke at length, touching his chest and pointing with his chin to Io and me, and toward Sestos, and once pretending to draw a bow.

Drakaina told Pasicrates, "He says he won't do what you ask as a slave, that a slave remains a slave only as long as he's watched. If he goes back to the People from Parsa, he will be a soldier again, and as a soldier he won't do what you ask unless you free Latro, and Io too. He says you can force him to go to the city, but that once there he won't deliver your message—only tell lies."

Even Pasicrates smiled at that.

"For myself," Drakaina added, "I remind you that I am the person sent by your regent to the barbarians—not this black man. Not even you."

"Yet another messenger may be useful, particularly one who speaks their tongue. His price is too high, but I imagine it can be lowered."

I said I was willing to go into Sestos if he wished me to.

Pasicrates shook his head. "If you were lost permanently, how could I explain to the regent? No, you must stay with me until the city capitulates and we return home."

Catching my eye, the black man motioned toward the tower, then spoke to Drakaina.

She said, "He desires to show you what he has been building."

I said, "And I want to see it. Come along, Io." Though I did not say so, I suspected the black man wished to put himself under the protection of the man called Hypereides. I do not remember him, but Io seemed to like him, and it appeared likely the black man was right in thinking he would fare better with him than with the Rope Maker.

"You know everything about siegecraft," Pasicrates said as we came near the tower. "Explain this to me."

I told him that since he could see it himself, there was very little to explain. It was a tower on wheels, built of wood. The back was left open to reduce its weight, but the front and sides were covered with planks to keep out arrows, and with leather to prevent the planks from being set ablaze. Before the tower was pushed against the wall, the leather would be soaked with water by men using rag swabs on long poles. In addition, leather buckets of water would be hung in the tower, to be used by the men inside.

He said, "Our enemies will put their finest troops opposite this tower."

I answered, "Yes, but good fighters will be put in the tower too."

The black man had gone around it as we spoke. Now he reappeared, bringing with him a bald man in a leather cuirass. The bald man seemed astonished to see us, then smiled broadly. "Latro and little Io, by the Standing Stone! I didn't think I'd be setting eyes on you again till we got back to Thought. How did you get here? Is that fellow Pindaros with you?"

He patted Io's head, and she embraced him and seemed for a moment too moved to speak.

"I don't suppose you remember Pindaros the poet, do you, Latro? Or his wench Hilaeira either."

The Rope Maker stepped forward. "I am Pasicrates, son of Polydectes. I am here as the representative of Prince Pausanias, son of Cleombrotus, Victor of Clay and Regent of Rope."

"Hypereides," Hypereides said. "Son of Ion—" Io whispered afterward that he meant he was of the Ionian people and proud of it, and that Pasicrates is a Dorian. "—commander of the *Europa*, the *Eidyia*, and the *Clytia*. Only my ships aren't in the water right now." He jerked his head toward the west. "They're beached, and most of my men are here working on these things."

Pasicrates said, "I'm told you sold this slave to a hetaera in your city."

"That's right, to Kalleos." Hypereides paused, looking from Pasicrates to Drakaina, as though wondering whether either were out to make trouble for him. "Not legally, of course, because women in my city can't hold property. Everything's in the name of a man she calls her nephew. She pays him so much a year for that."

"We are more reasonable in Rope—we don't love lies. Latro and the child are our regent's now, given him by your hetaera."

Io yelped, "He was supposed to pay!"

"Then he will, you may be sure. But in Rope, children who speak out of turn are whipped for it. Remember that." Pasicrates had never taken his eyes from Hypereides. "As the strategist of the Rope Makers here, I'm interested in your tower, Commander. How could you make it so the top was level with the top of the wall, when you couldn't measure the wall?"

Hypereides cleared his throat. "With all due respect, Strategist, neither one of those is exactly true. We want the top higher than the wall, so we can put bowmen there to shoot down on the enemy. And we could measure the wall. We did. Come around to the front here." He led the way and pointed upward. "See that door? It swings down, and it'll be level with the merlons. There's a stair in the back, as you probably saw, so all our men will have to do is run up the steps and step off onto the wall."

"It must have taken a brave man to carry a measuring pole to the base," Pasicrates said, "even late at night."

"Oh, no." Hypereides's mouth twitched with amusement. "I measured it myself, and in broad daylight too. First I had a bowman—there he is. Come here, Oior."

A big, bearded man in loose trousers shambled over. He had a hammer in his hand and there was no bowcase at his back and no quiver at his waist; yet I knew the bald man was correct, for the bearded man had the look of a bowman.

"We tied a thread to an arrow," Hypereides continued. "Oior shot the arrow so it stuck in the ground at the foot of the wall. Then we cut the thread and pulled the arrow in so we could measure the thread. That gave us the distance from the place where Oior stood to the base of the wall."

Pasicrates said, "Which is *not* the height of the wall, unless you were very lucky."

"No, certainly not. Then we stuck a sword in the ground so it was exactly a cubit high. When the shadow of the wall touched the place where Oior had stood, we measured the shadow of the sword and divided the length of the thread by the length of the shadow. The answer was the height of the wall: forty-seven cubits."

Oior the bowman smiled at me and touched his forehead in greeting.

When we returned to Pasicrates's tent, he sent Drakaina and Io away, then held out his hand. "I see you're wearing your sword, Latro," he said. "Give it to me."

I unfastened the catch of my belt. "You're welcome to look at it," I said, "as long as you mean me no harm."

"Give it to me," he said again.

The very flatness of his voice told me what he meant to do. "No," I said. I refastened the catch.

He whistled. I suppose he must have decided I required correction before we left to make our circuit of the walls and perhaps even before we called upon Xanthippos, because his slaves appeared at once, one carrying two javelins and the other a whip, a scorpion of three tails. They entered through the back of the tent, and Pasicrates moved to block the front, his hand upon his sword hilt.

"These men may kill me," I told him, "but they will not beat me."

I recalled that he had said a woman sold me to the regent. "And if they kill me, what will you tell your master?"

"The truth," Pasicrates murmured. "Sestos did not fall, you were lazy and insolent, I tried to discipline you, and you resisted."

His hoplon leaned against the tent wall near the entrance. With a practiced motion, he slipped his arm through its leather loop and grasped the handle. "Now take off that sword, and your cloak and chiton, like a sensible man."

I said, "No one thinks you Rope Makers sensible men."

"And so they are our slaves, or they soon will be." He glanced at the slaves that were truly his. "Keiros, Tekmaros, don't kill him."

Neither was well equipped to capture an armed man alive, and what happened next would have been ludicrous, had it not been terrible. The slave with the scorpion advanced first, lashing the air to make a savage sound he must have hoped would frighten me. I stepped forward and slashed at the rawhide lashes. He jumped back and in so doing impaled himself on one of the javelins held by the man behind him.

The terrible thing was not that it killed him, but that it did not. With the head of the javelin in his back, he remained alive, bleeding and gasping like a fish on a gig as he dropped the scorpion and flailed about with his arms.

I caught it up—and as I did so, saw that Pasicrates was almost upon me. Its stock was of some heavy wood, and the lead-tipped lashes looked as though they might easily entangle a man; I threw it at his legs.

He was too quick for me. The stock rang against the bronze facing of his hoplon. I swung Falcata in the downward stroke that is most powerful of all. Again he was too quick, raising his hoplon to block her blade; but it bit the bronze like cheese, cut the hoplon to its center, and leaped free as a lynx springs from a rock.

Pasicrates screamed. It was a high, shrill cry like a woman's, though he thrust at me like a man even as he screamed, and made me skip aside.

The wall of the tent was at my elbow then; this scroll lay on my pallet not far from my left hand. I stooped to pick it up. That saved me, I think. A javelin passed so near my head that the sound was like a blow. Blood streamed from my ear.

The javelin had pierced the side of the tent. A slash laid it wide. I stumbled out and ran east, past the tents and through the little fields toward Parsa and Persepolis—toward the heart of the Empire, though I cannot say how it is I know the names of those places.

When I had reached the hills and could run no more, I found this hollow in the rocks and stopped to rest, the pulse pounding in my head like the laughter of some great river in flood. Soon the gray clouds hanging over the land parted. The sun appeared, a crimson coin set on the horizon behind me. I staunched the blood from my ear with moss, wiped Falcata's smeared blade on fallen leaves, and unrolling this scroll read enough to learn that I must write.

Writing has given me time to catch my breath and listen for pursuit. There has been none. When the moon rises, I will run again. It is important, so very important, that I do not forget I am fleeing, and what it is I fly from. "I have to remember things for you," the child, Io, told me as we wandered among the soldiers and siege engines of Thought. I wish she were with me now.

# FORTY-ONE

## *We Are in Sestos*

THE GODDESS SENT ME HERE, and it was no dream. How easy it would be to write that I dreamed, as so many have written in so many other places. Yet I know I did not, for I dreamed before the goddess came.

It was a dream of love. The woman was raven-haired, or so it seemed in the moonlight, with eyes that flashed with desire. How she clutched me and drove my loins into her own! A lake, dark and still, mirrored silver stars; all along the shore men in horned and leering masks capered with women crowned with the vine, to the thudding of timbrels and the rattle of crotali.

Then I woke.

The woman had vanished, the instruments fallen silent. My torn ear burned and throbbed. The stones stood about me, hard and dark. The air was cold, heavy with snow. I heard the wind muttering among the oaks, and I knew it—though I do not know how—for the thought of Jove, the god who rules the gods and cares little for men. It seemed to me that he was mad, black thoughts repeating one or two words again and again as they brooded upon revenge.

I sat up, and the night was like any other. A wind walked among the trees, and an increscent moon hung low in the west. Far off a wolf howled. My limbs were stiff with cold, but I felt no desire to roll myself in my cloak again; I felt instead that I should rise and fly from some danger, and though I no longer recalled what it was from which I had fled earlier, I sensed a menace that was no less now. Stretching, I looked down to find this scroll, which I recalled having pushed into a hiding place among the rocks.

At once I gasped and nearly cried out, staggering backward from the lip of an abyss beside which I had slept only a few moments before. It seemed a pit without a bottom, or at least without any bottom the silver radiance of moon or stars could ever reach. Trembling, I cast a stone into it and listened. I heard nothing, though I strained to hear for many thuddings of my fearful heart.

Though perhaps my stone is still falling, falling always and without end, something moved in the abyss. If it lacked any termination, still it had sides; and blurs of white and palest green, tiny and remote, swarmed over them as ants may creep across the walls in a sealed tomb. Sometimes it appeared that they flew from one side to another, flitting like bats and flickering like rushlights.

"You would find me," someone behind me said. "I have come already."

I turned and saw a girl of perhaps fifteen sitting on a stone behind me. Her gown was woven of somber autumn foliage, yellow, gridelin, and russet, and a stephane with an ebon gem was on her brow. Though she sat with her back to the moon, I could see her face clearly; it seemed hungry and ill, like the faces of the children who sell their bodies in the poor quarters of cities.

"Soon you will wonder what became of your book," she said. "I will keep it for you; now take it, and leave my door."

When she spoke, I was more afraid of her than of the abyss; perhaps if I had not feared her so, I could not have done as she instructed me.

"I have rolled it tightly for you, tied it, and pushed your stylus through the cords. Put it through your belt. You have much to do before you write again."

I asked, "Who are you?"

"Call me Maiden, as you did when we first met."

"And you're a goddess? I didn't think—"

She smiled sourly. "We still meddled in the wars of Men? Not often now; but the Unseen God wanes, and we are no longer lost in his light. We will never be wholly gone."

I bowed my head. "How may I serve you, Maiden?"

"First by taking your hand from your sword hilt, to which it has strayed. Believe me, your blade is powerless against me."

I dropped my hands to my sides.

"Second, by doing as I instruct you, and so relieving me of the

necessity I laid upon myself for Mother's sake. You recall nothing of
this, but I have promised to reunite you with your comrades."

"Then you've been kinder than I deserve," I said, and nearly stammered from the joy that flamed in my heart.

"I act for my mother, and not for you. You owe me no thanks. Nor
do I owe you any. If you had accepted your beating like any other slave,
my task would have been easy."

"I am not a slave," I said.

She smiled again. "What, Latro? Not even mine?"

"Your worshiper, Maiden."

"Smooth-tongued as ever. No man outreaches his gods, Latro, not
even in falsehood."

"You said that you've promised to bring me to my own people,
Maiden. If that was a falsehood, slay me now."

"I will keep my promise," she said. She licked her lips. "But I
hunger. What payment will you give me, Latro, when I do as you wish?
A hundred bulls to smoke upon my altars?"

I shook my head. "I'd slaughter every one, and singing, if I had
them. I have nothing beyond what you see."

"Your book, your sword, your belt, your sandals, and those ragged
clothes. And your body, but I will not ask you for that; it will be mine
soon enough, no matter what. Would you heap my altar with the rest?"

"With everything, Maiden."

"And Io?"

I asked, "Who is Io?"

"A slave. She says yours. Will you give her to me freely?"

I nodded, though I sickened to nod. "You have only to show her
to me, Maiden."

"Then I will not ask you for her. Nor for your book and sword and
the other things. I ask an easier sacrifice instead: a wolf."

"Only a wolf, Maiden?" Now my spirit leaped for gladness. "You
are too generous, too merciful!"

"So many have said. Yes, a wolf. The wolf is sacred to my mother,
as you would know had you not forgotten it. Furthermore, I will see
that this wolf comes to you, and I will place my sigil on it so that you
will know it."

"And I won't forget?"

She pointed, and though the hill stood between us and the rising sun, when she pointed I knew that it was there. "In summer, when the days were long, you lost the dawn before evening. Days are shortened now; when the wolves howl again, you will yet remember me and this: The wolf will attack you, yet you will not fear it. He is the one."

"As you command, Maiden, and gladly."

"Not so gladly when the time comes, perhaps. But first you must return to the walls you fled, return with the dawn. Will you do that?"

"It's dawn now," I told her. "Can I run so fast? I will if I can."

"Your foes seek your life. Be wary. As the sun rises, you will see a woman and a child walking hand in hand. Draw your sword and give it to the child. Do you understand?"

I nodded. "I will do just as you've said, Maiden."

"Then when you find the wolf, grasp its ear, cut its throat, and speak my name. Go now, do that, and my promise will be fulfilled."

The city was far out of sight to the west; yet I saw it, its gray walls, grim with a hundred towers, rising high above the tents of the besiegers. I sprinted toward it, and it vanished; but I continued to run, leaping stones and loping across fields of stubble until I reached in truth the tents I had seen falsely through the eyes of the goddess.

Here soldiers woke and spat like other men, goaded by the braying of the trumpets—buckled on their armor, took up spears and hoplons marked with the inverted ox of Thought, and formed ragged files that were soon straightened by the curses of their enomotarches. Some looked at me curiously, and I waved this scroll above my head so they would think me a messenger; no one stopped me.

The tents ended. I reached a place where houses and shops had stood outside the walls. They had been burned, though whether by the besiegers or the besieged I cannot say. There were towers and sheds on wheels, and ramps of clay and wood. Worse, the tumbled stones and tiles of the ruined houses threatened to trip me with every stride. Once I noted a dented pan among the ruins, and once a scattered string of coral beads. I thought then of the misery of poor women I would perhaps never see.

Soon I was within bowshot of the walls. An archer there kindly told me so, sending his shaft whizzing past my eyes to bury itself in the blackened ground to my right, so that I returned this scroll to my belt and ran wider.

Already the sun was well above the horizon behind me. The Maiden had said I was to give my sword to the child "as the sun rises," but it seemed to me it was impossible that day. Yet I continued to run, or rather to trot, circling the walls in search of the woman and the child.

The temptation always was to go too near, for by curving my path more sharply I could have decreased its length. Twice more archers loosed at me, their long-flying arrows falling at last almost at my feet.

I had made a half circle when I saw them—a woman in a purple gown and a child in a torn gray peplos, hand in hand, so deep in the shadow of the wall that the soldiers on it might have slain them with stones had they wished.

At the same instant a wounded man shouted, drew his sword, and dashed toward me. I marveled at his courage, for he had lost his left forearm not long before; the stump was still bandaged below the elbow, and the bandage was still gay with his blood. I had drawn my own sword before I remembered the words of the Maiden, who had perhaps desired that I fight this one-armed man without it. That seemed no more than just, for surely he was still weak from his wound. I ran to the woman and the child then with all the speed I could command, extending my sword to the child hilt foremost.

She accepted it readily; but when I turned, others were sprinting after the one-armed man. One fell with an arrow through his throat, but two more caught the one-armed man, wrestling his sword from his hand and pulling him to safety. As I watched them, I was bathed in gold. The sun had risen above the city wall, bringing a second dawn.

Still other men, shieldmen in armor, dashed from the wall to take us. They dragged me, with the woman and the child, into a doorway so deeply set that it was like a tunnel ending in a narrow door. When this door swung back, we were in the besieged city. Houses of two and even three stories were set thickly along the narrow street, many with their backs formed by the wall. The men who held us seemed not otherwise than the men outside who warred on them; but with them were soldiers not like them at all, soldiers whose curling beards were black instead of brown, and who wore loose trousers of yellow, blue, and green.

They bore us to the citadel and took the woman from us, and with her my sword as well. Now we are shut up in this guard room, where at Io's urging (for this child is the slave girl I told the Maiden I would sacrifice if she wished it) I write my account.

# FORTY-TWO

## *Though Not Without Aid*

I HAVE DEFEATED THREE MEN, guards of the satrap from Susa. They were Hellenes, though in Sestos the Hellenes do not govern themselves, as Io explained when I had finished writing of our capture. So it is, she says, wherever the Hellenes live on this side of the Water.

"All the better for them," I said, "assuming that the men of Parsa are wise and just. These Hellenes are proud, grasping, and turbulent; brilliant, perhaps, but without any real feeling for the duties of the citizen and the majesty of the state."

She agreed, then asked in a whisper whether I thought someone was listening.

"No," I said. "I speak my mind—the simple truth."

"But I'm a Hellene myself, master."

"I was considering the men. The women are better, perhaps, yet wanton."

"You only say that because you saw them in Kalleos's house, mostly. Do you remember her? Or Phye? Or Zoe, or any of the others?"

I shook my head. "I only know how these Hellenes have seemed to me." I sought to take the sting from my words. "Their children are beautiful and very kind."

She smiled. "I'm the only one you've had much to do with. But maybe you're right anyway about the men and women. What do you know about the People from Parsa?"

"It was they who commanded the soldiers who brought us into this city; but though I feel sure I've seen them before, I can't remember where."

"I saw them back in Hill. They don't talk like we do, and they keep their women out of sight even more than the people do in Thought.

And I saw one on the wall yesterday. That was how I knew how to get Drakaina into Sestos."

I asked whether Drakaina was the woman in the purple gown, and Io nodded.

"She wanted to get inside so she could talk to the People from Parsa for the regent, but she didn't know how. Only yesterday, you and she and Pasicrates walked around looking at the towers on wheels, and I saw a man from Parsa on the wall watching her. The jewels on his cap and in his rings caught the light, so I knew he must be an important man, and from the way he looked at Drakaina I knew that if she ever came near the wall he'd have soldiers come out and get her. Then you fought with Pasicrates and ran away, and I thought I ought to go in with her, so that maybe I could get him to help you. The Rope Makers will probably kill you if they ever catch us again."

"Who's Pasicrates?" I asked, not liking to hear that I had run from him.

"He's the head Rope Maker out there," Io told me. "Or he was. I'll tell you about him if you want, then you can read about him in your book. We're going to have plenty of time, I suppose."

Io had no sooner spoken than the door swung wide. I expected to see soldiers like those who had brought us here, perhaps with an officer from Parsa; but these were all barbarians with long trousers and cloth-draped heads. I found I knew already what sorts of faces they would have and how they would be armed. Yet because I did not know I would recall those things until I saw them, I will write something of them here.

Their hands and faces are the only parts of their bodies they do not cover; and sometimes they cover even their faces, pulling up the cloth that conceals the neck to keep dust from the nose and mouth. Instead of sandals they wear shoes (which I think must be very uncomfortable) so that no part of the foot can be seen. Among the Hellenes bright colors are worn often, but garments are all of one hue save perhaps for a band at the edge. The People from Parsa have half a dozen different colors in the same cloth. Even soldiers like those who came for us do not wear much armor.

Their spears are no taller than the men who bear them. Instead of a pointed grounding iron that can serve as a second spear head if the shaft breaks, they have a round weight at the butt. It is wise of them to make them that way, I think, because so short a spear would be useless after the shaft had broken; but the weight should permit the soldier to reverse his broken spear and use it as a mace. This weight shifts the point of balance to the rear, just as the grounding iron does.

The men of Parsa always have their bows and bowcases. I think they must be fonder of the bow than any other race; surely no race could be fonder than they. Their bows are of wood and horn bound with sinew, and they bend backward when unstrung. Their arrows are hardly longer than a man's forearm and have iron points. Some have blue feathers, some gray. They are carried in the bowcase with the bow.

Their swords are short and straight, with tapering blades sharpened on both sides. Those of the soldiers who came for us have bronze lions' heads on their pommels, and that of Artaÿctes, to whom they brought us, has a golden lion's head. It is very beautiful, but the truth is that all these swords are hardly more than long daggers—good for thrusting but for nothing else. Some of the men from Parsa do not even carry swords. They have long-hafted axes instead, and that is what I would choose myself in preference to such a sword. The men who bear these axes wear a knife at the belt.

Artaÿctes is of graying beard, with eyes even harder and darker than is common among his countrymen. Because he wears a jeweled cap and many rings, I decided it was he whom Io saw upon the wall. The woman Io had called Drakaina sat at his right hand, not cross-legged as he himself sat, but with her fine legs to one side and bent at the knee to show their grace. When we came, she drew the end of a many-colored scarf across her nose and mouth.

He addressed her in a language I did not know, and she bowed her head. "Once my lord has spoken, the thing is done."

As the Hellenes speak, he said, "Your tongue is more supple than mine, in this speech particularly. They do not comprehend ours?"

"No, my lord."

"Then explain to them why they have been brought into my presence."

Drakaina turned so it appeared that she looked from the window of Artaÿctes's audience chamber, yet I saw her eyes were on me. "I told my lord what you did to Pasicrates and said you could no doubt kill three ordinary men. He has a guard of Sestians beside his own soldiers, and three have volunteered to fight you. Not with spears, but with hands bare, as contestants fight in the pancratium. Do you know that event? Only weapons are barred."

I was about to ask what I had done to Pasicrates (whom Io had told me I had fled) when Artaÿctes clapped his hands and a sentry ushered in the three. All were as tall as I am, well-muscled men at the height of their strength.

Io protested, "This isn't fair!"

Drakaina nodded agreement. "You're right, but the men of Parsa don't like boasting. I'd forgotten that. When they hear a boast, it's a point of honor with them to make the man perform accordingly, even when it was spoken by another. I believe my lord thinks too that Latro has been my lover, though we both know it is not so."

Io said bitterly, "By no fault of yours."

I was watching the three. If the leader could be killed, it would take the heart from the others. Often a leader stands between his followers, but in battle the place of honor is the right flank. As I took off my sword belt I muttered, "Maiden, aid me now."

At once the door of Artaÿctes's audience chamber opened again, and two more men entered, both as naked as the first three. Neither was large, but the first was so handsome and well shaped in every limb that every other man must have seemed deformed in his presence. The other was older, yet strong still, sun-browned and grizzled, with cunning eyes. Neither made any move to help me, each standing motionless beside the door, his arms at his sides. The three who faced me did not so much as look at them.

Artaÿctes said, "You are three set at one. Kill him and return to your duties."

The Sestians to my right and left stepped forward so that with the third they might enclose me. I knew that was death and edged to the left, so that the man there would have to fight me alone, if only for a moment.

He grappled, and I struck him with my fist below the navel and in the face with the crown of my head. He reeled and fell backward, his nose gushing blood.

At once the older man flung himself upon him, face to face as lover kisses lover. Until then I had not been certain the rest could not see the two who had come last, but when I saw them I knew. I circled and feinted, sure delay would favor me.

Nor was I wrong. The grizzled man rose, his mouth crimson with blood, and seized one of my opponents from behind. Still the man did not see him, yet his movements were slower.

"I am Odysseus, son of Laertes and King of Ithaka," the grizzled man whispered. "We need more blood, for Peleus's son."

"I doubt it," I told him, for I had seen that the remaining Sestian watched my eyes and not my hands.

When the fight was over, Drakaina smiled—I could see her lips through the thin stuff of the scarf. "My lord Artaÿctes feels the news I've brought is too important to remain caged here. Furthermore, there isn't food enough in the city for it to resist much longer—the people are boiling the straps from their beds."

Artaÿctes spoke some angry word, but Drakaina did not look chastened.

"He hoped for relief before this. It hasn't come; so he will go, taking his own people and those from the far lands. He plans to leave the Hellenes here, knowing they'll negotiate a surrender that will spare their houses and their walls. When he's conveyed my news, he'll get an army from the Great King and return to crush the barbarians, if they're bold enough to remain. I've told him you've sold your sword to the Great King, and he's just seen you're a fighter to be reckoned with. He asks if you'll go with him to Susa, where he expects to find the Great King."

I nodded, adding, "Yes, certainly."

Speaking for himself in his harsh accent, Artaÿctes asked, "Are you not of the Hellenes? You look as they."

"No, my lord."

"Then prove it. Let me hear your native tongue. The Hellenes will learn none but their own."

I did as he said, swearing in the tongue in which I write these words that I owed no allegiance to Thought or any such city. I do not think Artaÿctes understood me, but he seemed convinced. He took my sword from behind the scarlet cushions on which we sat and handed it to me.

"We will go by night," he said. "The barbarians will be asleep, save for a few sentries. No one must know. The people of this city tell all they learn to Yellow Horse, no matter how often they swear their loyalty. You are to ride beside me and carry this woman with you. See that she is not harmed." By "Yellow Horse" he meant Xanthippos, but he broke his name as I have broken it here.

When we had left the brightly hung audience chamber, Drakaina said, "Before we go, you must be armed. Wouldn't you like a shield and spear besides your sword? What of a helmet?"

Io told me, "You had round things for your chest and back when I met you, master."

I nodded. "A shield and a helmet, certainly, if there's going to be real fighting. No spear. I'll take a couple of javelins instead."

The armory was in the lowest part of the citadel. I asked for an oblong shield of medium weight, but those they had were hoplons, round and very heavy, or peltas shaped like the moon and very light.

"These honor my goddess," Drakaina said, holding up one of the latter. "It's the kind the javelin men in Thessaly use."

I told her that leather over wicker would stop only arrows and slingstones.

"That's because that's all they have to worry about," she said. "They stay well away from the spears."

I shook my head, knowing that if there is any fighting at all tonight, it will be hot work. I will not be able to run from the spears.

"Here, sir," the armorer said. "Try this. It's the smallest hoplon in the whole place."

It is a cubit and a hand across (I have just measured it), and faced with bronze, as I believe they all are; but there is wood and a leather lining behind it; and as he said, it was the lightest.

Io called, "Here's a nice helmet."

"Nice for a Hellene, perhaps," I told her. "But I don't want the men from Parsa to think I'm a Hellene in the dark."

The armorer snapped his fingers. "Wait a moment, sir. I believe I've got just what you need." He returned carrying a helmet shaped like a tall cap. As soon as I tried it on, I knew it might have been made for me.

Io said, "I've heard people talk about the Tall Cap Country, where they wear caps like that. And the bowmen on Hypereides's ships had them, but theirs were foxskin. I didn't know they made helmets the same way. Is it far from here?"

"Across Helle's Sea," the armorer told her, "and a good way by land after that; it would probably take you three or four days. Do you have a boat?"

Io laughed and said, "I'm not going," which I thought singularly ill omened.

I got a cuirass as well—not one of the heavy bronze corselets the shieldmen wear, but one of many layers of linen stitched together. It should give a good deal of protection while weighing not much more than a warm cloak. The javelins were easiest of all, for the armory had any number of good ones.

"The satrap has assigned me a house," Drakaina said when I had collected all the equipment I needed. "I'm going there now to get some sleep before tonight. It wouldn't do for him to see me with circles beneath my eyes." She hesitated. "You would be welcome, but I don't know that it would be wise."

I told her I wanted to go up on the wall and have a look at the country.

"As you wish, then."

The armorer said, "I could show you around, sir. Oschos's my name."

Io told him, "My master has no money."

"But he's been talking with the satrap," Oschos answered, smiling. "So perhaps he will have." To me he said, "Our citadel's built right into the wall, sir, on the east side, so you can start from here and go right around, passing through the guard towers."

I studied the plain and the hills beyond as we walked along the wall. The Hellenes will expect any escape to be made to the south and west, so Artaÿctes says. A short march that way would bring us to a place from which we might easily cross the strait by boat, evading the blockading ships. He means to try the northeast instead, making over-land for the port cities of a sea called the Propontis. Because Oschos was with us, however, I could not give more attention to that direction than to any other; and so I studied them all, and even the harbor, where the ships of Sestos cant their scorched masts through the soiled water.

When we left the wall we passed a marble building guarded by eunuchs, out of which some slaves were carrying chests and baskets. "What's that?" Io asked.

Oschos looked respectful. "The house of our satrap's women."

Io remarked that it looked more like a tomb.

"It was one," Oschos told her. "I hear that he uses them whenever he can. He feels a gynaeceum without windows is more secure, and who can doubt it?"

When we were alone here Io commented, "I wouldn't like to be Artaÿctes when he dies. The gods below aren't going to like his putting his concubines in a tomb."

"Who are the gods below?" I asked her as I hung up my new shield. The truth was that I felt I already knew one at least.

"The gods of the dead," she told me. "There's quite a lot, really. Their king is the Receiver of Many, and their queen is Kore, the Maiden. They have a whole country of their own under the ground, Chthonios, the world of ghosts."

Now I write and Io sleeps. When night comes I will ride with Artaÿctes and the People from Parsa, perhaps to the world of ghosts, because I have pledged my honor. But I will leave Io here, as she herself prophesied. Perhaps I shall never see her again. A moment ago I brushed her hair from her brown cheek, wondering whether there was ever a face dearer to me than hers; and though I cannot be sure, it seems impossible. How she would laugh at me, if she were to wake and find me weeping for her!

# FORTY-THREE

## A Soldier of the Mist

LOST IN THE NIGHT and its shifting vapors am I. Already I have nearly forgotten how this night began.

I lay on a pallet in a cold, dark room with a single high window, a window having narrow steps and a vantage for an archer beneath it. I think I had been asleep; a child, a girl, slept beside me.

A lovely woman came for me, and with her a hard-faced spearman. I must have known that they would come, for I rose at once and put on my cuirass and helmet by the light of the spearman's lamp, thrust this scroll through my belt, and took up my hoplon and javelins. I think I knew where we went and why, but that too is lost in the mist. "We will let Io sleep," I said to the woman. "She'll be safe here."

The woman nodded and smiled, her finger to her lips. Before she died, she said her name was Eurykles.

We hurried down dark and narrow streets reeking of ordure and joined a throng of silent people before the gate. The woman led me to the front, saying, "Artaÿctes and his guards will be here at any moment. Then we'll go."

I asked her who the rest were, but men on horseback pushed their mounts through the crowd before she could answer. The chief among them, a bearded man on a white horse, spoke in a language I could not understand; and to my amazement another man, who grasped his saddle cloth, spoke after him just as I write these words. This is what they said:

"In the most holy, most sacred name of the Sun! My people, does our situation seem desperate to you? Reflect! Here we have been penned like coneys, with scarcely enough to eat and without even clean water to drink. When next the Sun, the divine promise of Ahura Mazda,

mounts his throne, we shall be free, every one of us, and once more in
the Empire.

"So it shall be if we act like men. Those who fight must press ever
forward as they fight. Those who need not fight must turn back and
fight to aid their brothers. Horsemen, do not ride off, leaving your
brothers on foot to fight alone. Surely Ash will know of it! And I will
know of it too, and what I know I will soon tell the Great King. Rather,
ride at the flanks of those who press your brothers on foot, and protect
my household."

More was said, but the spearman tapped me on the shoulder and I
listened no more. He led two horses, and he handed the reins of a champ-
ing gray stallion to me. The woman said, "Can you ride?"

I was not sure. I answered, "When I must."

"You must tonight. Mount, and this man will help me up."

I leaped onto the gray's back and discovered that my knees knew
something of horses, whether my mind retained it or not.

Grinning, the spearman clasped the woman about the waist and
lifted her until she sat behind me. Though I have forgotten so much, I
still recall the flash of his teeth in the dark and her arm about my waist,
and the musky, flowery smell of her that was like a summer meadow,
with a serpent among the blossoms.

"At last I know why the People from Parsa put their women in
these trousers." Her voice was at my ear, ecstatic with excitement. "For
a thousand years they have not known but that they might have to gallop
off with them next day." Someone shouted an order, and the gates swung
toward us. "Stay with Artaÿctes," she said. "The best troops will be with
him."

As we rode out, the mist from the harbor crept in, meeting us half
a stade from the gate. Covered carts rumbled behind our horses. The
woman said, "Now the enemy knows. If the wheels weren't making so
much noise, you could hear their sentries shouting already."

Indicating the carts, I asked why they were here.

"For Artaÿctes's women. His wife and her maids will be in the first,
his concubines in the others." She hesitated, and I heard how sharply
she drew breath. "But where is he? Where are his guards?"

A few dozen foot soldiers with oblong shields followed the carts, and before them marched one who bore an eagle on a staff. My heart nearly burst at the sight of it (as it does now at the thought), though I could not have said why.

There was a shout from a thousand mouths. I swung about in the saddle to see the wide hoplons and long spears of the enemy break through the mist, and above them a black cloud of slingstones, javelins, and arrows. They had waited only until the last foot soldiers were clear of the gate, knowing perhaps that the Hellenes inside would close them against our retreat. Their phalanx was a hedge of spears.

"Go!" the woman cried. "He's tricked us! He must think I'm a spy—he's leaving the city some other way."

Before she had finished, I had loosed the reins and dug my heels into the gray's ribs. It sprang forward like a stag. In an instant, we had passed between the last cart and the soldiers who followed the eagle; but the mist held another phalanx as terrible as the first. I turned the gray aside and lashed it with the reins as I saw a third phalanx wheel to block the road; for there was a narrowing space between it and the second, and in that space only a scattering of archers and slingers.

Fearsome as the close-drawn shieldmen were when they fronted us, they could do nothing as we thundered past their flanks. One of my javelins I cast left, the second right, and though I did not see my foes die, each must have taken its toll. A bearded archer nocked an arrow meant for me, but we were too swift; I felt his bones break beneath the gray's hooves.

Horsemen followed me, iron-faced riders from Parsa with singing bows. We turned as one and caught the phalanx from behind, scourging the soft back of that monster of bronze and iron, felling its shieldmen like wheat before the reapers. Falcata scythed their spears and split their helmets, and they died, falling onto the dry yellow grass under a sky suddenly blue.

That is all I can recall of that time. When I lifted my head, a rolling mist had covered the lake. Somewhere the woman I had lain with screamed. As I struggled to rise, my hand touched a crooked sword half-buried in the mud. Not certain even that it was mine, I stumbled to my feet and limped among the dying and the dead in search of her.

I found her where the bodies lay thickest. Her feet had scattered gems that twinkled in the starlight, and a black wolf tore her throat.

Its forepaws pinned her to the ground, but its hind legs stretched useless behind it, and I knew its back had been broken.

I knew too that it was a man. Beneath the wolf's snarling mask was the face of a bowman; the paws that held the woman were hands even while they were paws. Ravening, the wolf dragged itself toward me. Yet I did not fear it, and only fended it from me with the point of my sword.

"More than a brother," it said. "The woman would have robbed me." It did not speak through its great jaws, but I heard it.

I nodded.

"She had a dagger for the dead. I hoped she would kill me. Now you must. Remember, Latro? 'More than brothers, though I die.' "

Beyond the wolf and the woman, a girl watched me—a girl robed with flowers and crowned. Her shining face was impassive, yet I sensed her quiet pleasure. I said, "I remember your sacrifice, Maiden, and I see your sigil upon it." I took the wolf by the ear and slit its throat, speaking her name.

I had come too late. The woman writhed like a worm cut by the plow, her mouth agape and her tongue protruding far past her lips.

The Maiden vanished. Behind me someone called, "Lucius . . . Lucius . . ."

I did not turn at once. What I had thought the woman's tongue was a snake with gleaming scales. Half-free of her mouth, it was thicker than my wrist. My blade bit at its back, but it seemed harder than brass. Frantically it writhed away, vanishing into the night and the mist.

The woman lifted her head. "Eurykles," I heard her whisper. "Mother, it's Eurykles!" With the last word she fell backward and was gone, leaving only a corpse that already stank of death.

The man-wolf was gone as well. The man lay in his place. When I touched him, his beard was stiff with blood, his back bent like trampled grass. His hands thanked me as he died.

"Lucius . . ." The call came again. It was only then, too late, that I sought for him.

I found him beside the broken eagle. He wore a lion's skin, but a spear had divided his thigh and a dagger had pierced his corselet of bronze scales. The lion was dying. "Lucius . . ." He used my own speech. "Lucius, is it really you?"

I could only nod, not knowing what to say; as gently as I could, I took his hand.

"How strange are the ways of the gods!" he gasped. "How cruel."

*(These are the last words of the first scroll.)*

# SOLDIER OF ARETE

And there came one to Xenophon as he was offering sacrifice, and said, "Gryllus is dead." And Xenophon took off the garland that was on his head, but ceased not his sacrifice. Then the messenger said, "His death was noble." And Xenophon returned the garland to his head again; and it is the tale that he shed no tears, but said, "I knew that I begat him mortal."

—Diogenes Laertius

# FOREWORD

THIS SCROLL IS IN POOR condition and contains various lacunae. "Latro" seems not to have written for a week or more following the departure of his party from Pactye. The Thracian winter may well have been the sole cause; although papyrus will endure for thousands of years, it falls to bits on being wet. Its fragile nature is only too well illustrated by this example, which has been severely damaged toward its center. By that, we have lost a considerable portion of the text, presumably dealing with the arrival of the *Europa* at Piraeus. A third hiatus, apparently resulting from morbid depression, follows his description of the ceremony of manumission at Sparta.

The horsemanship of the ancients has been much maligned by modern scholars unable to conceive of a rider retaining his seat without stirrups. They would be well advised to look into the history of the Plains Indians, who rode like ancient cavalrymen and like them employed lances, bows, and javelins. (The light, long-hafted axes used by the Persian cavalry would be instantly approved by Geronimo or Cochise.) In my opinion the Indian who fired his .45–70 Springfield from the back of his galloping pony—and this was done frequently—performed a feat more difficult than any demanded of ancient horsemen.

The reader should be aware that the horses of the ancient Greeks were unshod and were rarely gelded—never, if they were to be used in war. Though they were small by modern standards, the lack of stirrups made mounting difficult. (In fact, it may well be that stirrups were originally mounting devices, adopted when selective breeding had at last produced larger animals.) The cavalryman employed his lance or pair of javelins to vault onto his horse's back. Some horses were trained to advance their forelegs to render mounting easier.

As this account makes abundantly clear, modern historians are mistaken in rejecting the Amazons as legendary. Ancient writers record their invasion of central Greece in the time of Theseus (c. 1600 B.C.) in circumstantial detail, while the funeral mounds of fallen Amazon leaders dotted the route from Attica to Thrace. In any event, it should be obvious that among nomads a determined 120-pound woman might be a more valuable fighter than a man of half again her weight, equally effective with the bow while tiring her mount far less. It should not be necessary to point out that women warriors are found throughout history, or that our own age has more than most.

Pankration was the ancient equivalent of the martial arts. Only biting and gouging were forbidden, and the fight continued until the loser acknowledged his defeat. Students are cautioned that not every athlete shown striking another with his fists is a boxer. Boxers' hands were bound with leather thongs.

This scroll is of particular interest in that it contains the only known example of the prose of Pindar, after Homer the greatest Greek poet.

# PART ONE

# ONE

## *I Will Make a New Beginning*

ON THIS FRESH SCROLL, which the black man has found in the city. This morning Io showed me how I wrote in my old one and told me how valuable it had been to me. I read only the first sheet and the last, but I mean to read the rest before the sun sets. Now, however, I intend to write down all the things that will be most needful for me to know.

*Latro* is what these people call me, though I doubt that it is my name. The man in the lion's skin called me *Lucius,* or so I wrote in the first scroll. There also I wrote that I forget very quickly, and I believe it to be true. When I try to recall what took place yesterday, I find only confused impressions of walking, working, and talking, so that I am like a vessel lost in fog, from which the lookout sees, perhaps, looming shadows that may be rocks, or other vessels, or nothing—hears voices that may be those of men ashore, or of the tritons, or ghosts.

It is not so with Io, nor, I believe, with the black man. Thus I have learned that this is the Thracian Chersonese, this captured city, Sestos. Here a battle was fought by the Men of Thought against the People from Parsa by which the chief men of the latter hoped to escape. Thus says Io, and when I objected that the city seems fit to stand a lengthy siege, she explained there was not food enough, so that the People from Parsa and the Hellenes, too (for it is a city of Hellenes), starved behind their walls. Io is a child, yet nearly a woman. Her hair is long and dark.

The governor of the place assembled all his forces before one of the chief gates and put his wives and female slaves (of whom he had many) in tented carts. There he harangued his men, saying he would lead them against the Men of Thought; but when the gates were unbarred, he and his ministers went swiftly and secretly to another part of the wall and let themselves down by straps, thinking to escape while the battle raged. It was for naught, and some are captives here.

As am I, for there is a man called Hypereides who speaks of me as his slave—the black man also. (His head, which is round and very bald, reaches to my nose; he stands straight and speaks quickly.) Nor is this all, for Io—who calls herself *my* slave though this morning I offered to free her—says King Pausanias of Rope claims us, too. He sent us here, and a hundred of his Rope Makers were here until just before the battle, when their leader was wounded and they (having little liking for sieges and expecting a long one) sailed for home.

It is winter. The wind blows hard and cold, and rain falls often; but we live in a fine house, one of those the People from Parsa took for their own use earlier. There are sandals beneath my bed, but we wear boots— Io says that Hypereides bought such boots for all of us when the city surrendered, and two pairs for himself. This Chersonese is a very rich land, and like all rich lands it turns to mud in the rain.

This morning I went to the market. The citizens of Sestos are Hellenes, as I said, and of the Aeolian race—the people of the winds. They asked anxiously whether we planned to stay all winter, and told me much of the danger of sailing to Hellas at this season; I believe this is because they fear that the People from Parsa will not delay in recapturing so fertile a country. When I returned, I asked Io if she thought we would stay. She said we would surely go, and soon; but that we might come back if the People from Parsa try to retake the city.

Something quite unusual happened this evening, and though it has been dark for a long while, I wish to make a note of it before I go out again. Here Hypereides writes his orders and keeps his accounts, so there is a fire and a fine bright lamp with four wicks.

He came while I was polishing his greaves and had me buckle on my sword and put on my cloak and my new patasos. Together we hurried through the city to the citadel, where the prisoners are kept. We climbed many steps to a room in a tower, in which the only prisoners were a man and a boy; there were two guards also, but Hypereides dismissed them. When they were gone, he seated himself and said, "Artaÿctes, my poor friend, it is in no easy position that you find yourself."

The man of Parsa nodded. He is a large man with cold eyes, and though his beard is nearly gray he looks strong; seeing him, I thought I understood why Hypereides had wanted me to accompany him.

"You know that I've done all I could for you," Hypereides continued. "Now I require that you do something for me—a very small thing."

"No doubt," replied Artaÿctes. "What is this small thing?" He speaks the tongue of Hellas worse even than I, I think.

"When your master crossed into our land, he did so upon a bridge of boats. Isn't that so?"

Artaÿctes nodded, as did the boy.

"I've heard that its deck was covered with earth for its entire length," Hypereides continued, wondering. "Some even assert that the earth was planted with trees."

The boy said, "It was—I saw it. There were saplings and bushes at the sides so our cavalry horses wouldn't be afraid of the water."

Hypereides whistled softly. "Amazing! Really amazing! I envy you—it must have been a wonderful sight." He turned back to the father, saying, "A most promising young lord. What's his name?"

"It is Artembares," Artaÿctes told him. "He's named for my grandfather, who was a friend to Cyrus."

At that Hypereides smiled slyly. "But wasn't all the world a friend to Cyrus? Conquerors have a great many friends."

Artaÿctes was not to be disturbed thus. "What you say is true," he said. "Yet all the world did not sit over wine with Cyrus."

Hypereides shook his head ruefully. "How sad to think that Artembares' descendant drinks no wine at all now. Or at least, I wouldn't think they give you any here."

"Water and gruel, mostly," Artaÿctes admitted.

"I don't know whether I can save your life and your son's," Hypereides told him. "The citizens want to see you dead, and Xanthippos, as always, seems to favor the side to which he is speaking at the moment. But while you still live I think I can promise you wine—good wine, too, for I'll furnish it myself—and better food if you'll answer one small question for me."

Artaÿctes glanced at me, then asked, "Why don't you beat me until I speak, Hypereides? You and this fellow could manage it, I imagine."

"I wouldn't do such a thing," Hypereides said virtuously. "Not to an old acquaintance. However, there are others. . . ."

"Of course. I have my honor to consider, Hypereides. But I am not unreasonable—nor am I so stupid that I do not guess that Xanthippos sent you. What is his question?"

Hypereides grinned, then grew serious once more, rubbing his hands as though about to sell something at a good price. "I—I, Artaÿctes—desire to know whether the noble Oeobazus was in your party when you let yourself down from the wall."

Artaÿctes glanced at his son, his hard eyes so swift I was not sure that I had seen them move. "I see no harm in telling you that—he will have made good his escape by now."

Hypereides rose, smiling. "Thank you, my friend! You may trust me for everything I have promised. And more, because I'll see to it that both your lives are spared, if I can. Latro, I must confer with some people here. I want you to go back to the place where we're staying and fetch a skin of the best wine for Artaÿctes and his son. I'll tell the guards to let you in with it when you return. Bring a torch, too; it will be dark before we go back, I think."

I nodded and unbarred the door for Hypereides; but before his foot had touched the threshold, he turned to put another question to Artaÿctes. "By the way, where did you plan to cross? At Aegospotami?"

Artaÿctes shook his head. "Helle's Sea was black with your ships. At Pactye, perhaps, or farther north. May I ask why you are so much interested in my friend Oeobazus?"

But Artaÿctes's own question came too late; Hypereides was already hurrying away. I followed him out, and the soldiers who guarded Artaÿctes (who had been waiting on the wall for us to leave) returned to their posts.

The wall of Sestos varies in height from place to place as it circles the city; this was one of the highest, where I think it must be a hundred cubits at least. It commanded a fine view of countryside and the sun setting over the western lands, and I paused there for a moment to look at it. Those who stare at the sun go blind, as I well know, and thus I kept my eyes upon the land and the sun-dyed clouds, which were indeed very beautiful; but as chance would have it, I glimpsed the sun itself from the corner of my eye and saw there, in place of the usual sphere of fire, a chariot of gold drawn by four horses. I knew then that I had glimpsed a god, just as—according to my old scroll—I had seen a goddess before the death of the man who called me Lucius. It frightened me, as I suppose the goddess must have also, and I hurried down the stairs and through the streets of Sestos (which are gloomy and very cramped, as no doubt those of all such walled cities must be) to this house. It was not until I had found a skin of excellent wine and bound together a handful of splents to make a torch, that I understood the full import of what I had seen.

For what I had seen was merely this: although the sun had nearly reached the horizon, the horses of the sun had been at a full gallop. It had seemed so natural that I had not paused to question it; but as I reflected upon the sight, I realized that no charioteer would drive at the gallop if he were close to the place at which he intended to halt—how could he stop his team without the gravest danger of wrecking his chariot? Indeed, though only two horses are hitched to the chariots used in war, all soldiers know that one of the chief advantages of cavalry is that horsemen may be halted and turned so much more readily than chariots.

Clearly then, the sun does not halt at the western limit of the world, as I have always supposed, to reappear next day at the eastern in the same way that fixed stars vanish in the west to reappear in the east. No, rather the sun continues at full career, passes beneath the world, and reappears in the east just as we should see a runner dash behind some building and reappear on the opposite side. I cannot help but wonder why. Are there those living beneath the world who have need of the sun, even as we? This is something I must consider at more length when I have the leisure to do so.

It would be a weary task to set down here all the thoughts—most half-formed and some very foolish—that filled my mind as I made my way through the streets again and mounted the stairs of the tower. Artaÿctes's guards let me in without caviling, and one even fetched a krater in which to mix water with the wine I had brought. While they were thus occupied, Artaÿctes drew me aside, saying softly, "There is no need for you to sleep badly, Latro. Help us and these fools will never learn you bore arms against them."

His words confirmed what I had already gathered from my old scroll—that I had once been in the service of the Great King of Parsa. I nodded and whispered that I would certainly free them if I could.

Just then Hypereides came in, all smiles, carrying six salt pilchards on a string. There was a charcoal brazier to warm the guardroom, and he laid the fish here and there upon the coals where they would not burn. "One for each of us, and they should be good eating. Not much fruit this time of year, or much food in Sestos yet after the siege; but Latro can go out and try to find us some apples when we've finished these, if you like. And some fresh bread, Latro. Didn't you tell me you'd seen a bakery open today?"

I nodded and reminded him that I had bought bread when I went to the market.

"Excellent!" Hypereides exclaimed. "It'll be closed now, I'm afraid, but perhaps you can rouse out the baker with a few thumps on his door." He winked at Artaÿctes. "Latro's a first-rate thumper, I assure you, and commands a voice like a bull's when he wants to. Now if—"

At that moment something so extraordinary occurred that I hesitate to write of it, for I feel quite certain that I will not believe it when I read this scroll in the days that are yet to come: one of Hypereides's salted pilchards moved.

His eyes must have been sharper than mine, because he fell silent to stare at it, while I merely assumed that one of the pieces of charcoal supporting it had shifted. A moment later, I saw it flip its tail just as a hooked fish does when it is cast onto the riverbank; and in a moment more all six were flopping about on the coals as though they had been thrown alive into the fire.

To give the guards credit, they did not run; if they had, I believe I would have run as well. As for Hypereides, his face went white, and he backed away from the brazier as if it were a dog with the running disease. Artaÿctes's young son cowered like the rest of us, but Artaÿctes himself went calmly to Hypereides and laid a hand upon his shoulder, saying, "This prodigy has no reference to you, my friend. It is meant for me—Protesilaos of Elaeus is telling me that though he is as dead as a dried fish, yet he has authority from the gods to punish the man who wronged him."

Hypereides gulped, and stammered, "Yes—that's—it's one of the chief reasons they insist that you—that you and your son—They say that you stole the offerings from his tomb and—and—plowed up his sacred soil."

Artaÿctes nodded and glanced toward the fish; by that time they had ceased to jump, but he shivered as if he were cold just the same. "Hear me now, Hypereides, and promise that you will report everything I say to Xanthippos. I will pay one hundred talents to restore the shrine of Protesilaos." He hesitated as though waiting for some further sign, but there was none. "And in addition I will give you soldiers from Thought two hundred talents if you will spare my son and me. The money is at Susa, but you can keep my boy here as a hostage until it is all paid. And it will *be* paid, I swear by Ahura Mazda, the god of the gods—paid in full and in gold."

Hypereides's eyes popped from their sockets at the magnitude of the sum. It is well known that the People of Parsa are rich beyond imagining, yet I think that few have dreamed that anyone other than the Great King himself could command such wealth as this offer of Artaÿctes's suggested. "I'll tell him. I'll— In the—no, tonight. If—"

"Good! Do so." Artaÿctes squeezed Hypereides's shoulder and stepped back.

Hypereides glanced at the guards. "But I'll have to tell him everything that's happened. Latro, I don't imagine you fancy any of those fish—I know I don't. I think it's time we went home."

I will return to the citadel now—perhaps something can be done to help Artaÿctes and Artembares.

# TWO

## *Artaÿctes Dies*

THE HERALD'S CRY BROUGHT ME from my bed this morning. I was pulling on my shoes when Hypereides rapped on the door of the room I share with Io. "Latro!" he called. "Are you awake?"

Io sat up and asked what the trouble was.

I told her, "Artaÿctes is to be executed this morning."

"Do you remember who he is?"

"Yes," I said. "I know I spoke with him last night, before Hypereides and I came home."

Just then Hypereides himself opened our door. "Ah, you're up. Want to come with me to see them killed?"

I asked him who was to die, other than Artaÿctes.

"His son, I'm afraid." Hypereides shook his head sadly. "You don't remember Artaÿctes's boy?"

I cast my mind back. "I have some recollection of seeing a child last night," I told him. "Yes, I think it was a boy, a bit older than Io."

Hypereides pointed a finger at her. "*You* are to stay here, young woman! Do you understand me? You've work to do, and this will be no sight for a girl."

I followed him out into the street, where the black man was waiting for us; and the three of us set off for the sand spit on which the Great King's bridge had ended. It was there, as half a dozen heralds were still bawling (and as half Sestos was busy telling the other half) that Artaÿctes was to die. The day was overcast and windy, with gray clouds scudding along Helle's Sea from the First Sea in the north.

"This weather reminds me," Hypereides muttered, "that we must all have new cloaks before we leave here—you particularly, Latro. That rag of yours is hardly fit for a beggar."

The black man touched Hypereides's shoulder, his eyes wide.

"For you, too? Yes, of course. I said so. For all of us, in fact, even little Io."

The black man shook his head and repeated his gesture.

"Oh, ah. You want to know about our voyage—I was about to tell you. Get us to where we can see what's going on, you two, and I'll give you all the details."

By that time the people from Sestos were crowding forward and Xanthippos's troops were pushing them back with the butts of their spears. Fortunately several of the soldiers recognized Hypereides, and we were able to claim a place in front without much trouble. There was nothing to see yet but a couple of men digging a hole, apparently for the end of a timber that they had carried to the spot.

"Xanthippos isn't here," Hypereides commented. "They won't be starting for a while yet."

I asked who Xanthippos was, and he said, "Our strategist. All these soldiers are under his command. Don't you remember Artaÿctes mentioning him last night?"

I admitted I did not. The name *Artaÿctes* seemed familiar, which was natural enough since the heralds had been shouting it as we came; then I remembered telling Io that I had spoken with someone called Artaÿctes the night before.

Hypereides looked at me speculatively. "You don't remember the fish?"

I shook my head.

"They were pilchards. Do you know what a pilchard is, Latro?"

I nodded, and so did the black man. I said, "A smallish silvery fish, rather plump. They're said to be delicious."

"That's true." (People in the crowd were shouting, *"Bring him!"* and *"Where is he?"* so that Hypereides was forced to raise his voice to make himself heard.) "But pilchards are oily fish—fatty fish even when salted. Now I know that both of you are sensible men. I want to put a question to you. It's of some importance, and I want you to consider it seriously."

Both of us nodded again.

Hypereides drew a deep breath. "If some dried and salted pilchards were cast onto the coals of a charcoal brazier—with a good fire going— don't you think that the sudden melting of all their fat might make them move? Or perhaps that oil dripping from the fish onto the coals might spatter violently and, so to speak, toss the fish about?"

I nodded and the black man shrugged.

"Ah," said Hypereides. "I'm of one mind with Latro, and Latro was there and saw them, even if he doesn't remember."

Just then a roar went up from the crowd.

The black man pointed with his chin as Hypereides shouted, "Look! Here they come—worth a round hundred talents apiece, and about to be slaughtered like a couple of goats." He shook his head and appeared genuinely saddened.

The man must have been close to fifty, strongly built and of medium height, with a beard the color of iron. One saw at once, from his dress, that he was a Mede. His son appeared to be fourteen or so; his face was as unformed as the faces of most boys of that age, but he had fine, dark eyes. The man's wrists were tied in front of him.

With them was a tall, lean man in armor who bore neither a shield nor a spear. I saw no signal from him, but the heralds cried, *"Silence! Silence, everybody, for Xanthippos, the noble strategist of Thought,"* and when the chattering of the crowd had been muted a bit, he stepped forward.

*"People of Sestos,"* he said. *"Aeolians! Hellenes!"* He spoke loudly, but as if this commanding voice were natural to him. *"Hear me! I do not come before you to speak for Hellas!"*

That surprised the crowd so much that it actually fell silent, so that the birds could be heard crying above Helle's Sea.

Xanthippos continued, *"I wish that I did—that we were come at last to a time when brother no longer warred against brother."*

That drew a resounding cheer. As it died away, Hypereides grinned at me. "They're hoping that we've forgotten they were fighting us not so long ago."

*"Yet speak I do—and I am proud indeed to speak—as the representative of the Assembly of Thought. My city has returned to yours the greatest blessing that any people can possess—liberty."*

Another cheer for that.

*"For which we ask only your gratitude."*

There were shouts of thanks.

*"I said I could not speak for the Hellenes. Who knows what Tower Hill may do? Not I. Who knows the will of the wild folk of Bearland? Not I again,*

*O citizens of Sestos. And not you. Those few Rope Makers who were here took ship before your city could be freed, as you know. And as for Hill, who does not know how savagely its spears seconded the barbarian?"*

That brought a growl of anger from the crowd. Hypereides whispered, "Strike again, Xanthippos. They're still breathing."

*"Many of my brave friends—and they were friends of yours, never forget that—lie in the great grave at Clay. They were sent there not by the arrows of the barbarians but by the horse of Asopodorus of Hill."*

At this the crowd gave a little moan, as though a thousand women had felt the first pangs of labor. I reflected that it might well be true, that in years to come men might say that something new had been born today on this narrow finger of the west thrusting eastward into Helle's Sea.

*"And yet my city has many more sons, men equally brave; and whenever you may have need of them, they shall come to you with all speed."*

Wild cheering.

*"Now to the business at hand. We stand here, you and I, as servants of the gods. I need not recount to you the many crimes of this man Artaÿctes. You know them better than I. Many have counseled me that he should be returned to his own country upon the payment of a rich ransom."* It seemed to me that Xanthippos darted a glance at Hypereides here, although Hypereides appeared insensible of it. *"I have rejected that counsel."*

The crowd shouted its approval.

*"But before justice is done to Artaÿctes, we will act as only free men can—we will hold an election. In my own city, where so many urns and serving dishes are made, we cast our votes on shards of broken pottery, each citizen scratching the initial of the candidate he favors in the glaze. In Sestos, I am given to understand, your custom is to vote with stones—a white stone for yes, a black one for no, and so forth. This day, also, you shall cast your votes with stones. The boy you see beside him"*—Xanthippos pointed to him—*"is the blasphemer's son."*

There was a mutter of anger at that, and a man on my left shook his fist.

*"You of Sestos alone shall determine whether he lives or dies. If you will that he lives, move aside and let him flee. But if instead it is your will that he die, stop him, and cast a stone. The choice is yours!"*

Xanthippos motioned to the soldiers standing with Artaÿctes and his son, and one whispered in the boy's ear and slapped his back. Xanthippos had assumed that the boy would try to dash to freedom through the crowd; but he ran away from it instead, down the narrowing finger of sand and shale toward the sea, I suppose with the thought of swimming when he reached the water.

He never did. Stones flew, and a score of men at least got past the soldiers and ran after him. I saw him fall, struck on the ear by a stone as big as my fist. He got up and staggered a few steps more before being struck by half a hundred. Although I hope he died quickly, I cannot say precisely when it was that his life ended; certainly many stoned his body long after he was dead.

As for his father, after he had watched his son die, he was laid on his back upon the timber and spikes were driven through both his ankles and both wrists into the wood; when it was done, the timber was set upright in the hole that had been dug for it and rocks and sand piled around it to keep it so. Some of the women present flung stones at him also, but the soldiers forced them to stop, fearing that their stones would strike the five soldiers Xanthippos had stationed to guard him.

"Come," said Hypereides. "The real action's over, and I've a good many things to see to. Latro, I want you to buy us those cloaks we were talking about. Can you manage that if I give you the money?"

I told him I would, if there were cloaks for sale in the city.

"I'm sure there must be. Take him and Io with you so that they can pick out their own. Nothing too grand, mind you; they would only get you into trouble. Get something bright for me, though. Not red, because that's what the Rope Makers wear—not that anybody would take me for a Rope Maker, I imagine. Not yellow, either; the yellow ones fade so quickly. Make it blue or green, rich looking if they have something like that, and suited to my height." He is half a head shorter than the black man and I. "And make certain it's thick and warm."

I nodded, and he handed me four silver drachmas. The black man touched his shoulder and pretended to tug at a rope of air.

"Ah, the voyage! You're right, I promised I'd tell you about that. Well, it's simple enough. Do both of you know about the Great King's bridge?"

I said, "I remember that the heralds said this was where it ended.

I imagine that the Great King's army must have marched up the same road we came down to get here."

"Right you are. It was a bridge of boats, scores of them, I would think, all tied together by long cables, with planks laid over their decks to make a road. It was here for nearly a year, according to what I've heard, before a big storm finally broke the cables."

We nodded to show we understood.

"The People from Parsa didn't fix it, but they stored the cables here in Sestos. They must have been very costly, and of course they could be spliced if the Great King ever ordered the bridge rebuilt. Xanthippos wants to take them back to Thought to show off. They should cause quite a stir, because nobody at home has ever seen cables anything like their size." Hypereides held out his arms to indicate the circumference of the cables, and even if he was doubling their diameter, they are very large indeed.

"Well, as you can imagine," he continued, "the first thing that everybody's sure to ask is who made them and what happened to him. Xanthippos had me look into that, and I found out that the boss was a fellow called Oeobazus, one of the barbarians who let themselves down from the city wall with Artaÿctes. And last night, when you and I talked to him, Latro, Artaÿctes said that they had intended to go north, maybe as far as Miltiades's wall. Xanthippos would like to have this Oeobazus to trot out for the Assembly as well as the cables, so we're to go after him as soon as *Europa*'s ready."

I asked when that would be.

"Tomorrow afternoon, I hope." Hypereides sighed. "Which most likely means the day after. The men are touching up her caulking now, and they ought to be finished today. Then we'll have to load the stores. But there's still some to get, and I'm not getting them by standing here talking to you two. So go and see about those cloaks, like I told you. When you've done that, pack up everything—we may not come back here, I don't know."

He hurried off toward the docks after that, and the black man and I returned to Sestos and the house in which we had slept to fetch Io.

We found it empty, however.

# THREE

## *The Mantis*

HEGESISTRATUS INTERRUPTED ME, BUT NOW I write again. It is very late now, and all the others are asleep; but Io has told me that soon after the sun rises I will forget all that I have seen and heard today, and there are things that I must set down.

When the black man and I returned to this house and found Io gone, I was anxious about her; for though I cannot recall how it is I came to have such a slave, I know I love her. The black man laughed at my gloomy face and said by signs that he thought Io had followed us to see Artaÿctes killed, and I was forced to admit he was probably right.

Accordingly we left the house again and went to the market. Several of the shops fronting on it offered cloaks for sale. I bought rough, undyed ones for the black man, Io, and myself, new cloaks made without washing the oil out of the wool and woven so tightly they would shed rain. I knew that such a colored cloak as Hypereides wanted would be costly, so we bargained for a long time over ours, the black man (who is a better bargainer than I, I think) speaking much to the shopkeeper in a language I do not understand. I soon realized, however, that the shopkeeper knew something of it, though he feigned otherwise. And at length even I was able to catch a word or two—*zlh*, which I believe is "cheap," and *sel*, "jackal," a word the shopkeeper did not like.

While they were haggling, I was searching for a cloak for Hypereides. Most of the brightly dyed ones seemed too thin for winter to me. At last I found a thick, warm one of the right length, bright blue, woven of fine, soft wool. This I carried to the shopkeeper, who must have been very tired of arguing with the black man by then. I showed him our four silver drachmas and the four cloaks, and explained that the four drachmas were all the money we had.

(That was not strictly true, as I know the black man has some money of his own; but he would not have spent it for the cloaks, I feel sure, and he probably did not have it upon his person.)

If he would let us have all four cloaks for the drachmas, I said, well and good—we had a bargain; if he would not, we would have no choice but to trade elsewhere. He examined the drachmas and weighed them while the black man and I watched him to make certain he did not substitute worse ones. At last he said that he could not let all four cloaks go at such a price and that the blue one alone should bring him two drachmas at least, but that he would give us the gray cloaks we wanted for ourselves for a drachma apiece if we would buy it.

I told him we could not spare the smallest cloak, which we required for a child—after which we went to a different shop and started the entire process again. It was only then that I realized, from things that the second shopkeeper let drop, just how nervous such merchants here have become because they do not know whether the soldiers from Thought will go or stay. If they stay, these shops may hope for very good business indeed, since most of the soldiers have some plunder and there are a few who have a great deal. But if the soldiers go home and the People from Parsa return and lay siege to the city, the shops will have no business at all, because everyone saves his money to buy food during a siege. When I understood this, I contrived to mention to the black man that we would sail tomorrow, and the price of the green cloak I was examining dropped considerably.

Just then the keeper of the first shop we had visited came in (the owner of the second looking as though he hoped someday to murder him) and said he had reconsidered: we could have all four cloaks for the four drachmas. We returned to his shop with him, and he held out his hand for the money. But I thought that he deserved to be punished for making us bargain so long; thus I began examining the cloaks yet again, and while I was looking at the blue one I took care to ask the black man whether he felt it would do for Hypereides on the coming voyage.

The shopkeeper cleared his throat. "You're sailing, then? And your captain's Hypereides?"

"That's right," I told him, "but the other ships won't put out when we do. They'll be staying here for a few days more at least."

Now the shopkeeper surprised me, and the black man, too, I think.

He said, "This Hypereides—is he bald? Rather a round face? Wait, he told me the name of his ship. *Europa?*"

"Yes," I said, "that's our captain."

"Oh. Ah. Well, perhaps I shouldn't tell you this, but if you're going to get that cloak for him, he'll have at least two new ones. He came in after you left and gave me three drachmas for a really choice scarlet one." The shopkeeper took the blue cloak from me and held it up. "That one was for a bigger man, though."

I looked at the black man and he at me, and it was plain that neither of us understood.

The shopkeeper got out a waxed tablet and a stylus. "I'm going to write out a bill of sale for you. You can put your mark on it. Tell your captain that if he wants to return the blue cloak, I'll show him the price and give back his money."

He scratched away at the tablet; and when he had finished, I wrote *Latro* alongside each line in the characters I am using now, keeping it close so it would be sure to blur if he held a heated basin near the tablet to erase it. Then the black man and I carried the cloaks here and packed everything. I hoped from moment to moment that Io would return, but she did not.

When it was done, I asked the black man what he intended to do, and he made signs to show me that he was going to his room to sleep awhile. I told him I would do the same, and we parted. After a few moments, I opened the door of my room as quietly as I could and crept out just in time to see the black man slipping out his own with equal stealth. I smiled and shook my head, he grinned at me, and together we walked back to the sand spit where the Great King's bridge had ended, in the hope of finding Io.

That at least was the black man's only motive, I believe; as for me, I confess I went with a double purpose, for I meant to set Artaÿctes free should the opportunity present itself.

As we drew near the place, we met the last idlers from the crowd returning home; several told us that Artaÿctes was dead. One seemed a sensible enough fellow, so I stopped him and asked how he knew. He told us that the soldiers had pricked him with their spears without result, and at last one had driven the head of his spear into his belly to determine whether his blood would spurt; it had only leaked away like water from a sponge, so it was certain that the action of the heart had ceased.

The black man made signs then, urging me to inquire about Io. I did, and the man we were questioning said that only one child had stayed behind, a half-grown girl who was with a lame man. I did not think that Io could be considered half-grown (I remembered her well from having spoken to her this morning), and as we hurried along I asked the black man whether he knew of any such lame man. He shook his head.

Yet it was Io, and I recognized her at once. Only she, a boy, the soldiers, and the man the idler had mentioned remained with the corpse of Artaÿctes. The man with Io was leaning on a crutch, and I saw that he had lost his right foot; in its place was a wooden socket ending in a peg. This was tied to his calf with leather strips like the laces of a sandal. He was weeping while Io sought to comfort him. She waved and smiled, however, when she saw us.

I told her that she should not have disobeyed Hypereides, and though I would not beat her for it, Hypereides might. (I did not say this to her, but I feared that if he beat her too severely I might kill him. Then I myself might well be killed by the soldiers from Thought.) She explained that she had not meant to disobey, but had been sitting on the step when she had seen the lame man; he had seemed so weary and so sorrowful that she tried to comfort him, and he had asked her to go with him because both his crutch and the tip of his wooden foot sank in the sand. Thus, Io said, she had not gone to see Artaÿctes die—which was what Hypereides had forbidden—but to assist the lame man, a fellow Hellene, which Hypereides had certainly not ordered her not to do.

The black man grinned at all this, but I had to admit there was some justice in what she said. I told the lame man that she would have to return to the house with us now, but that we would help him if he, too, were ready to go back to Sestos.

He nodded and thanked me, and I let him lean upon my arm. I admit that I was curious about him, a Hellene who wept for a Mede; and so when we had gone some small distance, I asked what he knew of Artaÿctes, and whether he had been a good man.

"He was a good friend to me," the lame man answered. "The last friend I had in this part of the world."

I asked, "But weren't you Hellenes fighting the People from Parsa? I seem to recall that."

He shook his head, saying that only certain cities were at war with the Great King, some of them most unwisely. No one, he added, had fought more bravely at the Battle of Peace than Queen Artemisia, the ruler of a city of Hellenes allied with the Great King. At Clay, he said, the cavalry of Hill had been accounted the bravest of the brave, while Hill's Sacred Band had fought to the last man.

"I'm from Hill," Io told him proudly.

He smiled at her and wiped his eyes. "I knew that already, my dear; you have only to speak to tell everyone. I myself am from the Isle of Zakunthios. Do you know where that is?"

Io did not.

"It's a small island in the west, and perhaps it is because it's so small that it's so lovely, and so much loved by all its sons."

Io said politely, "I hope someday to see it, sir."

"So do I," the lame man told her. "That is, I hope to see it once more at a time when it will be safe for me to go home." Turning to me, he added, "Thank you for your help—I believe the road's firm enough for me now."

I was so busy with my own thoughts that I hardly heard him. If he had really been a friend of Artaÿctes's (and surely here no Hellene would lie about that) it seemed likely he knew Oeobazus, for whom we would soon be searching. Furthermore he might help me rescue him, if rescue were necessary. Crippled as he was, he could be of no great use in a fight; but I reflected that there is always more to a battle than fighting, and that if Artaÿctes had been his friend, Artaÿctes had perhaps found him of service.

With these thoughts in mind, I offered him the hospitality of the house Hypereides had commandeered, mentioning that we had plenty of food there and some good wine, and suggesting he might sleep there tonight if he wished, with Hypereides's permission.

He thanked me and explained that he was not short of money, Artaÿctes having rewarded him generously on many occasions. He was staying with a well-to-do family, he said, where everything was comfortable enough. "My name is Hegesistratus," he added. "Hegesistratus, son of Tellias, though Hegesistratus of Elis is what I'm generally called now."

Io said, "Oh, we've been to Elis. It was on the way to—to a place up north where King Pausanias sacrificed. Latro doesn't remember it, but the black man and I do. Why do they say you're from Elis, if you're really from Zakunthios?"

"Because I'm from Elis, too," Hegesistratus told her, "and most recently. Our family has its roots there—but this is no story for a little maid. Not even a maid from Hill."

"I'm Latro," I told him. "You already know who Io is, I imagine. Neither of us knows our friend's name—we don't speak his language—but we vouch for his character."

Hegesistratus met the black man's eyes for a moment that seemed very long to me, then spoke to him in another tongue (I think in that which the black man had used to the shopkeeper); and the black man answered him in the same way. Soon he touched Hegesistratus's forehead, and Hegesistratus touched his.

"That is the speech of Aram," Hegesistratus told me. "In it, your friend is called Seven Lions."

We were nearing the city gate then, and he asked me whether the house I had mentioned was much farther. As it happened, it was on the next street after the wall, and I told him so.

"My lodgings are on the other side of the marketplace," he said. "Might I stop, then, and take that cup of wine with you? Walking makes my stump sore"—he gestured toward his crippled leg—"and I would be very grateful for the chance to rest it a bit."

I urged him to stay as long as he wished, and told him that I would like his opinion of my sword.

# FOUR

## *Favorable Auspices*

HEGESISTRATUS HAS BEEN ON THE wall observing birds. He says our voyage will be fortunate, and he will come with us. Hypereides wanted to know whether we would find the man we seek, whether we would bring him to Xanthippos, and how the Assembly would reward us for it; but Hegesistratus would answer none of these questions, saying that telling more than one knows is a pit dug for such as he. He and I spoke together awhile, but he has left now.

An odd thing happened while the black man, Io, and I sat at wine with him; I do not understand it, so I shall record it here exactly as it took place, without comment, or at least with very little.

As we chatted, I became more and more curious concerning my sword. I had seen it lying in the chest this morning when I put on a clean chiton and again when the black man and I packed; but I had felt no curiosity about it at all. Now I could scarcely remain at my place. At one moment I feared it had been stolen. At the next, I felt certain it possessed some peculiarity upon which Hegesistratus's comments would be deeply enlightening.

As soon as he had mixed the wine and water, I rose, hurried to my room, and got out my sword. I was about to give it to him when he struck my wrist with his crutch and it fell from my hand; the black man jumped up brandishing his stool, and Io screamed.

Hegesistratus alone remained calm, never rising. He told me to pick up my sword and return it to the scabbard. (Its point had sunk so deeply into the floor that I had to use both hands to wrench it free.) I felt then as though I had wakened from a dream. The black man shouted at me, indicating the wine, then spoke loudly to Hegesistratus, pointing at me and toward the ceiling. Hegesistratus said, "He wishes me to remind you that a guest is sacred. The gods, he says, will punish one who, having invited a stranger, harms him without cause."

I nodded.

Io whispered, "Latro forgets. Sometimes—"

Hegesistratus silenced her with a gesture. "Latro, what were you going to do with that sword?"

I told him that I had wanted him to examine it.

"And do you still?"

I shook my head.

"Very well," he said, "in that case I will. Draw it again and put it on the table, please."

I did as he asked, and he laid both hands upon the flat of the blade and shut his eyes. So he sat for a long time—so long that I had rubbed my wrist and drained my wine before he opened them once more.

"What is it?" Io asked when he had withdrawn his hands.

He shivered a little, I think. "Are you—any of you—aware that divinity can be transmitted, like a disease?"

None of us spoke.

"It can. Touch a leper and you may discover that you have leprosy. The tips of your fingers whiten, or perhaps the spot appears on your chin or your cheek, because you scratched them with those fingers. So it is with divinity. One finds temples in Riverland in which the priests, when they have served their god, must wash and change their clothing before leaving; this though the god, in most cases, is not present." Hegesistratus sighed. "This has been handled by a minor deity, I think."

He looked his question at me, but I could only shake my head.

"Have you killed with it?"

I said, "I don't know. I suppose so."

Io told me, "You killed some of the Rope Makers'—" then covered her mouth with her hand.

Hegesistratus asked, "He killed Rope Makers? You may tell me—I assure you that I am no friend of theirs."

"Just some of their slaves," Io explained. "They caught us once, but Latro and the black man killed a lot of them first."

Hegesistratus sipped his wine. "That was far from here, I take it?"

"Yes, sir. Back in Cowland."

"That is well, for the dead may walk. Particularly those slain with this blade."

I looked around, for I had heard Hypereides's step. He was surprised to see Hegesistratus; but when I had introduced them, he greeted and welcomed him.

Hegesistratus said, "I hope that you will excuse me for not rising. I am lame."

"Of course, of course." The black man had brought a stool for Hypereides, and he sat down. "I'm not getting around very well myself. Been tramping my legs off all over the city."

Hegesistratus nodded. "And there is another matter about which I owe you an apology. A moment ago my friend Latro called me Hegesistratus of Zakunthios. That is true; I was born there and grew to manhood there. But I am properly Hegesistratus, son of Tellias—"

Hypereides started.

"And I am better known as Hegesistratus of Elis."

Hypereides said, "You were Mardonius's mantis at Clay. You told him not to advance—that's what I've heard."

Hegesistratus nodded again. "Does that make me a criminal in your eyes? If so, I am in your power. Both these men obey you, and one has a sword."

Hypereides drew a deep breath and let it out. "Mardonius is dead. I think we ought to let the dead lie."

"As do I, if they will."

"And if we're going after revenge, we'll have to enslave just about everyone in this city. Then who'd hold the place against the Great King? Xanthippos himself said that."

I had poured him a cup of wine, and he accepted it. "Do you know what the Assembly wanted to do to Hill?"

Hegesistratus shook his head.

"Level it! Sell the people of Cowland to the Crimson Men! I'm in leather—in peacetime, I mean. Can you imagine what that would have done to the leather trade?" Even though it was cold, Hypereides wiped his face with his hand as if he were sweating. "It was the Rope Makers who prevented it. Well, the gods know that I'm no friend to the Rope Makers—what are you snickering at, young woman?"

Io said, "You used the same words he did, sir. Just before you came in. That's lucky, they say."

"Why, so it is." Turning back to Hegesistratus, Hypereides asked, "Isn't it? You ought to know, if anybody does."

"It is," the mantis said. "It is always fortunate when men agree."

"You've got a point there," Hypereides conceded. "Now look here, I'm the skipper of the *Europa,* and we're close to sailing—we should cast off around midmorning tomorrow. How much would you charge me to see what the gods have to say about our voyage, and maybe give warning of any special dangers we may face?"

"Nothing," Hegesistratus replied.

"You mean you won't do it?"

"I mean no more than I say—that I will do it and charge you nothing. You intend to go up Helle's Sea after Oeobazus?"

Hypereides looked amazed, and so, I confess, did I.

Hegesistratus smiled. "There is no mystery here, believe me. Before he died, Artaÿctes told me you had been asking about Oeobazus, as Io will verify."

I told Hypereides, "The black man and I went back when we were through packing. Artaÿctes was dead, and there was no one there but Hegesistratus and Io, a boy, and the soldiers. That was how we met Hegesistratus; he was mourning Artaÿctes."

"As I still am," Hegesistratus added. "And of course you thought that it might be useful to talk with someone who knew Oeobazus by sight. You revealed that quite clearly while Io was bringing our water and this really excellent wine. Very well. He is a Mede—not a man of Parsa, though we Hellenes often call them Medes, but a true Mede—of thirty-five or so, rather taller than most, a strong man and a superb horseman. There is a long scar on his right cheek, only partially concealed by his beard; he told me once that he got it as a boy when he tried to gallop through a thicket. Now may I ask Hypereides why he was trampling around Sestos? I would have thought that most of the things his ship requires would be easily found, or else clearly impossible to obtain. What is it that appears possible, and yet proves so elusive?"

Hypereides said, "Somebody who speaks the dialects of the northern tribes, knows their customs, and will come along with us. Either Oeobazus is safely back in the Empire and out of our reach, or he's being held in one of the civilized cities to the north—which ought to be easy—or he's in some barbarous kingdom on this side of the First Sea. So that's where we may run into trouble, and I'd like to be ready to deal with it."

Hegesistratus stroked his own beard, which is black, curly, and very thick, and said, "You may have found him."

He took leave of us then, and while the black man prepared the second meal, Io drew me aside. "Master," she asked, "were you really going to kill him?"

"Of course not," I said.

"Well, you looked like it. You came in so fast with your sword, and you looked like you were going to split his head. I think you would have, if he hadn't been so quick."

I explained that I had merely wanted him to see it, but she looked unconvinced and asked me many questions about the things the black man and I did today. Describing them reminded me that I had not yet shown Hypereides the cloaks we bought, so when I had satisfied Io's curiosity, I got them and showed them to him. He seemed pleased with them, and most of all with his own; but he said nothing about the scarlet cloak, and I thought it would be unwise to inquire about it.

After we had eaten, Io brought me this scroll and urged me to write down everything that happened today; she said she felt sure that we would want to refer to it later. I have done so, giving everything of any importance that was said in detail and in the words the speakers used, as well as I can write them in my own tongue.

As I wrote before, Hegesistratus interrupted me. He wanted to know where Io and I had been when we had been captured by the Rope Makers, and when I could not tell him, he woke Io and spoke to her. Afterward he said he was going onto the wall to observe the flights of birds; it was dark, when birds seldom fly, though there are some kinds that do, I know. He was gone a long while, but when he returned he spoke with Hypereides, telling him that the word of the gods was favorable and that he would go with us if Hypereides wished it. Hypereides was delighted and asked him many questions, of which he answered only two or three—and even these in ways that told Hypereides very little.

At last, when Hypereides had returned to bed, Hegesistratus sat with me before this fire. He said he wished that he could read this scroll. I told him I would read it to him if he liked, and added I had another in my chest that was full of writing.

"Perhaps I will ask you to do that soon," he said. "Io tells me you do not remember, and I wonder how much you are aware of it."

"I know it," I said. "At least, I see that others remember the days that are gone. That seems strange to me, and yet there are certain things that I remember, too—my father and mother, and the house where we lived."

"I understand," he said. "But you do not remember how you were befriended by Pausanias of Rope?"

I told him I recalled Io's saying that we had been to Elis when we went with King Pausanias to sacrifice, and asked if this Pausanias was a real king.

Hegesistratus shook his head. "No, but he is often called that. The Rope Makers are accustomed to having a king as their leader; since he is their leader now, they call him a king. In reality he stands regent for King Pleistarchos, who is still a boy. Pausanias is his uncle."

I ventured that if Pausanias had befriended Io, the black man, and me, he must at least be a good man.

At that, Hegesistratus stared long into the flames, seeing more there (I think) than I did. At last he said, "If he were of any other nation, I would call him an evil one. Latro, if you do not remember Pausanias, do you perhaps recall a Tisamenus of Elis?"

I did not, but I asked Hegesistratus whether this Tisamenus was a relative of his, since both were said to be "of Elis."

"Only a very distant cousin," Hegesistratus told me. "Both our families are of the Iamidae; but they have been rivals since the Golden Age, when the gods dwelled among men."

"I wish this were the Golden Age," I said, "then I might go to some god, and he might make me as others are."

"You are less different from them than you believe, nor is it easy for men to earn the gratitude of the gods; and they are not much prone to it."

My heart told me he was right.

"Io has told me that you see the gods already. So do I, at times."

I confessed I had not known I did.

"Often I would be happier if I could forget what I have seen as quickly as you do." Hegesistratus paused. "Latro, I think it likely that Tisamenus, who hates me, has charmed you. Will you permit me to break his charm, if I can?" He swayed from side to side as he spoke, as a young tree may sway in a breeze that is strong yet gentle. He held up both his hands, their fingers splayed like the petals of two flowers.

Now, though I recall what he asked me, I do not remember my answer. He is gone, and the small knife I brought to sharpen my stylus is smeared with blood.

# FIVE

## *Our Ship*

THE *EUROPA* SAILED FROM SESTOS today, when the sun was already halfway down the sky. We could have gone much earlier. Our captain, Hypereides, found one thing wrong, then another, until at last the lame man who seems ill came aboard. Then there was no more such faultfinding.

We rowed out of the harbor. It was hard work, but pleasant, too. Once we were well into Helle's Sea, we hoisted sail; with this blustering wind in the west, there is no need to row. The sailors say the eastern bank is the Great King's, and should the wind blow us too near it we will have to row again. As I began to write this, we passed three ships of the same kind as ours. They were returning to Sestos, or so it appeared, and had to row. With all their oars rising and falling, they seemed six-winged birds flying low over the wintery sea.

Io came to speak with the black man and me. She warned me many times that this scroll will fall to bits if it becomes wet; I promised as many times to put it away in my chest as soon as I have finished writing. I asked about the man with the crutch. She said that his name is He-gesistratus; that the black man and I know him (the black man nodded to this), and that she has been nursing him. They have laid him aft beneath the storming deck, where he is out of the wind—he is asleep now. I asked what his illness is, but she would not tell me.

The kybernetes has been going down the benches talking to the sailors. He is the oldest man aboard, older I think than the lame man or Hypereides, small and spare. Much of his hair is gone; what remains is gray. He came to our bench, smiled at Io, and said that it was good to have her on board again. She told me we once went around Redface Island on this ship, but I do not know where it lies. The kybernetes made the black man and me show him our hands. When he had felt them, he said they were not hard enough. Mine are very hard—I can see I have been doing a lot of manual work—but he said they must be harder than they are before I can row all day. We will have to row more, he said, so that we will be ready for it if ever we must row for our lives. Io told me he is an old sailor who knows more about ships and the sea than Hypereides, although Hypereides knows a great deal. Hypereides paid for this ship (because the Assembly of Thought made him); thus he is our captain. I said he seemed a clever man to me—perhaps too clever. She assured me that he is a very good man, though he knows a great deal about money.

I should say here that the black man and I have the upper bench on the port side. It is an upper bench, Io says, so that we can sit together, and it is near the prow because the best rowers are at the stern, where all the others can see them and take the beat from them. The black man, who sits nearer to the sea, is a thranite—a "bench-man." I am a zygite—a "thwart-man." This is because the black man rows against the parodos, which is like a balcony hung from the side of the ship. I row against the thwart, or rather against a thick peg in it. When the ship is under sail, men can be stationed on the parodos to keep the ship from heeling too much; but when we row, anyone who walks along it must step over the looms of the thranites' oars.

I should say also that the men below us are thalamites. It means "inside-men," I believe. Their oars pass through holes in the side of the ship, and there are greased-leather boots around their looms. One of the sailors was punished earlier (I do not know for what reason). The shield-men bound him to a thalamite bench with his head out the oar hole. He must have felt as if a bucket of cold seawater were being thrown in his face each time he drew breath. He looked repentant enough, and cowed enough, when they untied him.

The black man was gone for a while. When he came back, I asked where he had been, but he would only shake his head. Now he sits staring at the waves. There are leather curtains along the railing to keep out spray, but they do not come as high as our heads.

———

We came to shore to spend the night here, hauling our ship onto the beach. We built fires to warm ourselves and to cook on—there is plenty of driftwood—and I am writing by the light of one now, while everyone else is asleep. This fire was nearly dead, but I have collected more wood. A moment ago one of the sailors woke, thanked me, and went back to sleep.

There is a tent for Hypereides, the kybernetes, Acetes, and Hegesistratus. If it rains, we will make more from the sail and the battle sail; but now we sleep beside these fires, rolled in our cloaks and huddled together for warmth. When I asked where we were going, Io said to Pactye, where the wall is.

I woke and saw a woman watching our camp. The new moon was high and bright, so that I could see her quite clearly, standing just beyond the shadows of the pines. Two of Acetes's shieldmen were on guard, but they did not see her, or at least did not pay heed to her. I got up and walked toward her, thinking that she would vanish into the shadows when I came too close, but she did not. I cannot have lain with a woman in a long time; there was a tremor in my loins like the shaking of the sail when we tried to steer too near the wind. There are no women on our ship save for Io.

This woman was small and grave and very lovely. I greeted her and asked how I might serve her.

"I am the bride of this tree," she said, and pointed to the tallest pine. "Most who come to my wood sacrifice to me, and I wondered why you—who are so many—did not."

I thought I understood then that she was the priestess of some rural shrine. I explained that I was not the leader of the men she saw sleeping on the beach, but that I supposed they had not sacrificed because we had no victim.

"I need not have a lamb or a kid," she told me. "A cake and a little honey will be sufficient."

I returned to the camp. Tonight the black man, Io, and I ate with the four in the tent, the black man having prepared our food; thus I knew that Hypereides had honey among his stores. I found a pot sealed with beeswax, kneaded some of the honey with meal, water, salt, and sesame, and baked the dough in the embers of the fire. When both sides

of the cake were brown, I carried it to her, with the honey and a skin
of wine.

She led me to the foot of the pine, where there was a flat stone. I
asked her what I should say when I laid our offerings there. She said,
"There are rhymes men use, and others favored by their wives and daughters; but all of them have forgotten the true way, which is to present
what is offered without speaking a word."

I set the cake on the stone, poured a little honey on it, and set down
the pot of honey beside it. Opening the wineskin, I poured some on the
ground.

She smiled and sat down before the stone with her back to the bole
of the tree, broke off a piece of the cake, dipped it into the honey, and
ate it. Bowing, I offered her the skin of wine; she took it from me and
drank deeply of the unmixed wine, wiped her mouth on the back of her
hand, and motioned for me to sit across from her.

I did, believing I knew what would soon come, but unsure how I
might bring it about, since the altar stone lay between us. She returned
the skin to me, and I swallowed the hot wine.

"You may speak now," she said. "What is it you wish?"

A moment before I had known; now I knew only confusion.

"Fertility for your fields?" She smiled again.

"Have I fields?" I asked her. "I do not know."

"Rest, perhaps? We give that as well. And cool shade, but you will
not want that now."

I shook my head and tried to speak.

"I cannot take you to your fields," she told me, "that lies beyond
my power. But I can show them to you, if you like."

I nodded and sprang up, extending my hand to her. She rose, too,
the wineskin upon her shoulder, and took it.

At once bright sunshine covered the world. The trees, the beach,
the ship, and the sleeping men all vanished. We walked over furrows
of new-turned earth in which the worms yet writhed. Before us went a
man with grizzled hair, one hand on the plow, an ox goad in the other.
Over his bent back, I saw a garden, a vineyard, and a low white house.
"You may speak to him if you like," the young woman said, "but he
will not hear you." She took another swallow from the skin.

"Then I will not speak." I wanted to ask her then whether these fields were indeed mine, and if so why the old man plowed them; yet I knew they were, and that the garden, vineyard, and house were mine as well. I even guessed that it was my father who plowed.

"It will be a good harvest," she told me. "Because I am here."

I asked her, "How did you do this? Why can't I stay?"

She pointed to the sun, and I saw that it was almost at the horizon; already the shadows were long. "Do you wish to see the house?"

I nodded and we went there, passing through the vineyard on the way. She plucked some grapes and ate them, putting one into my mouth. It tasted sweeter than I had thought any grape could, and I told her so, adding that the sweetness must have come from her fingers.

"It is not so," she told me. "These grapes taste sweet to you because they are your own." In the thick shadows under the vines I could see stars reflected in water.

Something that was neither ape nor bear crouched beside the doorstep, hairy and uncouth, yet possessing an air of friendship and goodwill, like an old dog that greets its master. Its eyes held golden sparks, and when I saw them I remembered (just as I remember now) how I had seen them dance about the room once when I was small. This hairy being did not move as we approached it, though its golden eyes followed us as we passed.

The door stood open, so that we entered without difficulty, though I felt we would have passed through it just as easily if it had been barred. Inside a kettle bubbled on the fire, and an old woman sat with her arms upon an old table and her head upon her arms.

"Mother!" I said. "Oh, Mother!" It seemed to me that the words had been snatched from my throat.

"*Lucius!*" She rose at the sound of my voice and embraced me. Her face was aged now, lined, and streaked with tears; yet I would have known it at once anywhere. She clasped me to her, weeping and repeating, "*Lucius, you're back. You're back! We thought you were dead. We thought you were dead!*"

And all that time, although my mother held me in her arms as she had when I was a child, I could see across her shoulder that she slept still, her head cradled in her arms.

At last she kissed me and turned to the young woman saying, "*Welcome, my dear! No, you must welcome me if you will, and not me you. This is my son's house, not mine. Am I—are my husband and I—welcome here?"*

The young woman, who had been drinking from the skin while my mother and I embraced, swayed a trifle but nodded and smiled.

My mother rushed to the door, calling, *"He's back! Lucius is home!"*

The plowman did not turn, guiding his plow and thrusting at one of his oxen with the long, iron-tipped goad he carried. The sun had touched the muddy fields; I could see our beached ship in the darkness at the bottom of the furrows, so that it seemed that this farm, lit by the dying rays of the sun, hovered over a benighted world that the toe of the plow had reached.

"We're going now," the young woman said thickly. "Aren't we going to make love?"

I shook my head, one arm around my mother and my other hand clutching the frame of the kitchen door. They melted as clotted honey does, warmed in one's mouth.

"Well, I do," she said.

The last glimmer of sunshine faded, and the air grew cold. Through dark boughs I saw the sea, our dying fires, and the ship lying on the beach. The young woman pressed her lips to mine; I felt then that I drank old wine out of a cup of new-turned wood. Together we sank to pine needles and fern.

Twice I lay with her, weeping the first and laughing the second time. We drank more wine. I told her that I loved her while she vowed she would never leave me, each laughing at the other because both knew we lied and that our lies were without harm and without malice. A rabbit blundered into the moonlight, fixed us with one bright eye, exclaimed, *"Elata!"* and fled. I asked if that was her name, and she nodded while drinking deep from the skin, then kissed me again.

Far off at first, then nearer and nearer, I heard the sound of dogs coursing deer. Vaguely I recalled that many who by some ill stroke of fortune have found themselves in the path of such a hunt have been torn to bits by the hounds. I wished then that I had put on my sword before I carried our offering to the tree. Elata was sleeping with her head in my lap, but I rose—nearly falling—with her in my arms, intending to carry her to one of the fires on the beach.

Before I could take a step, there was a crash of splintering limbs. A stag bounded from the shelter of the shadows, saw the fires (or perhaps only winded the smoke), and sprang back, nearly knocking me down. I could hear its labored breathing, like the bellows of a forge, smell its fear.

Elata stirred sleepily in my arms as the stag dashed away, and the baying of the hounds sounded closer than before; I set her on her feet, intending to lead her to the fires. She kissed me and pointed, announcing with drunken solemnity, " 'Nother man coming to see me from your ship."

# SIX

## *The Nymph*

ELATA RETURNED A MOMENT AGO, pleading with me to ex-
tinguish this fire. I would not, though the rest are only embers. I
know she has lain with Hegesistratus, and after that, I believe, with one
of Acetes's shieldmen. Now she has washed in the stream where we draw
our water; but when I suggested that she dry herself at my fire, she
seemed afraid and asked me to put it out, kissing and begging while
one hand crept under my chiton.

I am very tired; if Elata wishes to lie with a man again, she will
have to choose another one. Yet before I sleep, I must write about the
woman (Hegesistratus calls her a goddess) with the piebald hounds.
What she said and what Hegesistratus said may be important tomorrow.

The goddess was young, less voluptuous than Elata and more beautiful—I feel certain she has never know a man. There were others with
her, beautiful women also. Them I could not see as well, because they
shunned the brilliant moonlight in which the Huntress shone so boldly.

But first I should tell of her hounds; we saw them before the Huntress and her retinue. Having no sword, I had snatched up a stick. When
I saw those hounds, I understood how foolish that had been—a reed
would have been of equal service. Each was as big as a calf, and there
were twenty at least. Leaning heavily upon my arm (and in truth I do
not think she could have stood alone) Elata saved me. The fierce hounds
fawned on her, snuffling her scent and licking her fingers with their
great, rough tongues when she stroked their heads. I did not venture
any familiarity with them, but they did not harm me.

Soon the Huntress appeared with her silver bow. She smiled at us,
but her smile was without friendship; if her hounds had brought the

stag to bay, her smile would have been the same, or so it seemed to me. Yet how delicate she was! How lovely!

"The man who forgets." Thus she named me; her voice was a girl's, but there was the shout of a hunting horn in it, high and clear. "You will not have forgotten me." Then she touched me with her bow. At once I remembered how I had met her at the crossroads, though at first, and at the last, she had been both older and smaller, flanked by huge black dogs of another breed. I recalled, too, that she was a queen, though she looked so young; and I bowed to her as I had before.

"I see that you've debauched my maid." Half-smiling, she pointed. I replied, "If you say it, Dark Mother."

She shook her head. "Call me Huntress."

"Yes, Huntress, if that is what you wish."

"You would furnish my pets some sport, perhaps. Would you like a running start? I might permit you a stade or two." Her nymphs were clustering in the darkness behind her; I could hear the silver chimes of their laughter.

I said, "As you wish, Huntress. The end will be the same." Yet the fires on the beach were not much more than a stade away, and I wondered whether I might not snatch up a brand. With fire in my hands and the sleeping sailors roused, the hunt might take a different turn.

A new voice, a man's, called, *"Latro?"*

"Over here," I said, hardly raising my voice.

*"Is there someone with you?"*

I nearly smiled at that. The Huntress answered, "Surely you know us, mantis."

Hegesistratus was nearer now, so that it seemed to me that he must certainly have seen the Huntress in the moonlight; but he said, "Is that a woman by the tree?" Though he had the help of his crutch, he could walk only with difficulty over the dark, uneven ground. I dropped my stick and extended my hand to him; he took it, and at once bowed his head before the Huntress. The Hellenes do not kneel as we do, nor prostrate themselves like the peoples of the East; yet it seems to me that there is more honor for the gods in the bent heads of men who will not kiss the dust for anyone.

"Whom do you serve, Hegesistratus?"

He murmured, "You, Cynthia, should you wish it."

"And you, Latro? Will you serve me again, if I ask it?"

My bowels had turned as milk does in a churn, and the arm with which I supported Elata shook; but I reminded myself that this uncanny woman had given one memory at least back to me—that of my earlier meeting with her. (I have forgotten it now, though I recall that I remembered it not long ago; and I recall still what I thought and said of it.) "You're a queen," I told her humbly. "Even if I wished to, how could I refuse?"

"Others have sometimes managed it. Now listen, both of you. No, by my virginity! Hear me, all three of you."

The girls in the shadows gasped.

"Latro named me a queen. Soon you'll meet another—you may rely upon me for that. She has a strong protector, and I intend to make use of him to flush a boar; all of you must aid, and not oppose, her. But when the moment comes, the slut must lose. It will be at my brother's house—you know it, mantis—and thus you should be on friendly soil. Press on, north and west, until you meet her. The queen will save you, if you don't turn south."

Hegesistratus bowed and I assured her we would do our best, although I did not understand anything she had told us. One of her huge hounds was snuffling Hegesistratus's feet. She glanced at it and said, "Yes, take that scent well."

She told Hegesistratus, "Latro has all the qualities of a hero save one—he forgets instructions. You must see to those. My queen must win in order that the prince may be destroyed—and thus this queen must not win."

He bowed lower still.

"You bring victory, Latro, so you must drive for my prince. If you succeed you'll be rewarded. What is it you wish?"

"My home," I told her, for my heart was still bursting from the sight of it.

"What? Barley fields, pigpens, and cowsheds? They aren't mine to give. I have it—do you remember what it was you asked of Kore?"

I shook my head.

"It was to be reunited with your friends. She granted your wish, sending you to some of them at least. They were dead or dying, as was only to be expected since Kore is the Queen of the Shades. I shall return you to your friends also—but to living ones, for I have no interest in the dead."

Hegesistratus whispered, "Yet you are she who brings sudden death to women."

I was so happy I scarcely heard him. Releasing Elata, I fell to my knees. "Huntress, you are too good!"

She smiled bitterly. "So many have said. You are content, then, with your reward?"

"More than content!"

"I'm delighted to hear it. You shall be punished as well, for what you've done tonight to my maid, losing for a while at least what you're pleased to call your manhood." She advanced toward Hegesistratus; though she was hardly taller than he, she appeared to tower above him. "As for you, you shall not choose your reward. Your filthy longings are known to me, so there is no need of it—that soiled child shall be yours for the present, though Latro has been there before you."

Hegesistratus was already supporting Elata as I had a few moments before; he murmured his thanks.

"But you may have her only until you come this way again," the Huntress warned him. "Whenever you do, she shall be free to reoccupy her home."

At her final word, all were gone—the Huntress herself, her pack, and the maidens of her train; only the mantis, Elata, and I remained in the darkness beneath the largest pine. For a long moment I thought I heard the wild baying of the hounds, far and faint; but even that faded.

Hegesistratus was too lame to walk well over the stones and the slippery carpet of fallen pine needles, and Elata was still too drunk. In the end I carried her down to the beach while he held on to my arm. As we went, I begged him to explain what had taken place—to tell me who the Huntress was and just what power she wielded. He promised he would; but he would not do so then, leading Elata far away from the fires instead. Near the water, where the sand was moist and packed by the waves, he could walk well enough.

Thus I wrote as I did, beginning with the time I noticed Elata watching us. When I had finished writing of the stag, Hegesistratus returned and spoke with me as he had promised. While we talked, Elata returned as well, and washed herself in the stream.

I asked Hegesistratus who the Huntress was, and added that he seemed to know her.

"Only by reputation," he told me. "I had never seen her before. You have, obviously."

I could no longer remember the time, but I felt that was correct and told him so.

"She is a goddess," he told me. "Could you think her an ordinary woman when you spoke to her?"

"I thought her a woman," I said, "because that was how she appeared to me—but certainly not an ordinary one. Is her name Cynthia?"

"That is one of them," Hegesistratus told me. "She has a great many. Do you know of the Destroyer?"

I shook my head and said that from the sound of his name I did not wish to.

"You are sadly mistaken, forgetting how many things should be destroyed—wolves and lions, for example. Why, he even kills mice."

At that, some memory called through the mist that seems to fill the back of my head, and I said that though there might be no harm and even some good in the destruction of mice, I was far from sure I would wish to see all the wolves and lions dead.

"You would if you kept sheep or goats," Hegesistratus told me practically, "or even cattle. Do you have many cattle? The goddess implied you did."

I said that I owned a yoke of oxen at least, if the vision Elata had shown me was true. After that I had to tell him all about it—how she had returned me to a place she had said (and I had truly felt) was my home, and all that we had seen and done there. When I asked how she had accomplished it, he admitted he did not know and wondered aloud if such things were still in her power. I asked whether she was a witch.

"No," he said, "that is a very different thing, believe me. She is a dryad, a kind of nymph."

I said, "I thought that only meant a bride, a marriageable young woman."

Hegesistratus nodded. "Since you are a foreigner, that is easy to understand. Of all the unseen beings, the nymphs are nearest us; they are not even immortals, although they are very long-lived. Our country people both fear and love them, and as a compliment to a girl, her swain may pretend to believe her a nymph in disguise. From such frivolity, 'nymph' has become a commonplace compliment."

I said, "I see. It would seem that another way in which they are much like us is that they, too, must obey the Huntress, whom you say is a goddess."

"She is," Hegesistratus affirmed. "She is the sister—in fact more than a sister, the twin—of the Destroyer, of whom we just were speaking. He is one of the best of the Twelve, a true friend to men, the patron of divination, of healing, and of all the other arts. His sister . . ."

Seeing his expression I said, "Is not quite so friendly, I take it."

Just then Io came to sit with us, rubbing her eyes but full of curiosity. "Who's that woman?" she asked Hegesistratus. "I woke up, and she was lying next to me. She says she belongs to you."

Hegesistratus told her that was true.

"Then you'd better find her some clothes, or there may be trouble when the sailors wake up."

I sent Io to bring Elata's gown, which had been left under the pine.

Half to himself, Hegesistratus said, "I wish there were a place on the ship where she would be out of sight. I hate the thought of them ogling her." I pointed out that he need only put her forward of the first bench, at which he chuckled. "You are right, of course, when the men are rowing; but most of the time they are not."

I said, "Even when they're not, only those nearest her will be able to see her clearly, because the ship's so long and slender. But is what the sailors are going to want from her so different from what you want?"

"My filthy desires, you mean. That was what the goddess called them."

I nodded.

"She also indicated that you had the nymph before me."

I forbore telling him that I had her twice, and apologized, mentioning that the Huntress had not yet given him Elata when we had lain together.

He sighed. "Nor would I have her now if you had not. As for those filthy desires of mine, only a woman would call them that, and not very many of them. I lost my wife, you see, some years ago; and it is not easy for a lame man far from home to find a new one. Or for any man alive to find as good a one, for that matter."

I asked, "Doesn't the Huntress have lovers of her own?"

Hegesistratus shook his head. "She has had a few—or at least men or gods who wanted to be. But they all came to bad ends, and quickly. There is a story . . . I don't know whether it's true."

I urged him to tell it anyway, for though I am so tired, I know how important it may be to learn as much as possible about the Huntress.

"All right. She is the daughter of the Thunderer—I don't think I've mentioned that—and according to this legend, at the age of three she came to him and asked for as many names as her brother, a bow and silver arrows, to be queen of the nymphs, and a great many other things; and when he promised to grant all her wishes, she asked that she might be full-grown at once, like her parthenogenetic sister the Lady of Thought, who was of age when she sprang from her father's head. That, too, was granted her, and it is sometimes said that because of it she has never grown up in truth."

I suggested that the same thing could be said of this Lady of Thought, and Hegesistratus agreed. "Neither one has ever had a real lover, as far as anybody knows. But the Lady of Thought, at least, does not insist upon virginity in others. It may be that she is not a whole woman, just as certain men are not whole men, because of the way she was born."

Io returned then to report that she had found Elata's gown and covered her with it. She said also that there was a large animal moving among the trees; it had frightened her so much she had snatched up the gown and run. Hegesistratus and I agreed it was probably a cow, but she seemed doubtful. He asked for her help in protecting Elata, to which she readily consented after receiving my permission. I suggested that the boy might help as well, but they both insist that there is no boy on our ship.

Now I see the first faint light of dawn.

# SEVEN

## *Oeobazus Is Among the Apsinthians*

HEGESISTRATUS SAID, "IT IS BOTH bad news for us, and good. But I confess that I would not change it if I could. The news might so easily be worse."

Our captain nodded, rubbing his bald head, as I believe he must often do when he wants to think.

Io, who had gone with Hegesistratus to watch Elata, asked them, "Who are the Apsinthians?"

But before I write the rest of the things that were said today in the cookshop, I should write here who these people are and so forth, though perhaps something about them is written elsewhere in this book already. (I have been looking, but have found only a little.)

This town is called Pactye; it is on Helle's Sea. When I was unrolling my old book—because I wished to find how I came to own a slave—I found a passage recounting an oracle of the Shining God in which he told me: *But you must cross the narrow sea.* A short time ago I asked Lyson (he is one of the sailors) whether Helle's Sea was narrow. He says it is very narrow. I asked then if there was a sea narrower still somewhere, but he does not think so. He said also that we have never crossed it, but only sailed up its western coast. He says that the eastern shore is governed by a satrap of the Great King's, and we would be captured or killed if we crossed.

Nevertheless, I think that this is the sea I must cross if I am to be healed as the Shining God seems to have promised me. Here is something else I wrote (I know the hand is mine) in that book: *Look under the sun if you would see!* Since I am not blind and have no wish to be a mantis like Hegesistratus, it must mean to see the past. That is the thing I cannot do; yesterday and all the days behind it seem wrapped in mist. I asked Io whether she, too, was blinded by mist when she tried to look back. She said that the mist was there only when she tried to remember the years when she was small; that seems strange to me, for they are the only ones I have not lost.

Hegesistratus the mantis is forty or a little younger; he limps and has a curly beard. His wife, Elata, is very lovely—wanton, too, I think. He never leaves her unless he must, and then my slave watches her for him. Since I have no need of her now, I have no reason to object.

It was Io who told me most of the things I know about these people. She is my slave, of eleven or twelve, I would guess. I should ask her how old she is; surely she must know. I think she must be somewhat tall for her age, and her little face is lovely; her long brown hair looks almost black.

There is a black man, too. He is my friend, I think, but I have not seen him since we tied up. He spoke with Hegesistratus in a foreign tongue and went to the market with the others. But when Hegesistratus returned, with Elata and Io, this man was not with them. He is tall and strong, his hair curls more even than Hegesistratus's beard, and his teeth are large and very white; he is about my own age, I would say.

Our trierarch is Hypereides. He is a hand's breadth below my height, bald (as I said), and exceedingly lively, talking and hurrying here and there. I polished his armor before we docked, and he wore it when we landed. It is very good armor, if I am any judge; and perhaps possesses a spirit, for when I polished it, it seemed a tall woman with a shining face stood behind me, though when I looked, she was not there.

I should mention also that I have a sword. Hypereides had me wear her when we went ashore. I did not know where she was, but Io showed me this chest (I am sitting on it) and my sword was in it. She is a fine one with a leather grip and a bronze guard, and hangs from a bronze belt such as men wear. FALCATA is written on her blade in the characters I use. It was while I was getting her that I found my old scroll in this chest.

Hypereides told us the Apsinthians' land lies north and west of the Chersonese. That is good, because it is farther from the Empire; but bad, too, since we cannot reach it in our ship without sailing back down Helle's Sea in the direction we have come and rounding the tip of the peninsula.

Little Io wanted to know what Oeobazus was doing among the barbarians. Hegesistratus shrugged and said, "He may not have gone there freely. If you force me to guess, my guess is that he was captured and carried there—the barbarians in this part of the world are forever fighting, raiding, and murdering each other, and robbing and enslaving anyone who ventures too near their territory without an army the size of the Great King's. But all I actually know is that I came across a barbarian who swears that another barbarian—a man he knows well and trusts—told him the Apsinthians have such a captive."

Our captain pushed away his greasy trencher. "But you can learn more, can't you? Can't you consult the gods?"

"I can consult the gods indeed," the mantis acknowledged. "How much the gods will tell me . . ." He completed his sentence with another shrug.

"Just the same, we shouldn't make any definite plans until you do. What'll you require?"

While they talked about that, Elata showed me the bracelet that Hegesistratus had bought her. It is Thracian work, or so she said. The gold is crudely yet cleverly shaped into bunches of grapes and grape leaves, from which peep two eyes with blue stones at their centers; and the whole is bound together by the twining grape tendrils. Io says it reminds her of the big tree half-smothered under wild vines at the place where Hegesistratus found Elata, though I could not remember the place even when I studied the bracelet.

Hypereides said, "Go with them, Latro. Do as Hegesistratus tells you."

I was surprised, not having paid a great deal of attention to their talk; but I stood up when Hegesistratus did. Smiling as she drained her wine, Elata asked, "Are we to come, too?"

Hegesistratus nodded. "There is a sacred grove near the city; we will use that." To Hypereides he added, "Are you sure you do not want to be present?"

"I wish I could—not that I'd be of much help, but because I'd like to know as much as possible as soon as I can. But if we're going to sail around Cape Mastursia, there's a lot I have to attend to first."

"Your absence may affect the result," the mantis warned him.

Hypereides rose. "All right, I'll join you later if I can. A sacred grove, you said? Who's it sacred to?"

"Itys," Hegesistratus told him.

As we left the cookshop for the wet streets of Pactye, Io asked, "What did you and Hypereides do, master?" I described our morning (we had visited officials and haggled with chandlers, mostly, and on several occasions I had run back to the ship with messages), and asked about hers. She told me she and Elata had gone shopping while Hegesistratus talked with various barbarians around the marketplace. "There are Crimson Men here," she said, "the first ones I've seen since we left the Great King's army. Hegesistratus says they're waiting for the ships from Thought to leave Helle's Sea so they can sail home." Her bright black eyes discovered an open door, and she pointed. "There's some right there. See them?"

I did, four swarthy men in embroidered caps and beautifully dyed crimson robes arguing with a cobbler. One of them noticed that I was looking at him and waved. *"Bahut!"*

I answered, *"Uhuya!"* and waved in return.

"What did you say to him?" Io asked.

*"My brother,"* I told her. "It's just a friendly greeting you give someone you're on good terms with, particularly if you're in the same trade, or both foreigners in the same place."

She looked up at me intently. "Master, can you speak the language of the Crimson Men?"

Hegesistratus halted momentarily and glanced back at us.

I told Io that I did not know.

"Well, think about it. Pretend I'm a Crimson Man—one of their daughters."

"All right," I said.

"Over there, see that big animal? What is it?"

I told her, *"Sisuw."*

*"Sisuw."* Io was delighted. "And—and him back there. What do they call him, master?"

"The boy in the colored cloak? *Bun* or—let's see—*nucir.*"

Io shook her head. "No, I meant the old man. I didn't even see the boy. Where is he?"

"He's seen that we see him," I explained. "But he's still watching us around the corner of that cart. He's probably just curious."

"I think that you really can talk the way the Crimson Men do, master. At least a little bit, and maybe pretty well. I know you can't remember, but one time you told me that *Salamis* means *peace*."

I confirmed that it does.

"So I ought to have known already from that," Io said, "and it's something I'm going to have to find out a lot more about." Despite what she said, she has not asked me any more questions concerning that language; nor did she even speak again, I think, while the four of us walked the ten stades or so to the sacred grove, contenting herself with silently chewing a lock of her hair and often looking behind her.

At the city gate Hegesistratus bought a little wine and a pair of pigeons in a wicker cage, remarking that they would make us a good meal after our sacrifice. I asked him how one read the entrails of such birds. He explained that it is really not much different from reading the corresponding organs of a heifer or a lamb, save that the shoulder bones are not consulted; but that he did not intend to divine in that fashion today. I then asked how he would question the gods, and he said that I would do it for him. After that I asked nothing more, because the girl who sold us the pigeons was still near enough to overhear us.

The leaves of the grove have turned to gold, and most have fallen. It must be a lovely spot in spring, but today it seemed forlorn. Nor do I think that Itys receives frequent sacrifices from the people of Pactye— surely they would build him a temple, if he did. When I poked among the ashes of the last fire before his altar, I found them soaked to mud by the autumn rains.

"But we must have fire," Hegesistratus declared. He gave me a coin and sent me to a house from which smoke rose to buy a torch.

"Don't many people come between now and the good weather," the untidy old woman I found cooking there declared as she tied a double handful of dirty straw around a long stick of kindling for me. "And mostly them that does come wants me to give their fire to them for nothing."

I assured her that she would be rewarded by the gods for such a pious act, and mentioned that having given her money, I expected my straw to be well doused with oil.

"You mean lamp oil?" The old woman stared at me as though it were a foreign commodity practically unheard of in this part of the Chersonese. "No use wasting *lamp oil* on this—why, I've got you some nice grease here that will burn every bit as good. Well, I don't give away much fire for nothing, I might as well tell you. Not unless they're kin to me." She paused, brushing back her straggling gray hair. "Once I did last year, though, because of how the poor mother was all by herself and crying so. Are you the one that's lost your child, young man? How old was it?"

I shook my head and told her that I did not think any of us was missing a son or daughter.

"That's what everybody comes for, mostly—children strayed or dead. Dead, mostly, I suppose. When there's lots of people, they get their fire from each other, naturally."

Her grease was old enough to stink, but it took fire with a roar when she thrust the end of the torch into the flames under her pot. I inquired about Itys, whose name was not familiar to me, and she told me that he had been eaten by his father.

The sailors are talking excitedly among themselves—I am going over to ask them what has happened.

# EIGHT

## *The* Europa *Sails at Dawn*

THE KYBERNETES TOLD ALL THE sailors that he will cast off as soon as it is light enough to see, and Hypereides sent Acetes and his shieldmen into Pactye to collect those who have not yet returned. When the ship puts out, I do not think that Io and I will be aboard—or the black man, either. I should ask about that when I have finished writing.

The sailors say the Crimson Men's ship has slipped out of the harbor. Earlier this year Pactye was ruled by the Empire, and Crimson Men traded here freely, they having been subdued in the same fashion. Now the Great King's armies have withdrawn, and the citizens of Pactye do not know whether their city is to be independent (as it once was), or subject to Parsa or another place. When Hypereides and I conferred with the councillors, they warned us that there must be no fighting with any of the people of the Empire while we were here, for fear Pactye would suffer for it later. Hypereides promised there would not be; but now that the Crimson Men have left the harbor, they are fair game; and since they spent the summer trading around the First Sea and the Euxine, they should be carrying a rich cargo. The sailors say that if the Crimson Men merely cross Helle's Sea to some port still in the hands of the Great King (Paesus being the most probable place), we can do nothing. But if they try to run down Helle's Sea and along the coast to return to their homes in Byblos, there is a good chance that the *Europa* will catch them. A trading vessel such as theirs can sail by night as well as by day, while *Europa* will have to anchor almost every evening to take on fresh water. But a trireme like *Europa* is a much faster sailer; and when a fair wind is lacking, it can be rowed faster than any trader can sail.

Now I must write about the boy. Hegesistratus, Elata, and Io had laid a small fire while I was gone, using the driest wood they could find. I lit it, and as soon as it was burning well Hegesistratus told us the legend of Itys, son of Tereus, who was a king of Thrace.

This King Tereus was a son of the War God and an enemy of Hill. Thus when Hill went to war with Thought in his time, he came with an army to the support of Thought. There he wooed and won Princess Procne, the daughter of King Pandion. When the war was over and her husband returned to Thrace, she accompanied him and there bore him Prince Itys. All went well until her sister, Princess Philomela, visited the court; Tereus fell madly in love with her and, after picking a quarrel with Queen Procne, banished her to a remote part of his kingdom.

When Princess Philomela resisted his advances, he arranged that it should be reported that Queen Procne had lost her life during an incursion by a neighboring tribe. Believing that she would become his queen, Philomela submitted; but in the morning Tereus cut out her tongue to prevent her from revealing what had taken place, for he did not wish the succession of Prince Itys, whom he loved as dearly as a bad man can love a son who bears his face, endangered by a son borne by Philomela.

The maimed princess was then sent home to her native city. Although this occurred before the age of letters, it does not seem to me that the loss of speech alone can have kept her from telling others what had been done to her, for such things might readily have been communicated by gestures, as the black man talks with me; and surely her father and many others must have wondered to find she could no longer speak. But how many women who have tongues, similarly wronged, have held their peace from shame! Doubtless Philomela, cruelly forced to silence, felt as they did.

Soon, however, she learned that her sister was still alive and living once more with King Tereus as his wife; and that was too much. Many months she spent in making a royal robe for her sister of the finest stuffs, and into it wove pictures relating her sad story.

With the most admirable courage she returned to Tereus's court, and there displayed her robe to him before presenting it to her sister. No doubt she had held it some distance from the king's eyes, so that the pictures could not be seen clearly; but when Procne examined it in her chamber, she understood at once all that had happened, and with her own hands she murdered their son, Itys. Together the sisters butchered the unfortunate boy, roasted his flesh, and served it to his father that night. Gluttonous and unsuspecting, Tereus emptied the dish; and when he had pronounced it good, they revealed to him that he (like the Time God, Kronos, said Hegesistratus) had devoured his heir.

With drawn sword Tereus pursued the sisters. But Cynthia, who avenges the wrongs of virgins as her own, changed him to a black vulture, Procne to a nightingale, and pretty Philomela to a swallow, a bird whose tail has been cut away in the same way that Philomela's tongue was; thus it is that the one sings only when it cannot be seen, while the other flies too swiftly to be caught; for their foe pursues them always.

And so it is also that Itys, slain by his mother to avenge the crime of his father, brings help to children, who suffer for reasons they are too young to understand.

When Itys's history was finished, Hegesistratus had me stand between the altar and the fire. Murmuring invocations, he cut the necks of the pigeons, scattered their blood upon the flames, poured a libation of wine, and fed the fire with fragrant herbs. When these things had been done, he sang the paean of Itys, with Io and Elata for his chorus.

The fumes of the fire made me want to sneeze and sleep; as if in a dream, I saw the youth Io had pointed out, a boy coming into manhood, with the first sproutings of his beard apparent on his face. His cloak was costly and of the east, his black hair elaborately dressed. There were rings of gold in his ears, yet his manner was furtive; and he appeared surprised when I pointed at him and asked why he had come to our sacrifice without taking part.

Just then Hegesistratus asked if I remembered who he was, and I replied that he was Hegesistratus, the mantis. He asked whether I could run as fast as he; when I declared I could, he asked whether I might not run faster, and I acknowledged it was so. He asked if I also recalled the kybernetes, and whether I thought he could outrun him. I answered that he could not, and he asked me why.

I said, "Surely you know."

"Yes," he told me. "But I must discover if you do."

"Because you're lame. You were wounded by the Rope Makers, or so you told me once." When I said this, Io looked surprised; I do not know why.

Hegesistratus asked, "And where was I wounded?"

"In the thigh."

He nodded. "What do you think of my new winter boots? Are they well suited to running? Both of them?"

I glanced at them and assured him that they appeared to be of excellent quality (which they did). "But like all footwear they're better for walking than for running. Every man runs his fastest in bare feet."

"That is well said," Hegesistratus admitted. "Now, Latro, do you still see the boy you spoke to a moment ago?"

Elata winked and pointed him out to me, though that was not necessary. I told Hegesistratus that I indeed saw him still.

"Ask him how Oeobazus fares."

I cannot say how the boy came to have word of Oeobazus, nor how Hegesistratus came to learn of it, unless someone mentioned the boy to him this morning in the market. But I called, "Boy! Stand nearer our fire. What can you tell us about Oeobazus, the Rope Maker who rove the cables of the Great King's bridge?" I knew who this Oeobazus was because the mantis had talked of him with our captain in the cookshop.

"Oeobazus is not a Rope Maker," the boy replied. "He is a Mede."

"But you know him," I insisted.

He shrugged. "He is a Mede. We can't trust them as we do our own people."

Hegesistratus told me, "You must repeat everything that he says, Latro." And so I did. When I had finished, Hegesistratus said, "Ask where Oeobazus is now."

It was not needed, for the boy could hear him as well as I. He shut his eyes for a moment. "He is on a horse."

"He rides," I told Hegesistratus.

The mantis stroked his jaw. "Is he alone?"

"No," the boy replied, addressing me. "Many ride with him, tall warriors with lances. A hairless man who looks very strong holds the noose about his neck." Seeing that Hegesistratus had not heard him, I repeated all this.

"His hands are bound?"

The boy nodded. "The cord is passed through the girth of his horse."

"*Latro!*"

Startled, I looked around and saw our captain, Hypereides, who had just come up. He waved, and I waved in return, getting my chest full of smoke in the process. I fell to coughing, and had to leave the fire.

Hegesistratus called a greeting and moved to a place from which Hypereides could see him. I do not know what happened to the boy; I have not spoken to him since. When Hypereides drew nearer, he asked how our sacrifice had gone and whether the omens had been favorable.

"Very much so," said Hegesistratus, "provided we follow the advice of Itys."

"Wonderful!" Hypereides crouched before the fire to warm his hands. "And that is . . . ?"

"You and your crew must round Helle's Cape to rendezvous with us on the Thracian coast. We—Itys specifically indicated the four of us here, and your black slave—must track Oeobazus in Thrace."

Hypereides winced. "I'll be sorry to lose you."

Smiling, Elata said, "Let us hope the separation will not be a long one."

He nodded gloomily at that and stared into the fire. "As regards myself—and *Europa* and the crew—I can understand Itys's advice well enough. We certainly can't abandon the ship, and if Oeobazus is in Thrace—"

"He is," Hegesistratus told him. "Itys confirmed it."

"Then the only thing we can do is report it to Xanthippos and get there as fast as we can. But the five of you will be running a terrible risk." He glanced over at Io. "The child must go, too?"

Io said, "If Latro's going, I have to go with him."

Hegesistratus nodded. "Yes. She must."

"All right, she can go. She and Elata won't actually be in as much danger as you and Latro and the black man." Hypereides sighed. "They'll give you two fighters, at least. They're both good—at least I've seen the black man fight myself, and a poet, Pindaros was his name, told me one time that he meant to compose some of his verses about Latro. You won't be able to do much in the way of fighting yourself, I'm afraid, with that wooden foot and your wound only half-healed."

(It was only then that I saw that Hegesistratus's right foot, which I had supposed booted, was indeed no more than a wooden peg; and I resolved to kill him when I can.)

He would not agree. "My wound's closing fast, and though I might not be of much use in a phalanx or on the storming deck of your warship, put me on horseback and I'm as good as any other man."

Hypereides stood up, rubbing his hands. "Horses cost a lot of money. You'll need at least—"

Hegesistratus waved the offer away, saying that he would pay for them. But after we returned to Sestos, the black man drew him aside and took him to see five horses. This I know because I followed them, though they did not see me. Surely it was to buy these horses that Hegesistratus sent the black man away, and that was long before we went to the grove of Itys. Besides, the boy with whom I spoke was not Itys, or so I think, but merely a common, living boy, perhaps from some foreign ship. Nor did he say the things that Hegesistratus told Hypereides he did.

Hegesistratus is betraying us, and for it I shall kill him when the ship has gone.

Io came to me just as I lay down to sleep, saying that she was cold. I wrapped us both in my cloak and laid hers over us. When I asked her age, I heard her hesitate before answering as she pondered the greatest age I might accept. I will not write here the age she gave me, for I know it to be false. It was not long before I discovered what she wished, and I would not give it to her, though many would, I think. I asked whether she was glad we were going to Thrace with Hegesistratus and Elata, and she said she was. When I asked why, she said that Thrace is on the road to Hill, and Pindaros is probably in Hill, and that the best thing for me would be to find Pindaros, who might take me to some place where I would be cured. When I heard that, I was happy that I had written so carefully all that was said of this Pindaros.

Then I slept for a time. When I woke, Io was weeping. I asked why she wept, and she said it was because she had been a temple slave in Hill, and if she returned, she would surely be punished very severely. I asked her whether my own home was in Hill, though I did not think it was. She confirmed that it was not, only hers. If that is so, I have no desire to go there. I will travel the world until I find a place where the people know me and tell me I am of their blood.

Nor will I put Io in more danger than I must.

# PART TWO

# NINE

## *Elata Says*

I MUST READ THIS EACH morning when I rise, and write each day before it is too dark; thus it will become a habit. Though I forget that I am to do it, I will do it still.

This morning, when I saw the three women, I did not know their names, nor why they danced. The others were still asleep when Elata returned to our camp. I did not know then that she was one of our party; but she told me that she was, and after I had counted our horses I knew that it was true. Besides, the others accept her as I have seen since. She told me that she danced alone because she loves to dance, and riding leaves her stiff and sore.

But I had seen the other dancers. I praised their grace and asked her where they had gone. She said then that they are the river's daughters, and that their home is in the river—she offered to take me there if I wished so that I might see it for myself. One who wears the belt of manhood, as I do, should not be afraid; but I was as frightened as a child when she said it, and I would not come with her.

She laughed at me and kissed me; and even though she is so small, it seemed when I held her in my arms that she was larger than I. She says this river is the Melas, the boundary of the country of the Apsinthians.

I asked then why they danced, and she said it was because the rains had come. "You don't remember how much wine I drank the night I met you, Latro. I drank because I was burning with thirst." She smiled at me, her head to one side. "Now the rain has returned, and it is the season of growth. Would you like to lie with me again?"

I was still frightened, but I nodded. Just then one of the sleepers stirred, and she laughed and backed away. Perhaps she was only teasing me, and I have never lain with her. Yet I feel it is not so.

The sleeper sat up, rubbed his eyes, and said, "Good morning, Latro. I am Hegesistratus. Will you help me with my boots?" I said I would if he required my help; and he told me he did, that they were very difficult to pull on, and that I helped him every morning. I feel sure this is true, though I do not remember it and his boots slipped onto his feet easily enough. He said that he would be happy when the warm weather returned and we can wear sandals again. So will I; boots are very uncomfortable whether one walks or rides.

The girl woke then. She says her name is Io, and she told me something of the rest and where we are going. She said that we hope to take prisoner a Mede called Oeobazus for the city of Thought. I nodded at all she said; but I know that there is not much love for Thought in my heart, and a great deal of sympathy for this man Oeobazus.

The black man rose and went to wash in the river. Because I was afraid for him, I went with him and washed, too. Elata came with us, perhaps because she feared I would tell him of the other dancers, for she held her finger to her lips when he was not looking. She let her gown fall to the ground and dove into the rushing waters, but the black man and I only waded in up to our waists, and Io (who had come with us, too) merely washed her hands and feet.

Last of all, Hegesistratus came, I think because he feared for Elata; but because he had come, he had to take off his boots and wash his feet. When he had dried them, he put on his boots again without my help. I do not know what this may mean. Can it be a sign of submission to assist a comrade, a man older than myself, in pulling on his boots? I cannot believe it—those who submit walk beneath a yoke.

I, too, was afraid that I would mention the dancing women, and so I told the black man and the rest about the rider I had seen, a big man with a lance on a big horse.

"That will be an Apsinthian," Hegesistratus said. "He may even be a scout of their king's, though it's more likely he was just a petty aristocrat out hunting. When we ford the river, we will be in their country." He smiled sourly and added, "I would imagine that a few of them will welcome us to it before the day is over." I asked him then whether the Apsinthians hunted with lions as other men do with dogs, and he assured me that they do not. The beast that ran beside the rider's horse seemed a lion to me, but I did not speak of it then.

The sun that had shone so brightly at dawn soon hid behind clouds, and a thin rain fell. We had to ride a long way upriver to find a ford; and though hoofprints proved it a ford indeed, its water was higher than the horses' bellies. The rain stopped soon after we had crossed, but the sun did not return. In the cities, the market must have been full by the time we reached a place from which we could see the ashes of our fire across the noisy river.

The black man had been leading us, but when we halted for a moment to look at the thicket where we had slept, he turned back and spoke long to Hegesistratus in a tongue I do not understand. Hegesistratus explained that he had urged that we ride west from each ford in future instead of returning to the coast as we have been doing.

"It would save a great deal of weary riding," Hegesistratus conceded, "and it is certainly true that we are beginning to run short of food; but it would also greatly increase our likelihood of becoming lost, and we might even wander out of Apsinthia and into the country of the Paetians to the north. We can steer by the sun and the stars whenever the god grants us clear weather, but we are not apt to see much of that for some time to come."

The black man pointed to the sky to show that he knew where the sun was, though its face was veiled.

Hegesistratus said, "Until now, we have tried to stay near the coast so we can meet the *Europa* at the queen's great temple at the mouth of the Hebrus. Yet we must locate Oeobazus first; and should we reach the Hebrus, we can follow it to the temple. So let us vote upon this matter. Those who wish to do as Seven Lions has suggested, raise your hands."

The black man's hand shot up, and I raised mine as well, because I feel that he is my friend. Io held up hers, too, I think out of loyalty to me; and thus it was decided.

When we rode on, I looked for hoof marks where I had seen the rider, for near them I hoped to discover the footprints of the animal that had bounded beside his horse as well, and from them to decide whether it had been a dog, as Hegesistratus had said, or a lion, as I had thought it. It is not safe to try to distinguish between these by size alone, for the great hounds of Molossis leave imprints as big as a small lion's; but the claws can be seen in front of the toes in the track of a dog, while in the pug mark of a lion they are not to be found. The hoofprints of the rider's steed were equally invisible, though I discovered the pug marks of a lion.

Here the shoreline is low, almost flat, and often muddy, so that we did not always ride within sight of the sea; when we did there were no islands in view, though I cannot say what a summer day might have shown. We ate the first meal without dismounting; but we halted here where there is good water, hobbled the horses, and built a fire to cook the second. We had finished our bread and olives and were deciding whether to set up our tent when Io saw the riders.

She shouted and pointed. It was dark enough by then that they could not be seen at once if one had been looking into the fire; but after a moment I made them out against the trees that grow beside the stream—nine men on horseback armed with lances. Hegesistratus rose and greeted them in the Thracian tongue while I made sure my sword was free in the scabbard and the black man groped for his javelins. I should write here that Hegesistratus and I, as well as the black man, each have a pair of well-made javelins; Io says Hegesistratus bought them for us in Pactye, a city to the east and south. Hegesistratus has one of the light, long-hafted war axes of the Medes also, inlaid and footed with gold. The black man has a knife with two edges; it, too, appears to me of their making, though its fittings are only bronze like those of my sword.

When Hegesistratus spoke again, he raised his cup, so that I knew he was offering to share our wine. One of the Thracians replied. I could not understand him, but his tone told me that he had refused. I whispered to Io that she could be of no help to us and instructed her to go to the sea. She nodded as if she intended to obey and left the circle of firelight, although I do not think she went far.

Soon the Thracian horsemen trotted over to us. The one who had spoken to Hegesistratus spoke again. Hegesistratus hung the wineskin on his lance, and he lifted it until the skin slid into his hands. He drank the unmixed wine and passed the skin to the man beside him. Hegesistratus gestured toward our small pile of possessions, I think to show that we had no more wine.

The Thracian pointed toward the black man with his lance and spoke again.

"You must put down your weapons," Hegesistratus told him, and he did, sticking their heads into the soft earth. I thought then how simple it would be to kill the Thracian with a single cast, for my own javelins were not far from my hand. With their leader dead, the rest might ride away, or thus it seemed to me. Yet I did not act.

He rode to where Elata watched us, and indicated by a sign that he wished her to stand nearer to the fire where he could see her better. When she only shook her head and trembled, he managed his big horse very skillfully, so that its broad chest crowded her closer and closer to it.

At last her foot touched one of the burning sticks, making its end move in the flames and sending up a cloud of red sparks. She screamed, Hegesistratus shouted at him, and another Thracian urged his mount forward and thrust at Hegesistratus. The black man's javelin struck him below the eye. The point seemed to sprout behind his ear like a horn. I should have cast my own then; but I stabbed the leader—up and beneath the ribs—instead, and severed his head as he fell. This I wondered to see, for I had not known my blade was so good.

At this the other Thracians galloped off and wheeled with leveled lances. I ran for my horse, hoping there would be time to take off the hobble before their charge. I found him freed already, and bridled; Io held his reins. As I sprang onto his back, the thunder of the charge began.

It was not the Thracian lancers who charged. All in an instant, as a storm roars out of the night, long-haired riders boiled around us, one galloping through our fire and scattering its coals, so that she seemed to leave a trail of flame, as a torch does when it is thrown.

I rode after them and had a singing arrow sting my ear for my pains; nor did I shed any other blood, for all the Thracians who were not dead had run by the time I reached the point where they had received the charge. A woman (whom I believed a man) writhed beside a corpse, blood bubbling from her mouth as she gasped for breath. (Even before I dismounted, I could hear the sucking of the wound in her chest—a horrible sound.) I tore her tunic to bandage her and bound the wad of wool with strips of rag. It was while I did this that I found she was a woman, for my fingers brushed her breast. Her friends returned before the last knot was tight, but when they saw that I was trying to help her, they did not interfere.

We tied her cloak to the shafts of two lances and carried her to the fire. Hegesistratus has sewed her wound with sinew wet with wine. I know that he does not think she will live, nor do I. Elata says that she will surely live, however.

Elata has smeared my ear with warm pitch to stanch the blood; and now Io weeps for me, which I do not like. I have told her it is not blood from a nick that kills a man but the will of the gods. The black man laughs at us both and stands very straight with his chest thrown out because these women have never seen such a man as he.

Now everyone is asleep, save for Hegesistratus and one of the women, with whom he speaks. The horses stamp and nicker, frightened by the smell of so much blood. Surely the Thracians will return and bring with them others—but not before dawn, I think.

# TEN

## *The Amazons*

THE WARRIOR WOMEN BURN THEIR dead. This and a great many other things I have learned about them from Hegesistratus, who speaks their tongue. He says it is not the same as Thracian. I asked how many he speaks—for it seems to me that I have only this one in which I am writing and the one I speak to Io and the others, though she says I have at least one more. He answered that he speaks all tongues, and perhaps it is so; Io calls him a mantis and does not wish to tell me more about him. The warrior women think the black man uncanny; and I know that Io thinks the same of the lovely Elata; yet I think that Hegesistratus is stranger even than the warrior women.

He names them breastless* ones, and so do Io and Elata, so I will call them that as well. Io says that we were told of them last summer by a wicked woman called Drakaina, though I cannot remember it.

If Pharetra dies, the others will halt and build a pyre for her. We need not halt, too, unless we choose, Hegesistratus says; but it seems to me that it would be foolish to leave them. We are sure to encounter more Thracians, and it would be better to fight them together if we must fight. I have spoken about this with the black man, and he agrees. Hegesistratus and Elata will certainly not go without us.

The other Amazons have made a litter for Pharetra and slung it between two of the captured horses. This morning when I rode beside her, she smiled and spoke to me. When I shook my head to tell her I did not understand, she showed me by signs that she wanted me to help her out of her litter; but I would not. Her hair is nearly the color of my own, though I think more touched with red. Her wound has made her

---

*In Greek *amazos,* "without a breast."—GW

face white and thin, so that it seems that the high bones beneath push
through her cheeks, as stones rise in a plowed field after rain.

All these Amazons are tall and strong. They have only the left
breast, and a flat white scar where the right breast should be; their tunics
have a single strap, worn so that it covers the scar. I asked Pharetra about
this. She made many signs until I said, "You need only one to nurse a
single child?" She nodded to that, so she must know at least a few words
in the language of the Hellenes.

I asked her name. She spoke it for me, but I cannot say it as she
does. Pharetra, "bowcase," is as like it as any word I know, though she
laughed at me when I called her that. Now we are going to move on.

We have ridden through the Thracian town and camped here, in this
muddy field beside the river. Everyone is angry about it—I, too. We
met the Thracians after the first meal; Io says most of them look like
those we killed last night. I have read all I wrote about that but learned
only a little. I must write less about what has taken place and more
about the things I see.

The highest Thracians have tattooed cheeks and gold rings, and so
much gold on their bridles that their mounts are burdened by it. There
were at least a hundred. We could not have fought them with three
men and a few women, but Hegesistratus and the queen spoke to them
and made peace. He says he is not certain it would have been possible
if the Thracians had not wanted to show the women to their king. He
says also that some know the speech we use, though they feign otherwise;
we must be careful of what we say. He asked permission for us to gather
wood for a fire, but they say there is none here (a lie) and some will be
brought us. Thus I must write quickly, while the light lasts.

It is young rye we trample here, and plainly not all these Thracians
are horsemen, for we have seen many peasants on foot. The horsemen
are the landowners, perhaps, and their attendants. Certainly many are
rich.

The lance seems their chief weapon. Their lances are half again as
tall as a man and no thicker than a spear; I would find them awkward,
but they handle them very well. The swords I have seen have only one
edge, like Falcata, and long tapering points. Some have bows, but theirs
do not look as good to me as the bows of the Amazons. The Thracians

wear cuirasses of linked rings or quilted linen, however, and some have helmets, while the Amazons wear no armor at all.

The Amazons' bows are made of layers of horn and wood bound with leather. Each keeps a lump of black beeswax in her bowcase with which she rubs her bow to keep it dry; they wax the bowcase also, and all have beautifully made bowcases of boiled leather. Pharetra let me look at hers. There was a compartment for the bow, a hollow bone to hold strings, and a quiver for her arrows. A griffin on the front of her bowcase has slain a man—not drawn or painted, as I would have thought such a picture would be, but molded into the leather. I would guess that the images were cut into wood, and the boiled leather hammered into the depressions while it was still hot and soft. Each arrow is as long as my forearm from the end of the longest finger to the elbow—a cubit and two fingers. The tips are iron and seem too slender to me.

Her sword looks very odd. It is crooked like mine, but sharp along the outer edge. If someone were to take a leaf-shaped sword and cut away half the metal down the blade, what remained would be something like the swords of the Amazons. I can see, however, that such long, light blades might be useful on horseback.

A peasant has brought firewood in a cart. With a fire on which to cook the second meal, all of us feel better, I think. Hegesistratus paid for the wood—two obols, which seems very dear to me. He told Elata that the peasant promised to bring wine and a young goat, so we may have meat later. Io says it has been a long time now since we have had a good meal. Some meat will be good for Pharetra, too.

Hegesistratus has told me that the Thracian town is Cobrys, and the king's name is Kotys. Some of the people we passed in Cobrys looked like Hellenes to me, though no doubt most of them were Thracians. A dozen horsemen guard us, sometimes gathering in twos and threes to talk until their commander scatters them again. I will eat with the others and pretend to sleep; later I will see how watchful these Thracians are.

Not wishing to reveal what I planned, but anxious to learn how dangerous it might be, I asked Hegesistratus to tell me what Fate has in store for me. He smiled and agreed that was perhaps as good a means of passing the evening as we would find. Io was eager then to have her future foretold as well, and he promised he would do that also, provided that she would assist him with mine.

When she agreed readily, he got a small mirror from his bag and polished it with salt, poured out a libation to the Goddess of Love (mirrors are under her care, as he explained), and had Io take a brand from the fire. Sitting with his back to the fire, he watched the stars in his mirror for a time, or so it appeared to me. It is not clear tonight, but not wholly clouded either; wisps of cloud come and go, sometimes passing across the face of the moon, and often across the face of her who holds it.

When he was satisfied that everything was correct, he taught Io a simple prayer and had her walk in circles around him as she recited it, holding high the brand and matching her steps to the words. Elata crooned a different invocation, a sighing, nearly inaudible sound that seemed to fill the night, like the soughing of the wind. Soon four of the Amazons were clapping to keep the time, while a fifth strung her bow and plucked the bowstring, sliding one finger up and down. The black man tapped a stick of firewood with two others.

"Swords," Hegesistratus muttered. "I see swords. You are in great danger that will become greater yet, many swords, long and sharp."

I asked whether I would die.

"Perhaps. Yet I see gods about you, many smiling. Nike accompanies you always. The Destroyer smiles upon you—" He dropped the mirror. Io halted her march, and the others fell silent. Elata hurried to his side.

"What did you see?" I asked him.

He shivered, picked up the mirror, and turned it so that its polished side lay facedown. "My death," he replied. "All that is mortal dies—I should not have let it master me."

It was clear that he did not wish to say more, and I said nothing to force him to.

At length he continued, "Nike is with you, as I said. You see the gods, or so Io has often assured me."

I told him I did not know.

"You do not see her because she stands behind you. Perhaps if you were to look into a mirror, as I just have, you would see her then. But you may not look into mine."

I said, "I don't want to."

"Good." He wiped his brow with his finger, flinging the sweat onto the ground before him. "Let me see—what else was there? You will travel far. I saw the Boundary Stone beckon, and he is the patron of travelers. The Lady of Thought and the Huntress were playing draughts, which means that each will use you in the game if she can."

The queen, who had been listening as though she understood most or all that Hegesistratus said, now asked a question in her own tongue. She is no taller than the others, and I think not much older than I; but she has eyes like cold seas, and all the rest hurry whenever she speaks to them. Hegesistratus calls her Hippephode, the cavalry charge.

Now he shook his head. "No, I did not see the War God." To me he added, "She said that you possess his virtues—*arete*, as we would say. She felt he might be inclined to defend you, and it may well be true; I did not see everything."

Io said, "But you said the Destroyer smiled at him. That's good, isn't it? The Destroyer gave him good advice the time he came to our oracle in Hill. I used to remember what it was, but I'm afraid I'd get it wrong."

The mantis nodded slowly. "He is often a friend to men. I have sometimes wished that his twin were more like him, although she is occasionally friendly toward women, and especially toward girls like you. And certainly she has been a good friend to me—a very generous friend indeed." He clasped Elata's hand as he spoke.

I asked what advice he had for me, based upon what he had seen.

He shrugged. "Like all who are in great danger, you must be bold, yet not overbold. It is those who are daring but not rash who live through dangers. If possible, you should go to Dolphins. The greatest of all the Destroyer's oracles is there, and if you consult it and make the right sacrifices, he may have something very useful to tell you. Will you write that in your book? And read it, too?"

I assured him I would.

"Beware of women, and of the learned, whether women or men. They will advise you in their own interests, not yours, if you allow it. But that is a warning such as I might give every man."

I nodded, for I understand very well what he meant, though he is a learned man himself.

"Be careful not to offend those who favor you, and do what you can to gain the goodwill of those who do not. Hunting may please the Huntress, for example, and study the Lady of Thought, or favoring her city. Or sacrifices of the proper kind—though nothing is sure."

Io asked, "Now will you do me?"

"No," Hegesistratus told her. "Or not this evening, at least."

Just then the peasant who had brought us firewood returned leading a young he-goat and carrying a jar of wine. The mantis poured out a few drops of the new wine to the Destroyer; and the black man (who was very clever about it) dispatched the goat, skinned it, and cut it up for us more quickly than I would have believed it could be done. With his fingers he told us that he wished to keep the skin to make a drum; everyone agreed that he should have it.

Pharetra sat up to eat and drink with us; surely that is a good sign. When I asked when she had been hurt, Io said it was last night when we fought these Thracians. Io and Elata take good care of her, and the Amazons seem happy to let them.

After we had eaten, the Amazons sang; only Hegesistratus understood their words, I think, but they have wonderful voices—so fine that our guards drew nearer to hear. (They wear foxskin caps; their cloaks are divided and cover their heels.) At last everyone except Elata and I lay down to sleep. The fire is nearly dead, and though it is so cold, I will not add more wood; that would only frighten Elata and make it easier for our guards to see me.

When I wrote of the Amazons, I should have said that they lack bronze bits for their horses. Theirs are of rawhide, and though I cannot remember, it surprised me very much; thus I do not believe I have seen such bits before. Their reins, too, are rawhide, their saddle pads of sheepskin, not greatly different from ours.

Hegesistratus is lame and has a curly beard, very black; Elata is smaller than the Amazons and very beautiful, and Io is still a child. It is written here that we are to find Oeobazus. Hypereides the Trierarch sent us. I asked Hegesistratus and Io before they slept, and both confirm it. This land is Apsinthia, in Thrace.

I have tried to write until Elata slept as well, but I am tired and this fire is almost out. Perhaps she will not sleep tonight at all. Another rider has joined our guards, a larger man than the rest. That is bad, the dog very bad, perhaps. I am going to lie down, but stay awake till Elata sleeps and the fire is out.

# ELEVEN

## *Ares and Others*

K ING KOTYS, OEOBAZUS, AND CLETON—I must remember them all, or at least remember them when I read this, and remember to read it frequently.

I had not meant to sleep, but sleep overpowered me. When I woke, the moon was low, and only the glow of embers showed where our fire had been. Elata was gone; Io, Hegesistratus, the black man, and the Amazons sleeping. I could not see our guards, but I heard their horses snort.

Though I can no longer recall yesterday morning, I know we were not prisoners of the Thracians then. I remember how I saw them riding across the plain. Perhaps we should have fled, but they would surely have pursued us, and it seemed better to fight on unwinded horses if we had to fight, and to make peace if we could; thus we are here.

There is little cover near our camp, so I waited until the moon was down, then crept over the new rye toward the Thracian city, keeping low in the furrows. They surely expect us to try to flee it, thus that seemed the best way. Once a rider passed close, but he did not see me. I took my sword, but left my two javelins behind. All this time I wondered about Elata, thinking that perhaps the guards had lured her away from our camp, raped, and killed her.

There are few stone buildings in the city, and its wall is toward the sea. The houses closest to us were humble, built of wood and wattle and roofed with straw. In several streets, not one showed a light.

Thinking that such poor people would not be likely to sound the alarm unless their own lives and property were threatened, I called softly at a door; and when no one came, I thumped it with the pommel of my sword. At last an angry man answered. I could not understand him, but using the speech of the Hellenes, I told him that I was a Hellene and a traveler; and I asked him to take me to the house of someone of my own nation, where I could find lodging.

I do not believe he understood anything I said, but perhaps he recognized the tongue I spoke. In any event, he unbarred the door. He had a club, but let it fall when he saw Falcata. He led me almost to the docks, where there was a house—Cleton's—larger than most; then he pointed to the door and ran away.

A woman opened when I called. I do not know her name, but she is a servant of Cleton's, I think, a Thracian. She did not want to let me in. She was frightened, but once she understood that I could not speak Thracian, she woke her master.

Cleton is short and fat and gray of beard, but not lacking in courage, I think, for when he came, it was with an angry face and a heavy staff; nor did he lay it down when he saw my sword. His hours of business, he told me, were from the opening of the market until nightfall. If I wished to speak with him, I could do it at his warehouse, and now I must go.

"I cannot see you then, noble Cleton," I replied (for his servant had mentioned his name), "because I am guarded. Do you think I always go about in a dirty chiton, with muddy knees? I had to creep like a lizard to visit you here."

He stared at me, then ordered the woman to go back to bed. "You don't have to worry about her," he assured me. "She only knows three words: come, go, and spread your legs. You're no Ionian, though you talk like somebody from Thought. Where are you really from?"

"I can't remember," I said.

He laughed. "Well, there's many another lad that's had his troubles. You don't have to give me your name, son. What is it you want from me?"

"Nothing but information," I told him. "Where is Oeobazos the Mede?"

"That's common knowledge," he said thoughtfully.

"Not to me. I don't speak Thracian."

Cleton shrugged. "It's a barbarous language. I used to think I didn't know it very well myself, because I had so much trouble with shades of meaning. Later I realized they couldn't do much that way either—it's a language for yelling at people. Would you like some wine?"

I nodded, for it seemed clear that Cleton's friendship was worth having. He leaned his staff in a corner and led me to a larger room where there were benches and a table.

"We eat inside a lot here," he said. "The weather's awful. So's the wine, but because of the war it's all I've got. Do you know if the Great King's coming back?"

I said, "I have no idea."

"I hope so—the army bought everything I had, last time. Paid well, too. Have a seat, won't you? If you'll excuse me for leaving you, I'll fetch the wine."

It occurred to me, of course, that he had gone to get help; but there was nothing I could do about it except listen, which I did. He was soon back with wine, water, a mixing bowl, and two cups.

I said, "If Oeobazos's whereabouts are known to everyone, there's no reason you shouldn't tell me."

"Yes, there is," he explained as he handed me my cup. "So far I've had nothing in return. What have you of value to tell me?"

I thanked him and asked what might be of value to him.

He shrugged again. "You could start by telling me where they're keeping you, and what you've done."

"Nothing that I know of," I said. "We're being held in a field, inland, not too far from the city."

"There's more than one of you, then. There must be—they wouldn't hold one man in a field. How many are there?"

"Thirteen."

"That's an unlucky number, don't you know that? There are twelve Olympians, and they never permit a thirteenth. When the wine god came, the hearth goddess resigned to make room for him. It's not pleasing to him to make a face at your host's wine, by the way. It may be bad, but it's the best I've got."

I said, "It isn't the wine—what we drank tonight was far worse. It's that I read tonight that I see the gods, and yet I know nothing about them."

"Neither does anyone else, son—don't let them fool you. Who are the other twelve they're guarding, and what brings you to Cobrys?"

I explained that we were not a single group, but two that had been traveling together. "My companions and I were sent by a captain from Thought," I told him. "His name is Hypereides. Besides myself, there are Hypereides's mantis and his wife—"

"Wait a moment." Cleton held up his hand. "Did you say Hypereides? What does he look like?"

I did not know, but I sensed that if I confessed it, I would learn nothing more. I said, "A thousand people must have seen Hypereides—he's a very well-known man. What would it prove if I were to describe him?"

Cleton said, "You prove to me that Hypereides sent you, and I'll tell you where the Mede is. What does Hypereides want with him?"

"He's been ordered to find this Oeobazus and bring him to Thought," I told him. "I can't tell you more than that. As for proving that Hypereides sent me, his ship's to meet us at the mouth of the Hebrus. You might send someone there and ask him. I'm called Latro, and his mantis is Hegesistratus."

Cleton's eyes flew wide. "Hegesistratus of Elis? The man with the wooden foot?" I was too stunned to reply, but he took my silence for assent. "You're traveling in fast company, son. Very fast indeed. Do you know who Hegesistratus of Elis is?"

I said, "He's Hypereides's mantis, as I told you."

"And that's all you know. Yes, of course. Well, when the Great King's army came through here, he was Mardonius's mantis. I never actually saw him myself, but I heard quite a bit about him. The Great King held the supreme command, as you'd expect, but Mardonius was his strategist—some sort of relation, too—his son-in-law, I believe. So Mardonius's old mantis is working for Hypereides now?"

Having need of wine, I drained my cup. "If you say it."

"Hypereides does a little business with me once in a while. Horsehides, mostly. Maybe a bit of amber if the price is right. Say hello to him for me."

I promised I would.

"Is that all you want? Where Oeobazus is?"

"If you could procure our release, we would all be very grateful," I told him.

Cleton nodded. "I'll come out tomorrow and have a talk with Hegesistratus; then I'll see what I can do. Do you know where the temple
of Pleistorus is?"

I shook my head.

"Northwest of the city, up on the hill. These Thracians put all their
temples on hilltops, and Pleistorus's is the big one, because he's their
war god. We call him Ares."

I asked how far it was.

Cleton fingered his beard. "I haven't been up that way all that often,
son. I'd say maybe ten stades or a little bit less. There's a processional
road that'll lead you out from town—you know, smoothed down and
everything. You can't miss it once you get on that."

Yet I did, and I doubt whether Cleton himself has ever gone that
way by night without a lantern. The processional road he had told me
of began at the marketplace, as I expected, and gave me a smooth, well-
marked path out of the city, for it had gotten plenty of attention from
the spade, and there was a carved post on one side or the other every
ten or fifteen cubits.

The night was nearing that moment at which one feels that dawn
must come (though in fact it does not come) as I left the city behind
me; and as the processional way rose, lifted by the first low hill, I could
see the scarlet spark of our fire to my right. Someone had been cold
enough to wake up and put on more wood, obviously; I wondered who
it had been, and whether he had noticed that I was gone.

Then the processional way divided into two, equally wide as well
as I could judge in the dark, and without any indication as to which
led to the temple of Pleistorus. Thinking it would be prudent to stay
as near our camp as I could (for I hoped to get back before dawn), I
chose the one to the right. I had not gone far when I heard music, and
not much farther before my eyes caught the glare of torches.

I had scarcely time to take a step before the dancing girls came
whirling down the processional road. There were five, two clashing cymbals and two thumping tympana, followed by a larger group that included flutes and carried torches. The fifth girl, who bore no instrument,
halted her wild dance to embrace me. I cannot imagine that I have ever
been more surprised than I was then.

"Don't you recognize me, Latro? I know you forget, but is it as quickly as that? Come dance with us. Can you move your feet the way I do?" She took my hand, and in a moment more I found I was prancing along beside her, greatly handicapped by my boots.

"Step to your left, step to the right—turn and turn about. Left, right, right. You're getting it. Why, you're doing very well!" The others were dancing backward to watch, and though I could not see their smiles, I did not need to.

"You were sitting by the fire trying to write, not so long ago, and you couldn't keep your eyes off me. Don't you want to dance with me now?"

Between gasps I tried to explain that I had urgent business at the temple of Pleistorus.

"You're lost, then, poor boy. This goes to the temple of the Mother of the Gods—we're coming back from there."

Someone I at first took for one of the Amazons caught up with us then to tell us we could not dance at the head of the procession, and must wait until the king had passed.

Very happy to wait, I nodded and moved to one side of the road; but Elata laughed at him and said that she and her friends had been dancing at the head of the procession all the way from the temple. "Oh!" he exclaimed (his tones were like those of a deep-voiced woman). "Are there many more of you?" She said that there were, and he ran on to find them—but passed all four as if blind.

Before he was swallowed by the night, the larger group was upon us. Its dancers and musicians were mostly men and sensibly barefoot, clustered around a file of riders. Though it has been only a short time since I saw them, I cannot remember much about those who rode in the train of the first; his eyes caught mine, and I could not look away. Nor, I think, could he.

He was youthful and tall, broad of shoulder, mounted upon a milk-white stallion. Mail that shone like gold covered him from neck to sole, save for a breastplate in the likeness of a lion, and greaves terminating in the features of a woman, tranquil and grave; but it is his own face that I remember most clearly, its thick brows, piercing eyes, and heavy jaw. It was the face of such a man, I think, as might lead entire armies to the edge of the world and beyond.

After him, the other riders, and the strange dancers, came a rabble singing and carrying torches. I suppose that they were from the city, though I do not know. When the last of them had passed, I asked Elata whether the first rider had been the war god. She laughed at me just as she had at the womanish priest, assured me he was not, and told me that her friends had called him King Kotys.

By that time Dawn's rose-tinted fingers barred the eastern sky, and though I had hoped to visit the temple of the Thracian War God before daylight, I wanted far more to return to our camp while Hegesistratus still slept. Together Elata and I left the road, descended the sheep-nibbled hillside, and crossed fields and jumped water-filled ditches, guided now and then by glimpses of the fading fire, and at last by the towering white column of its smoke. Hegesistratus was still in this tent, rolled in his cloak. I plunged Falcata into his back.

At first I did not understand what I had done, and it was while I stood staring at his body that Hippephode and the black man over-powered me, seizing me from behind and wrenching Falcata from my hand. Hegesistratus has told them to keep me here, and not allow me to go outside; and though the black man has kindly brought me this book, with my stylus of slingstone metal pushed through its cords, he has also made it clear by many signs that he and the Amazons stand ready to kill me should I try to leave.

When I think back upon the night, I cannot understand why I desired so greatly to take the life of Hegesistratus the mantis. It was out of friendship for him, and not from any regard for Hypereides, the captain from Thought, that I sought Oeobazus—for I do not remember the captain save as a name in this book. Yet I wished with all my heart for the death of Hegesistratus, and I saw no contradiction in that.

Although I no longer desire the life of Hegesistratus, it seems to me that what I learned concerning Oeobazus, King Kotys, Ares, and the others may be of importance in the future. Thus I have written everything here, and I will try to remember to read it tonight.

# TWELVE

## *We Will Fight*

WHEN EVERYONE HAD SPOKEN, ONLY Elata voted to do as the king has demanded. We have eaten the second meal as usual; when the fire dies, Hippephode will give the signal. We will have to leave the tent behind, with a few other things; but that cannot be helped. I will take this book and my old book, thrusting them through my belt.

Though I have read my own account of all I did at dawn, the only things I recall are seeing Hegesistratus asleep before me, and stabbing him. Hippephode and the black man must have been watching, for one held each arm before I knew they were upon me. If I had fought, I think I might have freed myself; but I could only stand and wonder at what I had become, someone who murdered a friend and found himself prisoner of two others.

Then Hegesistratus himself came into the tent, and only a blanket lay at my feet, a blanket that had been pierced by my sword.

The black man brought this book, as I said. Hegesistratus would have come sooner to speak with me, I think; but a fat old man drew him aside. They talked long in voices too low for me to hear. The old man was Cleton. I cannot recall going to his house in Cobrys now; but I know I did, because I wrote about it here. And when I saw him with Hegesistratus, I recognized him and whispered his name.

When Cleton left at last, Hegesistratus and Elata entered the tent; Io followed, tiptoeing to escape their notice (though I doubt she did) and sitting silent in a corner for a long while before she spoke. Once I saw the tent wall move, so I knew that the black man listened, too, though doubtless Hegesistratus had spoken to him and the Amazon queen before Elata and I came back this morning.

When Hegesistratus had seated himself on the ground before me, he asked whether I were not surprised to see him alive and well, and I acknowledged that I was indeed.

"Do you understand," he asked, "that I am no ghost? Nor a phantom born of your imagination, nor any other such thing?"

I said I did, and added that I did not think myself much inclined toward either imagination or phantoms.

"But you saw a phantom this morning," the mantis told me. "And in fact you killed it, insofar as such a phantom can be killed."

When I said nothing, he continued, "Do you see me clearly now, Latro? I, having stepped in here from the bright sunshine outside, cannot see very well yet. Have your own eyes adapted to these shadows?"

I told him that I could see him perfectly, that I had been writing in this book earlier and had thought the light entirely adequate.

"Then as I entered, you will have noticed that I possess a physical peculiarity that is rather rare." He gestured toward his wooden foot.

"I saw that you're lame," I said, "but I don't consider it well mannered to speak of it."

Her face very serious, Elata told me, "Yet there are times when such things must be spoken of. Then it is inoffensive to do so. Hegesistratus has been mutilated; as I have told him, I love him all the more for that. What exactly is the nature of his mutilation, Latro?"

"He has lost his right foot," I said. "It has been cut off at the ankle. Did I do that?"

Hegesistratus shook his head. "You did not, but the person who did it is indeed present. I will speak of that in a moment. But first, what would you call this?" He tapped his peg.

"A wooden foot," I said. "A device to permit you to walk."

"Then I am a man with a wooden foot?"

"Yes," I acknowledged, "I would say so."

"You cannot tell me, of course, whether you have ever seen another foot like mine. But do you think such feet common?"

I said that I did not.

"In that case, I am *the* man with the wooden foot, am I not? I might be called that?"

"Certainly," I said.

"Do you hate me? On that account or any other?"

I shook my head. "Of course not, why should I?"

Hegesistratus held out his hands. "Touch me," he said, and I did. "I am real, you see. I can be felt as well as seen and heard. Now I want you to consider our situation. You are young and strong. I am twenty years your senior, and lame. You have no weapon, but you should hardly need one. By the time Elata's cries bring the others, I will be dead."

I told him that I had no desire to harm him—that I was sure he was my friend.

"Then let me tell you how I came to have this." He tapped his foot again. "I was born on the lovely Isle of Zakunthios; but my family originated in the city of Elis, on Redface Island. That is the southernmost part of the mainland of Hellas."

I nodded to show that I understood.

"Our family has always been closer than most to the unseen. For some of us it seems very close indeed; for others no nearer than for other men. Or other women, I should say as well, for the gift is given to them at least as often as to us men, though we men have gained greater fame from it. In me it has been very marked since childhood."

I nodded again.

"As my reputation grew, I was invited several times to come to Elis, our ancestral home. Year after year these invitations came, each more cordial than the last. I consulted the Fates, and each time I was warned not to go.

"After more than a decade of this, a message arrived that came not from the Assembly of Elis, as the previous letters had, but from Iamus, the head of our family. In it he said that no less a god than the Destroyer had thrust aside the veil of the years for him and shown him in such a manner as to inspire his complete confidence that I would one day succeed him, that our family would thrive with me at its head, and that I myself would be rich, and respected throughout Hellas. That being the case—and as I said, he had received such guarantees that there could be no doubt of it—Iamus urged me to visit him in Elis without delay. He is an elderly man, as I ought to have told you. His health is poor, and there were matters concerning certain family properties, and to be honest certain ingrained family quarrels, with which he was eager to acquaint me before Death came to him. He wished to give me his blessing also, and indeed the blessing of such a man is not to be despised."

Hegesistratus fell silent, as men often do when they try to speak of the decisions that have shaped their lives; and at last I asked, "Did you go?"

"No, not at first. I made a pilgrimage to the navel of the world instead, to Dolphins, where—as I told you yesterday—the Destroyer has the greatest of all his oracles. For three days I prayed and sacrificed, and at last, escorted by six priests, I entered the sanctuary of the pythia. My question was: 'If I go to Elis, as it appears that my duty demands, will I escape the danger awaiting me there?' The responses of the god are often cryptic, but this one was as straightforward as any petitioner could desire:

> "Though those most feared lay hold of thee,
> Thy own strong hand shall set thee free."

Hegesistratus smiled bitterly. "What would you have done in my position, Latro?"

"Gone to Elis, I suppose, and been as careful as I could."

He nodded. "That is what I did. The god's words could be interpreted in only one way, as my own good sense, as well as the priests, assured me: I would be beset by enemies of whom others were mortally afraid—in my foolish pride I supposed that these would be from some disaffected group within our family, for not a few are heartily afraid of us, although their fear is seldom warranted—but I would escape by my own efforts.

"And so this prophecy appeared fully reconcilable with the one Iamus had been given, while justifying the many warnings I had received. I went, met with the leading members of all the various branches of our family, and sensed no deadly hostility in any.

"Soon the Assembly invited me to officiate at the Italoan sacrifice, and to foretell, as the custom is, the future of the city from my scrutiny of the victims. So signal an honor could hardly be refused, and in fact I could see no reasons to refuse it, although I warned the magistrates that they might be sorry to hear all that I would tell them—this because I already had some notion of the future of that part of Hellas. They absolved me in advance from any blame and repeated their invitation.

"I performed the sacrifice, and the presages were as urgent and as unambiguous as any I have ever seen—the freedom of Elis was menaced from the south; only by the exercise of the greatest courage and prudence could it hope to preserve even a modicum of its ancient independence. I confess that in conveying this to its citizens I drew somewhat upon previous revelations that had been vouchsafed me; but the portents were so clear that I felt entirely justified in doing it. I left little doubt in anyone's mind as to whom these despots might be, for there was little in my own; and I stressed the urgency of my warning.

"If only I had listened to my own words, I would have fled Elis that night; as it was, I remained until the celebration was complete, spent the following day in thanking Iamus and various other members of our family, and in saying good-bye to everyone, and went to bed resolved to depart next morning.

"And so I did. A dozen Rope Makers reached our wall before dawn, the feebleness of their force a measure of the contempt of Rope for my ancestral city. Few though they were, Elis did not dare to resist them, knowing that the finest army in the world stood behind them. Our gates were flung wide; they marched into our city, hailed me from my bed, and carried me to Rope."

Seeing my wonder, Hegesistratus said, "Oh, there was nothing supernatural about it, I'm sure. Some spy had repeated my words to them, and they had acted at once, as they frequently do. Are you at all familiar with the place?"

Io spoke then for the first time. "We've been there, but I'm sure Latro's forgotten it. It's not much anyway."

Hegesistratus nodded. "There was a pretense—a very thin one—that I was merely the guest of one of their judges; thus I was detained in a private house. My legs were clamped in stocks of iron, and I was questioned for several days. The Rope Makers seemed to believe that someone had bribed me to divine as I had, and they were understandably anxious to learn the identity of my corrupter. When at last I convinced them that I had only spoken the truth, I was informed that I would be publicly disgraced, tortured, and ultimately killed, the following morning.

"That night one of my captors, feigning kindness, provided me with a dagger. Do you know that dishonorable custom of the Rope Makers?"

I shook my head; but I could see the dagger as if I held it in my hand, and I felt I knew what was coming.

"The doomed captive is permitted to take his own life, thus sparing Rope the opprobrium of having done away with some well-regarded person; afterward their judges can swear by every god on the Mountain that he died by his own hand. Some unfortunate slave is accused of having provided the weapon and duly executed—they killed one of their own kings, Cleomenes, in that fashion about ten years ago. I will never forget the sound of the door shutting and the heavy bar outside being set in place, nor the sharpness of the blade as I sat testing it with my thumb."

Io said, "But what about the oracle? Didn't you remember that the Destroyer had promised you'd be able to free yourself?"

"Oh, yes, of course." The bitter smile came again. "And I also recalled how often I had been warned against going to Elis, and how I had continued to ask, by this means and that, until I so wearied all the gods that I received a response that could be twisted into a favorable one, then hurried off. That is what we mortals do, you see; and subsequently we wonder to discover that our gods mock us. I grew up that night, child, and I hope your own maturation is a great deal easier.

"For a long time I simply sat there with the dagger in my hand, listening to the house go to bed. The Destroyer had been correct, of course, as he nearly always is: my own strong hand could free me, and in a very short time, too. All I had to do was plunge that dagger into my chest. But it is hard, terribly hard, for a man to end his own life; King Cleomenes could never strike deep, they say, though eventually he made so many shallow cuts that he bled to death.

"I thought of him sitting in stocks like mine—possibly the very same stocks, and in that very room—striking at himself and flinching, and in a few moments striking and flinching again; it started my thoughts down a fresh path, for I remembered how many animals I had sacrificed in my life, everything from small birds to bulls, always without flinching. And I recalled how slippery their blood had made the handle of my knife, particularly when I had dispatched three or four large animals at a time, as I just had at Elis. Leaning forward, I nicked both feet until my ankles were slick with my own blood; then I wrenched and pulled as hard as I could.

"In that way I was able to get my left foot out, but not my right.

Perhaps it was a little larger; or perhaps that opening was a trifle smaller—I cannot say. By now you know, of course, what I did next; I began to cut away that foot, one small slice at a time. Twice I fainted. Each time I awoke I cut away more, until at last I could draw out what had once been my right foot. So many sacrifices and the examination of so many victims have taught me something about the way an animal is put together; and despite all our boasts, man is only a featherless animal on two legs—if you have ever seen the skinned carcass of a bear, you know how like it is to a human body. I tied off the major blood vessels, trimmed away flesh I knew could not live, and bandaged the stump as well as I could with my filthy chiton."

Io asked, "Could you climb out the window then? I would've thought you'd be too weak."

Hegesistratus shook his head. "There were no windows, but the wall was only mud brick, as the walls of most houses in Rope are. With the dagger, I was able to pry out a few bricks. Rope itself has no city wall; one of its greatest boasts is that its shieldmen are its walls. Late at night, there was nothing and no one to prevent me from hobbling into the countryside, though every step was agony. In the morning I was found by a slave girl milking cows. She and a few of her fellow slaves concealed me in the cowshed until my stump was half-healed; then I made my way to Tegea, and from Tegea, home."

At this point in Hegesistratus's story, three Thracian lords galloped into our camp, all of them finely mounted, with gleaming armor and many gold ornaments on their bridles and their persons. They spoke for some time with Hegesistratus while he interpreted for Hippephode.

After they had gone, she called the Amazons together, and Elata came for Io and me. Hippephode addressed her women while Hegesistratus repeated the message the Thracians had carried to us from their king.

They had begun, he said, by affirming King Kotys's goodwill and offering various proofs of it: he had not killed us, though he had thousands of warriors at his disposal; he had permitted us to camp here close to his capital, had allowed us to buy food and firewood, and so forth. Now, they said, it was time for us to prove our own goodwill toward him and his people. We were to surrender our horses and our arms; and when we had done that, we would be taken before the king, who would listen to whatever requests we might make of him with a gracious ear.

After repeating this to Hippephode, Hegesistratus had asked for time in which to consider the matter, and had been told that if we had not turned over both our horses and all our weapons by tomorrow morning, we would be overwhelmed and killed.

When Hegesistratus had reported this, the black man spoke, and Hegesistratus translated his words for the rest of us, first in the tongue of the Amazons, then in that of the Hellenes. "If this king is indeed our friend," the black man had said, "why should he wish to take away our horses and our weapons? Every king wants his friends well equipped and his foes disarmed. So let us do this. Let us assure this king of our friendship, just as he has assured us. Let us swear to him that if there is any task he requires of us, we will do it—we will slay his enemies, and bring him anything he wishes, though it lies at the edge of the world. But he in turn must allow us to keep our horses and the weapons his service will require, tell us where Oeobazus is, let us take Oeobazus to Thought if Oeobazus is in his kingdom, and give the Amazons the horses they have come so far to get."

If I had known before why the Amazons had come to Thrace, I had forgotten it; but I do not think Io knew, because she looked as surprised as I felt.

Queen Hippephode spoke next; all the Amazons cheered her lustily when she was through, and Hegesistratus interpreted for us: "I agree with everything that Seven Lions has said, but I have one thing more to add. We Amazons are the daughters of the War God; and though we love him, he is a strict father, laying upon us laws we dare not break. One is that we never lay down our arms, lest we become as the daughters of men. We may make peace, but only with one who trusts our pledge; and if he will not trust it and demands that we break our bows, we must fight until we die. To the present day, no Amazon has ever violated this law, which was not made by women or by men, but by the god who is our father. King Kotys must be made to understand that we will not violate it either."

# THIRTEEN

## We Await the Attack

CLETON CAME BACK TO WARN us. This time I talked with him, as well as Hegesistratus, and I must tell about that here; if we live, it is something I may require. But first I will set down everything I had intended to write before Hegesistratus came to speak to me again.

When Hippephode had finished, he asked whether anyone else wished to be heard, and I said we need not ask King Kotys where Oeobazus was; he was in the temple of Pleistorus, the War God. I added that since this god was the father of the Amazons, they could ask him to let Oeobazus come with us. Hippephode promised they would, and I recounted what I had seen and heard the night before. Hegesistratus confirmed that Cleton had come as he had told me he would, and questioned him about Hypereides. Then we voted, with the result I have already recorded.

After that, Hegesistratus talked with Hippephode and the black man; that was when I wrote what stands above, laying it aside when he returned to speak with me again.

"We have been discussing tactics," he asid. "When morning comes, we will send the king a fresh message, offering to give him a hostage as a guarantee of our good behavior. That should at least postpone any attack."

I agreed that seemed an excellent plan, and asked who the hostage would be.

"We will offer to let him choose—any single individual he selects."

"Then he'll choose you," I told Hegesistratus, "if he's not a complete fool. Losing you would cripple us more than losing anyone else."

Hegesistratus nodded. "That is what we hope he will do. If I can meet him face-to-face, I may be able to accomplish a great deal—which brings me to the matter I wanted to tell you about, Latro. And you, Io." She had followed him to the door of the tent, where I was sitting.

"Before the Thracians arrived, I recounted something of my history to you. If I bored you, I am sorry; but I thought that you ought to know why the Rope Makers hate me, and why I hate them."

Io said, "I can certainly understand now why you hate them. But if you were just telling those people in Elis what the gods had told you to tell them, why should they hate you?"

Hegesistratus smiled. "If only everyone were as reasonable as you, there would be fewer quarrels. Unfortunately, men hate anyone who opposes them for any reason. And not only did I warn the Eleans against the Rope Makers, but I have warned many other cities since then—warned anyone who would listen whenever I had the opportunity, in fact. Furthermore, they were humiliated by my escape, and they know that I served Mardonius to the best of my ability.

"I said that the Rope Makers hate me; but there is someone else, a man who is not truly one of them, who hates me far more. Tisamenus of Elis is his name, and this Tisamenus is the mantis of Prince Pausanias, the Regent of Rope."

Io's expression when Hegesistratus pronounced these names was such that I asked her if we had encountered these people. She nodded without speaking.

Hegesistratus said, "Io has already told me that you have met them, although you do not remember it. She has told me, in fact, that Pausanias calls you his slave."

I think I looked angry at that, because he added hastily, "Without any right to do so. Io also told me that she believed you had written a good deal about your interview with Tisamenus in your other book—more, or so she thought, than you had told her. Would you be willing to read it to me?"

"Of course," I said. "But you called him Tisamenus of Elis and said that he was this prince's mantis. Is he a relative of yours?"

Hegesistratus sighed and nodded. "He is—a rather remote one, but of our blood nonetheless. I told you that there were family quarrels. Do you remember that?"

"Yes," I told him. "Certainly."

"The most ancient of all is that between the Telliadae and the Clytiadae—the sons of Tellias and the sons of Clytias, who betrayed him. I am of the Telliadae, as you know; Tisamenus is of the Clytiadae. He is of about my own age. Should I recount a little of his background?"

Io said, "I wish you would. I'd like to know more about him."

"Very well then. Although the Clytiadae are descended from the first Iamus just as we Telliadae are, they lack something of our reputation, and I have heard that the young Tisamenus showed few of the early signs that mark an authentic mantis. Instead, his chief ambition was to gain honor as a victor in the games—for he possesses extraordinary swiftness of both body and mind, and great strength for a man of no great size.

"Though he had married sooner than most, his wife bore him no children; and with that as an excuse, he borrowed sufficient funds from his wife's family to take him to Dolphins to consult the Destroyer. Once there, however, he took the opportunity to question the god about his whole future, and was assured that he should win five glorious victories."

Io asked, "You mean running races and so on?"

Hegesistratus shook his head. "No, though that is what he believed. As you perhaps know, the great games in honor of the Destroyer take place at Olympia, which is near Elis, every four years. Tisamenus enrolled himself as a contestant in no fewer than five events.

"It was the talk of Elis, as you may imagine, and word of it reached us on Zakunthios very quickly. An uncle of mine, my mother's brother Polycletos, asked that I look into the matter. I consulted the gods by half a dozen methods; the results were uniformly negative, and I reported that Tisamenus would win none of the events he had entered, which proved correct.

"But enough of this—I know I am taxing your patience. Let me say briefly that after the games Tisamenus soon discerned his true vocation and was taken into Pausanias's service, and that he has never forgiven me. Presumably the battles of Peace and Clay were two of the victories the god promised him, for Eurybiades, who commanded the combined fleets at Peace, is a subordinate of Pausanias's, while the regent himself directed the allied armies at Clay."

Hegesistratus fell silent for moment, his piercing eyes fixed on mine. "Here you must accept my word for what I tell you. It is possible for a mantis—if he is both skilled and powerful—to cast a spell that will force another to work his will. Are you aware of that?"

We both nodded.

"The magi, as the sorcerers of Parsa are called, are adept at it. I learned it from one of them while I was in Mardonius's service. Where Tisamenus has learned it, I cannot say; perhaps from a magus taken prisoner at Peace, though that is conjecture. But I feel sure that he *has* learned it; and if you, Latro, will read the applicable passage from your book aloud, I may discover something of interest."

Accordingly I untied the cords of my other scroll, searched it for the name of Tisamenus, and read aloud everything I found, beginning with the words, "In the regent's tent there was no one to meet me." One section Hegesistratus asked me to read twice. I give here precisely as it is in the older scroll:

"There is one more thing to tell, though I hesitate to write of it. A moment ago, as I was about to enter this tent Io and I share with Drakaina and Pasicrates, I heard the strange, sly voice of Tisamenus at my ear: *'Kill the man with the wooden foot!'* When I looked around for him, there was no one in sight."

Hegesistratus nodded as if to himself. "There it is. When I mentioned these spells, I ought to have told you also that the caster can—and often does—steal the memory of the event. I do not mean it is lost after a single day, as you ordinarily forget everything; rather it is forgotten at once, as soon as the event itself is past. In this case it appears that my cousin was not quite so skillful as he perhaps thought himself, for in you, who forget everything, some fragment of memory remained for you to record, though it seemed to you nothing more than a voice in the wind. Perhaps knowledge of your condition made him careless, or perhaps the very flaw that makes you forget everything permitted you to remember this."

Io said, "Tisamenus was really there, even if Latro didn't remember him being there as soon as he left—is that what you're telling us? Like you can't touch a ghost?" She shivered.

Hegesistratus said, "Latro's memory of him was killed, if you will allow it; its ghost vanished, as ghosts frequently do. When Latro, with

Prince Pausanias and a shieldman of Pausanias's bodyguard, returned from the cliff after viewing the ship that would take you both to Sestos, my cousin must have called Latro aside. I would guess that he took him to his own tent, though it is barely possible that the whole thing was done elsewhere, in some other place where he could feel certain he would not be interrupted. There he cast the spell, and as it happens we can be fairly sure of the very words he used: 'Kill the man with the wooden foot.' But there was a second spell as well; one to make Latro forget the first. It was intended, at least, to make him forget that he had spoken to Tisamenus without Pausanias present. I doubt that the regent would have appreciated having the man he was sending to the Chersonese employed for a private purpose by my crafty cousin, so the second spell—the spell of oblivion—would have been absolutely necessary."

Io had been chewing a lock of her hair; she spat it out to speak. "But I remember when Latro and the black man found us at that place outside the city. He didn't try to kill you then."

"Yes, he did," Hegesistratus told her. "Although you must understand that he himself did not realize what he was doing; he did not plan these acts. He brought me to the house Hypereides had commandeered, where his sword was. He saw to it that I was seated and relaxed, and he got his sword."

"But you hit it with your crutch! I remember. Latro, you looked like somebody who'd been woken up with a kick."

Hegesistratus told her, "That is a very good way to think about it. Under such a spell the charmed person moves as though in a dream, and scarcely seems to know that he walks and strikes in the waking world.

"There were a couple of oddities involved, by the way—one that helped my cousin, one that opposed him. It is difficult to force any man to act against his essential nature, you see. For example, if I were to cast such a spell on you, ordering you to pat your horse's nose, there would be no difficulty—it would be something you would have no rooted objection to doing, and you would do it. But if I were to tell you to kill someone instead, that might be another matter. I doubt that you have ever done such a thing."

Io shook her head. "I haven't."

"Latro, however, has been a soldier, and indeed from what you and the black man have told me, he was in the Great King's army when it marched down from Horseland. It is probable that he has killed a good many sons of Hellen; I was only one more."

I asked him, "What was it that worked against the spell? I'd rather hear about that."

*"Lingua tua,"* Hegesistratus said, using the very words that I write here. "Your tongue. Tisamenus did not know it, and so he had to cast his spell in one not your own, which is extremely difficult; I was surprised to find that he had succeeded as well as he clearly had.

"After I had reviewed everything I knew of the subject, and consulted with a certain friend who was hiding in Sestos—do not speak about this man to others, please—I returned, intending to remove the spell if I could. I found Latro writing; he had put his sword away again, but he had that little bone-handled knife he uses to sharpen his stylus, and when I attempted to take off Tisamenus's spell, he stabbed me with it." Hegesistratus touched his side. "The wound is still not quite healed, and perhaps it will always give me a twinge at times. But to continue, seeing how hazardous that was, I cast several spells of my own—one to make him overlook my wooden foot, for instance. Of course you know what happened to that."

"No," Io said. "I don't. What was it?"

"Then you were not listening when Latro spoke to all of us a short while ago. He recounted his conversation with Cleton, the merchant from Hundred-Eyed he discovered in Cobrys. He had mentioned my name to him, and Cleton, suspecting nothing, called me 'the man with the wooden foot.' "

I nodded. "And that made me want to return here and kill you. I practically forgot about Oeobazus."

"Exactly. But there are powers in the four worlds that are far greater than my wicked cousin, and one chose to protect me. Or perhaps chose to protect us both, for if you had killed me as you tried to, it is more than probable that either the Amazons or the black man would have killed you—people generally do not take kindly to someone, even another friend, who kills a friend while he is asleep. But as I started to say, I am protected by certain spells and charms, and it is most probable that one of the gods they invoke stepped in to save me."

Io said, "Then maybe they'll save us tomorrow."

I saw how frightened she was and hugged her, telling her that only those of us who fight are liable to be killed, and the worst thing that can happen to her is having to sweep the floors of some Thracian house.

# FOURTEEN

## *In the Cave of the Mother of the Gods*

T HIS IS WRITTEN BY THE light of our fire. Cedar is stored here for
the sacred fire, and the embers were still smouldering from a sacrifice. Io found the wood and puffed the embers while the rest of us
fought at the mouth. Three Amazons are missing, and two more are
wounded badly. The black man's cheek was laid open by a thrust; Hegesistratus sews it shut. No one knows what has happened to Elata.

It is raining outside.

I have just read what I wrote before sunset, and there is much more I
must write down. Cleton returned. Hegesistratus, Queen Hippephode,
the black man, Io, and I spoke with him, and he told us about the
prophecy.

"I went to the palace," he said. "I've done some trading for King
Kotys—very profitable for him—and I like to believe I've got some
influence. I had to wait quite awhile, but they brought me in to see him
at last.

"He was sitting at table with three noblemen, with his best gold
rhyton in front of him. Those drinking horns they have are symbols of
power, did you know that? If you've got one, you'd better be ready to
back it up. Well, I could see that he was a little drunk, which is unusual
for him. All the barbarians are pretty hard drinkers, but Kotys usually
carries it better than most of them. The way you reason with a king
(this is what I've found myself) is you tell him he's got a problem and
offer to take care of it for him—so that's what I did. I said I knew he
had all of you outside his city, some of you barbarians from the east
(because you always tell barbarians it's the other fellows) and who knows
what the tribe might do if there was real trouble? And some of you my

own countrymen that had just beat the Great King and all his Medes, and were liable to have an army on his doorstep any day.

"I said right away that I'd gone out here to talk to you, because it's always better to tell them yourself before somebody else does. I said what I'd heard was that you were traders, so I'd got my wagon and my best mules and come out here hoping to do a little business. I told him, too, that Egbeo's doing a fine job. Egbeo's in charge of your guards, see? I bribed him—not much—so I didn't want him to get into trouble.

"Then I said I'd found out you weren't really traders, but pilgrims and ambassadors from Thought, because Kotys knows all about Thought, it and Hundred-Eyed being just about the biggest trading cities up this way. I told him it looked to me like the whole thing could be wrapped up without hard feelings, so if he'd just have his key people cooperate with me, I'd try to take care of everything for him.

"Then he grinned and said, 'When the moon's high,' and all the nobles went *haw, haw!* I knew right then there was something up, so I said, no, I'd really been planning to go out here again and see about it this afternoon.

"He shook his head. 'Cleton, my friend, don't you trouble yourself about them anymore today. Go tomorrow. Then you'll have my permission to act in whatever way you think best.'

"I bowed three times and backed out, saying how happy I was to be of service, got the wagon again, drove up to the temple of Pleistorus, and asked to see Oeobazus. Kotys is high priest, but there's always somebody there, and they're priests, too. I knew a couple of them, and when I said I'd just come from the palace and was supposed to set some things up for tomorrow, they let me talk to him. Have any of you seen the place?"

None of us had, and we told him so.

"Well, don't expect a nice marble building like one of our big temples back home. It's pretty big, all right, but built out of this local stone—limestone, I guess—and it's pretty narrow, because the boys up here don't trust themselves with long spans. You have to go in at the front where there's a hall so that the most important ones can get out of the weather. Then the altar and so forth, and a great big wooden statue. In back of it is a nice curtain I got them from Sidon. Some of the nobles' wives have embroidered it with the god riding his horse.

His lion's running alongside, and he's got his lance in one hand and his wine horn in the other. They wanted to do Zalmoxis as a boar down in one corner, but there wasn't room enough for that, and besides, it would be mostly in back of the statue down there. So I told them just to do his front, his forequarters, if you follow me. His head—"

Hegesistratus held up one hand. "Were you able to speak to Oeobazus?"

Cleton nodded. "They've got him in a room in back. It's got a window, but it's way too small for anybody to get through, and there's a couple of bars in it. Kotys is going to sacrifice him."

I do not believe Hegesistratus is often surprised, but he was surprised by that; I saw him blink. Hippephode touched his shoulder and he translated for her, using a tenth as many words as Cleton had. I told Cleton I had not known that these people practiced human sacrifice.

"Only the kings do it." Looking important, Cleton clasped his hands behind his back and threw out his chest. "The king's sacrifice can't be like an ordinary man's, so the difference is that commoners and even nobles sacrifice animals like we do, but the kings sacrifice people. Usually they're captives from their raids. You've got to take into account that the king isn't just a regular man." He winked. "The king's descended from Tereus—lots of them are named for him—and *he* was the son of Pleistorus himself. Pleistorus is the son of Kotytto—that's our Rhea—and sometimes he's her lover, too. So when the king stands up there at the altar with his sacred regalia on and chops the head off a *human being*, you know he's something more. It's one of the ways he proves it, see?"

"When?" Hegesistratus asked.

"Tomorrow," Cleton told him. Hippephode knew that word; I saw the shock on her face even as I felt it on my own. No one said anything until Cleton added, "He moved it up—they weren't supposed to do it until next month."

There was another silence, and at last Io asked, "Does he know about it?"

Cleton nodded. "He was the one that told me, then I talked to the priests, told them I wanted to see it and so on. There's no secret about it, and in fact the priests have been trying to get the news out—sending out heralds and so forth—ever since Kotys ordered it. If you ask me, he's got this spring's oracle on his mind."

Hegesistratus grunted. "Then perhaps you had better tell us about that in some detail."

"Well, every year whoever's king up here sends an embassy to Lesbos, where they keep Orpheus's head in a vault underneath the temple of Bromios. You know about that? The head's still alive, or anyhow it's supposed to be. And in the way of thanks for the gifts the ambassadors brought it, it gives the king some good advice for the year that's starting. Generally it doesn't amount to much, stuff that boils down to beware of strangers but trust your friends and so forth. Only sometimes it'll make your hair dance across your head, and then pretty often the king will cut the throats of a few of his dear relations because of it."

Hegesistratus said, "I assume that this was one of those years. What was the oracle?"

"The exact words?" Cleton asked.

"That would be best, if you remember them."

"I couldn't forget them if I wanted to," Cleton told him. "It's announced every year at the festival, and this year half Cobrys reeled it off to you until you were sick to death of it." He recited something in singsong Thracian.

Hegesistratus pulled at his beard, his eyes half-shut, and addressed Hippephode in the speech of the Amazons. She stared at him, I noticed, before touching herself just below the neck. He shrugged and turned to us. "I am not sure I can render it in acceptable verse, but I will try.

> "Ill fare the strong when god, god smites,
> Then howl the hounds and wheel the kites.
> Doves stoop like hawks, and oxen gore,
> The child rides armed, and maids to war.
> Then Bendis seeks to halt the sun,
> But see how swift the lions run!
> The Lord of Battles, battle brings,
> And battle drinks the blood of kings."

When Hegesistratus was finished, I glanced at the black man and he at me so that when I spoke it was for both. "I don't see that it has anything to do with Oeobazus."

Io added, "Or with us. Aren't you going to explain it to us, He-gesistratus?"

"Later, possibly." To Cleton he muttered, "All this sounds extremely serious, my friend. Have you more bad news for us?"

"I think so," Cleton said. "But I'll let you judge it for yourselves. After I left the temple—this wasn't long ago, you understand—I had to go back to the city to catch the road that comes here. Well, I ran into Egbeo and thought they'd let you go, so I stopped him and asked. He said no, his orders had been to get everybody onto fresh horses, so he'd sent them off one at a time and gone last himself."

I told Hegesistratus, "They plan to attack us when the moon is high—it will give light enough for them to use their lances. There will be many more than our present guards, I imagine; and this King Kotys may very well lead them in person."

Hegesistratus shook his head. "Do you really think they may? I would have said that we could trust the king's word."

Cleton declared frankly, "Well, I wouldn't."

When all of us had thanked him for his information and good offices, and watched his mule-drawn wagon rattle down the road, Hegesistratus told me, "You are quite correct, Latro, I am sure. But although I do not believe our friend Cleton is a spy for the king, he may very well repeat what he has heard here to someone in the city. If he does, it may reach the king's ears, or those of one of his officers. We must get away tonight, if we can."

Seeing the questions in my eyes, he added, "I would like to consult the gods before I say anything further, and the Amazons have yet to beseech the father of their race."

He spoke briefly with their queen, then said, "Hippephode agrees that a horse would make a suitable sacrifice. Certainly it must be the worst we have, for under these circumstances we cannot spare the best. I believe the god—this god particularly—will understand. Perhaps one of the horses we took from the Thracians at our first encounter. Then I will leave it to you two"—he meant the black man and me—"to devise a plan for our escape, with Hippephode. You must be our strategists, and I shall be your mantis—though I will have to translate for you, I fear."

The Amazons built an altar of wood and earth and plunged a short sword into it. Meanwhile, the black man and I had washed the worst of the horses (which I thought still a very good horse indeed) and decorated it with such finery as Io and Elata could contrive. Hippephode performed the actual rite, slitting the horse's throat after what I assume were appropriate prayers and a hymn sung by all the Amazons. Hippostizein, the tallest, caught the blood in a basin, smeared some on the sacred sword, and threw the rest into the fire. Then the queen and Hegesistratus opened the paunch, and cast the heart and liver, with other organs and certain bones, into the flames. Hegesistratus watched them and the smoke with care, and scrutinized both shoulder blades before telling us what he had learned.

"There is bad news," he said, "but good news, too. We will not escape every danger threatening us unscathed; but it appears that in the end we shall obtain what we wish."

The black man gestured quickly toward Elata, Io, himself, and me, and then toward Hippephode and her Amazons.

"Yes," Hegesistratus said. "Both groups, not immediately—not tonight, I believe—but soon. Ares, at least, is pleased to grant his daughters' request."

The black man crept past the sentries as soon as the sun had set so that he might watch the road. We assumed that the Thracian leader would ride at the head; and though it would be well if he were the king, if he were not he would nevertheless be the best hostage. Io and Elata were to remain behind in our tent. The rest of us mounted as soon as we could be certain we would not be seen, hoping to attack before the moon rose—even the wounded Amazon sat a horse, insisting (so it seemed) that she was well enough to fight, when Hippephode ordered her into the tent with Io and Elata. Someone kissed me in the darkness, and I think it was she. Certainly it was a woman larger and stronger than Elata.

# FIFTEEN

## *I Would Go Now*

HEGESISTRATUS WILL NOT AGREE TO it, and I have promised to defer to him. We spoke in private and agreed that if something is to be done, it must be done quickly, and I am the one to do it. I told him I planned to go as soon as I finished; but he insists I rest first and sleep if I can.

This is because of the events he foresaw in the flames of our sacrifice—that though we would indeed secure Oeobazus, it would not be tonight. If we wait for dawn, he says, it will be easier to discover the other exit from the cave, if one exists. I had planned to leave through the mouth, for which night would be the best time and in fact the only possible time. Perhaps I should not have agreed, though there is as he says a wind from the mouth. I can see it carrying away the smoke.

I have just reread what I wrote before Hegesistratus came, and I find that I passed over something that should be set down before I forget. After our sacrifice, Io asked Hegesistratus about the spring oracle again.

He said, "I suppose that nothing less than a full, line-by-line exegesis will satisfy you; very well, I will attempt one. But you must realize that the king will have a sage of his own; and that this sage, having a sizable body of the pronouncements of this oracle to study, will understand it far better than I.

" 'Ill fare the strong when god, god smites' is the initial line, and the sole questions involved are the identities of 'the strong' and of the gods. It is not at all uncommon for oracles such as this to set a riddle in the first which is solved in the final line, and I believe that to be the case here; 'the strong' are the kings referred to in the last line. Do you follow that?"

Io nodded, and so did the black man and I.

"At least three gods are mentioned, though there well may be more. Those we can be certain of are 'the Lord of Battles,' that is, the War God; 'Bendis,' which is the Thracian name for the Huntress; and 'the sun,' which can only be her twin. Those three we can feel certain are involved.

"The second line runs 'Then howl the hounds and wheel the kites.' The wheeling kites would appear to indicate that many will die; kites feed upon carrion and wheel over battlefields. The question is whether 'hounds' refers to the many-headed dog who protects the principal entrance to the Lands of the Dead. Because Bendis is referred to so openly, I think them hunting dogs instead, and if I am right, the line means, 'There will be pursuit, and many will die.' "

Io said, "What does it mean about the child?"

"Be patient," Hegesistratus told her. "We shall reach that soon enough. The next line is 'Doves stoop like hawks, and oxen gore.' I believe this line may bear two meanings; the first and certainly the most obvious is simply that the orderly operations of nature will be suspended—there will be prodigies. Doves do not swoop down upon their prey like falcons in the normal course of things, and oxen are the most docile of beasts. But I think that we are being told here as well that specific individuals or groups whom we do not expect to fight will do so. Doves are of course birds sacred to the Goddess of Love, and when they appear in prophecy they most frequently represent fair young women—you will recall that when we sacrificed at the grove of Itys outside Pactye I told you about two princesses who were transformed into similar birds. The 'oxen' mentioned in the second half of this line are presumably peasants, though in this country, as in our own, the peasants are far from docile and often accompany their lords on their raids."

I told Hegesistratus, "The next line's the one that Io's so interested in: 'The child rides armed, and maids to war.' "

"Correct," he said. "Latro, you have an excellent memory when you have one at all. That is indeed the line as I gave it, but unfortunately there is very little I can tell you about it. 'The child' may possibly be the God of Love, the goddess's son; but as he habitually goes armed, and flies rather than rides, I have little confidence in that interpretation.

The Huntress is another weak possibility—passing at once to woman-
hood, she has remained a child in some respects; and it is true that she
often rides, particularly here in Thrace. But she, too, habitually goes
armed, so that this interpretation is open to the same objection as the
first one. Worse, she is named outright in the line that follows: 'Then
Bendis seeks to halt the sun.' She will act when 'the child rides armed,'
and thus she herself is unlikely to be the child referred to. What would
be the point in saying that she will act when she acts? I would guess
that this 'child' is someone with whom we are unfamiliar, possibly a
prince of this or a neighboring state.

"The 'maids' are in all probability the persons referred to as 'doves'
in the line above, and if that is correct, these two lines with the 'doves-
maids' pair constitute a smaller cycle of riddle and solution set within
the greater one. If 'the child' is indeed the Huntress, then the 'maids'
Orpheus has said will ride to war may well be the nymphs of her train—
but a far more probable solution has already occurred to all three of you;
I can see it in your faces."

The black man pointed emphatically toward the Amazons, and Io
and I named them.

Hegesistratus nodded. "And that, we can say with virtual certainty,
is the interpretation the king and his adviser have settled on. Consider
King Kotys's situation; he received this oracle in spring, nearly a year
ago, and it hints strongly that he himself may be killed, warning that
'when god, god smites . . . battle drinks the blood of kings.' Summer
finds the mighty forces of the Great King streaming through Apsinthia
in full retreat. Can this be what the oracle foretold? But the Great King
was not even wounded, and in any case Orpheus's oracle was given to
him, Kotys, and not to Xerxes, as we call him.

"Now, so near the year's end, warrior maidens—perhaps to Kotys
an unheard-of thing—appear in his kingdom. From what Cleton has
told us, we may be certain that the first party of Apsinthians we encountered knew of the oracle. They molested us and found themselves
attacked by maids riding to war; thus the second party, which agreed
to a truce and conducted us to Cobrys. Latro, you are King Kotys. What
will you do next?"

"Come here, I suppose," I said, "and see the warrior maids for myself."

"You would be running a grave risk," Hegesistratus told me. "As your adviser in all such matters, it is my duty to warn you that the events foretold may not occur until you yourself have encountered one— or perhaps all—of the portents. If you do as you plan, King Kotys, you may yourself bring about the very results you fear."

I nodded. "I think I understand. What do you advise me to do, Lord Hegesistratus?"

"First, send three trustworthy men to verify that these are indeed warrior maidens, as specified by Orpheus. Second, disarm them. If you attempt to destroy them, they are sure to resist; and their resistance may itself begin the war spoken of. But if you deprive them of their weapons and horses, they cannot 'ride to war.' "

Io shouted, "Wait a moment! I know he sent those lords who wore so much gold, and he wants us to give him our weapons and horses. But he gave us until tomorrow morning, and now you and Latro say he's really going to attack tonight."

Hegesistratus sighed. "Yes, I'm afraid he is. Cleton and the gods brought the same warning; thus we can be as sure of it as of anything. Although we did not say outright that we would not surrender our horses and weapons, we were playing for time, and he knew it. Now he means to take the wolf by its ears if he can. Kings may bleed, but a wound may be all that is meant, or the oracle may refer to other kings, not to him. Or the oracle itself may be false; the Bright God is said to spoil the oracles of Orpheus from time to time, and as we have already seen, he is certainly involved in all this, acting in opposition to his twin sister."

Io jumped up, too excited to sit still. "So was that why he moved up sacrificing Oeobazus? Because he wanted to get on the good side of the Lord of Battles?"

"Precisely. Let us consider the four final lines as one: 'Then Bendis seeks to halt the sun,/But see how swift the lions run!/The Lord of Battles, battle brings,/And battle drinks the blood of kings.' Bendis and the sun we have spoken of already. I would guess that 'the lions' are strategists or perhaps mighty warriors; they rush to battle. The Lord of Battles is of course Ares—or Pleistorus, as he is called here. All right, he is to bring battle, but someone will presumably be victorious. May it not be Kotys himself? The divine favor of Pleistorus is thus to be sought at once, and fortunately a suitable victim is at hand. Kotys will destroy the warrior maidens if he can, then urgently petition Pleistorus's favor."

That was all Hegesistratus said then, or if there was more, I do not remember it now. But when we spoke here in the temple—apart from the others and in the tongue I write, so that they could not understand us—he gave me a warning that may be of the greatest importance.

"You do not remember our conversation with the Huntress," he said, "but perhaps you have read of it in your book today?"

"I didn't," I told him, "but at the moment whatever she may have said to us is of no interest to me. You speak my tongue—tell me where my land lies."

Hegesistratus shook his head. "I would if I could, but I do not know. If we live through this night, I can consult the gods for you. Do you wish it?"

"How can you speak my tongue and yet not know where it's spoken?"

Hegesistratus seated himself beside me; this was before we talked about my going to the temple. "Because I am the man I am. Do you know of Megistias?"

That name signified nothing to me.

"He was the mantis of King Leonidas of Rope, and died with him. It was given to him to know the speech of every bird and beast, and thus he learned of many faraway things, though once he told me that most beasts, and all birds, concern themselves little with the doings of our kind."

I asked, "Could a bird tell me where my home lies?"

"I doubt it. In any case, I—who sometimes talk with gods—cannot converse with birds. Yet another power of tongues has been given me as that was given him; I know the speech of every man I meet, and of every woman. I cannot explain how I do it. Mardonius often used to ask me, but I could only ask in reply how it was that he could not. It is possible I never learned, as other children do, to speak our own tongue at all."

I believe that at that moment I could have fallen upon my sword. "It seems to be the will of the gods," I said, "that I never find my home."

"If that is indeed their will, you must bow to it," he counseled me. "Will you read the words of the Huntress?"

I shook my head.

"Then I will tell you. She promised you that you should be returned to your friends. I did not speak of it earlier because your slave girl was listening; but I tell you now. I advise you to read that part of your book, and also to read again that part which you read aloud this afternoon in the tongue of the sons of Hellen."

Here I will write of the battle. The moon was low in the east when we heard the black man's cry. At once we broke the circle of our guards, Hippephode leading her Amazons at my left, Hegesistratus at my right. Two were before us, but the Amazons' bows sang; though I forget everything else, I will never forget the whiz of the arrows. The bones of the Thracians broke under our horses' hooves.

The king's hand was upon his sword, but before it cleared the scabbard I was upon him; I pinned his arms to his sides and wrenched him from his saddle. A Thracian charged me—I recall the gleam of the moonlight on his lance head. I swung my horse about so that the king's body would receive the lance, and the Thracian raised it and galloped past. The king is very strong; he freed an arm and struck me in the face, so that it seemed to me that all the stars of heaven had rushed into my eyes; but I got one hand around his throat and choked him until he no longer tried to pull my arm away.

All this time I was riding north by west as we had agreed, driving my heels again and again into my horse's sides. He is a fine horse, but he could not outrun the Thracian horses with two heavy men upon his back. The black man, Hegesistratus, and some of the women reined in until they rode beside or behind me. The black man held a javelin still, and with it he killed the first Thracian who would have overtaken us, turning in the saddle and casting it hard and well when the Thracian was very near. The arrows of the Amazons rid us of more, the men tumbling off their horses, or their horses falling under them; but there were too many.

Suddenly I felt that we were flying. I looked down and saw the silver bow of the moon below us, so that it appeared we had leaped above the sky. It was only one of the ditches with which the Thracian farmers drain their fields, and my horse had jumped it before I knew it was there. He stumbled on the farther side; I almost fell, and nearly dropped the king.

In a moment more, I knew that I must, or die. The man on my right was not Hegesistratus but a Thracian, his lance poised high for a thrust. I would have thrown his king at his head if I could; but though I lifted him well, I could not make such a throw from horseback. The king fell between us, and the lancer pulled up, as I knew he would. I could cast my javelins then. One I killed, I think; one I missed.

I do not know how we found this sacred cave. We rode into the hills, then along a road, because it was only there that our horses could gallop. I heard a voice: *"Latro! Latro!"* It was the black man, and though it seems that he seldom speaks, he was shouting. The road ended at the mouth; it glowed crimson in the night, lit by the embers of its altar fire. It is too low to ride through, even if the rider lies on the neck of his horse, though the chamber is much loftier a short way in.

When I reached the black man and the others gathered at the mouth, the black man dismounted and led his horse inside, waving for the rest of us to follow. A young priest rushed at him with a sword; the priest's thrust would surely have killed him had it been a finger's width to the right, but the black man caught his wrist and cut his throat.

Elata is no longer with us; we left her behind in the tent. I believed that Io was there as well until I saw her among the Amazons (this was before she built the new fire for us). I told her she would have been killed had she met one of the Thracians face-to-face.

"I did, and on foot he would have been nearly as big as you, but on our horses we were about the same. I stuck him in the neck."

Several Thracians rushed into the cave on foot, but Amazons killed two with arrows, and the rest fled back out the mouth.

I asked Io where she had found her sword.

"The queen gave it to me," she said. "Queen Hippephode."

I told her, "She shouldn't have, Io, and you shouldn't have taken it."

She had finished wiping the blade (far more thoroughly than it required, and on the hem of her own peplos) and had knelt to blow on the embers, pretending to pay very little attention to what I was saying. "I asked her. I told her I couldn't shoot a bow, but I can ride as good as anybody, and you'd need everybody to protect you if you were going to steal King Kotys. She asked me if I knew what it meant, going into a battle, and I said I'd seen lots of fighting, I'd just never done it. Then she looked through her things and gave me this sword."

"She wouldn't give you her own sword, surely."

"It belonged to an Amazon who got killed before they met us. That's what she said."

I wanted to take it from her, but how could I disarm her when I knew we might be fighting for our lives again very soon?

"I guess she still feels bad about her friend that died," Io said, "because she was crying when she gave it to me. I didn't think they cried."

And that is all I will write now. I must sleep a little—Hegesistratus has promised to wake me at dawn. Except that Io told me she had taken the young priest's robe, thinking that she might make a chiton from the unstained part. "He's been cut," she told me. "Like they do with yearling bulls." She pointed to her own groin.

# SIXTEEN

## The Horses of the Sun

THE WHITE HORSES PHARETRA AND I stole are stabled with our own; and indeed (like the sun itself) they seem to wash every shadow. Queen Hippephode says that we must not slaughter them, no matter what happens, and Hegesistratus agrees; but the Thracians do not know that.

I had been asleep. I believe this was the sleep I spoke of when I last wrote on this scroll, saying, "I must sleep a little—Hegesistratus has promised to wake me at dawn." But it was not Hegesistratus (he is the mantis, and has a wooden foot) who woke me, but the Men of Thrace.

No, not even them in truth, but the sentry in the mouth of the cave. She shouted that they were coming, and I woke at the sound of her voice. I saw her draw her bow and let fly before she ran back toward the sacred fire. She nocked another shaft, turned, and shot again without ever breaking step; I would have thought such bowmanship beyond the reach of mortals, but I saw it and write only what I saw.

The Thracians ran in through the narrow mouth, but by that time I was on my feet, and this sword—FALCATA is written on the blade—was in my hand. Those in the van were highborn, or so I should guess. They had fine helmets, well-painted shields, and costly armor, of scales sewn to leather. Behind them were many peltasts; some had helmets, and each two javelins.

I believe that the Thracians would have been wiser to form a phalanx with their lances, but they had left them outside and came raggedly, sword in hand. I myself killed only two of the Thracian lords. After the fight, I would have claimed the mail shirt of one; but Falcata had spoiled both, cleaving the bronze with the flesh. There was a third with an arrow through his eye, however; Queen Hippephode and her Amazons presented me with his mail. I am wearing it now.

I cannot tell how many peltasts I killed. There were many dead; but the black man fought with the priest's sword, it would be difficult to distinguish wounds left by Falcata from those of Hegesistratus's ax, and some of the Amazons used their swords, I think. Hippephode fears all may exhaust their arrows, but those shot in this battle they reclaimed, or most of them.

In the cave's gullet, three peltasts could front me, and no more; I cut down several, while the bows of the Amazons thrummed like lyres. When the peltasts fell back to cast their javelins, the Amazons slew many more with arrows, and the javelins grazed the stone, which is so low in places that I must stoop to walk there. We laughed at them.

When the fighting was over, and the Amazons had honored me with this armor, we decided that Hegesistratus should approach the Thracians crying a truce, for we had not wood enough to burn all the bodies. Besides, we agreed that if Hegesistratus could meet with King Kotys, he might make some agreement that would be to our benefit, since the War God was plainly on our side, and had in fact favored his daughters so greatly in the battle that not one had received a serious wound.

Hegesistratus talked with the king, and afterward everyone began dragging the bodies of the dead Thracians to the mouth of the cave, where the living Thracians were to claim them. That was when I stole away, though it was not yet dawn.

A hundred steps from the sacred hearth, the cave was darker than the blackest night. I very much regretted that I had not brought a torch, though I knew I could not have made one without drawing attention to myself; the black man would have insisted on coming, though his cheek pains him so much, and perhaps the queen would have wanted to send some of her Amazons as well. So many, I felt certain (and Hegesistratus had agreed), would only weaken the rest by their absence, and could accomplish no more than one; if Oeobazus were to be rescued, it would have to be by stealth, for we had not force enough.

Yet as I crept along, I feared that I might forget; and in this, too, Hegesistratus had concurred. At his suggestion, I had thrust this scroll through my belt. I had promised him that if I discovered another way out of the cave, I would stop and read it as soon as there was light enough.

As I have written already, I wore the armor the Amazons had given me; I should write also that I had Falcata, the helmet of one of the lords I had killed, a pair of javelins, and a pelta; for I had thought it would be well for me to look as much like a patrician of Thrace as I could. Of the helmet and javelins, I was soon exceedingly glad, because the first saved my head from many a knock, and I probed the uneven stones before my feet with the iron heads of the second; but I had to cast the pelta aside, for twice I had to climb in order to keep the faint draft I felt full on my face. I was counting my strides and had counted one thousand two hundred seventeen when I heard the roaring of a lion and the snarl of another.

To meet such a beast in that blackness would mean my death, I knew—and yet I was not willing to go back, and tried to turn aside instead; but though I left what seemed the larger passage, I heard the lions before me still. Many times I wondered what had brought them so deep into the hill; though I knew they often slept in caves by day, I had not thought they would willingly enter one so far.

When I had counted more than two thousand steps, I glimpsed light. Then I felt myself a fool indeed, because the answer to the riddle seemed plain: the lions had not gone so far into the dark, but rather had made their den in the very place I sought, the opening through which the draft blew. And though I had no liking for lions even by day, it seemed likely that a few stones and a shout or two might permit me to slip past them. Not many wild beasts will face an armed man by choice.

As the light grew brighter, and the rocks and slippery mud over which I had groped my way so long appeared, I recalled the promise I had made Hegesistratus; but though I took this scroll from my belt and untied the cords, I could not distinguish the words, and had to walk farther before I could sit down upon a stone and read everything I wrote yesterday, beginning with "I would go now." And even then, I was not actually within sight of the mouth.

At last I read of the oracles of the ox and the child and how each had been fulfilled, all of which I believe I recalled at that time, as well as my writing about them, although I have forgotten those things now.

After that it was time to face the lions in earnest. I rolled this scroll up again, put it in my belt as before, and advanced with a javelin in each hand.

Soon I met with an illusion so extraordinary that it ought to have forewarned me of what was to come, though in fact it did not. To my left there rose a pillar of the kind sometimes found in caves, lofty and damp. Stretching from the stone beneath my boots to the stone over my head, it glistened like pearl; but I am not sure I would have paid much heed to it if it had not at first appeared otherwise to me. For when upon approaching it, I had merely glimpsed it from the corner of one eye, it had seemed to me not a natural object at all, but rather just such a column as is often seen in the houses men build for the gods, columns of white marble or wood painted white.

When I took my gaze from it and walked on, it again seemed to me a thing made by hands, so that I stopped, turned back, and stared.

After that, I felt I traveled not in the cave but through a broken and tempestuous landscape, where rock and mud alternated with smooth walls and floors, and they with sallow grass and the bright blue skies of droughty summer. The sharp stone teeth of the cave seemed simultaneously a forest of columns and a thicket of spears, all echoing to the roaring of the lions who waited for me outside.

For they were outside, beyond even this new, smaller, and more circular mouth. For a moment or two, when I had seen that they were not in the cave at all, I had come to doubt their very existence. Was it not more likely that the sounds I had heard were nothing more than the rage of rushing water? The roar that of a waterfall? That I, who saw a portico where none stood, who felt that there were a hundred men at his back, then looked to find himself alone, had dreamed the lions as I had so much else?

Then a lion stalked before the mouth of the cave, snarling, tawny in level sunshine, with a mane as black as his exaggerated shadow. One javelin poised above my head, I hurried forward.

The sun had just risen over the hill I left. Before me lay a narrow and rocky defile with a stream running along its lowest point; what I saw there was like—and yet utterly unlike—what I had anticipated. I had expected to find several lions, the sons and daughters of the black-maned beast that I had caught sight of through the mouth of the cave, and a mature lioness, perhaps with cubs. I indeed counted no fewer than four lions; but all were huge males, as large as that I had first glimpsed—and in fact the four were so much alike I could not have said which I had seen first.

And though there was a lioness as well, she wore a woman's shape. Tall and strong, more massive of limb than the largest of Hippephode's Amazons, she regarded the stony lips of the cave from the elevation of a silver chariot no horses drew. Her face showed unmistakably her strength and her unswerving purpose; her large eyes burned yellow and fierce—eyes that might adore, thus they seemed to me, or thirst for blood. All of which was august enough; yet there was something more extraordinary still (while still more beautiful) about her appearance, a thing that in the whole time I spent with her I never dared to ask about and never fathomed: it appeared that a second sun rose behind her, between her broad back and the rugged wall of the defile, splendid light enfolding her in a mantle brighter than the purest gold.

"Come." She motioned to me. "I have need of you." In her hand was a large tambour, and though her fingers did not appear to brush its head, its taut skin shook with each thudding of my pulse.

I hesitated.

"You fear my lions." She whistled, and all four bounded to her. She stroked their muzzles, scratching their chins and ears as if they were so many puppies; but when their amber stare fell upon me, I recalled that they were truly lions.

"Much better." She nodded as I edged nearer her. "Do you know who I am?"

I shook my head again.

"My name is Cybele—to you, here, at this time. My priests would tell you that I am the greatest of all gods." She smiled; and seeing her smile I knew I loved her. "But their priests say that of most gods."

"Do you hear my thoughts?" I asked her, for it seemed that she had read them.

"When they are written upon your face? Certainly. Do you not kneel even to a goddess?"

"Not when there are lions present, Cybele."

"They are less than kittens to me—and to you, for as long as I protect you. Do you remember driving such a cart as this? Tell me what you are doing here."

"No," I said, "I don't. The Thracians—King Kotys holds a Mede called Oeobazus. He will be sacrificed to Pleistorus, and I must find the temple and save him if I can."

"You are children," Cybele told me, "you and that foolish seer with the crutch. He thinks to fancy the immortal gods as bettors fancy horses. Your black friend owes me a blood price, by the way. He slew one of my priests, a most promising young man."

I said, "I didn't see everything, but I've been told that your priest was promising to kill him at the time."

"He will not be permitted to pay in jests, although his are somewhat more amusing than yours." Cybele waved a hand, and her lions bounded away, scrambling up the sides of the defile until they had gained the hilltops; she rose and stepped down to stand beside one of the chariot's tall, slender wheels. "Get in," she instructed me. "Take up the reins."

Slowly, I advanced and did as she bid. The chariot seemed higher than I had thought and lighter than I would have believed possible, as if its gleaming sides weighed nothing. There were four pairs of reins, a set for each horse; I looped them through my fingers in the proper way. And though only empty harness lay upon the ground before me, in those trembling strips of leather I touched the fire of four mighty hearts. "Yes," I told Cybele. "I've done this."

"Then listen to me."

I put the reins down and turned to face her, discovering that her eyes were now at the level of my own.

"If you do as you've planned, you will be killed. Not by me, directly or otherwise; but you will die. I can show it to you if you like—how you'll be found out near my son's temple, your flight, the lance through your back, and all the rest. It will seem as real as this to you. Do you wish to see it?"

I shook my head.

"You're wise. All deaths before death are for cowards—let them have them. Very well. You do not recall your meeting with the usurper, and that is my doing, though you do not recall that either."

"She promised to reunite me with living friends," I said. "Hegesistratus and I were talking of it not long ago."

"But he did not tell you her price, although he knows it." With an expression of contempt, Cybele waved that price aside, whatever it had been. "It does not matter; she would only cheat you in the end. And the end, you may be sure, would be long in coming. I can be cruel as well as kind, but my pledge is a pledge, even as my punishment is punishment. I have saved your life today, for you would have done as you planned and died for it if I had not been here. Now I ask *you* to reward *me*. Will you do it?"

"Of course," I said. "And willingly."

"Good. The Mede will be your reward—do as I tell you, and he will drop into your hand like ripe fruit. The usurper warned you that you would soon meet a queen. Have you met one?"

"Yes, I have—Hippephode, Queen of the Amazons." I blurted out a sudden realization: "Why, they must be your granddaughters! They're the children of the War God, and he's your son."

"And what does Queen Hippephode want? Do you know what has brought her to this land?"

"Sacred horses from the Temple of the Sun. She has brought precious gems and gold—so Hegesistratus told me—with which to buy them."

"This king will no more sell them than free your Mede—but we will force him to both. Do you know where the temple lies?"

I was not sure which temple she meant, but since I knew the location of neither, I shook my head.

Cybele smiled again, the smile of one who laughs inwardly. "The sun will show it to you. When you're clear of this gorge, look toward it. The temple will be directly beneath it. Look under the sun."

I said, "I understand."

"That is well—so does he.* His sacred herd grazes in the Meadow of the Sun; it lies between us and the temple. You must drive the horses around the temple. There you will strike the processional road. Turn right at every forking, and you should reach the entrance of my own temple. Lead the sacred herd into it and hand them over to the queen, and you shall have the Mede, living and whole. That I promise you."

---

*Latro appears to have spoken Greek to the gods he encountered. If so, the word he used may have been μανθάνω, whose literal meaning is "I learn." The god of the sun was also the patron of learning and prophecy.—GW

"Aren't the Horses of the Sun guarded?" I asked, and added, "Surely you must know there are armed Thracians at the entrance to your temple."

I wish I could describe her look as she replied; there was love and sorrow in it—rage as well, and towering pride and many other things, too, perhaps. "Why do you imagine I have chosen you?" she asked me. "If a child might do it, would I not send a child? Nor shall you be without assistance. The three whom you will meet first will be your auxiliaries, worthy of your trust because they come from me. Go now."

# SEVENTEEN

## Sworn Before All the Gods

KING KOTYS'S OATH WILL SURELY bring destruction upon him and his nation, should he break it. One of the Amazons' best horses was our sacrifice, a red heifer the sacrifice of the Thracians. The terms: Hippephode may choose four, for which she must pay the price agreed. We must bring the rest, unharmed, to the temple of the War God, where Oeobazus the Mede will be handed over to us, also unharmed. We will leave Apsinthia, with the Mede and the four sacred horses, unmolested.

The exchanges are to take place tomorrow, then we will go. Meanwhile, food and wine are to be brought to us. We have no need of water—there are many pools in the depths of this cave, which Hegesistratus has told me the Thracians say is a path to the Country of the Dead. The Amazons and I watered the horses from one such pool. Io helped us.

I asked Hegesistratus about Cybele before I wrote of her. She is surely a mighty goddess—she saved me and will save the Mede. Hegesistratus says she is numbered among the friends of men, and was once accounted the greatest goddess, mistress of all the beasts, though Cynthia contests it with her as she does other things. The Queen of the Dead is Cybele's daughter, and I made sure both were among the gods to whom the oath was sworn.

Yet I distrust King Kotys. There was fury in his eyes when he looked at me. There was triumph in my own, I think, for it was I who brought the Horses of the Sun here as Cybele commanded me, with the aid of Pharetra and the lion. There is a boy with us called Polos, who says that he helped us, too, and certainly he ran in behind the last horse, and may well have been driving it before him. Hegesistratus thinks Polos may be a spy for the Thracians; but he wishes to let him stay so that the Thracians will know that we do not violate our oath.

It was the ceremony that interrupted my writing, but just now I read what I had written; I still recall all those things. Certainly my encounter with Cybele was more important than the capture of the sacred horses—but were not the horses captured at her command? Meeting her was more important to me, but to her it was our taking of the White Horses of the Sun, for if she had not desired it, she would not have appeared to me as she did, perhaps. Thus I should write of that, too, before I sleep.

I have been watching the women walk to and fro before the fire, when I should have been writing. We have a big fire now, because some peasants came with more firewood, and hay and grain for the horses, and the cave is cold. One of the Amazons found iron spits in a small chamber not very far back, and she and two others are building supports for a spit so that we can roast our meat that way. Her name is Badizoe.

Their limbs are round—how gracefully they walk!

The lion was the first; I had not gone more than two stades from the defile where I had spoken with Cybele when he stood in my path. I knew the goddess had sent him—he was one of hers—but it was very difficult to approach him without fear. I said, "Come with me," and he walked at my heels like a dog, though I did not dare touch him. At that time I could not see the Temple of the Sun because of the trees.

Pharetra was the second; we found her just where the trees ended and one could see the white horses on the hillside, nearer the temple. Although I did not know her name, I knew her for an Amazon by her fine bowcase and bowman's eyes. She embraced me, and I her, but she released me and backed away very quickly when she saw the lion. It was some time before I could convince her that the lion would not harm her; but I knew it would not, since both had been sent by the goddess.

We crouched behind bushes, the lion on my left, Pharetra on my right; I asked how she came to be there, but though it seemed she understood my whispered questions, I could not always follow her replies. The mantis spoke with her when we returned, and he says that she fell from her mount in the battle and hid from the Thracians.

She pointed to the sacred horses and sucked in her cheeks like Hippephode's, counting four fingers.

I asked, "Your queen requires four of those white horses?" I said it because Cybele had told me that the horses were to be Hippephode's.

Pharetra nodded, pointing to herself and me.

I said, "You suggest that we take four and bring them to her." I spoke slowly, and when I had held up fingers to make the word "four" clear, Pharetra nodded enthusiastically.

I shook my head, pointed to the horses, and drew a circle in the air to show that I had been instructed to bring *all* the horses to her queen. When Pharetra did not seem to comprehend, I counted them—twenty-five. I opened and closed my hand five times, then drew the circle again.

She stared at me and shook her head, then shrugged.

I was looking at the herdsmen. There were five, all noble Thracians whose bridles and persons flamed with gold. They had swords and lances, but no helmets; and only one wore armor. The question was whether to proceed against them at once or wait for the third helper Cybele had promised. I know that even the best of gods do not mean all that they say, and we were three now; it seemed possible that the third who was to help us was myself. I was going to suggest that we approach a couple of Thracian lords who appeared deep in conversation when we heard the quick triple drum taps of a cantering horse.

It was Elata, though I did not know her then; she was the third. She rode up to us on a handsome bay colt, and the noble herdsmen saw her. Everyone rides in Thrace, so I would not have imagined that the sight of one slender girl on horseback would have alarmed them, and perhaps it did not. But one rode toward us as if to learn what she wanted.

It might have been wiser to wait, and attack him while he suspected nothing—or even to have mounted Pharetra on the colt. Surely she would have been a lighter burden, one better suited to such a young animal. As it was, I did neither. Elata slid from the colt's back, and I leaped onto it and jabbed the colt's sides with my heels. It was foaled for a charger (I wish it were here with us now), and though it was so young and carried a man in armor, it shot toward the Thracian like a dagger from the hand; only then did I realize that Elata had been riding without reins.

That did not really matter; the bay colt knew its business. The roaring of the lion behind it would have terrified any other horse, and perhaps the colt did not seem frightened only because it was already galloping as hard as it could. My first javelin struck the noble herdsman square in the chest and tumbled him from his saddle. The lion raced past, easily avoided the second Thracian's lance, and pulled him down.

Pharetra was sprinting toward the sacred horses. My knees and my hand on its neck directed the colt after her; the three remaining Thracians were on the other side of the herd. Neither of us had to fight them, as it turned out. They dropped their lances and galloped away as fast as cowards can.

I saw Pharetra mounting a milk-white mare and followed her example—exchanging the bay colt (who was slackening then) for a white stallion, the biggest of the sacred horses. For a moment I feared he might throw me off, for I did not know whether the sacred horses were ever ridden, and it would be no easy task to break a full-grown stallion of such great size; but though he was as fiery as the storm, he wished to run, not to buck. Off he flew, and the rest of the herd after him just as I had hoped. We had the last stabled here in Cybele's holy cavern long before the Thracians arrived to demand them back.

Thus our situation is as I described when I began; we are eleven—twelve, if Polos is counted among us. Of those fit for battle, there are only seven—Hippephode, Pharetra, and two more Amazons; Hegesistratus, the black man, and me. Two other Amazons are badly wounded; Elata and Io tend them, but I do not believe either could be of service in a battle. Elata would not fight, though perhaps Io would. The boy has a sling and a little bag of stones for it; he promises to teach her the art.

When the Thracians came, Hegesistratus discovered that the noble herdsmen who fled reported that Pleistorus took the sacred herd. (I wish we had Cybele's lion still so we could deceive them in the same way again.) Hegesistratus told them he did it because he desires that Oeobazus be given to us, and that he is angered with King Kotys because the king wants to sacrifice him to overawe the people, and not for the glory of Pleistorus. I asked Hegesistratus whether the Thracians had believed it, and he told me he thought they had.

———

Just now when Io got more wood for the fire, she discovered a bundle of arrows concealed among the logs. There was a letter in the bundle, which she read aloud to us: "May the Stone favor him who does this! These cost-two owls. Europa's man may repay me. I send him greetings."

Hippephode says that they are not very good arrows, but ten thousand times better than no arrows. All the Amazons have full bowcases now. The black man says he can use a bow; he wants to borrow that of one of the wounded Amazons; but she will not let him take it. Hegesistratus says these arrows were hidden in the wood by Cleton, a friend in Cobrys. I think that Cobrys is the chief town in this part of the world.

I am sitting near the mouth so I can write by daylight, but not so near as to give some Thracian bowman a clear shot at me, I hope. It is time for the first meal—Io and the black man are preparing meat. Hegesistratus begs information from the gods; he fears that the king may have sacrificed Oeobazus despite his oath.

Io came here to speak with me a few moments ago. She began by telling me that she was my slave and that she had been a most faithful servant to me for nearly a year. She told me that she understood that I forget this between the setting and the rising of the sun, but she assured me that it is so.

I told her that though I may forget, as she said and indeed as I myself sense, I knew that she was a good child and a true friend, for my heart warms whenever I see her; but that I could not believe she was my slave, because I love her too much not to have freed her.

Then Io asked me about Elata, and from her tone I knew that she had come to the matter that truly concerned her. I thought she was afraid Elata might betray us to the king, so I said that I was certain she would not. Cybele, I explained, had promised me the help of three trustworthy allies, and these had been the lion, Pharetra, and Elata. Since Cybele wished Queen Hippephode to have the sacred horses, it was hardly likely that she would send someone who would betray us.

"Have you asked Pharetra about Cybele's sending her? Did the goddess appear to her or anything?"

"No," I admitted. "But Pharetra didn't mention anything of that sort when Hegesistratus asked how she had become separated from us in the battle—or if she did, Hegesistratus didn't tell me. Besides, suppose that Cybele had told her not to speak of it. We'd be putting Pharetra in an awkward position if we asked her about it."

Io shrugged. "I guess so. What do you think about Elata otherwise? Is she an ordinary girl?"

"Certainly not," I said. "She's much more lovely than most women. I may forget things quickly, Io, but I know that."

"Do you want to lie with her?"

I considered my answer. It seemed certain that a truthful reply would give Io pain; and yet I could not help feeling that lies, though told from the kindest motives, do more harm than truth. At last I said, "I suppose I'd have her if she wished it; but she's shown no sign of wanting me to, and Hegesistratus told me this morning that she's his."

"The black man has had her," Io said.

"If that's true, it lies between him and Hegesistratus," I told her. "I only hope it can be settled without bloodshed."

"I don't think Hegesistratus knows. I didn't tell him."

"Do you want me to do it?" I asked. "I wouldn't tell any man such a thing unless I'd seen it myself."

Io shook her head.

"Then what's the point of our talking about it? Besides, if Hegesistratus is a mantis, he has no doubt discovered it for himself. It would be very difficult to conceal unfaithfulness from a mantis."

"I don't think he's tried to find out about that. I think he's afraid of what he might learn—like that time when you and Elata came back together in the morning."

It had begun to rain, a light drizzle that dripped from the lips of the cave, a few steps from where we were sitting. I rolled up this scroll and tied it with the cords as I considered my reply. "Hegesistratus is a wise man, Io. He makes mistakes, no doubt, as even wise men do. But he is wise nevertheless, and I think his wisdom shows in what you have just said."

"But do you think Elata's just a common girl? Except for being so pretty?"

"What do *you* think her, Io?"

"I don't know," Io answered.

"Why are you so concerned about her?"

"Because of Pharetra. You like Pharetra—I know you do."

I admitted it. "But that doesn't mean that I don't love you, Io."

"Well, just a few days ago, Pharetra was nearly dead. One of these barbarians had put his lance right here"—Io touched her own ribs—"and you could even see the big cut in back where the point came out. She was spitting up lots of blood, and she could hardly breathe."

I said that I found that very hard to believe.

"So do I," Io declared. "So do the rest of the Amazons, I think. She was hurt the first night we fought the barbarians. Then they brought us to that field where they made us camp, and we spent the next night there. The night after that was when we fought them again and you tried to steal their king."

I shook my head to show that I had forgotten it, as I have.

"And Hippephode didn't want Pharetra to fight, but she did. And today she was well enough to help you steal all those white horses." Io paused, her eyes upon my face.

"Master, you were with Hegesistratus when he got Elata. I want you to look in your book and find the place. It was one night between Sestos and Pactye. Will you open your book again, and read me what you wrote then?"

I read it to myself first, however; and when I had finished, I told Io that I wanted to consider the entire matter further. This woman Elata is a nymph, or so I wrote. If the rest do not know it, she would surely be angry if I revealed it.

Hegesistratus says the Mede is still alive; he caught sight of him in his mirror, staring at our hill from the narrow window of the room where he is confined. Hegesistratus thinks someone has told him we are bargaining for his life. He says Cleton may have smuggled a letter to him.

I wish that I could smuggle such a letter to Pharetra, but I write no tongue but this. If it were not winter, I would at least send Io with a flower, though I had to face down a hundred Thracians to get it.

# EIGHTEEN

## *Pharetra Is Dead*

SHE LAY BESIDE ME WHEN Hippostizein woke me. I could just
see her face in the firelight. I kissed her cheek before I rose, though
she slept on.

I think I remembered her, though I did not remember where I was,
or who the people I saw sleeping nearer the fire were. The tall woman
who had awakened me picked up this sword, whispering, *"Guard,
guard."* Thus I knew that this sword is mine. I buckled it on and followed
her. She led me away from the fire, through the darkness to the cave
mouth, where a sentinel darker than the night stood guard. He had a
long sword and a pair of javelins; when he grinned at me, I knew that
we were friends. He embraced me and I him, and we wrestled for a
moment.

I asked them whether we had enemies who might try to come into
the cave, first in this tongue, then in the one the woman had used.
Neither understood this one, as well as I can judge, but both clearly
understood the second, nodding vigorously and pointing down the road
that begins at the entrance to the cave. I said that if anyone tried to
enter, I would shout and wake the rest, and that seemed to satisfy them.
They went back into the cave.

I went outside and watched awhile from there, for though the night
was cold, the cave was colder. It had been raining not long before; the
ground was still wet, and water chuckled here and there down the rocks.
When I had been outside for a long time (or at least so it seemed to me)
a dog began to howl far away. Surely a man with a sword should not be
afraid of a howling dog, yet I was frightened, feeling that a horrid thing
stirred in the darkness. That was when I returned to the cave, wrapping
myself in my cloak and standing well inside where the howling sounded

very faint. Though I smelled the smoke of the fire, I was cold. I paced
up and down to warm myself.

Soon there was another step—the harsh tramp of a leather boot
followed by taps that made me think of a blind man feeling his way
with his staff. The man who came to the mouth was not blind, however,
but crippled; he has lost a foot and walks with a crutch. He is called
Hegesistratus, "Leader of the Host," but I did not know that then. He
greeted me, calling me *Latro,* as all these people do, then went outside
as I had. I did not see him again for a long time.

At length the night covering was drawn from the world. The howling ceased, and the tall woman came again, and the woman who had
slept by me with her. I touched my chest and said, "Latro?" They nodded
and told me their names, Pharetra and Hippostizein, though they did
not say them precisely as I have set them down. I write them as Hegesistratus and the girl say them, not having letters for the other.

The tall woman and I went into the cave, where the children were
bringing water from the depths and the lame man mixing wine in a
krater. The black man handed me a cup; I recall that very well, and how
I dropped the cup when Pharetra cried out, so that it smashed on the
stone, splashing my boots with wine.

She was dead when I reached her, lying beneath the bodies of peltasts. I fell on my knees, letting the Amazons and the black man rush
by me while I lifted them from her; an arrow had gone through her
throat. I picked her up and carried her back into the cave, though it
was filled with smoke; the image of the Mother had fallen over onto the
sacred hearth, its ancient, dry, paint-daubed wood burning fiercely and
making too much smoke for the wind from the earth to carry away.
Deeper in the cave, the horses were stamping and whinnying.

Falcata is my sword; she split the old image like kindling. I heaped
the pieces on the fire until the flames whipped in the wind and licked
the stone ceiling. I took away Pharetra's sword and bowcase and laid her
on the fire.

The Thracian lords came calling for a truce; we allowed two into the
cave. Hegesistratus spoke for us, telling them that we could take their
lives without incurring the displeasure of the gods, because they had

broken the peace made yesterday. (When I have written, I must read this and learn of that.)

They said they had not broken it, that it still stood. The peltasts who killed Pharetra this morning did so without a lord, they said, out of the hate they feel for us; they also said that their king will punish those who live, and that he has appointed riders to protect us.

Then they accused us of burning the holy image of Kotytto. Hegesistratus said that we did not destroy it intentionally, we having no wish to give offense to any god and having sufficient wood—no doubt it was knocked over in the excitement following the attack. He offered them silver to pay for the carving of a new image, which they accepted.

The leader of the women spoke through Hegesistratus, saying that the sacred horses had been frightened in their dark stalls beyond the fire. Two ran and fell, as she said, and we have had to kill them.

When they heard that, the lords of Thrace looked grave and declared that we had violated our oath. Hippephode (that is her name) became extremely angry, shouting at them in the tongue of Amazons. Hegesistratus wanted to let both return in safety to their people; but Hippephode's women seized them, putting swords to their backs.

After that, Hegesistratus and Hippephode spoke together for a long time, and only a moment ago it was decided that we shall let one leave but keep the other. If the king of Thrace honors his agreement today, we will return the lord to him. But if he does not, we will kill him.

While I was reading about the sacrifice and oath yesterday, the children came to speak to me. The girl is Io Thabaikos; the boy, Polos. The girl is my slave, she says, though she kissed my cheek like a daughter and I held her on my lap. She is the "Io" who helped water the horses yesterday, as I just read. I asked if Polos was my slave, too.

She laughed. "No! He's mine—I'm teaching him to talk."

The boy grinned.

"Isn't he the son of one of these women?"

Io shook her head. "They don't keep them. If they have a boy, they take him to his father. Usually the fathers are Sons of Scoloti. You don't remember the Sons of Scoloti, master, but there were some on Hypereides's ship. They have long beards, and one had blue eyes. They're very good bowmen."

I said, "I don't care about the Sons of Scoloti right now, Io. Tell me about Polos."

"Well, he knows more about horses than anybody else in the world. If Polos had been back there with the horses, those two wouldn't have fallen over the ledge."

The boy seemed to understand her; he nodded solemnly.

"He can't be Hegesistratus's son even if that young woman's Hegesistratus's second wife," I said. "Hegesistratus speaks the way we do. Who does he belong to?"

"Me," Io said. "I told you, master."

I shook a finger at her and made her leave my lap. "Don't answer me with jokes. Where are his father and mother?"

Io shrugged. "Northwest of here someplace—that's the way he points. I don't think he lives with them anymore."

The boy shook his head. *"Enkilin."*

"They live in the hills," Io translated. "Show him what you found, Polos."

Shyly, the boy groped in the ragged sheepskin he wore and produced a small leather sack. When I held out my hand for it, he loosened the thong and poured a tinkling flood of little gold coins into my palm.

I whistled. "This is a considerable sum of money, Polos. Where did you get it?"

He looked at Io as though seeking permission to answer, or perhaps only to speak as Hellenes do. "From a dead man."

Io said, "One of those you killed, master. He thinks that because you killed him, you should have the money."

I considered that for a moment. "Perhaps we could share it? Half for you, Polos, and half for me?"

The boy nodded enthusiastically.

"But Io must keep my half for me—otherwise I'll forget it, as she knows very well. And neither of you should show how much you have in any civilized place, or you'll get your throats slit for it. Understand?"

We counted the coins into two piles. There were eighteen, each about the size of the end of my smallest finger. Io ran to fetch a rag, into which she knotted my nine. Polos returned his to the sack and gave that to her as well.

I asked, "How many peltasts would you say attacked us this morning, Io?"

"A lot. They had a lot more than we did."

I nodded. "But how many is a lot?"

"Twenty or thirty, maybe."

"Could there have been eighteen? We might guess better if we knew the number of their dead—did you and Polos count them?"

Io said, "I suppose there could have been. I counted the ones you killed. Seven."

We went to look at them; there were eleven dead altogether. The man who had carried the coins wore a helmet, and had worn a ring until someone took it. He saw me, even as I saw him, but there was no hatred in his stare. "Io," I said, "Hegesistratus thinks Polos may be a Thracian spy. What do you think? Can he be trusted?"

Before she could answer, Polos lifted both hands, shook his head violently, and dashed toward the back of the cave. Io told me, "He doesn't want to hear any secrets. I suppose it's because you might think he told if somebody found out."

"If he doesn't want to hear secrets, we can take it he's no spy. But who can we trust? Trust absolutely?"

"The black man."

"All right. What about Hegesistratus and his wife? The queen?"

Io shook her head.

"Why not?"

"Well, the queen has her own people to look after. And she has to do what her god told her—bring the Shining God's sacred horses to his big temple in the south, and all the rest of it. She'd have to put those things ahead of us."

"Very good. And Hegesistratus?"

Io looked uncomfortable. "To start with, he cares a whole lot more about Elata than I've ever seen any man care about any woman. When you read about her in your book, you wouldn't tell me what it said. Do you remember it now, master?"

"No, but I'll read it again when I have the chance. That was to start with. What's the rest?"

"He worked magic for the barbarians—I mean the People from

Parsa, not these barbarians here—and you fought for their Great King, master, and so did my city."

"And the black man?" I asked.

Io nodded.

"Then we were all on the same side; that's not a very good reason to distrust someone, Io."

"But now he's working for Hypereides, and so are we. And Hypereides fought *against* the Great King. That's an awful lot of changing around."

"Perhaps," I said.

"Besides Hegesistratus hates the Rope Makers as much as he loves Elata. I don't like them myself, but they're the friends of Hypereides's city."

"All right," I told her, "that's quite enough. Go and get the black man."

"Can I say something first, master? I promised Polos that I would."

"Certainly," I said, "if it's important. What is it?"

"Well, master, Hegesistratus and Queen Hippephode have been deciding what we're going to do, just about always. But you're the one who really ought to. That's what Polos says and I think so, too. The Amazons are all good fighters—I didn't know women *could* fight like that till I saw them. The black man's really wonderful, and Hegesistratus is like a wounded lion. But it's not any of them that the Thracians are afraid of. It's you. I was in back of you this morning with my sword, and I could see their faces. Polos says they call you 'the hero,' and it means Pleistorus is inside you even if you don't know it."

When she fell silent, I asked, "Is that all?"

"You see the gods sometimes, master. You really do. Once you saw the King of Nysa and touched him, and then I could see him, too. He was old and he looked like the black man—but . . ."

"Go on."

"One time before the Shining God gave me to you, I went to the theater back in Hill. It costs a lot, but sometimes a rich man will buy seats for poor people, and that time my old master did and let us in first. The actors wore masks, but the people in the play didn't know."

"You aren't making a lot of sense, Io," I said. "I think perhaps you'd better bring the black man now."

Suddenly defiant, she stood up very straight, her eyes on mine. "You can beat me if you want to—only I know you won't. How long do you think we could stay in this cave if you weren't in here with us? I know Apsinthia's just a little hole-in-the-corner barbarian kingdom, but the king's still got hundreds and hundreds of soldiers, and maybe thousands."

Then she was gone, before I could order her to go. I have written this while I wait for her to return with the black man.

# NINETEEN

## *My Duel with the King*

OEOBAZUS THE MEDE, THE BATTLE at the temple, the strategist from Rope and Cleton's other news—I must set down all of these, for we will soon sleep and I will forget them.

When I cast back my thoughts to morning, I see the women's heads on the lances, their long, dark hair dripping in the rain. Lordly horsemen in gilt ring mail flanked us, and the first pair bore the heads on their lances. Yet though we were few, and our equipment not so fine, I soon saw they feared us.

Hippephode rode in front on the Destroyer's white stallion—that was how we started, I think. Hegesistratus came after her, and Elata close behind him. Then the black man and I, and the children, with Polos on a white colt; then the white horses without riders, and last, the rest of the Amazons, driving the horses ahead of them.

But the women's heads made me angry; and so when I saw that the Thracians were afraid, I rode past Queen Hippephode and the rest until I was between the Thracian lords who held the lances, and asked in the tongue of the Hellenes where they had found the heads and whose they were. The lords would have had me believe that they could not understand my words, but I saw clearly that they did, for they flushed with anger.

"We thought you warriors," I told them, "but warriors would never boast of killing women—warriors kill men, and bring their women home to warm their own beds. Do you trim your lances with infants' heads, also? Or do you believe it more manly to impale the whole infant upon the lance head?"

They said nothing and looked to right and left, unwilling to meet my gaze. "When a boy hunts," I told them, "he kills a bear cub and says he has killed a bear, never thinking that the day will come when he will meet a bear. Then he will have need of his little spear."

Hegesistratus called to me to be silent.

"I will be silent," I said, "if they will give us the heads of these women so that we may burn them honorably."

At that one of the Thracian lords spoke with Hegesistratus in their own tongue, and Hegesistratus told me they had agreed to give us the heads when we reached the temple of the War God and permit us to burn them on the sacred hearth. Thereafter I kept silent, but I urged my horse forward so that I rode before the Thracian lords who held those lances.

At the temple, it seemed at first that the Thracians' word was good. The king waited for us there, dressed in golden mail and a rich cloak; behind him rode an old man with a white beard, also richly dressed, and many glittering lords of Thrace. All of them sat excellent horses. When the king saw me, he looked angry, and when he saw the boy riding one of the sacred horses, he looked angrier still; but the Thracian lords spoke with him, and both he and the old man nodded. Then the women's heads were taken from the lances, and though the Thracians held them by the hair, the Amazons who received them cradled them in their arms. There was already a fire in the sacred hearth. Queen Hippephode spoke to the Amazons as Amazons speak, lifted her arms in prayer to the War God, and conversed for a brief time with him. After that the heads were set upright in the fire, and fragrant wood heaped upon them.

When they were consumed, the king addressed the Thracian lords who had come into the temple with him. In a low voice, Hegesistratus repeated what he said to the Amazons; and Polos did the same for the black man, Elata, Io, and me, though he speaks the tongue of Hellenes worse even than I.

*"Listen to me! You know what we promised. Who has ever called our vows worthless?"*

The king had a fine, deep voice and piercing eyes. It was strange to listen to Polos's halting speech instead.

*"We have sworn that they shall go in peace. No one shall so much as offer them insult—though our charge would scatter them like chaff. There shall be no war!"*

Then all the Thracian lords repeated his words.

*"The gold they give us for the Sun's sacred horses shall go to the temple of the Sun. Thamyris shall receive it."* Here he glanced at the old man. *"And they shall go in peace!"*

Again all the Thracian lords echoed his words. After that, the old man and some of the lords went behind the curtain at the back of the temple and led out Oeobazus the Mede. Hegesistratus and the black man sighed, and Io said, "Well, finally!" He is tall and strong, with a scar that rises out of his black beard; his face is darker than Hegesistratus's, but not so dark as the black man's.

Then the king spoke again, but Polos did not translate his words for us because he had run to look at Oeobazus's sword and bow, which had been brought forth. Nor did Hegesistratus repeat to the Amazons anything that the king had said, because he and Oeobazus were embracing. When he spoke to Oeobazus, it was, I suppose, as the Medes speak; but I understood a few words, and from those and his manner knew he was telling Oeobazus that he would present us when there was time for it.

Oeobazus took up the weapons that had been returned to him, and we deserted the temple's fire for the chill drizzle outside. There Queen Hippephode pointed out the sacred horses she wished to take, choosing the stallion she had ridden and three others, all of them fine animals; an Amazon slipped a bridle onto each. Hippephode counted gold into the old man's hands—a great deal of it, or so it appeared to me. The king questioned several of the pieces, biting them to test the goodness of the metal; when the last was passed, a peltast brought the old man scales with which he weighed the gold. I could not understand what he said, but it seemed clear that he had announced himself satisfied.

Here was the crisis, and all of us must have known it. The black man sprang onto his horse. Hegesistratus was no more than a moment behind him, vaulting into the saddle with his crutch as I think he always must. But in the tongue of the Hellenes, and almost as a Hellene might have said it, the king told us, *"Wait!* We have promised you shall go in peace. However, if one of you should choose battle instead, in that there can be no violation of our pledge."

I knew then that many of the lords of Thrace understood the tongue of Hellenes, for they stirred at his words and some laid their hands upon their swords.

Hegesistratus said loudly, "We do *not* choose to fight. Let us leave in peace as you swore."

The old man spoke to the king as Thracians speak, his voice low and urgent. It seemed to me that he, too, called for peace; but the king shook his head angrily.

"This does not concern you," he said to Hegesistratus, "nor any of your party save one." Although he spoke to Hegesistratus, he looked at me. "The rest of you may begin your journey, if you like. He, too, may go in peace, if he wishes. We have said it. But if he desires instead to meet us with arms—as one hero meets another—he need only tell us."

Hegesistratus called sharply, "He does not desire it. Mount, Latro!"

"Yes," the king told me. "Mount! You will need a lance. Someone bring him one—a good one."

Though I do not believe that the king had confided his plan to his counselor, one of the Thracian lords at least must have known what he intended to do; without an instant's delay, he was at my side holding a new lance.

I would not take it. "You have called yourself a hero," I told the king, "and I know that what you said is nothing more than the truth. Only a fool fights a hero, unless he must." I went to my horse to mount; but one of the Thracians pricked its flank with his dagger, so that it cried out and danced away from me, its eyes rolling with pain and fear. The Thracian who held the lance thrust it in my face.

Hippephode confronted the king then, a woman taller even than he; anger flamed in her cheeks and blue ice flashed from her eyes. I do not know what she said, but she pointed toward the lowering sky, then to the temple, and at last to sky again, and her voice was like the snarl of a panther. The black man urged his horse forward as though to join her, but many hands tore him from the saddle and threw him to the ground. The king turned away from the Amazon queen again and again; always his eyes were upon me.

I said, "What sort of fool are you, who tell your people that we are to go in peace, and break your word with the next breath? Don't you know that it is thus that kings lose their thrones?"

"Take it if you can!" he shouted, and spat in my face. At that moment, the lance was thrust at me again, and I did as he said.

At once everyone fell silent. Those who had held the black man released him; he stood, wiping mud from his clothing and his person, his wounded face a mask of rage.

Hegesistratus rode to where we stood, and no one stopped him. The king said, "If you would speak to us before we fight, dismount!"

Hegesistratus nodded. "Out of the respect I have for Your Majesty." He slid from his horse, keeping hold of his saddle until he could brace himself with his crutch. "King Kotys," he said, "you have sworn before your gods and ours that you would let us go in peace. Do so now, before battle drinks the blood of a king. It may be they will forgive you."

"If that is all you have to say," the king told him, "be silent or we will stuff your mouth with dung."

Hegesistratus turned to me, his voice so soft that I could scarcely hear him. "Do you know how to use a lance, Latro?"

I said, "I don't know, but I doubt that there's a great deal to learn." The Thracian lords grinned at that, pulling their beards and elbowing one another.

"He has a helmet. You had one yesterday, but you seem to have left it behind. Do you want one now?"

I shook my head.

The king said, "You have your lance. Mount!"

I asked him whether we would fight on the hillside.

"No." He pointed. "Ride to that thicket, turn, and meet my charge."

Hippephode had been speaking swiftly to Hegesistratus; now he said, "The queen asks a favor of you: she wishes you to take her horse. Your own is badly unsettled and is, as she says, too small."

I thanked Hippephode and mounted her white stallion, still the holy steed of the Sun. A disordered mob, we streamed to the base of the hill; there some of the Thracian lords made the rest stay back, with Hegesistratus, the Amazons, the black man, and the others. The king reined up perhaps ten cubits before them. "No quarter will be given," he told me. "Do you understand?"

I said that I did not think I could kill a man who begged me for his life, but I would try. Then I rode down the misty valley to the trees he had pointed out. They were half a stade from the bottom of the hill, perhaps.

A lion roared as I wheeled the stallion. At the sound of his challenge, other lions roared to my left and right, hardly a bowshot from us.

The stallion reared, pawing air. Afraid the king's charge would find us unprepared, I shouted into the stallion's ear, digging heels into his sides and flourishing the lance overhead to make it clear we had to fight whether lions roared or not—though their terrifying voices rose behind us like the tumult of an army.

He sprang forward. I felt the earth quiver beneath us; the roaring of the lions and the thunder of his hoofbeats filled all the world.

I glimpsed the king at that moment, I know. He was urging his mount forward, his lance poised. Rain more violent than any we had seen that day intervened, washing the king, the throng of riders behind him, even the hill of the War God's temple from my sight. It cleared almost at once; and when it was gone, the king had turned from me as if charging the lords of his own court, or perhaps the Amazons. There was a swirl of men and horses, and a shriek that pierced the rain and freezing mist with astonishing immediacy, as though we were already in the midst of that wild melee.

Swords flashed; there was a confused shouting.

A moment more, and we were part of the fight indeed. I do not know whether I could have halted the stallion with a rawhide bit; I was so stunned by what I had seen that I scarcely tried. I could have killed half a dozen lords of Thrace then if I had wished, but I did not, lifting my lance instead and leaving them unscathed.

Yet a battle had begun. Before me two Thracians struggled knee to knee—a third stabbed one from behind. The black man rode past like a whirlwind, his pelta cut nearly through and his sword red with blood. Hippephode called her Amazons to her, her voice a trumpet. I tried to rein the white stallion toward them, ducked a thrust from a Thracian whose squealing mount was pinned between two others, and hacked wildly at the lance shaft; it was only then, with Falcata already in my hand, that I realized I had dropped my own lance and drawn her.

Someone shook my shoulder. It was Hegesistratus, with the Mede at his elbow. *"Run!"* he shouted. *"Get clear!"* Then they were gone. Before I could cleave a Thracian's helmet, the man threw down his sword and raised his hands. As I passed him I caught sight of Io and Polos, galloping off into the mist. I rode after them.

There is not much more to tell, and in any event our supper is ready. After what seemed a very long ride, I overtook Io, who explained that she and Polos had become separated. We rode on until even the stallion was exhausted and at last, long after this short day had grown dark, halted at this farmhouse. Io has money that she says belongs to me. She offered the man and his wife a small gold coin—at which their eyes grew large indeed—if they would feed us well, let us pass the night here in safety, and say nothing. Soon after that Polos joined us, leading three riderless horses. One is mine, and it had my scrolls and stylus still in its saddlebags. Io showed them to me and told me about the record I must keep.

I was reading how the mantis escaped from Rope when a wagon driven by a fat old man rattled into the farmyard. The farmer—who seems just such a man as the peltasts who came to the temple with their lords—swore he had seen no strangers today; but Io called, "Cleton!" and brought him in to share our wine. He says the king is dead; the old man, Prince Thamyris, rules the city. A strategist from Rope has come in a warship with many soldiers, demanding news of Oeobazus and of us.

# TWENTY

## *Raskos*

THE WOUNDED MAN CAME BEFORE sunrise; we three were sleeping on the floor. I sat up at his knock, and the girl, Io, sat up, too. I told the boy—his name is Polos—to unbar the door. He would not and looked frightened. I did not want to leave the warmth of my blankets; I tossed fresh wood upon the fire and asked who was there.

"Raskos!" he replied.

Then the farmer came out of the room where he had slept with his wife and opened the door.

Raskos came in. He had a pelta and javelins; I threw off the blankets at once, thinking that I might have to fight. He spoke to the farmer, who laughed, made a fist, and tossed his thumb into his mouth. He waved toward a stool by the fire, and though I could not understand what he said, it seemed that he was inviting Raskos to sit down.

Speaking in the way the Hellenes do, Polos whispered, "He's not drunk." He was shaking so much I put my arm about him, at which he breathed violently through his nose, which I think must be a habit of his. He is ten, I would say, or perhaps a year or two older. He has reddish hair and dark eyes.

Raskos spoke more, mumbling and looking around as though he had never seen the house before, often repeating the same words. Io asked what he was saying, and Polos told her, "He says he was lost in the snow."

I went to a window and opened the shutter. It had indeed snowed during the night; snow a little thicker than my thumb lay over everything, so that all the bushes and trees appeared to be covered with white blossoms, bathed now in moonlight.

Raskos was beseeching the farmer, whose name was Olepys, or

something of the sort. I was about to close the shutter when I saw people walking up the road. Three of them were carrying a long and apparently heavy bundle upon their shoulders, and when one pointed toward the house, it was plain that they intended to stop.

But I was too full of my own thoughts to pay much attention to these travelers then. As I latched the shutter, I asked Io, "Do you remember what Cleton told us? I've been considering it, and since we're all awake, I think it would be best if we got an early start."

She said, "Do you want to send Polos into the city to talk to this Rope Maker?"

I shook my head, for I knew that no strategist was apt to tell the truth to a ragged boy. "The first thing is to locate Hegesistratus and warn him that the Rope Makers are here. We know that they've learned about him, and they probably want to kill him."

"Maybe they have already," Io speculated gloomily. "I know you don't remember it, master, but a few days ago Hegesistratus was trying to read the future for you and saw his own death. It sounded as if it was pretty close."

I was about to tell her that we ought to warn Hegesistratus just the same, if we could, when someone tapped at the door.

It was a weeping woman in a dark cloak. Straggling hair, loose and disordered, hung about her shoulders, and her cheeks were streaked with tears; with her was another, younger woman. The three men who carried the bundle waited a few steps behind them, looking uncomfortable. Two were hardly more than boys.

Io jabbed Polos with her elbow, and he told us, "She says her husband's dead. They're going to the burning. They want this man to come."

"This man" was the farmer, who smiled at the woman, shook his head, and pointed to the stool beside the fire, though there was no one there.

The woman only sobbed the louder, at which the farmer's wife came out of the room to comfort her. "*Ai Raskos!*" the weeping woman cried. "*Ai Raskos!*"

The farmer shouted at her then, and when she paid no heed to him, at the three with the bundle, who shook their heads and would not meet his eyes. In a moment they laid the heavy bundle in the snow and removed some of the cloths; it was a man's body, and though it was too dark there upon the moonlit snow to be sure, it seemed to me that he looked very much like the one who had awakened us.

The farmer got a brand from the fire and held it above the dead man. His beard was marked with two gray streaks. His nose looked as if it had been broken. An eye stared at us from under a half-open lid; although I wished someone would close it, I did not try to do it myself. An ax or heavy sword had severed his left shoulder, cutting through almost to the final rib.

After a great many whispered instructions to his wife, the farmer replaced one of the youths who had carried the body, and all six trudged away. I made certain the children cleaned their teeth and washed their faces and hands, then went out to saddle our horses, who had passed a comfortable night in the shed with the cows; we had a big white stallion, a white mare, and four others. "Thanks be to whatever god governs horses," I said to Polos, who had come to help, "that this mare's not in season."

He grinned. "Oh, if we let them cover her a few times, it would be all right. It's the Earth Shaker, the Sea God. He's the Horse God, too."

The white stallion had been rolling his eyes and baring his teeth at me, but Polos calmed him with a touch. "Which one are you going to ride?"

"My own." I pointed to the one who had worn my saddlebags the night before.

"How do you know that he's yours?" Polos asked. "Io says you forget from day to day."

"This isn't from day to day," I explained. "It was late when you brought these horses, and the sun isn't properly up yet."

Polos thought about that for a moment as he saddled Io's small, docile chestnut. "Do you remember fighting King Kotys yesterday?"

I admitted that I did not know I had ever fought a king, and added that since I was still alive I appeared to have won.

"You didn't really fight. He ran away, and then his people killed him for running. Should I call you Latro, or can I call you master like Io does?" Polos paused. "Io's your slave, did you remember about it?"

I shook my head. "I'll free her, then, so that she can go home to her father and mother. If you're not my slave, Polos, you shouldn't call me master. I'm sorry to hear that this king was a coward; I suppose some kings are, but one doesn't like to think of them like that."

"I don't think he was," Polos told me, "but it's not the kind of thing I know much about."

I laughed at his solemn little face and mussed his hair. "What is?"

"Oh, horses and goats and dogs—all kinds of animals. And the weather. I'm a wonderful weather prophet."

"Really, Polos? What will today be like?"

"Sunny and windy, at first. The sun will melt this snow, so that the ground gets all muddy. But after that thick clouds will come, and the day will end too soon."

I sighed, reflecting that he might have been speaking of me, though it did not seem that he intended it.

"Master—Latro—I'll do anything you say."

"All right," I said, "but why are you telling me? Have you disobeyed me? Did I beat you?"

"No," Polos told me. "I've always done everything you told me, although you haven't told me much. But I wanted to say that I thought you were wrong about some things, and I don't want you to be angry with me."

I said we would see about that when I knew our disagreement.

"I think I ought to call you master. If I don't, lots of people will ask why I'm with you. But if I do, they'll think I'm your slave, like Io."

I led him back into the house so that we could toast our stiff fingers at the fire; it gave me an opportunity to consider what he had suggested. "Suppose I were to die, Polos. You say I fought a king yesterday, and if it's true, I may very well die today. Won't my heirs—if I've got any— claim you? You might have to spend the rest of your life as somebody's slave."

Polos shook his head, a little mule. "If the king couldn't kill you yesterday, master, who's going to kill you today? And besides, if you have heirs, they're probably nice people. There are lots of people—not very nice people at all—who catch boys and girls that don't belong to anybody."

Io came in, and I asked her whether she had given the woman the money she had promised her after the farmer left.

"Not yet," Io said. "Not until we're ready to go, because we might need something else. Do you remember why we're going, master?"

"To find a man called Hegesistratus, if we can."

Polos asked me, "Do you remember him? What he looks like?"

I shook my head.

"Or why we want to find him?" Polos persisted.

"Because the Rope Makers want to kill him." I asked Io, "Hegesistratus is a friend, isn't he? When I pronounced his name, it seemed a friend's in my mouth."

There was a knock at the door. From the other room, the woman shouted something.

"*Raskos!*"

Io told me, "Don't open it!" as I drew my sword.

I had to, if I wanted to go on calling myself a man; but I had not time enough to explain that to Io. Sword high, I opened wide the door with my left hand.

There was no one there. The sun had just risen, and long purple shadows fled from every little ridge of wind-driven snow. The footprints of those who had carried the body to the door—and carried it away— were half-filled with snow already; so was the formless depression where the body had lain. There were no newer, fresher tracks.

"Io," I said, "you can speak the way these people do, can't you? A little?"

Io nodded. "It's Thracian, master—we're in Thrace. I've picked up a bit, and Polos knows it."

I said, "Then, Polos, you must warn the woman that Raskos may come back. Do you understand me? If he does, she mustn't open the door. She must tell him, through the door, that he is dead."

Polos nodded solemnly.

"The snow's fallen since he died, I think, and changed the landmarks he knew. Snow's something one usually finds only high up on mountains, so if he comes again before it melts, she must tell him— without opening the door—exactly how he can reach the spot where his body will be burned."

When Polos had spoken with the woman as I told him and Io had given her a coin, we rode off. "Just before that happened"—Polos jerked his head to indicate the farmhouse—"I was going to tell you I thought you ought to ride the white one. You rode him when you fought King

Kotys, and I don't believe he'll give you any more trouble."

I shook my head. "He had a hard day, yesterday, I imagine. Didn't I ride him a long way, Io?"

She nodded. "A very long way, master. We were both really tired when we stopped here, and so were the horses." Each of us was riding one and leading another.

Polos asked, "What if somebody wants to fight with us?"

"Then I'll get on him," I promised. "And he'll be better rested for not being ridden now."

Polos looked from me to the big white stallion, considering. "You *are* heavy."

"Of course I am, and I'm wearing a sword and mail."

"Oeobazus has a sword with a gold hilt, but I think yours must be better."

I asked who Oeobazus was.

Io told me, "The Mede we made the king free. Really, you made him, mostly. You've been keeping up your new book really well, so there ought to be a lot about it there. But probably you shouldn't try to read it while we're riding, especially in this wind."

"All right," I said, "I won't."

Polos asked, "Sometime will you show me how to fight with a sword?"

"You've seen him," Io said. "I know you were watching us the last time. You saw what my master did."

"I was watching," Polos admitted, looking at me. "I saw what he did, but I don't know how he did it. Four men came at him together, and I thought he'd be killed, but he killed them, one after another. There can't be many swordsmen like him."

I had to confess that I no longer recalled the incident he described.

"But you know how to do it. What would you do if you were faced with four together?"

"Get away," I told him, "if I could."

"But if you couldn't?"

I turned the problem over in my mind, seeing soldiers with spears and swords who were not actually there, but who had once, perhaps, stood before me in that way. "Determine which is the leader, if you can," I told Polos. "One is always the leader when there are four, the

one the rest would be ashamed to have see them run. It's very likely
that there aren't really four trying to kill you. One is trying to kill you,
and three are trying to help him. Disable him at once, if you can. Killing
him is good, of course; but a deep cut in his sword arm or his leg may
be just as good."

We stopped at a solitary house; Polos talked to the people there
and told me that they said they had seen no strangers, and that he felt
they were telling the truth. I spoke loudly: "They haven't seen Hegesistratus?" I did it hoping that Hegesistratus would hear me and know
my voice, but no one answered.

On the road again, I said, "Your sword must be a part of you, Polos.
Do you understand that?"

He nodded. "But when I held your sword last night, it didn't want
to be."

"Falcata's too heavy for you," I told him, "and you haven't handled
her nearly enough. It's good to have a good sword, but it's better to
know the sword you have and keep it sharp. Some scabbards dull the
blade, because they're lined with hard wood; some of them even have
bronze where it rubs the sharp part of the blade. If you've got a scabbard
like that, sell it and get another—only leather or wool should touch the
edge."

Polos nodded; I could see he was thinking about what I had said.

"And yet you must always remember that it isn't the best sword
that wins, but the best swordsman."

A man carrying two javelins was walking some distance ahead of
us—a man who, as nearly as I could judge, left behind him no tracks.
I asked Polos about horses, knowing them a subject that would occupy
Io as well, and learned much.

# TWENTY-ONE

## *The Strategist from Rope*

A LEADER OF THE INVINCIBLE armies of the Silent Country demands that the Apsinthians hand over to him any foreigners they hold—so the wounded peltast told Badizoe, and the villagers beg us to go before it becomes known in Cobrys that we are here. They beg us, I say; but they dare not make us go. They fear us too much, though we are only myself, the two women, and the children. All their fighting men are gone, having been summoned to the city a few days ago.

Badizoe came to tell me that she had made use of their fear to get news as well as this food; I asked what she had learned, and called Io here to hear it. Io says it is more than we found out from Cleton, but not very much different. We asked Badizoe how the villagers came to know these things, and she said that a man wounded in yesterday's fighting has been permitted to return to the village. When she heard of it, she made these women take her to him. Elata goes with her, speaking first as one nation, then as the other. Here is what she says he said.

King Kotys is dead. He challenged a Hellene but fled him. When his nobles saw it, they cut him down, though others sought to save him. Thamyris and those who tried to save the king have barricaded the palace.

While the rest planned their assault, the strategist from Rope made port. He has the lambda of Rope upon his hoplon and wears a scarlet cloak. With him are shieldmen from Pylos. He told the lords that if they do not do as he says, it will not matter who is king in Cobrys— he will return with an army and burn the city. He spoke with the Thracian lords outside, where the wounded peltast overheard him, then went into the palace.

We are going now. Badizoe wants to find her queen and the rest of the Amazons, and Elata to find Hegesistratus the mantis. Io thinks it would be best for us to go with them, and so do I.

Everyone is asleep save for the boy from Susa. All fire is holy to him; often he prays to this one, but at times he wanders beyond the firelight searching for a place to rest. There is surely something wrong with him; I doubt that I have ever met a boy before—or anyone not wounded— who could not rest. I think that Polos knows what is wrong, but Polos will not tell me. The boy's name is Artembares.

I have been reading in this how a litter was constructed for Pharetra and slung between two horses. I cannot remember Pharetra, but when I read her name, I seem to feel her hand touch mine; surely she was lithe and lovely beneath her fiery hair. I know I loved her, even though I have forgotten her.

The gods own this world, not we. We are but landless men, even the most powerful king. The gods permit us to till their fields, then take our crop. We meet and love, someone builds a tomb for us, perhaps. It does not matter—someone else will rob it, and the winds puff away our dust; then we shall be forgotten. For me it is no different, only faster; but I have written in my scroll how Pharetra smiled at me. For as long as the papyrus is preserved she will be here, though even little Io is only brown dust sobbing down the night wind with all the rest.

But having read it, I know that for my own sake tomorrow I must write what I recall now: how we came to the new village and took their wine and the pig, then camped here, far away, because we feared their numbers, though we could not let them see that. I was tired and cold, and drank deeper than I should, perhaps; and Elata more deeply still. Then Badizoe and Io were afraid I would violate her while she slept— as I would have, if only they had not been there, and Polos watching. As things were, I was extremely angry with them both. I could have killed them, but I was neither so angry nor so drunk as that, and if I had struck Io, Badizoe would have drawn her sword; then I would cer- tainly have killed her. I lay down, pretending to sleep; but the pretense was quickly real.

When I woke, Io and Badizoe slept, too. I tried to awaken Elata by kissing her, and with such caresses as men give women; but each time she stirred it made the hills uneasy. I heard our horses speaking as one man speaks to another; and though I lose so much, I have not forgotten that horses cannot speak; and so I let Elata sleep on, and began to read, as I have said.

But first I heaped what wood we had left on the coals and, discovering a dead tree, lopped its limbs with my sword and moved Elata away from the fire so that she would not be scorched while she slept.

It may have been the brightness of the flames that brought the boy. He asked if he might warm himself, and I, seeing that he was alone and harmless, said he might. When he had watched me reading for some time, he said, "I know you don't worship the way we do—you say that Hephaistos is the god of fire, and he's not even one of your greatest gods. But do you object if other people believe something else?"

I said, "That depends on what they believe, I suppose." We were both keeping our voices low so as not to awaken those who slept. "You're from Parsa, aren't you? I know that you people pray to Ahura Mazda by building fires on your mountaintops, and I have no objection to that."

He smiled; it was not until he did that I saw how sad his face was. Then he abased himself before the fire in the eastern way and spoke to his god in a tongue I do not know.

By the time he had finished, my eyes were smarting. I laid down this scroll and asked if he was lost.

He nodded. "That was why I got on the ship. You were on it, then Hegesistratus came aboard, too, so I thought perhaps it would take me to Susa. You must have visited our country. Have you ever been to Susa?"

"I can't remember," I told him. "I forget a great deal."

He moved closer, fearful, it seemed, that he would wake Io, although she slept on. "So do I. No, I can remember a lot, but I can never remember anything important. Is that how it is with you?"

"No," I said. "I can remember only a few things—how Polos and Io drove the pig, for example; that's Io beside you, and him on the other side of her. He gathered those pine boughs to make them a bed. Nothing important, as you say. I've been reading this to find out how I came to be here, and I've learned that I came to find Oeobazus, a Mede; but he's not with us now. Do you know him?"

"Certainly I know him," the boy said. "You asked me about him once before, and you and the other barbarian asked my father about him when we were in the tower. Have you forgotten that?"

"Yes," I admitted. "I'm afraid I have."

"You didn't ask my father that time, really. It was the other bar-barian, the short one. Do you remember how you tried to free us?"

I told him I was sorry to learn I had not succeeded.

"There were guards with us in that room in the tower. One heard a noise and went to see what it was. He never came back, and when the other went to look for him, you came in. You had cloaks and helmets, and you wanted us to put them on. You said that once we were outside the citadel we could hide in the city till the barbarians sailed away. But my father said the people there—I don't remember the name of that city."

"Neither do I," I told him. "Go on."

"That they might—would hurt us if they found us. And he said Yellow Horse would look everywhere for us because he had promised him so much for our freedom. He thought Yellow Horse was going to accept the money and let us go. My father's very rich." The boy tried to look modest. "He'll reward you, I'm sure, if you take me to him."

"So you wouldn't come with me? What happened then?"

"Nothing." The boy fell silent, staring into the flames. "You left, more soldiers came, and we went to sleep. Will you come back to the ship with me?"

"What ship?" I asked.

"The one you were on before—you and the little girl and the peri."

I do not know what that word means, but he glanced toward Elata when he said it. I said that I did not think I could go back to the ship with him until we had found Oeobazus.

"He's over there," the boy said, and pointed.

"How do you know?" I asked.

"The same way I knew where he was when you asked me before. Don't you remember? You wanted to know where he was, and I told you he was riding a horse, with his hands tied."

Polos sat up then. I told him I was sorry we had awakened him, that we had tried to talk quietly.

He said politely, "You didn't wake me up. I was thirsty."

I began, "This is—"

"Artembares the son of Artaÿctes," the boy from Susa told me. He is older than Polos, and at least a head taller, I would think.

"Artembares," I repeated.

Polos would not look at him, though I saw his eyes roll. "When did he come? Did you call him?"

"Certainly not," I said. "He was cold and saw the fire; he asked if he could sit here until he got warm, and I said that he could."

"He spoke to you first?"

"Of course," I said. "What is it that's bothering you so much, Polos?"

Artembares said, "I spoke first here at your fire, but you had spoken to me already at another fire, when you asked about Oeobazus. I don't like to speak to people who haven't talked to me first." He hesitated. "It doesn't seem right."

Polos announced, "I'm going to the stream to get a drink," and I gave him some wine to mix with the water so that he would not become ill. I asked whether he had met Artembares before, and he shook his head and ran away.

Now I am going back to sleep.


I have been talking with Oeobazus, who speaks the tongue of Hellenes better even than Artembares. He came to me while I was sharpening Falcata with the farmer's stone and told me his name, saying that though he knew that all of us had fought to save his life, he also knew that I had done the most, and that he wished to thank me for it.

"It's not our custom," he said, "to spend many words—not even on great matters. But for as long as I live, you've only to call on me whenever you need my help."

"You may spend few words," I told him, "but no man could have said more."

He smiled at that and held out his hand, and I took it. I believe we were both somewhat ill at ease; after a moment he chuckled, indicating the whetstone. "I see you've blunted your sword on the necks of our enemies."

"No," I said. "I did it last night, chopping firewood. I thought I'd find her edge wrecked this morning, but it's hardly worse than it was—this is a very good blade." That reminded me of Artembares, who had come to our fire just after I split the last of the deadwood. I said, "There's somebody of your nation with us, a boy from Susa. Have you met him?"

Oeobazus looked mystified and shook his head.

Io had been listening; she said, "My master forgets. You said the mantis told you about him before we got here."

"Yes, he and I had a long talk yesterday. Your master may forget me, and I'll understand if he does; but I'll never forget him."

"Did he tell you, too, that sometimes he sees things other people don't?"

Oeobazus nodded.

"Sometimes people think they're not real, but once I saw the same thing he saw. I think it depends on what each person means by real."

Oeobazus smiled at her. "Spoken like a true Hellene! I've listened to your wise men argue such things all night—and never reach any conclusion. For us, there are only truths. And lies. We don't trouble ourselves about unreality."

"That's good. Just after we woke up, my master said he'd found a boy from Parsa who knew where you were, and he was going to guide us. Badizoe and I wanted to know where he was, and my master said he'd already gone as far as the next hilltop, and he pointed. We could see a young stallion there, kind of red brown and about half-grown, only we couldn't see anybody riding him. And when we asked Elata, she just laughed. But that horse led us right to you."

Oeobazus fingered his beard, which is black and very thick. "Perhaps you should ask Hegesistratus."

"I have," Io told him, "only when he was through answering I didn't know what he'd said."

"Or Seven Lions. He tells me he knows your master better even than you do."

Just then the black man himself dashed into the shed where we were talking, pointing with his chin and talking very fast to Oeobazus, who appears to understand his tongue; Oeobazus told us, "He says that there's a chariot coming, and the rest of the Amazons are following it."

We all ran out to look. Hegesistratus and the lovely Elata were already there, and Badizoe galloping off to meet her queen. A Thracian was driving the chariot, but the man who rode beside him looked like a Rope Maker, a tall soldier in a scarlet cloak. As they drew nearer he waved and shouted, "Noble Hegesistratus! Latro! By every god, it's good to see you both!"

# TWENTY-TWO

## *There's Where We Camped*

I O TOLD ME, "I'LL BET if we went over and hunted around for it, we could see exactly where we built our fire. Look, our altar's still there."

I admitted the place seemed familiar, though I could not actually recall having been there.

"The Amazons were with us then," Io said.

They left after the first meal, half a dozen strong women, of whom two are badly hurt. They took all the white horses, and they have a guard of Thracians sworn to ride with them as far as the fords of the Hebrus. Hegesistratus says the Hebrus is the western border of Apsinthia. They bear tokens from three lords here to other lords, their kinsmen in Cicones. Besides these, their queen has a letter written with this stylus upon a strip of white lambskin by the strategist from Rope; it declares them to be under the aegis of King Leotychides and Prince Pausanias the Agid Regent.

"I'll miss them," Io told me. "You won't, master, but I will. And I miss Polos—I miss him a lot. Do you remember him?"

I shook my head, for I did not.

"He was just a boy—a Thracian, I guess. Anyhow the way he talked sounded a lot like Thracian. He was younger than me, but it was nice to have somebody around who was about my age."

I told her I hoped we would someday live in a place where there were other children, and a wise woman who could teach her all the things that women must know.

"I learned a lot, just watching the Amazons," Io declared. "Queen Hippephode liked me, and Hippostizein and Pharetra tried to be nice to me because they liked you. I didn't like Pharetra because you looked so silly every time you saw her—then she got killed, and I felt so bad.

I still do. You don't remember her now, do you, master?"

"I do a bit," I answered, because I sensed the knowledge in me, though the mists hid it. "What did she look like, Io?"

"She was almost as tall as you, with great big cheekbones." Io pulled up her own cheeks to show me. "She had red hair and lots of freckles, and her legs weren't quite straight, I think from riding so much."

I sighed, as I sigh now. "She sounds very beautiful."

"Well, I wasn't trying to *make* her sound like that!"

"No," I said, "but you couldn't hide it." Then I leaned from my horse to Io and kissed her cheek.

"Anyway"—she wiped her face—"that reminds me that I have to talk to you as soon as we're by ourselves. About him"—she gestured swiftly toward the chariot—"and Hegesistratus, too."

"All right," I said. I decided then to write down all that we had said, and I now have.

We are in a fine big house in Cobrys, the property of one of the lords who have sided with Thamyris. There are servants, though I doubt that they are to be trusted. When we had given our horses over to them to be watered, fed, and stabled, Acetes drew Oeobazus aside, and me with him, and told us that he was not truly a strategist from Rope, as he has told the Thracians. All the others had recognized him, of course, and would have smiled at our amazement. I am glad they did not see it.

Oeobazus said, "I wondered why Hegesistratus was so cordial. He hates the Rope Makers."

"I'm not very fond of them myself," Acetes admitted, "but I understand them better now. It's great sport to be one."

At the second meal, we had to act as though he were a Rope Maker for the benefit of the servants; but when it was finished, he sent them off and we gathered before the fire to drink the harsh wine of the country and crack nuts.

"Hypereides is staying here, too," he told us. "He has the room next to mine. The rest of you will have to sleep in here, but I daresay you've slept in worse places."

Everyone laughed and agreed we had.

Oeobazus voiced the question that was on my own lips: "Who is Hypereides?"

"The captain of our ship," Acetes told him. "He's the one Xanthippos told to fetch you. The rest of us are just working for him, one way or another."

Io said, "Well, I wish he were back here now. I'd like to see him, and he shouldn't be out so late."

"He's bargaining about food and wine for the voyage home," Acetes explained, "and doing a bit of trading on his own account on the side, if I know Hypereides. Don't worry your head about him—he can take care of himself."

Oeobazus asked, "He sent out Hegesistratus with Elata, and Seven Lions—the black man—and Latro with Io, is that correct?"

Acetes and Hegesistratus nodded. Hegesistratus added, "We met the Amazons by the favor of a certain goddess. They were on an errand for the War God, but we could have accomplished nothing without them."

Oeobazus nodded, mostly to himself, I think. "I ran across a tribe years ago who believe that the War God's none other than Ahura Mazda—Ahura Mazda incognito, as it were. Perhaps they're right. How did you know where to look for me?"

Acetes grinned. 'Hegesistratus here sniffed you out, or so Hypereides says. What I don't understand is what you were doing here. You can't have been heading for Media or Parsa."

Oeobazus shook his head. "I was going to Thought."

"To Thought!"

"Yes." The Mede seemed to hesitate, looking around at our faces. "Hegesistratus, you're the only person present who knows me at all well. What do you know about me? Tell them, and me."

"You are a brave soldier, a superb horseman, and a skilled technician.* You were Artaÿctes's adviser on fortifications and siege engines."

"And nothing else?" Oeobazus pressed him.

Hegesistratus fingered his beard. "Let me see. You are a Mede, and though you told me once that you have an estate near Ecbatana and a

---

*I assume "Latro's" abbreviation TC indicates Lat. *technicus*. Presumably the word Oeobazus employed was Gk. τεχνίτης, which would have been immediately recognized by a speaker of Latin. In translating such terms, it is often impossible to escape the appearance of anachronism.—GW wife, you also told me—on a different occasion—that you have no heir. And there is this: you were practically the only man at Artaÿctes's court who never asked me to read his fate."

"We once had three sons." Oeobazus's expression had grown sad. "Fine young men, all of them. They entered the Imperial Army. Noblemen of my nation, you must understand, go into the king's service as a matter of course; anyone who did not do so would be highly suspect."

Hegesistratus said, "Certainly."

"The king—Xerxes, the Great King, as you call him—planned an expedition against the barbarians of the north. You have all met their warrior women now, so you know what they're like—wild horsemen who follow their herds. One may defend oneself against them, but to attack them is like attacking smoke; they fight and flee, then circle back, having neither cities nor crops to lose. The expedition was bound to be a travesty, and everyone realized it save the king. But Susa was crammed with supplies that would be sent north to the army at need."

No one spoke. I glanced around at the boy from Parsa, who was sitting beside Elata well back from the fire. He seemed to be listening attentively, though I could not see his expression.

"Spring came, and the army camped about the city wall," the Mede continued. "My sons were with it, cavalrymen all of them; and so was the king. Artaÿctes presented me to him, praising me as the man who had contrived so much storage for his supplies. The king was pleased; he smiled and offered to grant me a boon, as a reward for my service. Greatly daring, I asked that one of my sons be permitted to remain with me."

Oeobazus fell silent until Io asked, "Didn't he do it?"

"Yes, he did. He nodded and smiled again, and promised me that all three would be left behind in Susa. Next morning, when the army marched north, my sons lay beside the road with their throats cut, so that every soldier who passed might see with his own eyes what happened to those whose—" Oeobazus stood up, and seemed for a moment to wash his face in his hands. "I apologize. You asked why I was trying to get to Thought, and instead of the straightforward reply to which you were entitled, I've inflicted this rigmarole on you. If you'll excuse me now, I think a quiet ride around the city might help me sleep."

When the door had shut behind him, Acetes cleared his throat and spat into the fire. "He really ought to have somebody with him, but you can put me down for an idiot if I see how we can do it."

. A boy's voice from the back of the room called, "I'll go, sir. He won't see me."

I turned around to look, as did everyone else. It was not the richly clad youth from Parsa (as I had expected), but a boy a good deal younger, clothed in a ragged sheepskin.

Io shouted, *"Polos!"* as he slipped out the door; a moment later we heard the clatter of hooves as he galloped away. Io was on her feet. "Master—"

"Absolutely not!" I caught her arm and forced her down again.

"I just wanted to ask him where he'd been," Io explained. "I haven't seen him since last night."

"He was with us before?"

Hegesistratus told me, "Yes, in the Great Mother's sacred cave. This morning you said he had been talking with you beside your fire last night, but had gone for water and never returned. I suppose he must have followed us."

. Elata, who I think must seldom speak to more than one, now said, "He makes himself useful whenever he can and bears a happy heart— I'm glad that he's decided to stay with us. But, Io, your master's right. The night streets of this troubled city are no place for a young girl."

The black man nodded emphatically.

Hegesistratus refilled his cup. "They will be back soon, I think; if either was going into danger, I did not sense it. Io, this seems to me a good time for sharing nuts and telling ghost stories, not worrying about absent friends. You told me a fine one on the ship—how your master was present when a necromancer raised a dead woman, remember? I know he cannot recall it, and I doubt that the others have heard it; so why not tell it again?"

Acetes exclaimed, "That! By the Maiden, I've never been so frightened in my life. Io wasn't there. I suppose she got it from the poet— he was from Hill, too. You don't do that sort of thing, do you, Hegesistratus?"

"Necromancy?" The mantis shook his head. "I have laid a ghost or two, and I questioned one once." He swirled the wine in his cup and peered into it, seeing more in the flickers of firelight reflected there than I would have, I think. At last he said, "Our ghosts are becoming worse, have you noticed? It used to be they were no more than lost souls who had wandered away from the Lands of the Dead, or perhaps never reached them, spirits no worse dead than they had been alive, and frequently better. Such were the ghosts of which my masters told me when I was younger; such, indeed, were those I myself encountered as a young man. Now something evil is moving among them." He paused again. "Have any of you heard about the things that happened to Captain Hubrias? Do you know about the White Isle?"

Acetes shook his head; so did the black man, Io, and I.

"It was two years before the war, so he told me. His ship was off the mouth of the Ister, becalmed in fog, when the man at the masthead called down that he heard music and the beating of many wings. They had been talking on deck, I imagine, but after that they listened, and they heard the same sounds. Soon they realized that what they had taken for a thicker bank of fog was in fact an island with white stone cliffs and a beach of white sand. Hubrias told me he had sailed those waters since he was a child, and he knew perfectly well that there was no such place—but there it was."

Io asked, "What did he do?"

"Nothing, really," Hegesistratus continued, "until a man in armor appeared upon the beach. He waved and shouted for them to send a boat; Hubrias assumed he wanted to be taken off, so being curious about the island, he had four of his crew row him over. He soon realized, however, that this man was more than a common soldier; he was as handsome as a god, Hubrias said, and looked as strong as a bull. As soon as they had sand under the bottom, Hubrias jumped out and saluted him, assuring him that he and his ship were ready to serve him in any way he wished.

" 'I am Achilles,' the ghost informed him, 'and I require a favor from you.' As you may imagine, Hubrias told him that he needed only to name it. 'Then go to the temple of Athena Ilias,' the ghost told him. 'There you will find a slave called Chryse. Buy her from the priests and bring her to me.'

"Hubrias swore he would, naturally, and jumped back in the boat as quickly as he dared. Just as they were putting out, the ghost told him, 'She is the last of Priam's line—treat her with honor!'

"They sailed to the Troad with fair winds all the way, and Hubrias located this girl; she was about fourteen, he said, and had been keeping house for one of the priests. He paid a stiff price for her and lodged her on his ship in as much comfort as a ship permits, requiring her to do no work. He told her that she was intended as a gift for the king of an island in the Euxine, and she promised quite willingly always to speak well of him to this king."

Acetes asked, "What happened when he got back to the island?" I myself was wondering whether Hubrias would be able to find it a second time.

"Off the mouth of the Ister they met with fog again." The mantis shook himself and emptied his cup, tossing the lees into the flames. "But this time there was a good wind. Hubrias said they had to reef their sail again and again; even so they nearly ran aground on the White Isle. The ghost was there, waiting for them on the sand; and standing beside him was the most beautiful woman that Hubrias had ever seen. It had been over a year when I talked with him, yet his eyes lit up still each time he tried to describe her to me. There was something in her that beckoned to you, he told me. You knew she was the proudest woman in the world—and the most humble. There was not a man alive, he said, who would not have laid down his life for her, and been happy to do it.

"He had tricked out this Chryse in amber beads and so on, and they put her in the boat and rowed her over. She knelt to the ghost and the woman—who was a ghost as well, no doubt—and they clasped hands when they saw her.

" 'My friend,' the ghost told Hubrias, 'you have served me well. Go in peace, and I promise you will not go unrewarded.' Hubrias said that after that he could not seem to make an error in navigation, or even do a bad trade. He paid silver and was repaid in gold, as the saying goes. If he wanted to go south, the wind was in the north; and when he was ready to come back, it was in the south. He was already a local magnate when I spoke with him. He owned an estate near Tower Hill and was thinking of buying another."

"Well, that doesn't sound like such a bad ghost to me," Io said. "I don't think I'd have minded meeting that one."

Hegesistratus shrugged. "Perhaps not. But as Hubrias was sailing away, he heard a scream. He turned then, he said, and looked behind him. The ghost was holding Chryse above his head by an arm and a leg, while the beautiful woman watched. Chryse screamed again, calling Hubrias by name, begging him to return and save her. Then the ghost tore her apart."

I heard the long *O-o-o-h!* of Io's indrawn breath before Elata laughed. "Is that really true?" I asked Hegesistratus. "Did it actually happen?"

He shrugged. "I did not see it. But I myself talked with Hubrias, and I believed him. No player from Thespiae could have looked as he did when he described the woman, or sweated as he did when he described the death of the slave girl. Acetes, tell us about the raising of the dead woman in Thought. Was that as bad?"

Acetes had just crushed a walnut between the heels of his hands; he picked at the meat as he spoke. "Worse. I've seen a man killed by a bear, and I don't think that what your ghost did to the slave girl could have been much worse than that. This was. We'd all gone to a hetaera's—Hypereides, the kybernetes, the poet, a couple of other fellows, and me. Latro belonged to this hetaera then, and he was on hand to keep us in line. There was lots of good wine and some of the best food I ever ate, and the girls were real lookers—"

Someone—I suppose that it must have been the black man—had barred the door after Oeobazus and the boy had left. Now someone pounded on it, and I heard the boy shout, *"Let us in!"* The black man and I hurried over, lifted the bar, and pulled open the heavy door. Oeobazus and Polos stumbled into the firelight, half-carrying a fat old man with blood streaming down his face.

# TWENTY-THREE

## *At This, My Zygite Bench*

I MUST FINISH WHAT I began writing last night. I have just now reread it all, and I confess that I think myself rather foolish for having recorded Hegesistratus's story in as much detail as I did; but the time we spent about the fire, between the time the Mede left and the moment when he and Polos returned with Cleton, seems very precious to me; I think that Io and I cannot have had many such moments, times of comfort, free from danger. Perhaps that is why Io speaks of Kalleos's house in Thought as she does. Kalleos was the hetaera Actes mentioned, she says.

The old man was nearly unconscious when Oeobazus and Polos carried him in. While Hegesistratus and Elata saw to his wound, Acetes, the black man, and I questioned Oeobazus. He said that he knew Cleton because Cleton had come to see him while he was a prisoner in the temple of Pleistorus. He had seen him standing in the street arguing with half a dozen Thracians. There had been a woman servant beside him holding a lamp—its light had attracted his eye. He had just recognized Cleton when one of the Thracians cut at him with a sword. The woman had dropped her lamp and fled; and the boy—Oeobazus had not known his name—had dashed up to help. Together they had lifted Cleton onto Oeobazus's mount and brought him here.

"He'd said he was a friend of your master's," Oeobazus told me, "and I know he was a friend to me while I was imprisoned—the only person who offered me any hope."

"He was," Hegesistratus confirmed, glancing up from binding Cleton's wounds. "Or rather, I should have said he is. I don't think this is going to kill him."

Elata nodded, and winked at me.

"The sword was not heavy enough or the arm strong enough—whichever way you care to put it. The blade bit into the bone, and deeply, too; but a skull is thick this high above the ear."

Cleton (whose name I had heard by that time from Oeobazus) muttered, and Elata held a wine cup to his lips. "He's dry—it's how I often feel as the vine laps my roots. He must have water to make new blood."

He drank all the cup held, and we laid him before the fire. That is when I wrote what I did, starting when Io showed me our old camp; for she had said (this as we whispered among ourselves and listened for the old man's rasping breath) that he had come to see us there, speaking to me as well as to Hegesistratus. I asked her whether I had written of that and whether she thought I should read it now, but she said she had overheard everything that had been said and would tell me at need.

After a long time, Cleton spoke to Hegesistratus and the black man, who helped him sit up. That was when I ceased to write. They set him beside the hearth, with his back to its warm stones.

"They took Hypereides," he told us. This was the captain mentioned earlier.

"Who did?" Acetes demanded.

"Nessibur and Deloptes."

Hegesistratus said, "Do not excite yourself—that can only do harm. Do you know where they have taken him?"

"To the palace."

"I see. Oeobazus has indicated that there were more than two Thracians confronting you when he caught sight of you—six at least. I take it that the rest were retainers of these two?"

Cleton nodded wearily.

Hegesistratus turned to Acetes. "In that case, those he names are certainly two of the aristocrats who sought to protect King Kotys. Presumably they slipped out of the palace through a side entrance."

Cleton nodded again.

Acetes said, "They got him from your house, fellow? How'd they know he was in there?"

Cleton's clouded eyes went from his face to Hegesistratus's, from Hegesistratus's to mine, from mine to the black man's, and at last to Elata's. I thought then what a terrible thing life is, in which a man grown old and weak may find that some ill-considered act of his has doomed a friend. "I told them," he said. "I told Thamyris. He sent them . . . they said so."

Acetes cursed and asked Hegesistratus, "Do you understand the political situation here?"

"Not as well as he does," Hegesistratus told him. "Perhaps not even as well as you do yourself. You've been to the palace and talked with Thamyris, I know. I never have."

"And I'm going back, as soon as I can get my men together. Will you come with us?"

"Certainly," Hegesistratus told him. Oeobazus, the black man, and I nodded together.

Io had squeezed between the black man and me; now she asked Cleton, "You were a spy for this Thamyris, weren't you? Besides for Hypereides—and you seemed so nice!"

At that Cleton managed a smile and took one of her hands in his. "I've tried to be," he assured her. "Honestly, I have. I sent you more arrows. Did you know that?"

Io nodded.

"Do you think I could have done that without friends among the Thracians? That I could live and trade here at all?" His hand left hers to grope for his cup. Elata held it for him.

When he had drunk he said, "I gave you good advice, child. I did. Kotys was a hothead, but Thamyris had his ear—sometimes anyway. Didn't want the Mede killed, afraid the Amazons might kill Kotys, wanted to let everyone go."

Hegesistratus said, "The other aristocrats must hate him, if he was so near the throne—most of them at least. I would guess that those standing with him now are family connections, sons and cousins and so on."

Cleton nodded again. "Nessibur's his grandson. Deloptes is a nephew."

Hegesistratus pursed his lips. "And who do the others want crowned? A younger brother of Kotys?"

"His son. He's only three."

Oeobazus told us, "But now Thamyris has my unknown friend to bargain with. He'll threaten the rest with phantom armies from Hellas—make them appoint him regent for the young prince, perhaps."

Cleton spoke to Io and me. "Hypereides came to see me this afternoon. We're old friends, done business together for years. This time he needed wine, I had it. We struck our bargain, and I told my people to take the wine to his ship. He promised he'd bring the money tonight."

Acetes said, "So when he left, you told Thamyris he'd be coming back."

"Sent word to him," Cleton whispered. "Told him the Rope Maker's man of business would be in my house. Maybe . . . trading rights. Keep the others out."

I said, "But Thamyris didn't come. He sent the two lords."

Cleton sighed, and sipped from his cup again. "I didn't expect him to—just send somebody who could bargain for him. But they wanted to take Hypereides back to the palace, and he wouldn't go. Said he'd come in the morning and bring the Rope Maker. I think they thought he was lying. Maybe he was, maybe he felt they couldn't win."

I nodded.

"They got him and bent his arms back. I followed them out into the street, tried to explain to them that he was my guest, my customer."

Io said, "And they tried to kill you."

Under his breath Acetes added, "And probably believe they have— that they've killed their own agent. They're desperate. These are players who have to win the next throw."

Io asked, "What are we going to do?"

Acetes straightened up. "Get the men together, go there, and get him out."

I asked how many he had.

"Shieldmen? Five, and two bowmen."

"Cleton, do you have hoplons and breastplates among your goods? Helmets and so forth?"

His head moved less than a finger's width. "Yes, four."

"Four of everything?"

Again the feeble motion.

"Good. Acetes, find out where they're stored, arm the four largest sailors, and teach them how to behave like shieldmen—they probably know already. Take Hegesistratus, this Mede, and the black man with you. When you reach the palace, insist that they let everyone inside."

Acetes nodded. "You're right—that's just what a real Rope Maker would do."

"I'll join you if I can't get in. What's it like?"

I felt Io's grasp tighten on my hand.

"You'll have to slip past the Thracians outside first," Acetes warned me.

"I know, but how is the palace laid out? Where might they keep Hypereides?"

Cleton gasped for breath. "Square. Hear me, son. I've been in it many times. . . . A wall, not too high. No towers. Inside's courtyard, stable in back. Palace square, too. Hall and kitchen . . . ground. Sleeping rooms up steps . . . captives down. Underground. Turn right, five streets."

Hegesistratus tried to remonstrate with me, but I brushed him aside and got out the door before even the black man could halt me.

The streets were dark and oozing with filthy mud, so that I had to walk slowly. I had not gone far before I nearly collided with a woman, but it was not until she spoke that I realized she was Elata.

"Latro," she said, "stop, and listen to me. Do you know I cure?"

"Of course," I told her. "I saw you helping Hegesistratus with Cleton tonight."

"And I would cure you, Latro, if I could. I can't, but I do understand how utterly you forget. I think I'm the only one who does, even now, though Io knows better than the rest. You don't remember who Hypereides is, nor do you care. Nor should you. My tree is old already, yet it and I will live for a great many seasons after Hypereides is dead and forgotten. You must guard your seed, Latro. Tonight you're risking it for nothing. Why?"

I did not understand what she meant by her tree, for women do not have that; but I told her, "I am doing it so that I will never be as Cleton is tonight. Let that be enough for you." I kissed her and ordered her to go back before someone harmed her. I, too, had drunk a good deal of wine; yet though she had chewed resin to sweeten it, her breath tasted of more.

A man rode past. He stared, and I saw he wore a helmet and bore a lance; I was glad that he did not stop. I hurried on and had nearly reached the palace when Io overtook me.

"Master!" she called, and caught at my cloak.

I spun around, my fist up. "Have I ever struck you, Io?"

"I don't remember," she said. Then, when I lifted my fist higher, "Yes, master, once or twice. It doesn't matter."

"I should strike you again now. You could have been killed, and now I have to take you back."

"Good." She sounded happy. We turned and began to retrace our steps. "You're the one who would have been killed, master, don't you know that? I'll bet there are a thousand Thracians in there with this Lord Thamyris, and your being dead wouldn't help Hypereides one single bit."

I told her, "If you follow me again, Io, I won't bring you back; I'll take you with me. That will be safer, I think, than leaving you in the streets of this barbarian town alone."

"You ought to stay in the house with me, master, or go with the black man and Acetes."

"I can't do that."

"Why not?" she asked. "Nobody'd blame you."

"But they'd know, Io, what I had set out to do, and that I had not done it—had not actually tried. While I myself would not know. I would see how they pitied me, as at times I've seen it today; and I would not know why." Quite suddenly there was a rush of moisture to my eyes, as if some veering wind had carried smoke to them. I did not weep, since men do not do such things; yet my eyes streamed, no matter how quickly I blinked. Today I must guard myself against this self-love, for surely it and wine were what unmanned me.

I believe a tear may have struck Io; she looked up quickly and said, "I can go the rest of the way alone, master. I'll be all right."

"No," I said, and shook my head, though perhaps she could not see the gesture.

When we reached the house, I had to pound on the door with the pommel of my sword before Elata lifted down the bar for us. Io threw her small body into my arms, and I kissed her as I had kissed Elata, knowing her a woman, however young, though I had thought her only a child before. "I won't run after you again," she promised. I nodded and did not tell her how much I hoped she would—how frightened I was.

Recalling the man with the lance, I chose not to follow the dark street I had walked down before, this time turning right at the first corner, then left at the next turning. When I did, I saw that a fire had been built in the middle of this new street, almost to the palace. Several men were standing around it, and it seemed to me that they were warming their hands.

# TWENTY-FOUR

## *The Boar*

THE GREAT BEAST IN THE shadows was what struck everyone's fancy—so much is clear. I have listened to Hypereides, the mantis, the Mede, Acetes, and the shieldmen; and every one of them spoke of it. The mantis wanted to know how I had entered the palace. I had simply climbed the wall, which had not been difficult, and I told him so.

But first I described how the black man had saved me when I circled the watchfire. That made Hypereides happy and the black man, too. He showed us how he had snapped the Thracian's neck before he could draw his sword. I did not tell anyone that he had run ahead of me hoping to stop me; it would make Hypereides like him less. Nor did I say anything at all concerning Elata or Io. I told him instead of the other things that I did before pulling off my boots and making my dash for the wall. They are lost now, no doubt, with our horses and a great many other good things that we left behind us in the house. I remember that I considered discarding my cloak as well; now I am glad I did not, but I could not have climbed the wall wearing my boots.

Polos desires me to tell him many things about swords; I have explained that I must write this first. I will strive to be brief.

The black man had warned me I might be killed, pointing at the dead Thracian and to me, and opening and shutting his hands to indicate how many Thracians he felt might be within the wall, which was a very great number indeed. I did not dare answer him aloud for fear the other Thracians would overhear me, and so I spoke as he, with my fingers, saying it might also be that they were few and I would kill them all.

He grinned at that—I saw his teeth flash in the darkness. Then he went away; he is my brother.

Though my hands had spoken so boldly, they trembled when I crouched in the shadow of a house to take off my boots. Because they stood against a cold sky bright with stars, I could see the Thracians upon the wall, the black outlines of their helmets and the sharp heads of their javelins. If I were to talk to Polos of swords and fighting now, as he wishes, I would tell him how important it is to stand for a time in the place of your enemy; I do not believe any man can win who does not do that, save by the favor of a god. Thus I supposed myself Thamyris and penned within the palace wall.

The lords siding with me I could not station upon the wall, because they would not consent to it; they would mount the wall only if there was an attack. On the other hand, I would require a force of picked men who would rush to counter any such attack. Very well—the lords would be that force. Peltasts could guard the wall through the tedious watches of the night, and sound the alarm.

But I, Latro, knew that peltasts are simple men, however hardy— just as I myself am a simple man. Simple men would keep their eyes on the men around the fires.

Thus I needed a distraction that would draw their eyes to a fire some distance from me. If the black man had remained with me, I would have asked him to provide it. As it was, there was no one to help me except the dead Thracian. Crouching very low, I dragged him to the back of the wood piled for the fire I had been skirting when he discovered me; there I stood a log upright and drove his knife into it. I was afraid someone would hear me, but the men around the fire were talking and the fire crackling. It was not easy to make his flaccid hand grasp the hilt, but by slipping the pommel into his sleeve I managed it.

Then I went quickly to the other side of the palace, not by shunning the light of each watchfire in turn, as I had before, but by going a short distance into the city (so that I kept well away from all the fires) and returning to the wall again. Soon, I knew, someone would go for wood and discover my dead man, and he would be filled with amazement when he saw that this man had (as it would appear) fought with a log and died. He would want the others to see everything that he had seen— and the peltasts upon the wall would hear him.

I had expected to wait for some time; but though everything happened, I think, as I had anticipated, I had scarcely reached a house near the palace wall before I heard shouts. Hesitation would have doomed my plan, for the peltasts would quickly return to their posts. I dashed to the wall and began to climb.

The top was the most hazardous point; I leaped as soon as I saw a roof below me, though I had no means of knowing how strong it might be. When I struck the thatch, I heard a pole snap under me, and the thatch sagged; but it muffled the sharp crack, save for the horses beneath. I slid down the roof and dropped to the ground, and though that distance was considerable, the courtyard was muddy and soft; I knew I was safe for a time then, since the men upon the wall were certain to look outward.

The palace stood dark before me. Hidden by the shadows of its broad eaves, I traced its wall, my fingers groping the rough ashlars. Soon they discovered a deep-set doorway, and within it a low and narrow door, of wood bound with bronze. Softly I put my shoulder to it, pushing with all my strength. It budged less than a hair's width; but when I relaxed, it seemed to me that it swung toward me, though only very slightly. Groping, I found a ring at one side. I pulled; the creaking of the hinges startled me so much that it has not been until this present moment, while I sat writing this, that I realized how foolish I had been.

Not long ago, I wrote that one must stand in one's enemy's place; but I myself had failed to do it when I hoped (as I had) to enter by some window. Thamyris would have been a fool to bar his doors—it would only have impeded his lords as they hurried to defend the wall. In the same way, the king who had built the palace would not have had its doors open inward; such doors only obstruct those who would rush out, and they are easily broken by rams.

I found myself in a smoky corridor lit here and there with cressets. Halfway along its length, there was a door on either side, and I saw that a wide chamber, more brightly illuminated, awaited me at the end.

One of the doors was barred within. The other gave access to a dark room where bundled lances, spears, and javelins leaned in corners, and wooden figures wore helmets, swords, and leather shirts much like my own, heavy with scales and plates. From one I borrowed an oval shield faced with bronze, and after stumbling over a sheaf of javelins, I severed the thongs with my sword and selected two. I understood then that the gods intended I should fight for my life—why else would they thus equip me? I took a helmet as well (I have it still), a high one with an august crest like the spread fingers of a webbed hand.

When I left the storeroom, Thamyris was standing at the end of the corridor as though waiting for me. "Come," he said, and motioned to me.

I did not know who he was, for if I had seen him before I had forgotten it; but I did as he asked. He vanished from the end of the corridor as soon as he saw I obeyed him; and when I entered the megaron, he was seated upon his throne. Though the megaron reeked of smoke, another scent underlay it. Some time passed before I recognized that second odor.

"Come closer," he said. "Have you come to kill me?"

I told him that I certainly had not—that I did not even know who he was.

"I am Thamyris, son of Sithon," he said. He was old, his long beard faded to a solemn white, though his glance still held a spark. Something huge twitched, though only very slightly, in the shadows behind him.

"I'm called Latro," I told him, "and I've come here to kill no one— only to free your captive, the Hellene. Give him to me and allow us to leave unmolested, and I swear we will do no one here the least harm."

"You are called Pleistorus in this land," he told me. "By many other names in others. As for your Hellene, I care nothing for him—he was the bait that hooked you, nothing more." He clapped his hands, and two armed men stepped from the shadows. When I saw them, I thought that it had been one of them I had seen move. "Bring in your foreigner," he told one. "He may be of further use."

The man addressed hurried away; the other waited beside the throne with sword drawn.

"This is my grandson Nessibur," the old man on the throne said, nodding toward him. "He will succeed me as King of Thrace."

I congratulated him.

"Are you not going to say that I am not yet so much as king of Apsinthia? Or that Apsinthia is only one small kingdom among fifty?"

I shook my head and told him I knew nothing of the matter. The truth was that I was not thinking of it at all, but of the name he had given me. I have since asked Io, who says that it is only the name of some Thracian god.

"*Latro!*"

It was the prisoner, a bald, round-faced man whose hands were bound behind his back. Seeing that, and thinking it best to act boldly, I shouldered the lord who had brought him aside and cut him free.

"Thank you," he said. He shook his hands and slapped one against the other. "I'd like to have one of those javelins of yours, but I'm afraid I couldn't hold on to it."

The man who had brought him asked whether his sword should be returned to him.

Thamyris laughed. The laughter of old men is often shrill cackling, I know; yet there was something worse in his, the wild mirth of those who have felt the hand of a god. "Why not," he asked, "when he cannot grasp it? Pleistorus, were you not about to tell me that Thrace—and even the Apsinthian throne"—here he struck its armrest loudly with his open hand—"is beyond *my* grasp?"

I shook my head again, adding, "I've no desire to be rude, Thamyris, and don't know whether Apsinthia, or Thrace, is beyond your grasp or within it. If they are what you wish, then I wish you well in them."

The captive said, "You're Lord Thamyris, sir? My own name is Hypereides. I hail from Thought, but I've been assisting the noble Acetes, the strategist appointed by Prince Pausanias, the regent of Rope—the Rope Makers are our allies, as I imagine you know already. I assure you I'm not a spy or troublemaker of any kind, and I have friends here who'll be happy to vouch for me."

Thamyris spoke as if he had not heard him. "We Thracians could be masters of the world. Do you know that?"

I said, "I'm sure you breed many valiant men."

"None but the Indians are more numerous"—he leaned toward me—"none but the Rope Makers more warlike. Were we united—as we shall be—no nation on earth could resist us!"

Hypereides said quickly, "But you'll need allies, Thamyris. What you have here is cavalry and light infantry. It's good, I know. It's very good. But you're going to need heavy infantry, too, and a navy. Now the best phalanxes are the Rope Makers', as everybody knows. And the best ships are ours, as we proved at Peace."

Thamyris leaned back as old men do, staring at the smoke-blackened ceiling. At last he sighed. "You are still here. I shall have you gutted with your own weapon as soon as Deloptes returns with it. Disemboweled by Pleistorus, if I can arrange that, and I imagine I can." He rose with these words and came down from the throne to stand before me.

"You are reputed to be overlord of every battlefield. You are not. After so many years, I—we—have found him." Briefly, fingers like claws caressed my jaw below the cheekpieces of my helmet, before coming to rest upon my shoulders. "If you were what you say, you would slay this foreigner for me with his own sword, the moment that it was brought to your hand. You know *he* would, but you do not know I know it. Learn that I do."

He seemed strange to me—not like a man, but rather a doll manipulated by another. I said, "Very well, I am the master of all battlefields, if you say it. In the person of that master, I tell you no strategist worthy of his command kills those who might readily be brought to fight for him."

That was all Thamyris said and all I said, because at that moment the wide door at the head of the megaron was thrown back. A peltast ran in and knelt to him, still grasping his javelins; he spoke in a tongue I do not understand, and Thamyris replied in the same way.

The peltast objected, and indicated the door through which he had come, expostulating. He was somewhat younger than I, and I could see that though he did not wish to disagree with the old man, he felt he must.

Thamyris shouted at him; then Nessibur spoke, stepping down from the dais. There came a guttural grunt from the shadows, at which Thamyris trembled, though he did not seem to know it. He called loudly and clapped his hands, and half a dozen well-armed men filed in to stand at either side of him. Nessibur left with the young peltast, I suppose to arrange whatever difficulty had brought him.

Just then Deloptes returned, carrying Hypereides's sword, a bag of coins, and some other things. Hypereides tied the bag to his belt by the thongs and slung his sword about his neck in the fashion of the Hellenes, who seldom wear the sword at the belt.

"Your master is at our gate," Thamyris informed Hypereides. "Nessibur will admit him; and if you die before his eyes as a man ought to, you will have the satisfaction of showing him that his nation is not alone in its boasted courage."

"And if I live," Hypereides replied, "I shall show that mine is without peer—as it is—in overcoming adversity."

Thamyris turned to me. "Take his sword, Pleistorus, and take his life. Or lose your own."

I exclaimed, *"It's a boar!"*

I did not intend to speak thus aloud, but the words escaped my lips before I could shut them in. Although Hypereides stared at me as if I had suddenly gone mad, what had actually happened was that I had at last identified the pervasive odor underlying the smoke of the megaron: it was not the stench of a pigsty but a deeper, harsher smell, ripe with musk—the smell a hunter may catch when one of those great brutes is brought to bay.

# TWENTY-FIVE

## *Farewell to Thrace*

IO CALLED ME AFT TO watch its coastline vanish behind us. When I told her I had been writing, she wanted me to return to it at once; but I stayed with her until nothing could be seen save the wake of our ship and the gray sea. It is winter and the season for storms, the kybernetes says; but I do not think we will have one today. The sun rose in bright gold at dawn; and though the wind is chill, it serves us well, and the sun is golden still.

As soon as I had placed the boar's scent (so I was upon the point of writing when Io called to me) I could also make out the beast itself, huge and black as night, where it lay in the dusky area behind the dais; its chin rested flat upon the stone floor, but it watched our every movement with eyes that shone as red as embers.

When I said I smelled a boar, several of the men protecting Thamyris spoke; and though I could not understand their words, I sensed that they had understood mine.

"Is it chained?" I asked. "They can be dangerous."

If he replied, I did not hear him. I went to examine the boar more closely, and the Thracians who had come at his order stepped aside to let me pass.

The boar rose as I approached it, and I saw at once that it was not chained. For an instant its eyes left me for Thamyris, and he shouted an order. My attention was upon the boar, not on him or the men beside him; but I spun about when I heard a sword drawn. Hypereides had pinned the Thracian's arm—another's hand was on his hilt.

I cast both javelins, and the distance was so short that I could not miss. If the remaining four had come at us as one, we would have been killed immediately; as it was, I had to shelter Hypereides with my shield as much as I dared, for he had none of his own. We were driven back, as was to be expected; but to be driven back from the place where we were, was to be driven toward the boar.

*"Run!"* I told him, and together we fled along the wall of the megaron, for I hoped to put the boar between our attackers and ourselves. It turned toward us, as I had feared it would. Falcata stabbed deep—but in the side of the neck, not over the eyes as I had intended; and for that bad thrust we might have died.

We lived instead, as Hypereides had foretold. The enormous boar recoiled from my blade, scattering the remaining Thracians like so many birds and opening one from groin to throat with its fearsome tusks. (Its shoulders were higher than theirs—this I saw.) Thamyris drew his sword and rushed upon us like a madman, and Hypereides ducked beneath his cut to kill him.

What would have happened next had we, the three remaining Thracians, and the boar remained pent in the megaron, I cannot say; the great door opened once again, and through it dashed a pack of piebald hounds. For an instant, they foamed like the sea about the boar, so that it seemed to me they would surely drag it down and tear it to bits; but it shook them aside and fled through the open door. Outside I heard the shouts and shrieks of those in the courtyard, and the baying of the hounds.

Then boar and hounds were gone.

Of the rest of the battle I write but a little, for though many a wound must still bleed, all I recall of it is scattered and confused. Acetes had come, and (so he explained to us a few moments ago) had persuaded Nessibur to admit his shieldmen and Hegesistratus, Oeobazus, and the black man, as well as himself; but before he had called for a truce and advanced to the wall, he had given a pledge to the Thracians besieging the palace that he would open its gates for them if he could. He did this, as he himself conceded, upon the advice of Hegesistratus, who had pointed out to him that he could not lose by it, for he need not unbar the gates unless he wished the aid of the Thracians outside them.

It would seem that when the boar dashed into the courtyard, someone there—whether a Thracian or a Hellene no one can say—threw wide both gates, perhaps merely in the hope that it would run out; at this the Thracians outside rushed in, believing that Acetes had fulfilled his pledge.

Nessibur is dead, they say, and with him all who sided with Thamyris except a few peltasts. With much gold, Acetes received the daughter of a noble Thracian, who offered to buy a girl from him in addition. The gold has been divided, the greater portion among our crew, but much also to Hypereides, Hegesistratus, the kybernetes, Oeobazus, the black man, and me. Mine I have hidden in my chest. Some was in coins of many sorts, most in ornaments, rings, buckles, and the like; thus the division was by weight.

We might have had much more gold, I think, had we remained in Thrace; but all of us were eager to go. It was for Oeobazus that we came, Io says, and we have him. We sailed in such hurry that many useful articles were left behind. In justice to Io, I must add that I do not think anything can have been left by her. She brought a sword she says the Amazons gave her, a sling Polos made for her, my clothing as well as her own, this scroll and my old one, and other things. I still have the helmet I took from the palace, though my shield was so deeply cut I left it behind.

I was talking to Polos, who asked many questions about the boar; all the Hellenes have been chattering about it. I brought him to Hegesistratus, who told us that in Thracian art a boar is the foe of Pleistorus; this foe is called Zalmoxis, and is often shown as a bear instead. Hegesistratus and Polos say Pleistorus is the god to whom Oeobazus was to be sacrificed. Hegesistratus could not explain why Thamyris had a boar in the megaron, except by saying what everyone says: that besieged men are unlikely to turn out any animal that can be eaten at need.

Polos wanted to know whether Hegesistratus had seen the boar, and whether it was as big as everyone is saying. "I did," Hegesistratus told him, "and it was as large as they are saying now. However, it was not as large as they will say it was when we reach Thought."

I think that a very good answer indeed.

Perhaps I should not trouble myself with such trivialities, but I have nothing better to do than write, though some of our crew are bailing or shifting the supplies in the hold to better the trim of the ship. Thus I will set down that we who were in the battle at the palace are the envy of the rest. Hypereides has told the four sailors to whom Acetes gave helmets, hoplons, and breastplates that they may keep them as the reward of their valor. These represent a great deal of money, but Acetes told Cleton we would pay for—rather than return—them. Hypereides plans to bill the priests on the high city for the full amount; because he is bringing Oeobazus, they will not refuse him.

After I wrote last I went privately to Hegesistratus to ask him about the hounds; it puzzled me that no one mentions them. He said he did not see them; he heard their baying, but thought himself the only one who had. I assured him I had heard them, and seen them. He says they are Cynthia's; she is a goddess to whom both of us are indebted. He was fervent in her praises—even more so when I described to him how her hounds had chivied the boar.

Elata challenged us to swim, though the sea looks so cold. (This is the one these Hellenes call the Water.) The kybernetes had a sailor tie a long line to the sternpost, letting it trail after the ship so that swimmers could catch hold of it, should it appear they might be left behind. When Hegesistratus took off his clothing, I saw that he had been wounded several times, some very fresh; he says he received those when he and I fought alongside the Amazons. (Io says these women gave her the sword. It seems very strange to me that women should also be soldiers.)

Hegesistratus pointed to the oldest wound and asked whether I remembered it. When I admitted I did not, he told me that he received it from an assassin in Sestos. I cannot recall Sestos, though I know that there is such a city on Helle's Sea.

Everyone stared at Elata when she took off her gown. She did not seem to mind, but soon grew chilled and dove into the sea; Hegesistratus untied the thongs that hold his wooden foot and dove after her. They called for me to join them, but I do not think Hegesistratus truly wished it; though no one swam with them, they swam together for a long time. When they returned to the ship, they sat very close together and wrapped themselves in both their cloaks, saying that though the sea is cold, the wind is colder.

———

The kybernetes says that this island is Sign-of-Thrace; it is called so because it is a day's sail from the Thracian coast. Everyone says we have been in Thrace, though I cannot recall that either. Io tells me I have written much about it in this book.

There are fine ports on this island, Hypereides says, but this is only a fishing village. We do not wish to dock at one of the ports because no one knows whether these Hellenes remain loyal to the Empire; here we count two men for each villager. Besides, these poor people care nothing for the Empire, and it nothing for them. Hypereides, Io, and I are going to sleep here tonight; this is the largest house in the village. It is good we have a house to sleep in. We would be very uncomfortable, I think, if we slept outside, even if we slept around a fire built in a sheltered spot.

As things are, we have been roasting fresh thrushes, which is very pleasant. Kroxinas, whose house this is, netted them a few days before; his wife plucks them for us, and we roast them on green sticks.

Kroxinas has as many questions as Polos, it seems, but he asks them mostly with his eyes. When he can no longer hold one back, he asks Io. Hypereides answers, usually. Kroxinas asked what had brought our ship to Thrace so late in the season, and Hypereides told him we came to set the son of King Kotys firmly upon the throne of Apsinthia.

Kroxinas had heard of Kotys, but had not known he was dead. (All this was greatly complicated by the fact that Kotys' son is named for his father.) Hypereides said that now that the Empire is crumbling, it is the task of Thought to bring the rule of law to the islands of the Water and the lands along its coasts. His talk has made me think that the Great King must need me now more than ever.

Io added, "There was a big battle—my master and Hypereides were right in the thick of it."

Kroxinas and his wife were as eager to hear about it as I, and Hypereides obliged us. I will set down here only the meat of what he said, omitting a good deal.

"After King Kotys was murdered by his nobles, his mother's brother, Thamyris, tried to take the throne. He was getting on in years and had been chief adviser to his nephew—a good one, from all I heard—but now he wanted to be king himself. We had been patrolling Helle's Sea against the Great King, but as soon as Xanthippos got word

of it, he sent us off to Apsinthia right away. The Thracians are afraid of
the Rope Makers; so since we didn't have any with us, I bought a scarlet
cloak for Acetes in Sestos. When we got to Thrace, he pretended he was
a strategist from Rope and the rest of us were allies and auxiliaries from
their league. That got the nobles supporting the prince on our side
pretty quickly, and I was able to find out what was going on, even
though the whole situation was still badly confused at that point.

"With Thamyris surrounded and the other Thracians afraid of us,
I didn't think anything of going around Cobrys alone. I had my sword
for footpads—which a man isn't allowed to wear back in Thought—
and like I said, the city was friendly. I didn't even wear armor. What I
should have done is taken Latro and the black man with me; they're my
bodyguards, but I didn't think I needed them.

"Well, I got quite a surprise. I was sitting around in the house of
a friend of mine, telling a few jokes and talking about business, when
in comes a couple of high noblemen. Their faces were practically blue
with tattoos, and by the stone I'm glad I won't have to look at those
again for a while! Each had half a dozen henchmen with him, every one
of them armed to the teeth. 'King Thamyris wants to talk to you,' they
said. 'We've come to escort you to the palace.'

"I know what barbarians are like, and I could see I wasn't going to
get out of that palace until I bought my way out, so I said I'd come
tomorrow and pretended to be drunk. They weren't buying any, though.
'Our orders are to bring you,' they told me. They threw me down and
tied my hands behind my back, and off we went.

"Latro here found out about it and came to the palace to try to get
me out. They brought me in and told me they were going to make Latro
kill me; it was just a threat to bring us around, of course, but I didn't
like it and neither did he.

"Thamyris had a pet boar. It's one of the shapes Zalmoxis is supposed to take, so I imagine it was a sacred animal of some kind. I don't
suppose you've ever been to Riverland, Kroxinas, but believe me, the
country's full of them. Then, too, we've got owls in Thought, as you
likely know; they're the sacred birds of our goddess, and her priests feed
them.

"So to change the subject, Latro said, 'That's a lovely pig you've
got there,' and went over to have a look at it. Thamyris must have

thought he meant to harm it, so then everything turned upside down.
He had half a dozen retainers with him, thinking that was enough to
hold us, I suppose; but we killed a couple as quick as you could snap
your fingers and were getting the upper hand of the rest when Latro saw
that the boar was set to charge. 'Run,' he yelled to me, and believe me,
we ran! That was the biggest boar you ever saw in your life, and it went
for those Thracians like we went for the Great King's ships at the Battle
of Peace."

Io asked, "Isn't that when Acetes came?"

Hypereides nodded. "That's right. Acetes had heard about what had
happened to me, too, and he led the loyal Thracians' attack. If he hadn't,
they probably would've killed Latro and me sooner or later. We had the
wildest battle you ever saw; no formations and 'each man stand shield
to shield for his city' stuff—this was the kind of real knock-down fighting old Homer tells about. I haven't had so much fun since Fennel
Field."

Kroxinas, who had listened openmouthed, asked Io, "What became
of Thamyris? Did they cut off his head?"

"Yes, as a matter of fact that's exactly what they did," Hypereides
told him. "Cut it off, stuck it on the point of a lance, and put it up at
the palace gate for everybody to see. But only after I'd killed him with
my own hand."

Io nudged me as though to say, "I bet it was you, master."

I said, "I've been talking to Hegesistratus about the boar. No one
ever killed it, he says."

Hypereides shook his head. "A hundred people have asked me what
became of it, but I don't know."

Kroxinas's wife murmured, "Don't you think the boar might have
been Zalmoxis himself? We're Hellenes, but we have people who worship Zalmoxis here." She shivered. "I don't think the baby prince's uncle
would've tried to be king if he hadn't been promised it by some god."

Io told Hypereides, "Pleistorus doesn't like Zalmoxis. In Thrace we
saw pictures of him sticking Zalmoxis with his spear."

Hypereides laughed. "Well, Pleistorus didn't come around to help
us. I wish he had—we could have used him."

# PART THREE

# TWENTY-SIX

## *In Cimon's Garden*

COMFORTABLY SEATED IN THE SHADE of an apple tree, the great men received us. Hypereides had described them to me already; thus I knew that the tough-looking, round-headed, blunt-featured man was Themistocles, and the tall, fine-looking, younger man Cimon, our host. Xanthippos we have met previously, so Io says, though I do not recall him. At any rate he greeted us as friends, and Cimon's servants brought stools for us.

"We've asked you here to discuss the death of Oeobazus," Themistocles began. I saw that he watched Oeobazus himself for his reaction, and so did I. There was none.

After a moment, Xanthippos chuckled. "Not many dead men have borne the news of their own demise with such equanimity, Oeobazus. You are to be congratulated."

The Mede's white teeth flashed like a sword in the thicket of his beard. "If you mean you're going to kill me, I've heard that in other places."

Themistocles shook his head. "I said only that you were here to talk about it. It took place quite some time ago. You were sacrificed by the Thracian barbarians to—what is it they call him?"

"Pleistorus," Hegesistratus prompted him.

Themistocles cocked an eyebrow. "He's one of their major gods? In that part of Thrace?"

Hegesistratus nodded. "Very much so."

"Good. That was the end of you, Oeobazus. Most certainly you never came to Thought or any other part of the Long Coast. Since we can clearly no longer call you Oeobazus, what would you like us to call you instead? Not by one of your family names, please."

The Mede thought quickly, or perhaps had been warned that some such question would be asked. "Why not Zihrun? I believe I'm entitled to that."

Xanthippos smiled, as did Hegesistratus and the black man. Seeing that no one else understood, Xanthippos explained, "It's 'Life chose me.' Certainly that's a good name for you, Zihrun. You're not unwilling to return to the Empire?"

At that Cimon spoke for the first time. There is nothing extraordinary about his clear, pleasant voice, and yet there is something very extraordinary about being spoken to by Cimon; I think it must come from the level gaze of those gray eyes. He said, "We won't tell you how dangerous this is for him. You're not children."

I looked around for Io, for she is indeed a child still, though she might say otherwise; but she and Elata had wandered away among the trees, perhaps feeling it more decent to leave men's talk to men. Polos was helping in the stable.

"Well put." Themistocles nodded. "We'll have to talk more about this in private, Zihrun—who you're to see and what you're to tell them, everything we need to learn. I'm going to impress the importance of your death in Thrace on everyone here in just a moment. But first we owe you more of an explanation, and more in the way of assurance, than you've had yet. What do you know of our politics?"

"That your people are themselves your king," the Mede said. "That you're their war leader, their highest-ranking strategist, called the polemarch. Beyond those, nothing."

"And you, Hegesistratus?"

"A foreigner's knowledge, and out of date at that. I am eager to learn."

"Then I'll explain to both of you, as quickly and simply as I can. If I show any prejudice for my own party or my friends, my colleagues here will correct me, you may be sure. I ask you to notice—to begin with—that I'm outnumbered."

Xanthippos shook his head and cleared his throat. "Hardly. Hypereides is your man, and a speaker of considerable eloquence, as I've several times been forced to admit."

Themistocles grinned; it made me like him. "There you see it— that's how we do it here. Among you Medes, I'm told, there are many

men so honorable that everyone trusts them. We're not like that at all—
we never trust one another. So what we do instead is make sure that
each side's represented, so that every rascal's got two worse looking over
his shoulder. Hegesistratus knows all this, of course. We Hellenes are
all the same.

"The Rope Makers—we'll be talking about them soon—would tell
you they have two kings so each can keep the other honest. We have
two political groups instead—the shieldmen's party and the naval mob.
I'm head of the naval mob. Xanthippos and Cimon are leaders of the
shieldmen's party. That means that when we say we're behind you,
you've got the pledges of both sides."

The Mede nodded.

"We have our differences," Themistocles continued, "serious and
profound differences. You said earlier that our people rule themselves.
It's actually the case only when my own party's in power."

Cimon shot him a glance both censorious and humorous.

"I represent the working poor, who make up the majority in our
city just as in every other. My people want jobs as seamen, stevedores,
and dockyard workers. They make our pottery and so on, and they know
that for them to eat, Thought must trade. That means we get the ship-
owners—like Hypereides here—and most of the merchants and man-
ufacturers, too."

Cimon glanced at Xanthippos and said, "Allow me to speak for our
side, Themistocles. I'll begin by warning Zihrun and the rest that not
everything you've said is true. And, Zihrun, you're not to suppose that
because we're shieldmen, we think that Thought could live without
ships, although Themistocles and his friends sometimes talk as if it could
live without soldiers. Nor does Themistocles, as he tried to imply, represent all poor men who work. Wholly untrue! No men work harder
than those who must plow and sow, tend and guard the herds and flocks,
harvest and thresh the grain, prune and manure the vines, and trample
the grapes. If you were to go into our Assembly, Zihrun, you would
find that those vital workers, without whom we would all starve, support
our party to a man. And should Themistocles challenge that, I will show
you two score of them here and let you speak with them yourself.

"Although we are proud to champion the interests of these hard-
working citizens, and their wives and children, they're by no means our

only supporters. You yourself, Zihrun, and you, noble Hegesistratus, are yourselves far from their lowly, though absolutely necessary and valuable, class; nor would anyone count either of you among the naval mob's surly loiterers. You're men of breeding and learning, and it is we and not Themistocles, who is a man of mean birth and small education (though I scruple to say it), who represent the best families in Thought."

Themistocles fidgeted upon the stone bench in a way that showed him eager to speak, and Cimon rose as if to make sure he retained the floor.

"Nor are those all. The virtue of a city does not reside in its best families; however excellent their stock, they are too few. Nor does it lie in the poor, who cannot fight unless some other feeds them. No, it is in the craftsmen, the skilled artisans, the worthy merchants, and the independent freeholders that true *arete* is found. *They* are the defenders of the city, and even Themistocles cannot deny that they are ours."

Themistocles applauded derisively.

"You will say now that it was not defended when the Great King came, and you will be right. Our sheep and our goats and our cattle were driven off, our horses stolen, our poultry and swine devoured, our crops destroyed, the tombs of our ancestors and the temples of our gods desecrated, and our city burned to the ground. All that is perfectly true. All that took place because the resources of our city were unwisely diverted from its army to the ships. And none of it can be permitted to take place again, or we shall be ruined utterly. The land *must* be defended! If the Long Coast were an island, you would hear me speaking in support of Themistocles. It is not."

Themistocles rolled his eyes. "Are you through at last, young man?"

"Why, no." Cimon sat down again. "My career has scarcely begun, and I intend to be polemarch myself before I'm through. But I've said what I had to say for the present, if that's what you mean."

"Good." Themistocles leaned toward us with the look of a man never more in earnest. "Then let me say that you spoke the truth when you said I was of humble birth—I am. My grandfather was a silver miner, and my father also worked in the mines for a time. As for learning, isn't it a matter of what a man learns? What do you Medes learn, Zihrun? You're an educated Mede, as my young friend pointed out. What does a Mede's education consist of?"

"One learns how to honor the gods," the man we had called Oeobazus told him, "most of all, how to honor Ahura Mazda, who is the god of gods; and to ride, to shoot with the bow, and to tell the truth."

Themistocles nodded as though what he had heard had merely confirmed what he had already known. "A very good education, I would say. Cimon here can play the lyre quite well, and he's a fine singer. You'll hear him tonight, I feel sure. As for me, I know how to make a city great."

Hegesistratus began, "You spoke of the Rope Makers—"

Themistocles silenced him with an upraised hand. "And I shall have much more to say about them soon. But before I do, I must make certain that our friend from the east understands one thing. It's that though we differ, we are alike in our devotion to Thought. As you may know, we have the custom of ostracizing politicians—Xanthippos, Cimon, and I are all politicians, you understand—who are considered too divisive. We send them away, without dishonor, for a specified number of years. But when the Great King's army came, I called all those who'd been ostracized home and gave them commands. They served the city well, as I knew they would.

"Xanthippos, Cimon, are you with me in everything we're doing today? Do you agree that all of us shall work for the good of Thought?"

Both nodded, and Cimon added, "We do."

"Do you pledge yourselves to hold in strictest confidence everything we say here today, provided I share whatever I can learn with you? To do everything in your power for Zihrun and the rest? And particularly for—" Themistocles glanced toward Hypereides.

"Latro," Hypereides supplied.

"For Latro?"

Both nodded again. Xanthippos said, "You have our hands on it, all of you."

"And mine." Themistocles paused; the warm breath of spring sighed in the newly green boughs, and though birds trilled there, it was so quiet I could hear the men taking down the wall beside the road talking at their work.

"I'm afraid that's as much assurance as we can provide you, Zihrun," Themistocles said, "but it's better than the word of a king. If I fall from power—and I will eventually, you can be sure—Xanthippos or Aristides will become polemarch. Aristides couldn't be here in person—Cimon's his representative. But I swear there isn't a man who walks on earth less likely to betray somebody it's his duty to look out for than Aristides. There're a few of us who're just as honorable as any Mede, and he's their chief. Notice that it's me, his enemy, who says that. I think he's wrong about a lot of things. I believe he's misguided, and the whole Twelve know he's pigheaded. But if the shieldmen have sworn to protect you, and they have, Aristides would die to save you.

"Now listen to me, all of you. I'm not going to threaten you—I know free men can't be checked long by threats. But if this were the Empire or any other tyranny, you might very well be strangled tonight to keep Zihrun safe. Hypereides, didn't you say Latro's got a bad memory?"

Hypereides nodded. "He forgets everything in a day or so."

"Then he must learn to forget faster. Any of you who still remember what Zihrun used to be called must forget it at once." Themistocles pointed toward the black man. "Hypereides says you don't speak our tongue, but you seem to have understood what I've been saying. What's the name of that man beside you, the one with the beard?"

"Zihrun," the black man told him.

"Hegesistratus, why did Hypereides send you to Thrace?"

Hegesistratus answered smoothly, "To assure King Kotys and his people of the continued friendship of Thought. King Kotys—that particular King Kotys—is now deceased, alas. But his son, a child dear to the gods, has his crown. And his son's advisers have sent many tokens of their goodwill."

Themistocles nodded, satisfied. "What about you, Latro? Why were you sent to Thrace?"

I told him quite honestly that I had not known I had ever been there.

Hypereides said, "Don't any of you forget. If anybody asks you about Oeobazus, we heard he was sacrificed to Pleistorus. We didn't see it ourselves because we weren't there at the time. It's just what we were told."

Xanthippos glanced at the sun, as a man does who wishes to judge just how much of the day remains. "I think we can get on with it,

Themistocles. Latro, are you and your friend aware of your legal status here?"

I told him I could speak only for myself, but that I had assumed we were foreign visitors. I knew we were no Hellenes.

# TWENTY-SEVEN

## *Io Weeps*

WHILE I WAS WRITING WHAT stands above this, Polos came wanting to talk of chariots and horses. I made him wash, then spoke with him as he wished.

Io has brought a bouquet of apple blossoms. Not many have opened yet, she says, but she found a few; and some of them that Elata broke in the bud opened while she held them, which seems strange. I explained to them that we are going to Rope tomorrow with Themistocles, and that has made Io very unhappy. She says the Rope Makers are cruel men who cannot be trusted, and indeed Hegesistratus says the same; thus it may be wise to record here everything else we said under the tree.

Xanthippos and Hypereides explained to the black man and me that under the laws of Thought we are Hypereides's slaves, having been given to him as prisoners of war by the city of Tower Hill. (I must ask Io about this.)

"I was planning to sell you to Kalleos," Hypereides said, "and I wrote her a bill of sale. I was to get five parties in return, with up to ten guests. But since I've only had one so far, you haven't actually changed hands, understand?"

I nodded, and so did the black man.

"I can see you don't like the idea of being slaves, and I don't blame you for that, I wouldn't myself. What we've worked out here—Xanthippos, Themistocles, Cimon, and me—is a legal mechanism for freeing you both. It's simple for the black man, but for you things get complicated because Prince Pausanias is claiming you."

He glanced at Themistocles for confirmation; Themistocles nodded.

"Some of Pausanias's men took you away from Kalleos, see? And while we were in Sestos, she applied to him for compensation and got it. You can understand the prince's position—he paid for you in good faith, and we've got you. He feels we ought to return you to him."

On behalf of the black man and myself, I told Hypereides that he would have neither of us long.

"That won't be necessary. I said we'd worked something out—weren't you listening? I got word of this the day we landed, and I talked to Xanthippos about it as soon as I'd let him know about—about our trip to Thrace."

Xanthippos smiled. "You see, Latro, I believe strongly in assisting those who have assisted me, and Hypereides had a great deal to say about what happened in the palace, though perhaps we shouldn't speak of that here. I enlisted Cimon in your cause—he has some useful connections in Rope—and Hypereides enlisted Themistocles. You mustn't imagine that Pausanias is an ordinary Rope Maker. He represents the old Lacedaemonian aristocracy, or what's left of it, and he's both a reasonable and a magnanimous man."

Seeing that Xanthippos had finished, Hypereides said, "So here's where we stand. I'll free the black man for two minas, the money to be paid whenever he has it. Is that all right?"

The black man hesitated, then nodded.

"And I renounce any claim on you, Latro. So does Kalleos—I talked to her about it today and paid her a little something. Themistocles is going to Rope, where they want to honor him for what he's done in the war. You'll go with him—Io, too. When you get there, Pausanias will free you and declare you a resident of Rope—not an actual Rope Maker, you understand, but an alien living there and a free man. You'll be his subject, of course; he's the Agid Regent. But you'll be nobody's slave."

I asked if I would be permitted to leave Rope to search for my home.

Cimon said, "Certainly, at any time. It's only the Equals* who can't leave without the permission of the judges. As an alien resident, you'll be able to travel and even to trade; and if anyone anywhere tries to harm you, you'll be able to claim the protection of your city."

The polemarch, who had been watching me narrowly, asked, "Will you do it? Come to Rope with me?"

---

*The *Homoioi,* who could vote in the assembly and hold office. Latro seems to have been declared a *perioikos,* a "neighbor."—GW

I shrugged. "Would you, in my place?"

He actually seemed to consider it for a moment, rubbing his heavy jaw, then nodded.

"Hegesistratus? Will you advise me?"

"Reluctantly. I know you don't remember it, but you read a fairly lengthy passage from your old book to me once. In it the regent told you that you were no longer to be his slave but his friend."

I felt then as though a heavy burden had been lifted from my shoulders.

"He sounded sincere, or at least it seemed you thought he did," Hegesistratus continued, "and it is only fair for me to tell you that. Nevertheless, my advice is that you should not go."

Then I wished to ask Io, but I—a grown man taking counsel with others—was ashamed to ask the advice of a child. I asked the black man instead, and he spoke to Hegesistratus.

"Seven Lions wishes to learn whether he is now free," the mantis said.

Hypereides nodded. "I have to give you a paper, and you have to sign one. But those are just formalities."

The black man spoke again, and Hegesistratus said, "Then he advises Latro to go, provided Themistocles permits him to go as well. Themistocles?"

The polemarch nodded. "Certainly. Will you come, Latro?"

"Yes," I said. "You have my word on it."

Cimon, particularly, appeared to relax after I had spoken. He smiled and gave me his hand.

"Which leaves no one but Elata and me to be disposed of," Hegesistratus said, "and we should not be much trouble."

Just then one of Cimon's household slaves came and spoke briefly to Cimon, who said to Themistocles, "Simonides is here, with the others. He says they've brought everything."

"Good. We'll start in the morning. Hegesistratus, I hope you understand that my party can't make further use of you here. You were with the Great King, so we'd be handing Xanthippos and Aristides a weapon. Your connection with Hypereides is ended."

"I understand, and I regret it," the mantis said. "It has been a fortunate connection for me."

"And for me," Hypereides put in. "I regret it, too."

Themistocles asked, "Any bad feelings? Do you think you've been misused in any way?"

"No, I do not," Hegesistratus assured him. "Precisely the contrary."

"Hypereides says you have sufficient funds. If that's not the case, I can arrange something."

Hegesistratus waved the offer away. "Doubtless you would tell Zihrun that no Hellene can refuse money, but the truth is that we are quite comfortable. We will take passage on a ship bound for Zakunthios as soon as I can find a decent one; I have a house there. After that, to Dolphins, perhaps."

Cimon came here to speak with me. He began by asking the children the name of the Mede. I had already told them about that, and both answered, "Zihrun, sir." He asked whether they were certain, and they repeated, "Zihrun," after which he sent them away, saying we wished to be alone.

When they had gone, he began by thanking me for agreeing to go to Rope as Prince Pausanias had asked. "It would have put me in a very embarrassing position if you hadn't," he told me. "We had men standing by to overpower you if necessary—Themistocles insisted on it—but how would it have looked, when I'd persuaded the prince to free you? And Themistocles's gang might have used the entire business against me; they were my men. If he were to report that we had stolen the slave of a citizen, that slippery trader would back him to the hilt."

I said that if his men had succeeded in overpowering me, I would certainly have been grateful to Hypereides for anything he did to free me.

"I suppose so. There's actually a fairly strong argument for holding that you're a free man already, do you know that?"

"No," I told him. "But I'd like very much to hear it."

"You two were captured by the Rope Makers after the Battle of Clay," he explained. "Nobody disputes that. The Rope Makers handed you over to Tower Hill for some reason, and their people gave you to Hypereides. You were mercenaries, weren't you? You and the black man?"

I said that I thought so.

"All right. But a couple from Hill were captured with you; and you have that little slave from Cowland. It turns out that the man was Pindaros, son of Pagondas, a member of one of their leading families who's been making a name for himself as a poet. He's claiming that at the time you were captured you were not employed by the barbarians directly, but by him on behalf of his city. If that view were accepted, we'd have to send you back to Hill under the terms of the peace Rope forced upon us."

I jumped up, I confess, when he said this, and strode back and forth exulting. I did not feel myself a slave even when we met under the tree, and now that feeling has been vindicated.

"The question was how much pressure this Pindaros could get the oligarchs of Hill to bring on behalf of a mercenary," Cimon continued, "though no matter how much they brought, we couldn't have given in to it. Their city's unpopular here, and it would have severely damaged our relations with Rope. As things stand now, I've chalked up a minor diplomatic triumph. Aristides and Xanthippos acknowledge it. Xanthippos and his son are staying over for dinner, by the way; so are Hegesistratus and his wife."

I said that I was glad of that, for I am by no means eager to be parted from Hegesistratus, and Io and the black man like him, I know.

"Themistocles and his retinue will be there, too, of course. We'll eat in the courtyard; I think we've seen the end of the rains for another year. Then tomorrow you'll be traveling with Themistocles. I wish I could come along with you—I like Rope—but it wouldn't look right. I came here, really, to caution you about Themistocles."

I said that I realized he was a powerful man here.

"He is, and a crafty one. Do you remember how he asked the mantis about the Thracian god?"

I nodded. Though I know I forget, I have not yet forgotten that.

"His mother was a Thracian, just as mine was. He knows the country backward and forward; he even speaks a little Thracian to the ambassadors sent by their kings. If you lie to him about Thrace, or try to hide anything, he'll know it."

That did not seem to be the right moment to explain that I have forgotten Thrace, so I held my peace.

"And I wanted to give you this letter. Do you read our tongue? You speak it well."

I shook my head.

"Then I'll read it to you. It's to one of the judges—his name's Cyklos." Cimon took the letter from his chiton and read: *"To Cyklos son of Anthes, Cimon the son of Miltiades sends his greetings. Latro, who bears this, deserves well of you and of us. Shield him from every harm, good Cyklos, lest we are both disgraced."*

I thanked Cimon for this introduction and asked him to add a request that the judge help me return to my home, which Cimon has promised to do. He will have a servant bring me the letter again, and I intend to roll it up in my old scroll.

That is all of importance that has happened today, though I might add that this farm of Cimon's is indeed a beautiful place. The house is a double square, with many rooms. There are three large barns besides the stables, all limed as white as the house and in excellent repair. The garden I described earlier I think very lovely, but the meadows beyond it are at least equally so. Over their rich grass the foals romp as joyfully, and almost as awkwardly, as Polos himself. When I talked with the laborers taking down the wall, they said that Cimon's father had been a great man; there was no need to tell me—I had seen it already. The stones from the wall are to be carted to Thought and cast into the marsh between Thought and Tieup, where Themistocles and Cimon wish to build a long wall to defend the city. I asked how Cimon intended to keep travelers from stealing his fruit. The laborers said that he will allow them to take it.

# TWENTY-EIGHT
## *Mnemosyne*

T HE MISTRESS OF MEMORY HAS given me what is surely the strangest adventure any man ever had. It has not returned to me the time I so much wish to recall; but Simonides thinks that through it I may retain the day just past, and many of those to come.

We dined in the larger court—a great throng. Cimon, our host, reclined at the head of the table, Themistocles to his right and Xanthippos on his left. With Xanthippos were his son, a good-looking youth who wore a cap throughout the meal, and his son's tutor, Damon, a quarrelsome old man. With Themistocles was the white-bearded Simonides of Ceos, whom Hypereides calls the greatest poet alive. Hypereides may say that if he wishes, but I have not forgotten what Cimon said of the poet Pindaros, who declares me a free man; and it seems to me that no poet can be greater than the one who announces to a man that freedom is his right.

Hegesistratus reclined next to Simonides, I should say, and Hypereides next to him. I was next to Damon and thought it bad luck when I heard how he contradicted everyone, but soon noticed that he argued with no one who did not speak. I kept silent and was safe. The black man was at my left—I could not wish better company.

Hegesistratus, as I saw, soon fell into conversation with the poet, so that the two of them seldom spoke to anyone else, though many times they glanced across the table at me. Little Polos helped serve and ate at the foot of the table, but came trotting up so often to tell me something he felt I might wish to know or to ask me some question or other, that everyone was soon laughing at him and he became a general favorite, Pericles swearing that on one occasion he had galloped around the table in both directions and bumped into himself.

A fine lyre was brought after the meal, as Themistocles had predicted. Hegesistratus played and sang beautifully, at which the black man spoke to me with his fingers of another time, when we had sung with many women; he struck his chest and flourished an imagined spear, so that was certainly a great day. Simonides played very well, chanting his own verse. Pericles played and sang nearly as well as Hegesistratus. His tutor would not sing, though Xanthippos says his voice was once very fine. He played the lyre, however, better than anyone else. Cimon sang last and with the best voice; when he had finished, all of us shouted his praises and pounded the table with our cups.

Servants came and took away most of the dishes. As soon as the table was clear, the dancers entered and performed upon it. There was one who brought five daggers she made stand upright on their pommels. She danced among them with great skill, and when we thought she could do no more, leaped from the center of the circle into the air, turning backward so that she landed on her hands with her feet high above her head. Everyone shouted, and she rolled off the table like the wheel of a cart.

Hegesistratus touched my shoulder then, whispering that he wished to speak to me. I left the table and went with him into a small room where Simonides sat. He asked whether I recalled Cimon's saying that it was here, upon his own estate, that the Thunderer had fathered the muses. I assured him I did—it had been said just before the singing began—but I knew neither the Thunderer nor the muses.

"The Thunderer is the father of gods," Simonides told me, "Zeus Maimaktes." I understood then that he is the god my own father called the bright-sky father.

I asked about the muses, but Hegesistratus waved it aside. "The important thing," he said, "is that it was here—at least, according to Cimon, that the god found Mnemosyne, the Lady of Memory. Simonides is a sophist and a famous teacher as well as a poet. Did you know that?"

I shook my head.

"One of the skills he offers to teach his students is that of memory. His own is perhaps the most famous of all time; it is said that he forgets nothing."

"Which is not true," Simonides told me, "although it brings me many students, of whom you may be one. What I've proposed to Hegesistratus is no more than that we visit the spot tonight and offer a sacrifice to Mnemosyne. Afterward I'll give you a lesson in the art of memory, and I can teach you more on the journey to Rope. It's possible that with training you may come to remember a good many things that you've forgotten. Or if not, you may at least cease to forget so much. Will you do it?"

I agreed gladly—this has surely been a fortunate day—and Hegesistratus spoke to Cimon regarding what we planned and got a kid to sacrifice, a donkey on which he rode (for he has lost one foot), and a servant to guide us. The place was nearby, though it did not seem so because we soon left Cimon's fields and woods behind and climbed a rocky hillside by a winding path. From the cleft rock where the small altar top lay upon three half-embedded stones as though by chance, Cimon's big house had dwindled to a few golden sparks.

The servant had brought wood for a fire and a fire box full of embers. Simonides recited the invocation, and I held the kid while he cut its throat. Afterward we skinned it and burned the heart and liver; when Hegesistratus had poured the libation, we roasted a few pieces of flesh over the fire.

"Now, Latro," said Simonides, "tell me truthfully. Do you really wish to remember?"

"Very much," I told him.

"Then close your eyes. Do you desire to remember so much that you would perform a great deal of work in order to do it?"

"Oh, yes," I said.

"Then you must think of a very large building. We're going to erect this building in your mind. We will not merely look at it as we looked back at Cimon's house while this man kindled the fire, but come to know it as only men who build may. Each stone and ornament must stand distinct in your mind."

I felt the hill tremble beneath me, as if a creature larger than any wild ox had risen to its feet. Opening my eyes, I saw a huge woman, twice the size of any man, emerge from the depths of the narrowing cleft, which seemed too small to have contained her. Her long, fair hair was braided, and the braids, as thick as my arm, were entwined and bound with gem-heavy cords of many colors. Her face was racked with grief, her gaze upon far-off things.

"No, Latro," Simonides said, "I want you to keep your eyes closed."

Feeling certain that the giantess meant us no harm, I shut them again.

"We must have a site for the palace we are going to build," he continued. "You must imagine this place. Think about it." After a long time he asked, "Have you done so?"

I nodded.

"Describe it to me."

"It's where the desert begins," I told him, "at the margins of the last fields."

"Look to the north," he instructed me. "What do you see?"

"Desert. Yellow sand and red stones."

"Is that all? Look to the horizon."

"I see a low line of rock. It seems darker than the stones nearby."

"Very good. You're facing north, are you not? That's the direction in which I told you to face?"

I nodded.

"Since you're facing north, east is toward your right; turn your head and tell me what you see."

"More desert. Rocky hills like this that climb higher and higher. The sun peeping above them."

"Excellent. Since you're facing north, south lies behind you. Look south, over your shoulder, and tell me what you see there."

"Sand," I said. "Yellow sand lying in waves like the sea. A man is leading three camels, but they are very far away."

"Better and better. Look to the west now, along your left arm."

I did as he told me. "Fields of barley and millet, and the mud huts of peasants. Beyond is the river, and beyond the river the setting sun."

"How many huts do you see?"

There were four, and I told him so.

"Do people live in these huts?"

"Yes," I said. "The men who till the fields live in them with their families."

"Good. It may be that we'll meet some of these people by and by. Look now toward the spot where your palace is to stand. What's the first thing you will do when you begin to build your palace?"

"Clear away this sand," I told him, "so that my palace may rest upon rock."

"Good. We'll clear it now. I've sent a thousand men with spades and baskets, and they've taken away all the sand. Do you see the naked rock?"

I nodded.

"It must stretch very far—as far as the hills you saw. If it does not, we'll have to bring back the men with spades. Does it stretch very far?"

"Yes," I said, "very far indeed." I felt the warm wind on my face and wondered to behold such a mighty work.

"Now you must lay your foundation. These blocks may be of rough-hewed stone, but they must fit well. Lay this foundation now. Does it extend across a great distance?"

"Very great."

"Then you're ready to lay the floor. It must be of smooth marble, white, but veined brown and black. Into each slab some glyph has been cut, and no glyph is like any other. The first four have a circle, a triangle, a square, and a cross. Do you see them?"

I nodded again.

"And there are many, many other shapes, too. Some are like the heads of animals. Some depict the whole creature. Some are like the footprints of men or birds, while some resemble leaves. There are many straight lines, but also many lines that waver or bend. Walk slowly across them—a long way—studying each glyph. Have you seen two that are the same?"

"No," I told him.

"That's well. Now we're going to approach the palace, but in order to approach it we must leave it. Look toward the west. Do you still see the river there? Is it a wide river?"

"Very wide. I can scarcely glimpse the trees on the other bank."

"Good. Walk west to the river, please. All the way to the river, until the water laps your feet. Is the riverbank clothed with grass?"

It was not, but covered with thick black mud.

"Good. Turn now. Face the east; lift your eyes and look back at your palace. It's very high, isn't it?"

It was, with a hundred lofty arches and airy galleries, and course upon course of pillars, each towering colonnade thrusting a hundred carved capitals above the last.

"Walk toward it. Now stop and look to your left and right. What do you see?"

There were fields of grain rippling in the wind.

"And before you?"

An avenue lined with statues.

"What are these statues? Describe them."

Lions with the faces of men.

"No. Only the one nearest you is a lion with a man's face—that's what's deceived you. If you look more closely, you'll see the rest are somewhat different. Describe the statue facing the one you've already described."

A winged lion, with the head and breasts of a woman.

"That's correct. Walk forward a little, just a couple of steps, and describe the statue beyond the lion with the woman's head."

I did as he directed. It was a winged bull with the head of a bearded man. Facing it across the avenue stood the image of a powerful man with the head of a bull.

"Good."

It seemed to me that I heard the tones of old Simonides in the sobbing wind; for a moment I marveled, knowing as I did that he was not where I was but north of the sea. I decided that he was surely dead now, and it was only his ghost I heard, somehow separated from his tomb and searching for it.

*"Look back now toward the lion with a man's face. Study it carefully. It shall be the conservator of your name. The stone is soft. Take out your knife and carve your name, Latro, in the right foreleg of this statue."*

I did as the ghost had said, though I feared some guardian might appear to kill me for it. As I fashioned each careful letter, I wondered how I had come to this place from far Hellas. Long ago I had eaten a good dinner there, listened to music, and climbed a hill. After that, everything was wrapped in mist.

"Turn around, so that you face the lion with a woman's head and breasts. . . ."

I did. She rose, spreading mighty pinions that would have outreached the yard of a trireme. "Surely you know *me*, Latro." Her voice was the purring of a huge cat.

I shook my head.

"I am your mother, and your mother's mother. For me and by me you stole the horses of the sun, that they might be returned to him. I am she who asks what walks upon four legs at sunrise, upon two at noon, and upon three at evening. And all who cannot answer me, at evening die."

# TWENTY-NINE

## *The Palace Walls*

ITS THOUSAND COLUMNS, ITS THRONGING statues and pictures, still rise around me—I have never remembered anything so vividly. So I told Simonides when he asked, a few moments since, what I was writing. He asked me several trifling questions, some of which I answered, and some of which I could not. Overall, he appeared pleased.

To tell the truth, I feared I would forget the palace when he interrupted me; that has not occurred, however. Thus I will take a few moments more to write that this is a lovely morning. Hegesistratus and his wife, and Zihrun the Mede, set out a short while ago. The black man and I, with Cimon, Hypereides, Io, and some others, walked a few stades along the road with them to say our good-byes. Io and the boys lagged behind as we returned to Cimon's house; and I, seeing she wished to speak to me, lingered also and fell into step with her.

"Master," Io said, "there's something I've got to tell you. You've probably written this in your book already, but maybe you ought to write it again. And if what the old man's teaching you will really help you remember, remember it."

I said that I would certainly try, if she thought I should.

"We were all in Thrace—I know you don't remember, but it's true. We were in Kotytto's sacred cave, where there was the big painted statue of her that got burned up later the same day. A lot of Thracians were outside, and you were guarding the way in for us. You told me you heard a dog outside, and Hegesistratus went out, and the Thracians didn't try and stop him. You and me and the black man talked about that, but we didn't really decide anything. I don't know if you asked him about it later."

"Nor do I," I told her.

"I know, but I thought I ought to remind you. Did you hear the dogs last night?"

I had not, and I shook my head.

"I did, and so I thought you should know and write it down, just in case you should meet Hegesistratus again when I'm not with you."

"Aren't you coming to Rope?" I asked. To which she replied that she was, but that the Rope Makers are not nice people.

I could not recall the taller boy's name, but I remembered Polos from the second meal the night before, so I asked whether he would come with Io and me. He nodded, and so did the older boy.

We have a cart drawn by mules to carry our food. My chest is in it, and so are some things of Io's. Simonides drives the cart because he is too old to walk far. Themistocles has said that anyone who becomes tired may ride on the cart as well, but it sways and jolts. Only the Median boy rode this morning; Io and Polos walked with me. Now we have stopped at a farm for the first meal. I should add here that two of Themistocles's slaves are with us—their names are Diallos and Tillon. I am wearing my sword, though my helmet and the other things are in the cart. The road will be safe enough, Themistocles says, until we get to Bearland.

I have just read what I wrote this morning; I should finish it, though I do not believe I could ever forget the winged lion-woman.

When she asked me her question, I remembered Hegesistratus and how he had ridden the donkey—but at other times walks with a crutch. So I said, "It is a traveler, Gaea. When he begins his journey he rides a horse, but the horse dies, or is stolen, or must be sold for food. After that, the traveler has to walk for himself, and by evening he is footsore and limps along with a staff."

She smiled as she leaped from her pedestal to stand beside me. "That's a good reply," she said, "even though you lack the advantage of lameness. I've always thought it was his lameness that gave Swollenfoot his clue." Though she stood on four legs and I upon two, she was so huge that she still looked down into my face, as she had from the pedestal.

I asked whether my answer was a correct one.

Gaea only adjured me to follow her, in order that she might show me the palace. "Poor Mnemosyne's one of my daughters," she said. "She doesn't get a lot of sacrifices."

I asked who Swollenfoot had been.

"A man who was too good. His father maimed his feet when Swollenfoot was a baby; he was always a little lame thereafter. Yet he was a wonderful fighter, like you. Shall I tell you his answer?"

"Please."

"He said it was a mortal, crawling upon hands and knees in the morning of life, soon walking erect, then at last—like your traveler— with a stick. If you ever get to Hill, they'll tell you that in my despair at his response I threw myself from the wall of their fortress and perished on the stones below. You'll observe that I'm winged." She chuckled.

I ventured that the mere solving of a riddle, and a rather easy one, hardly constituted a basis for suicide. All this time we were walking side by side down the avenue of statues, which were of a thousand different kinds, and approaching the doors of the palace. These, as we neared them, loomed higher and higher.

"The truth is that I returned to my element. Doesn't it trouble you to find earth winged? I'm not often considered a deity of the air, like the Lady of Thought."

"No," I said. "The sophists believe that the earth is a sphere." I paused in the hope that she would confirm or deny it, but she did neither. "A sphere is the only perfect shape, or so I've been told, no doubt by Hegesistratus or Simonides. In other lands, people believe that the earth is flat and say that it floats upon an endless sea, or that it's supported on the back of a great turtle, who swims in such a sea."

"Continue," she ordered me.

"I hesitate to speculate in the hearing of one who knows the truth."

Gaea looked at me, and though her face was the face of a woman, her eyes were the eyes of a lioness. "She is eager to hear your speculations."

"As you wish. It is soon seen that such explanations fail to resolve the question. If I slap water with my hand, it does not remain in the air but quickly falls to earth. Thus though the sea exists, it too must be supported in some way. Besides, a man who swims in the sea finds that the earth lies below it. It is true that he comes at last to such a depth that he cannot reach earth; but if another comes, a better diver, this other diver reports earth still. Plainly, then, the sea is held like water in a bowl, deepest at the center, but hardly endless at the center. And in fact a bowl that was endless at any point could never be filled."

"Continue," she said again.

"If I continue, Gaea, will you tell me the significance of your riddle?"

"No, you shall tell me. But continue."

"One who observes the sun at evening sees that it moves no more slowly at the horizon than it did when crossing the sky at noon. Similarly, it rises in full career. Where, then, does it halt? Plainly it does not halt, but circles and recircles the earth without cease, as do the moon and the stars, of which the same things might be said. If the sea proposed by some existed, the sun, the moon, and the stars would plunge into it and their lights would be extinguished; but that doesn't occur. All these things show that the proposed sea, upon which the earth is said to float, doesn't exist. As for the sea on which we sail, it's supported by the earth, and not the contrary.

"I said that water falls to earth. What doesn't? Birds, clearly; otherwise they would be killed. If you startle a bird from a bush, it may perch upon another—but it may not. And anyone may see for himself that eagles and vultures need not alight except to eat and drink, for they remain upon the wing without effort. What supports the earth? What supports these birds? The earth flies; Gaea is winged."

"Well reasoned," she said. She remained silent after that until we reached the stair that led to the entrance arch of the palace; then she asked, "Why do you think I said I devoured all who could not answer my question?"

I ventured to say that the earth devoured all men at last.

"Not those who understand my question, Latro. Isn't your traveler upon the journey of life? Say yes, or I'll devour you at the end of your days."

"Yes," I said as we mounted the stair.

"Explain."

"In the morning of life," I said, "a young man goes forth as though mounted, because he is carried upon the shoulders of his parents. By midday their support has vanished, and he must walk for himself. In the evening of life, he can hold up his head only because he is supported by the memory of what once he was."

As I spoke the final word, Gaea's vast wings roared behind me and I felt a wind as violent as a storm at sea; by the time I turned, she was already very far above me. Higher she rose, and higher still as I watched openmouthed, until she was little more than a dark speck against the overarching azure dome, and I felt certain she would soon disappear into the cloudless sky. But at last she settled upon a cornice of the topmost battlement, where she remained motionless and appeared to have become again a mere figure carved from the reddish stone, as she had been when I had first seen her.

Alone and wondering I entered that great palace. Its rooms were spacious indeed, but filled with little more than light and air. While I wandered from one to another, seeing here, perhaps, a single red-glazed urn displaying the capering black figures of satyrs, and there an iridescent enameled beetle rolling a great golden sun toward some corner of an empty chamber, I sought the meaning of Gaea's riddle. Why had she asked it of Swollenfoot? And why of me? Why had she offered to show me this palace of memory, yet deserted me as I was about to enter?

When I had walked through many empty rooms, I came upon a statue of a young woman dancing naked among daggers, her marble limbs so delicately poised that I hesitated to touch her for fear she might fall. At length I did, and she fell, shattering upon the many-figured floor.

I looked up from the ruin of this statue and found that I was staring into the wrinkled face of Simonides. His hand was on my shoulder. He asked if I was well.

I apologized for having nodded, and added, "That was a very strange dream!" The truth was that the desert palace seemed far more real to me than the windy night or the rocky hilltop where we sat about our fire. Hegesistratus and Simonides urged me to recount my dream, which I did.

That is everything I have to write about it, except that this morning a slender young woman Io had not named for me took me aside and told me she had dreamed of me the night before. I was flattered (as no doubt she intended I should be) and asked to hear her dream.

"I was dancing in an empty hall," she said, "watched by no one but you. At the end of my dance, when I stood on one hand surrounded by my daggers, you pushed me, and I fell on one and died." I gave her my word I would never do such a thing. Her name is Anysia.

Today, as we walked, I told Io about my dream—although not about the dancer. Io was excited, most of all (I think) because I still remembered so clearly all that I had seen and said. She asked what Hegesistratus had said about it, but the fact is that he had said next to nothing.

I have not yet told this to Io, and perhaps I will not; but while writing of my dream, I have thought of yet another answer to Gaea's riddle, and perhaps this one is more nearly true (for me, at least) than any of the rest. It is that a young man such as I am undertakes the journey of life as if on horseback, ever hurrying forward. As he grows older he comes to realize that it is but a pilgrimage to the grave and walks more slowly, looking about him. When he is old, he may take up his stylus and begin to write of what he has seen; if so, unlike other men, he is not devoured by the earth in which his body lies when life's journey is done, for though dead he still speaks to the living, just as it seemed the shade of Simonides still spoke to me outside that vast building in the desert.

When he talked with me this morning before Cimon's house, he asked first about the statues. I described that of Gaea to him, but when he asked what it signified, I could not say. He said that by that image, which at any moment might take wing, I was to know that my thoughts would be lost if I failed to give each into the guardianship of some image within or without my memory palace.

We have stopped here for the second meal, and here we will pass the night. I have taken the opportunity to read all that I wrote during the past three days. Of Cimon's banquet, and our offering to Mnemosyne after it, I recall nothing; yet the memory of the palace remains before my mind's eye, more vivid even than that of the house in which I was born. I see the man-faced lion with *Latro* cut in its foreleg, and the now-empty pedestal where once Gaea crouched, the mighty doorway, the strange, bare rooms, and all the rest. It would be remarkable indeed if a man could remember only his dreams, but the truth is that I can remember no other dream than that.

# THIRTY

## *Tower Hill*

ADEIMANTUS'S CITY IS THE FINEST in all Hellas, according to Io. Simonides confirmed it as we sat over wine with Adeimantus and his sons. Themistocles laughed and told Adeimantus that when Simonides was staying at his house in Thought, he liked nothing better than to rail against the citizens of Tower Hill, seeing only greed in the fine marble, silver, and gold everybody else admires. "And yet," finished Themistocles, "this man who can't bear to see others living in a beautiful city has had his own ugly old face painted by Polygnotos."

Simonides laughed as loudly as anyone. "I've done no more than follow the course of wisdom I profess to teach. All of you will concede, I think, that when other things stand equal, the best-looking man will get the most support from his fellows and the most votes in the Assembly."

Everyone nodded.

"Well, then," Simonides continued, "it must follow that the finest city will get the most support from the rest as well—if other things stand equal. And since Tower Hill's a rival of my friend Themistocles's city, and I can't malign its wide streets and imposing buildings, I criticize the morals of its citizens. That I can do with perfect justice even though I know so little about them—the morals of citizens everywhere being atrocious. As for this face of mine, I can't do a thing about it. But in time to come, I'll be judged not by my face but by my picture, which is perfectly beautiful. Fifty years from now everybody will say I was the leading figure of the age."

Adeimantus commanded the ships of Tower Hill at the Battle of Peace. It was he who opposed the ships from Riverland, which everyone says were the best the Great King had. The walls of his house are adorned with captured shields and weapons, and the figureheads of ships he destroyed. The wrecks washed ashore at a place called Crommyon; he had his men saw off the figureheads there. He presented one to every captain who served under him, he said, and kept the rest for himself.

Because these weapons and figureheads looked familiar to me, I asked Io whether we have ever been to Riverland; she says we have not. Adeimantus said he had never visited that country either, but that people are mistaken to envy the Great King his possession of it, though it is the oldest and most revered in the world. "The men who fought so hard for a foreign king will fight against him harder still," he told us. "The whole nation rose against the Medes after Fennel Field, you remember. And it will rise again."

If the hearts of the men of Riverland are as dark and proud as their crooked weapons and painted shields lead me to believe, I feel sure Adeimantus speaks no more than the truth. The black man confirms this, if I understand his gestures, saying that men like himself—his own nation, in fact—held sway over Riverland for a long while, but eventually its populace drove them back to their own country. He says also that he has been there, but he and I did not know each other then; it is a fine place.

There will be a play tonight. All of us, even Io, are to have seats.

A man with one hand has come to speak with Themistocles.

Io came to warn me of this man—thus I wrote quickly that he had come, then stopped to hear her. His name is Pasicrates. He fought me in the Troad, Io says, and it was I who cut off his hand. I tried to explain to her that war is war. A soldier rarely hates the men he fights, and when the fighting is over, he is happy to sit down and hear how things were on the other side.

Just then the man himself joined us, followed by Simonides and little Polos. I doubt that there is any need to describe him, since I will surely know him by his missing hand, which it seems I cut off somewhat above the wrist. But he is strikingly handsome in the fashion of Hellenes, with darting, intelligent eyes. He is smaller than I by half a head, perhaps; but if he is as quick and strong as he appears, he must have been a very dangerous opponent.

"Good evening, Latro," he said. I had stood when they came into the room, and he embraced me as I might have the black man. "You don't remember me, I know, but we're old friends as well as old foes."

I said I hoped that he, as well as I, could forget any past enmity.

He laughed and held up the stump of his left forearm. "You made it hard for me to forget, but you're going to be one of us, and my life in battle may depend upon your comradeship. So I'd better forgive you, and I do."

I wanted then to hear how we had fought, but I did not ask for fear it would reawaken past resentments.

"You're coming to Rope? You mean to accept Pausanias's offer?"

I know we are on our way to Rope, thus I said, "I'll decide after we get there."

"He wants you for the games, did they tell you about that?" Pasicrates left for a moment and returned carrying stools for Simonides and himself; when the old man was settled, Pasicrates sat down beside him.

Io had shaken her head when he mentioned games, so I said, "I know nothing of games. Does this mean I'm going to have to fight someone?"

"Exactly. Boxing, wrestling, and the pankration—they're the things I told him you'd be good at. You might do for some local meet in the footraces, but you couldn't possibly win at Dolphins, no matter what Pausanias thinks."

"Dolphins?" Io asked. "Is that where we're going?"

Pasicrates nodded. "If your master will agree to do as the regent wants."

"The big games for the Destroyer," Io told me. "They have them every four years. They're always two years after the ones at Olympia, and girls can watch as long as they're not married. Isn't that right, Simonides?"

The old sophist smiled and nodded. "It would be a great honor for you, Latro. One that you might never forget."

"I've never been to Dolphins," Io said. She added firmly, "But I'd really like to go."

"Then we will," I promised her.

Pasicrates and Simonides left us soon after that to prepare themselves to go to the theater. Pasicrates had brought neither clothing nor sandals, and Simonides was going to lend him some, though he warned him that they would not be up to the standards of Tower Hill.

"He seems to be a fine man," I told Io when they had gone, "but I think he hates me."

"He does," Io said. "We'll have to be really careful around him. You, too, Polos. He's the kind who hits boys."

Polos asked, "Did you cut off his hand with your sword?"

I shook my head. "How did it happen, Io?"

"I wasn't there," she told us. "But Pasicrates tried to beat you—I mean with a whip, because you were supposed to be the regent's slave. You wounded one of his real slaves with a javelin, and then you must have fought him, because you split his shield with Falcata, and it went right down through his arm. He yelled something terrible—that was the first I knew anything about it. There were a hundred Rope Makers besides the slaves, and all of them came, but you got away. I didn't see you again after that till I was walking close to the wall with Drakaina— you ran up to us, and all of us got taken into the city, which was what we wanted anyhow."

The Median boy had entered silently as she spoke, and I told him there was no reason he and Polos should not use the stools Pasicrates had brought.

Polos rolled his eyes and shied; Io told him, "It's really there, what- ever it is. If Latro touches it, then we'll see it, too."

"I see him a little already," Polos said, "but I don't want to see him any more than I do right now."

I asked Io what they were talking about, but the Median boy spoke—impolitely, I would say—while she did, so that I did not hear her. "There are so many people living in this house. Have you met the others?"

I said I had been introduced to our host and his sons, and seen some of his servants.

"Soldiers from Kemet, and they're very angry." The Median boy turned on his heel and left.

Polos relaxed and took a stool. "He's like Latro—only he can't remember he's dead. I think that his thoughts must always stumble there."

I asked where Kemet lay, but neither knew. I must remember to ask Simonides. I have cut it across the chest of the hawk-headed man.

Polos asked, "Do you *have* to be very strong to fight with a sword?"

I told him it was certainly better to be strong, but better still to be quick.

"If the strongest man's the quickest, too, does he always win?"

Io said, "Or woman, Polos. Remember the Amazons? I've got a sword, too, and I've killed my man."

"No," I said. "Not always."

"Who does? And how could Io kill a man? She's said that before."

I considered the matter, knowing what I needed to say but unsure of how to make my point. The fluting notes of a syrinx floated through the window, and I looked out; three small boys were coming down the street, one tootling the pipes while all three danced. Some dignified-looking men had stopped to laugh and cheer them.

"Look," I told Polos and Io. "Do you see those boys?"

Io said, "They're playing Pan-and-satyrs. We used to do it back in Hill."

"I want you to study them. Pretend that they're men, not boys, and that they're fighting with swords instead of dancing. Can you do that?"

Both nodded.

"See how they move. A sword fight is a kind of dance, even if the fight's on horseback. Look at them carefully—which is going to win?"

Io said, "The one with the pipes," and Polos nodded.

"Why?" I asked them.

Polos said, "Because he dances the best."

"That's right. Why does he dance better than the others?"

They only stared at me, so I sent them off to find three sticks, each a trifle shorter than my arm.

When they returned, I showed them how to hold their sticks like swords instead of axes, with the thumb at the top of the grip. "An ax is a good weapon, but a sword is a better weapon. If you hold your sword like an ax, you'll chop with it like an ax. A sword slashes and thrusts— you must be a butcher boning a carcass, not a woodchopper cutting down a tree. Don't either of you understand yet why the boy with the pipes danced best?"

"I do!" Polos said. "Because he had the pipes."

Io nodded. "He knew in advance what he was going to play, but the others couldn't know till they heard the notes."

I told them, "That's the one who always wins a sword fight. Now each of us ought to have something for the left hand. It's always very unwise to fight without something in your left hand. A shield's best; but if you don't have one, use something else, a knife or even another sword."

Io got her cloak and wound it about her left arm. "You did this sometimes in Thrace, master. A couple of times it got cut, and I had to sew it up for you, but the blade never went through to your arm."

"If you were to lay your arm on the windowsill, any sword would cut through the cloth and bite bone," I told her. "Very few will do that in a battle, however, though possibly Falcata might. It's one good reason for getting the best sword you can and always keeping it sharp. You should let a little more cloth hang down to flutter before your opponent's eyes."

Polos said, "I don't have a cloak. Should I buy one here?"

"Yes, buy one tomorrow—though not for that reason. But you must fight now, not later. What are you going to do?"

He picked up his stool and said, "I'll pretend this is my shield."

I told him, "You don't have to pretend. A stool makes an excellent shield."

Io said, "You used to fight the Thracians with a javelin in your other hand, master. I think they thought you were going to throw it, but you never did."

I nodded. "Because if I had, I would have had nothing for my left hand except my cloak. But you can never be sure such a thing will not be thrown—your opponent may believe it will end the fight, or see something else he can use. If Polos were to throw his stool, for example, he might snatch up this other one.

"But now that you have your swords and shields, you must forget about them for a moment. Do you remember that I said a sword fight was a sort of dance?"

They nodded.

"I said it because you must move your feet in the right way without thinking about them. If one of you were going to teach me a dance I didn't know, I'd have to think about moving my feet—but I wouldn't be a good dancer until I didn't."

Polos performed a little dance to test himself.

I told them, "An untrained sword fighter will nearly always favor one foot. Usually it's the left, because the left hand's got the shield. He'll step forward with that foot and drag his right foot behind it. For people like you two, who're liable to be a lot smaller than those you fight, that's a great advantage. You take a step back and cut at his leg. You don't have to wait to see it—it'll be there. Just make a quick cut that brings your point well in under the edge of his shield."

I had them practice this, tapping my calf with their sticks while I used the other stool as my shield.

"Now that you know how that's done, you know also that you mustn't advance your left leg like that," I told them.

Io added, "And why Acetes's shieldmen wore greaves."

"That's right," I said, though I do not remember who Acetes is. "And they didn't wear just one, did they? Didn't each man wear two?"

Io and Polos nodded.

"That's because a good fighter uses both his legs, and uses them equally. The next thing you have to learn is never to move one leg only. Whenever you move one leg, you must also move the other; and you mustn't favor the left leg over the right—or the right over the left."

So we passed the time until Simonides came to lecture the children about proper behavior in the theater.

# THIRTY-ONE

## *From the Tomb*

WE CAME UP THE HILLSIDE along a wide white street. Now the men from Riverland have gone, and so has the Median boy. The sky is light enough already for me to write. Soon we will leave, too; Themistocles says our road runs west to Stymphalos, then south through Bearland.

Last night we went to see a play. I do not know whether I have been to a theater before—perhaps to one somewhat different from this. It seemed strange to me, but not entirely so.

Our seats were at the bend (the best place) and well down in front. The long benches are curved like a horse's hoofprint. The acting floor is in the center with the actors' tent behind it. Pasicrates sat next to me until the black man changed his seat to sit between us—I think because Io asked it.

The jokes concerned the doings of the city, yet many amused us just the same. The actors wore masks, contriving to change the expressions of these wooden faces by varying the angles at which they poised their heads and covering certain parts of the masks with their hands, which I thought very fine. These masks are carved in such a way as to make this possible, of course.

It was pleasant to sit in comfort on a warm evening and be thus entertained; but from time to time my gaze left the actors and wandered away to the stars, seeing there the Ram, the Hunter and his Dogs, the Seven Maids toward whom so many temples look, and many other things. The cold moon-virgin appeared to warn me it was to her land we were bound; and as she spoke, Io whispered in my ear, "When we get back I'll have to tell you the story of the White Isle, master. I feel like I've just seen it." Then I could not help wondering what the watching gods thought of us, with our clever masks and our jokes. What we think of crickets, perhaps, whose singing we hear with pleasure, though some of us smash them with our heels when they venture into sight.

After the play, the gaudy litters that had carried them to the theater awaited Adeimantus and his sons, Themistocles, and Simonides. The rest of us trooped after them, but the black man soon drew me aside. There are many wineshops here where one may drink and crack nuts, and trade banter with attractive women if one likes. The rule, as several women told us, is that they may enter only the ones that permit them, and that they must pay the owner (often once such a woman as themselves) one spit each time they leave with a man. Most asked for six, explaining that they could keep only three, having to pay one to the proprietor (as I said), one to the city, and one to the goddess of this place. A skin of unmixed wine was very dear, so the black man and I drank mixed wine by the cup—this so weak in some of the shops that he pretended to drown and once told me with his fingers that he had seen a trireme in the krater.

In the third or fourth, we came upon a slender, dark-haired girl from Babylon who could speak the black man's tongue as well as the one I use among these people. The black man wished to go with her— and for me to come, too, for it is by no means safe to visit such places alone. Here was a difficulty: I liked neither the Babylonian nor the friend to whom she introduced me, while the Babylonian would have to pay double if both of us left with her. It would have been better if I had given her an additional spit, but we soon arranged that they would linger in the street; and I, soon after they had gone, would meet them there.

This settled, they left. I stretched, yawned, and gossiped a few moments longer with the Babylonian's friend, a skinny girl who said she was from Ithaca, drained the last cup and wiped my mouth, and wandered out.

I had drunk enough to heat my face and ears; I still recall how pleasant the night breeze was, and how I wondered why we had chosen to linger so long in the close, smelly wineshop. When I began to walk, I discovered that I was not as steady on my feet as I had expected to be, although I flattered myself that no one else would have observed it.

It appeared that the black man and the Babylonian had gone on without me; but I soon caught sight of them, deep in talk, a few doors off. I waved, and they made their way arm in arm down the street. I hurried after them, then realized that the black man would not relish my company and maintained a distance great enough to allow them some privacy. After a time, they left the narrow, dirty street for another narrower and dirtier still. I recall turning the corner to follow them.

It seemed then that a great wave overwhelmed the city, and I was tossed with many another among rushing waters. I could not breathe this dark water, and indeed I could scarcely breathe the air of the strand on which it left me at last; but it seemed I had no need to. I got to my feet, my body hardly heavier than a child's, and stared about with unbelieving eyes at the immense cavern in which I stood.

Its shadowed ceiling was as remote as the highest mountain peak. Through it here and there streamed vagrant silver light, much as one sometimes sees the sun thrust golden fingers through the chinks of a stormy sky; it did little more than emphasize the general gloom.

If the cavern was lofty, its height was as nothing to its breadth. In desolate plains, barren hills, and sullen meres, it stretched on, mile upon mile, in every direction, until at last all was lost in darkness. During the whole time I spent there, I never so much as glimpsed a bird, or a single bat, or indeed a beast of any kind, though once or twice I crossed their watery tracks, dim prints deeply impressed in the soft clay. Here and there, however, I saw wandering human figures, bent, naked, and alone.

I called to some. When none responded, I set out after the nearest, an elderly man whose painful, shuffling gait gave clear evidence that I would quickly overtake him. "Who are you, wise one?" I inquired, feeling it would be best to make some friendly overture before asking where this cavern was and how I could get out of it.

"I am myself," he grumbled, "just as you are yourself. Go. Leave me in peace."

"But what's your name?" I insisted.

He shook his head and shuffled forward. He would not meet my eye.

"I am . . ." I found that I could not complete the thought. Frantically, I searched my memory. "I'm called the mercenary," I said at last. "There's a statue—a lion with a man's face—that knows my name."

For the first time, he glanced at me. "Give me your hand." He clasped it between his own, which were as cold as snow. "You are not wholly gone," he told me.

I said at once that I would leave if my presence disturbed him.

"No, stay. When I lived, I was called Gortys. That is how we speak here, though it was not truly I that lived. The part of me which lived is now dead, and what you see is the part that never lived, hence cannot die."

I tried to draw my hand away; his freezing grasp had grown painful. "The child called me master," I said, "the one-handed man Latro, as I told you."

"I will come with you." He took my arm.

Some distance from us was a man wrestling a boulder almost as large as himself. I saw him squat, get his fingers under it, and lift it nearly upright before it escaped his grasp and fell. Having nothing better to say, I asked who he was and what he was trying to do.

"He is a king," the old man told me. "Do you see that hill over there?"

I nodded.

"Sisyphus must roll his stone to the summit and leave it there. While it remains in place, he will be released from his torment."

I watched him spit on his hands, wipe them on his thighs, and lift the stone again. "Who'll release him?"

"The god who condemned him."

I led the old man over to him, and it was a long and weary distance indeed, for the floor of that vast cavern was streaked with dark gorges too broad to leap that could not be seen until they gaped at our feet; most held sunken streams and were lined with slimy stones.

When at last we reached the toiling king, it seemed that he had advanced his boulder by no more than three strides. He was as naked as the old man whose icy fingers still clasped my arm, though his body was smeared with the ocher mud of the place; and his cunning face was beaded with sweat and sagging with fatigue.

"Are you permitted to accept help?"

He shook his head impatiently and bent again to his stone. "What would you want for your help?"

"Nothing," I told him, "but perhaps two of us could do it."

My hands were already on the boulder as I spoke. Together we rolled it forward, though it twisted in our grasp as though its center leaped within it. Dirty and wet already, my chiton tore as I heaved away; I tore it off and tossed it aside. In that moment the stone, which we had then rolled nearly halfway up the hill, slid from the king's grip.

I caught it, though I cannot tell how; and in an agony of frustration lifted it clear of the mud. Every joint in my body creaked, and it seemed that every bone was about to snap, but I staggered to the hilltop with it and slammed it down, embedding it in the soft soil around the spring.

For a moment it trembled there, like an egg about to hatch; then it split. The report was deafening, the rush of light from it blinding. I reeled and fell.

As I lay on my side in the half-frozen mud, I saw the faces of the black man and the Babylonian girl within the stone—faces wreathed in flames. The black man shouted something I could not understand and extended his hand to me. I helped the king rise, and together we clambered up and into the narrow, fetid alley I recalled.

The Babylonian had ten thousand questions, none clear to me thanks to my bewilderment and her accent. She and the black man held blazing torches. I took hers from her and dropped it into the hole from which the king and I had clambered.

For a moment I glimpsed age-blackened masonry, bones, a green sword, and armor rotten with verdigris; but soil from the alley was already sliding into the hole. I felt the ground give way beneath my feet and stepped hurriedly back. A crack shot up the wall above the hole. The Babylonian screamed, and the king and the black man pulled me away. With a roar like the storm's, the entire wall fell. We fled, coughing and wiping our eyes to free them from its choking dust.

The black man and the Babylonian—her name is Bittusilma—came to tell me they are married. When I raised my eyebrows, she explained that she is going with the black man, who wants to return to his home in Nysa. She will leave him when they reach Babylon, or come near it.

The black man spoke to her then, and she said, "He thought the chief man in your party wouldn't let me go with you, but he says he won't refuse now. He says you're his friend. You have to insist that both of us be allowed to come."

I promised to do my best.

"I was married to a captain," she told me. "He was killed here last year—then I couldn't get away. Hepta Leones* wishes me to tell you I'm his third wife."

Proudly the black man held up three fingers.

I questioned her about the pit in the alley. She said she and the black man had lain together for a long time; that was when they agreed to marry. They thought I was waiting outside. When they found me gone, they made torches with which to search the alley. I asked what had happened to me, wishing to hear how she would explain all she had seen. She said that when the king and I had entered the alley, the roof of a vault, "one forgotten perhaps for many years," had given way.

I should say here, too, that I spoke much with the king while we walked back to this house. It was he, he said, who had built the first tower upon the hill, thus founding this city, which he calls Ephyra. He described it.

He asked whether I knew of Asopus the river god; and I, not wishing to appear ignorant, told him I did. This river god, the king said, had ever been his friend. He is not a great god like the Twelve upon the mountain, and the king himself is—or so he says—a son of the storm king by a nymph whose father is Asopus; thus he and the god are related, and differ less in the respect due them than gods and mortals commonly do.

When the river god's daughter Aegina had been stolen, the king had witnessed it. He told the river god where the girl had been taken, and asked in return for a spring at the foot of his tower so that he and his men might never lack water during a lengthy siege—thus he was punished as he was. He told me that he had always hoped the river god would remember him and find some way to help him. He thought I was the aid the river god had sent. He asked what reward had been promised me, and I was forced to tell him that if I had been sent by the god—or anyone—I was not aware of it.

"I never gave anything away while I was among you," he said sadly, "and anyone who wished my help could have it—at a price. You have seen the riches I gathered by it."

---

*Usually translated, but here in the original Greek, perhaps to indicate Bittusilma's careful pronunciation.—GW

Bittusilma, the Babylonian, happened to overhear this and looked around. The king saluted her, whispering to me, "I know my own breed. If she plays you false, I'll ask them for leave to make her suffer for it." I do not know to whom he referred.

That was when we came to the house and found the soldiers from Riverland terrorizing everyone.

# THIRTY-TWO

## *For the Second Meal*

WE HAVE HALTED HERE NEAR the lake. Though we did not leave the city early, we put in a hard morning—even the black man rode on the cart before it was done—and ate the first meal long after the usual time. We did not go far after that, and Themistocles has chosen to stop here, where a cool wind blows from the water and there are good facilities for travelers. As we walked, Io talked of the hauntings last night, which seem to have disturbed everyone. I have read about the theater and how I assisted the king, but it seemed I did not write much about them; thus I have been anxious to speak with Pasicrates or Simonides, and when we sat to eat the second meal, I contrived to sit between them. Had Simonides or Themistocles told me to take a lower place, I would have, of course; but if Pasicrates had done it, we would have had words. No one did.

"This is the lake," Simonides remarked, "at which Heracles killed so many monstrous birds."

This interested the black man, who asked (through his wife) whether these were the same birds that visit his own country and war against the small men of the south.

Before Simonides could reply, Pasicrates announced proudly that this Heracles was an ancestor of his. It seems that he is related on his mother's side to the Agid royal family. "But I can recount these family matters for you anytime," he said to the black man's wife. "Ask your husband whether he has seen the creatures himself."

The black man nodded and spoke to his wife, who translated. "He has seen them flying over, and once he saw one some children killed."

Everyone except Pasicrates and the black man laughed loudly at that. Pasicrates was very angry, I think. Through his wife, the black man said seriously, "Sometimes these birds attack our children. We think it's because they think our children are the small men of the. south—that's the reason every boy in my land carries his own little spear. The long beaks of the birds are like spears themselves, and their necks are very long, too. They strike like snakes, and because they can fly, they're formidable enemies, though they won't often stay to fight a warrior. They fly very high—far beyond the reach of our arrows. If this man Heracles killed many, he was our friend."

Everyone wanted to talk of something else then, I think, so I asked Pasicrates whether he had been disturbed by the ghosts, as Io had.

He nodded. "I was awakened by someone's screaming—one of Adeimantus's daughters, I think. I sprang from my bed and found myself face-to-face with a tall man who had a barbed spear and a big shield. I remember thinking—even then—that it was exactly like the one on the wall; it had the same horizontal stripe. The man thrust at me. . . ."

Pasicrates fell silent, staring at the stump of his missing hand. Possibly I was mistaken, but it seemed to me that he went pale. At last he muttered, "It isn't much of a ghost story, I'm afraid, but then I didn't make it up. He jabbed at me with his spear, as I was about to say. Then spear and shield dropped to the floor. When I got a light for my lamp, I saw they were the ones that had been hanging on the wall of my room. I won't tell anyone about this back in Rope. They'd laugh at it, just as all of you laughed at the slaughter of the Stymphalian birds, which has occupied so many great poets and artists. But there may be more to it than appears—again, like the birds."

From the foot of our table Io said, "It *was* one of Adeimantus's daughters. It was Callia, and Polos saw them, too. What I don't understand is why they went away all at once."

The black man's wife said, "The man who'd fallen into the tomb with your master took them away. He was what people here call a magus. He asked your master if he wanted them exorcised, and when he said yes, he summoned them and left with them."

Pasicrates asked whether she had been able to see them.

She shook her head. "But as soon as he spoke, the house was quiet."

Io said, "Once when we were in a little place near Thought, there was a farmhouse that was terribly haunted, just all of a sudden. You don't remember wrestling Basias, master, but that was when it happened. The innkeeper told us about it."

Themistocles said, "Adeimantus felt that we brought them, though he was too polite to say so. Tell us about this magus, Latro. Was he actually from Parsa?"

I do not recall the man himself, but I remember what I read of him here; so I said that I had thought him a Hellene.

"That certainly seems more likely. How did you meet him?"

I explained that he had been trying to move a stone, and I had assisted him. "We were both very dirty by the time the job was done," I said, "so I offered to let him wash up at the house where we slept last night. I didn't think anyone would object. Was that Adeimantus's?"

Themistocles nodded.

Simonides told him, "Latro still has great difficulty in remembering anything for more than a day or so, although he's improving. There were earth tremors all over Tower Hill last night, it seems. I didn't feel them myself."

Io said, "That's what probably made the hole that swallowed my master and this magus. Isn't that right, Bittusilma?" To Themistocles she added, "Bittusilma saw it."

The black man's wife said, "It was a tomb. The people of that foolish town had forgotten where it was and built over it."

Simonides shook his head sadly. "A great stone rolled into the sacred spring at the summit of the Acrocorinth and split. It's clearly an omen."

Io sighed. "I wish Hegesistratus were here."

Pasicrates darted a glance at her and said, "Then read it for us, sophist."

Themistocles cleared his throat. "Simonides has favored me with his interpretation already. We'll reserve it, at least for the present, I think."

Pasicrates said, "In that case, O noble Themistocles, I'll favor you with mine. Tower Hill links Hellas—your mainland to the north with our own Redface Island to the south. The spring is the heart of Tower Hill. Its damming by the stone indicates that Tower Hill will be vanquished. The splitting of the stone, which permitted the spring to flow freely once again, indicates that Hellas itself shall be split in two. When that takes place, Tower Hill will flourish as before."

I did not wholly understand this, but I saw that Simonides and
Themistocles appeared uncomfortable; so I asked Pasicrates who he believed would vanquish Tower Hill.

"Certainly not Rope—it's our principal ally. If I thought your little
slave knew anything about the politics of her city, I'd ask her whether
Hill could be the one; but I've got to admit it doesn't seem likely. It's
an inland agricultural center like Rope. Hill wouldn't have much reason
to attack a seaport so far away."

Io asked Simonides, "Would it be the Earth Shaker who sent Tower
Hill this omen?"

He shrugged. "From a strictly rational point of view, it's alterations
in the courses of underground streams that cause the earth to tremble.
As far as we know, any god might make use of those tremors to send
an omen—certainly the Earth Shaker might. Or any of the chthonic
deities."

Io nodded, half to herself. "What about the ghosts?"

Simonides told her, "It's well established that disturbing tombs
frequently produces such manifestations; and many tombs must have
been disturbed last night"—he nodded toward the black man's wife—
"as we have heard."

Pasicrates said, "When I led the contingent sent by my city to the
siege of Sestos, I heard that the barbarians had ravaged many tombs,
taking not only the offerings left before them, but the grave goods, too.
I did not hear that any of them had been punished for it."

"What about the loss of Sestos?" Themistocles asked dryly.

"If you like," Pasicrates conceded. "Certainly it was a very strong
city, and it fell very quickly. I'm told that we had not yet boarded the
ship that took us home when we received word that the city had surrendered."

Io asked, "What do you mean, you heard?" I could see she was
afraid of Pasicrates, yet she spoke up bravely. "You were there. I was
there, too, and I remember you."

"I was ill," he told her. "My wound had brought a fever."

Themistocles said, "It was not you, then, who ordered the Rope
Makers home. Or was it?"

Pasicrates shook his head.

Polos asked, "You can't hold a shield anymore, can you?"

Pasicrates smiled at him and looked as though he wished to tousle his hair. "I can still use my shield—it was made for me by one of our finest armorers and has straps with buckles. I'll show it to you when we get to Rope."

That, I think, is all that was said at the table that I may need to know tomorrow. After the meal, Io said she was going to walk beside the lake and asked me to come with her. The shore is marshy in spots, and there are lofty reeds, though one sees also where these reeds have been harvested for thatch; there are many frogs. I asked Io whether she was afraid of the birds.

"No, master," she said. "Or maybe yes, a little bit." She had brought her sword.

"They're not here," I told her, "or at least not many, or there wouldn't be so many frogs. Water birds with long, sharp bills always like frogs."

Io nodded and sat down on a fallen tree. "Aren't your feet sore, master? We went a long way today, and you never once rode in the cart."

I admitted they were, but said that if she wanted to walk farther I would go with her.

"The truth is I don't want to walk at all, master. I only wanted to get you away so nobody could hear. I know you still remember what Pasicrates said about the ghost in his room. What do you think he was going to say when he stopped talking?"

I considered the matter for a moment. "That he was afraid. Most men would be afraid of a ghost, I think, and most would not be ashamed to admit it. Pasicrates might be."

Io spat out the hair she had been chewing. "I don't think so. I mean, he'd probably lie about that, like you say, master. But I don't think that was what stopped him. If he'd been going to say he was afraid at all, he would have said it when he told about hearing Callia screaming, or when he first saw the ghost." Io slid from the log and picked up a long stick. "Look, master. I'm the ghost. I have a spear and a big shield, and I'm going to try to kill you."

I snatched at the stick, which snapped between our hands.

"That's right," Io said. "You'd try to grab the shaft." She threw aside the broken stick and resumed her seat beside me on the log. "I think that's what Pasicrates did. He probably caught it, too—he's really quick."

"With his right hand? That would have been very difficult, Io. He would have had to reach across the ghost's shield."

She shook her head. "With his left hand, master. I think that was what he was about to say. He looked at the place where it had been, remember?"

"Do you mean that he was lying? He didn't see the ghost at all?"

"No, master. I mean that when he fought it, he had a left hand." She said nothing more, staring at the sun-bright clouds across the waters of the lake.

"A ghost hand, because the other was a ghost?"

"You don't remember Hegesistratus, do you, master? Did you read about him today?"

I told her I had not.

"He was a mantis, a really good one. He knew a whole lot about ghosts and gods, and right after we met him he said that people who'd been killed with your sword might be particularly likely to come back. It was you that cut off Pasicrates's hand, master. With your sword."

It is very late now, but I do not think Polos is asleep. I cannot sleep either, so I have lit this lamp. Far away, on the mountainside, someone pipes. When I lie down and close my eyes, I seem to see the capering figures that ring the majestic red urn in my memory palace—one of them pipes, too. I think that it is better I remain awake for a time and write more.

I should have written that this Pasicrates was waiting for Io and me when we returned. He said that he had errands in the town and asked me to tell Polos to obey him; Io shook her head, but after I saw the stump of his arm I did as he wished. When Polos returned tonight, he trembled and would not speak.

I went to the room where Pasicrates sleeps. He swore that he had not struck Polos. I saw that he hates and fears me very much, and that he hates himself, too, for that; I pitied him, though perhaps I should not have. I asked if we were not going to Rope, and if it was not his city—I felt sure it was, because he had said he would show Polos his shield there. When he said that we were, and it was, I told him I would kill him if he hurt Polos, though we stood in the marketplace of Rope. Once more he swore that he had not hurt him.

We woke Themistocles; he said I should not harm Pasicrates (which I knew already in my heart, I think), and sent me back to this room, where Polos and Io and I sleep with the black man and his wife.

The moon is high. I have read many sheets of this scroll—much about Hegesistratus and many times about Pharetra. My eyes burn and weep.

# THIRTY-THREE

## *Bull Killer*

THE GOAT MAN NAMED HIM—*Kain-Tauros*. Now I fear him, though he is only a boy, and smaller than Io. I drew her aside and asked her about him. She said he is my slave, at which my jaw fell.

"You forget, master. Do you know that? Usually you do."

I nodded, having found already that I could not recall how we came here.

"You were in a big battle. You were wounded." She guided my fingers to the scar. "Before we came here we were in Thought and then in Tower Hill, and before that we were in Thrace—that was where you got Polos. You got me last summer when we were in Hill."

I promised her I would free them both and let them return to their families; but she said she does not remember hers, and his is very far away.

After that I called him to me. I said that I could see he was not happy, that a slave's lot is never a happy one, and that if it was I who had enslaved him, I regretted it; in any case, I said, I would set him free whenever he wished.

He stared at me. His eyes are big with night, like Io's, and they soon filled with tears. He said that it was better for him to be the slave of a good man who would teach him, and feed and protect him, than for him to run wild and perhaps be caught by a bad one; but that I had not always protected him, that I had lent him to a bad man. He pointed this man out to me; it was Pasicrates, the one-handed man who ran so swiftly before his thigh was torn by the boar. I promised Polos I would never lend him to anyone again, and told him that if I forgot my promise he was to remind me. I asked what Pasicrates had done to him, but he ran away. Io says that she does not know. I think that she suspects, however; and so do I.

I have read what I last wrote in this scroll. There was no lake where we woke this morning; thus I believe I have neglected to write for at least a day.

This house is in Bearland, where no field is ever flat; its mountains rise all around us, many and steep but very green. No one plows here, which seems strange to me. The women work small gardens with wooden spades, and short hoes whose blades are the shoulder bones of sheep. Their men herd sheep and goats, with a few cattle and horses, and hunt. We, too, hunted today; it was then that I saw him. This is how it came about.

This morning, after Io had named those in our party for me, Themistocles instructed me to put on my helmet and mail. I wore my sword as well, and though I have no shield, I carried a pair of javelins. The black man was equipped much as I, with a long sword; but Pasicrates had not so much as a knife—Io says it is because he ran all the way from Rope to meet us.

We had not gone far before we found the road blocked by a landslip, which Pasicrates swore must have taken place since he had passed that way. If we had not had the mule cart, we could have clambered across the mud and stones, perhaps; but to clear them away would have taken many days. There was nothing for it but to turn back and try to find our way south by another route, one that Pasicrates did not know; and before the sun was higher than the mountains we were thoroughly lost.

Then Pasicrates urged that we turn back yet again, because the road seemed to become worse with every stade we walked; but Themistocles and Simonides wanted to press forward until we met a traveler who could advise us. Their words were becoming warm when Tillon noticed a ditcher at work and crossed the fields to him.

The argument stopped; and Bittusilma, by smiling at each in turn, got them to agree that we would take the ditcher's advice, whatever it should be. For a time all of us stood watching him as he spoke with Tillon and Tillon with him, though it was much too far for us to over-hear anything they said.

Before long Tillon returned, bringing the ditcher with him. "He was born near here," Tillon explained, "and he says he knows all the roads between here and the Silent Country—he's traveled a great deal. He says he'll guide us for his food and a spit a day."

Themistocles took out an obol and gave it to him. "Here's your first day's wage, to show I mean what I say. As this good man told you, we're on our way to Rope, and we're in a hurry—you'll get two more as soon as we reach the Silent Country."

The ditcher, who was muddied to the hips and still carried his mattock on his shoulder, took the coin and mumbled thanks.

"Now, do we go forward or turn back?"

"You're in a hurry, so you got to push ahead, the main road bein' blocked. There's other ways, but all about as bad as this or worse."

Themistocles and Simonides were triumphant; Pasicrates asked angrily about the road ahead.

"Worse'n this," the ditcher told him. "But we can get that cart through."

Simonides inquired about lodging for tonight, at which the ditcher shook his head. "There's gentry. I can show you where their houses is. Whether they'll take you . . ."

He led the way, and we walked beside him; we were soon well ahead of the rest of the walkers and the cart. "This is Latro, my master," Io told him. "I'm Io, and this is Polos."

He grinned and nodded to all of us. "Aglaus." He has lost several teeth.

Io ventured to ask whether his own master would not be angry with him for leaving his work.

"Happy to be rid of me," he told her.

"Where do you live?"

"You mean a house? Haven't got one."

"We don't either," Io said.

I explained that I was not a Hellene, spoke to him in this tongue, then asked whether he had ever encountered anyone of my nation.

He shook his head. "Not many foreigners comes to Bearland. What comes out's less than that."

"Bandits, you mean?"

He nodded. "The one-handed man, he's a real Rope Maker?"

Io said he was.

"They'll leave you be, then."

Polos asked who these bandits were, but Aglaus pretended he had not heard him. He asked Io, "Do you like that man with the money?"

"Not as much as I do my master and the black man, or Polos. But he seems to be a good man, and he's a friend of Hypereides's, our old captain."

Aglaus nodded, absorbing this. "The old man?"

"Themistocles is his master, I think. They don't *say* that, but it seems to me that's how it is. He's not mean, though, and he's really trying to help Latro."

"The lady?"

"I like the black man a lot, and he likes her."

"I'd heered there was people like him, but I never seen one till now." Aglaus chuckled. "I don't suppose it hurts. Wonder how we look to him."

"I don't know," Io admitted. "I never thought about it." She pondered the matter for a hundred steps or so. "I bet we look sick to him. Did you notice the scar on his cheek?"

Aglaus nodded. "Can't not see it."

"That's from a sword, and I was there when he got it. He lost a lot of blood, and he wasn't a whole lot darker then than my arm."

"That fella Tillon seemed all right. Who's t'other one?"

"Diallos. They don't do more than they have to."

Aglaus grunted. "And the Rope Maker with his hand gone?"

"Stay away from him."

"I see. You know any more Rope Makers?"

"Not very well," Io admitted. "Eutaktos and Basias, but they're both dead."

"Was they better'n him?"

"Yes, a little," Io told him. "No, Basias was a whole lot better. Eutaktos—well, Eutaktos was hard, but he wasn't mean. If somebody didn't do what he said, he'd beat them or whatever, but not because he liked it. It was just so they'd be afraid not to obey him the next time. And I think he liked money too much, but there are worse things."

I remarked that he had been a brave soldier.

"Do you remember him, master? Why, that's wonderful!"

I said that I remembered the sacrifice of the girl, and how Eutaktos had encouraged his men until he died.

"I wasn't there," Io said, wondering, "and I don't think you told me about it. Was that after Cerdon was bitten by a snake?"

I confessed I did not know.

"What happened when Eutaktos died?"

I remembered the Great Mother and the promises she had made the slaves, but I thought it best not to speak of it, and I did not. I wondered much, however, to find these things so clear in my mind when I recall only this day, my childhood, and the fight at the temple besides.

Not long afterward we overtook the men carrying the corpse. The dead youth—Lykaon was his name—appeared to have been two or three years younger than Pasicrates. His wound was horrible. All of us expressed our grief as the custom is, and Aglaus bowed very low to Lykaon's father.

"I've heard of you," this man told Themistocles. "I was in the army. So were some of my sons."

There was more such polite talk; I gave it scant attention, watching those who held the corpse instead, and those with them. There were seven in all, and they were studying us—Pasicrates, the black man, and me particularly—with equal intensity. Those whose hands were free fingered their javelins and the hilts of their big hunting knives.

Then the old man, whose son the dead youth was, spread his cloak upon the baggage in our cart and ordered them to lay the body on it. At that, everyone relaxed and smiled, and I found that I was smiling, too. I asked Io where we were going.

"To their house," she said happily. "We'll spend the night there and help out with the funeral tomorrow."

Themistocles had taken off his own cloak. He and the dead youth's father covered the corpse with it.

This house is old and very large; it has a tower, and there are other houses around it and a wall of stones about the whole, more than twice the height of a man. The dead youth's father is Ortygenes; he has eight living sons and a great many daughters. Aglaus says he has outlasted three wives.

One of the young men ran ahead to tell the many women here what had happened. They met us on the road wailing and tearing their hair.

Soon afterward, the eldest of Ortygenes's sons told Pasicrates, the black man, and me that he and his brothers, with some other men, intended to kill the boar that had killed Lykaon. All of us were anxious to go with them, and so was Polos; but I reminded him of the dead youth's wound and strictly forbade it.

We were far from the house when at last we heard the hounds— not the song of hounds on the scent, but the barks and sharp yelps by which hounds that have brought their quarry to a stand urge one another forward. Everyone began to run, and Pasicrates and the black man were soon far ahead of the rest of us. Though I ran as fast as I could, I was well behind, with one of Lykaon's brothers close behind me.

It shamed me that Pasicrates had outrun me. I do not like him, and I sense that he hates me—thus I sought some shorter route to the hounds and thought that I had found it. A moment more and I was alone, still in earshot of the chase but unable to see even the slowest of the other hunters. One check after another presented itself: first a tangle of thorn, then a sheer drop too great to jump. Very angry at my own folly and walking instead of running, I made my way slowly to open ground.

Then Fortuna, who had just played me so ugly a trick, chose to smile upon me. Not half a stade away and watching me through one eye stood a most promising bay colt; he trotted over at my whistle as though he had known me all his life. Though much of this countryside is too rough for horses, I saw immediately that here I might ride for two stades at least down the valley, and so be much nearer the boar than I was. I sprang onto the colt, and we skimmed the half-wild fields at a crackling gallop.

Now I must rely upon what the black man has told me about the hunt, with his fingers and speaking through his wife. The boar had taken shelter in an old wolf den, so that the hounds could not get behind it. Someone ran back to fetch fire with which to smoke it out; but as soon as he had gone, Pasicrates crawled into the den. If this is so, the Rope Maker must surely be the boldest man alive—and the most foolish.

The boar charged, as was only to be expected. Pasicrates's javelin caught it in back of the shoulder, leaving a raking cut along its ribs. The tusks that had torn Ortygenes's son made no more than a shallow gash across Pasicrates's thigh. Had the den been smaller, one or both would have died of course.

When the boar burst into the light, the black man was not the first, he says, to cast his javelin; but it was his that remained in the boar's body as it broke the ring of hounds and dashed into the forest.

And out of it, where I upon the bay colt caught sight of it with a score of hounds at its heels.

I cannot say whether the colt answered my hand or charged the boar of his own accord. My cast was lucky, as the sons of Ortygenes said afterward; but I was close when I made it, which is ever the mother of good luck.

At once the boar stumbled, and the hounds swarmed over it like so many ants on a dead beetle. All this was soon sponged from my thoughts by what came afterward; but now, as I write of it, I seem to see the boar again, the great, dark head with its flashing tusks lifted for the last time.

No one could tell me to whom the bay colt belonged, though several of the dead youth's brothers advised me to keep him until another claimed him. I dismounted, however, because I was eager to retrieve my javelin and (in truth) see whether it had pierced the boar's heart, as it had. With no one to watch him, the colt wandered away, though I would have caught and kept him if I had known of the injury to Pasicrates then.

The boar was gutted and its entrails thrown to the hounds, as the custom is. Someone felled a sapling, and we were binding the boar's feet over it when Pasicrates joined us, leaning upon the arm of the black man. He wished to know who had killed the boar—and was not much pleased, I think, to learn it had been I; he congratulated me nevertheless, and offered me his hand. I do not think I can ever have been very fond of him, but I came near to loving him at that moment. "I'll stay with you," I told him, "while they go ahead with the boar. Perhaps someone will bring one of Ortygenes's horses for you."

"No one has to stay with me," Pasicrates replied. "I can find my way back alone."

Then the black man, speaking with his fingers, told me to go with the boar and the men from the house, and to return with Themistocles's cart, if I could reach that spot with it.

I agreed and hurried ahead of those who carried the boar. That was when I glimpsed him trotting through the trees, Polos to the waist.

# THIRTY-FOUR

## *The Feast Is Over*

THERE WAS MUCH EATING, AND much wine drunk—far too much of it by me. I slept for a time, and woke to find myself stretched on the earth of the courtyard beside many another. It shamed me, and I rose and left this house and its proud wall behind me, and walked to the ford. There I was ill and washed, taking off my chiton and washing it, too, in the cold mountain water, wringing it out, and letting it dry awhile on a bush before I put it on again.

By then the sun was low, and I thought it best to return to this house. I spoke with Ortygenes, its owner; and afterward by the help of this lamp I read what I wrote yesterday. How I wish now that I had said plainly what it was I saw! Whom did I call "the goat man"? A goatherd? Surely I know the proper word for that!

This day was given over to the funeral rites of Lykaon, who was Ortygenes's son. Io helped the other women wash and perfume his body. There were thirty of them at least, when three might have done everything necessary with ease, but every woman in the place wanted to have a hand in it, and did. When it was complete, Lykaon was attired in his best clothes, with a fine green cloak and new sandals with white lachets.

Meanwhile, some of Ortygenes's male slaves had felled an old olive tree, a very large one already more than half-dead. Its wood was cut up and split, and every bit of living sapwood pared away. While the men were doing this, the children gathered many baskets of olive leaves and wove Lykaon's crown, of green twigs with their leaves still on them.

Ortygenes and his sons, aided by Themistocles and Simonides, the black man and me, and various others, prepared Lykaon's bed, first laying down very carefully a thick layer of pine kindling, then shaping the bed from the olivewood, with a hollow down the center to contain the leaves. (Pasicrates did not assist us in this because his leg pains him too much.) Io, who had left the other women to supervise the weaving of Lykaon's crown, carried it in. It was not until this crown had been fixed on Lykaon's head, she says, that the coin was laid upon his tongue; though small and old and worn almost smooth, the coin was gold, which impressed her greatly.

When everything had been made ready, Lykaon was carried in by his brothers, with his father, his sisters, and all the other women following the body. His father and his brothers preserved a manly silence; but the women wept and wailed aloud, even Io and Bittusilma.

Each brother spoke in turn, recounting some incident which recalled Lykaon's courage, honesty, cleverness, good nature, and so on; most were brief, but two marshaled too many words. His father then described the portents that had accompanied Lykaon's birth, recounted the prophecies he had received concerning him, and explained how each had been fulfilled.

Simonides recited verses he had composed for the occasion, describing the sorrow of Lykaon's noble ancestors at his death as they received him into the Lands of the Dead. (Afterward I asked Io whether she had enjoyed this poem. She said she had, but thought it somewhat inferior to one that she had once heard at the rites of a sailor.)

Ortygenes spoke again after Simonides, explaining to all those present that Simonides was a famous poet from Ceos, and praising Pasicrates and Themistocles.

Pasicrates spoke only briefly, first assuring the people of Bearland of the friendship of Rope, then explaining that it had been because of his desire to avenge Lykaon that he had entered the den of the boar.

Themistocles began by speaking of the friendship of Thought for both Bearland and Rope. It was in those places, and only in them, he said, that the ancient virtues of the Hellenes had been preserved. Thus, he said, they must become the teachers of the rest of Hellas, reminding the people of the high ideals of their forefathers, ideals exemplified by the noble youth lying before us. There was, Themistocles said, in his train, a man who each day forgot everything that had passed the day before; yet even he did not forget the training he had received in his youth, and thus—though he could not be wise—he was honorable, just, and brave. (I did not know he was speaking about me until I saw the faces of so many others turned toward me and Io thumped my ribs with her sharp little elbow; then my blood rushed to my cheeks and I resolved to commit some unworthy act so that Themistocles would never speak of me in that way again. But in truth I feel already that I have committed many.) So is it with Lykaon, said Themistocles. He has drunk of the waters of forgetting, the last, merciful gift of the kindly gods that spares the dead so much care; but the education he received in this house as a boy remains with him, and because it does he will be received among the dead as a hero.

It was not given to men to escape death, Themistocles said, but to the immortal gods alone; for a man the sole question was whether his death brought good or evil to his fellows. Today the Long Coast, the Silent Country, and the Islands, too, were gathered in friendship with Bearland to mourn her son. If the barbarian was eventually vanquished for good, it might well be because of this.

After Themistocles had spoken, Ortygenes ordered the torch to be brought, and the full mourning of the women began. They keened, wept, tore their hair, and scratched their cheeks until they streamed with blood, mourning not only Lykaon but all their dead, and confided to his ears messages of love, comfort, and longing, to be repeated when he should encounter their lost ones among the shades. His father, Themistocles, and even my Io, had penned letters, and these were put into the bosom of his peplos.

Then the torch was applied to the kindling, which took fire with a crackling that soon became a roar; and Lykaon's final bed was curtained with red fire. The day was hot, clear, and nearly windless. How bravely the towering column of sable smoke rose into the blue heavens! All of us backed away; even so, many a hair was singed on one and another. Through the leaping flames I caught sight of the very face of Death, and quickly turned my eyes away to look instead at the green grass, the lowing cattle, and the gracious olive trees that are mine—though they are in fact Ortygenes's—for a brief while longer. Soon I shall be as Lykaon, perhaps far less mourned, soon remembered only by these scrolls.

The sacrificial beasts were a young bull, three rams, and three black he-goats. They were dedicated in good style to the chthonian gods and roasted upon Lykaon's funeral pyre. The boar we hunted yesterday was roasted, too; there was more than enough meat for everyone present. The black man told me I had killed the boar, which I had already forgotten. He says also that we saw a much larger boar in Thrace. No one succeeded in killing that one, however.

Aglaus stopped to speak with me, and I asked how old he is. He is in his thirty-second year, though he looks so much older—I think because his hair has begun to gray and he has lost some teeth. His father was called Aglaus also. He asked whether the letters I use were pictures. I explained that they are, *A* being the head of an ox and so on; but that I did not intend an ox now when I set down *A*. I showed him how to write his name in my own tongue, scratching the letters in the dirt.

He thought that the goat man was a certain god who lives in the mountains of Bearland. His name is All. I asked how he came to bear this strange name, and Aglaus said that he is the fourth son of Time and Earth, though his brothers do not recognize his claim to the fourth world, which is this one. The other three are the sky, the sea, and the Lands of the Dead, which lie under the earth. It is he who brings terror at noon to those who wake him from his slumber. I asked whether Aglaus had ever seen him. He affirmed that he had. Io, who had come to listen to us, says that this god aided the men of Thought against the barbarians at Fennel Field.

When Aglaus had gone, I asked Io about the letter that she had put into Lykaon's bosom. At first she did not want to tell me, but when I promised I would not tell anyone else, she told me it was to her parents. She does not know whether they are dead, but believes they may be. She said she told them she was well and happy and has a fine man, but that she misses them both very much. I wanted to ask her who this man is, but she was crying, so I comforted her instead.

Now only what I said to Ortygenes remains to be written.

I found him staring into the embers. There were many men around him, all asleep. He had a skin of wine and offered some to me, but I refused it. He asked whether I had ever seen his son alive. I could not remember, and shook my head.

"He wasn't as big as you," he said. "We hardly ever are. But the old blood ran true in him."

I said that everyone had told me what a fine young man he had been.

"Are you a Bundini?" Ortygenes asked. "Some tribe of the Getae?"

I could say only that I did not know; in any case, I do not think he heard my reply.

"Our line fought on the windy plain of Ilion," he told me, "but in his entire life my poor boy never saw anything beyond these mountains.

> " 'Some marks of honor on my son bestow,
>     And pay in glory what in life you owe.
>  Fame is at least by heavenly promise due
>  To life so short, and now dishonor'd, too.
>  Till the proud king and all the Achaean race
>  Shall heap with honors him they now disgrace.'

"Here's a secret—you'll forget it anyhow, what's-his-name says. Know who the Achaeans are?"

I admitted I did not.

"We are," Ortygenes said, "and I'm a king in hiding. You think we'll ever win our country back? We won't. Nations are like men— growing old, never young. My son had the misfortune to be a young man of an old nation. So did I, once. Yours is young still, whatever it is. Give thanks."

This morning we entered the Silent Country. Themistocles gave Aglaus money and dismissed him; but when we halted for the first meal, we discovered that he had been following us, which made the Rope Maker very angry. Themistocles permitted Aglaus to share our food, but told him to return to his own land after he had eaten, that we no longer required a guide and would not pay him anything more. Aglaus was very humble, saying he would serve us without pay, like a slave, and do whatever work Tillon and Diallos thought too hard. Themistocles shook his head and turned away.

Then Bittusilma and Io spoke to the black man and me. The black man has money, it seems, and so do I. (Io is keeping mine for me; it is on the cart.) They proposed that we should employ Aglaus as our servant, each giving him a spit on alternate days. The black man was doubtful, but I said that if he did not wish to do it, I would hire Aglaus myself to wait upon Io, Polos, and me; then the black man agreed to the arrangement Bittusilma and Io had originally suggested. Aglaus rejoiced when we told him, and I think even Themistocles and Simonides were happy, though they tried to appear otherwise. Tillon and Diallos welcome him now as a comrade.

I have said nothing, only nodding when Io explained the new arrangement to him; yet I welcome him, too, as something more. When he arrived, as we sat eating, I recalled a silver chariot. I remember standing in it and holding the reins, though no horses were harnessed to it. Perhaps it is only an imagined object in my memory palace, but I do not think so; it seems to me that it stands among rocks, not walls. If having Aglaus near helps me remember, I would pay him much more than a spit.

Tonight I read about Lykaon's cremation, and what Ortygenes said to me. When I had finished, I asked Pasicrates whether the people of Bearland were called Achaeans. He said that they were not, the Achaeans having been destroyed by the Dorians, his own tribe, who had slaughtered all their men and seized their women. Aglaus confirmed it—but looked (or so it appeared to me) rather too serious.

# THIRTY-FIVE

## *Cyklos of Rope*

THE JUDGE TO WHOM CIMON gave me a letter has welcomed me, with Io and Polos, into his home. I had forgotten the letter (as I have forgotten the man called Cimon) but Io says I showed it to her before I rolled it into my old scroll, and she told me what it was and gave it to me when I needed it. Cyklos is of middle height; though his hair is as gray as iron, no young man could stand more straight. I have not seen him smile.

I should set down here that the wounded Rope Maker who was with us ran ahead of us when we neared Rope, though it clearly gave him a great deal of pain to run. Nothing of that showed in his expression, and the strides he took with his right leg were as long as those with the left; but when he looked back to wave good-bye to us, his face was white. After seeing it, I watched him closely as he ran, and twice he nearly fell. Themistocles and Simonides had tried to dissuade him, but he said that it was his duty to announce us, and as long as he could do his duty he would do it. I offered to send Polos, who runs very swiftly, in his place; but he would not hear of that.

He must have reached Rope well ahead of us, for we received a magnificent welcome. All five of the judges had marched out of the city to meet us, accompanied by at least two hundred Rope Makers under arms. Their armor gleamed like gold in the bright sunshine. With them was the Women's Chorus, which I am told is very famous, playing and singing, and with the Women's Chorus, a score of lovely young girls who danced to their music.

The greatest welcome was for Themistocles, who was embraced by all the judges; but when each had greeted him and praised his shrewd leadership during the war (in which Io says the black man and I took part), they inquired about me and greeted me as well. I said that so far as I knew I had done nothing to deserve their goodwill, but that I would attempt to deserve it in the future, at which they appeared pleased. That was when Io passed me the letter, which she had taken from the scroll in my chest. Cyklos had already introduced himself, and I gave it to him.

In Rope we were first brought to the palace of the Agids. We did not see Prince Pausanias, who is said to be the greatest man here, but Simonides says that we will surely see him at the ceremony tomorrow. We were greeted instead by the white-haired Queen Gorgo and her son, King Pleistarchos, a boy about Polos's age. Gorgo told me that she recalled Io and me from our earlier visit to her city, and asked Io what had befallen the beauty who had accompanied us. Io said she had been killed at the siege of Sestos. Gorgo nodded, and said that she had foreseen that death, sudden and violent, awaited her. I must remember to ask Io more about this woman; I place this wish among the shattered fragments of the dancer.

I should write here, too, that the Agid palace is not a great structure like the memory palace in which I attempt to store all the things I may wish to recall, but only a commodious house of stone. This house of Cyklos's is not even stone, however—merely mud brick, and of moderate size.

Now I must write everything I have been told concerning the solemn ceremonies that are to take place tomorrow. Before I go to sleep, I will put this scroll in a prominent place so that I will be certain to read it in the morning; thus, I hope, I will be able to act well tomorrow, even though I must necessarily be separated from Io.

First, that they will begin at the rising of the full moon—that is very important here. Simonides and I spoke at length with Cyklos this afternoon; he told us that there had been great concern here lest we come late, in which case many features of the ceremony would have had to be eliminated. I lay between the paws of the panther: *Everyone must be in place before twilight brings the rising of the moon.*

Second, that about two thousand others will be honored with me, though I am to be their head and chief. In order to ensure that there are no mistakes that might offend the Triple Goddess, each of us is to be accompanied by a sponsor, a young Rope Maker who has already rehearsed the ceremony several times. Mine will be Hippoxleas, one of the youths attending Cyklos; he is as tall as I am, and I would call him handsome (though perhaps somewhat overheavy at the jaw), but Io does not like him. She said that he was of the same mold as Pasicrates, the one-handed Rope Maker who ran ahead to announce us. By this I thought she meant that the two were closely related, so I asked Hippoxleas whether they were brothers. He smiled and told me that they are only distant cousins, but good friends.

"You'll have the most difficult job of all," I warned him, "if I'm to lead the entire group. I forget, as Simonides told you."

He laid his hand on my shoulder in a friendly fashion and grinned. "Not at all, Latro. Think they'd give it to a simpleminded fellow like me if it were going to be too hard? No, it's the rest who drew the tough jobs." And indeed, of all the young men about Cyklos, only Hippoxleas seems to be looking forward to the great events of tomorrow night. I lay his name, *Hippoxleas*, just to the left of the wide door, at the foot of the doorpost.

Third, that our preparations will begin long before sunset. Following the first meal, all of us are to assemble on the bank of the Eurotas, north of the temple. There we and our sponsors will be able to practice by daylight all the things we will have to do in darkness. Io wants to come; Hippoxleas says there is no reason she should not, though she will have to stand among the spectators. That *we must go after the first meal*, I write upon the floor before the golden sun the blue beetle rolls.

Fourth and last, the order of events, because I do not know whether I will have an opportunity to write after the practice. Following songs by the Men's Chorus, there is to be a sacrifice on behalf of the entire Silent Country. It is assumed that the omens will be favorable, because the wishes of the goddess have been consulted upon several occasions during the past few days, and each time she has urged that the ceremony proceed.

After this sacrifice, there will be speeches honoring both Themistocles and those who are to receive residency; I do not know exactly how many, or who will give them. Then Themistocles himself will speak, honoring the Rope Makers, their auxiliaries, and their allies for the great part they played in the war.

Next he will be crowned with trefoil by the two kings. (It seems very odd to me that Rope should have two kings, but Aglaus and Io both confirm it. Polos knows no more of this place than I.) We must cheer very loudly as the wreath is placed upon his head. He will then be presented with gifts; as I understand it, each of the five judges, the kings, Queen Gorgo, and the prince regent will all make him rare and valuable presents, after which Themistocles himself will offer an unblemished white bull to the King of Gods. (This bull is one of the gifts he is to receive.)

Thus far I, at the head of those who will be freed and made residents of Rope, will have been merely an onlooker; but now we are to throw aside our clothing and bathe in the Eurotas. Each sponsor will carry perfumed oil with which to anoint us, as well as a towel and a new white garment. When all of us are freshly attired, we are to form a column, with Hippoxleas and myself in the lead. I am to stand at his right.

We will file past the temple of Orthia, where we will be given torches, and our sponsors offerings, by the priestesses. (The Women's Chorus will perform while these are distributed.) Then we will march to each of the temples of Rope in turn. The dancers are to go first and the Women's Chorus after them; we need only follow. We are to sing the refrains of all the songs—I am told that these refrains are short and easy, and that we will be drilled in them during the practice tomorrow. At each temple, a hundred men will make offerings. (These have already been told off; each group of one hundred will march as a unit.)

When we return to the temple of Orthia, I am to make my own offering together with all the men who have not yet made theirs. The prince regent, the five judges, and both the kings will pass among us, accompanied by priestesses. As each declares each man free, the priestess with him will place a crown of wildflowers upon that man's head. *I will be the first man freed by the prince regent,* who will be assisted by Queen Gorgo. *I must thank each briefly, humbly, loudly, and gratefully.* As soon as I have finished speaking, I am to throw my torch into the river.

By the time the last slave has been freed, the meat of the sacrifices should be done. There will be general feasting, and—as Simonides warns me—a great deal of wine.

In my avenue of statues there stands one of the Hydra; it has seven heads and four feet. I cut an event into each: *the first sacrifices, the speeches,*

*Themistocles's own speech, the presentation of gifts to him, his sacrifice, our cleansing, the distribution of torches and offerings, our march, my offering, the ceremony of manumission, and the drowning of the torches.*

Io asked whether I had seen the black man. We found him at a gymnasium near here, watching Hippoxleas teach Polos the Rope Makers' sword drill. Io showed us a small room without windows, on the other side of the court from the one in which Io, Polos, and I sleep. It holds only a pair of stocks, of oak reinforced with bronze and iron; there are bloodstains on the floor. Io and the black man found a place in the wall where it has been repaired. They say that a man we know was imprisoned here and escaped by breaking through this wall. Both warned me not to speak of it. We left that room without being seen by anyone, though one of those who attend Cyclos saw us as we crossed the court.

Io says she will be very happy to get out of Rope—she does not like it here. Nor do I, though after tomorrow it will be my city. Io asked me to ask Cyklos when we will go to Dolphins for the games.

We ate the second meal at the barracks of the mora to which Hippoxleas belongs. It was a long low shed, bare of everything except tables and benches. Io said on the way over that we had eaten in one of these when we were here previously, warning me not to taste the broth. I soon saw, however, that all the Rope Makers eat it with relish; I tried it, but found it bitter and salty. Hippoxleas told me where it gets its black color, but I do not believe him—there was much teasing of the black man and me, and even a little of Themistocles and Simonides. Bacon, onions, and barley boiled together made up the rest of the meal, though Hippoxleas says they seldom get bacon.

Later I sat listening to Cyklos talk to Hippoxleas and the other young men, although some did not like having me there. I would not call Cyklos a good speaker—his voice is not musical, and he seldom turns phrases—but the young men hung upon every word.

A slave brought wine and dried figs. I wanted to awaken Io and Polos so they could have some, but Cyklos shook his head and I did not. I have saved a fig for each, however.

Though they were couched in so homely a style, some of the things Cyklos told us seemed very striking to me. He talked of Cyrus, a barbarian king who conquered many nations. One of his counselors advised him to shift his capital to a place where the climate was milder and the land more productive. Cyrus refused, saying that soft lands bred soft men. Cyklos then spoke of the fertility of the Silent Country, which abounds in wheat, barley, and every kind of fruit. He asked how it could be that the Rope Makers were not as soft as their soil.

He spoke also of a law which makes a woman a widow as long as her husband remains abroad, asking first whether the law was fair to her husband, and then (when no one replied) whether it was fair to the woman herself. The young men debated the matter and concluded that it was fair to neither: a man should not lose what is his each time he leaves home; nor should a woman forfeit the security of her husband's name because she is separated from him. Cyklos explained the reason for this law; it was made for the benefit of Rope, which must have infants because it requires men. Though he did not say this, I wondered whether it was not made also so that men would not desire to travel.

Cyklos asked, "Would you leave your wife here, Latro, now that you know our law?"

I said that I would not, at which everyone laughed.

"You don't have to worry," he said. "The law applies only to us, not to you." But it seems to me that it has application to me whether these people rule that it applies or not, because I would surely forget a wife as soon as we were separated. And indeed, it is entirely possible I have a wife now, who supposes herself a widow.

"It's we Rope Makers who defend the city, you see," Cyklos said, "and not you neighbors, though we can call on you to fight at need. Did you see our mighty walls today?"

I said that I had not, and that I did not think this city had any.

"It is walled with our shields," he told me.

He yawned and stretched. "We'll have a lot to do tomorrow, I'm afraid—all of us will be up late." I rose with the others, but he motioned for me to sit once more.

When the young men had left, I said, "It's very generous of you to house the children and me as you have, but I'm afraid we must be a burden as well as an inconvenience. Soon, I hope, we should be on our way to Dolphins. I'm sure that you'll be glad to see us go."

He waved that aside, pouring a fresh cup of wine for me and one for himself. "Hippoxleas says you're a master swordsman."

I said I hoped that I had not boasted to him.

Cyklos shook his head. "He's been teaching your boy, and found that you've taught him a great deal already. Pasicrates said you cut off his hand; he thinks there's something uncanny about you. So does the prince regent."

I said, "I think I'm a very ordinary man."

"Then you're not—ordinary men never think of themselves that way. Themistocles tells us you forget. Tomorrow morning will you remember what I tell you now?"

I said that I would write it in this scroll and read it in the morning.

Cyklos opened the chest upon which he had been sitting and produced two wooden swords, tossing one to me. "No thrusting at the face, understand? Everything else is fair. Now try to kill me."

I cut at his hand. He parried very cleverly and sprang at me; I caught his wrist and threw him down, my wooden sword at his throat.

When he had risen and recovered his breath, he asked, "How is it that you don't forget what you know of the sword?"

I explained that knowledge and memory are distinct: "Words written remember, a seed knows."

"Can you drive a chariot? Four horses?"

I do not know whether I can or not, and I told him so.

"In the morning, Prince Pausanias is going to ask you to. In less than a day you'll be declared a resident of Rope, and thus a subject of His Highness. Will you agree?"

I said I would certainly agree to try, if the prince of my new city wished it.

Cyklos turned and paced the courtyard, no longer watching me. "We've lost a great deal of prestige," he said. "First it was Peace, then after Clay, Mycale and Sestos. But we'll soon sweep Themistocles from the board, which should help enormously. Then if we dominate the Pythic Games—we *must* win the chariot race—and move boldly against some city of the Great King's—"

I asked whether he intended to kill Themistocles.

"No, no," he said. "Honor him—heap him with honors and gifts. No one can blame us for that."

# THIRTY-SIX

## *Bloodstained*

TORN AND RUINED CLOTHING, CLOVEN armor, and the weapons of the heroic king hang in the hall of the prince's house. "These were King Leonidas's," the prince's son explained to us. "My father got them at the Gates when he brought Leonidas's body home. He was my grandfather's brother. Please don't touch anything, sir. My father doesn't permit it."

I took my hand from the dead king's chiton, Themistocles assured the prince's son we would not, and Io whispered, "You want to be a famous warrior? This's the price they pay."

Polos (at whom her whisper was directed) did not appear to hear her, staring at everything with wide, dark eyes.

Pleistoanax said, "All mortals die. Since I must die, I wish to do it as he did, face-to-face with my enemy."

I remarked, "He wasn't actually facing the man who killed him. He was struck from behind by a javelin."

Pleistoanax smiled. "I see you know his glorious history, sir. He had broken the barbarians' line and was charging their king. One of the king's bodyguards killed him, exactly as you say."

Themistocles was eyeing me narrowly. "I don't think Latro can remember Leonidas's history—if he ever heard it—or much of anything else. How did you know about that, Latro?"

"From this chiton. There's a lot of staining near the arms and around the hem, but it's fairly even on both sides; I'd say that someone hacked the arms and legs of the corpse. The wound that killed him left a circular tear in back, about a hand above the waist, and a small hole across from it in front."

Pleistoanax went to look at the chiton as I spoke, and I noticed he did not scruple to touch it. He is a tall boy not yet come to manhood, and rather too handsome for my taste.

"The weapon penetrated his backplate," I continued, "passed through his chest, and was stopped by his breastplate. An arrow wouldn't have pierced the bronze, and would have left a smaller hole. A sword would have left a broad cut in the linen, not a round tear—so would a dagger. A horseman's lance would have made a larger hole, and it would probably have gone through his breastplate as well." I was about to say that the tear left by a shieldman's spear would have been larger, too; but I stopped just in time and substituted, "A king of Rope would never have had his back to the spears.

"So it was probably a javelin," I concluded, "a strong cast by someone not far behind him."

A young Rope Maker with a hand missing had entered while I spoke; from what I read here this morning I knew that this must be Pasicrates. I greeted him by name, and though his face kept his secret, his eyes revealed his surprise. All that he said, however, was, "His Highness will see you, even the children."

"And I?" Pleistoanax raised an eyebrow, determined to show he was no child. I doubt that he is as old as Io.

The prince stood to greet us, in the most gracious possible fashion, embracing Themistocles, Simonides, and me, patting Io's head, and pinching Polos's cheeks. Although Io warned me against him before we came, I liked him at once. His face is rendered hideous by a scar that draws up the right side of his mouth, but no one can be blamed for such accidents.

"This is Tisamenus, my mantis," the prince said, gesturing toward the pudgy little man who had sprung to his feet when the prince rose. Seeing him, I told Io by my glance that she and I would speak about this later. She had described this rabbity little creature as a monster; the monster seemed ready to fawn upon Themistocles whenever he snapped his fingers.

"Sit down, all of you. You, too, Pasicrates. Since you're going with us, there's no reason you shouldn't hear this."

Themistocles cocked his head. "Cimon said something about Your Highness wanting Latro to represent Rope at Dolphins. Will you attend the games in person?"

"Yes, and take you with me if I can—that's why I asked you to come here this morning. It might make a good impression if we could mention it tonight at the ceremony."

Themistocles and the prince had seated themselves by then, so the rest of us sat down, too. Themistocles said, "I haven't seen the great games in quite a while—it's certainly tempting. Simonides here goes every year."

"My trade," the old poet explained modestly. "I celebrate the victors from Thought without asking for a fee, if they wish it; as a foreigner, I feel I owe it to the city that's received me so graciously. And there are rich fees to be picked up from the other winners, now and then."

Prince Pausanias winked at his son. "Suppose *I* won, poet? You wouldn't charge me, would you? Don't you—and Thought—owe us something for my victory at Clay?"

Simonides cleared his throat. "Indeed we do. Why, I'd say that we owe you every bit as much as you'd owe the Long Coast if Themistocles—an example taken at random—had won the Battle of Peace. Who was the fellow you Rope Makers put in charge of the combined fleets? I forget his name. Anyway, between the two of them, I'd have to call Peace your greatest victory, because it was the first."

Pausanias roared with laughter, joined in a moment by his plump little mantis and Pasicrates, and at last by Themistocles himself. Io whispered, "Themistocles was the real commander at Peace."

The prince wiped his streaming eyes. "Poor old Eurybiades! The triumph of a dozen lifetimes, and no one will accord him the least credit. If I win, Simonides, you shall compose my victory ode. Without payment, if you insist—but no one has ever called me ungrateful."

Simonides made him a seated bow.

"Our entry's only nominally mine, however. It's no secret, and you might as well know the facts at the outset. My aunt's the one who bred and trained our team. You've already met her, I understand."

Themistocles and Simonides nodded.

"She's got an eye for horses, and a way with them, like no one else I've ever seen; but you know the law—no married women, and a widow's accounted a wife still. Once wed, always wed, as far as the gods are concerned. We didn't think it was much of an obstacle at first. She'd give the team to Pleistarchos."

Themistocles said, "Sounds reasonable. What went wrong?"

"Pleistarchos, mostly. He can be just as stubborn as any other Rope Maker, and he insisted that if he was going to enter, he wanted to go to Dolphins and watch the race. I think he was actually hoping to drive himself, although he hadn't got up the nerve to propose that."

Themistocles chuckled.

"As you may imagine, my aunt wouldn't hear of it. Neither would the judges—they get nervous whenever one of our kings is out of the country, and who knows when the barbarians are going to try again?"

Themistocles said smoothly, "The war's over, if you ask me. A king of Rope is more likely to be in danger on Redface Island than away from it."

"My thoughts exactly—everything's getting back to normal. Take a look at this letter. The messenger arrived last night."

Themistocles glanced at the papyrus, then read it out loud: " *'Greetings, most royal Pausanias Kleombrotou, from your devoted servant Agis Korinthou! The spoils of war you entrusted to me I have entrusted to the honest Muslak Byblou upon the following highly favorable terms. Muslak has this very day delivered into my hand a full eight hundred darics for you as surety. Of what your goods bring, he is to retain every tenth coin, and no more. The other nine he shall render in a year, less the eight hundred darics already paid. Shall the gold be sent to you? Or ought I to trade with it? Tin is coming once more and we might do well in that.'* "

Io whispered to Simonides, "I thought they didn't trade."

Overhearing her, the prince said, "We don't, child—that is to say, Pasicrates here doesn't, nor do any of the Equals. But King Leotychides can and does both buy and sell on behalf of our city; and so do I, acting as I do in place of King Pleistarchos. Having heard that letter read, you can understand the dangers inherent in it. I find myself, without my knowledge or consent, dealing with a Crimson Man—in theory at least an adversary."

As we walked to this field, I asked Io whether she thought the prince's agent would really do business with the enemies of her people without his permission; the prince and Themistocles, strolling arm in arm, were too far in advance of us to overhear.

"They aren't the enemies of *my* city," Io said, "and I don't know a lot about them. But I know a lot about Pausanias, and I feel sorry for the Crimson Man." After we had taken a few more steps, she added, "I think he would. He'd know what Pausanias wanted—as much gold as possible, any way he could get it. And he'd know, too, that Pausanias couldn't say it was all right."

I had not thought of that. It made me admire this girl all the more, though I cautioned her against judging a maimed man by his scars—I think it must be his appearance that has turned her against the prince. She wanted to take my hand while we walked, but I pretended I did not notice and kept it closed so that she would not see the blood smeared on my fingers.

When we reached this place (seven stades, Pasicrates says, outside the city) only the chariot I am to drive was waiting for us. I took its reins and gave the team a little light exercise, without letting them reach their full speed or anything close to it. They seem good enough, responding well to the reins and the whip, but rather lacking the mettle I would have liked to see.

Polos told me it was marvelous to listen to me describe in so much detail how King Leonidas had been killed by a javelin. No one was near enough to hear us, so I confided to him that the javelin had not in fact been thrown—that the man who had killed Leonidas had stood above him with the javelin in his hands and driven it through the king's armor and into his back. (I do not understand how I have come to know this, and yet I am absolutely certain it is true.)

Polos looked puzzled. "Wouldn't the point have gone right through his breastplate, too? Couldn't you stick something with a javelin harder than you could throw it?"

"That's true," I said, "if you're only practicing, jabbing your point into a tree or something of that kind. But in a real fight, a thrown weapon always strikes harder. Something makes us hold back, if only a little, when we strike another man. To strike hard at the back of one who has already been knocked down is particularly difficult."

Although the blood appears fresh, it cannot be wiped away, ever on the papyrus.

I should say here that after I read, I carried this scroll with me in order that I could read and write when time allowed it. The queen and her chariot still have not appeared; thus I write. This is a very pleasant spot, a wide expanse of level, open ground, with a few large trees that shade the horses, and us, beside this clear, cool stream. The breeze is soft, the air wonderfully clear.

I thought I heard a shepherd piping and went to see; it was only Io, playing pipes she says Aglaus made for her. I saw that he had cut them from green rushes, cementing them with beeswax and binding them with split willow twigs. Io had named him for me this morning; now I asked whether she was not ashamed of our having a servant so poor and common looking, with many missing teeth, for I know women are often very sensitive concerning such things.

Io laughed and said we were about to get another, because Polos's milk teeth are coming out. Her own are nearly all gone. She grew serious, saying that she liked Aglaus very much though there was something about him that reminded her of Elata. I do not recall Elata; I tried to conceal it, but Io saw that I had forgotten her and told me that she is the wife of Hegesistratus of Zakunthios, another mantis.

"I liked her, too," Io said. "But I was afraid of her."

Polos shouts.

# THIRTY-SEVEN

## *The Dead Man's Stare*

H IS FACE AND OUTSTRETCHED HANDS appear to me whenever I close my eyes. He tries to speak to me, I know, yet I cannot
catch his words. I will write instead, though I had to beat Cyklos' slave
before he would bring the lamp; I will write until I fall asleep on this
stool, my back propped by the wall.

The queen and the boy they call a king came in her chariot. The
driver was a slave, short but muscular; a most cunning man, I think,
about horses. He wanted to know how much I had driven. When I told
him I could not be sure, he winked at me and thumped my shoulder
with his fist.

Queen Gorgo spoke with me. There cannot be two such women in
the world! She asked whether I recalled our meeting in the temple of
Orthia. When I explained that I sometimes forget, she told me gently,
"But you must remember our meeting at my house, yesterday."

"Of course," I told her. "No man could ever forget a queen so lovely
and so gracious." It was a lie, and I blushed for it even as the words left
my lips. As quickly as I could, I turned the talk to her horses, which
are all grays, very beautiful and finely bred.

"I think they're probably the best in Hellas," she told me. "We've
raced them against my nephew's before, and they've always won easily;
but now he says that his can't lose as long as you drive for him. Are you
going to cast a spell on my horses? Or on your own?"

I told her I knew nothing of such things.

She nodded slowly, and her eyes were sad. "You remind me of
Leonidas; you're a plain fighting man. You've something of his energy,
too, I suspect. It's a good thing for Rope that there are such men as you,
but not for your wives and mothers."

While I spoke with Gorgo, Polos had been scrutinizing her team. He told me how eager they were to run, and how confident of victory. Of the one I was to drive he said, "They know they aren't going to win. They only want to finish the race and go back to the pasture."

I asked, "How can they know they won't win? Did they tell you that?"

Polos shrugged, and appeared every bit as downcast as if he were one of the horses himself. "They only say that the man who drives always makes them gallop too fast, so that they're winded before the race is over."

I dropped to one knee, bringing our eyes to a level. "Tell them I won't ask them to do their best until the last stretch of the last lap. Nor will I shout until then. When I shout, the race will be practically over. Then they must show their heels, and afterward they'll be walked back to their pasture. Can you do that?"

"I think so. I hope they'll understand and remember."

We raced three times around the field, which was large, as I have said. The finish—and the start—was the great oak under which we had rested. Gorgo stood there to judge the race; she held up fingers to give us the count of laps, although that was not really needed. When her driver saw that I did not force my horses to their utmost, he took a comfortable lead and held it. I permitted him to do it, even though Prince Pausanias shouted for me to drive faster at the end of the first lap, and also at the second.

Perhaps I should not write it, but it was a great joy then to drive as I did—very fast and yet without any straining for more speed— through the clear, warm morning. No dust rose from the soft grass, and the tall trees and low walls of piled stones seemed to spin past us in a sparkling dance.

I do not know whether Polos can actually speak with horses; such things seem impossible to me. But as we swung through the third turn at the far end, I felt all four steady themselves for the final dash. We gained a bit on Gorgo's chariot then.

Half the lap passed . . . two-thirds. *"Now!"* I roared it with every shred of wind my lungs would hold and cracked my whip like lightning over the heads of the team. They bounded forward like four stags.

When we had brought both our teams to a halt, Queen Gorgo's

driver spat all the ugly words he could lay tongue to into my face—some of them words I have never learned. Until Pasicrates stepped between us, he pretended that he was about to strike me with his whip. Prince Pausanias paid less heed to him even than I, grinning at Gorgo, who much to my surprise smiled at him in return. As for pretty Io and little Polos, they fairly capered with delight; and even Themistocles and Simonides were wreathed in smiles.

Then Gorgo's driver threw himself at her feet, talking very fast and pointing to her team. I could not understand all that was said, but I knew that he was begging her to propose a second race. It is never good, as I explained to Io, to make a horse run twice in the same day, though it must often be done in war. Indeed, it is best to give a horse several days in which to rest after a hard run.

But the prince readily agreed to hold a second race before the first meal. Their drivers walked both teams until they no longer sweated, examined their feet, and at last permitted them to drink a little. I asked Polos whether our horses understood that they would have to run again. When he nodded, I asked him to explain to them, if he could, that it was not my doing, that when I had promised them they would be returned to pasture after the race, I thought it true.

Polos positively glowed with pleasure, saying, "They don't mind. They want to race again."

I would not have held them back if I could, but I did not urge them forward. Of their own will they thundered around the meadow, keeping pace with Queen Gorgo's until the final turn. Then, as her chariot drew well ahead of mine, it threw a wheel. Her driver fell, and was dragged half the length of the course by the grays. For a moment it seemed we would trample him, but my team answered, swinging right. He was stunned, however, and when I saw Pasicrates cut the reins from his wrist, I thought him dead; but before we left, he stood and walked.

We ate the first meal here. The food was not good, but Io says the food at the barracks is worse. We eat there at times, she says. She wants me to ask the queen to let us dine with her, though I have told her Cyklos would surely be offended, and rightly. Io asked Aglaus where the black man was, but he could only tell us that he had gone out alone shortly after we went to speak with the prince.

As I left with Hippoxleas to go to the practice, I happened to pass the room where the black man sleeps with his wife; and I overheard him addressing her, his voice that in which an officer gives his orders in battle. We had not gone far when both came running after us. Gasping, the black man's wife asked whether I could wear my sword when I was made a resident of Rope; and when Hippoxleas declared that all weapons were absolutely forbidden, she drew me aside almost rudely, while the black man prevented Hippoxleas from going with us.

"There'll be trouble tonight," the black man's wife told me breathlessly. "He wants me to wedge the table against the door, and not open until I hear his voice. He's going to the ceremony—he'll bring your sword with his, wrapped in his cloak. He'll throw it to you if you need it."

I told her to take Io and Polos into the room with her, but she said, "Aglaus can protect them better than I could, and he'd kill me if he found Aglaus with me."

I will say nothing of the practice; it was easy enough, and I cannot recall anything that need be noted here except, perhaps, that Queen Gorgo directed it.

After the second meal we assembled, as before, to await the rising of the moon. We stood in silence, as we had been taught at the practice; and on the rare occasions when anyone dared to speak, he was hushed at once by several young Rope Makers. The slave standing next to me in the darkness (a wiry little rogue from what I could see of him) nudged me once or twice as though to assure himself, as well as me, that this was no dream. I had overheard these slaves talking among themselves at the practice and knew they were those who had fought best in the war, chosen by their fellows.

The full moon rose at last, hailed by the deep tones of the Men's Chorus. There can never have been another so beautiful as that silver shield upon the arm of the goddess!

Hardly had the men's voices fallen silent than we heard the bellowing of the bulls. Trotting they came, one black and one pied, each with two strong men to hold the shining chain through its nostrils. Priestesses cast fresh logs on the fire, and when its flames shot twice the height of a tall man, King Leotychides dispatched both bulls, which knelt in reverence to the goddess as they died. Together, Queen Gorgo and Tisamenus (the prince's mantis) examined them, she announcing each finding in her strong, clear voice.

Afterward each of the judges spoke, praising Themistocles. It was while he was replying, loudly cheered by all of us, that I happened to bump slightly against the young Rope Maker who was to sponsor the wiry slave. It was far from violent, and indeed I doubt that he gave any heed to it; but my arm told me that he had a dagger beneath his cloak. I thought then that he had been warned as I had, and had felt it wise to bring a weapon, though he risked the displeasure of the gods.

Themistocles was crowned by Leotychides and Pleistarchos, and our voices echoed to the heavens. Surely there is no point in listing here all the gifts he received, for there were very many; but I will say that the prince gave him the finest of all, a chariot of silver, set with precious stones and drawn by the horses I drove twice to victory. That was the final gift, and I saw how widely his eyes opened when he received it. There is a certain look that a man wears when he finds he has risen to a height he never dreamed of, and Themistocles of Thought wore it then.

As for me, my face must have made my amazement plain, for Hippoxleas whispered, "Is anything wrong?"

I shook my head, and did not tell him that I recalled that chariot, having seen it elsewhere.

Aglaus touched my arm, and when I turned to stare at him, pointed out the black man among the spectators, with Polos and Io before him. The moon was higher now, and the sacred fire lit the whole scene; I could see the cloth-wrapped bundle the black man held, which he had been too prudent to bring close to the young Rope Makers.

We bathed in the cool waters of the Eurotas, as we had also at the practice, but this time we did not resume our old clothing; our guides consecrated us with a perfumed unguent and clothed us anew in white.

When this was done—and it did not take long—we formed our double column. There was considerable confusion, though we had practiced it again and again. I wanted to bawl orders as though upon the drill field, and I saw the same wish on the faces of Hippoxleas and a dozen others; still we kept silent, and it may be that the column shaped itself more smoothly because of it.

No doubt the march around the city should have tired us. I cannot speak for the rest, but I was not conscious of the least fatigue. The clear voices of the women, the graceful and ever-changing figures of the dancers, and the solemn scenes at temple after temple buoyed all our spirits, I think. In the flickering torchlight the carven faces of the gods smiled upon us. Lustily our voices answered those of the women as we praised each god in turn.

Sooner than I would have believed possible, our procession was over. Another temple, I thought, and it did not surprise me to find that it was upon the banks of the Eurotas, for the last two we had visited had stood there also. But it was the temple of Orthia, to which we had returned; and there I presented to an ancient image of the goddess the silver figurine Hippoxleas had carried for me, and cast away my guttering torch. Those who had not already made offerings now presented similar figures, though theirs were of lead. Mine depicted the goddess winged; wearing a tall headdress, she stood before her sacred tree. Those of the slaves that I saw were of beasts of the chase or small soldiers bearing bows or slings.

Prince Pausanius himself placed the crown of blossoms on my head, just as I had been promised he would. He seemed even more cordial than he had been in the morning, embracing me and twice instructing Hippoxleas to see that nothing evil befell me during the feast to come; each time Hippoxleas assured him that nothing would. It seemed strange to me that a man such as I, larger and (I believe) stronger than is common, should be cosseted like an infant. I could not but observe how brilliant the eyes of Queen Gorgo appeared; but such was my fatuity, and such the excitement of the moment, that it was not until the wreath was upon my head that I realized they were bright with tears.

When the feast began, Io, the black man, Polos, and Aglaus joined us. There was meat and wine in plenty, fruits and honey, honeyed breads and cakes—everything that anyone could wish for. We ate and drank our fill, and the black man collected figs and grapes, and a skin of good wine to take back to Bittusilma. By that time the scarlet moon rode low in the west. Half or more of the feasters had gone to their homes already, or so it seemed to me. I had forgotten the black man's warning, and so perhaps had he, though the bundle that held our swords lay at his feet. Not far off a hundred hounds or more coursed deer; their baying haunted the night whenever the noises of our feasting slackened.

There came a scream of anguish and despair—I hope I never hear such a sound again—and with it a running man, his chaplet of blossoms half-fallen from his head. He had one of the knives the priestesses had used, and though I could not be sure in the darkness, it appeared to me that he was drenched with blood. At once Hippoxleas rose as though to stop him, received the curved blade in his belly, and snatched away my crown of flowers. All this took place so quickly that I was still staring openmouthed when Hippoxleas lay dead at my feet.

A dozen daggers struck down the man who had killed him; the crowd surged about us, and I lost sight of the black man and the rest.

For what seemed to me whole days, I searched everywhere for them. I never found them, and when I felt that a new day should already have filled the sky, exhausted and more than half drunk, I decided to return to this house. I stumbled a score of times, but fell just once, when I tripped upon the legs of the expiring slave.

He, too, had worn a crown of blossoms; it lay in the dust not an arm's length from where he had fallen. Though his mouth ran with his blood, he struggled to make his speech clear to me, to forgive me, warn me, or tell me I know not what—or perhaps merely to beg my help; all the gods know how gladly I gave it. It was then that I recognized him, for in trying to stanch his blood, I had drawn him out of the shadows and into the moonlight. He was the slave who had driven Queen Gorgo's gray horses, and though I did him no harm, he will not let me sleep.

Since returning, I have learned that the one-armed man and some other Rope Makers had forced the black man, the children, and Aglaus to leave the feast, threatening the black man with the laws of Rope when he would not.

I am in a place besieged.

# PART FOUR

# THIRTY-EIGHT

## The Pythia

THE PRIESTESS OF THE GOD of Dolphins is very young. She appears kind.

I have written it, and do not know what more to write. But Kichesippos and my slave girl stand and stare.

They cannot read these letters, yet they know what letters are. If I make mere marks here, they will remonstrate with me, but what is there to say, and why should it be said? My slave girl slept with me. When we woke, the prince asked whether I had covered her. She said I had, but I know she lied. She fears he will bring me a boy.

Again. Io says I used always to do this, Kichesippos that it will make me well to speak of my disease, whether to him, or to the shining god of healing whose place this is, or merely to this roll of papyrus. When we hear ourselves, says Kichesippos, the gods hear us. That cannot be.

I asked Io what to write. She said I must write all that I remember. What I remember is only this: my mother's kiss before I slept. In my sleep I died and was swept into the Lands of the Dead, the dark kingdoms beneath the mountains. Long I wandered through the caverns where the nights to come are stored. There was much stone there, water, and mud; but nothing more. I heard the neighing of the horse of He Who Gathers, and the roaring of lions. At length I walked once more in the lands of the living, here in the pavilion of the prince; yet I know they come for me.

Io taught me her name; I thought her my sister, but she is my lover. The rest—the prince, Cyklos the judge, Kichesippos, the black man with the scarred cheek, his wife, the angry one-armed Pasicrates, our romping Polos, Amyklos, and Aglaus. There are more whom Io did not name, most of them slaves of the prince; and in the clear sunshine very many, for thousands gather here.

Pausanias and I went to the holy cave again. I write *again* because it seems from what Apollonios told us that we have been there before, though I do not remember it. The priests wear no sandals, and they are not to wash their feet. When I stared at them, the prince explained these things to me; he says, too, that they must sleep upon the ground, but everyone save himself does that here. We sacrificed, mumbled the many prayers, washed, did everything Apollonios instructed us to do. Then we entered the cave.

Its walls are damp and very high. Far above our heads, the narrow wedge of sky was nearly black. From it I knew we were in a place other than the lands of men; for when we had stood upon the mountainside, the sky had been bright with the glorious azure that is the most beautiful color of all. Here, then, the sacred fire of pine and henbane burned. Here, wrapped in preternatural gloom, the child-pythia sat her tripod behind a curtain of gauze. Apollonios had guided us no farther than the entrance; Anochos, the proxenos of Rope, waited behind him.

The prince spoke: "I have been promised victory, and yet my charioteer is ill, gripped by a dread that neither he nor I understands. What am I to do?"

No one made a sound or moved a finger after that—nor did, nor could, I. The thudding of my heart no longer echoed in my ears, and no breath stirred in my nostrils. Some distant voice drew out a single, melancholy note that neither rose nor fell.

In the depths of the earth the python stirred. I heard it, the rustles of its scales, the hiss of its exhalations soughing so faintly that I believed it far away until its head was thrust from the crevice beneath the lofty tripod. Scarcely to be seen, it wreathed the pythia in phantom coils.

She screamed. We started, for at her scream our breath and life returned to us. Her arms flew out, her head back so that I thought her neck must break; the voice of the prince issued from her throat. As a lancer unhorsed might wrench his eyes from the blade poised to take his life, I glanced toward the man himself; he was not speaking, but stared as astonished as I.

*"Thou art royal, royal be."*

Afterward Apollonios reminded us that no one but a priest could understand the ravings of the pythia, and recited for us the following verses:

> Not gems nor spears can forge a crown,
> What gods raise up, men drag not down.
> Though queens in rags, they queens remain,
> Gracious in aid, their favor gain.

When we had left that sacred place, the prince said, "You understood the words the pythia spoke, Latro. Tell me."

I was frightened and asked, "How did you know?"

"Because you know the servants of him who stands behind all gods, as I told you last year. And because I saw your look when Apollonios prepared to tell us what she had said. Now, what did she really say?"

I repeated the pythia's words to him.

"Interpret it for me."

I shook my head, and he slapped me hard enough to stagger me. "Be a man! Once you would have tried to kill me for that."

He berated me much more. I do not recall all that he said, and I would not set it down if I did, no matter what Kichesippos and Io may say. Perhaps he would have struck me again, had not Polos ridden up.

Upon seeing the prince, he slipped from his mount's back at once. "Your Highness . . ."

The prince whirled to confront him.

"Your Highness, when we were up north, Latro used to ride all the time. He liked to. I thought maybe—"

As a squall blows off at sea, leaving the rainwashed sun, the anger drained from Pausanias's scarred face; he grinned and ruffled Polos's brown hair. "I suppose it can't hurt, and this certainly isn't helping. Latro, do you want to straddle this bag of bones?"

I shook my head.

"Then you probably ought to. What a nag! Where'd you find him, Polos?"

"He belongs to my uncle, Your Highness. He's a very good horse, really he is."

"To the venerable Amyklos? Then I shouldn't be so hard on him."

The prince grasped the horse's jaw and skinned back its lips. "But he's an old horse, Polos—thirty at least. Nearly too old to work. Mount him, Latro!"

Polos dropped to his hands and knees so that I might step on his back, which made me itch to kick him. As soon as I was up he said, "I'll run alongside, Your Highness. I'll keep him out of trouble."

"Good!"

I let the old horse have his head, thinking that he would walk if he chose to move at all; to my astonishment, he darted away like a blooded racer, along the road, then into the trees and headlong down the wild mountainside, so that Polos was left as far behind as the prince. I heaved on the reins; at once the old horse slowed to a walk, and I let them fall to his neck. He whickered, and it seemed to me, almost, that he had spoken.

"You're welcome," I said. After that I sat looking at the pines and laurels through which we passed. It seemed to me that I could see their roots as well, the greedy fingers with which they tear at dead men's bones.

Soon we were joined by a riderless bay colt who appeared to enjoy the company of Amyklos's horse; and before long, our path—which I left entirely to the horses—began to climb; thus I rode up the mountain, always at a slow walk, for what seemed to me a very long time.

At last we reached a small temple of native limestone, in which stood the marble image of a maiden with a bow, and a real woman hardly less lovely. Leaving the shade of the temple, she extended her hands to me. "Dismount, Latro. You and I must talk awhile. Aglaus, will you look to the comfort of our guests, please?"

The gap-toothed servant, whom I had not noticed before, now stepped from behind a column to take the reins of my mount. As soon as I slid from his saddle, he let Aglaus lead him away; the colt trotted after them.

"There's a spring nearby," the pythia of this temple said. "Aglaus will fetch water for you if you wish it—but water, alas, is all we have. You did not bring your book?"

I shook my head.

"A pity. These are high matters we will discuss. I cannot speak of them yet, because all who must be present have not yet arrived. But you must promise, Latro, that you will write down everything. In fact I ought to do it myself—I drink too much, my husband says. But then I drink to forget."

I promised then that I would write as she advised (which I am doing now), for her touch had lifted my spirits a little; and I apologized for having brought no wine.

"We were lovers once," she told me, "lip to lip and lip to cup. Perhaps we will be so again. But not at present; not as you are today."

I nodded my agreement, for I have no desire to lie with any woman.

Soon Aglaus returned, bringing Polos and Polos's uncle, the long-faced old Amyklos. They had drunk at the spring and still wiped their mouths, flinging sparkling drops into the sunshine. I was conscious of my own thirst, but only as I might have been conscious of someone else's—it seemed pointless to satisfy it. The woman made them welcome, and they joined us in the shade of the temple.

"I hope you don't mind our taking you here," Polos said. "We're only trying to help you."

I told him that when he had invited me to step on his back, he had gone too far, that I would be old soon enough.

"What about sitting on my back to ride?" he asked.

I said I would not ask to do that for some while yet.

"But you already have, to steal the horses, and then to kill the boar."

I gave him an angry look, and he said, "I know you don't remember, but it's true! Tell him, Elata—you were there the first time."

The pythia said, "I can show it to you, Latro, if you want. You stole the horses of the sun, with the help of Polos, a lion, and a woman called Pharetra."

Embarrassed, the boy looked away. His old uncle laid a hand upon his shoulder. "You believe great warriors shouldn't weep. Can't you understand that the greatest must?"

When his nephew did not answer, he said, "You think highly of strength, Polos, and there's nothing wrong with that, because you're not strong yourself yet. But Latro can't think highly of it; he's strong, and so he's learned how little strength can do. You see, a boy can look up to a hero—in fact it's only natural at your age. But if that hero were to look up to himself in the same way, he'd be a monster, and not a hero at all."

When I had wiped my eyes, Polos told me, "I'm not ashamed of you, Latro. Really I'm not. You only remembered Pharetra because Aglaus is here."

That surprised me enough to awaken me for a moment from my despair. I feel sure my jaw dropped, and Aglaus himself looked as astonished as I.

Polos asked his uncle, "Is it all right if I tell him?"

"No, I'll tell him. You forget, Latro. We've talked about that before, so I know you know it. Gaea did it, as even young Io understands, and Aglaus is sacred to her."

My gap-toothed servant shook his head. "I don't mean any offense, sir, but nobody never told me that."

"You've been her lover since you were a boy, Aglaus, or so I'd guess. She returns your love, and perhaps loves you all the more because you don't know it."

A memory came to me, as though a singing bird had perched upon my head. "You've seen the god All," I told Aglaus. "You told me once."

"I've seen a few things," Aglaus admitted, looking hard at Polos and Amyklos. "Usually I've got sense enough not to speak about it to them that won't believe me. I told you 'cause you'd seen him yourself."

I nodded. "What are you doing up here, Aglaus? Don't you have work to do?"

"She brought me," Aglaus explained, pointing to the pythia. "She came while I was helping the cooks. Io knows her, and said for me to go with her and do what I was told, which is what I've done."

The pythia said, "This is a sanctuary of my mistress's. You call her a goddess, and I'm her servant—far more so than Io or Aglaus are yours. I've been sent into this quarrel to represent her interests. Amyklos, Polos, and Aglaus are here for her foe, Gaea, who took away your memory."

"Prince Pausanias asked the oracle," Polos said. "And the god there told him to have me get my uncle to help you. He's a famous healer."

Old Amyklos added, "I haven't been able to accomplish much, I'm afraid. That's why we're here."

"And I'm here," a new voice called, "simply because I'm a friend of Latro's."

The speaker emerged from the pines some way down the slope. He is muscular, of middle size, and has the eyes of a fox. "I doubt you remember me, but Sisyphus is the name. A driver you beat told me about this, and I thought I'd like a hand in it." He hesitated, then roared with mirth. "You won't see the joke, but it *is* funny."

The pythia murmured, "Now we can begin."

Learning from Polos that my long ride had lifted my spirits somewhat, Kichesippos walked with me to the town and back. Now he insists I write of it. The air was fine, the sun bright. A slave in the marketplace called me brother. I was ashamed and pretended I had not heard him. Later I asked Kichesippos. He says I was freed by the prince. They are Crimson Men, and their ship lies at Cyparissa. They will be sold with their goods, said to be rich, when more have come to watch the games. Kichesippos is himself the prince's slave; he says he does not wish freedom. The pythia, he says, is the slave of the god—and that is much the same.

# THIRTY-NINE

## *Diokles*

THE GYMNASTES HAS BEGUN MY training. Prince Pausanias wants me to box, and fight in the pankration, besides driving for him in the chariot race. Diokles talked with him, Cyklos, Tisamenus, Amyklos, and me this morning. Diokles is a head shorter than I. His beard is dark gray and bristling, and he spits often. He is training Pasicrates, too, for the footraces.

"I can see that he's strong," Diokles said. "What's the matter with him?"

The prince looked at Tisamenus, who shrugged. Old Amyklos said, "He's dispirited, and he can't remember, that's all. But exercise appears to help, not harm, him."

Diokles nodded sagely. "That's the way it usually is. What's he downhearted about?"

Tisamenus sighed. "You may leave that to us, sir. As you have been told, he does not remember."

Cyklos cleared his throat, the noise of one who feels that the time has come for him to take charge. "Our prince regent's mantis and this man, who I am informed is a noted physician, are treating these difficulties. It is for you to prepare his body for the contests."

Diokles nodded to show that he understood, though his eyes wanted to argue.

"It is vital to Rope that he do well. He must win at least one event and perform creditably in the rest—no excuses will be accepted. When will you enroll him?"

"Tomorrow, when the lists are opened, if he's got his fee."

The prince smiled. "Tisamenus has it. He'll go with you—there may be some difficulties. You can tell the hellanodikai that Tisamenus speaks for me and for our city. He'll explain to them that Latro qualifies in every way."

"I see." Diokles nodded to himself.

When we were alone, watching Pasicrates jogging around the track, Diokles asked in what way I did not qualify, and I told him I did not know.

"I'll swear you do," he told me. "You don't have to worry about that, see? I'll be behind you all the way. But I've got to know what we're up against. You're not from Redface Island, are you? You don't sound like it."

I said, "I think you're right."

"But you don't know? Huh! Can you wrestle?"

"A little, perhaps."

"That's good. A lot of wrestlers enter the pankration, but they never win. You talk to them and they'll tell you that once they get their grip on their man, it's all over. Fine. Maybe it takes them to the semifinals, see? Then they don't get their grip." He paused as if awaiting my reaction. "You know what it is, don't you? The pankration?"

I said, "I think I can guess from its name."*

"But you've never seen a match?"

"I don't know."

Diokles spat. "This is a great job, this is. All right, it's boxing, wrestling, and kicking. Can you box?"

"I think so."

"We'll find out. How about kicking?"

I said, "I suppose that anybody can kick."

Diokles spat, as before. "Take off those sandals. Don't put them back on till the games is over." He extended a hand at shoulder height. "Kick it, and kick hard. The harder you kick, the better I'll like it."

I kicked as hard as I could, but the end of my foot barely touched his palm.

"Try again!"

The result was scarcely better than before.

"With the other foot!"

This time I could not even touch his palm.

---

*All-power—GW

"Now hold out your hand for me."

I did as he said; the tips of my fingers were level with his eyes. His feet pumped like a boxer's fists: right-left-right, each kick higher than his head. At the third, I jerked my hand away.

"There's half a dozen kicks, and you're going to learn them all, with both feet. That's the first thing. I'll show you how you work out on the korykos."

Quite suddenly, he struck at my face. I blocked the blow with a forearm and backed away. He slapped at me with his other hand, and I blocked that as well. Swiftly his right fist jabbed at my waist; I knocked it aside.

"Now let's see you tag me."

When I had pinched his nose and smacked his face, he said, "You *can* box. The prince says he's seen you drive, and you're good. It's the only thing I'd trust him on, but I'd trust him on that—these blue bloods generally know horses even when they don't know anything else. The pankration's the problem."

Pasicrates was passing us just then. Diokles called, "One more lap— as fast as you can go—and then I'll give you a rubdown!"

Seeing Pasicrates sprinting around the track, I would have thought him fresh. He seemed to fly.

"He could win," Diokles mused. "We're going to write him up for stadion, diaulos, and dolichos. By the twins, I believe he's got a chance in all of them. Friend of yours?"

I said that I supposed he was.

"He says the girl's yours, but you and him are partners in the boy."

It seemed safest to nod, so I did.

"You leave them both alone till after, understand? I told him and now I'm telling you. Don't touch them, or anybody!"

Io sits watching me, but I will write no more.

Today, when I was very tired, Io led me to a grove in secret. The woman had wine, and had brought a cloth for us to lie on. I drank, and explained that I had no interest in her and no money. She laughed and rubbed my manhood between her fingers; but after a time we returned here.

———

Diokles sat down beside me after the second meal. He said, "Latro, I can't quite figure you out," and I told him he had no reason to.

"I've got to earn my fee." He spat. "The old judge, he thinks that if you don't win, they're not going to pay."

I nodded, knowing what he had said was true.

"Well, he's wrong about that. We're all hooked up with the oracle here, see? We've got to be. We have to make an offering every year after the games, and believe me it's a lot. But when somebody don't pay up, the priests go after him. So I'll get my money, and quick, too. Are you listening to me?"

I said that I was.

"But in your case—what's wrong with you, anyhow? Tell me."

I said that I did not know, then that it did not matter.

"Huh! Not to you, maybe, but it does to me. You want to win, don't you?"

"I suppose so."

"All right, then let me tell you something. In any event you can name, the ability a man's born with counts for a lot. That's a gift from the gods. Nobody can change it. Condition counts for a lot, too—it's very important. Then there's all the training he gets, and the tips from somebody like me who's done it here, done it at Olympia, done it at Nemea and Isthmia a dozen times. Things like that can make a big difference. But the most important thing is what's in a man's heart— whether he wants to win so much that he'll do whatever winning takes. You know the story they tell about Heracles and the cart?"

I did not, nor did I care to; yet I will set it down here because I must write something. (I am afraid that if I cease to write, I may throw myself upon my sword. There is a spirit in me that longs for it, and my hand strays to the hilt whenever I lay the stylus down.)

"This farmer," Diokles said, "had been trying to drive his cart along a narrow road, and it had slipped off into the ditch. 'Father Zeus,' he prayed, 'send me help, please! I'll never get this thing out by myself.'

"Just then, who should come along the road but Heracles of Hill, the strongest man in the entire world. 'Praise to Zeus,' said the farmer, 'who's sent you in answer to my prayer. Noble Heracles, won't you hoist this old wreck of a cart out of this ditch for me? You might help my oxen up, too.'

"But Heracles just laughed. 'Father Zeus hasn't heard a word you've said,' he told him, 'and I passed this way by pure chance. Now take your whip in your right hand and the ox goad in your left. Lay your shoulder to that wheel, and shout and curse your oxen with all your might. That's the only way that Father Zeus ever hears a man.'

"And it's a fact," Diokles affirmed. "I've seen men win, and boys, too, that didn't have a chance. Winded and out of it, and nine or ten strides behind, then beating somebody they had no business ever to beat. Some god sees them, see? 'Well,' he says, 'ain't he the plucky little 'un. I think I'll just puff him along a ways.' "

When I said nothing, Diokles finished, "There isn't any god going to do that for you. Not the way you are."

I spoke to him then of my feelings, as I have not spoken to anyone, not even little Io. I do not recall all the many, weary words I used, but what I said was this: that it seems to me that there is nothing to be found upon earth but treachery and hatred and the lust for blood and more blood. Man is a wolf to men, a vile predator that preys upon its own kind. I know that is true of me, however much I detest it. I know, as well, that it is true of everyone else, without exception; and that most of them do not even detest it as I do.

I ceased to write and, fearing my sword, shut it away in my chest; then I sought a lonely road, down which I walked for many stades. At length it seemed to me that another kept me company. At first I could not see him. After some while, there came a shadowy figure there, and at last a man who seemed as solid as I. I asked whether he was a ghost, and he freely acknowledged that it was so.

"You don't have to be afraid of me on that account," the ghost told me. "Most people are dead—you live ones are just sort of taking a holiday, and it'll soon be over. We'll laugh about all this then. Say, remember helping me with that rock?"

I did not, but I said nothing.

"They let me come because you did that. Our queen said it would be all right—they're a queer lot, sometimes. Did I ever tell you why she and our king were so down on me? It's a pretty good story."

The ghost waited for an answer, so I shook my head; he must have seen it in the moonlight.

He chuckled. "Well, back before I died, I decided I wasn't likely to care much for the Lands of the Dead; so I got my wife, Merope, to promise that no matter what anybody said she wouldn't bury my carcass, or burn it, either. Merope's a good girl—not too bright, or she'd never have married me; but once she pledges her word on a thing, that's the end of it. She'll do it if it kills her."

I said, "I see."

"You don't see *her*." He pointed toward a cluster of stars. "She's the one you can't see—the family's never forgiven her. Well, anyway, I died—being a mortal, you know—and Merope laid my body out and left it there, just like she'd promised. Pretty soon it was stinking up the whole palace, but Merope wouldn't let anybody touch it.

"As soon as it got ripe enough that people were kicking up quite a fuss, I went to our king. 'Let me return to the Lands of the Living,' I said, 'and revenge myself upon this faithless wife of mine who won't even give me a decent burial.' You see, I knew how seriously he takes these things.

"Well, to make a long story short, they let me out. I ran off and hid, and had a wonderful time until they finally fetched me back. I'm not going to do that this time, though—they might find me another rock."

His voice grew serious. "What I came to tell you, friend, was that we've been looking into <u>killing</u> Pasicrates."

"If you wish," I said.

The ghost laid a hand on my shoulder, and though it seemed that of a living man, it was as cold as ice. "Most of us agree it's an awfully attractive idea, but our seers tell us that it doesn't look as if it would be of any help to you until you're dead yourself."

"Which will be soon," I said.

"You're right, and that's precisely why you shouldn't rush things, my friend. Anyway, since killing him won't help, we're going to have to force him to let go. That Elata's a nice girl, by the way. She reminds me a lot of Merope, and she's on your side for old times' sake, as well as your having promised the Huntress that you'd fix the race. She got that mantis of hers to look into it for us, and he agrees with Amyklos. Amyklos is on your side because of his nephew, of course."

When I returned here, I found that someone had draped an old cloak across two stools as if to curtain the place where I would sleep. I thought nothing of it; but when I lay down, I found that a woman lay beside me.

"You've been mourning," she explained. "I've come to kiss your tears away."

How sinuous her body was, fragrant and smooth with perfumed oil! Perhaps it was that the ghost had brought me hope, perhaps only that she was somehow different; but though I had been able to do nothing with the woman with the wine, with her I was a man again.

Afterward, we walked hand in hand by moonlight. "I know you," she told me. "No wonder I had that dream! I'm in love with you."

Her name is Anysia.

"Diokles the gymnastes sent me," she said, and pressed some coins into my hand. "Here's what he gave. Return it to him—or keep it yourself if you like."

I slept well after she had gone, but not for long, I think. Now I am awake again; the sun is not yet above the mountaintops.

# FORTY

## *For the Sake of Days Past*

E LATA IS KIND TO ME, partly because I have promised the Huntress that a race will end as she wishes—or so the ghost said. After I read what I had written, I asked who Elata was. Io explained that we met her, and Hegesistratus her husband, in the north; Io called him a mantis, as the ghost had. Elata, it seems, was the woman with the wine of whom I wrote.

"They're here with a five-tests man from Zakunthios, and to consult the oracle. Zakunthios isn't big enough to have someone in every event, the way Rope does."

She wanted to know whether I recalled meeting with Elata in the grove. I admitted I did not, but said that I had read of it here, at which she blushed. "Elata thought she might be able to cheer you up," she told me, "so I said that if it would make you better it was all right with me. And you really *are* better, but I think it's the special food. Kichesippos had a big fight with Diokles about that, and Amyklos looked like he was getting ready to fight both of them. He says more barley and no meat at all."

I told her that I would eat whatever my physicians wished, if only it would help me remember.

"It isn't that now," Io said. "It's just to help you feel better, and I think it's working, a little. You're writing more in your book, and that's a good sign."

Io said, too, that this Hegesistratus is eager to see me but will not come to our pavilion. He is afraid of the Rope Makers. There is a truce everywhere in Hellas in honor of the games, but he does not trust them even so.

The Huntress is a goddess, Io says. She knows nothing of a promise

I made her, but she says I may have taken an oath at her temple in
Rope. The black man would not let Io and Polos go to the temple with
me.

He and his wife will accompany Pasicrates, Tisamenus, and me this
morning, when we go into Dolphins with Diokles to have our names
entered in the rolls. Now we are waiting for Diokles.

While waiting I have read about many past days. *"Pharetra, 'bowcase,' is as like it as any word I know, though she laughed at me."* My heart
leaped when I read that. What has become of her? Perhaps she died of
her wound.


Tisamenus came to speak with the black man and me. I know that Io
does not like him, but he seems friendly and polite, and everyone defers
to him because he is said to be an illustrious mantis. "Last night I
conferred with Trioditis concerning you," he told me. "She will do all
that lies in her power to aid you, provided you do all that lies in yours
to aid Rope. 'The queen must win,' she said, 'and thus the queen must
lose.' Does that convey any meaning to you?"

I shook my head, and so did the black man.

"I feel certain it is Queen Gorgo, her priestess, who must win,"
Tisamenus told us. "When you drive for our prince regent, sir, you will
represent her as well. The rest we must strive to understand.

"By favor of divine Trioditis you are improved," Tisamenus continued. "Your thoughts, I hope, haven't turned to the taking of your own
life?"

I did not reply, at which the black man stared at me.

Tisamenus said gently, "When the soul has been overwhelmed by
grief, sir, as yours has been, a man does nothing that he is not compelled
to do, for then he believes that nothing can help him. At such times,
he is no danger to himself or anyone else. But as the claws fall away,
hope—the final horror, if I may say it, from that deadly box the gods
packed for men—hope returns. It is then that his family and friends
must watch a man, because he's apt to think that by putting an end to
his life he'll put an end to his sorrows."

I confessed then that such thoughts had sometimes stirred in me.

"Never trust them, sir." Kindly, he laid his hand upon my knee.
"Trust me instead. I've trafficked with many ghosts, and they are less

happy even than we, and envy us. I've heard that while you crossed the barbarian lands you journeyed for a time in the company of Hegesistratus the Tellidian?"

I nodded, recalling what Io had said about him.

Tisamenus shook his head. "He is a great mantis, sir, and is now counted by some the head of our clan, though he dare not show his face in Elis. But he is consumed with malice, sir. I am his kinsman, and I find those words as bitter as gall in my mouth. Yet they are true. He is the sworn foe of Rope, and has said that he will destroy it, if it does not destroy him."

Here the black man made several quick gestures. I did not understand most of them, but one certainly represented a dagger plunged into his own chest.

"It's true," Tisamenus told us, "that Rope imprisoned him, and that he escaped as you describe." He heaved a sigh. "With what infinite patience the gods labor to teach us! We speak at times of a man who will stop at nothing; I have not infrequently spoken thus myself. And yet it never strikes us, when we must deal with such a man, that he will, in fact, stop at nothing."

Tisamenus pierced me with his eyes. "But he had slandered our city, sir—your own and mine. You forget, hmm? You haven't forgotten, I hope, that you've been proclaimed a resident of the most glorious city in Hellas?"

The truth is that I remember nothing of that, but out of politeness I said, "Certainly not."

"And I"—Tisamenus touched his chest—"I have been granted a like privilege. We're her adopted sons, sir, both of us. You will have heard before this, no doubt, that the noble Pasicrates desires to marry in order that he may adopt the little barbarian called Polos. Tell me, sir, who owes the greater loyalty to his father? Is it the son of his body, or one he has adopted?"

I said that I supposed the adopted son owed more, for his father had been his rescuer as well.

"Nicely reasoned, sir! Consider my position, then, if you will. I was in Elis, where I still maintain the house that once I shared with my wife, for the Italoan Festival. There, too, was my cousin, leveling the grossest insults and the vilest slanders against the very city that had a short time before honored me by making me her son. What was I to do? Sit silent and appear by my silence to consent? I essayed a response to his defamations, and was shouted down by men I had known—had numbered among my friends, in fact—since boyhood. In desperation, I dispatched a letter to our patron and another to my good friend Cyklos, both carried by the swiftest of my slaves. In them I recounted what I had seen and heard, and urged that they warn my cousin that he was making enemies of many who would greatly have preferred to be his friends. Would you not have done the same?"

I agreed that I would, though I would probably have gone to Rope myself to hurry things along.

"Just so, sir. As it happened, the prince regent had not yet returned to the city, but Cyklos dispatched several trusted officers to reason with my cousin. They came as a delegation, you understand, and not a military force. I believe there were five or six all told. Elis welcomed them, and when they found that nothing they could say would sway my cousin, they invited him to visit Rope, where he might speak with Cyklos in person, pointing out that he had never troubled to see for himself the modest place to which he had imputed so much evil. He demurred; they insisted, and at last, having received permission from the magistrates, placed him under restraint and carried him to Rope by main force. Do you know how criminals are commonly confined, sir, in Rope?"

I did not, nor did the black man.

"They are flung into pits, sir, and afterward their food is thrown down to them. Nothing of the sort, you may be sure, was done to my ill-mannered cousin. Instead Cyklos himself, one of the most distinguished men in our city, welcomed him as a guest in his own home, though he was later forced to confine him when he insisted upon leaving at once.

"As I was about to say, I think it likely that my cousin is responsible for the sorrow that oppresses you. It is more than possible that he has charmed you in some way. I wished to speak with you now because I have heard that he is here for the games. I trust that you recall his appearance? If not, your friend can point him out to you."

When I wrote that which stands above, I had no notion that we would in fact encounter this man, who seems generally to be called Hegesistratus of Elis, so quickly. Diokles came (which was why I stopped writing), and we went to the place where the judges of the games sit to receive those who wish to take part—we were a great throng, come as I soon learned not only from all parts of Hellas, but from every other place where the Hellenes' tongue is spoken.

In this courtyard in Dolphins many were examined at length, for the rule is that only Hellenes may compete. The black man's wife told me, in fact, that he had been anxious to take part in the stadion and the javelin throwing, but had been told that he could not, though he had offered to pay his own fees. We waited there for some while before we were permitted to address one of the hellanodikai.

This man knew Diokles and greeted him by name. Diokles in turn introduced the rest of us and explained that the black man understood that he would not be allowed to compete, but that he wished to study the way in which the games were conducted with an eye to establishing a similar event among his own countrymen. Pasicrates's name was entered on three rolls as soon as his fees had been paid.

"Are you a Hellene?" the hellanodikas asked after looking long at my face.

I said, "Certainly," and explained as Tisamenus and Diokles had instructed me that I had been made a citizen of Rope.

"That's bronze-bound, Agatharchos," Diokles declared when I had finished. "I got it straight from King Pausanias. I wasn't going to take him on until I did."

"I see." The hellanodikas fingered his beard.

"He will drive His Highness's chariot," Tisamenus told him. "I myself have been made a Rope Maker, as you may know already; I am commonly called Tisamenus of Elis. The noble Pasicrates, a Rope Maker by birth, will vouch for him as well, I feel certain."

All eyes turned toward the one-armed man, who said with the intonation of a serpent, "He is a resident of my city—but he is no Hellene."

At these words, I saw something I would never have thought to see. Tisamenus whirled and raised his fist to the one-armed man, who backed away with fear naked upon his face.

Deftly, Diokles stepped between them. "A little rivalry, Agatharchos. You understand."

The hellanodikas shrugged. "Better than I want to. Latros Spar-
tathen, if you're really a Hellene, let's hear you spout some poetry."

I confessed that I did not remember any.

"Come, now. You must know something. How about this:

> " 'For thee, my son, I wept my life away;
> For thee through Hell's eternal dungeons stray;
> Nor came my fate by lingering pains and slow,
> Nor bent the silver-shafted queen her bow;
> No dire disease bereaved me of my breath;
> Thou, thou, my son, wert my disease and death;
> Unkindly with my love my son conspired,
> For thee I lived, for absent thee expired.' "

Sorrow swept me away—a moaning wind. My eyes filled with tears;
I could only shake my head.

"Sir," Tisamenus whispered, "you must speak now, and speak poetry, or—Cyklos does not regard you kindly."

The palace rose before me, tier upon tier. Frantically I hurried from
image to image—a man with the head of a crocodile, another with that
of a hawk.

"Well?" the hellanodikas inquired.

I tried to repeat what he had said about the silver-shafted queen,
though I did not know then—and do not know now—what it meant.
For an instant, I seemed to glimpse her behind him, her smooth, fair
face aglow above his black hair. From somewhere or noplace the half-
remembered rhymes rose to my lips:

> "You golden lyre, Apollo's and the muses',
> Your tune commands the dance, your tone he uses,
> When master of the warbling choir,
> He lifts the crystal voices higher."

Faintly I heard someone shout, "What . . . ? *Latro!*"

> "You quench the bolt, the lightning's fearful fire,
> The eagle rests his wings, that never tire;

> To hear you shaken by your song,
> Fell Ares quits the spear-proud throng."

"Latro, it's me, Pindaros!" Though he is older than I by ten years at least, and smaller, too, he wrapped me in a bear's embrace and lifted me off my feet.

"Will drive for His Highness in the chariot race," muttered the hellanodikas as he wrote. "Boxer. Pankratiast."

Pindaros and the black man danced, swinging each other like stones in a sling.

# FORTY-ONE

## *The God Himself Shall Rule*

THUS IT WAS DECIDED AFTER much argument. Pharetra is going tomorrow, with her queen, Themistocles, Hegesistratus, and the rest. Meanwhile, a score of travelers arrive each time I draw breath; and it is the talk of the town—still more so of the great camp beyond it that spreads ever wider. When Pindaros invited us to join him over wine, I doubted that there was a drop left in Dolphins, or a single place to sit; but he guided us to the inn where he stays whenever he comes here.

"Which is every four years," he told us, "each time they hold the games. I haven't won as yet, but I have high hopes—very high—for this year. And it's good publicity."

Thinking him too old for the footraces, I asked whether he boxed. He and Diokles laughed about that. (Pasicrates and the mantis were not with us, though Pindaros had invited them both. Pasicrates would not stay, while Tisamenus, I would guess, did not wish him to speak with the prince alone.)

Over our wine, Diokles and Pindaros explained the structure of the games to me. There are to be trials of music as well as strength and swiftness. For a time I ceased this writing to ask Diokles about their order again, which Kichesippos allowed; this is to be relied upon.

- Singing to the lyre. Pindaros was set down for this when we finished the wine. The verses must be contestant's own, ones never heard before.
- Flute-playing.
- Stadion—a single circuit of the track. Pasicrates will run.
- Diaulos—two circuits. Pasicrates entered this as well.

- Dolichos—twenty-four turns. Pasicrates entered.
- Five trials—they are running, throwing a diskos, jumping, casting a javelin, and wrestling.
- Wrestling.
- Boxing—I will do this.
- Pankration—this also.
- Horseracing—the prince entered Argas; Ladas will ride him.
- Stadion for boys.
- Five trials for boys.
- Boxing for boys.
- Dolichos for boys.
- Diaulos for boys.
- Chariot race—I will drive for the prince.
- Lyre-playing—Simonides will do it.
- Running in armor—the last event.

On certain days there will be several events. For example, on the first Pindaros and the rest will sing in the morning, the flute-playing will begin after the first meal, and the stadion before sunset. All the boys' events (except the horserace) will be held on the same day, and on the last, the lyre-playing will be followed by the race in armor.

Io found us while we sat over wine, bringing the news that Themistocles of Thought had come, riding in a silver chariot. I do not remember this man, but Io and the black man say that we traveled with him to the prince's city; the Amazons will use his chariot if they compete.

I should write that I believed Bittusilma the black man's wife, but both swear there is nothing between them. Polos says this is because married women may not watch.

When we had drunk the wine, we went back to the courtyard where names are set down upon the rolls so that Pindaros might enter. There we met Themistocles, a burly, jovial man in fine clothes, and Simonides, an old man. He had come to enter the lyre-playing. Themistocles told Pindaros he had come only to see the sights, and explained how the black man and I had been freed, as Bittusilma had before. It was much the same. Then Pindaros told everyone how he had gone to Hill to get the money to buy our freedom—though we were never truly slaves.

When he returned to Thought, we were gone. He left money with a woman there and went back to Hill, where he asked the wardens of the city to make Thought free us.

As I heard all this, I thought better and better of him. I know that not everyone who shouts a greeting is in fact a friend, but I think Pindaros one. I asked if he would play and sing for me, to lift my sorrow from me. I know music has that power. He said he would if I would come to him this evening. Now I do not believe it will help, though Kichesippos says that it may.

There is much more to write; I will strive to be brief.

The Amazons arrived like stones through a window, stilling all babble. Heads turned; then we saw them, five, gaunt and far taller than most men, clad in grace and ragged skins but bearing beautiful weapons. My jaw fell with the rest—but that was as nothing, for the tallest turned aside to embrace me. We kissed, and a thousand throats laughed and cheered. My cheeks burn now as I write of it. This Pharetra was my lover in Thrace. When I learned of that, I went to speak to the judges with her and the other women; but the judges ran to get others, and we were left to wait.

That was when I saw the prize for the chariot race, which I had not noticed before. It is a tall red urn, the work of some excellent artist, filled they say with the finest oil and sealed with wax. But it is more: it is the urn from my memory palace, although when I walk into the palace in my mind, it stands there also—this seems very strange to me. Black dancers with beards, and the ears and tails of horses, caper around it.

The hellanodikai returned, a dozen at least, all of them shaking their heads. No woman, they insisted, could compete. That the queen is unmarried made no difference—no women at all. Nor could anyone compete unless he was a Hellene, and none of the Amazons can speak as the Hellenes do—or only a few words.

I had not observed that Io had left us, but now she darted through the crowd to us, bringing with her a handsome, limping man with a curly beard. Themistocles greeted him as a friend, the hellanodikai hailed him, and the Amazon queen embraced him. While he was speaking with one and another, Io told me that he is a great mantis—more

famous even than Tisamenus. He was with Pharetra, Io, and me in the
north.

He speaks the tongue of Amazons, and he assured the judges that
a very great god, the god of war, had sent these women; but the judges
still refused.

When he had heard them out, he turned to Themistocles and the
old lyre-player. These three spoke together very rapidly, but their voices
were too low for us to overhear them.

When all had nodded together, Themistocles stepped forward to
address the judges—or rather, to address everyone present while pretending to address them. His booming voice filled the whole courtyard.

"You must pardon my ignorance, friends," he began. "It's been
many years now since I attended these games."

The hellanodikai and several others assured him that they were
delighted he had come this year, for it seems he is a very great man
indeed.

"I have been informed that my dear friend Prince Pausanias of Rope
has entered the chariot race," Themistocles continued. "Tell me, does
he intend to drive his chariot himself? Will the reins be in his own
hands?"

At this several of the judges pointed to me and explained that I was
to drive on behalf of the prince.

"And that's the prize, that fine red jar there? Will Latro get it if he
wins? He's a fortunate man!"

The hellanodikai hastened to explain that I would not—that it was
actually the prince who was competing, not I.

"Oh," said Themistocles. "That explains it. I know Latro, and he's
no Hellene—"

They hastened to say that they had ruled I was a Hellene, and that
I had been permitted to enter two events.

"But not the chariot race," said Themistocles. "Clearly, it is the
prince who is the contestant in that. Tell me, is it lawful for a woman
*not* to enter?"

At this the judges looked perplexed indeed. They whispered among
themselves, then said that since women could not enter, it was of course
implied by the rules that they need not enter.

"Wonderful!" Themistocles rubbed his big hands together and smiled broadly. "But I might enter? I am both a man and a Hellene, and I have a fine chariot."

The judges said that they would be delighted to have him enter; there was no question of his qualifications.

"Then I'll do it," he told them. "Put down my name, please. I'm Themistocles Athanaios, and this woman is to drive for me." Here he pointed to Pharetra.

Afterward I kicked the korykos, instructed by Diokles. It is a pig-skin filled with meal, suspended by a rope. Agatharchos the hellanodikas came to watch me because my name is upon three rolls now. He told me that many who have been set down will be struck off when the judges have seen them practice, but I will not be. Diokles says that I am better, that he still does not approve of love in advance of the games, but that he made a good investment. I did not follow him; and though Io watches me as I write, I hesitate to ask her. I feel I— There are cliffs here from which a man might throw himself onto rocks or into the sea.

I have had a strange evening and a very strange dream. I will write here of what actually happened first; then if there is time, recount the dream; then if there is still time, how I feel now. That is most important of all, but I do not think it apt to change again, so I may write of it whenever I choose.

Io and I went to the inn where we had drunk with the poet. He welcomed us and, seeing how fatigued I was, suggested that I stretch myself upon his bed while he sang. I did, thinking all the while: thus it is for the dead—a rest from which they need not rise. It was then that I dreamed my dream.

The poet said, *"I'm afraid that's all for tonight. I don't dare strain my voice."*

At these words I sat up.

Io was crying. She hugged and kissed the poet, saying over and over how lovely his music and verses had been. As for me, I recalled not a single line. But I felt myself a hero who might raze cities or raise new ones; and so I grinned like an idiot as I embraced him, pounding his back while he pounded mine.

"I knew hearing me would help," he said. "If you hadn't an ear for poetry—yes, and a heart for it, too—you wouldn't have remembered that scrap of mine I heard you recite for the judges this morning. Not you of all men, because you forget everything; but the Shining God heals, Parnassos is his place, and he's our patron."

It was pitch dark when Io and I left the poet's inn for the streets of Dolphins; we had a long walk ahead of us, and I found myself wishing I had brought my sword.

"Pindaros must be the greatest poet in the world," Io told me. "And just think—he's our friend!"

I asked whether I had snored.

"Did you nod off? Master, you couldn't have—it was too wonderful. Besides, your eyes were open the whole time."

I said, "I was afraid I had, just for a moment. It seemed I'd missed a verse or two."

Io shook her head. "Well, you certainly didn't snore—I would have shaken you right away. And you're so much better! Even Diokles says so. It was not seeing Pharetra, wasn't it? You've been pining for her, but now that she's here you're all right again."

A new voice announced, "She is closer than you think," and the lame man hobbled through an archway, followed by the Amazon queen, Pharetra herself, and a slender woman whose floating hair did not even reach Pharetra's shoulder.

Io said, "Hegesistratus! Oh, I'm so happy! Latro's so much better now."

"And so he ought to be," Hegesistratus agreed. Pharetra slipped her hand into mine.

The queen spoke using the tongue of Amazons, which I do not understand; and Hegesistratus said, "We are going out to have a look at the horses. Would you like to see them, too? They will be racing against yours."

We went to the Amazons' camp, where the other three guarded their horses. They held up brands so we might see them. Surely there have never been better ones! They gleamed like flames in the torchlight, snorting and stamping. Io said how good it was of Themistocles to help the women as he has, and of the lame man to enlist Themistocles's help for them. The lame man only shook his head and spat into the fire. "He has become a friend of the Rope Makers," he told her. "For the good of the world, he must be discredited, and they destroyed." Afterward, he cautioned us to say nothing of this.

The lame man remained behind with the queen and the other women when we left, but Pharetra came with Io and me. A woman was in my bed; when she saw Pharetra, she attacked her with a little dagger. It woke the prince—Cyklos—everyone, but they were not angry and cheered the women as they fought. Pharetra knocked the dagger from the smaller woman's hand, caught her at last, and threw her into a ditch.

When everyone had gone back to sleep, Pharetra lay beside me, and though she is as large as a large man, her kisses were a woman's. I loved her very much. She speaks a few words of the Hellenes' tongue, and she told me that once she and I tended the white horses in a cave. She wanted to know whether I remembered Hippostizein, who died in the north. (I do not.) Late at night, she told me, fear comes upon her. If she loses when we race our chariots, her queen will surely offer her to appease their god. I held her very tightly after that. She woke me when she left, and thus I write here as I do, having carried this lamp outside and lit it from the embers.

This was my dream.

A boy stood beside the bed. When I turned my head to look, I saw he was younger than Polos. His feet tapped the floor, for they were those of a kid; horns budded from his forehead. "Come with me," he told me, and we went out into the mountain town, up a crooked street, then climbed steep slopes.

"You're a faun," I said. "Fauns bring dreams." Someone had told me that—I do not recall who.

He nodded, "I bring you." His kid feet climbed the rocks better than my human ones.

We reached a little temple where a fire blazed on the altar. Here is something very strange—a lovely woman made me welcome, and later I was to meet her waking. No doubt I had met her this morning, and she had lingered in my thoughts. Polos and Amyklos were there, both horses from the waist down. Polos frolicked between the temple and the trees. "Don't be afraid," he said. I told him that I wished to die, thus nothing held terrors for me. But the last was a lie.

Tisamenus and Pasicrates came, attended by my servant and conducted by a strange, sly man who grinned when he caught sight of me.

Hounds bayed. Later, when we admired the Amazons' white horses, the lame man asked whether I heard hounds. I did not, as I told him. I did not tell him I had heard them earlier in my dream.

"Take back your hand," the woman said to Pasicrates. "Take it back, if ever you hope for rest."

The one-armed man snapped, "He took it from me; let him keep it." Tisamenus murmured, "It's you, then. You're doing this. Now that I know it, I may break the charm."

"There is no charm," Amyklos told him. "Only hate."

"In that case he must die, sir." Tisamenus nodded his own confirmation. "Cyklos is weighing that already, because of—" He jerked his head toward Polos. "He's not one of them. Such loves are dangerous."

Aglaus said, "If you're harming my master—"

Pasicrates struck him in the throat. Aglaus fell, and did not rise again. At once Amyklos was upon Pasicrates, stallion and rider, too, knocking him off his feet and planting both front hooves upon his chest. Pasicrates stared up, pop-eyed, as Amyklos mocked him. "You preen yourself upon strength, swiftness, and courage. Look at me! Old, but stronger and faster than you are—or will ever be. And braver, too. What are all your boasted qualities compared to any charger's?"

Grim, the woman crouched beside Pasicrates. "Don't deceive yourself. Do you think this only a dream? Death here is death, and Amyklos could kill you easily. Those you call friends will find you dead where you slept. Your prince will have forgotten you long before the sun breeds worms in your corpse."

I helped Aglaus stand, then asked Pasicrates what he had done that had roused such wrath against us in these people; but he would neither look at me nor reply. Polos begged his uncle to allow Pasicrates to sit up. "You want me to love you," Polos told Pasicrates, "and I *want* to. Truly I do."

Something stirred in me, like a spider on its web.

"I *would* love you," Polos said. "I promise I will."

Standing next to the woman, I had bent over Pasicrates to speak to him. Now he reached toward me with his stump of arm; when he withdrew it, it was a whole one like my own. Far away, someone said, *"That's all for tonight. I don't dare strain my voice."*

———

I have watched the sun rise. I forget, I know, but I have not forgotten the night that crushed me like the horse-Amyklos of my nightmare; thus I write as I do, hoping that if it returns I will read this.

A man's life is indeed short, ending in death. If it were long, his days would be of small value. If there were no death, of none. Let him fill each day with honor and joy. Let him not condemn himself or another, for he does not know the laws of his existence or theirs. If he sleeps in death, let him sleep. If while sleeping he should meet a god, he must let the god decide how well or ill he lived.

The god he meets must rule upon a man's life, never the man himself.

# FORTY-TWO

## *Pausanias Rages*

IO SAYS THAT WHEN KICHESIPPOS came to speak about me, the prince struck him. I think it shameful to strike so aged and learned a man. So does Pausanias—I saw it in his face—but he struck him nonetheless.

"The gods toy with me." Thus he spoke to Tisamenus when he summoned us. "They give me the greatest victory in history and tear its fruits from my hands."

"The Hellenes should restore your goods to you," Tisamenus told him. "They're deeply in your debt."

"I can't ask that!"

"Of course not, Your Highness." Tisamenus rubbed his plump chin and rolled his eyes to heaven. "Yet some others might urge such gratitude—without so much as a hint from Your Highness, to be sure. Themistocles is here; and Simonides, the poet, is with him."

Here is what happened. I learned of it bit by bit, and the last only by going to the agora and speaking to the Crimson Men held there under guard. Pausanias entrusted the spoils of his victory to their ship; they had been promised a safe passage by Tower Hill, but they were overtaken and boarded by a ship from Hundred-Eyed, and towed to a port at the foot of the mountain. By this he has lost a fortune.

Their captain knows me. Muslak is his name. Not wishing him to see how I forget, I hailed him in return when he hailed me. *Lewqys,* he called me, and perhaps that is my name; surely no man is really named Latro.

He said, "I knew you'd come back when you could come alone. You didn't want the old man to know we're friends, did you? But we hoped you'd come sooner."

GENE WOLFE

I told him I had seen no point in returning until I learned their situation, though the truth was that I had no notion how I might help them. When one understands nothing yet must speak, it is best to question. I asked a great many. When I wanted to know whether he would return me to my home if I were to free him and his crew, and return their ship to them, his eyes flew wide. He swore he would. He assured me he knew the place, pointing to the west. *Luhitu* was the word he used. We spoke as the Crimson Men do, so that their guards would not understand.

I still do not know what can be done, but I know that for gold these Hellenes will connive at anything. Io has some, as I saw when she got out the coin I gave Aglaus.

The prince watched me box with Diokles. We wear himantes to protect our hands and do not strike hard. Diokles is quick and wary; as I explained to the prince, that is what is needed in practice.

"You seem cheerful enough today," he told me.

I showed him how Diokles tricks me with his left hand, and explained how much trouble that had given me. "So I've learned something new, Your Highness. I will forget where I learned it, I know. But I think not what I have learned."

He grinned and slapped my shoulder. His scars give him an evil face, but I do not believe an evil heart beats beneath it. "It was you that cured him, wasn't it, Diokles?"

Diokles spat. "He cured himself, Highness, by doing what I told him. I might have helped a little."

"I feel sure you did. I've been keeping track of Latro's physicians, or trying to. He's been cured by Kichesippos and Tisamenus (who had a wondrous vision last night, by the way). And by Amyklos, I'm sure, although he hasn't come around yet to claim the credit for it. Yes, and by his slippery little wench Io. That's four. And now by himself and you, which makes six. Is there anybody else? How about Polos?"

Recalling the dream of which I wrote at sunup, I told him, "Yes, Highness, by Polos and Pasicrates. But by Polos most of all."

"That brings my total to eight—I shall win the laurels for certain. But I wanted to ask both of you something about Polos. Latro, can you recall what Tisamenus told me concerning him this morning?"

"Certainly. That he should ride Argas for you."

"You have the ear of the gods, Latro, as I've said before—whether you know it or not. So do you agree?"

I shrugged. "Does Polos want to?"

"I haven't asked him."

Diokles spat again. " 'Course he does. He's asked me about the boys' events, wanting to get into everything. I had to tell him he couldn't, and those big boys would thresh him anyhow. But he's lighter than Ladas. That's always good. Besides, you never saw such a hand with horses."

Aglaus rubbed me while Diokles did the same for Pasicrates. "What a dream I had! You knocked me down, then helped me up."

I have forgotten my own dream, but I had read of it here. I asked whether he was certain it had been I.

"Sure, because I thought you'd hit me again when you lifted me. My neck's sore—that brought on the dream, I suppose."

Pasicrates remarked that such a dream seemed a good omen for a boxer.

"No more boxing for Latro," Diokles told him. He counted on his fingers. "He's only got four days till the real thing, and he mustn't carry bruises into it."

I should say here that no boxer would hit a man again after helping him rise—when a man has been knocked down, the fight is over. It is only in the pankration that a man knocked down may continue to fight.

Afterward, Pasicrates spoke with me in private. "I had a dream, too," he said, "but in mine it was I who struck Aglaus." I said nothing, and he continued, "When you saw how angry I was, you asked whether I wanted my hand back. I was angry at you—I suppose I struck Aglaus because he's your servant—and I said that since you had taken it you might keep it. I felt that if you returned it, I would have to end our quarrel, you see."

I said that if that was the case, I certainly hoped I had given it back to him.

"You did. We rode to your quarters, and you got it out of your chest. Your sword lay on top; under it were chitons and so on. You kept pulling things out and putting them on the ground. My hand was at the very bottom. I took it out and stuck it on my arm somehow."

He laughed, and I laughed with him. "I hope you helped me repack my clothes."

"I don't remember. But the truly odd part is that all day I've felt as if I really had it back: like a complete man again. I can do anything that anybody with two hands can, after all—except play the lyre, perhaps."

Tisamenus took me to the prince, and the three of us called upon Orsippos. Tisamenus says he is a warden of Hundred-Eyed and its richest citizen. At first, I could not understand why I had been brought to be stared at by Orsippos, who is fat and has lost hair at the crown. Later I realized that it is because the prince has bet with him and he wished to see me. Their bet on the chariots was doubled.

Though it made some other Rope Makers angry, Pasicrates and I marched side by side at the opening of the games; the ceremony was extremely impressive. Afterward, the Babylonian, the black man, and the children found us; and we remained with them in the stadium to hear a poet from Cowland. Pasicrates ridiculed his twanging accent at first, but soon acknowledged him the best of all. The hellanodikai were of the same opinion, awarding him the laurels. He is certainly a friend, as Io says he is, for he talked with us for a time though a hundred at least were waiting to speak with him.

The stadium is very fine; its lower seats are stone, though the upper ones are wooden. It is open at each end so that those who please the god may come and go. The oval track is exactly a stade in length—we marched around this. All the poets brought stools; they sat in the center, with their stools on the grass. The listeners left their seats to gather around their favorites. By the time the contest was over, the crowd around our poet was very large indeed.

I have begun to read this from the beginning. Today I read about Artaÿctes and his son, but learned little of use. I have told Aglaus that he must speak to me each day, privately, about the slaves in the market; and I have told him what he must say.

Pasicrates ran well but did not win; the prince was angry. At his command, Tisamenus and Diokles sought to have my name set down in the wrestlers' roll, but the judges would not permit it, saying it is too late.

This has been an unquiet night—laughter, I find, can be as hard to bear as any blow. Pharetra lay with me, and for a time we talked of bows and the like, she having visited the house of a man who deals in such things. His swords, she says, are fine, his bows not bad. I told her to find out whether he would sell her bows, arrows, and swords without asking why she required them. When she said she had nothing to trade, I explained that I would supply her with money. She has learned enough of Io's tongue to make herself understood.

The other woman came. She did not dare enter the pavilion but screamed at Pharetra, calling her a wild cow and many other names; she roused everyone. Pharetra chased her away, but even Polos laughed at us. I could not remain. I write this by the fire of a knowing man with a wooden foot. He has consulted the gods for me, and says I will do well in the games, and score my greatest triumph in the chariot race. I have been considering what I must do, and feel sure he is correct.

Today was the day of the diaulos, the most popular of all the footraces. Elimination heats were held in the morning, the great event at evening. Pasicrates ran so well that it seemed to all of us that he had won, but the judges ruled in favor of another. The distance between them cannot have been more than the width of a man's thumb.

Diokles taught me wrestling. He calls it the least useful part of the pankration, but says that I should know it as well as the rest. He taught me several valuable holds, but when we actually wrestled, I beat him easily.

The poet with many rings is composing an ode to honor the winner of the stadion; the man's city will pay.

A man from the Isle of Roses has won the dolichos. It was terrible to hear the blows and see Pasicrates's face afterward; I should have knocked the mantis and the old physician aside and stopped it. When it was over, he called Polos to him and kissed him, and embraced me as a brother. He limps, as I noticed after the race, when he thinks himself unobserved. Now the prince has sent him to Tower Hill, telling him not to return without gold.

This was the day of the five trials. I did not go to the stadium with the others but into the town, hoping to buy a stall for Aglaus. The market was empty, however, because everyone had gone to the games. I was ready to leave when Anysia invited me to share the first meal with her; thinking she would want money, I told her I would not lie with a woman until after the chariot race. She took my arm and said I need not, that she wished to speak with me. When everyone returned to eat, we ate, too; I found an old woman (cast in eye, south side of the agora) very ready to sell her little fruit stall. Later Anysia and I went to the stadium with the rest.

Here is everything Anysia told me before the first meal; it is certainly important if it is true, and perhaps even if it is not. She is from Thespiae, west of Hill, and lives by dancing. Tonight I watched her in the red glare of the torches—how like a goddess she appeared!

"I'm your true love," she said. "You forget, and so you can't really know love, but I love you and I'll never forget you. I'm as true a love as you will ever have. Do you think you love Pharetra?"

"I must," I told her. "My heart leaped when you spoke her name."

Anysia seemed to study me. "You probably won't believe me, but the Amazon you think is your Pharetra isn't. Your Pharetra died in Thrace."

I felt then that I had heard my own death sentence.

"There's a certain Amazon," Anysia continued, "who others may tell you is Pharetra. She's very tall and strong, and has brown hair. Do you know the one I mean?"

Io had described such a woman when we woke, calling her Pharetra.

"Her name's really Hippostizein. She was a comrade of your Pharetra, who was quite a bit shorter and had red hair. Seeing how you grieved and knowing you forget, your slave told you this woman was Pharetra, after she volunteered to play the part."

I said nothing.

"They laugh about it behind your back, no doubt, and think themselves extremely clever; but your slave girl, at least, has exchanged her happiness for yours. Or so I'm told."

I nodded, for I feel that I understand.

"As a favor to me, who've told you the plain truth, please don't beat her too severely—I've been beaten myself, a time or two. You can kill the tall one for all I care."

I shook my head, knowing that I would harm neither Io nor the tall woman. "How did you learn all this?"

"From someone I met last night. I'd danced a long time and was tired, but music woke me. I've never heard music like that. I followed it, hoping that I could get the piper to join us, and since I was thinking about how I'd dance to his music, I started to dance as I turned over the steps. When I spun around, this woman—Elata's her name—was dancing, too, following me. She's beautiful, and a wonderful dancer, by the way.

"When the music stopped, she asked why I'd been crying. I told her about you and all the awful things the Amazon had done to me, calling her Pharetra, which was what somebody told me her name was. And she—this Elata—explained that she'd known both of them in the north, and that Pharetra was dead. Your slave had talked to her husband about it, and he had the Amazon kiss you."

We spoke a good deal more, she telling me much concerning a dancer's life that I will not set down here. She said that she loved me. I told her I could not marry her, or anyone, until I found my home; and that even after I found it, I might be in no position to marry. She said she wanted my love, not my property—this is a new idea for me, I think. At first she assumed that I forgot with every cup, and when I had proved that I remembered everything we had said in the market, that I recalled much that I do not—how the tall Amazon she calls Hippostizein had pushed her into some water, for example.

I, too, will call her Hippostizein, for I think that Anysia spoke the truth. But I need her if I am to free the friends who know where my home lies, and thus I must say nothing to her. I did not speak with them today for fear their guards would become suspicious.

Polos came to watch me exercise the horses. As Diokles and I rubbed them down, he asked me to explain *arete*. "I know Ares is the war god here," he said, "like Pleistorus. But this isn't war. How can anybody say that the man who runs fastest shows his *arete*?"

"It isn't the man who runs best who runs from the enemy," I told him, "and sometimes you want your men to run. When they do, you'd like to see them escape so they can fight again, on better terms or from a better position."

Diokles spat. "War isn't all blood and death, lad. And it isn't always the biggest army that wins. Pretty often it's the one that drills the best, and keeps its armor clean, and stands up best to long marches on short rations. Old Ares isn't some kind of monster, see? Think of him as a plain man that wants to win the war and get back home to Aphrodite. He's for training, discipline, and fair play with the men. And he whistles when he loses just like he whistles when he wins."

I asked Diokles then whether other events are to be held on the day of the chariot race; he said not. Thus my friends will be left in the market, perhaps, to wait the return of the crowd—at least I must hope so. Wrestling tomorrow, but I must go to Cyparissa to see the ship. I have ordered Aglaus to remind me of it. I should not have mentioned the ship to the dancer, but she cannot have guessed what I plan.

The road to the coast is steep, and narrow in many places. All that is good, but I could wish it not so long. It will be dark, or twilight at least. The ship is unguarded, moored with a single cable. It will be hard to conceal my sword—perhaps it can be tied beneath the chariot. I must try this.

There are marble seats above the wooden ones. I saw them and the watchers there, when I stunned the last man; but when I pointed them out to Io, she could not see them, though a woman there waved to us.

The prize was a beautiful dish full of the finest figs. I gave them to everyone who wanted one and presented the dish to Prince Pausanias, who was very pleased. He put his arm about my shoulders—a signal honor. He won a large sum by betting on me.

The judge has drawn up a deed for me by which I give the children to the poet from Hill. I signed it and left it with him; thus Io at least will return to her city. The all-power fighting is tomorrow.

They say the Amazon will drive the horses of the sun, but it is I who will drive like the sun himself. When I cut the harness, we will have four riders; the rest must fight on foot.

# FORTY-THREE

## *Pindaros of Thebes*

MAKES THIS OFFERING TO THE Shining God, his patron, ever the patron of letters, whom he dares call his friend. The pythia has asked him to do this so that it may be known how the god worked his will.

A queen out of the north brought to the god's games his own flashing horses, deep-chested and headed like bulls, with fiery eyes. About the track they thundered, behind them the brightest gift of the merciful Lacedaemonians, lent by Neocles's son, ship-commanding Themistocles. A second turn. Lo, the Dorian chariot holds the pace stride for stride. Crowned still with the sacred boughs of Daphne—fairest daughter of the river—the conquering pankratiast guides it, Latros of Sparta (whom once I conducted as the god directed me) smiling upon the god's virgin handmaid. Five others are crusted with the showering dust. At the sight the cheers of the Hellenes ring loud, like the beating of bright shields.

As a skillful hand strokes the strings, the god's servant, the dark spearman's daughter, restrains her eight-reined team, forewarned of the fast-approaching turn. By a head—a neck—half a length, the mighty four, speechless slaves of Heracles's heir, best in battle, outreach them. So Latros drives. So drove Diomedes, when heroes mourned the son of Menoetius—but drove a straight road.

Before Latros a thousand scatter as quail, war-tried heroes who crushed the barbarian upon the Boeotian Plain, frightened as children, fleeing like the sad Asteria before the earthshaking steed of Poseidon, parting as the wave before the prow of *Argo*. None pursue the flying Latros, for none can.

Now what need of speed or dust? What envious hopes strain after

the argent chariot of the gray-eyed Athena? This lordly urn, the gift of
the god, her servant receives, presents in his turn to the virgin queen—
thus is peace forged between Theseus's foes and Theseus's city. Hippephode receives it glorying, joyful in duty done, speaks by the lamed son
of Elis, great in counsel, of the road home. Advised by him and royal
in bearing as in deed, she dedicates it, emptied of rich oil, to the Shining
God upon his holy mountain—the god's forever.

Scarcely has the daughter of war spoken than the voice of war
sounds. Dull is he whose lips malign the line of Heracles, whose strength
lingers even in fostered sons. Like his mighty club, speeding Latros has
struck the sacred city. In freezing Colchis, Jason sowed the dragon's
teeth, brought forth from the furrow hundreds armed and fierce for
battle. So was it with him who was once my charge. He from tumbled
apples and pomegranates in the marketplace brought forth sharp swords,
loud-voiced bows, and quivers rich in arrows. And from the slaves of
the Argives, soldiers.

At once the Argives, sworn foes of Lacedaemon, call for the aid of
Lacedaemon's manly sons, mighty in brazen battle, against the defilers
of the sacred peace. Declaring he has no guilt in the matter and credited
because of the gold he lost on the race, the Lacedaemonian prince mus-
ters his dreaded guards and marches in tardy pursuit.

No man dare say the immortal gods have had no hand in this. Io,
my slave, wise beyond her years and full payment for all the good I
sought to do Latros, led me to the limping Hegesistratus, the tongue
of the Amazon queen, where he sat grieving his lost wife. "I have failed
Cynthia." Thus he groaned in my hearing. "Before you, you see a corpse,
foul already with the stench of death. The silver chariot would be overheavy, and Latros bore the victory always. Nor would the woman who
had desired him so long dare to defeat him, now that she had his love.
Bribed, I swore to serve the deity of my enemies, but could not serve
her well. My end I foresaw in distant Thrace—her slaves shall wrest me
from my island home, and five swords send me down to death."

Mantic Tisamenus, Iamus's child, gave me this scroll and the other,
this as he said for the wide-shouldered pankratiast. "He implores the
mercy of the Shining God, ever generous. In these the ill-starred Latros
gives the offended god his life—all that he has had." The queen of the
one-breasted daughters of war has urged that these be added to the urn

she has given. His priests consent. Tomorrow she will sacrifice before setting out for her own land, well content.

Themistocles of Athens will not be welcomed when he returns to his violet-crowned city, so many of his fellow citizens say, alleging that he has sold himself to Lacedaemon, however hotly he denies it. His cupfellow Simonides grinds away at the rhyming mill as before.

The Spartan regent is cried up for his sagacity everywhere, and talks of marching against the Sons of Perseus. All know now that the ship Latros took carried his cargo, and it is said that at his command his Lacedaemonians shunned the Phoenician steel, by their well-considered hesitancy obstructing the narrow way so that others could not join the battle. In this way, so runs the tale, the shrewd prince gained ten times over what he lost. But some to whom I spoke in Cyparissa report that as the vessel bore Latros and the slaves away, a slender woman with a bow stood at his side. These do not scruple to name her Artemis, the argent twin; that it was a chariot of silver that triumphed no one can deny. Whether this be truth or empty fable, it is certain that Pausanias the son of Cleombrotus is accounted twice a hero among the stratagem-loving Greeks.

As for this poor servant of the Shining One, the patron of the muses, he and his slave will return to their own seven-gated city—or perhaps journey to far-distant Sicily, rich in flocks, as the grave emissaries of glorious Hieron, splendid in victory, importune. If that be so, he prays the blessing of Ino, white keeper of the chambers of the sea among the daughters of Nereus. Permit us to voyage in safety, O lovely Ino, to that great city, Syracuse, the precinct of Ares.

# GLOSSARY

*(Soldier of the Mist)*

The principal proper names in Latro's account are identified here. A few (such as "Lands of the Living" and "Shining God") have been omitted when their meaning seems obvious. Certain other terms that could pose difficulties for his readers are defined as well.

*Acetes*—The commander of the armored soldiers (hoplites) on Hypereides's trireme.

*Acharnae*—A village roughly midway between Thought and Advent, but farther inland than either.

*Acheron*—A river flowing through both the Lands of the Living and the Lands of the Dead.

*Advent*—A small city near Thought, allied with it. The most famous temple of the Grain Goddess, the Royal House, is there.

*Aea*—The capital of Colchis, an ancient barbarian kingdom far north and east of Thought.

*Aegae*—A small city on the northern coast of Redface Island, the home port of the *Nausicaa*.

*Aesculapius*—The god of healing, an ancient physician deified.

*Agamemnon*—An ancient king and hero.

*Agathocles*—A famous musician of Thought.

*Agids*—The older royal family of Rope.

*Ahuramazda*—Ahura Mazda. Literally, Wise God or Wise Lord; the chief force for good in a mythology in which evil occupies an equal place.

*Alcmene*—The mother of Heracles.

*Amompharetos*—An officer (roughly a colonel) in the army of Rope.

*Anadyomene*—One of the names of Kalleos's goddess; it means "Sea-Born."

*Angra Manyu*—The evil god who opposes Ahura Mazda.

*Antaeus*—A Libyan giant, a son of Gaea.

*Apia*—The name given Gaea by the Sons of Scoloti.

*Apollodoros*—A famous choirmaster.

*Aram*—A country lying between the Cities of the Crimson Men and Babylon. Its language is understood in most parts of the Empire.

*Archilichos*—A poet and freebooter.

*archimage*—Great magician.

*Areopagus*—A hill in Thought, the site of murder trials.

*Argiopium*—A village near Clay.

*Argives*—The people of Hundred-Eyed.

*Argolis*—A peninsula southwest of Thought, to which wealthy families fled when it became apparent the Great King's army would capture their city.

*Artabazus*—The wily general who took command of the Great King's army following the death of Mardonius.

*Artaÿctes*—The governor of Sestos, appointed by the Great King.

*Artemisium*—The northernmost point of Goodcattle Island.

*Artimpasa*—The name given the Triple Goddess by the Sons of Scoloti.

*Asopus*—A god of rivers, the father of numerous nymphs. Live coals are discovered in the beds of his streams, which are also called Asopus.

*Auge*—The Huntress. This is the name by which she is known in Bearland; it means "bright light."

*Basias*—An ouragos in Eutaktos's lochos.

*Bearland*—A primitive mountainous area in the middle of Redface Island. It is technically independent of Rope.

*Boat*—A volcanic island in the Water. The metal-workers' god maintains a forge there.

*Boreas*—The god of the north wind.

*Budini*—Fair-haired barbarians inhabiting a densely forested tract northeast of the plains now held by the Sons of Scoloti.

*Celeos*—An ancient king of Advent. The present Royal House is built upon the ruin of his palace and takes its name from it.

*Cerdon*—One of the many slaves who work Pausanias's estate. Cerdon talks with Latro beside the fire on the evening of his capture.

*chalcis*—A bird that never wakes, but flies in its sleep. Its proximity induces sleep in others.

*Chersonese*—The peninsula separating Helle's Sea from the Water.

*Chios*—An isle of the Empire, peopled by Hellenes.

*Chthonios*—The underground Land of the Dead.

*Cimmer*—The eponymous founder of the barbarian tribe displaced by the Sons of Scoloti.

*Circling Isles*—A group due east of Redface Island; they form a rough oval.

*Clay*—A small city near Hill, allied with Thought. It gives its name to the battle in which Latro was wounded.

*Copais*—A large lake northwest of Hill; its waters enter the Lands of the Dead.

*Coronis*—A princess of Horseland, the mother of Aesculapius. The literal meaning of her name is "crooked horned." A more plausible meaning is "of the broken tower."

*Corustas*—A strategist of Tower Hill.

*Cowland*—The area northwest of the Long Coast. It is dominated by Hill.

*Crimson Country*—A coastal strip to the northeast of Riverland, dominated by the cities of the Crimson Men.

*crotali*—Musical rattles normally consisting of tuned lengths of bone or hardwood suspended at one end from a handheld frame.

*Delian*—Usually the Shining God, but also his twin the Huntress; from their place of birth.

*Demaratus*—The rightful claimant to the younger (Eurypontid) crown of Rope, now in exile at the court of the Great King.

*Demophon*—An infant prince whom the Grain Goddess wished to render immortal by bathing in fire. Her good intentions were frustrated by the arrival of his mother. Priests of the Grain Goddess at Advent must be of his family.

*Dog's Tail*—A sand spit extending from the island of Peace.

*Dolphins*—A mountain town on the mainland west of Tower Hill. Its oracle is the most famous in the world.

*Drakaina*—A lamia. Her name means "she-serpent."

*Eleonore*—One of the courtesans employed by Kalleos. Her name means "merciful."

*Eleusis*—Advent.

*Enodia*—A name of the Dark Mother; it means "of the roads."

*enomotia*—A military unit of 24 men and an officer. Roughly, a platoon.

*Ephesos*—A coastal town of the Empire, inhabited by Hellenes; it is a short distance north of Miletos.

*Euboea*—Goodcattle Island.

*Eumolpides*—The leading family of Advent—once its royal family.

*Eurotas*—A river on Redface Island. It flows almost due south and empties into the sea. Rope is on this river.

*Eurybiades*—A strategist of Rope.

*Eurykles*—A sorcerer and self-appointed priest of the Dark Mother. Kalleos's lover.

*Eutaktos*—A lochagos (roughly a captain) in the army of Rope.

*Euxine*—An extensive inland sea northeast of Helle's Sea. It is linked with Helle's Sea by the First Sea, and is far larger than both.

*Falcata*—Latro's sword.

*Fennel Field*—A battle in which Men of Thought repelled a seaborne invasion by the Empire.

*Fingers*—Dectuplets borne by Gaea, five boys and five girls. They are friendly to metal-workers and magic-workers.

*Gaea*—The eldest of all goddesses, worshiped by the aboriginal inhabitants of Redface Island and in many other places. The lion is her cat, the wolf her dog; she is also associated with pigs, cats, snakes, and bulls. She once spoke at Dolphins, but has been driven out by the Shining God. Her name means "earth."

*Gates to the Hot Springs*—A point in the northeastern coast of Cowland where cliffs wall the beach. A traveler walking north reaches thermal springs soon after passing them.

*Gello*—A freedman formerly employed by Kalleos to keep order.

*Goodcattle Island*—A long, narrow, rocky island northeast of the Long Coast.

*Gorgo*—The most distinguished woman in Rope, a princess, the widow of its heroic King Leonidas, the mother of its boy-king Pleistarchos, and the chief priestess of Orthia.

*gridelin*—The color of dried flax, a light gray-violet.

*Gulf*—A body of water west of Tower Hill, open to the sea only at its western end.

*hebetic*—Suggesting Hebe, the goddess of youth. Suggestive of a youthful cupbearer at a banquet. (Hebe is a cupbearer to the elder gods.)

*Helle*—The long-ago princess who gave her name to Helle's Sea by drowning in it. Her name presumably means "daughter of Hellen."

*Hellen*—The eponymous ancestor of the Hellenes.

*Helle's Sea*—A narrow strait between the Water and the First Sea. Sestos is on Helle's Sea.

*Heracles*—An ancient hero possessing great strength, who purged Hellas of monsters and was made immortal after his death.

*Heraclids*—Royal or aristocratic persons descended from Heracles.

*Herodotos of Halicarnassos*—Called "the father of history." He titled his book *Historia*, which means "inquiry."

*Hilaeira*—The young woman who joins Latro, Pindaros, and Io at Lake Copais. Her name means "brightness."

*Hill*—The dominant city of Cowland. It is walled, and has seven gates.

*Hippocleides*—The epitome of insouciant indifference. One of the eighteen suitors of an heiress, he performed a comic dance at their betrothal party. On being told by her father that his absurd capering had cost him his marriage, Hippocleides replied that it made no difference to him and continued to dance.

*Hippagretas*—Lochagos of the City Guard of Tower Hill.

*hoplon*—A circular shield of wood lined with leather and faced with bull's hide or bronze. A letter or symbol identifying the soldier's city is usually painted on the face—a club for Hill, for example.

*Horseland*—Thessaly, the country north of the Gates to the Hot Springs, famous for its cavalry.

*Hot Gates*—The Gates to the Hot Springs.

*Hundred-Eyed*—A major city on the east coast of Redface Island.

*Hypereides*—A leather merchant from Thought, and the captain of the *Europa*.

*Hysiae*—A village on the road from Thought to Hill.

*Hysiai*—A town on the road from Rope to Hundred-Eyed.

*Ialtos*—An officer in the army of Thought.

*Iamus*—The founder of a family of prophets.

*Ilissus*—A stream of the Long Coast; it empties into the Strait of Peace near Tieup.

*Ino*—An ancient princess of Hill, the stepmother of Helle and Phrixos. She is worshiped in many places on Redface Island. Her name probably means "my daughter."

*Io*—The child slave who attaches herself to Latro at Hill. As she tells Latro, her name means "joy."

*Island Sea*—A landlocked sea east of the Euxine.

*Issedonians*—A barbarian tribe of the remote northeast.

*Ister*—A great river emptying into the Euxine.

*Kalleos*—A hetaera of Thought. Her name means "my beauty."

*Kallidromos*—The mountain whose cliffs form the Gates to the Hot Springs.

*Keiros*—A slave belonging to Pasicrates.

*Kekrops*—The sailor killed by the Neurian.

*Khshayarsha*—The Great King.

*Kichesippos*—Pausanias's slave physician.

*kopis*—A heavy, curved, single-edged sword having its edge on the inside of the curve. Latro's sword appears to be a kopis. A large knife of similar pattern, used by hunters to skin and cut up game.

*Kore*—The Queen of the Lands of the Dead, Gaea's daughter. Her name means "maiden."

*Lalos*—One of Kalleos's cooks.

*Lar*—A household spirit.

*Latro*—A wounded mercenary.

*Lebadeia*—A small city west of Lake Copais, the site of the oracle of Trophonius.

*Leon*—Kalleos's other cook.

*Leonidas*—A heroic Agid king. A small force under his command fought to the last man at the Gates to the Hot Springs. Gorgo is his widow.

*Leotychides*—The King of Rope who commanded the combined fleets at Mycale. He is from the younger (Eurypontid) royal family.

*lochagos*—The officer commanding a lochos. Roughly, a captain.

*lochos*—A military unit of one hundred men.

*Long Coast*—A more or less triangular peninsula extending from the mainland between Peace and Goodcattle Island; Advent, Tieup, and Thought are on this peninsula. Its name is probably derived from the long and relatively straight coastlines of its eastern and southwestern sides.

*Lycurgus*—The chief author of the legal code of Rope. He was a prince of the younger (Eurypontid) royal family.

*Lyson*—A sailor assigned to guard Latro and the black man.

*Malea*—A rocky cape, the southernmost point of Redface Island, famous for storms.

*Mardonius*—The commander of the Great King's army killed at the battle of Clay. A man of great strength and courage, he led the Great King's bodyguard in person.

*Medes*—A nation closely related to the People from Parsa but subject to them. Because the Medes are more numerous, they are often confused with the People from Parsa.

*Megara*—A small city on the eastern side of the isthmus linking Redface Island with the mainland.

*Megareos*—Captain of the *Eidyia*.

*megaron*—The public room of a type of ancient palace. (The word is sometimes used for the palace itself as well.)

*Megistias*—King Leonidas's seer and sorcerer.

*Miletos*—A coastal city of the Empire, inhabited by Hellenes.

*Molois*—A stream in Cowland.

*Mormo*—A servant of the Dark Mother.

*Mycale*—The battle in which that fraction of the Great King's navy which had survived the battle of Peace was burned.

*Myrrha*—A Cypriot princess, mother of the most handsome of men.

*Naxos*—An island in the Water, belonging to the Empire.

*Nepos*—Captain of the *Nausicaa*.

*Neuri*—A tribe of barbarian sorcerers and werewolves.

*Nike*—The goddess of victory.

*Nysa*—The black man's country, south of Riverland.

*Oior*—A bowman aboard *Europa*.

*Orthia*—The Huntress, called so in the Silent Country. The famous wooden figure from which this name is derived originally represented Gaea. It means "upright."

*Oschos*—An armorer of Sestos.

*ouragos*—The second in command of an enomotia. Roughly, a platoon sergeant.

*Parsa*—The country of the Great King, the location of Persepolis and Susa.

*Pasicrates*—Pausanias's runner.

*Patroklos*—An ancient hero, slain at the siege of Ilion.

*Pausanias*—The Agid regent of Rope.

*Peace*—An island south of the Long Coast. Also the largest town on the island, the narrow channel separating the island from the mainland, etc.

*pelta*—A light shield in the form of a thick crescent, of wicker covered with leather.

*Persepolis*—The capital of the Empire, largely a governmental and religious center.

*Phanes*—An eastern god, said to be the creator of the universe. This name means "revealer."

*Phrixos*—Helle's brother.

*Phye*—The most important courtesan employed by Kalleos. Her name means "tall."

*Pindaros*—The poet chosen by the citizens of Hill to guide Latro.

*Pitana*—One of the villages making up Rope.

*Pleistarchos*—The Agid boy-king of Rope.

*Pleistoanax*—Pausanias's son.

*Polycrates*—An ancient king, long famous for good fortune.

*Polyhommes*—A priest of the Grain Goddess at Advent.

*Propontis*—The First Sea. It links Helle's Sea with the Euxine.

*Redface Island*—A large island south of the mainland, linked with it by an isthmus. The Silent Country and Bearland are regions of Redface Island. Tower Hill is on the western side of the isthmus.

*Rhoda*—One of the courtesans employed by Kalleos. Her name means "rose."

*Riverland*—Kemet, the most ancient of all nations.

*Rope*—The dominant city of the Silent Country. Its soldiers are said to be invincible.

*Sabaktes*—A servant of the Dark Mother.

*Sacred Way*—The road from Thought to Advent.

*Samos*—An island of the Empire, inhabited by Hellenes.

*Saros*—The gulf or sea separating Argolis from Peace. (Also a ruined city on the coast of Redface Island that once controlled this sea.)

*Scoloti*—An ancient barbarian king.

*Selene*—The bright aspect of the Triple Goddess. The others are the Huntress and the Dark Mother.

*Semele*—A princess of Hill, mother of the Kid.

*Sestos*—A walled city on Helle's Sea.

*Silent Country*—The fertile portion of the Eurotas valley. It is guarded by mountains to north, east, and west; its southern side is protected by a swamp. The Silent Country is dominated by Rope.

*Simonides*—An elderly poet and sophist. He wrote the verses inscribed at the Hot Gates.

*Solon*—The chief author of the legal code of Thought.

*Spercheius*—The river separating Cowland from Horseland. It was forded by the Great King's Army on its way to the Hot Gates.

*Spu*—The bowman killed by the Neurian.

*stephane*—A gold or silver headband, widest across the forehead.

*Susa*—The largest city in Parsa.

*taksis*—A large infantry unit of variable size. Roughly, a division. Its commander is one grade below a strategist.

*Tekmaros*—A slave belonging to Pasicrates.

*Teleia*—The queen of the gods.

*Teuthrone*—A fishing village on the coast of Redface Island.

*Themistocles*—Thought's most famous and influential politician and strategist.

*Thoe*—The youngest of the Nereids. Her name means "swift."

*Thought*—The chief city of the Long Coast and the intellectual capital of Hellas.

*Thygater*—The woman reanimated by Latro and Eurykles. Her name means "daughter."

*Tieup*—The chief port of Thought.

*Tisamenus*—Pausanias's seer and sorcerer.

*Tower Hill*—The richest city in Hellas. It is on the gulf, on the west side of the isthmus. Tower Hill built and controls the skid used to take ships across the isthmus.

*triacontor*—A small warship, rowed with 30 oars.

*Trioditis*—The Triple Goddess: Selene, the Huntress, and the Dark Mother.

*Triple Goddess*—Trioditis, the twin sister of the Shining God. Fundamentally a deity of night, she is particularly associated with dogs, which bay at the full moon, course game under the crescent moon, and rush unseen at benighted travelers on the dark roads of Hellas.

*trireme*—A large warship, rowed by 170 oars.

*Trophonius's Cave*—One of the many entrances to the Land of the Dead.

*Umeri*—One of Latro's comrades.

*Water*—The sea east of Hellas. It contains the Circling Isles and many other islands.

*Xanthippos*—The strategist in charge of the siege of Sestos, an aristocratic soldier-politician from Thought.

*Zoe*—One of the courtesans employed by Kalleos. Her name means "life."

# GLOSSARY

## (Soldier of Arete)

See *Soldier of the Mist* for the following terms: Acetes, Aram, Artaÿctes, Asopus, Basias, Bearland, Budini, Cerdon, Chersonese, Clay, Cowland, Dolphins, Drakaina, Eurotas, Eutaktos, Falcata, Fennel Field, Gaea, Gorgo, Helle's Sea, Hill, Hypereides, Iamus, Ino, Io, Ister, Kalleos, Kichesippos, Kore, Latro, Leonidas, Leotychides, Lyson, Mardonius, Medes, Nysa, Parsa, Pasicrates, Pausanias, Pindaros, Pleistarchos, Pleistoanax, Riverland, Rope, Sestos, Simonides, Susa, Themistocles, Thought, Tisamenus, Triple Goddess, and Xanthippos.

*Achaeans*—An ancient tribe, displaced by the Dorians.
*Achilles*—A leader of the Achaeans at the siege of Ilion.
*Adeimantus*—A magnate of Tower Hill.
*Aegospotami*—A small city on the eastern coast of the Chersonese, near its midpoint.
*Aeolians*—A tribe of Hellenes inhabiting the northern coast of Asia Minor.
*Agatharchos*—An official of the Pythic Games.
*Aglaus*—The poor laborer employed as a guide by Themistocles in Bearland and later as a servant by the black man and Latro.
*Ahura Mazda*—The supreme god of Parsa.
*Amazons*—Barbarian priestesses of the War God.
*Amyklos*—A centaur famous as a healer.
*Anochos*—A citizen of Dolphins employed by Rope to represent its interests there.
*Anysia*—An acrobatic dancer in the troupe engaged by Cimon.
*Apollonios*—A priest of the oracle at Dolphins.
*Apsinthia*—The barbarian kingdom just west of the Chersonese.

*Ares*—The god of war.

*arete*—The virtues of a soldier, ranging from cleanliness and love of order to courage in the face of death.

*Argas*—Prince Pausanias's racehorse.

*Artembares*—The young son of the governor of Sestos under the Great King.

*Artemisia*—The warrior queen of Halicarnassos.

*Asopodorus*—The commander of the cavalry of Hill at the Battle of Clay.

*Athena Ilias*—A goddess who aided the Hellenes during the siege of Ilion.

*Badizoe*—An Amazon; her name means "slow march," or "walk" when applied to cavalry.

*Bittusilma*—The Babylonian who attaches herself to the black man; her name means "house of perfection."

*black man*—Seven Lions, the soldier from Nysa who cared for Latro after the Battle of Clay.

*boiled leather*—Cuir-bouilli; leather hardened by immersion in very hot wax.

*Byblos*—The sacred city of the Crimson Men, said to be the oldest city in the world; it lies north of Sidon.

*Cape Mastursia*—The tip of the Chersonese.

*Ceos*—A small island off the southeastern end of the Long Coast.

*Cimon*—An aristocratic young politician famous for hospitality; pronounced *Keé-mone*.

*Cleombrotus*—An Agid prince, son of Anaxandridas and brother to Cleomenes and Leonidas.

*Cleton*—A merchant from Hundred-Eyed long resident at Cobrys.

*Clytias*—The founder of the pro-Laconian branch of the Iamidae.

*Cobrys*—A port on the Thracian coast; the capital of Apsinthia.

*Crimson Men*—Traders from the eastern shore of the Great Sea, from the color of their robes and the dyed cloth they sell.

*Cybele*—A name under which Gaea is worshiped in the east.

*Cyklos*—One of the five judges of Rope.

*Cynthia*—The Huntress, born in a cave on Mt. Cynthus.

*Cyparissa*—A small port at the foot of Mt. Parnassos.

*Cyrus*—The first Great King, founder of the Empire.

*Damon*—Pericles's tutor, once a famous singer.

*Deloptes*—A Thracian nobleman.

*Diallos*—A slave of Themistocles's.

*Diokles*—The professional employed to train Latro and Pasicrates.

*Elata*—A dryad of the Chersonese; her name means "pine."

*Elis*—A small city near the western tip of Redface Island.

*Europa, the*—The trireme commanded by Hypereides.

*Fortuna*—The goddess of chance, now commonly called Lady Luck.

*Getae*—Barbarians of the northern forests; the Budini are a tribe belonging to this group.

*Hebrus*—A river of Thrace.

*Hegesistratus*—Mardonius's seer and sorcerer.

*Hellas*—The country of the Hellenes, a peninsula extending south into the sea.

*Hellenes*—The sons and daughters of Hellen, linked by a common language.

*Hieron*—The tyrant of Syracuse.

*Hippephode*—The queen of the Amazons; her name means "cavalry charge."

*Hippostizein*—The tallest Amazon; her name means "trooper."

*Hippoxleas*—A Silent One, reporting to Cyklos.

*Hubrias*—A merchant captain of Hundred-Eyed.

*Huntress*—An aspect of the Triple Goddess.

*Iamidae*—A clan of prophets, descended from Iamus.

*Ilion*—A ruined city of the Troad; it lies on the Asian coast south of Sestos, near the southern outlet of Helle's Sea.

*Kemet*—Riverland; the black land.

*Kotys*—The name of numerous Thracian kings.

*Kotytto*—A name under which Gaea is worshiped in Thrace.

*Kronos*—The king of the old gods; he prevented the heavens from further influencing the development of life on earth.

*kybernetes*—Sailing master.

*Lacedaemon*—That portion of the Silent Country anciently governed by Rope; the lambda on the Rope Makers' hoplons derives from this name.

*Lewqys*—*Lucius,* as pronounced by a Crimson Man.

*Luhitu*—Possibly a garbling of *Latium.*

*Melas*—A river of Thrace.

*Miltiades*—The victorious commander at the Battle of Fennel Field and the builder of the wall across the Chersonese.

*Mnemosyne*—A titaness; her nine daughters are the goddesses of astronomy, comedy, dance, geometry, history, poetry, rhetoric, song, and tragedy.

*Molossis*—The region between the Acheron and the Arethon; it is famous for its huge dogs, which are widely exported.

*Muslak*—A merchant captain of Byblos.

*Nereus*—Among the old gods, the sea god.

*Nessibur*—A Thracian nobleman.

*Oeobazus*—The Median engineer who built the bridge of boats across Helle's Sea.

*Orpheus*—A shaman killed by the Thracian women; his head was cast into the Hebrus, still pronouncing the name of his lost wife.

*Orsippos*—A magnate of Hundred-Eyed.

*Pactye*—The northernmost city of the Chersonese, just south of Miltiades's Wall.

*Paetians*—The Thracian tribe north of the Apsinthians.

*Pandion*—An ancient king of Thought.

*Parnassos*—A lofty mountain north of the Gulf; Dolphins is on this mountain.

*peltast*—A foot soldier armed with a pair of javelins and a pelta.

*Pericles*—Xanthippos's teenage son.

*Perseus*—The father of Perses, and thus the founder of the nation of the Great King.

*Pharetra*—The Amazon loved by Latro.

*Philomela*—A princess of ancient Thought; her name means "lover of song."

*Pleistorus*—A name under which the War God is worshiped in Thrace.

*Polos*—The young centaur sent to Latro by Gaea.

*Polygnotos*—A famous painter of Thought; Cimon's sister Elpinice is rumored to be his mistress.

*Priam*—The last king of Ilion.

*Procne*—A princess of ancient Thought; her name means "firstborn."

*Protesilaos*—The first hero to die at the siege of Ilion.

*pythia*—The Destroyer's virgin prophetess, probably about fifteen.

*Pythic Games*—Contests held at Dolphins every four years in honor of the Destroyer; they include competitions in music and poetry as well as footraces, boxing, etc.

*python*—Gaea's sacred serpent, slain by the Destroyer; it haunts the oracle he wrested from her.

*Raskos*—A peltast killed by Latro.

*Rhea*—The mother of the gods. A name under which Cybele is worshiped in the west; it means "earth."

*Seven Lions*—The black man.

*Sicily*—A large island west of the Gulf.

*Sidon*—The capital of the Crimson Men; the king of Sidon is the commander of the Great King's navy.

*Sisyphus*—The first king of Tower Hill.

*Swollenfoot*—A king of ancient Hill.

*Syracuse*—A great city established by colonists from Tower Hill.

*Tegea*—A small city in Bearland.

*Tellias*—The founder of the anti-Laconian branch of the Iamidae.

*Tereus*—The name of numerous Thracian kings.

*Thamyris*—A Thracian prince; King Kotys's chief adviser.

*Thespiae*—A small city in Cowland.

*Thrace*—A vast barbarian country stretching from the eastern bank of the Nestos to the western shore of the Euxine.

*Tillon*—A slave of Themistocles's.

*Troad*—The area once controlled by Ilion, including the Thracian Chersonese, Mysia, and Phrygia Minor.

*Xerxes*—Khshayarsha, the Great King, ruler of the Empire.

*Zakunthios*—An island west of Elis.

*Zalmoxis*—A shape-changing shaman deified; his name is presumably derived from the Thracian word *zalmo*, "skin."

*Zeus*—The king of the gods.

*Zihrun*—The alias adopted by Oeobazus.